LEGENDS OF
GRAVENSTONE

The Secret Voyage

A Novel By:

Alex Aguilar

ISBN-13: 978-1-9833-0769-0

For us, the dreamers with no voice.
Never stop fighting...

A special thanks to
Peter Crowley & Mattia Turzo.

Neither one of you knows me.
But your magnificent music saved me from
Writer's Block more times than I can count.

TABLE OF CONTENTS

Foreword

My name's Jack Barlowe.
It is my name and mine alone.

Nothing in the world has been more misunderstood than a troubled mind. Many are often quick to mark people as 'mad', 'radical', or 'loose in the head' simply because one's opinion does not match with theirs.

But the mind was destined to doubt, destined to wonder, destined to question every aspect of life. Of course, upon doing so, the mind tends to drift into troubled territory and a person may find themselves questioning the truth, seeking some form of meaning in a world where there is none to find.

It is because of this that people often become lost…

Whether they're lost in their work, in their beliefs, or in a barrel of ale, people seek only a way to soothe their minds from the cruel reality that the world has no true significance. The world simply *is*. And we are but specks of dust drifting with it, always have been.

It is because of this that, when the atrocities of the world burden the mind, I find it often helpful to remind yourself of your name. Simple as it may seem, it is the one thing that nobody can take from you. They can beat you down to nothing, take away your hope and pride, make you feel like you're nothing but an utter waste of space on this earth…

But you will always have your name. *Always.*

It is a minor reminder that, while there may be millions of people out there, you will always be *you*. It is a reminder of your singularity. And it's quite remarkable how something so trivial can often lift you when your spirit is drowning in despair.

Trust me, I would know… I remind myself every miserable morning…

My name's Jack Barlowe, I say to myself. *And I'm the world's greatest storyteller.*

Or at least, I *used* to be… These days, hardly anyone outside of this village knows my name, and those that do haven't many great things to say about it. For someone who was once acquainted with folk of great regard, many would say I have shit luck to end up in this piss-pot. And the rest, well… *They* figure I'm just some crazy old man with delusions of grandeur…

But *I* know who I am… *I* know what I've lived through…

I may not be in the same league as the Queen Savior or the Guardian Knight, but I was there when the whole mess happened. And that's more than anyone in this wretched village can say for themselves.

The world was a different place when I was a young lad. I can hardly recognize my own face when I look at my reflection some days. My eyes are about the only familiar image of the life I once had. The rest of me, sadly, has deteriorated along with my mind.

1

Some mornings, in fact, it takes me a moment to remember my name.

And it is a moment that terrifies me, truth be told…

This morning's by far the worst. I'm lying there face down on the floor of my humble little cottage, my eyelids shut and my body aching from head to toe. My throat feels hoarse and my wine-tainted lips are painfully dry. If it were up to me, I'd sleep the whole bloody day. But that damn market's up and running and the chattering outside is growing by the minute.

The throbbing in my head forces me awake, but I can't bring myself to move just yet. I manage to open one eye; the other's pressed against the wooden floorboards. The first thing I see is an empty glass bottle, just inches from my face, and the wiry legs of a black beetle crawling inside of it.

I hear a sudden knock on my door; a gentle knock, like that of a nervous child. The only response I can muster is a soft groan as I lie there and hope my untimely visitor will give up and leave before I gather the energy to say *'piss off'*.

But no such luck… Instead, the knock gets louder…

"Mister Barlowe!" a girl calls from the outside.

Damn it all to hells…

Reluctantly, I rise to my knees. I feel last night's dinner crawling up my throat for a moment, and so I take a few deep breaths to ease it back down.

"Mister Barlowe!" the annoying little rat keeps calling for me.

Does she not realize what time it is…?

"He's not in there, stupid!" says another voice, this one more muffled.

"It's 2 hours 'til mid-day. Where else would he be?" the girl replies. Her gentle knocks turn into a persistent thumping. "MISTER BARLOWE!!"

I stumble to the door and open it. The sun's light burns my eyes like hells' fire. And I can see the silhouette of the tiny redheaded thing standing there on my doorway. With a hand pressed against my forehead, I say the first thing that comes to my mind.

"Quit that bloody knockin' if you want to keep that hand of yours, girl…"

My words are hardly coherent through my slurring, and what *should* have been intimidating instead comes across as laughable. I leave the door open and walk gently towards my armchair. As usual, the children allow themselves in.

"*Told* you," I hear the girl say as she closes the door behind her.

As I sink into my chair, I can tell from their scowls that they hate the smell of incense and liquor in the room. And yet they keep coming back, gods know why. It's as much a mystery to me as the reason behind those silly little hats the schoolhouse made them wear. The girl asks if she can open a window, but I harshly decline, telling her I very much like a dim atmosphere in my home. Instead, I allow her to light a few of my candles.

Once I force myself back to my senses, I recognize my three visitors right away. A redheaded girl about ten years old, her freckled cousin that looks just like her except for his shorter wiry hair, and their close friend, an elf boy with sharp ears and blue skin the color of the sea.

"Little rats!" I groan at them. "Don't you know it's ten years bad luck to wake a sleepin' man?"

"I've never heard such a thing," the redheaded boy says. "Ten *years?*"

"Aye," I say to him. "*Fifteen* if he's hungover."

The elf boy chuckles under his breath. "Which is, in your case, *always?*"

"Shut it, lad..."

While the boys laugh, the girl sets her rucksack down on my bedspread, which happens to be merely three feet from where I had passed out.

"Shouldn't you lot be at the schoolhouse?" I ask, pretending to be rude. Truly I hardly remember the last time I had a visitor that wasn't one of these three. Isolation isn't good for the mind... You start talking to the walls or pretending the mice in your kitchen are people...

"The schoolhouse?" asks the elf boy, his silver eyebrows arched with confusion. "But it's the seventh day."

"What?" I sit there slightly baffled. "No it's not... it's the *fifth.*"

"It's the *seventh,*" the girl says, and it is *her* word I take for granted. She's always been, after all, the most honest of the three.

"Piss off... is it *really?*" I lean forward and press my hands against my temples.

"Are you feeling well?" the human boy asks. "You look a bit ill."

"He's hungover again," the elf boy says. "Fetch him some water."

"Never mind the water!" I say to the elf boy. "Fetch me that bottle over in that corner there..."

He obeys. And I thank him silently for not forcing me to get up from my chair.

"We came to hear about Queen Magdalena!" the girl says excitedly, as she settles a pillow on the wooden floor and sits near my chair.

"Piss off!" her cousin says, taking a seat next to her. "No one cares about the bloody queen. *I* want to hear the one about the thief & the witch!"

"To hells with the lot of you!" the elf boy says as he fumbles through a cluster of half-empty bottles. "Mister Barlowe *promised* he'd tell us about the Guardian this week!"

"Fine," the girl sighs. "But while you're at it, will you at least tell us a bit about the first-ever Lady Knight?"

"No one cares about the Lady Knight!" says her cousin.

"*I* care!"

"You would!"

"Will the *both* of you shut your arses?!" I snap at them. It's not that I hate them, but the pain in my head only gets worse with every one of their shouts.

"Is *this* it?" asks the elf boy as he hands me a bottle of Roquefort liqueur.

"No," I reply, snatching the bottle from the boy's hands. "But it'll do…"

I drink from it as if I were drinking apricot juice. A few specks dribble down my bushy grey beard and I hear the children giggle. The liqueur burns my throat, fuels me, gives me the energy that I need to continue. I set the bottle down and take a deep breath. Without looking at my reflection, I can guess that my eyes are a frightening red. But the children don't seem to pay it any mind. Hells, they've been visiting me every seventh day for the better half of a year, they ought to be used to it by now.

In a moment of reticence, I glance down and smell the inner side of my shirt. As I suspect, it reeks of sweat and ale… Not to mention, the clothes I'm wearing are so old and worn, I look like a beggar. I start to wonder why these kids look at me that way every time they come to visit. While the rest of the village looks at me like a madman, they look at me with nothing but wonder in their innocent little eyes.

"I brought you a cantaloupe!" the girl suddenly says to me.

"I didn't ask for food…"

"But me mum says you'll die soon if you don't eat! Besides, your cooking is rubbish."

"Watch your tongue there, ginger…"

"*Wynnifred!*"

"I don't care," I say to her as I take another gulp from my bottle.

Truthfully, however, hers was the only name I *did* remember… If you asked me to name the other two, I'd die before I could tell you. The three of them are sitting about four feet in front of my chair, their attention fixed solely on me, begging me to fuel their imagination with my stories.

"Now… where was I?"

"You were going to tell us about the Guardian!" the elf boy says eagerly, brushing his shaggy silver hair out of his view.

"Can't you just give us a *bit* about the Lady Knight?" Wynnifred asks.

"Oh will you *shut it* about the bloody Lady Knight already!?" her cousin shouts.

"She once rode a fire-breathing dragon!" she says. "The *Guardian* never did that!"

"Don't be daft! Dragons are not real!"

"Actually they *are*, I heard the Guardian was *eaten* by one!" the elf boy intervenes.

"That's a load of shite!" the redheaded boy says. "The Guardian was *decapitated*."

"No, he wasn't!"

"He *was!*"

"Well which was it, Mister Barlowe?" the girl asks.

"Bloody hells, can you lot just *whisper* for a bit?" I say, groaning as my head throbs something awful.

"You're daft!" says the boy to the elf. "But not dafter than my sister Wren... *She* thinks it was poison that killed 'im..."

"Bollocks, all of it!" I finally say as I take another sip, this time a smaller one. "Now... the lot of you can sit there and shout at each other all day *or* you can listen to *me*."

The look of bewilderment in their little eyes returns. They get comfortable in their places and listen attentively as I take my last gulp and begin.

"What you fail to realize, children... is that it's all the same story," I say to them. "The Guardian wasn't always the Guardian, y'see... Much like the Queen wasn't always the Queen..."

"And what about Blackwood?" asks the redheaded boy.

"Oh that sneaky bastard was a thief since birth, I'm sure."

The children chuckle amongst one another, looking at me with anticipation and delight. Frankly, it's moments like these that I truly live for... Moments when I ceased to be the drunken madman, the beggar, the laughingstock of the town... I wasn't just that '*poor old fool*' that peasants judged and guards frowned upon. I wasn't a doomed halfwit that people were scared of someday becoming. I was the ever-knowing Jack Barlowe, a man that was once known as the greatest storyteller that ever lived.

"So where exactly did the Guardian Knight come from?" asks the elf boy.

"Patience, lad," I reply with a grin. "You'll find out in due time... For I know the perfect story for you all... A story filled with adventure and horror and wonders beyond your wildest dreams... The story of a ragtag group of misfits brought together by fate and roped into a voyage that would ultimately change the world, as they knew it... A group of misfits so different yet more alike than they cared to realize... A group of misfits that would one day become *legends*..."

I

The Humble Days

In a world filled with magic and wonder, there was once a place called Gravenstone. Rich, verdant, and full of life, this wondrous nation was as replete with beauty as it was with myths and tales of grand adventure. Conflicts over power, unexpected allegiances between foes, voyages filled with peril and death, the rich history of Gravenstone had it all.

For many centuries, it was the only land known to exist, until great voyagers sailed the Draeric Sea and discovered the nations of Qamroth, Ahari, and Noorgard. But Gravenstone was where it had all began. Every race to ever exist, in one way or another, could trace their roots right back to this mystifying land.

The year was 1121, in the age of silver, when Gravenstone was home to a vast array of life. But with the beauty of diversity comes the inevitable tension and conflict, and over the years the inhabitants of this land succumbed into a pit of turmoil and disorder.

It was said that, in the beginning of time, the Gods of Nayarith ruled the earth. It was said that they were the ones who created every race that lives today. The myth, should it be true, proclaimed that there had been nine gods to walk the land. And every one of them created their children in their own image. The god of humans created them all in different shades of brown, just as the dirt from which they came. The goddess of the elves drew specks from the great seas to create her children, and so their skin varied in tones of blue, some as pale as a chicory flower and others as dark as the midnight sky. The same went for the god of the green-skinned orcs, who created them from the leaves of the earth, as did the god of the goblins. And soon after, the gnomes were born, their goddess creating them to be smaller and more nimble than humans. And, of course, then came the minotauros, the pixies, the ogres, and the nymphs. The gods left their children to live in harmony, in the land they had themselves created, and drifted to the skies, where they could watch over them for all eternity.

Truth or myth, it was a philosophy that, over the centuries, had influenced a great many humans in power, from ministers to historians, even kings. But the greed and vanity of humans and their inability to match the traits of their sibling races had become a burden.

The strength of the orc, the agility and speed of the elf, the wings of the pixie… The idea of there existing a race more powerful was something that humans could not bear. It gave way for great unrest that ultimately led to an uprising. Humankind increased in numbers and power, thus leading to a clash among the races known as the Great War.

After a decade of mayhem and bloodspill, humankind won the war.

They proclaimed that any creature whose race was anything but human was to be banished into the Woodlands, a land of darkness and peril, and prohibited from ever setting foot in human realms... The price for breaking this law was certain and inevitable death.

Our story takes place approximately 250 years after the Great War, during a time in which life seemed simple and mundane. As with any other land, there were inevitable quarrels, yet never one as immeasurable and with as much loss of life as the Great War had been.

Gravenstone was split into two kingdoms. To the east was the kingdom of Vallenghard, ruled by King Rowan of Val Havyn.

To the west was the kingdom of Halghard, and it had been ruled by King Frederic of Morganna for many decades until his unexpected passing. They say the man had died in his sleep, though many whispers in the king's court spoke of foul play.

And lastly, in the center of the land, separating the two kingdoms was the vast green forest known as the Woodlands. It was a place that, after centuries of isolation from humankind, became a forbidden terrain through which not many souls would dare cross and the few that did were lucky to escape with every one of their limbs still attached, if they escaped at all.

Our story begins, as most stories would, with a particular group that dared to question the ways of the world. A group of brave souls that would transform it all.

Just beyond the blue hills, two miles south of the grand royal city of Val Havyn, there stood a humble village known as Elbon, which consisted of a strand of farms and rich fertile land that stretched for miles in every direction.

It had always been customary for the villagers of Elbon to work and harvest for six days of the week and rest on the seventh. On this particular seventh day, there was an eerie silence as the cold, humid breeze of dawn filled the air. The sun was starting to show its first light, but unlike any sunrise in the previous six days, there was hardly any sign of life throughout the village.

That was, of course, until there was...

The sound of leather boots spattering along the muddy trail, still damp after the rainstorm, began to wake the sleeping cattle as two young children no older than 12 ran through the village heading south. Despite the cold breeze, sweat was dripping down both their faces, stinging their nervous little eyes. Young Margot was leading the way, her twin brother Melvyn a few steps behind her, panting heavily as they made way for their mother's farm.

While key to the wealth of Val Havyn, the farmlands of Elbon and the many peasants and farmers that it was home to were rather deprived when compared to the grandiosity and elegance of the royal city. There was more wealth and capital to be gained and more people of nobility in the city, while the townsfolk of Elbon dressed in whatever rags their humble professions could acquire them.

Perhaps the major difference was the architecture of the city. The sheds and cottages in Elbon, most of which were made of wood, had been hand-built by some ancestor not many generations back and were no match for the graceful structures found in Val Havyn, where almost every dwelling was made of the finest stone and wood, painted white, with rooves made of thick auburn brick.

Val Havyn was the capitol city of Vallenghard and home to his majesty, King Rowan. Every other city and village in the kingdom was governed by a Lord of high nobility, entrusted personally by the king himself. There was already life in the royal city on this particular morning, as the seventh day was the busiest in the marketplace. Merchants from every village and keep nearby were already approaching the city gates for their weekly routine, unaware of the activity that was taking place just two miles south.

The young twins reached the first set of cottages. Young Margot was glancing back every other second and still she outran her brother by several yards. For one unfortunate moment, the boy overestimated himself and took the wrong step, where he lost his balance and stumbled into the damp soil. Margot ran back, grabbed hold of the boy's sweaty hand, and pulled him up.

"Come *on!*" she said, careful not to shout.

In the distance, they could see the two horses galloping after them. The twins spared not one second. They ran quicker, unaware that they were even capable of it, until reaching the wall of a wooden cottage where there lived a one-eyed woman that had grown deaf over the years.

"Climb! Now!" Margot lent her brother a hand. The boy hopped onto a barrel of foul-smelling water and climbed to the roof. Now, young Melvyn was not as fast a runner as his sister was, but he certainly did excel in climbing. He reached his hand out and pulled his sister up, as the two horses trotted into the village; their riders were two men dressed in rags and leathers.

"Where'd they go?!" the larger man asked his long-haired, bearded companion.

"You lost 'em?!" his companion shouted.

"*Me?* You were the one who spotted them!"

"Yes, but *you* were ahead o' me!"

The twins lay on the roof, trembling and sweating with exhaustion, as the two riders came to a halt just underneath the cottage.

"They can't have gone far!" the larger man said.

"Well come on, let's get this over with!" his companion replied, turning his horse and riding in a slightly different direction. The larger man followed, much to his disdain, and kept his eyes wide, inspecting every cottage and shrub around him for any sign of movement.

The twins took a moment to catch their breath, looking up at the clear gray morning sky. Margot turned to her brother, wiping her untidy black hair out of her face.

"How far d'you suppose we are?" she asked.

Melvyn gazed into the distance. He could see their mother's farm as clear as day. "A half-mile?" he guessed.

She nodded. Once they were breathing normally again, the twins gripped each other's sweaty hands once more, both trembling from the adrenaline still pumping through their veins.

"All right," the girl sighed anxiously. "Let's go!"

The largest farm in Elbon was in the southern outskirts, surrounded by steep green hills and only a half-mile from Lotus Creek. It was great in size, though not necessarily in luxury or wealth. Crops grew in vast portions, which resulted in a great amount of work, too much for the humble family that owned and tended the land.

And so, the young farmer made way for the barn on this seventh day, ready for yet another hard day's labor. There were no grievances, no complaints, nor even a grumble.

A blessing from the gods, his mother would say when the fields were kind to them. *Leaving the harvest in the ground for the rodents would be most ungrateful.*

The breeze in the air was warming up.

The birds were chirping their spring morning melodies.

The sheep had awakened for their morning meal and their keeper was gathering his gear in the stables. The smell of fresh horse feces inside the stables was enough to repulse anyone, but the young keeper had grown used to it. He was the first to wake in the brink of dawn and often the last to leave the fields at the end of a long day, the eldest son of the woman that owned the farm.

His name was John Huxley.

And, truth be told, he was not very special. He only *believed* that he was, which was far more dangerous. While he was loved by many and hated by few, the lad would often find danger as if he had a knack for it. At just 23 years of age, he had attained a good many wounds and scars, and still it seemed as if the lad was eager for the next one.

Every scar tells a story, Old Man Beckwit, his mentor, would often say. *But you, you dumb bastard, are turning into an old book that no one cares to read anymore.*

But there was no stopping John Huxley, for the young sheep farmer had an inconceivable spirit unlike any farmer in Elbon; he only lacked the guidance. His father used to say that John had his mother's heart, and that was most certainly true. But he also had his father's grit, and this made the lad dangerous.

To this day, in fact, many believe him to be the cause for all the chaos... He was, after all, the reckless bastard that crossed blades with the notorious thief Hudson Blackwood, something that not many men would have the guts to do.

But John Huxley did it... He drew his sword when nobody else would.

It was because of him that the infamous thief was captured to begin with, which in turn led to the disbarment of a well-regarded knight, which in turn led to a legendary voyage that would in turn lead to a great battle. And that very battle was only the beginning of a much greater story, one that would change the course of the world, as we knew it.

In the humble days, however, John lived a simple life, only ever *dreaming* of someday leaving Elbon for more adventurous endeavors. Every day, he'd wake up early to feed the sheep, milk the cows, collect the eggs, and water the herb garden for his mother. Then came the long hours under the sun, picking corn from the fields.

He was in the barn that morning, hoisting a heavy leather sack of farming equipment over his shoulder, when he was suddenly startled by the rickety wooden door. Two children ran inside, a boy and a girl, both covered in dirt and sweat. They struggled to catch their breath, as the girl shut the door immediately behind her.

"Help us!" the boy said agitatedly.

And not a second later, they heard the horse hooves just outside the walls of the barn. The horses bellowed as the riders came to a halt right at the doors, their boots casting shadows beneath the doorframe as they dismounted.

Margot and Melvyn hid behind the young farmer, who remained puzzled yet vigilant. Thick whispers outside argued over who should attempt to go in first. And it was at that moment that John understood what was happening. He removed the leather bag from his shoulders and set it down at his feet, as the barn doors began to rattle. He felt young Margot's hand gripping his sleeve; she was shaking and her breathing had quickened once again.

"They found us," she said.

Suddenly, the doors were kicked open and two men stepped into the barn, both with blades strapped to their belts but neither one reaching for it just yet. They walked heedlessly about, each in the other direction so that the young farmer wouldn't know where to turn. The larger man chuckled, revealing his relatively clean but uneven teeth.

"We've no business with you, farmer," said the smaller, bearded man. "We're just here for them children."

John Huxley said nothing, only grinned at their self-assurance, silently accepting the challenge. He tilted his head slightly to the left, speaking to the young girl but keeping his eyes locked on the two men. "Back door," he mumbled at her. "I'll handle these two."

The twins stepped back, leaving John to confront the men alone.

But the bearded one sighed and turned to his companion.

"Fetch them, will ya, Henrik?"

Henrik took slow, heavy steps towards the children, his thick arms swinging at his sides, causing him to appear more intimidating. But before the large man could reach them, there was the sound of hissing metal, followed by Margot gasping with surprise. John Huxley had reached into his bag and was now holding a rusty blade up at Henrik, who stopped in his tracks.

"Larz?" the husky man craned his neck towards his companion.

The bearded man smirked and took careful steps towards the farmer, unsheathing his own blade, which was sharper and more burnished. "You sure you want to do this, lad?"

John said nothing still, only kept his feet planted firmly, smirking at the two men as if he simply couldn't wait to swing his blade.

Henrik took back a few of his steps and unsheathed his own blade, standing on the other side of the farmer, closing in on him. "Think you can handle two blades at once?" he snickered.

And this time John couldn't help himself. "Try me," he said, giving his neck a good crack.

Larz attacked first, his black hair swaying in the air with every swing. Henrik gave them a few moments, looking for an opportunity to run towards the children; when he tried, however, John darted ahead, rolled on the dirt, and blocked his way.

The twins scattered towards the rear of the barn, heading towards a pair of doors next to a stall where a scrawny mule drooled over a bucket of water. Melvyn tried to kick them open but they wouldn't budge. When they glanced back, they saw their pursuers locked in combat with the farmer. A small cloud of dust had gathered inside the barn, as John Huxley dodged and blocked every single attack. Larz and Henrik made brief eye contact, both out of breath and with the same stunned expression in their faces.

"The key! Where's the key?!" Margot yelled.

John dodged a powerful strike from Henrik and stumbled about as he reached into his pocket and threw a small key made of copper at the twins. Margot caught it and opened the door, pushing her brother out first. The brief distraction was enough for Larz to land a small cut on John's left arm. They stopped for a moment.

John examined it... A flesh wound, but the sting of it made his skin throb all the same. He looked up at Larz, whose smirk then turned into a nervous scowl.

"Oh shit," Larz said.

Margot and Melvyn were outside for 5 seconds at most, before the backdoor of the barn nearly broke off its rusty hinges. Larz stumbled out and fell onto the mud, groaning in pain, his sword now out of his reach. The twins stared in disbelief, as the sound of metal clashing against metal grew nearer.

John stepped out of the barn first, taking careful backwards steps as Henrik attacked him ferociously. But the farmer did not look tired at all. He didn't even need to look at his sword, his eyes concentrated on his opponent, as if he could read his every move through a stare. Larz struggled to his knees, a hand pressed against the back of his waist as if keeping his spine in place. He reached for his blade a fraction of a second too late. A small pair of hands picked it up.

Larz found himself looking up at the eyes of young Margot, who was holding the thin sword up at the man's chin. She struggled to grip the heavy wooden handle, but there was a determination in her eyes that amazed the man.

"Certain death," she said, her brother standing at her side with a less convincing glare. John Huxley managed to disarm Henrik and did the same with his blade as Margot was doing to Larz. The farmer and the girl made brief eye contact and smiled. The two men were exposed and defenseless. It was over.

That was until John's expression changed drastically.

"Behind you!" he shouted.

Margot gasped when she felt a heavy hand on her head, followed by a blunt dagger pressing against her neck. She had failed to see the old man hiding behind the shrubs next to the barn. From the corner of her eye she could see his long grey hair falling over her shoulder, as he spoke into her ear.

"I'm afraid it *is* certain death, my dearest," he said. "But for *you*."

Margot dropped the blade and sighed.

"*Damn* it all to hells," she said. "*So* bloody close…"

The old man lowered his dagger gently, his lips curving into a grin. As usual, his faithful companion stood at his shoulder, a one-eyed crow with tattered wings and a hefty appetite. "Certainly close, my child. But even '*close*' can get you killed," the old man said, and then gave John a glance. "And besides… You cheated."

Margot smiled. "Actually it was *Melvyn* who asked John for help. *I* kept quiet."

"Did *not*!" Melvyn argued, to which his sister replied by sticking her tongue out.

John put his blade away and held a hand out for Larz. "Sorry about the whole door thing."

Once on his feet, Larz began moving his arm in circles, holding on to his shoulder with an expression of pain on his face. "You should be, you reckless bum. It was a tad bit overdramatic," he said, before clearing his throat and frowning. "But also… I'm sorry 'bout the cut. You alright?"

"John Huxley," said Old Man Beckwit as he walked over with his cane. "Too eager to wait for your turn, eh? Meddling into your brother and sister's training won't help *them* a bit, y'know?"

"Ask your goons who stumbled into whose cabin," John said, grinning as if the whole thing had been no more than a messy card game. He was already tearing a piece of cloth from an old shirt he'd hung at the entrance of his barn, using it to wrap his forearm and stop the bleeding.

"So how'd we do, Mister Beckwit?" Melvyn tugged at the old man's robe.

"It took 'em nearly an hour to find us," said Margot as she cleaned the mud from her boots. "And did you see how *fast* I was running, Mister Beckwit?" young Margot asked.

The old man chuckled as he fed his crow a handful of breadcrumbs. "Sure did," he said. "You've gotten faster, that's for certain. We still caught you in less than an hour, though."

"Yes, but *nearly* an hour!"

"Still less."

* * *

An iron pot hung over the fire, casting clouds of grey vapor into the air as the water came to a boil. A woman scooped a mugfull out of it; her hand was so rough and callused that she hardly felt the sting of the heat anymore, hadn't for several decades now.

She sprinkled in a handful of leaves from her garden, stirring it into a tea, as she rubbed her eyelids and yawned. Her black hair was a tangled mess and she wore the same shabby blue housedress that she'd worn for the past two days.

Another day's labor awaits, she told herself, and then sipped from her tea as if it were laced with red spindle.

Her name was Adelina Huxley, and she was the keeper of the largest farm in Elbon.

She was a kind woman with an immeasurable heart, rather soft-spoken and timid, the type of person that would blend into the shadows and remain unnoticed to a stranger. But those that knew her well knew that she was not one to be messed with, for the woman hid within herself a deep inner fury. The only unmarried woman in Elbon, she was, and she was fiercer than a wolf mother when it came to caring for her pups.

Don't mess with Mother Huxley, they'd say. *She may look feeble... but she'll gut you if you mess with her children.*

And it was certainly true... When it came to the safety of her young ones, no act was too cruel for her. Her children were like treasure, and the woman's love for them knew no bounds. They were, after all, the only thing she had left in the world, other than her farm. Her husband had been taken by a fever, and for several months after that she was known as the Huxley Widow. That was, of course, until that fateful winter's night when a group of bandits from the southern hills tried to invade the farm.

The story said that Adelina had seen them coming from a distance, and so she dragged her children into their humble little cottage and they barred themselves in. The bandits, stubborn as they were, had tried to force their way in. There were six of them.

Adelina Huxley killed every single one, with every failed attempt of theirs to break inside. She had used a hatchet, a few sharp nails, a pot of boiling stew, and a couple of kitchen knives. They say it took but one hour before all six raiders were lying dead somewhere in the surrounding yard.

All six were killed. Not a single one made it inside their home. She'd fought to keep her family safe and she'd fought to the death. And from then on, nobody ever called her the Huxley Widow again.

John was the eldest of four.

There was his sister Robyn who, at the young age of 17, was a daring and courageous soul. Having only been 7 when she held a knife in her hand to help her brother and mother fight off the bandits, she had grown up with very little fear and an unmatched loyalty for those dearest to her, the kind of girl that wouldn't hesitate to protect a pet ferret from a junglecat should the moment call for it. All she ever needed was her bow and a handful of arrows. Her beloved bow, which she had made out of the branch of an old elven tree from the city of Kahrr five winters past, was the most precious thing she owned and with it she felt invincible. It was her brother John that had taken her to Kahrr with him, and it was he that helped her carve the bow, which she decided to name *Spirit*. It was the first and last time she had traveled so far from home.

The youngest of the Huxleys were the twins Margot and Melvyn who, even at their age, had an unmatched thirst for knowledge. So intelligent, they were, they could outwit even some of the adults in Elbon. In fact, Adelina swore that if the twins one day learned to read, their tongues would be nearly as dangerous as Baryn Lawe's, the mad preacher of Val Havyn. The Huxleys were not by any means wealthy, but Adelina made sure they never had to skip a single meal. She'd raised her children on her own and she'd taught them to survive; taught them that even in the darkest moments, there was always hope, it took only a little effort to find it.

John approached the cottage that morning, after his squabble in the barn, only to find his mother hauling a pile of vegetable sacks onto a wooden cart tied to their finest mule.

"There you are," she said to him. "What was that?"

"What was *what?*"

"You know what. The clutter."

"Oh 'twas nothing," he kissed his mother in the cheek and took the vegetable sacks from her arms, then proceeded to do the hauling himself. "Just a littl' bat scaring the horses," he lied.

She glanced at his bandaged arm. "A bat did *that?*"

John shrugged and attempted a smile, but his mother was not very pleased.

"When will you learn to leave that wretched blade of yours alone?" she asked, her eyes full of worry. "It's gotten you into enough trouble."

"Nothing wrong with learning to use one," he insisted. "Besides, it was only Larz and Henrik. They couldn't hurt a wounded sheep if they tried."

"Someday, John," she said, shaking her head in subtle disappointment. "Someday, you'll find yourself crossing blades with someone who won't play as nice as Larz and Henrik."

"I'm sure I will," he hauled the last of the sacks. "Which is why it's best to prepare, yes?"

Adelina crossed her arms, unamused. Truthfully she was thankful for the guidance that Mister Beckwit gave her children when it came to self-defense. She only wished her eldest wasn't so bloody reckless. "I need you to haul the produce into the city this morning," she said to him.

"Is it *my* turn?"

"It isn't. But your sister Robyn's refusing to wake and help. One of these mornings, she'll be waking up to a bucket of ice water and gods know I've warned her far too many times."

"I'd say give it 5 minutes and if she doesn't wake, give it a go," he said in a teasing manner.

"Go on now. We'll be working late today, it looks like," she said as she went and fetched a wheelbarrow. "If we don't get these crops out now, the rodents will get to them first."

The young farmer gathered his things and prepared to leave for the city.

"And John?" his mother called. "Leave that cursed blade of yours here, will you?"

* * *

Val Havyn was a city of great reputation and even greater beauty. Every street was made of cobblestones. Every dwelling was made of stone and wood, painted white, with red bricks lining every roof, and cleverly designed lanterns hanging from every corner of every street.

It was like stepping into an entirely different world for John Huxley. He left his mule and cart tied in the usual stable by the city gates. Before walking away from it, however, he noticed a parchment nailed to the wall of the stable with the word '*Wanted*' painted in red. Below it was the black and white portrait of a mysterious-looking man with long wavy hair, a black hat with a rim, and a pair of unfriendly eyes.

Another wanted thief, John thought, and shrugged it off, seeing as no wanted man in their right mind would step foot in such a distinguished city.

And so, as he walked through the lively streets, John took in the fresh air and the daily sights the city had to offer. It was a tendency that he told no one about and yet his mind couldn't help but yield to it. As leisurely as could possibly appear, John observed.

A woman selling fried sweetened dough in the corner of a traffic circle, across from which an elderly puppeteer staged shows for bystanders, children, and vagabonds.

A dog pacing and sniffing the ground near a vegetable stand where there sat a woman with a sea-colored dress drinking a cup of hot tea spiked with rum.

A merchant selling blankets shouting his lungs away into the ears of onlookers, tourists, and peasants going about their day.

A boy carrying a basket of baked goods, who may or may not have been having a shouting contest with the blanket merchant.

By the time John finally reached the crossroad where there stood the old but well-admired Nottley's Tavern, he had seen four dogs, nine children, a knight eating a fried pig's foot, a woman chopping firewood, three men that *all* swore their venison meat was the best in the city, and six peasants that claimed to have been robbed and needed 10 coppers for a carriage ride back to their village; a request John found absurd, considering carriage rides never costed more than 5 coppers.

Nottley's Tavern was on the corner of Dreary Lane and another street whose name John never made a note to remember. Dreary Lane was known for being a street in which sellswords and mercenaries, thirsty for a good fight, would loiter with hopes of being hired for a job, typically by a tourist in need of protection or a merchant looking for an escort off to a place where they probably shouldn't be eyeing to begin with.

Any time John traveled to the tavern, his mind was elsewhere reminiscing on the countless moments in which his father would make the same comment about the notorious Dreary Lane and how though it was tied to a certain reputation, it was in reality named after a man known as Patryk Dreary who was merely the proprietor of every business in that particular block about a century prior.

It was nearing noon when John walked through the tavern doors and already there were herds of men staggering about with a pint of ale in their hands. It was hard to construe who had recently arrived and who was still there from the previous night.

"Good day, Mister Nottley," John said to the man behind the wooden counter.

"Is it now?" replied Nottley.

John placed the brown sack of vegetables on the counter with a smile. "Delivery for you."

Nottley took a peek inside, so as to inspect there was nothing missing. He then looked up at John with an unfriendly glare and said, "Tell Missus Huxley I'll pay her in a couple o' days."

"Oh… I'm sorry," John cleared his throat as he took a moment to find the proper words. "But we can't really allow that… We require payment up front."

Nottley continued to clean his silverware, as if John was no longer there.

There was a loud burp. It had come from a man sitting at the bar, a few feet away from John, gulping down the last of his ale. The man had on a long fading grey coat and a black hat with a jaggedly round rim, covering up his unkempt grey hair and thick, bushy beard.

John cleared his throat, reminding Nottley of his presence.

"Mister Nottley," he called. "I said we require immediate payment for a share of crops…"

Nottley looked back up at John. "I heard you the first time, lad," he said. "And *I* said to tell your mother I will pay her soon."

There was a loud tap. The very obviously inebriated grey man nearby slid his cup over to Mister Nottley, who was able to catch it just in time before it fell off the edge of the bar. "One more," the man said, and John could smell the foul stench coming from his breath.

"You sure you have the coin to pay for it?" asked Nottley.

"I said one more, mate."

John took the opportunity to reach for the bag of vegetables still sitting on the bar. But before he could retrieve it, Mister Nottley slammed his hand down and held on tightly to the brown cloth. At that same moment, a lanky young man approached the bar. He had short fuzzy brown hair and was dressed in raggedy brown clothing and an apron tied around his waist.

"We have a bit of a situation, sir," the young man said to his warden. "Mister Rodrick just vomited all over himself. Whole corner reeks like rotten pork now. At least I *believe* it was pork…"

"Then take care of it," Mister Nottley responded with a glare so sharp, it made John wonder whether the man would have slapped the lad had it not been for the crowds in the tavern.

"I will, sir. But he claims it was the duck we served him that made 'im sick."

"Bloody hell, boy…"

"I *know*, I thought the same. How *could* it be when it so obviously smells like pork?"

"Get out of my bloody sight!" Nottley snapped at him. By then, the man may as well have been shouting.

"R-Right," the young man stuttered. "Morning, John."

"Morning, Cedric," the farmer said, before the boy scurried off with a wet towel in hand.

Suddenly, John preferred the smell of the grey man's breath to that of the approaching fumes of the Rodrick man's vomit.

The boy's right, John thought silently. *The rotten fumes do have a more pork-like scent.*

The boy known as Cedric was an orphan that Mister Nottley had taken in as his ward. Cedric thought very highly of his warden, with him having been the only guidance the boy had while growing up. He was lodged in the basement of the tavern, and worked as a servant to the clientele, consisting mostly of merchants and beggars who made enough for a pint of ale. Cedric didn't know his age and Nottley cared far too little to keep track, but the young man was in his late teenage years and his innocence and naivety unquestionably showed it. His warped, chipped front tooth, along with the brown scar running down the left side of his lip and chin were evidence that the lad had faced his own deal of troubles in his short life. That, or his guardian was keen on physical discipline when there was liquor involved.

"Anything else I can help you with?" Nottley asked John, who remained insistent that he wouldn't leave without payment. He was prepared to confront the old tavern keeper, but not the loyal crowds surrounding them. And the fact that he had left his blade at home did not help either.

"You know," the grey drunken man sitting at the bar spoke suddenly, breaking the silence. "You ought to just *pay* the boy…"

As the man sat up in his stool, Mister Nottley and John glanced at him; there was both bafflement and a slight but very noticeable awe in the tavern keeper's eyes.

"*You* ought to mind your own business, you old bum," Nottley said. Two very obviously inebriated men suddenly approached the bar, standing over the shoulders of the grey man.

"A problem, Mister Nottley?" one asked, his breath far worse than the grey man's.

"None at all," Nottley replied. "Seems like the man's had enough, that's all."

"You heard the boss," one of the drunks placed a heavy hand on the grey man's shoulder. "Pay up what you owe 'n' get goin'."

There was a long pause, as the grey man looked up at Mister Nottley. Cedric watched from a distance, nervous that his guardian would release his anger on him, should anything in the tavern become damaged. In fact, by then, many eyes around the tavern were looking in their direction. John wondered whether it was wise to make an attempt for the bag again and walk out. It wouldn't have mattered to him if he didn't need the money for the week's supplies.

When he finally decided to reach for it, he was startled by the sound of wood screeching against wood. The grey man stood up from his stool, causing it to slide back as he struggled to stand straight from the many pints of ale he'd consumed.

"I decide when I've had me share," said the grey man, with a threatening expression on his face. "Now I asked you to serv-"

He was silenced by a glass bottle shattering against his skull. He fell unconsciously on the wooden floor, right upon the feet of a large, heavily-built man in his forties, with a dark complexion to his skin and short bushy black hair on his scalp. His name was Thaddeus Rexx and he was a blacksmith in the city.

After a brief silence, Mister Nottley gave him a nod. "Thank you, Thaddeus…"

Thaddeus Rexx nodded back. "Not in the mood for a riot this morning," he said, throwing what was left of the broken bottle of whisky on the floor and walking back to his table. He was a rather intimidating man, and while he had no friends nor any particular alliance to Mister Nottley, he did share a bond with the orphaned Cedric.

Nottley stood there silently for a moment, part of him envious that his moment was stolen. "Cedric!" he shouted across the room. "Clean up this mess."

"We'll drag 'im out of here for a pint of ale each," one of the drunken men said.

"No," Nottley grunted.

"*Half* a pint each?"

"Done."

They began by emptying the grey man's pockets. Then, one of them pulled out a brown coinpurse and threw it at the tavern keeper before dragging the old man's unconscious body out of the tavern doors. Nottley pulled 5 coppers from the stolen purse and tossed them at John.

"Now get the hell out of here," he said, and John obeyed.

The young farmer couldn't help but feel a shred of guilt upon seeing the two drunks landing continuous punches on the old man just outside the tavern.

"For your sake, we best not see your face in Mister Nottley's tavern again," one of them spit on the beaten man's back before heading back inside. The old man had by then regained some consciousness and despite his age, he appeared to have taken the punches rather lightly.

John should have helped, and he knew it. The remorse in his chest urged him to approach the man, now lying filthy in a puddle of mud and feces near a row of horses that had been tied up for a rest.

"Are you all right, sir?" John leaned in nervously.

The old grey man lifted himself to his knees, spitting out chunks of blood.

"Just taking a rest," he said with a chuckle.

John held out his hand to help the man up, but he refused to take it. He simply remained there on his knees, chuckling softly like a madman. Then, with a surprising amount of energy, the man leapt to his feet and gave his neck a good crack.

"Bloody hells," he groaned, and then stretched his arms up until they also cracked. "Ahh, that's the spot."

Unsure of how to react, John eyed the man up and down. He looked like a typical vagabond and he smelled like one too. But there was something peculiar about the man, something that wasn't entirely clear at first glance. "You took quite a beating there, friend," John said to him. "I thank you for what you did back there."

"Didn't do it for you," said the man, chuckling once again. He removed the hat gently from his head and set it down. Then he gripped the grey hair on his head and gave it a good yank, pulling it right off. John was stunned for a moment.

A tumble of black wavy hair fell onto the man's shoulders. And with the same approach, the man pulled off his feathery grey beard, revealing a thin layer of black scruff on his cheeks and jaw. It was as if he had shed off thirty years of age in a matter of seconds. He turned his grey coat inside out to reveal the black leather lining on the inside, clearly sewn on that way purposely.

He had transformed himself into a completely different man, no older than thirty. Looking back at John, with a bleeding lip and a swollen eye, the man held out his arms at his sides as if presenting his final appearance and asked, "How's it look, mate?"

The man had a particularly suave accent and a voice that was moderately deep but with a sharp edge to it, which seemed to fit perfectly with his provokingly mischievous manner. "Thought I'd switch it up a bit," he said. "The 'old man' get-up was starting to itch something awful."

John knew he had seen that face before, though he didn't quite remember when or where. The swelling from the beating the man took had perhaps made him harder to recognize. And so John stood there in awe, as he watched the man in black fade away into the city streets.

Val Havyn had many blacksmiths, but only two worth remembering.

One of them was Thaddeus Rexx, who was a skilled yet rather unmotivated man, the type who'd settled with something he was good at rather than something he *loved*. Having never had a family of his own, he made his living by day and spent nearly every evening drowning in ale at Nottley's Tavern.

The second blacksmith most renowned, mainly by merchants, was an older gentleman of lesser status. His weapons and armor were molded from the finest iron and steel and handled with such care, for which he was well compensated. His name was Willem Amberhill, and he was a good man. But life hadn't been too kind to him, and after having nearly died during the Plague of Red Tears, he had grown weaker and more prone to disease over the years. He had three daughters and a son who was killed by bandits on the outskirts of the city many years past.

Evellyn Amberhill, at 23 years of age, was his eldest daughter.

She loved her father dearly and she admired the care he would put into his work. Since she was a girl, she admired his work and assisted him in any safe way possible. It was not until the day she burned her left hand with a scorching hot blade that she heard him raise his voice for the first time.

"I told you never to touch anything!" he had said. "You don't know what you're doing!"

But, as clever as the girl was, she responded with, "Then *show* me how…"

The man was blinded by pride at the time. His son, who was expected to continue his legacy, died before learning to craft anything, not that the boy ever cared. And so eventually, the girl's persistence won her father over.

By the age of 13, Evellyn Amberhill could forge her own daggers.

By 15, it was gauntlets and boots. And by the time she was 18, Evellyn and her father could garner merchandise at twice the usual rate, for there was nothing the woman couldn't craft or find a way *to* craft.

However, fate would not be so kind to the Amberhill family.

The old man had recently fallen ill and business had slowed once again. There was no mother, at least not anymore; the Plague of Red Tears had taken her. The middle sister, whose name remained unspoken in the Amberhill home, had run away with some squire boy at 15 and was never heard from again. And Alycia, the youngest of the sisters, ran the household and tended to their father's care, while Evellyn worked day after day to provide for them.

On this particular sunlit day, John Huxley approached the Amberhill household with a far too obviously eager expression on his face and a sack of assorted vegetables tugged under his arm. From several blocks away, one could hear the high-pitched echoing stings of hot iron being struck. Evellyn held a wielding hammer in her right hand and was smashing it against what looked like the roots of a soon-to-be elegant chest armor. Sparks flew out of the scorching hot plate with every powerful strike. With her back towards the street, she did not see the farmer standing there, straightening himself up somewhat nervously.

"Hello there," he called out.

Evellyn had the hammer in midair when she turned her head and saw him. There was a hint of surprise in her eyes. "John!" she said, as the hammer slipped from her hand and onto the wielding table.

"Good day, Missus Amberhill," John said with a smile and a head bow.

"*Tiring*, yes. Good? That remains to be seen," Evellyn said, wiping the sweat from her forehead. She smiled back at John, and there was that usual shade of red rushing to her cheeks, which she would often blame on irritation from standing too close to the fire.

"Any day is good when blessed by your company, Evellyn," John said.

Evellyn chuckled as she struggled to maintain eye contact. She removed the pin that was keeping her hair out of her face, and down it came, a tumble of red waves that reached her waist. Her fair skin was stained grey with charcoal residue and she smelled of both iron and lilies all at once. John couldn't help but lose himself in her luminous green eyes; the only part of her that glistened in the daylight while the rest of her was tainted by that hard morning's labor.

"You're too kind," she said.

"Is your father home?" he smiled. "I've got some vegetables from this week's harvest for him." he held out the brown bag in front of him. A silence followed. Evellyn looked down again, though this time in a way that expressed a trace of discomfort and perhaps even shame.

"What's wrong? Does he hate potatoes?"

"No, it's not that," Evellyn muttered, smiling only for a moment. "I don't think we can purchase anything this week, John… Business has slowed since father's been ill, and… well…"

John raised the clip that held the small wooden gate in place and allowed himself into the welding yard. "That's not a problem," he said.

"No, John," she tried to protest.

"It's really quite all right."

"No, we can't take it. We'll simply skip this week."

"Don't be silly."

"John, don't," she said, standing in between him and the door to their cottage.

The young farmer had known the blacksmith's daughter all his life. When they were children, John would travel into the city with his father, hoping to see her if only for a mere moment, and for endless spring and summer days, the city streets were their playground. When she was alive, Evellyn's mother would often pay Adelina Huxley a visit, and young Evellyn would hop in excitement as she and John would lose themselves in the green fields, using wooden sticks as swords and fighting like knights.

Every moment John looked into her eyes, he saw the same girl he'd known his whole life. And Evellyn, in return, saw the same in him. Their mothers would often mention the possibility of joining their houses by marrying the two. After the deaths of John's father and Evellyn's mother, however, the connection between the two families was somewhat lost. All they had left now was this. Occasional encounters, brief conversations, and a lifetime of memories long forgotten.

"Fine," John said. "How about you take this now and pay us when you can?"

Another silence. Evellyn wiped her hands with a wet rag and moved away, allowing John to enter the cottage. She couldn't help but watch him as he made his way inside. He was a good man, she knew. Had fate not been so ill to them, he would have made a good husband. Part of her did not wish to lose the friendship they'd built over the years, and yet another part of her knew that there were not many good people left in Vallenghard… but John Huxley was certainly one of the few good ones.

The young farmer set the bag on a wooden nightstand next to the bed where Willem Amberhill rested. His youngest daughter, Alycia, sat nearby. "He just fell asleep again," she said.

"That's all right," John kneeled in front of the chair and spoke softly, so as to not allow Evellyn to hear. Little did the farmer know that Evellyn was standing close to the doorway right outside the room. John reached into his pockets and pulled out 5 coppers, the very same coins that Mister Nottley had paid him, and wrapped them in Alycia's hands.

"Take this and purchase some aloe root from the apothecary on Merchants' Square," he said. "A nice tea and he'll feel much better in no time, you'll see."

Outside, Evellyn waited.

John Huxley walked past her on his way out and said, "Until next time, Missus Amberhill."

"John?" she called out. He turned, but before he could speak she threw her arms around him and held him tightly. As her red hair brushed against the thin layer of stubble on his face, he caught the scent of lilies that he had always known her to have, and he couldn't help but embrace her back. They held on for a few moments longer.

"Thank you," she said.

* * *

"Burn the harlot!" shouted a middle-aged man with either a heavy Halghardian accent or plenty of missing teeth.

"Slice her head off!" yelled another.

"Throw her in a ditch!"

A herd of peasants moved in unison toward the wooden platform of the gallows near the city gates. John Huxley was on his way back to his cart when his eye caught the bundle of wavy raven-colored hair being pushed through the crowd towards the steps. People were throwing garbage and spitting on the woman, who remained helpless and held down by ropes at her wrists.

Among the crowd, a young boy carrying a large basket of baked goods was fighting to keep his balance; he was pushed back by an old man that rushed to the scene as if someone was giving away free samples of liqueur. John was able to catch the boy in time before he dropped his basket.

"S-Sorry sir!" the boy said nervously.

"Careful now," said John. "What is happening here?"

"A witch, sir," said the boy, his eyes wide and eager. "The Davenport brothers just got back from a trade in the city of Wyrmwood. They found her resting place not too far from 'ere. She was practicing dark magic…"

"Was she?"

"That's what they said, at least."

John had not encountered many witches in his life. He had encountered none, for that matter, but had seen mere portraits of wanted witches posted around the villages and cities where he had traveled to in his short life. He watched in awe as they brought the woman up to the wooden stand. Much to his surprise, she was a woman who couldn't have been older than 30. Her dark hair was greasy and slightly tangled, and the choppy ends stopped right at her chest. She was pale and her eyes radiated, even from afar, the color of a warm autumn sunset. She had on a raggedy dress the color of smoke, with traces of crimson red cloth patching up a few tears.

"She doesn't look much like a witch," John said.

"That's what makes 'em dangerous," said the boy, as he looked up at John.

"Have I seen you before, sir?"

"You may have," John said, keeping his eyes locked on the witch.

A middle-aged man stepped up to the wooden platform, where the Davenport brothers were holding down the witch by both arms; her hands were wrapped in what looked like brown leather, with rope holding said leather in place.

"What's that on her hands?" John asked the boy.

"That there's ogre skin," the boy replied, and it was clear that it gave him great pleasure to be able to relay the knowledge to an adult. "Ogres are immune to dark magic, ye see? That's why witches kept them as slaves during the Great War. An ogre's skin will keep a witch from using any magic, they say."

The middle-aged man on the wooden platform raised both his hands into the air, urging the citizens to lower their voices. John recognized him immediately. The man was known throughout the city as a prophet of the Gods, more specifically the god of humankind. Many had even said he could perform miracles. His name was Baryn Lawe. He was dressed in grey robes and wore a phony smile that conveyed his pride and vanity, to an extent that John couldn't help but scowl at the sight of him.

"My fellow Val Havyans," the false prophet shouted, and almost immediately folks were clapping and cheering him on.

"*Val Havyans?*" John grunted, soft enough to not attract attention. "Since when is *that* a proper term?"

"I don't like him a bit," the boy frowned.

"I can't say I blame you very much."

Baryn Lawe paced around the platform, soaking in the attention of the citizens the way he always did on such public displays. "This woman that stands here before us… has been accused of practicing witchcraft on our kingdom grounds."

The peasants began ranting once again, yelling insults and spitting at the ground so as to demonstrate their hatred towards the witch, who was so frightened and distressed that her left eye started twitching.

John said nothing, but continued to watch in astonishment.

Baryn Lawe raised his arms once more. The villagers slowed to a silence. The man knew plenty of tricks, John gave him that much. He knew the appropriate tone of voice to use and when exactly to pause for a more dramatic effect; a trick he often overused and yet no peasant doubted.

"The question here remains!" Baryn continued. "Shall we surrender this atrocious beast to the king's royal guard… allowing for the possibility of their mercy?"

The villagers shouted their insults once more.

"Will we allow this monster to walk freely, endangering the lives of our children?!"

More shouts echoed throughout the city. The crowd started to grow, as more citizens scattered into the scene from their homes.

"What exactly, I ask you today, should we do with this monstrous being?!" Baryn shouted at the crowds, who responded with only more anger and disgust.

John felt a knot building at his throat. "They're not going to kill her, are they?"

"You're surely not from around here, are you?" the boy responded.

Baryn Lawe turned to the Davenport brothers. He made brief eye contact with the witch, who kept a stern look of both hatred and sorrow and said not a single word. Her left eye, however, couldn't avoid that nervous twitch.

"The people have spoken," Baryn said. "Hang the witch…"

The crowd shouted in a false sense of triumph. John Huxley did not pretend to know what justice was, but he was sure this was not it. The Davenport brothers dragged the witch towards the noose and wrapped it around her neck. She had a terror in her eyes as she looked at the mad crowd, begging them for mercy.

"We've got to do something," John said, wishing he hadn't left his blade at home.

"Careful, sir," the boy held John back by the arm. "You don't want to anger them more."

And so John could do nothing but watch in agony. He longed for the courage to stop the repulsive citizens from murdering the innocent woman. He could hardly stand to watch, as the noose was tightened and the brothers gave Baryn the signal that she was ready for the hanging.

"For the good of our kingdom," the mad preacher said, as he gripped the handle that would release the wooden vent under the witch's feet.

Suddenly, there was a loud drumming sound that echoed from afar. The citizens turned, almost in unison, as a pair of guards announced an incoming presence at the city gates. Even Baryn Lawe stopped in his tracks, though John guessed it was mostly due to his loss of attention. There was a long silence; the only sounds in the air were that of iron-plated boots marching on the cobblestones.

Then, a majestic figure stepped through the gates; a knight in bright silver armor riding atop his white horse as he led a small squadron of soldiers into the city. Every pair of eyes in the crowd was locked on him. He held his helmet at his side as he rode silently towards the scene.

"That man there is S-"

"I know who he is," John interrupted the whispering boy. "Sir Viktor Crowley, the knight commander of the royal guard."

Even the young witch had her eyes locked on the knight, her entire body trembling as the noose itched at her neck.

Sir Viktor Crowley held his head up high. His golden wheat-colored hair was slicked back, just reaching the back of his neck. His face was clean-shaven, and though he had a few scars here and there, the image of him was as regal as they came. A less impressive knight rode beside him, a husky man with short brown hair and a beard that was too patchy to be striking. His name was Sir Jossiah Biggs, and he was another knight of the king's court.

They rode into the square, their confused eyes locked on the gallows and the woman standing on them, wrapped in the noose.

"What is the meaning of this?" asked Sir Jossiah Biggs.

The crowd was silent, as if expecting the mad preacher to answer for them all.

"Sir, it is an honor to be blessed with your presence," Baryn bowed at the sight of the golden knight Sir Viktor Crowley, ignoring Sir Biggs's less majestic poise.

"You were asked a question, peasant," Biggs snarled at Baryn.

"Pardon me, sir," the preacher said. "This wretched woman was caught red-handed in her resting place practicing the dark arts." The crowd began ranting once more, cheering for their elected representative.

"And who might you be?" Sir Biggs asked.

"I'm Baryn Lawe, sir. I stand here before you, representing the people of Val Havyn. This murderous wench is guil-"

"We heard you, Mister Lawe," Biggs interrupted again. "And in what way, may I ask, were you granted the authority to make such judgment?"

"I have the authority of our god, sir. Surely you must understand that in cases such as these, when the safety of our civilians and their children are in danger, we must take necessary precautions to ensure that these murderous beasts will not bring harm to our city."

"Has the King been informed of such matters, Mister Lawe?"

The preacher chuckled derisively. "Surely we mustn't bother his majesty with such harebrained matters. Nonetheless, the word of our god speaks above any laws set forth by men. Therefore, I believe it necessary to ac-"

"Pardon me...?" a smooth yet powerful voice asked.

Baryn Lawe froze where he stood. There was the sound of steel-studded boots hitting the cobblestones as Sir Viktor Crowley stepped off his horse, followed by a long silence. The knight handed his helmet to Jossiah Biggs, who was his second-in-command.

"What did you just say...?"

Baryn felt the sweat build at his temples. "I-I said... We mustn't bother his majesty with..."

"No..." Viktor interrupted him, pacing towards him. "*After* that."

Baryn struggled to speak as Viktor took slow steps towards the wooden platform. From afar, John noticed the golden crest imprinted on the back of the knight's armor. The crest was that of an eagle with its wings spread open as if preparing to take flight.

"Pardon me, sir," Baryn said. "I did not mean to offend."

"He asked you to repeat yourself," Sir Jossiah Biggs spoke, still atop his own horse.

Baryn gulped with anxiety before turning his gaze down with shame. Then he opened his shivering mouth and said, "I was merely speaking for our god, sir... Forgive me..."

Sir Viktor Crowley walked up the steps and unsheathed his sword as he approached Baryn. He held the tip of it a mere centimeter away from the preacher's chin.

"Listen here... Mister Baryn Lawe," Viktor spoke slowly, with a stern and hardening tone. "Never spit on our king's name in my presence again." They locked eyes for a mere moment, before Baryn could no longer hold his gaze and shut his eyes, his jaw still trembling anxiously. Viktor removed his sword from Baryn's jaw and turned his gaze to the young witch. Many had known the knight to be a man of trivial pride, yet he was revered as a heroic figure, not only among the citizens, but all throughout the realms of Gravenstone. Where there was a threat to its people, Viktor Crowley was there. And though his egotism had rendered him vain at times, there was no doubt that the man had honor and stood for justice above all else.

"The witch will come with us," Viktor said, sliding his sword back into place. "She will be held on trial before the king's court." He gazed back at Baryn Lawe before finishing his verdict, "...the *proper* way."

The crowd began to disperse. The young witch was relieved from the tightness of the noose and was lifted onto the saddle of Sir Jossiah Biggs's horse.

Viktor Crowley leapt back onto his white stallion and began to ride away, leading the soldiers to the king's palace, leaving the people behind to whisper and gossip about what they'd just witnessed. John Huxley couldn't keep his eyes off Viktor; to him, that was the man he wanted to someday become.

"That man is a legend," the boy spoke again.

"That he is," John said with a smile of wonder.

"Why do you suppose they call him the Golden Eagle?"

"Well... Not many have witnessed it," John said. "But those that did say that many winters ago, a dragon from the great plains of Belmoor made its way to Merrymont once while the king was there on duty. Viktor was a mere inexperienced soldier at the time. The dragon was destroying everything around it, including the Lord's castle. There was very little hope the city would stand, and therefore the guards were transporting our king away when the dragon caught sight of them. Viktor was almost 20 meters high above the western tower when he saw the beast below..."

"Did he shoot at it?" the boy asked.

"There was no time to shoot at it... He jumped from the tower with his sword unsheathed. At that height, no man could have survived that jump… But Viktor Crowley did… He soared through the air and landed right on the dragon's head. The blade pierced through its skull, killing it instantly."

The two of them watched Sir Viktor Crowley ride away in admiration.

"Someday, I want to be a knight," the boy said.

John smiled warmly down at him, for it was a dream they both shared.

"Perhaps you will," he said. "What was your name, kid?"

"Thomlin, sir."

"John Huxley," the farmer replied, shaking the boy's hand. "'Til we meet again."

* * *

"Focus," said Old Man Beckwit.

Robyn Huxley's hand trembled as it gripped the leathered handle on her wooden bow. She held on firmly to the arrow with her right hand as she felt the tight string digging into the flesh in her fingers. One of her eyes was closed; the other was locked on the wooden stand where her brother John had painted a round black target.

"Don't shiver," the old man whispered.

She obeyed.

With a loud exhale she let go of the string and scowled at the sight of her arrow piercing through the wood almost a foot away from the center of the target.

"Now," the old man sighed, pacing back and forth around her. "Where do you suppose you went wrong?"

"I let go of the arrow too quickly," she said, looking down in disappointment.

"Wrong," he replied. "In fact you held onto it for far too long. Anyone trying to kill you would have done it long before you shot it. Anything else?"

"My stance was wrong?" asked the young woman.

"Are you asking me or are you answering?"

"I'm answering."

"Your stance was fine. Anything else?"

Young Robyn considered it for a moment, while Mister Beckwit continued moving slowly in circles around her. She had always wondered why the old man would insist on pacing when he used a cane, though she found it too rude to ask. Mister Beckwit's loyal crow was resting on the wooden fence nearby, squawking at her every mistake as if it was laughing at her.

"All right, I know what it was," she finally said. "I had an eye shut."

"Did you?" the old man asked. "I didn't notice. In that case, you did *two* things wrong."

Robyn groaned with frustration. "What was it, then?"

"It's simple," he said, before coming to a halt at her side. "You doubted yourself."

The old crow suddenly wailed and flew over to Mister Beckwit's shoulder. In secret, Robyn hated that bird. More so, she hated how it seemed to only coo towards her or when in agreement with its master, as if having a conscience of its own. She found it oddly startling.

She also found it intriguing, however, to see a crow with only one eye. Not only was it missing, but there was a scar running vertically across the eyelid and down to the crow's feathery cheek as if someone had sliced it with a blade. Often she tried to imagine how the crow could have gotten such a scar, but once again she found it too rude to ask.

"But I've hit the target before," Robyn said. "I *know* I can do it. I'm just tired, that's all."

"Is that so?" Mister Beckwit asked. He reached down and dug through his rucksack. His black crow stood vigilant, as if anxiously waiting to see what its master would do next. Mister Beckwit pulled out two small sacks and held them close to his chest as he limped back towards young Robyn.

"I want you to hit these sandbags now," he said. "*While* they're in the air."

"But I-"

"But nothing. You said you've got it. If that's the case, let's make it more interesting, yes?" The old man threw the first sandbag up into the air. Robyn swore she had it, but the arrow missed by about a foot.

She pulled out another arrow. Mister Beckwit allowed her a brief moment before throwing the second bag. When she missed again she threw the wooden bow angrily onto the dirt.

She couldn't help but turn and look at it when it hit the ground, as she did every time she tossed it angrily somewhere. Her sister Margot, lively as she was, called out the glance once and Robyn had said it was to check it wouldn't hit someone or tip something over. In reality it was because young Robyn regretted every time she threw the bow and glanced with hopes that it wouldn't break.

She turned to the old man, the resentment clear in her eyes.

"Now what did you learn there?" he asked her.

"You don't have to humiliate me," she scowled at him.

Odd as it seemed, she wasn't nearly as angry about the sandbags as she was at the fact that if it hadn't been for the old man, she wouldn't have tossed her bow.

"Why of course not, young Robyn," Mister Beckwit said. "I'm simply trying to show you what you fail to see. Any old fool can learn to hit a still target with practice; it'll take 'em a week or two at most. But when you shoot to kill, or to save your own life... why that is a whole new thing altogether, my dear. You'll find that you don't shoot where the target currently *is*. By the time your little arrow hits that spot, it will be there no more. You must aim for the spot where your target is *heading* to."

Young Robyn said nothing. She gave his words a moment's thought before picking up her beloved elven bow *Spirit*.

"You've got spirit, young Robyn," the old man said.

"I know," she smirked, wondering if the old man had caught on to the irony.

"It's as clear as day, it is," he went on. "But your greatest weakness is your doubt, girl. You can have doubt in many things, but let it *never* be in yourself."

He paused as he heard the incoming sounds of a mule and carriage.

"Speaking of self-doubt," the old man spoke softly, just loud enough for Robyn to hear. Once again the crow squealed in agreement, causing the young girl to chuckle. "Greetings, John."

"Mister Beckwit," John hopped off the cart and turned to his sister, "And the queen of sloth herself! Bit late for your training, isn't it?"

"Is it sloth if the reason you're late for training in the first place is that you were up late training on your own?" Robyn replied as she aimed another arrow at her target.

"Lazy *and* a liar. This one's promising, Mister Beckwit. Hang on to her," John teased.

Robyn's arrow struck the hard wood, only it was nowhere near the target. She turned to her brother with embarrassment and said, "Don't you dare say a word. I've got this."

Her brother kissed her forehead and hugged her, before turning to Mister Beckwit and his loyal crow.

"Brought something for this one," John said, reaching into his satchel and pulling out a small piece of cloth tied by a thick thread. He unwrapped it, reached in, and pulled out a handful of dry crickets. He held his palm out at the crow, which paid him no mind. It squeaked a few times and moved further away from John's hand, standing nearly at the edge of the old man's shoulders.

"What's the matter? Does he not like crickets?" John asked.

"Oh, he just has a hard time trusting others," Mister Beckwit replied. After allowing John to pour the dry insects back into the bag, he took it from his hands. "That's very kind of you," he said.

"Have you done your chores yet, Robyn?" John asked his sister.

"I will in a moment," young Robyn replied, aiming another arrow at her target.

"You know how mother gets, now…"

"I'll *get* to it. Just let me concentrate."

Upon gazing at the arrow a foot away from the center of the wooden target, John chuckled softly, turned to Old Man Beckwit and said, "At this pace, the wolves will have eaten *all* our sheep by the winter."

There was the swift sound of wood being struck. John, the old man, and even the crow turned their attention towards the arrow, this time sticking out only a mere inch from the center of the board. Robyn smirked and squinted her eyes. Rather than pride, the girl felt an overwhelming need to break down the boards and shoot strictly at sandbags until she never missed one again.

"Maybe not *all* your sheep," the old man said with a subtle grin, his crow once again squawking in agreement.

II
A Test of Valor

Nearly a hundred miles west of the kingdom of Vallenghard, deep in the heart of the Woodlands, a mercenary captain sat in his tent biting into a piece of half-cooked venison, slobbering all over his ragged shirt as he washed down the meat with ale. He was a large man and some could even call him intimidating, but through it all one could still see that he had the bearings of the soldier he had once been.

He was a killer, of course. But he was a killer with honor, something many of his men lacked. His most major flaw, aside from his bent nose, was the trust he gave his company; the man was oblivious to the extent of their greed. He was well aware that some of his men had joined merely to quench their dire thirst for blood, and still he tried to place his morals aside for the sake of the gold. Little did he know, however, that on this particularly misty night he would come to the most inopportune realization that his merry little band of sellswords was never *his* to begin with.

The Rogue Brotherhood, they called them; a network of mercenaries that existed for nearly a century. They hid within the Woodlands, where no civilian would dare enter, and there they raided until a company in need of numbers sought them out. Those that knew of them feared them, for the rogues cared not for who they killed, only how much they'd be paid to do it. There were nearly a hundred men in the camp that night, most of whom were resting while others kept watch, huddled near a dimly lit fire.

From a distance, an even larger company was approaching them, and when the captain's second-in-command caught sight of them he rushed to the largest tent in the camp, the only tent marked with the symbol of the Brotherhood; a red scorpion with its pincers aimed up and its sharp tail curved upwards. Every member of the Brotherhood had the same mark tattooed on his or her left wrist, and it was a mark that struck fear in the hearts of many in the realms of Gravenstone.

"A company approaches, captain," said his second-in-command.

The captain raised a brow. It was well past midnight, which meant no sane man should have been leading his troop through the Woodlands, not if he cared to keep the numbers.

"How many?" the captain asked, wiping his lips with a handkerchief.

"Two, maybe three hundred."

"Banners?"

"None, sir."

The captain rose from his seat. He left his red captain's coat by his tent's entrance, next to his weaponry, and when he walked outside the frosty night air hit his chest like a dagger. The sash he wore as a belt and the leather sheath of his dagger were the only red things in his attire. His second-in-command, on the other hand, was fully armored in thick leathers dyed a dark auburn red, the known color of the Brotherhood.

"Shall I call for reinforcements, captain?"

Through the fog, the approaching troop was merely a sea of shadows, but it was large enough that the captain grew nervous. "Gather a squadron. Tell the rest to stay on alert."

"Aye, sir."

Suddenly, the captain caught sight of the sigil… There was only one flag at the very front of the march, but one was enough to send shivers up the man's spine. The symbol was of two hands locked in a handshake, with a pair of crossed blades behind them.

"Malekai…?" the captain called nervously.

The captain's second-in-command glanced back, his hand placed on the handle of his curved blade. "Yes, sir?"

There was a look of subtle distress in the captain's eyes, as if he had seen a face from the past that he preferred had gone unseen. "Stay near my tent," he said. "And whatever happens, don't try anything unless I give the word."

"Aye, sir," Malekai said with a head nod, before the captain rushed back to his tent and started lacing his leather armor back on.

The marching troop reached the Brotherhood's camp within minutes. They were a mixture of men and orcs and perhaps a dozen goblins lounging in the back of some of the carriages. They did not wear any type of uniform, suggesting most of them had been recently recruited. The man that appeared to be leading them dismounted his horse and walked into the camp first. He was a monster of a man, thick and muscular like an orc, and though he was dressed in furs and brown leathers, he had little need for armor; his brute strength and chilling figure was enough to deem him menacing.

Malekai Pahrvus, the captain's second-in-command, was standing at the camp's entrance with ten men surrounding him, and there they waited until the giant man stepped into the light of the torches. When he did, Malekai recognized the man instantly.

Harrok Mortymer, the Butcher of Haelvaara, in the flesh. Many of the members of the Brotherhood felt the sudden impulse to take a bow.

"Greetings, good sir," Malekai spoke first.

As Harrok the Butcher took slow heavy steps into the camp, some of the men couldn't help but shiver. And then, as if he wasn't menacing enough already, the Butcher spoke, his voice a frightening growl. "Who is your captain?" he asked.

The image of the Butcher was one that could petrify a man. He stood at six and a half feet in height, his eyes were pale grey, and his frizzed hair looked more like tangled threads of yarn rising out of a thinning scalp and falling over his shoulders. He wore a mask over the bottom half of his face, a piece of black leather that covered his disfigured jaw, and the leather was studded with the sharp teeth of a silver wolf. No one had seen the Butcher without his mask since the day he was struck by a warhammer to the jaw during the Battle of Haelvaara, or at least no one that did had lived to describe what remained underneath.

"Yes, it *is* a lovely night, isn't it?" Malekai said dismissively, but the Butcher was not the least bit amused by the man's banter. "The name's Malekai Pahrvus, at your service. Second-in-command to the captain of the Rogue Brotherhood."

"Your *captain*," the Butcher took an intimidating step forward. "Where… is… he…?"

Malekai gave it a moment's thought before deciding the numbers were not in their favor should a fight erupt. Instead he turned to one of his comrades, a bald man with tattoos on his scalp, and said, "Tell the captain Ser Harrok Mortymer is here to see him."

"No," the Butcher said.

Malekai and the rest of his mercenaries turned their heads.

"Not me," he said. "My *lord*…"

Behind the Butcher, a ghostlike figure dressed in black smiled underneath his hooded cloak.

The captain knew very well what was at stake. When he laid eyes on the sigil, he knew that one man would fall on this night. He poured the last of the ale into his tankard and began gulping it down as he breathed heavily through his nose, his eyes glowing with angst and torment.

"Sir?" one of his mercenaries peeked his head inside the tent.

The captain didn't even bother turning around.

"Let 'im in," he said, his eyes fixed on the dagger resting on his desk. He took a deep breath and closed his eyes, ready to face whatever horrors were in store for him.

A dark figure stood at the entrance, examining the entirety of the tent with only his eyes. Without looking back, the captain could sense the man's presence, only adding to his torment.

"Hmm… Is *this* how the captain of the infamous Rogue Brotherhood lives?" the man spoke, his voice confident and firm and eerily menacing. "I must say I'm rather underwhelmed…"

The captain set his half-empty tankard next to his dagger and took one last heavy breath.

The visitor began to pace with a demeanor so calm and a posture so fine that one would guess he was a man of nobility. The night was humid and misty, and yet the man's clothes were dry and unwrinkled. He wore a long black coat made of wool and leather, decorated with a graceful silver design on the edges, collar, and wrists. His hair was just as dark as his clothes and it flowed neatly down his sides and back, and his facial hair was neatly trimmed with great precision, reacting sharply against his pale skin.

"It's been a rather slow year," the captain responded, turning around and gazing into those startling black eyes.

"I'm sure it *has* been," the visitor replied as he walked carelessly towards the captain's chair and helped himself to a seat. The captain scowled subtly, having no choice but to sit on the old wooden chair on the opposite side of his own desk.

"But you'll be glad to hear I'm here to change that for you," the man continued. "You know very well who I am... In fact, you must have known for minutes now, considering your tankard's half-empty and your armor looks like you laced it in a hurry, and quite sloppily I'm afraid."

The captain's expression was hard to read, as it always was, and though his dagger was closer to his visitor than it was to him, he tried his best to remain at ease. "I know who you are," he said. "And I can imagine why you're here."

"Good," the visitor responded, leaning forward and extending his hand over the table.

The captain felt a dash of adrenaline as the visitor's hand brushed past the dagger and instead grabbed the tankard from the table uninvitingly.

"That ought to save me some time," the visitor said, resting back comfortably on the chair and sipping on the last of the captain's ale. "I must admit I am rather impressed by your work, captain. Your men are skilled, to say the least. And a good thirst for carnage is never something I can easily ignore."

The captain's attention was fixed on the man and nothing more, examining his every move and becoming more and more unsettled by the second. "The brotherhood is already under contract," he lied, and his visitor saw right through it.

"I don't want you to work for me," he said. "What I am interested in is more of an alliance, really."

There was a brief moment of silence, and the tension between the two men was starting to become rather obvious. The visitor leaned forward and placed his hands on the captain's table, far too close to the dagger than the captain was comfortable with.

"I'll be needing your men for a little task... A little errand that's waiting for me in Vallenghard. We march to the royal city of Val Havyn in the morning and I will need men with skills such as those of the Rogue Brotherhood to carry this out."

"We're not interested."

"I'm afraid I wasn't asking, captain..."

There was another moment of silence, and this time the captain was far too plagued by the tension to not point it out. "You don't scare me, Baronkroft..." he said sourly.

The visitor's lips curved into a subtle grin at the sound of his name, almost as if it pleased his ears to hear it. And then the captain rose to his feet and stood by the entrance of his tent.

"I'm afraid our business is done here," he said.

Lord Baronkroft nodded, shrugged his shoulders, and stood up. With a sigh, he walked towards the outside, but came to a sudden pensive halt right in front of the captain. "Just for my own curiosity," he said. "Would a blade to your neck scare you?"

"Try it 'n' I'll slice your hands off..."

"Hmm," Baronkroft grinned. "I shall take that as a no."

"Leave... *Now*."

Lord Baronkroft took one step towards the outside, before pausing and taking back that step. "One more question... How about a blade to dear old *Celia's* neck?"

The captain became instantly petrified. His hands were suddenly sweaty and shivery, and though he was fully armored he felt frail and defenseless.

"Would *that* scare you, captain?" Baronkroft asked, stepping even closer to the man until their faces were mere inches apart. "Or how about a blade to Celia's neck while she's forced to watch her dear old mother Dahrla get dismembered...? Would *that* scare you, captain?"

The captain could hide it no longer, and though his eyes were fixed on Lord Baronkroft, the concern in them was far too vivid. He could smell the ale in the lord's breath as he gawked into those black soulless eyes of his. The sight alone was nauseating. He wanted to kill him where he stood, but his dagger was out of his reach. Still, upon hearing the man's words, the captain couldn't bring himself to move a single finger or speak a single word without hesitating.

Baronkroft leaned in even further, much to the captain's discomfort, and spoke in a soft eerie whisper. "Do I have your attention now, you old limp bastard?"

The captain's throat was dry and hoarse. "You're full of shit," he said.

Baronkroft reached into the inside of his coat. "I figured you'd say that," he said as he pulled something out of his pocket and tossed it at the captain.

It was cold and moist and soft and rough, all at once.

It was a woman's finger with a copper ring still attached to it.

The captain's fury got the best of him. He looked back into Baronkroft's bleak gaze and grabbed hold of his collar, shouting "You murderin' son of a bitch!"

But Baronkroft's smile did not fade.

It was then that a towering figure entered the tent and pulled the two men apart, grabbing the captain by the neck and hoisting him two feet into the air.

"Ahh, thank you, my dear Harrok!" Baronkroft said with a wild chuckle as he adjusted the collar of his coat. "Always there when you're most needed, as usual."

The captain gasped for air as he looked down at the dreadful image of the Butcher.

"Captain, I'd like to introduce to you my supreme commander and most trusted friend Harrok Mortymer, otherwise known as the Butcher of Haelvaara," Baronkroft said. "You ought to be *thanking* him, really. After all, he did just save the lives of your sister and niece. Only the gods know what I would have done, should you have made me bleed. I get rather impatient when people lay their hands on me."

The captain's face began to redden and tremble as the Butcher tightened his fist around his neck. Lord Baronkroft took a moment to examine the sight of the vulnerable captain and smiled once more, as if it pleased him.

"Take him outside," he said to the Butcher. "And tie the old bastard up."

* * *

It was the evening of the seventh day, which meant a majority of the civilians of Val Havyn were in a tavern somewhere getting one last round of drinking in before the start of another week, during which they would probably be drinking some more.

It was a typical seventh night inside of Nottley's Tavern.

A drunken peasant woman sat laughing hysterically as she watched her husband stuff his mouth with as many biscuits as he could without vomiting.

A middle-aged man was playing a mandolin and trying hard not to stumble as three inebriated peasants huddled around him, swaying back and forth and singing along to his song.

A boy that couldn't have been older than eighteen was wiping tables and serving rounds of drinks to ungrateful customers that would consistently scowl at him.

A large blacksmith with a tedious posture and a sorrowful grimace on his face sat at the bar, gulping his ale like water. Of all the customers in the tavern, he was the only one that didn't scowl when the boy wiped the counter in front of him. In fact, it was one of the few moments in the night during which he actually smiled.

"Hard night, eh?" he asked.

"When isn't it?" young Cedric replied. "Another ale?"

Thaddeus Rexx nodded and the boy poured him another tankard.

"Anything interestin' happen this week, lad?"

"Nothing of the sort," Cedric said. "Well, 'cept for that old bloke this morning. Which, um... Thank you... for taking care of 'im, I mean."

Thaddeus said nodding, but merely raised his tankard and smiled at the boy, before pouring ale down his throat.

"He looked familiar, though, didn't he?" Cedric said. "His eyes did, at least…"

"He was pissed off his brains, lad. Most men you speak to every day are pissed, that's all you saw."

There was the sudden sound of wood breaking and glass shattering.

A fight had broken out near the man with the mandolin.

"Bloody hell…" Cedric scurried towards them.

A small crowd of people gathered around the two men wrestling on the floor next to a broken chair. "Gents, please…" Cedric tried to separate them, which only resulted in swings thrown his way and protests from the eager drunks watching it all.

Cedric stepped back. He wasn't fond of bruises, and the boy had borne enough in his life. He allowed for the men to grow tired before trying to separate them again. But it was too late. Jasper Nottley's voice towered over the crowd's chanting.

"What the bloody hell is going on here?!" he said, tying his trousers up as he stepped out of a room and a flustered woman twenty years younger than him followed behind.

Cedric turned to his warden and tried to calm him. "Sir, I've got it handl-"

Mister Nottley swung his palm and slapped the boy across the face without thinking twice. "I'm gone *five* minutes 'n' you can't help but get clumsy, boy?!"

Thaddeus Rexx leapt from his seat, his hands in a fist at his sides. But he remained in place, watchful that the tavern owner wouldn't try hitting the lad again. The drunken woman with the biscuit-eating husband scoffed and whispered, "*Only five minutes, eh?*" just loud enough for Nottley and the girl to overhear.

By then, the tavern had gone almost silent. It caused Nottley a touch of discomfort and so the man adjusted himself, ran his fingers through his hair once and said, "I'll give a free round to any man that carries these two out of here."

The same two men that dragged the old drunk that morning rushed to the scene and carried the two wrestling men out of the tavern. Mister Nottley glanced at Cedric angrily one last time. "One of these nights, boy," he aimed a finger at him. "One of these nights I'm throwing you out on your arse. See who cares for you *then*."

And, with that, Nottley walked back into his room and closed the door behind him. The man with the mandolin began playing his music again and the customers carried on as if nothing had happened. Cedric fought back the tears in his eyes, it was evident from their color and glow. He wiped the table where the two fighting men once sat and began to gather the shattered glass and the pieces of wood that were once a chair.

He paused briefly to place a hand on his left cheek, which was now a deep shade of pink. He sighed and allowed for a single tear to flow; a tear that he wiped within seconds. It was a moment that nobody seemed to notice, or was far too inebriated to care. All except for *one* man.

As Cedric gathered the wood, another pair of hands joined in.

A pair of rough, callused hands with a dark complexion.

Thaddeus Rexx said nothing. He simply helped the boy clean.

And young Cedric felt something he rarely ever felt.

He felt he had a friend.

* * *

"Listen here, gents… and listen good!" Lord Baronkroft said.

The captain of the Rogue Brotherhood was lying on the dirt, sweating and shivering, with his hands and feet tied to two horses on opposite ends.

The Brotherhood mercenaries were gathered around the scene, half of them at ease and the other half restless with their hands gripping their weapons. They watched in awe as their once honorable captain laid stripped of his armor, a broken man beaten half to death. The half of them that cared for the man were well aware that they were outnumbered, and they all had heard of the name Baronkroft in the past.

And so they had no choice but to stand and watch. They stood in a row at the camp's entrance, a wave of crimson red contrasting against the brown and green colors of the forest, while on the other side Baronkroft's army glared forebodingly at them.

"There are but *two* types of men in this world," Lord Baronkroft went on, making eye contact with every Brotherhood mercenary in the camp, one by one. "The first man is the one without fear… The man who takes action for a greater good… The man who fights to move forward and takes a thousand lives if necessary to achieve the unachievable."

The rogues listened attentively to the lord's every word.

The captain was hardly alive. One of his eyes was black and swollen and smeared in his own blood. His torso throbbed as the horses pulled him, his back pressing against the cold dirt and muck. He turned towards his men, but all of them were fixed on Baronkroft and the expression in their faces was beginning to worry him.

"Today, gentlemen, is the day we find out whether you all are the first man… or the *second* man… the one who gets slain for getting in the way," Baronkroft paused briefly and examined the eyes of the raiders. He smiled, satisfied with what he saw. "Gentlemen, what I am offering you is a future truly worth fighting for. A future in which there are no tyrants and no greedy kings or lords. All of us standing side by side as equals, all of us sharing the earth like brothers and sisters… Join me and you will know what it is like to live like gods…"

"Give it up, Baronkroft," the captain interrupted, spitting out specks of blood with every word. "The brotherhood will *never* serve you."

Baronkroft turned his head slowly and menacingly towards the fallen man.

"Pardon me, did you say something, captain?" he asked, approaching him.

The Butcher of Haelvaara gave his men a glance and they, in return, gave the horses a lash. The two horses began to pull, and the captain's screams echoed throughout the camp as his limbs stretched in opposite directions, pulling his muscles and bones in ways they were not meant to be pulled.

Lord Baronkroft kneeled, slowly and carefully so as to not smear his stainless clothes on the humid dirt. "It's all right, old man," he said. "Just let it all out… That's it… You know, I was a weak and unworthy man just like you once. Until the day I decided *not* to be."

"You're no man… You're a monster," the captain spoke through heavy, painful breaths. "You will never have the brotherhood and you will never have *me*…"

"Oh, captain… you poor, self-centered bastard. Haven't you figured this out by now?" Baronkroft asked. "I don't *need* you. I *never* did… I need *them*…"

Baronkroft turned his gaze towards his supreme commander and gave him a simple nod. Harrok the Butcher drew his axe, and with one powerful swing, the captain of the Rogue Brotherhood was no more.

Specks of the captain's blood stained Baronkroft's face and yet he welcomed it with a grin. The rogue mercenaries did nothing. There was no time to act. They stood and watched as their captain's head rolled away into the mud. Some of them had grins on their faces while others couldn't bear to look at the headless body. Baronkroft rose to his feet and turned to them all, his hands extended out in front of him.

"What say you, gents?" he asked.

The silence lingered for a few moments.

While many of them drew blank stares, unsettled and unsure of what to feel, a great majority couldn't help but admire the lord's brute nerve. Any man that wasn't afraid to behead a company's captain right in front of said company was a man not to be taunted with; and for men like those of the Brotherhood, Baronkroft certainly seemed like a man potentially worth following.

The first man to step forward was the most unlikely of them all. But Malekai Pahrvus had always been a daring man. With his head held up high and his weapon still sheathed, he stepped confidently towards the lord. "What's the task?" he asked.

Baronkroft drew a handkerchief from his coat pocket and wiped the blood from his face. "Pardon me?"

"The task you speak of," Malekai said. "In Val Havyn… What is it, exactly?"

Baronkroft didn't answer immediately. Instead he got closer to the red mercenary, keeping that grin on his face. "You were the captain's second-in-command, were you not?" he asked. "Tell me, kind sir… What is your name?"

"Malekai," he replied. "Malekai Pahrvus." He was a seasoned man of dark complexion, with hazel eyes and long brown dreadlocks decorated with beads. And he had a look of unsatiated hunger in his eyes that was almost as eerie as Baronkroft's.

"Tell me, Malekai Pahrvus… Will you step forward and lead your men as we march to the royal city of Val Havyn and retrieve the key to our salvation?"

Malekai remained silent for a moment. He turned his eyes from his fallen captain to his comrades in red. They looked at him expectantly, almost as if welcoming his authority. His lips curved slowly into a grin. "Our captain may have been a fair man," he said. "But we all knew he was weak… Weak all over, both in body and in mind."

Baronkroft examined the red mercenary. He had a way of reading people in ways no other person could. And when he looked upon Malekai's eyes, he was more than pleased with what he read. "A rather callous way to speak of the man you so keenly followed," he said. "Cruel, yet honest."

"Call me what you wish. This world wasn't meant for the weak," Malekai said, before he turned back at his company of red mercenaries one last time. By then, the few of them that were restless had grown calmer and their weapons were sheathed in place. After enough approving gazes, he sighed in anticipation, gave the lord a head nod and said, "The Brotherhood will join you, Lord Baronkroft… But I must warn you, our price is not negotiable."

"Understood," Baronkroft said. "I admire a man with a bit of backbone. Should make for a very fine captain."

The look on Malekai Pahrvus's face was one of hunger and grit. It was a face the previous captain could never carry. And it was a face that pleased his new company of mercenaries to an extent that was daunting, to say the least.

* * *

The whole mess started in Val Havyn, on the 13th day of spring.

It was a sunny and humid day, and the streets of the royal city were crawling with merchants. It began like any other working day; the market opened at first light, warm scents oozed from every chimney, and more members of the royal guard were patrolling the streets, keeping a watchful eye for thieves and scoundrels.

It was nearing midday when the smoke began to rise over the sea of rooves.

Nobody had seen it coming. One moment, the skies were clear and bright, and the next they were tainted by a virulent black cloud. And the curiosity and temptation was far too grand for a reckless young lad like John Huxley.

At this rate, most of our harvest will rot before we sell it, his mother had told him. *We must bargain.*

John made an unprecedented trip into the royal city's market that day and he planned to be back in time for supper. But fate had a different plan for him altogether. He would not make it home that night at all. He tied his mule at the stables and climbed off the cart, and he noticed immediately that something wasn't right. Citizens were running amok, crying devout nonsense and shouting to the city guard for help.

"Pardon me, sir?" John tried to pry.

"Move away, boy!" the man shoved him aside, nearly causing him to lose his balance.

"Excuse me, ma'am?" he tried again.

But it seemed everyone was far too busy panicking to pay him any mind. *What in all hells...*

He walked in the opposite direction from everyone else. And it was then that he caught a glimpse of the smoke. There was no time to think; he left his family's produce in the cart unattended and ran along a very familiar path that led to a very familiar crossroad.

When he made the turn on Dreary Lane, he felt the intense wave of heat against his face. Nottley's Tavern was engulfed in flames. People were stumbling out of the doors, shrieking with fear and putting out the flames on their clothes, as the walls and roof of the tavern began to fall apart and the fire spread to the nearby dwellings.

John froze where he stood, unsure of whether he should run inside to help or walk away.

And it was then that a boy stumbled to the floor right at his feet, baked goods scattering out of his basket. "Thomlin?!" John grabbed the boy's arms and lifted him to his feet.

"John!?" the boy wiped his dirty hands on his apron. "The fire's spreading! We must go!"

"Are there any more people in there?!" John asked worriedly. He stood on the cobblestone road, civilians all around him sprinting away from the flames, when suddenly an old wooden stool broke through the tavern doors. Thomlin hid behind John, but no longer tried to back away as his curiosity was peaked.

And then they saw him... A man dressed in black stepped valiantly out of the tavern and pressed his back against the wall of it, the only wall that wasn't yet swallowed up by flames. He wore a dark leather overcoat and a black hat with a rim, covering most of his slightly unclean face. He showed no sign of fear of the fire; in fact, he appeared to be smiling.

"Is that... who I *think* it is?" asked Thomlin, flustered at his inability to recall a name the way he was so keen on doing. John said nothing, but recognized the man instantly as the stranger that had taken a beating the previous morning.

"Out of the way!"

A group of guards sped by, shoving John and Thomlin aside and sprinting towards the tavern. At that same moment, a large peasant was running *out* from inside the tavern with an axe in his hand and a lit cigar in his mouth. The man in the black hat stood by the doorframe and surprised the running peasant with a punch in the face, before giving him a chance to swing his axe. The peasant was knocked unconscious immediately. Somehow, however, the man in the black hat managed to snatch the lit cigar from the peasant's mouth. He took a puff and then flicked it out in front of him. It landed on the cobblestones and a roaring trail of flames burst into the air, creating a barrier between him and the incoming guards.

John then saw the dripping oil lamp on the ground nearby and realized the man in the black hat was no common crook; he knew exactly what he was doing. The guards walked around the barrier of fire, but by then the man was nowhere to be found.

Suddenly, the sound of horse hooves began to ring in their ears.

John narrowed his eyes and noticed, in the distance, a group of knights galloping towards them up Dreary Lane. And then, through the smoke, he saw the figure of the man in the black hat crouching on the tavern roof, dangerously close to the flames.

The first guard galloped at full speed into the scene; the man in the black hat hopped down and landed on his horse. The guard was knocked off the saddle and the man took his place behind the reins.

"Whoa," young Thomlin couldn't help but say. "He's *good*."

The man in the black hat rode past them on the stolen horse. He locked eyes with John for a mere second before he turned onto one of the city's busiest streets. And it was at that very moment that John realized where he'd seen the man's face. It was drawn on the '*Wanted*' portraits all over the city.

"Stop that man!" Cedric yelled as he stumbled out of what was left of the tavern.

John Huxley felt the world slow down all of a sudden.

He watched as the man in the black hat rushed to his escape.

He thought of his mother, of all the times she'd lectured him about his mischief.

He thought of Robyn and the twins, and the kind of example he'd set for them.

He thought of Mister Beckwit and of all the times he'd said '*Think before you draw your blade*'.

And yet there he stood, watching as this criminal dodged and outsmarted every guard that crossed his path. And he simply couldn't stand by and watch it happen…

John's feet decided to move before he gave them permission to.

Before he knew it, he was running back to his cart.

"Sir?!" Thomlin shouted. "Sir, where are you going?!"

The young farmer hopped on the cart and began sifting through the produce, onions and ears of corn scattering all over the ground.

"Sir?!" Thomlin approached him.

Suddenly John pulled his rusty grey blade out of the pile. He unsheathed it and gave it a good twist with his wrist, his lips curving into a smile.

"By the gods," Thomlin's eyes widened. "You're not going after him, are you?! He's *dangerous*!"

But John Huxley was well aware that the man was dangerous; it was what drew his attention to begin with.

"Sir?!" Thomlin shouted. "Sir!"

"Go home, kid," John said, and then darted towards the danger like an eager swordsman.

Many yards north, in the heart of the city market, the thief rushed through the streets and alleyways on the stolen horse, desperately trying to lose the guards that were trailing him. He startled many of the citizens, galloping through the stands and causing a mess to deceive the guards.

John Huxley climbed onto the red rooves of the city dwellings, using the height to his advantage, just as Mister Beckwit had trained him to do since childhood. He ran, jumping from roof to roof, following the thief's tracks as best he could.

He found him near Merchants' Square, galloping towards the western city gates.

But a swarm of guards had gathered together and formed a shield wall, blocking the road. The thief, however, did not slow down by any means. He appeared to be enjoying himself. With a grin, he held his right hand out and somehow managed to snatch a tankard of ale from a nearby table; the man sitting there was knocked back on his chair, his bowl of stew splashing all over his chest.

As John ran closer, he couldn't help but observe.

The thief drank what was left of the ale and threw the tankard over his shoulder. He then removed one foot from the saddle and raised it up onto the horse's back. He did the same with his other foot and began to stand little by little as the horse continued to run at full speed.

No man should be able to do that, John thought to himself.

And yet there it was.

The thief held tightly onto the reins as he approached a nearby dwelling with a balcony. He jumped off the speeding horse, grasped one of the bars on the balcony and hoisted himself up. The guards began to shoot arrows, but the thief vanished into the windows of the premises before any of them struck him.

John looked ahead, realizing the thief was in a dwelling that was about ten roofs away. He smiled and picked up his pace.

The thief closed the balcony windows and took a moment to catch his breath and observe his surroundings. He found himself in a dusty old room that may have been used for lodging guests at one point but now appeared to be used for storage. The walls were bare, save for the spider webs on every corner. There were no stairs, only a small latch on the wooden floor that was raised open and a wooden ladder connecting the room to the first floor of the dwelling, which happened to be a saloon. Without thinking twice, the thief closed the latch and dragged a large cabinet over it. The music and the chattering voices beneath his feet continued as if nothing was happening above them.

Think, now… No distractions…

As he scanned the room, he looked for anything that could possibly aid him. He saw a lit lantern on a wooden nightstand.

A bundle of rope in the corner of the room atop a wooden chest with a steel lock.

Empty wine bottles on the floor, most of them broken.

About a dozen pieces of furniture covered with old, moth-ridden sheets.

A lumpy old bed in the middle of the room with a single filthy pillow.

On the floor was a pair of steel cuffs connected by a four-foot long chain, and several rats brushing past it, scavenging for food and crumbs.

Suddenly his eyes found what he was looking for. Something shiny drew his attention from atop a hefty wooden cupboard. It was a rapier with a double-edged blade and an acute tip.

He reached for it, unsheathed it, examined its roughness and stability…

It'll do, he thought.

And then a sharp noise suddenly startled him. The window he'd closed a minute prior shattered into pieces. The thief turned and saw a young man hopping in through the broken glass. He had short hair the color of wheat and was dressed in raggedy farmer's clothes. The cleanest thing he wore was a brown leather vest with mismatching buttons sewn onto it. They said nothing at first, only locked eyes with one another, as the young man shook the crumbs of glass from his shoulders and began to pace slowly and carefully around the room.

"That's not yours to take," John Huxley said.

With a smirk, the thief caressed the glistening blade as if it were made of the smoothest silk. "You mean *this*?" he asked. "But it sure does bring out my eyes, don't you think?"

The way he held the blade was almost admirable, gracefully and delicately, as if holding a docile yellow-tailed dove; if one could use a dove to kill a man, that is.

"The saloon is surrounded," John said, trying his best to look like a proper swordsman. "Put your weapon down and you won't be harmed."

The thief's smirk then faded into an ominous glare that sent a chilling rush up John's spine.

"Is that so?" he asked, sliding the stolen blade back on its sheath and tying it to his belt as he spoke, remnants of his smirk still lurking in the corner of his lips. "So... Indulge me, mate. You mean to tell me that the royal guard is on the hunt for a fugitive and when they've finally got him ambushed, they send... a *peasant* to fetch him?"

John couldn't help but feel a sting in his chest upon the thief's disdainful question. It wasn't his words, exactly, but rather the assumption of his lack of skill based merely on his profession. "I'm a farmer," he said, attempting a threatening glare of his own but coming across as more perturbed than anything else.

"Oh, a *farmer*!" said the thief mockingly. "Well *forgive me*, your highness."

"Put the sword on the floor," John ordered him.

"Yes, your grace, would you like it sheathed or unsheathed?"

"Don't mock me," John said, becoming more alarmed by the second. He realized there was a possibility that he'd made a terrible mistake. The thief did not react kindly when confronted. And yet here John was, not only confronting him but doing so while the thief was *armed*.

Suddenly, the mutters beneath the floors grew into muffled shouts and persistent thumps.

"Listen, you," said the thief, taking slow backward steps toward the window on the opposite end of the room. "I'd love to stay here and listen to some of your breathtaking farming stories, I'm sure they're a hoot. But I'm afraid I'll have to be trotting along now."

As the thief opened the window to escape, John's rebellious hand succumbed to the temptation and unsheathed his rusty blade. "I'm sorry," he said. "But I... I can't let you..."

The thief froze. The pounding under the cabinet grew harder and harder, and the angry voices appeared to be growing in numbers. There was no doubt anymore. The royal guard had taken over the saloon. And it was starting to agitate the thief.

"Do you know who I am?" he asked John, stepping away from the window.

"Does it make a difference?"

"Yes, it does," the thief's tone was serious once again. He had this way of keeping his mockery locked in place, ready to release it at the spur of any moment. John knew he was dealing with a dishonest man, and although he believed there existed men whose dishonesty had some reasoning behind it, the thief's eyes appeared almost impossible to read.

"You're Hudson Blackwood," John said. "You're the wanted thief."

"Is *that* what they call me here?" Hudson snickered. "That's rather disappointing. They call me a wanted *murderer* in Halghard."

"You were the one who set fire to Mister Nottley's tavern," John accused him.

"Oh, that place was falling apart on its own anyhow. It reeked of piss and vomit. I reckoned I was doing the city a favor."

"That is *not* for you to decide…"

The whacking on the wooden hatch grew louder as the guards began to splinter through it.

Hudson began to feel a rush of unease, as he knew his time was running short.

"Listen here, mate," he said hesitantly. "In a moment, one of two things *will* happen. Either I will jump out that window and go on about my affairs and we'll pretend we never had this conversation."

John stood his ground, at times seeming even slightly intimidating.

"*Or* we can go the alternate route," Hudson continued. "Which will end with me *killing* you and *then* jumping out the window and going on about my affairs. And let's face it, mate. I *will* kill you, given your profession, given mine, and given the fact that you're threatening me with that sad little kitchen knife."

John felt his hand shiver for a moment. His mother's words echoed in his mind all of a sudden: '*Someday, you'll find yourself crossing blades with someone who won't play as nice as Larz and Henrik.*'

And yet he couldn't help but yield to the thrill of the challenge.

"If you're so sure, why don't you draw your weapon?" John tempted fate for a bit, and during the two seconds of silence that followed, he felt something he hadn't felt since the night of the raid on the Huxley farm; the uncertainty of whether or not he would live to see another day.

Hudson Blackwood sighed and with an eye-roll, said, "Have it your way, then."

The thief was faster than John anticipated. He grabbed the first moth-ridden sheet to his left and threw it at John, briefly blinding him, then jumped atop the old bed and drew his sword.

Their blades crossed for the first time, and the hissing steel echoed throughout the room. The thief was dangerously quick and his strikes were robust and powerful. John felt a sting in his wrist with every attack he blocked. He stepped back, and the thief hopped down from the bed and kept swinging. John had never moved so quick in his life. Mister Beckwit's farmhands Larz and Henrik could never match the thief's speed, even if they fought him together.

They pressed their blades against one another and paused for a second, locking eyes once again as each one tried to outgrip the other. When their blades slid loose, John took the chance to swing first and managed to rip a two-inch gap on the front of Hudson's coat.

The thief paused for a moment and gave the farmer a look that spoke more threateningly than any words he could possibly invoke. Then, with a loud growl, he swung with an even greater force, causing the farmer to duck and move away rather than try to defend himself.

Thinking so quick was impossible. After every attack, John was already dodging another. He realized then that he was no match for the thief, and still he refused to run away from the fight. Suddenly, in an unlucky moment, the rusty blade slid from his hands and fell to the floor. He ducked, slid on his knees to fetch it, and nearly lost an eye as he managed to block the thief's downward swing, the rapier reaching just an inch from his face. Their blades collided several times again before Hudson's skill overtook John's and he disarmed him again.

And this time, John's reach came too late.

Hudson held his blade up to the farmer's neck.

"You did this to yourself, mate," he said, then prepared to cut.

But the sudden sound of splintering wood startled them. The cabinet was pushed aside and the small hatch on the floor creaked open. A guard peeked his head inside. Hudson kicked with his right foot and the guard ducked back down.

The thief then felt a sudden cold sting in his right hand, followed by the sound of clanking metal. When he turned, he saw that his wrist had been cuffed to a chain, and on the other cuff was the farmer's left wrist.

"It's over, thief," John said. "You've got no way out."

Hudson Blackwood was known for many things. He was not, however, known to surrender under pressure. With the strength of a wolf, he swung his fist and struck John in the jaw, right at the perfect spot so that he would faint from the blow. Hudson caught John before he fell to the ground, and then hoisted his unconscious body over his shoulder.

"The thief's getting away!" one of the guards shouted from under the hatch.

Hudson grabbed the lantern from the nightstand and dropped it a mere foot away from the guard's head. The lantern shattered and the oil splashed all over the floor, catching fire instantly. The guard backed away from the open hatch and Hudson made way for the window.

The window led to an alleyway between dwellings. There was another swarm of guards marching in from one end of it. But the thief then noticed a wooden cart just ten feet underneath the windowsill and the peasant that owned it was preoccupied conversing with a beautiful seamstress. The unattended cart was full of hay and had two horses tied to the reins.

What a bloody convenience, Hudson thought with a grin.

* * *

In the vast green hills of Vallenghard, a mere five miles west of the royal city, a company of about two hundred riders had gathered, awaiting orders from their commanders. Half of them were dressed in matching red leathers while the rest wore furs, suggesting they were accustomed to warmer climate. For many miles, they had ridden together, and yet they refused to interact.

The Rogue Brotherhood was simply following orders, but they were kept in the dark through most of the journey. Who was this foreign company of humans, orcs, elves, and goblins? Why were they in Gravenstone and how did their commander manage to sneak them past the cities at the shores? Other nations had granted freedom to nonhuman races, but the law in Gravenstone was strict and the penalty for breaking it was death. And yet here they stood, in the kingdom of Vallenghard, a kingdom of humans, fearlessly marching through the open hills with an army so diverse it could have been spotted from a mile away.

Whoever this Lord Baronkroft was, there was one thing they knew for certain...

The man had no fear... None whatsoever...

Malekai Pahrvus, the new captain of the Brotherhood, was discussing the plan of attack with the Butcher of Haelvaara while the company waited impatiently at the base of the hill. Among them, a trio of orcs from Lord Baronkroft's troop grumbled and snickered among one another, eyeing the Brotherhood mercenaries up and down as if they were of lower ranks.

"What in all hells are we waitin' for?!" asked one of them. "We've been sittin' for hours."

"I thought we was here to attack. What's with all the yappin'?"

"Lower yer voices, will ye?"

The largest of the 3 orcs was the smartest of the bunch. He kept quiet at the appropriate times and talked only when he had to. The other two, on the other hand, were impatient and crude and had no clue how to be subtle.

"Why'd we hire the human filth anyway?"

"Look at 'em. Bunch o' scrawny bastards."

"I said lower yer fuckin' voices..."

Captain Malekai Pahrvus approached the herd of soldiers on horse. He was calm and determined and though he wasn't smiling, it was obvious that he was enjoying the power that fate had placed in his hands.

"Attention, gentlemen," he said. "The royal city of Val Havyn is just ahead of those hills... I want every able-bodied man to prepare to march. The rest of you will stay here and look after the horses and prisoners."

There was a sudden tension among the crowd, in particular among the trio of orcs that stood near the front. They began whispering and shooting glares at Malekai.

"What did ye just say...?" asked the largest of the 3 orcs, with a glare so menacing that Malekai had to choose his words carefully.

"This here's Gravenstone, lad. We cannot risk th-"

"My name's not 'lad'," the orc interrupted. "It's Okvar... the Destroyer."

Malekai hesitated. He glanced at his company of red mercenaries, all of whom were prepared to fight for him should things get out of hand. He knew that the Brotherhood was serving *him* and not Baronkroft. And if he wanted to keep it that way, he would have to show no sign of weakness.

49

"Pardon me, *Okvar*," he cleared his throat and returned the glower right back at the orc. "But it seems I didn't make myself clear… We need every able-bodied *man* to march with us to the royal city."

Malekai took a moment to eye the orc up and down.

"Tell me… are you a *man?*" he asked him daringly.

Okvar clenched his teeth with rage and gripped his axe, preparing to dismount his horse.

At that moment, however, a deep voice broke the tension. "Easy now, brothers…"

Lord Baronkroft was on foot, walking so confidently that he had no need for a horse to be intimidating. "I believe what our new friend, Captain Malekai, is trying to say… is that folks here are a bit… shall we say, *reserved*. They don't take well to outsiders. One look at the color of your skin and they'll be rushing to fetch the guards."

Okvar was not happy, but he kept quiet all the same and let go of his axe.

"Are we ready?" Baronkroft asked the captain of the Brotherhood.

"Say the word, sir," Malekai grinned. "And we march."

"Excellent… Let's not waste another moment, then…"

The troops began to make way for the hills, about a hundred of them, all of them human. The rest had no choice but to stay put and await their commander's safe return… All of them except for one stubborn orc with a thirst for a good fight.

Okvar turned to one of his two comrades, making sure to keep his head down and not be overheard. "Make yerself useful," he said. "And go find me a good helmet…"

* * *

John Huxley had grown accustomed to waking up in the same dusty room, his back resting against the same lumpy bedspread for nearly twenty years. On this particular day, however, he was awakened by a tugging on his wrist and the tapping of his head against the wood of a moving carriage. He found himself sitting next to the wanted thief Hudson Blackwood, who held the reins in his hands as they traveled at full speed through the busy streets of Val Havyn.

Needless to say, the farmer was wide awake within seconds.

"Are you out of your damn mind?!" John shouted over the sound of horse hooves and screaming citizens diving to avoid the moving carriage.

"Make yourself useful, mate! Distract the blokes!" Hudson shouted back.

"Distract *who?!*"

"Behind us!"

John turned back, only to see a force of about six or seven guards speeding after them. He felt the sudden urge to hop out onto the cobblestone roads until he realized his wrist was still cuffed to the thief's.

"Stop the cart!" he demanded.

"Not happening," the thief didn't even turn to look at him; his eyes were fixed on the road and more importantly on the approaching bridge under which vagabonds slept at night and merchants set up shop during the day.

"Stop the cart *now*!"

"Keep shouting, mate. It's working," the thief said, referring to the frightened horses pulling them faster ahead. For a moment, John shuddered at the sight of a distracted child munching on an ear of corn in the middle of the road. Luckily, a woman with the reflexes of a wildcat pulled the child away just in time before the horses trampled over him.

"This is it, mate," Hudson Blackwood said, taking a peek behind them. "As soon as we cross that bridge, we jump!"

"Are you mad?! I'm not going anywhere with you!" John protested.

"I'm afraid you've got no choice."

"The guards are after *you*, not me!"

"Are they now? Because if I were a guard, all I'd see is a wanted thief and his companion rushing to make an exit."

"You're insane," John said in disbelief.

At that moment, however, an arrow struck the wood of the carriage. Had the backrest not been there, it would have hit John in the back. His eyes widened. The thief said nothing; his point had been made.

The carriage reached the bridge. Hudson dropped the reins, rose to his feet and yanked at the chain, pulling a staggered John Huxley along with him. They stood on the wood along the edge of the carriage, before the thief locked eyes with the farmer and gave him a nod.

"Now!"

And so they jumped, landing on the cloth above a fruit stand where a one-legged man sat smoking a pipe of tobacco. They rolled off the cloth, Hudson landing on his feet with an agility that could only be gained with years of thievery. John, in contrast, slammed into the floor on his side. He groaned in pain.

"This way, mate!" the thief said, but then his wrist jerked him backwards.

John, stubborn as he was, planted his feet firmly on the ground, his eyes showing no sign of jesting. "As I said before," he said, adrenaline pumping heatedly in his veins. "I can't let you go."

All around them, worried eyes stared and chatty lips murmured.

The thief sighed and rolled his eyes once more and with the swiftness of a fox he drew his blade again. Despite his sneering demeanor, his wide eyes and sharply curved eyebrows made for quite the intimidating stare when the moment called for it.

"You either do as I say or I'll chop your bloody hand off, mate. Your move."

John Huxley reached for his rusty blade, but panicked when he felt nothing but the leather of his belt. Nearby, a woman shouted for the guards. The thief wasted not another second and swung his sword again. John stepped back, dodging every incoming attack. The chain that kept them together was just long enough for a cushion of space between them. John was pushed further and further back until he felt his ankle thump against the wood of the fruit stand, where the one-legged man had fallen asleep with the lit pipe still on his lips.

Hudson panicked and poked his weapon forward.

John moved, the blade missing his chest by a fraction of a second. But the movement caused him to lose his balance and his back pressed against the fruit. Then he looked up… There, he saw the black silhouette of his blade on the cloth above, outlined by the light of the sun. It may have been the adrenaline that gave him the speed but before he knew it, John had grabbed the thief's arm and swung it upward.

Hudson's rapier poked a hole through the cloth, and when he pulled back he broadened the tear and John's sword slid through the gap. John caught it and unsheathed it just in time.

A crowd began to gather around them, as the farmer and the thief clashed swords again and again. But both of them were equally as tenacious and though the thief had the advantage of speed, the farmer's skill in defense was keeping him alive.

An arrow sped by, missing the thief by just a hair and piercing through an oversized melon on the fruit stand. Both John and Hudson paused in their tracks, their blades still touching, and realized there was a formation of guards lined up on the road with bows in hand and arrows held back at the ready.

"Oh shit," the thief said.

John had a slight moment of panic. He turned to the thief and mirrored his every move.

Together, they stepped onto the wood and hopped over the fruit stand, just in time for the sea of arrows to miss them. The fruit's nectar splattered over the road with every arrow that struck.

"This way, mate!" the thief pulled the chain.

They crawled towards an empty alleyway nearby and began running.

* * *

"Mum!" Robyn Huxley said, rushing agitatedly through the cottage's front door. "Mister Beckwit is out front asking for you! It's about John!"

Adelina was by the wooden fence a mere 5 seconds later, greeting the old man, only this time she didn't carry her usual affable smile. The first thing she noticed was the concern in Mister Beckwit's eyes, and then she felt her stomach turn at the sight of the black cloud of smoke in the distance.

"What happened?!" she asked.

"You need to get over there. Now!" said Beckwit, "Seems your son's a bit of an imbecile."

"Did something happen to him?!" Robyn asked worriedly, wiping the black curls away from her sweaty brow.

"Robyn, get back inside!" Adelina said, but young Robyn remained within proximity so as to purposely overhear.

"Larz and Henrik just got in. They said the wanted thief Hudson Blackwood's been spotted in the city… Last they saw, our dear John was… well, he was running after him…"

"He *what*!?"

"Mum, I *must* go with you!" Robyn argued.

"Robyn!" Adelina shouted. Robyn cringed for a moment. "Stop arguing with me, girl, and do as I say! Ready a horse. I'm going into the city. *Alone*!"

* * *

This is it, John Huxley thought. *There's no coming back from this…*

Every muscle in his body fought the urge to continue. Every breath had felt like his last. Never in his life had he been persecuted by the royal guard. Never had he had to dodge so many arrows or climb so many rooves.

Hudson Blackwood was a wanted man and John had made the stupid mistake of cuffing himself to him, without considering the very real possibility that he would tangle himself into the thief's mess. It was scary enough to have to flee for your own life and have your heart nearly implode from the thrill. What was perhaps scarier for John, however, was the realization that he was slightly enjoying it.

The two men stopped to catch their breath at an empty alley behind an inn. John was sitting with his back against the wall while Hudson was on one knee, rinsing his wrist with a jug of water that he had snatched from a drunken man, while the drunken man was busy trying to haggle his way out of an unpaid debt. As the thief poured the water, he tried desperately to slide his hand out of the steel cuff. His aggression was only causing his skin to irritate and there were traces of blood smearing out of a cluster of scabs that were possibly already there before that day; the thief had so many hidden wounds, it was hard to tell.

"You won't break out of that unless you purposely shatter your own wrist bone," John said.

Hudson grunted and shot him a menacing glare. "If I were you I'd keep my mouth shut, mate," he said. "If it wasn't for *you*, I'd be out of this bloody city by now."

"I'm sorry," John said. "But I couldn't let you escape. It's against my principles."

"*Principles?*" Hudson snickered. "Pardon me. Didn't realize you were both a farmer *and* a moron."

"Piss off…"

"The man that owns that tavern is a pontificating, malignant arsehole that beats his ward. So tell me, how does *that* settle into your principles?"

John raised a brow suddenly. "How can you tell he beats him?"

"How can you *not*, mate?"

John stammered. The thief's words were sending a knot to his throat. "W-Well… I don't believe a man being an arsehole gives you the necessary judgment to burn down his tavern."

"I know it doesn't. That was for stealing my coin purse." Hudson pulled out a lockpick, no bigger than his little finger, and began working at the lock on the cuff. John took a moment to examine the thief. The portrait of him on the city streets was accurate to an extent; they hadn't quite gotten his eyes right.

The portrait made him out to look intimidating and ruthless.

In person, Hudson's eyes were those of a conflicted man. A man that had seen his share of troubles in his life and made every wrong decision. Not that he didn't learn from those decisions, he certainly did. He learned that humankind was wretched and cruel and he found little reason to be any different in return.

Suddenly, there was a loud clink and the cuff snapped open. Hudson let out a soft chuckle and threw the cuff at John, who was both staggered and conflicted about his next move. The thief rinsed his wrists once again, sighing cleverly with relief.

"I'll let you off with a warning this time, mate," he said. "You're not exactly worth my precious time and I'm sure you've got plenty of exhilarating farming duties to get to anyhow." He removed his black hat and shook what little dust had gathered since the last time he had cleaned it, which, in this particular instance, was merely an hour ago.

"But I *will* say this," the thief continued. "There's a fine difference between being brave and being reckless, mate… Do us all a favor and *learn* it, will you?"

John rose to his feet, chain and cuff in hand and subtle hesitation in his eyes. Hudson turned towards the main road, but his feet came suddenly to a halt. The alleyway was suddenly blocked by a barricade of spears and about a dozen men in heavy armor. Another dozen approached them from the other end of the alley, surrounding them both.

"Oh dear…" Hudson said with a hint of concern.

The guards closed in on them, their weapons ready to strike if the thief tried anything.

"Listen, gentlemen," Hudson cleared his throat. "If this is about that cottage window back there… *He* broke it." He aimed at John with his thumb.

Behind the guards, on the main road, another man in armor leapt off his white stallion. The guards made room for him, bowing their heads with respect as the man walked past them. He was tall and blonde, and somewhere in his late forties. The design on his armor made it clear that he was of higher authority. John recognized the knight immediately upon seeing the golden emblem of the eagle on his back.

"Well now," Sir Viktor Crowley said. "If it isn't the infamous thief Hudson Blackwood."

"In the flesh, old mate," Hudson said, taking a bow and then eyeing the golden knight from head to toe. "And who are *you*, the king's jester?"

Sir Jossiah Biggs, who stood nearby, unsheathed his sword and growled at the thief's mocking remark, before Sir Viktor stopped him with a mere hand signal.

John's hands were in the air as were the thief's. The guards had stepped closer with their spears up, hardly giving the two any space to move.

"And *you* are?" Sir Viktor asked, looking in John's direction.

The farmer froze and his throat went dry instantly. He'd felt slightly uneasy standing just *yards* away from the golden knight two mornings prior. But now that Viktor was just three feet away, the unease was nearly unbearable.

"Um... John Huxley, sir... John Huxley of Elbon."

"Mister Huxley," Sir Viktor greeted him with a handshake, and then glanced at Hudson with a spiteful glare. "I believe we owe you our gratitude... You've aided us in the capture of a very dangerous man..."

Hudson kept his eyes locked on Sir Viktor Crowley. Had the circumstances been a bit different, he would have considered fighting off the knight in combat; after all, they both were quite gifted with a blade. He knew, however, that Crowley wouldn't hesitate to order his beheading. And so the thief had no exception but to yield.

Now, rumors in Val Havyn had the tendency of spreading like wildfire, and this particular instance was no exception. Crowds of peasants were staring from a distance, attentive and alert. Within minutes, John Huxley's name had been spoken more times than King Rowan's had when it came out that the king had passed out nude on the shores of Lotus Creek behind his palace.

"Remove the cuffs from Mister Huxley," Viktor motioned to his men. "And see to it that he gets his reward and a warm meal for his service. As for Mister Blackwood... lock him in the dungeons until the king returns. Do try and keep him in one piece."

Hudson was suddenly struck by a sharp blow to the back that brought him down to his knees. Two guards began punching and kicking him, while another grabbed and cuffed his hands. The thief had his face pressed against the cobblestones and though he tried to hide it, there was a very real pain and anguish in his eyes. For a moment John resisted the urge to turn back and help the man to his feet. But it was too late. The thief had been caught.

A sweaty guard who looked rather unfit for his profession greeted John and removed the cuff from his wrist. "This way, sir," he said.

When they reached the main road, every pair of eyes was on John Huxley. Peasants were aiming their fingers at him, whispering gossip at one another, spreading the word about the brave farmer who drew his blade at the infamous thief Hudson Blackwood. Among them was a curious boy holding a basket of baked goods.

"Thomlin!" John said eagerly.

"Sir!" the boy smiled and stepped forward.

"Is he with you?" the guard asked.

The farmer nodded and, out of fear, he lied.

"Um, yes… Yes, actually. He's my squire."

The guard raised a brow and glanced back and forth at the two of them. He wasn't convinced, but seeing as the crowd of peasants was starting to grow in abundance, he shrugged and said, "Very well…"

And so it happened that, on that 13th day of spring, the farmer and the boy were escorted to Val Havyn's royal palace, unaware of the bloodshed that would take place there that afternoon.

III
Captives

John Huxley and the peasant boy named Thomlin sat in an elegant courtyard, surrounded by beautiful lush gardens with paths made of flat stone. The flowers were everywhere, a stunning assortment of blue and white amid patches of green. There were outdoor corridors all around the courtyard, with tall stone columns wrapped graciously in leafy vines, which also crawled along some of the lower walls surrounding the gardens. There were 4 fountains, one in every corner, and a sandstone statue of a young King Rowan at the very center of it all.

John and Thomlin felt the warm breeze of the afternoon hit their faces and they were struck with the sweet scent of honey and roses rather than the stench of the fertilizer John had grown so accustomed to. The chairs they were sitting in were patted with the softest cotton they had ever felt. For the two of them, such material was rare and would, if at all, be used for wardrobe worn only on special occasions such as a village feast in Elbon or Val Havyn's autumn festival. In the King's castle, however, such material was used for chairs, curtains and even table covers; the thought of it made the both of them feel considerably out of place.

A pair of servants walked out of the palace with trays in hand and approached them. They set the trays down on the garden table and unveiled a banquet that could have fed four people in either of their households. Twice.

Roasted duck with steamed vegetables and an entire plate of syrupy, assorted fruit. Another servant approached and poured wine into two tankards made of copper.

"My thanks," John said, as the servants took a bow and walked away.

The farmer and the boy looked at one another, without moving a single muscle. It wasn't until they heard the wooden door close behind the servants that they both threw themselves into the food, as if eating for the first time in a week.

"I owe you so much, sir," Thomlin said, his eyes closed, savoring the tangy spice of the roasted bird wing on his plate.

"You owe me nothing. Just eat."

They chuckled loudly together, their mouths full of the finest food they'd ever tasted. Never had they been surrounded by such lavishness, and though they felt a touch of discomfort, it wasn't enough to prevent them from gulping it all down. Coming from a family of farmers, John seldom had the luxury of eating a full meal with more than a simple main course and water to ease it down. Suffice it to say, he would certainly not miss an opportunity like this.

Suddenly, the loud sound of a door being thrown open against the brick wall caused John to switch focus to an approaching guard. He was approximately John's height, but at least twenty years older. He had short fuzzy brown hair, a patchy beard, and a grimace that looked like it was permanent. His expression showed disapproval and his eyes a false sense of authority.

As he reached the table, John realized the guard's armor was far more elegant than most guards. The king's emblem on the man's chest armor made it clear that he was not simply any guard, but a knight of the king's court.

The knight drew out and tossed a black leather sack at them. John was just able to catch it after setting down his fork. Based on the weight and the sound it made as it hit his hands, he realized the sack was filled with gold.

"I believe this is rightfully yours," the knight said with a tone that could have been friendlier. "You're both to return to wherever you came from after you've finished your meal."

"Yes, sir," John said. He tried his best to sit up straight the way a man of class would sit.

"I heard that you single-handedly brought down the thief Hudson Blackwood," the knight said unexpectedly. Somehow, his tone gave John the impression that the knight did not want to be there and much less speak to a man of such lower authority. Yet it was the knight who chose to remain standing, towering over the table as if speaking down to a rival rather than an ally.

"Well, I wouldn't exactly say single-handedly," John said, unsure of how to respond.

"Yes, I wouldn't say that either," the knight replied. "And yet it's all everyone in the city's talking about; the farmer from Elbon that refused to allow a wanted thief to escape… Figured I had to meet you in person."

John and Thomlin made eye contact once more. The sensation in John's chest was a mix of discomfort and thrill. After all, it wasn't exactly fame that the young farmer wanted.

Recognition, perhaps…

Since before he could remember, John Huxley had always been scared of his own triviality. To die without having made the slightest difference in the world was something along the lines of his greatest fear. To die without having accomplished anything. He wanted to be remembered, if only by a few, as someone who knew his purpose.

Perhaps that's what John wanted. *Purpose.*

He simply lacked the guidance with which to find it.

"I wasn't aware, sir," John said nervously, clearing his throat with the last of the wine.

"Well… Enjoy it while it lasts, Mister Hoxxy," the knight said.

"It's, um… It's *Huxley*…"

"Yes, I'm sure it is… It's a shame no one will remember after a week, anyhow."

And with that, the knight walked away holding his head up high as if it was him who had single-handedly fought a skilled criminal. His words had stung John, but they weren't enough to bring the farmer's joy down. Thomlin smiled at him.

"If you're the one who captured him," the knight turned around before stepping into the palace. "Then who's the boy?"

John and Thomlin looked at one another, trying to devise a lie through a stare.

"I'm Thomlin, sir. I'm his f-"

"*Nephew*," John blurted out.

Sir Biggs looked back and forth at the two… At John's fair complexion, blonde hair, and blue eyes contrasting against Thomlin's chestnut-colored hair and dark brown skin.

"Peasants," the knight muttered with disdain as he slammed the palace door behind him.

The silence was only brief. John couldn't help but chuckle under his breath.

"A man with that form and bearing can only be Sir Jossiah Biggs," the boy said.

"I've seen him," John nodded. "He was there when they nearly hanged that witch two days ago, wasn't he?" John felt a sense of relief at the fact that the man's demeanor was about the same with everyone else and not simply him.

"Sure was," Thomlin said. "Something tells me if Sir Viktor Crowley hadn't been there, he would have allowed the hanging."

"Hmm… D'you know why he was ever knighted in the first place?"

"Honestly?" Thomlin shrugged. "I haven't the slightest idea."

* * *

The day was warm enough outside, but the dungeons below the grounds of the king's palace were cold and filthy. The walls and floors were made of grey bricks and stones, molded and placed together with such craftsmanship that it was hard to believe the palace had been built by humans.

Of course, it *wasn't* built by humans. It was built by a workforce of elves and orcs. But it had been many centuries since, and it was quite easy for a king to lie about such matters.

On one particular chamber in the dungeon, there was a long corridor with individual cells on each side and steel doors on both ends of the corridor that worked as a passageway between the guard barracks and the palace gardens. This was where prisoners were kept who were awaiting the king's verdict, before they were moved to the main dungeons, a place where not many would ever come out of.

Inside an exceptionally small cell, a young woman sat on the stone floor, finding the bug-infested cloth-matted bedspread too unpleasant to sleep in. She leaned back against the wall and though her eyes were closed, she had not slept in days; at least not for longer than a few minutes at a time. Her hands were wrapped in decaying ogreskin, held together by chains.

It was said that long before the Great War, during a time when witches lived among the rest of the populace in every city, they would use ogres as their servants. In order to spare any accidents, the witches had cursed these grey giants, making them entirely immune to magic. And so they remained that way over the centuries, generation after generation. The curse was so powerful, however, that even after death the ogres' skin was immune to a witch's magic and, when exposed to it, a witch was incapable of conjuring the most minimal spell.

Syrena, the young witch of Morganna, was no exception.

No one in Val Havyn had seen her do anything that came close to magic, and yet they were more than eager to hang her in broad daylight at the first accusation. Suffice it to say she was angry, and though part of her wanted to be rid of the ogreskin and enact her revenge against every civilian of Val Havyn, a greater part of her wanted simply to be free and as far from the kingdom as she could manage to run.

For 3 decades she'd been alive, and already she'd seen enough to rid her of any hope for a simple life; one that didn't involve struggling to stay alive, at the very least, was all she really wanted. Yet she hadn't known many people that didn't want to capture her, kill her, or have her way with her merely for a touch of the exotic. And anyone living such a cruel reality would grow to despise humankind just the same.

After hours of peace and silence, Syrena was forced back to her senses when she heard the steel door open and the sounds of footsteps walking down the corridor, approaching her cell. She knew the guard was a mute, for it was the same guard that had thrown her in her cell when she was first brought there. The voice she heard *had* to have been coming from whatever prisoner was being dragged in.

"Y'know, for a man of your size and weight you've got quite a soft grip, mate," she heard the prisoner speak, with a tone that wasn't cordial but not exactly stern either.

This was followed by the guard's abrasive grunt and the prisoner's voice responding with, "Ahh, *There* it is! *Now* I feel like a proper crook."

They stopped at the cell next to Syrena's, though she wasn't able to catch a glimpse of either man. She heard the doors opening, followed by the clinking of metal and the rattling of chains. The guard had removed the prisoner's cuffs... and this sent a rush of anger into the young witch's chest.

"One last question, mate," the prisoner said. "When will lunch be served?"

The large, hairy guard grunted angrily and slammed his fist against the steel bars of the cell. A punch like that could break a man's knuckles, but the guard did not wince a bit.

Hudson Blackwood smirked.

"Easy there, handsome. Wouldn't wanna crack your pretty little bones."

The witch was silent. Sitting in that position wasn't exactly comfortable, but she feared if she moved a single muscle, the chains in her wrists would rattle and give her away. She waited for the sound of the chamber door slamming to sit up straight, hiding within the sounds of the echoing hall.

Almost by impulse, the thief began to look and dig around his cell like a hound in search of a scent. He flipped the bedspread over and kept his eyes peeled for anything sharp that might help him unlock the cell door. He was a man that, in his life, had found himself in many cages and dungeons and ultimately came to the realization that there was always a flaw. Grand or small, the man was an expert in using that flaw to aid him in his escape. He looked all around, touching and knocking gently on the walls.

But he felt nothing. No airflow or opening. Just perfectly smooth stone.

He grunted, like an animal in a cage, unaware that a startled presence was eavesdropping through the wall. The unexpected sound of his growl caused Syrena to become curious about the man. There was only so much she could tell from a few words and a grunt; she sensed he was on the younger side, not exactly seasoned, but not naïve either. After all, a man who would speak to a king's guard the way he did was either a lunatic or knew exactly what he was doing.

Then, something caught the thief's eye. There was one flaw after all, but one that he wasn't sure would be of much help to him; an opening between the brickstones on the wall of his cell, connecting to the next, at about his knee's height. He chose to ignore it for a moment as he paced and gathered his thoughts.

Meanwhile, the witch's curiosity overcame her and she peeked through that very opening. Her heart was beating fast and she tried to breathe gently, anything to help remain undetected. She saw a man dressed entirely in black. Not a villager or a peasant, but an outsider, like herself. His smooth black hair fell to his shoulders and his scruffy face had a few imperfect scars, which despite his young age gave him a hardened look; the look of a man that has had to fight to survive on more than one occasion in his life.

The thief suddenly lifted his head up, narrowing his eyes as if he'd heard something in the distance. Syrena stopped breathing and moved slowly away from the opening. But it was too late.

"Who might you be?" he asked abruptly, his deep voice echoing in the silence of the dungeon.

She said nothing, hoping he would doubt his ears. Little did she know she was underestimating the aptitude of a skilled thief. When she decided to peek through the small gap in the bricks again, she found herself looking at the man's knees. He began to kneel, as if to take a peek himself, and she backed away with a soft whimper, pressing her head and back against the wall.

"Ahh. Keeping me guessing, eh?" he said, less threateningly than she had expected. "That's alright, frankly I don't care who you are. But do me a favor, mate, and look around your cell. See anything sharp? A rock, a twig, anything?"

She hesitated to answer. But her eyes moved almost unwillingly, inspecting every corner of her cell.

"Nothing," she said, and the man proceeded to sigh with frustration.

"That would have been too easy," he said.

She heard his back sliding against the wall as he sat and leaned back. Had there been no brick between them, their backs would have been touching. They remained silent for a moment, both of them lost in thought. The witch was unused to any reaction from a man that wasn't an attempt to hurt or kill her. She found herself with an odd feeling in her chest, and within that, the inability to speak a single word.

But the thief, much like her, was a solitary soul.

He sat there silently, contemplating on the many times he had escaped a prison cell. But this was Val Havyn, the capital of Vallenghard, and Hudson Blackwood was in no ordinary dungeon. This was the king's castle. Certainly, he had been foolish enough to think it was anything but inescapable. But the thief always did enjoy a challenge.

A question lingered in the back of his mind, however, and he was far too distracted and curious to let it go unanswered. "Why are you in chains?" he asked.

Syrena hesitated again, a bit embarrassed that her attempt at subtlety was no match for the thief's attentiveness. "How did y-?"

"I'm a cunning thief with an exceptional ear," he interrupted, as if to speed the conversation along. "*Your* turn. Why are you in chains?"

She looked down at her wrists, bound tightly by the metal cuffs pressing against the reeking ogreskin. Her hesitation faded. Perhaps it was the protection of the brick wall. Perhaps it was the somewhat affable tone in the thief's voice. She did not know why, exactly, but she answered him with as much honesty as he had answered her.

"I'm a witch…"

He didn't respond at first, which made Syrena uneasy.

But an idea, or perhaps the seed of one, planted itself in the thief's mind upon hearing her speak those words, and the feeling in his chest was far too familiar. It was almost like a pattern, the thief thought. First, there was the feeling of hopelessness and denial. Then came the necessary thought process of putting together a perfect plan. And finally, there was the part he favored best. The part where the seed of said perfect plan was planted and everything happened to fall into place in his mind.

He found himself smirking as he leaned his head back against the wall.

"A witch, eh?" he said. "How very interesting."

* * *

Princess Magdalena of Val Havyn was just as tenacious as her father. She was a young woman of 19 with fair skin, blonde hair, and a mind that was as promising as should be expected from a future queen.

"I don't *care* what father says! I have the right to choose!" she said, pacing angrily and rapidly away from her handmaiden.

"Please, m'lady… the king asked that you appear presentable for Sir Darryk. He paid for the finest tailor in the city to make this for you."

The princess stormed through the elegant and vibrant palace corridors, unsure of where exactly she meant to go. The library, the garden, *anywhere* she didn't feel confined. Brie, the princess's personal handmaiden, was following her majesty, holding an elegant red gown specially crafted for the princess's figure and complexion.

"I am the princess of Vallenghard! I can choose who I will or will not look presentable for."

She was beginning to lose her patience again, and though Brie was simply following the orders of her king, young princess Magdalena had half a mind to ask a guard to escort the handmaiden to the kitchen with the rest of the servants.

"Your father's company will arrive at dusk, m'lady. We haven't got much time to prepare."

"Good!" Magdalena said, coming to a halt and facing her handmaiden directly. "Then come dusk, I can *personally* tell Sir Darryk that I am simply *not* interested in this marriage arrangement."

"Your father only wants what is best for the kingdom," Brie replied, unable to look her princess in the eye and instead looking down at her feet; her worn out slippers looked tattered and sad compared to the princess's elegantly ornamented shoes.

"I couldn't agree more," said the princess. "That is indeed *all* he cares about. Never mind what is best for his own daughter." She turned and headed for the nearest door. She opened it and, as if it was her first time walking through the palace, she was thrown aback a bit as she felt the sudden breeze of the nearing dusk. She found herself in the palace courtyard, surrounded by the lusciously colorful garden, when she suddenly noticed a young man dressed in farmer's clothes and a boy villager sitting at the table in the center of the garden.

All of their eyes met at once.

John Huxley and Thomlin leapt to their feet almost immediately, both in shock, having been caught off guard by the presence of the graceful princess. Thomlin's eyes had opened wide and his impulse to whisper his knowledge out loud got the best of him.

"That's Princess Magdal-"

"I *know* who she is," John shushed him.

As the princess approached the table, both John and Thomlin made a poor attempt at a bow.

"Pardon me, who are you? And what is your business here?" asked the princess.

"I-I'm John Huxley of Elbon, your majesty. This is my, um... *nephew* Thomlin," the farmer lied, startled by the sudden interrogation.

The princess shot him a doubtful look as she compared the two of them.

"Your majesty asked what is your business here," Brie, the handmaiden, spoke.

"Brie," said the princess, giving her a look of displeasure. "I'd like a moment, please."

Embarrassed, the girl removed herself and headed to the servants' quarters, dragging along the red gown as if it were old laundry. The princess turned back to John and the boy, her eyes still waiting for a proper answer.

"I-I was invited here by Sir Viktor Crowley, your majesty," John said with a hesitant stutter, soon after realizing the silence had dragged for too long. "As a reward for assisting in the capture of the wanted thief Hudson Blackwood."

"He's been caught?" asked princess Magdalena, intrigued by the idea of a farmer capturing a notorious thief.

"He has, your majesty," John replied, his blue eyes meeting Magdalena's. He had only ever seen the princess from a distance whenever he traveled to Val Havyn and the princess happened to be out in the city streets. He'd never before noticed the beauty of her eyes; they were nearly as green as the lush garden surrounding them.

"M-My apologies for intruding," John said, realizing he had no more business in the king's palace. "My nephew and I will be on our way."

But before the young farmer could gather his belongings, a screaming guard barged suddenly out of the palace doors, grasping the attention of them all.

"Retreat!" the guard shouted. "Into the palace! NOW!"

"What is the meaning of this?" the princess asked.

"Quick, your majesty! You must take shelter before they find you!"

"Before *who* finds me?!"

"Hurry, now! They're comi-"

The guard could not finish. An arrow pierced into the back of his neck and struck through the front. The princess couldn't help but yelp in shock as the guard fell to his knees, blood gushing down his neck. John glanced in the direction the arrow had been shot from. Above the courtyard, there was a beautiful stone bridge that connected one side of the palace to the other, and standing over the edge of it was a man with a bow in his hands. He had dark brown skin, adorned dreaded locks of hair, and hunting armor made red leather. But the most frightening of his qualities was his odious smile.

Captain Malekai Pahrvus whistled loudly.

And before John had time to react, a horde of about 20 men entered the courtyard. About a dozen of the men were also dressed in red leather, the rest were in rags and furs, and all of them were armed.

The princess, the farmer, and the boy all glanced at one another with distress in their eyes.

And John, by impulse, unsheathed the rusty blade strapped to his belt.

"Behind me, your majesty!" he shouted, stepping in front of Magdalena and Thomlin.

The invaders were walking straight towards him, laughing and spitting, drawing their weapons and preparing for a fight. A rush of fear ran through the farmer's body, but his determination exceeded it and he remained in place, scanning the yard for anything that might aid him in combat.

"There she is," one of the men shouted, aiming his axe at the princess. "That's the one we want!"

Magdalena stepped back against the statue of her father, her arms extended back so as to protect the peasant boy Thomlin. John Huxley shielded them both. He knew there was a very real chance that he would die in that courtyard. At that very moment, however, one of the palace doors swung open and slammed against the brick walls.

Sir Jossiah Biggs stormed out and shouted, "Onward!!"

Two more doors opened and about a dozen men marched into the courtyard, dressed in steel armor and wearing King Rowan's sigil on their chests. They drew their blades and began fighting off the invaders. What had been a peaceful courtyard soon turned into a riotous battleground and at the center of it all was her majesty, princess Magdalena.

Unwilling to stand by, John threw himself into the fight, shielding the backs of the king's guards. Swords and axes clashed all around, and though John was keeping himself alive, there was a feeling in the back of his neck that he hadn't experienced during training.

It was a feeling of distress. An urge to survive.

He was afraid. But the thrill of it was keeping him intact.

One of the invaders caught sight of princess Magdalena and walked towards her. Thomlin tried stepping in front of her, but the princess locked her grip on the boy's shoulder and kept him in place behind her. When the man reached them, he snatched Magdalena by the wrist and smiled. Only he didn't attack; instead he began pulling her away.

John was fighting alongside the king's soldiers when he saw what was happening.

Magdalena tried to resist, and though the man was not exactly large in size, his violent demeanor frightened her. Thomlin tried to help, pulling on the princess's sleeve in the opposite direction.

John ran towards them, his nerves plucking at the back of his neck, consuming him, overcoming him. Before the red invader could drag them any further, John blocked his path and sunk his blade into the distracted man's chest. The man turned to look the young farmer in the eyes. He was no one in particular, just another mercenary of the Rogue Brotherhood. To the rest of his comrades, the man was not particularly skilled or renowned, and his face was to be long forgotten within weeks.

To John Huxley, however, this was the face of the first man he would ever kill.

The farmer stood there, unable to speak or move, aside from the nervous shiver in his hands. The man slid away and fell dead on the ground, leaving red smears on the blade's sharp edge. Magdalena and Thomlin both looked at John in shock, neither one of them having seen many men die at such close proximity in the past, and yet already having seen enough for a lifetime.

There was a sudden growl coming from above. One of the invaders jumped from the bridge and landed on the statue of King Rowan. John, the princess, and the boy backed away and witnessed the menacing figure above. Whoever it was, he looked more like a beast and less like a man.

Then he removed his helmet… and a few of the king's guards were stunned at the sight.

It was an orc, green-skinned and yellow-eyed, growling as he sunk his axe into the statue's head. Orcs hadn't been seen in the city in centuries, and the shock of it all distracted some of the guards long enough to cost them their lives.

"This way!" the princess shouted, and led the farmer and the boy down one of the outdoor corridors. They darted out of the way as bodies fell and weapons clashed against each other. But before they could retreat into the safety of the palace, a dark figure stepped into the end of the corridor and blocked their path. It was a man, a frighteningly large one, with a mask over his disfigured jaw.

He began walking towards them. And John prepared himself for the fight of his life.

"Careful, John!" Thomlin said.

Princess Magdalena, unwilling to yield, picked up an axe from a dead man's hands. It was heavier than she had expected, but the adrenaline allowed her to lift it. They stood next to each other, ready to face their incoming enemy; a drop of sweat ran down John's face as the man became larger and larger with every step. He didn't think twice about confronting the wanted thief Hudson Blackwood. The Butcher of Haelvaara, on the other hand, was sure to slay him with one strike.

The Butcher reached them. And when he did, he swung his battleaxe down.

John didn't move a single muscle. He was suddenly petrified.

Instead, the princess blocked the strike. The axe fell from her hands and the Butcher landed a slap across her cheek. She fell. And the Butcher wasted not a single second before he swung at John again.

The axe, however, was suddenly blocked by a silver longsword.

A tall, blonde-haired knight in gold-lined armor stepped in front of them, his sword locked with the Butcher's axe. Their weapons clashed, again and again, their skills matching each other's. The Butcher had no choice but to step back as the valiant Sir Viktor Crowley moved forward, unwilling to yield.

John helped Magdalena to her feet.

"Go!" Sir Viktor shouted at them. "The three of you. Go. Now!"

The Butcher gave his axe a powerful swing that sent the knight stumbling backwards.

But Sir Viktor was never one to surrender. He found his footing, then lunged forward and attacked, again and again, until the Butcher was distracted enough that the princess slid away into the palace, dragging John and Thomlin along with her.

Furiously, the Butcher landed a heavy kick on Viktor's chest, one that dropped the knight to the ground, and roared angrily; a nearby red mercenary whistled as if the roar had been an order. And then a black stallion galloped suddenly into the courtyard. Before Viktor Crowley had regained his stance, the Butcher mounted the stallion and trotted away, heading towards the guard barracks.

Viktor Crowley gritted his teeth.

"Follow that horse!" he shouted, but the Butcher was already out of sight.

John and Thomlin had no time to admire the beauty of the king's palace. The elegant red and blue patterns that adorned the walls, ceiling, and tiled floors were blurred as they ran through an elegant hall, their focus set on finding a way out.

The princess, acquainted so well with the palace as she was with the palm of her hand, led the way to the guards' barracks, which was a vast open field behind the palace surrounded by two-story lodgings made of wood where the royal guard was housed. There was no grass in the field, only dirt, which made it more efficient for training, and spread throughout the field there were racks of weaponry, targets, and training equipment.

It's beautiful, John thought to himself. *Perhaps more beautiful than the palace itself.*

The ran across the field of dirt and out the black gates, which led them out to a grassy slope, and just ahead of them was a wide river flowing south through the green valley known as the Blue Hills. The view was like an image pulled right out of a dream.

"Is that Lotus Creek?" Thomlin asked through heavy breaths.

"If it is, it runs all the way down to Elbon," John said.

"Can we get there by swimming?"

"Not unless you survive the falls," the princess said.

"*Falls?*"

"Two of them. If the first one doesn't kill you, the second one undoubtedly will."

The sudden sound of a galloping horse startled them. The Butcher of Haelvaara had caught up, and he left a group of his men at the gates to block the path. Five more horses followed, the first one ridden by Captain Malekai Pahrvus of the Rogue Brotherhood. Three of the other riders were red mercenaries and the last one was a mysterious figure hidden under a dark hood.

They were trapped.

The Butcher was the first to dismount. But John's attention was on the Brotherhood mercenaries. The Captain was armed with two blades and his eyes spoke of malice and mischief. He whistled and ordered his men to approach first.

"We should go, your majesty," Thomlin suggested, tugging at the princess's sleeve.

"No! We can't just leave him!" Magdalena stood her ground, suddenly wishing she had kept the axe from the courtyard. John felt his chest pounding from the unease. As horrified as he was with the notion of death, John realized this was to be his ultimate test of survival. A test in which, if he failed, he would pay with his own head.

He thought of everything Mister Beckwit had taught him.

He thought of Sir Viktor Crowley, of the bravery that it must have taken to dedicate his life to moments like these.

He thought of the thief Hudson Blackwood; of what *he* would do.

He felt a shred of guilt, almost. He did not respect the man. But he respected his skill and determination, and even his wit. It was a bit of a shame a man like that should have to be imprisoned.

But as much as he respected each one of them differently, John Huxley was his own person.

He wasn't wise like old man Beckwit. He wasn't valorous and distinguished like Viktor Crowley, nor was he as daring as Hudson Blackwood.

He was John Huxley of Elbon, stubborn and foolish and with more spirit than any farmer ever to set foot in Val Havyn. And so he threw himself with every ounce of courage he had left. He fought harder and faster than he ever had with Larz and Henrik.

The Brotherhood crooks took turns attacking John, though it was more to tease the lad rather than out of respect for combat. But John didn't step back. He blocked every attack he could and kept his stance, taking careful and balanced steps, glancing attentively in every direction. The Butcher and Malekai were watching as if they had staged the whole thing for their own amusements. Neither one of them moved until one of their men fell to the ground wounded and John moved to attack the next.

Princess Magdalena threw herself into the grass and snatched the injured man's weapon, a thick curved blade that looked like it had been crafted somewhere overseas. Then, with a deep breath, she finished the deed.

Meanwhile, John glanced back and forth between the other two men, his blade held up in defense. They paid no mind to the princess, shrugging her off as delicate and defenseless, and so she used it to her advantage.

John stumbled, barely missing an incoming swing.

But, as one of the red invaders had his back to the princess, she swung the blade down at his neck. The man shrieked with pain and fell to the grass. And he princess yanked the weapon out and the man's blood spattered all over her elegant shoes. She stepped forward for another strike, but then a large heavy hand grabbed ahold of her wrist.

She looked up at the Butcher's pale grey eyes. And the monstrous man tightened his grip until her wrist cracked; she yelped in pain as the blade slid from her hand. The princess couldn't see it, but the Butcher was smiling beneath his teeth-studded mask.

Thomlin, acting on impulse, scratched and pulled at the Butcher's forearm, attempting to loosen his grip on the princess, but Captain Malekai Pahrvus landed a swift punch that knocked the boy unconscious. The Butcher then placed a hand on the princess's face, his palm covering her entire jaw. She tried to escape his grasp, but it was useless. She felt her chest tighten as she wheezed for air, and so the Butcher squeezed unyieldingly, blocking her breathing entirely.

John screamed, as several flesh wounds on his arms and legs began to slow him down. There was only one man left, but he was unharmed and therefore faster than the farmer.

Malekai whistled again. And John became distracted enough that the red raider disarmed him and landed a heavy kick to the knee. John fell to the ground. He was so relentless he tried to stand immediately, and his wounds began to bleed even more. The red raider paced around him, landing kicks and punches every few seconds, and snickering while at it.

"All right, enough," Malekai said. "Hold him up."

The red raider obeyed, grabbing John by the hair and lifting him to a kneeling position.

"It's over, peasant," the captain said. "There's no use fighting." He then drew a dagger and used the tip to hold John's chin up.

"Stop!" a loud, thundering voice spoke. Every pair of eyes moved towards it.

The dark hooded figure climbed off his steed and approached them. He walked towards the wounded farmer, the studs on his boots clinking with every step. He was a tall man, a little over six feet in height, and was built well, though not as large as the Butcher. When he removed his hood, his black hair flowed down freely to his chest and back and he had hair on his face that was trimmed with great precision.

He knelt on one foot over the grass. And they took a moment to look at one another.

Lord Baronkroft into the farmer's naïve blue eyes and John into the lord's mystifying black ones. He noticed a strange shade of red where it should have been white, surrounding the lord's pupils.

"Who are you, boy?" Baronkroft asked.

John panted heavily through the blood seeping through his teeth. From the corner of his eye, he could see the Butcher hoisting the unconscious princess onto his shoulders. And Captain Malekai did the same with Thomlin.

"Don't hurt them," John pleaded. He had two or three cuts on his legs and several across his arms and chest, and his eye was starting to swell from the beating. "Please… don't hurt them…"

"Oh, I wouldn't dream of it," Baronkroft replied, gently yet disturbingly. "The princess must look as regal and presentable as she can… if she is to be of any use to me, that is."

The words only made John's chest thump faster and stronger. "What d'you mean?"

But Baronkroft said nothing, only kept his eerie smile. The Butcher threw the unconscious princess over the black stallion and then reached for the unconscious boy in Malekai's arms.

"Hang on," Malekai protested with a raised brow. "What about the Brotherhood's payment?"

The Butcher shot Malekai a menacing glare.

"Patience, Captain," Baronkroft interjected. "We're not in Drahkmere just yet…"

"We never agreed to go to Drahkmere… We agreed to help capture the girl…"

"Then we can settle your payment when we meet at the camp, good sir."

At that moment the Butcher dug into his horse's saddle and pulled out a large brown coinpurse, and he tossed it at Malekai and grunted, "That should shut you up."

Malekai grimaced, but he took the coinpurse anyway and tied it to his belt.

The Butcher sat on his steed, the unconscious princess and boy in front of him. "My lord?"

"Retreat at once," Baronkroft said. "I will join you soon enough."

They obeyed him, and soon the only two souls present by the creek were the lord and the farmer, whose weak state was keeping him from moving much.

"Who… are you?" John asked weakly.

The way Lord Baronkroft curved his neck was almost inhuman.

He looked more like a walking corpse possessed by someone; or perhaps, something. The expression on his face was blank and his profoundly disturbing eyes were wide and unblinking, as if he was seeing something the farmer could not see.

"It makes no difference who I am… but what I am," he said. "I am what your kingdom fears… what your *king* fears… For far too long this world has been cursed. For far too long it's been plagued by the filth of mankind…"

Baronkroft then used a single finger to raise John's chin upwards, forcing him to look into those dead eyes of his.

"Remember this face, boy… For it is the last face your little peasant eyes will ever see," he said, his lips curving into a grin again. "I am Lord Yohan Baronkroft… And soon the world will know my name." The lord's ominously slow demeanor made it hard to imagine him in combat. Even so, his appearance was haunting and his voice had a way of sounding calm yet earsplitting all at once.

Dusk had come, and the last light shone upon his dreadful face. And it was then that John noticed something peculiar. The redness in the lord's eyes began to fade and his face began to regain some of its humanity. And the lord blinked and blinked again, as if waking from a deep sleep.

"It's a shame," he said, his eyes gazing suddenly the horizon. "To lose something so precious… I'll be sure to provide her majesty with the upmost comfort on her final days."

Something grew suddenly in John's chest. Part of it may have been anger. Part may have been fear. All that he knew was that he wasn't dead just yet. And the least bit of force could make all the difference. Baronkroft curved his neck and looked down at the frail farmer again. The expression on his face was different this time; it was as if he hadn't seen or met the young farmer before that moment, only recognized him. And as he came out of this daze, he seemed almost unsure of his next approach.

"You've fought bravely, young lad," he said, his voice with a slightly augmented tone this time. "But you do not have the bearings of a knight. Tell me… what kind of man sacrifices his own life for another, without getting paid to do so? What do they call you?"

But John's mind was elsewhere, looking desperately for a way out.

"John," he responded, simply to buy himself more time. "John Huxley of Elbon…"

"Ah… Just as I thought," Baronkroft said grimly. "No one… No one but a boy in a world of men."

Then, something strange happened. The fear left John's chest entirely. The anxiety no longer had any control of him. If he was to die, he wanted to at least be in control of his own death.

"M'lord!" someone shouted in the distance.

Baronkroft turned and saw the last of his men fighting off the king's guards at the gates. And it was in that slight moment of distraction that John found his window of opportunity. With his eyes closed, the farmer spread his arms and threw himself backwards. He rolled on the muddy grass and fell into the river.

Stunned and thrown aback, Lord Baronkroft leapt to his feet and stepped forward, but the river's current was faster than he anticipated and John had already been carried away several yards. And so, with a groan, the lord leapt on his horse. He looked angry, like a boy who had his first blade taken away from him. "Filthy street-rat," he muttered, and then rode away in the opposite direction.

Down the hill, John tried to grab on to something; a rock, a patch of dirt, a tree root… But the river's current was far too strong and he had no choice but to embrace it.

If the first fall doesn't kill you, the princess had said, *the second one undoubtedly will.*

Great, John thought to himself.

All he had to do, then, was be sure to survive the first fall.

* * *

"So… what brings a witch to Val Havyn?" Hudson Blackwood asked as he drew imaginary patterns on the brick floor with his finger.

"You mean *who* brought me here. I wouldn't come here on my own if you paid me to," Syrena said. "The Davenport brothers of Falkbury, they called themselves."

"Never heard of them," Hudson said. "Just a pair of *sons of whos*, I presume."

"Really? They sure made themselves out to be high and mighty."

"Yes. Typical thing for a *son of who* to do. Believe me, I've met plenty."

The witch found herself smirking at the thief's finesse. They had been sitting for hours in the same position, and her legs were aching severely. But something about being in close proximity to another human being kept her from moving away from that position.

"And you?" she asked him through the small gap. Syrena's voice was soft and shaky and had a slight Halghardian root, as if she had lived in a vow of silence for years and her tongue had grown unaccustomed to formulating words. In fact, she had grown so used to the inner voice in her mind that she had, in some form, forgotten what her actual voice was like. But the accent was there; it was apparent in the way she pronounced her O's and rolled her R's.

"What *about* me?" asked the thief.

"How did the renowned Hudson Blackwood end up locked up in a dungeon?"

"I'm a thief, darling. I've gotten used to being locked up in dungeons," he answered. "I like to think of it as free room and board while I decide where the wind might take me next."

They sat silently for a moment. She tugged at the ogreskin in her wrists for the thousandth time, as if it would be looser than it was when she checked 5 minutes prior. Suddenly, the door to the dungeon opened and the large, mute guard ran down the long corridor towards the door on the other end.

"Why the hurry, handsome?" the thief asked.

As the guard sped by, he growled and punched the steel bars again.

"May I have my hat back when you get a chance, mate?" Hudson shouted, but the guard was gone by then. It left both the thief and the witch pensive. It wasn't the sweating and panting of the guard that startled them, at least not as much as the bloody axe in his hand.

Syrena closed her eyes, resting them, choosing to ignore what she had just seen.

For the first time in days, she felt she just might be able to get some sleep. The thief's company was not exactly warm, but it was company that was keeping her from losing the last of her sanity, and that was all that she needed. The thought of not having to stand alone against an entire city of witch-hating peasants was calming her, if only for the time being.

"Something very bad is happening out there," Hudson muttered.

"Good," said Syrena. "Better out there than down here."

* * *

When he fell down the first waterfall, the rocks had missed him by an inch. But the impact of the fall was enough to render him unconscious. The creek dragged his unconscious body about a half-mile south before the dirt took him. The water had washed the excess of blood in his wounds, but each one remained exposed to the cold wind.

John Huxley struggled to open his eyes as the river water splashed on the right side of his face as it was pressed against the earth. He was alive, though he wasn't sure for how much longer. As he sat up and regained his consciousness bit by bit, he found himself alone, surrounded by green trees and sharp rocks. The river could have taken him halfway to Roquefort, for all he knew.

The only thing he was certain of is that he was alive.

He noticed the blood oozing down the side of his head and wondered which of the rocks had been responsible for it. He also noticed he had lost his old rusty blade somewhere in the water. Or perhaps he had dropped it before he fell into the river, at some point before...

Then it struck him suddenly...

Princess Magdalena... And Thomlin...

The last thing he remembered was their unconscious bodies being carried away by the Butcher and that ghost-like man with the haunting eyes. He tried to remember the man's name, but his memory was failing him. He pressed both hands against his temples.

Not now, he told himself. *One step at a time.*

He gazed around, unsure where to begin his journey back to Val Havyn, or if it was even safe to do so. He couldn't follow the river north; the climb would be impossible with his injuries. He cleaned his face and wiped the dirt from himself before rising to his feet, when something caught his eye.

The waterfall was near. Its height gave him the impression that it was the first, not the second.

He approached it. The wound on his leg made him walk with a limp.

Up ahead he could see, through the falls, an opening in the earth, dark and hollow. A cave… The river's flow made its way inside…

A passageway out of the castle perhaps, John thought to himself. *If so, that could have been useful earlier.*

His mind was hazy and his body ached, much like it did after a hard day of labor.

He knew the sewers of Val Havyn were connected to a net of caves that ultimately all led to Lotus Creek. But he had no particular knowledge of what caves led where, or if any were safe to walk through.

He stepped through the curtain of water and found himself staring into a dark abyss as he stood at the cave's mouth. John felt a breeze coming from it. The cave led somewhere, and if it were consistent, it would take him north.

Perhaps it was his condition, but the farmer did not object. Over the span of just one day, he had survived a fight with a wanted thief, a battle in the palace courtyard, and another fight against hired swords in which the odds were dishonestly against him.

What else could possibly happen, he thought to himself.

And then he stepped into the cave.

* * *

Merchants' Square in Val Havyn was always replete with peasants, travelers, and civilians of every class. On that particular evening, however, the square was unusually loud and teeming, as the crowds gathered to welcome back their beloved King Rowan. Adelina Huxley had barely managed to squeeze through the crowds before an angry guard with fowl breath yelled at her to step away from the palace gates.

Something was wrong, she could tell. The guard looked about as anxious as a soldier before battle.

"My son is inside!" she said, but it made no difference.

The guard and his companion had their shields and spears up, blocking the gates. And Adelina's nerves only peaked when she stood to the side and heard the guards snickering about whether the boy was even still alive. She felt helpless, to such a degree only a mother could feel. She'd heard the news about John, about how he had succeeded in capturing the wanted thief Hudson Blackwood.

She'd heard John was taken to the palace, along with a peasant boy.

But that glimmer of hope only lasted for the better half of an hour. News of the attack on the king's palace had spread to every block of the city by nightfall and when it reached Adelina's ears, she shivered. She got to Merchants' Square as fast as her feet would allow it and found that the palace was surrounded by guards at every six feet.

"Heard about your boy," said a rough voice behind her, startling her. It was Mister Jasper Nottley, spitting out a chunk of old chewing tobacco on the road.

"What did you hear?"

"Rode all around the city chained to that murderin' thief Blackwood," said Nottley.

"Where is he?" she asked him, not hesitating for a second.

"Don't know. I ain't his nursemaid. All I know is he walked in there to claim his reward and never walked out."

Mister Nottley's last remark sent a chill up Adelina's spine.

"Any news of the attack?" she asked.

"Word 'round here's the Rogue Brotherhood invaded the palace. No one saw a thing. One moment they were inside the palace and the next they were gone. Vanished. Didn't raid a single shop in the city, just the palace."

There was a pause, as Adelina took the news with as much buoyancy as she could muster. But the man's unsympathetic tone only burdened her further.

"Why are *you* here?" she asked him.

"Blackwood burned what was left of my property," the man said with a scowl. "The king will arrive any moment now. I'm here to claim payment for the damages that filth cost me."

"Raiders just invaded the king's home... You think he'll have time to worry about your tavern?"

Mister Nottley ignored her and spit once more.

Adelina scoffed and paid him no more mind. She kept her gaze on the palace gates. The guards were still laughing and snickering among themselves, and it causing a feeling of dread in the woman's heart. She knew her son well. And though she knew he was a brave young man, much like his father before him, she could not deny John's imprudence.

For a moment, she felt a rush of anger...

Too many times she'd warned him... Too many times she'd told him to put his old blade down...

Too many times she'd asked him to look the other way and yet the lad seemed only to *look* for a good threat. Had he given it a second thought before confronting the wanted thief alone, he would not have been taken to the palace. He wouldn't have been roped into the whole damn mess. He would have been at home safe and unharmed.

But the lad has no interest in 'safe', she thought to herself. *It's simply not enough for him. It never will be. And he can't help what's in his blood...*

"Missus Huxley?" a soft voice called. A bundle of auburn red hair glistened under the light of the lanterns as Evellyn Amberhill pressed through the crowds. Adelina embraced her the way a mother would embrace her own daughter.

"Oh, my dear," Adelina cried. "It's so good to see you…"

"Any word of John?" the blacksmith asked.

"Not yet…"

Then there was the sudden sound of trumpets in the distance.

"Well," Mister Nottley said. "Our king has arrived."

The loud horns were almost inaudible as Adelina became distracted… A familiar figure walked out of the palace doors, heading towards the gates. The knight's silver armor, lined with gold, had loosened and the golden shape of the eagle on his back and front was hardly discernible under the smears of dirt and blood.

The man himself was as grandiose as he had always been. His golden wheat hair was untidy from battle and there was sweat on his face, surely, but not a single trace of his own blood was on him. When he reached the gates, the guards greeted him with respect and made way for him. Adelina and Evellyn were both within earshot and could hear the man's voice, almost as majestic alone as the man himself.

"Orders, sir?" the guard with the reeking breath asked.

"Stand by," Sir Viktor Crowley said. "The trespassers have retreated."

"Shall we send word to the princess that King Rowan has arrived, sir?"

"I'm afraid that won't be possible," Sir Viktor said, sighing deeply as if still regaining his strength. The guards looked at one another, both in uncertainty and concern. Adelina listened closely for any word of her boy. But the look on the golden knight's face spoke of greater worries.

"She's been taken," Viktor said, a look of terror on his face as he realized the true severity of the situation. "The princess has been taken…"

* * *

A sharp hissing sound resonated throughout the Blue Hills of Vallenghard.

A steel axe was being thoroughly sharpened with a whetstone, and the hands that held said stone were callused and rough and olive green in color. With every brush against the steel, there came a mild grunt, as if the orc was doing it as a means to relieve a hidden inner strain.

For those that hadn't seen enough of the Rogue Brotherhood, he was quite a menacing sight. It wasn't often that one saw an orc riding in a company of humans, and it certainly showed. He tended to be distant and withdrawn, spending more time with his axe than he did with his fellow human mercenaries.

The *Beast*, they called him. And he hardly ever spoke unless it was under his breath.

His trousers were made of red leather and matched his company's uniform, but his arms and chest were often exposed. His thick forearms were strapped with a pair of brown gauntlets, onto which he slid a set of daggers for easy access, two on each gauntlet. The afternoon was crisp and light, and so he allowed for the cool breeze to aerate the red scar across his chest.

The scar consisted of three lines, running diagonally from the tip of his left shoulder across his chest and ending at his lower right abdomen. No one knew how he had gotten that scar, only that it had to have been something large. Something vicious and hungry.

From afar curious eyes were watching him, examining him.

The Beast knew it, but he chose to ignore it.

As the only orc member of the Brotherhood, he was the only one from his company who had stayed behind in the hills, surrounded by strangers from overseas, many of whom looked like him. It felt odd to him, to see orcs and elves marching so leisurely amongst men. The Brotherhood hardly left the Woodlands and when they did they never took *him*, for orcs had no business in human realms. Even talking about such a contentious thing could cost you your life.

"What do ye make of the bloke?" asked a nearby voice, a nasally one with a snort after every sentence.

"Hard to say," replied a deeper, gruffer voice. "He don't seem to fit in with the lot."

"He's in a troop of human scum, *'course* he don't fit in."

"That's *his* choice."

"What if we talk to 'im?"

"Piss off. *You* talk to 'im."

"He looks strong. Might make a good guard dog. Y'think Okvar will like 'im?"

Gruul grunted. He hardly ever liked anyone, even his own kind, and so he was much less intrigued by the Beast. "We ain't here to make friends," he said to his comrade. "Just stick with the plan. We keep our heads down 'n' slip away when we find the chance."

"I *know* the plan," replied Murzol, a lanky orc with a lazy eye and a trace of snot underneath his nostrils. "But we don't know these lands."

"Neither does *he*. Look at 'im. He's a wild one."

"Yes... I s'ppose he don't talk much," Murzol mumbled distractedly. When Baronkroft decided to hire the Brotherhood, they had expected a company full of humans. At no point had it crossed their minds that they would have an orc riding with them. Not to mention Murzol, while often dull, was well aware of the growing tension between Gruul and their defiant comrade, Okvar. And he was starting to seek desperately for another plan, should the first happen to fall apart.

"But what if we need another sword by our side?" he insisted.

"You want 'im so bad, *you* go talk to the big bastard," grunted Gruul, as he sat and bit into a roasted oversized squirrel.

Suddenly, there was a sound coming from a row of shrubs nearby, like that of rustling leaves. Murzol noticed it, but Gruul had no more interest in talking. Instead, the lanky orc observed as the Beast stood up and walked towards the sound, his freshly sharpened axe held ready.

There was movement within the tall shrubbery. The Beast sniffed the air but caught no scent, and his yellow eyes were squinting for a better look. And it wasn't until he was some ten feet away that he saw them, a pair of eyes staring at him from within the leaves.

A pair of worried yellow eyes… They were begging him to keep quiet…

The Beast came to a halt, his red-laced boots sinking into the mud.

There was hesitation in his eyes. From such a close distance, whatever was hiding in the bushes would have made an attempt at his life by then. Except it didn't. And so the orc softened his grip on his axe. The pair of eyes blinked slowly and carefully at him.

What are you…? He wondered.

He released a brusque sigh. He felt his shoulders ease from the tension and his breathing had slowed again; that was, until he heard the snort behind him. It startled him and he raised his axe into the air, ready to strike.

"Oi! Easy… easy there, big fella," said the lanky orc Murzol, cowering down with his hands raised above his head. "I just wanna talk to ye…"

The Beast said nothing. He kept his stance and gave Murzol a ferocious glare.

Then there was a rather unexpected sound. It was high-pitched and shrill and it was coming from the bushes. It was the sound of a crying infant.

Murzol's eyes lit up like wildfire. Both him and the Beast glanced towards the sound and followed it… There, crouched within the leaves, was an orcess. She was pressing her child against her chest, wrapped in a bundle of cloth, and she was dressed in robes that covered her from neck to toe and a grey shawl that enclosed most of her hair, save for a flew traces of black around her forehead. She was terrified; it was obvious in the way her sharp fangs were quivering against her upper lip as her jaw shook with distress.

"What have we here…?" someone asked. Gruul was suddenly standing there behind Murzol and the Beast, his eyes determined and hungry. "What a beauty," he said, and he gave his lips a lick. He tried to step forward, but then a heavy red-laced boot sunk onto the earth in the way of Gruul's path.

The Beast said nothing still, only faced Gruul with a hostile glower.

"Step aside, lad," Gruul said, but the mercenary orc said more with a stare than he could have with words. Meanwhile, Murzol saw an opportunity and took it. He ran and grabbed hold of the orcess, who in return swung her arm to punch him, nearly dropping her weeping child.

The Beast growled and stepped towards Murzol, his axe ready to strike.

A voice, however, caught them all by surprise. "Hey! What's goin' on here?!"

A hand seized the orcess by the arm, ignoring the fact that she needed it to properly hold her child. It was a hand that was dark blue in color, like a starless sky at midnight.

"We saw 'er first," Gruul argued.

"It doesn't matter, does it?" the elf replied. Though his skin was darker than most elves, his hair was just as silver and his luminous eyes were as red as blood.

"Stay out of this, Jyor," Gruul warned him.

"Or you'll do what exactly?" the elf taunted him.

"She's *my* prize! You've *no* right."

"Baronkroft's orders were clear... *All* of the prisoners stay together," replied Jyor, his hand still gripped tightly around the shivering orcess's wrist.

"Please," she suddenly yelped. And everyone turned to look at her at once. "I-I... I go to city of Kahrr," she said, and it became clear that she wasn't used to speaking their language. "I *go*... Please..."

But Jyor, the elf, showed no sign of mercy in his eyes. He may have been shorter and much thinner than any of the orcs, but he was also faster than they were. And he was as fierce as a wildcat when challenged. "I'm locking her up with the rest," he said, locking eyes with Murzol. "Now let go of the bitch."

He then glanced at the Beast, who by then appeared more like a bystander.

"And *you*... Put the axe down, lad. It's no use causing trouble..."

The Beast walked away. He held his axe still, just in case, but he retreated into the darkness of his tent. And when he did, the orcess became even more flustered, having seen something in the eyes of the Beast that she hadn't seen in the eyes of the other orcs or the elf. Something like compassion.

"N-No... please," she kept begging.

"Talk again and you'll earn yourself a lashing," Jyor warned her, and then pulled her towards the rest of the prisoners. Gruul and Murzol tried to protest, but something in the distance caught their eye. At the top of the hill, a company of horses approached them. And standing at the very front was the hooded figure of Lord Baronkroft. To his right was the monstrous man known as the Butcher, and to his left was the Captain of the Rogue Brotherhood, Malekai Pahrvus.

Gruul and Murzol stepped back and allowed for Jyor to drag the orcess away. They walked back towards their fire and sat on the dry grass.

"I want that elf's head," Gruul muttered softly.

"Baronkroft will have *yours* if ye try it," Murzol snorted.

"To hells with Baronkroft. That orcess is *mine*."

"Hmm... What about the bloke?" Murzol asked again, his narrowed gaze aimed at the Beast's tent. "I think he's got some pluck, don't ye?"

"Fuck the bloke," Gruul said with growl. "He ain't true... Trust me, I sees it in his eyes. He's *soft*... He may as well be a human."

IV
A Rescue Brigade

The princess's handmaiden sat nervously in a wooden stool, rocking back and forth. When the attack happened, the royal servants had retreated to the nearest common room and locked themselves in. There was nothing for them to do but wait. Wait and hope that the royal guard could successfully drive the invaders away.

The king and his troops had journeyed to the southern coast of Vallenghard two weeks prior to the attack, where the city of Roquefort had been under threat by Aharian forces from overseas. Vallenghard prevailed and what little enemy forces had been left retreated and sailed back to their homeland. And as a show of gratitude for the king's aid, Lord Augustus Clark of Roquefort had offered his only son's hand in marriage to Princess Magdalena.

Sir Darryk Clark was a known man in Roquefort, but not really anywhere else. Princess Magdalena had never met him, and had little interest in marrying him. And when the letter had arrived in Val Havyn, she had not taken it lightly. Her father, in a desperate attempt to keep his kingdom intact, had agreed to the proposal without her consent. And he had sent word that Sir Darryk was to journey back to the royal city with him to start the arrangements for the grand ceremony.

The circumstances, however, had changed. King Rowan had no idea that he would come home to a missing daughter. And Sir Darryk had no idea of the cruel trick that fate had played on his bride-to-be.

The palace kitchens were cold that day, but that had very little to do with why the princess's handmaiden was trembling. There were rumors circulating all around. The optimists swore that the royal guard had drawn the invaders out. The rest of them knew better, well aware that the palace was dangerously unguarded and the odds did not favor the small force the king had left behind.

When Sir Jossiah Biggs barged into the kitchen to announce both the retreat of the invaders and the arrival of the king, there were sighs of relief all around. "You may return to your duties," Jossiah said.

The chattering began instantly. Smiles grew on the servants' faces but Brie, the princess's handmaiden, frowned still, examining the unusually stern expression on Sir Jossiah's face. Though his presence had the tendency to make her feel uneasy, she grew just enough courage to speak to him.

"Is the Princess back in her chambers?" she asked.

His reaction was not a pleasant one. He simply glared at her, his eyes speaking more than his words ever could. *You abandoned her*, they said. And the handmaiden couldn't bear to look at him any longer. She turned and headed for the door.

Thump.

She came to a halt. The kitchen was now empty, save for the knight and the handmaiden. And the sound was coming from a steel door on a far corner of the kitchen floor. The knight drew his sword and motioned Brie to follow him.

Thump. Thump.

"Where does that hatch lead?" Biggs asked softly.

"The kitchen cellar, sir," Brie replied.

"*And?*"

"The sewers…"

She placed her petite hands on the handle and gripped it. She and the knight made eye contact, as if to confirm they were both ready. Biggs nodded, his sword at the ready, and then the handmaiden lifted the steel hatch.

A pair of blue eyes was looking up at them.

Though Jossiah Biggs had his sword high above his head, the young man did not wince, mostly due to his lack of energy. He was wounded and exhausted and could hardly stand straight.

"Mister Huxley," Sir Biggs said, uncertainty in his eyes. "Well I'll be damned…"

* * *

Sir Darryk Clark waited patiently outside of the king's assembly room.

He was a decent man; a young handsome swordsman with brown skin and black curly hair. His armor was made of black steel, distinctive of Roquefort's army's uniform. And he looked confident in it, knowing very well that his skills were limited to being a knight, for he was a rubbish diplomat.

He sat in that elegant palace corridor, shaken from the news of the princess's capture and feeling more out of place by the minute. He could hear the rage in the king's voice inside the assembly room, a muffled yet thundering voice that nearly shook the paintings along the walls.

Suddenly a loud tapping approached from around the corner.

A middle-aged woman in an elegant turquoise gown walked past the young knight. She wore silver jewelry in her fingers and wrists, and her thick black hair was brushed away from her face, tied with a silver pin at the back. Her skin was just as smooth and brown as Darryk's, and her eyes were just as vibrant, only hers were as wide as an owl and horribly intimidating.

Sir Darryk stood from his seat out of respect, and it was obvious that he was both flustered and pleased to be meeting her. "My Lady," he said with a bow.

The Lady looked at him as if she had only just noticed he was there, as if she was not used to knights reacting so affably towards her. And it wasn't until she saw the crest of Roquefort in his chest that she realized who the young man was.

"You're Sir Darryk Clark," she said, her austere voice just as intimidating as her glare. "The one who was promised to the princess… Are you not?"

"Yes, my Lady," he replied, attempting a friendly grin.

Her name was Lady Brunylda Clark, the Treasurer of Val Havyn, and she was the only blood relative that the young man knew in the entire city.

"What a pity," she said, her face blank and her eyes firm. And then she turned and headed for the king's assembly room. Sir Darryk, unsure of how to respond, simply sunk to his seat again.

King Rowan's temper had always been short, but the fury in his eyes on this day was strong and vivid. His royal advisors sat around the long rectangular table at the center. And when the door to the assembly room opened, every pair of eyes turned to gaze at Lady Brunylda.

"Where is he?!" the king shouted.

"It's a pleasure to see you too, your majesty," she replied fearlessly, bowing her head and walking towards her chair. "He should be here shortly…"

The king slammed a heavy fist down into the table. "Where in all hells is Crowley?!"

Three knights of the king's court were sitting on one side of the table. Lady Brunylda sat across from them, next to the palace minister. The rest of the advisors consisted of nobles and township lords, most of whom had never held a sword in their lives and all of whose names the king would often interchange unintentionally.

For this, along with the fact that most of the advisors were merely interested in gaining profits from neighboring cities rather than the safety of their own, the king valued highly the opinions of his knights over those of his court, including the Lady. But on this day, King Rowan could hardly stand to look at his knights. He'd shouted at them all for the better part of an hour, as he waited for the two knights that he had left in charge of guarding the palace.

"How could you let this happen?! All of you?!" shouted the king, his voice resonating throughout the assembly room. He was a large man, on the heavier side, with a thick coat of brown hair that flowed neatly to his back and a rich beard that was fit for royalty. Traces of grey were beginning to show on his scalp, and his skin was rough and dry from days on the road.

"It was an unexpected attack, your majesty," Lady Brunylda replied. "I suggest we keep calm, an-"

"Keep calm?!" the king stepped towards her, his voice rising. "*Calm?!*"

"Fending off intruders is the duty of the royal guard and its knight commander," the Lady argued, her voice rising along with the king's. "If anyone is to be held accountable here, it's Sir Viktor Crowley and certainly *not* your advisors."

"I believe we should wait to hear what Sir Viktor has to say before anyone holds *anybody* accountable," said Sir Hugo Symmond, a tall thin knight with chestnut-colored hair and a remarkably impressive mustache.

"So *where* is he, then?!" the king shouted, slamming his fist down again. "Where in all hells is Sir Viktor Crowley?!"

Outside the assembly room, at the end of the corridor, a door swung open and in walked a knight of middle age and rough demeanor. Sir Darryk Clark rose to his feet again impulsively. The knight, who appeared to be heading towards the assembly room, came to a halt when he reached Darryk.

"Who are you?" Jossiah Biggs asked abruptly.

"Sir Darryk Clark of Roquefort, sir," the young man answered in a nervous stammer.

"The lad that was to marry the princess? My condolences," Jossiah grunted. "Head to the servants' quarters, lad. Ask for a young woman named Brie. She will show you to one of the guest chambers. We might be in for a long night."

"Yes... If it's all the same to you, sir," Darryk interrupted. "I would prefer to stay here in case his majesty requests my presence."

"His majesty is far too concerned with other matters, lad."

"Right... But if it's all the same to you."

Biggs made a gesture that wasn't of approval but not entirely of displeasure either. He examined the young man. Inexperienced, perhaps, but he had a firm posture and eyes that conveyed determination, if not confidence. "Sir Darryk, you said your name was, yes?"

"Yes, sir."

"Be careful where you place your loyalty, lad," Jossiah said. "Your devotion's admirable, but sometimes a man must make his own decis-"

But Jossiah didn't have the chance to finish his thought. The door at the end of the corridor swung open again, and in walked the majestic figure of the Golden Eagle of Vallenghard, Sir Viktor Crowley, only his stern demeanor had changed into a more brittle one. He looked less regal and more human than before. He breathed deeply and approached the assembly room door.

"I expect he heard the news," Viktor said, perturbed by the muffled screams just behind the door.

"Good thing you kept your armor," Jossiah muttered.

"What a bloody disaster," Viktor sighed, after which he glanced quickly at Darryk as if he hadn't seen him when he entered the corridor. Sir Darryk had never met the renowned Viktor Crowley in person; now there he was, a mere three feet from the legend, and yet he might as well have been invisible.

"Very well," Viktor said, taking one last deep breath as he stepped towards the assembly room. "Into battle..."

The two knights slipped into the assembly room, and instantly all eyes turned to them.

King Rowan's shouting ceased all of a sudden, and there was a silence in the room that nearly hurt to listen to.

"Your majesty," Sir Viktor Crowley took a bow, and soon his second-in-command Jossiah Biggs did the same. The king took slow, heavy steps towards the two knights. Sir Viktor stood at the front, while Jossiah stood behind him trying his best to look hardhearted while inside he had shriveled like a pup.

Viktor straightened himself.

"It is an honor to have you back in Val Havyn, your maj-"

King Rowan landed a heavy blow to Viktor's jaw.

The golden knight felt his neck crack as his head was knocked to the side with the punch. The advisors in the room suddenly lowered their gazes with discomfort. The only eyes that couldn't bear to look away were those of Lady Brunylda Clark and Sir Hugo Symmond.

Viktor had nearly lost his balance. He straightened himself once again and looked back into the fiery eyes of his king, who stood a mere foot from his face. As he wiped his chin he realized his lower lip had busted open, traces of red beginning to dribble, and his greasy hair had been brushed over his face. But he kept his gaze fixed and his stance firm.

"Explain yourself," the king said bitterly. "*Now.*"

Sir Viktor cleared his throat. "The attack was unprecedented, sire…"

"There were *dozens* of you, Crowley…"

"I'm afraid there were more of *them*, sire… We don't know how they got in. But there were men blocking nearly every path. We did our best to draw them out, but…"

The king's eyes spoke of more than just disgrace. There was a shimmer that wasn't there before.

I trusted you, they said. *I trusted you with her life.*

"What he says is true, your majesty," Jossiah Biggs added. "I was there when th-"

"Shut your damn mouth, Jossiah," the king interrupted, his eyes still fixed on his right hand knight.

The silence lingered a bit longer.

Sir Viktor's eyes would lower and rise repeatedly, like a scared child being lectured by his father. Only it was a lifelong friend he was facing, and somehow Viktor found it to feel worse.

"Your majesty," Sir Hugo Symmond broke the silence. "If Sir Viktor says they were outnumbered, I trust the royal guard did everything in their power t-"

"Fuck my royal guard!!" the king shouted with a sharp brusqueness in his voice, breaking his stare with his right hand knight and turning back towards everyone else in the room. "Seems I'm in dire need of a *new* royal guard if they can't be trusted with the safety of their future queen!"

"Your majesty," Lady Brunylda spoke. "While Sir Viktor should be certainly held accountable, I believe we should focus on th-"

"You will speak when spoken to, Lady Clark," the king shouted, shifting his attention back towards Viktor. "You! Where have they taken my daughter?!"

"I-I'm afraid I..."

"Quit stammering, you old fool, and *answer* me! Where have they taken her?!"

"I'm not sure, sire. She was led to safety and we thought sh-"

"You *thought*?!" the king interrupted. "To hells with your fucking thoughts! I need *answers*! Why can't *anyone* in this room tell me where these bastards came from or where they've taken Magdalena?!"

"They held no crest, your majesty," Sir Viktor spoke again. "A great part of them were members of a guild of mercenaries known as the Rogue Brotherhood. They operate within the Woodlands, but it seems they were open to foreign contracts as well."

The rage in the eyes of King Rowan suddenly turned into horror. "The Brotherhood...?" he asked.

The long silence that followed seemed to sting by the second.

A knot grew in the king's throat; the king hadn't felt a knot so painful since he heard word that his third wife died during labor. But even then, the king had had a shred of hope. He was given a daughter, a piece of his queen. And with the child he'd found the will to continue.

"Is she..." King Rowan struggled to speak. "Is my daughter dead...?"

Viktor had no answer for his king. He simply stood there with an uncertain frown as he observed his king's eyes grow diluted and weak. The only sound in the room came from the crackling in the fireplace. King Rowan, the most powerful man in Vallenghard, found himself defenseless; his forces weakened and his only kin taken. He sighed, and his silence spoke of despair and hopelessness. His hands tightened into fists and his face began to redden. Though the man was heavy and of middle age, he had the strength and energy of a lion and would often fight alongside his men in combat. Suffice it to say, had the table at the center of the room not been as grand, the king would have torn it to shreds with his bare hands.

"Sire... I'm truly... *truly* sorry," Sir Viktor said as he stepped forward. "I... I've failed you... And I don't deserv-"

"Leave..." the king said abruptly.

Sir Viktor's discomfort was insufferable. He knew there was nothing left to say, for any words would only anger his king further. "Yes, sire," were the only words he could muster, before heading for the door.

"The *both* of you..."

Both Viktor and Jossiah glanced back at King Rowan.

"Leave my palace..." the man said. "*Now.*"

The two knights looked at one another briefly and turned back to their king.

"Sire?" Viktor asked, perplexed and thrown aback.

The king took another step towards them, the fury vivid in his glare.

"My daughter may be dead because of you," he said. "You haven't just failed me... You have failed your *kingdom*. And you don't deserve to wear that crest... Now the *both* of you... Remove your armor, return your weapons, and get out of my palace..."

Sir Viktor felt a pressure building up in his chest. There was pain in his eyes; so agonizing he could hardly ignore it. "Sire, I can assure you I-"

Suddenly and without hesitation, King Rowan unsheathed his sword and swung it over his head. He plunged the sharp edge onto the headrest of his own chair and it sunk about three inches deep into the oak. He looked at the Golden Eagle, breathing heavily with rage.

"Listen here, Viktor Crowley," he said. "If you were any other man, that sword would be on your neck at this very moment. The only reason why it *isn't* is because of what you did for me... A life for a life... Consider our debt settled... Now do as you were ordered and get the fuck out of my sight..."

And with that, the golden knight's legacy was shattered, his reputation diminishing before him. There was nothing he could have said that would have changed his king's mind. Viktor Crowley left the assembly room, his friend Jossiah Biggs following behind him.

Two men. Not knights, nor even soldiers.

Only two men inside a royal palace they would never set foot in again.

* * *

John hardly felt the sting of the needle by the time the handmaiden was stitching the last wound on his arm. As reckless as the lad was, he had grown used to bruises and cuts over the years. And it certainly helped that the girl had a gentle hand. The stitches were carefully and skillfully sewn, so much so that the young farmer couldn't help but remark upon her skill.

"My sincere thanks," he said to her. "Was your mum or dad a healer?"

Brie, the princess's handmaiden, couldn't resist the cackle under her breath.

"Never knew my dad," she said. "And my mum was a seamstress."

"Oh... She must've been a very good one, then."

They sat in a room that was unlike the rest of the elegant palace. There was no paint on the walls, only bare brick, and there were wooden rectangular tables all around. John felt more at ease there than he did in the palace courtyard. Yet something about having his wounds tended to in the same place where the servants ate supper made him feel uncomfortable.

"Where did you learn to fight?" Brie asked curiously.

"Mister Abner Beckwit of Elbon," John replied, biting his lip and grunting as Brie sunk the needle into a part of his forearm that was still sensitive. "He, um... He actually used to be in the king's royal guard, Mister Beckwit... 'Til the day his parents died from the Plague and he had to choose between selling his family's farmland or tending to it."

"A noble act, I'd say."

"Yes, well... Why anyone would prefer to wield a pickaxe over a sword baffles me."

"Is there something wrong with not wanting to wield a sword?" Brie asked, causing John to stammer suddenly.

"N-No, I... I only meant... It doesn't get much better for us farmfolk, is all," he said. "Many can only dream of having what it takes to be in the royal guard. He was lucky. Anyhow, I'm sure the scarred muscles in his leg might have had something to do with his decision."

"How was he wounded?"

"Don't know. He never would tell us that particular story. But don't let the old man's limp fool you. He's as quick with a sword as he is with an insult. All in good form, of course."

Brie chuckled, cutting the remaining string at the edge of John's wound. But her smile did not last very long. Her lips curled back down faster than John could examine the damage on his arm.

"Is it true, what they say...?" asked the handmaiden. "Has Princess Magdalena really been taken?"

John had nearly forgotten about it all. The exhaustion was keeping him from focusing on more than one thing at a time. His frown returned, and with it the dread of having failed not only Sir Viktor Crowley but, in a sense, the entire kingdom. The handmaiden waited patiently for an answer, but she knew what that answer would be based on the farmer's expression alone.

At that moment, there was a pulsating echo heard throughout the corridor just outside the kitchens. A door had been swung open in the distance and the voices of two men, one seemingly angrier than the other, were approaching. At first, the voices were muffled. Slowly, however, John's ear began to pick up traces of a frenzied discussion.

"What a fucking disaster... The *nerve* of the man," the first man spoke.

"Simmer down, old friend."

"I've got three words to say to you. *King Rowan's Curse.* Same deed, just two decades late."

"I said hold your damn tongue!"

Brie set aside the sewing kit. Her hands were moist from the blood on John's wounds, and so she wiped them on her already tainted dress. "My apologies, I'll shut this," she said as she headed for the door.

"Wait," John stopped her, his head in a tilt and his attentive ear held out.

At the end of the corridor, the two men walked briskly along the servants' quarters.

Viktor Crowley had removed most of his armor but the steel plates on his boots remained, having had them made especially for him by a Val Havyn blacksmith whom Viktor could only remember as bearing the family name Rexx. The man wore a brown shirt that was wrinkled and stained with sweat and traces of dry blood that wasn't his. He looked less regal this way, like a well-built peasant.

Jossiah Biggs, on the other hand, still wore his armor entirely, just the way it had been left after fighting off the invaders, as if the denial of his expulsion was keeping him from removing it. Both of them still carried their swords, however, for once a soldier was knighted their weapons were commissioned and gifted to them, and they would become almost a *part* of them.

"How can you ask me to do such a thing after what just happened?!" Jossiah spoke heatedly and unreservedly. "Come to your senses, Viktor, this isn't just an outburst. This is real!"

"I am perfectly aware of our circumstances, old friend," Viktor said, coming to a halt and facing his once second-in-command. "And believe me, I've lost just as much as you have today. But there are eyes and ears behind every one of these walls!"

"Ahh, *let* them hear it!"

"Now is *not* the time to act rash, Jossiah. Now is the time to pull ourselves together and figure a way out of this."

"There is no *this*, Viktor. What part of that do you not understand?!"

There was a soft thump as a nearby door tapped against the brick wall.

The two men turned towards it suddenly, both gripping their swords as was usual of them for the first two or three hours after a battle. A wounded young man stood at the doorframe of the servants' dining room, his blue eyes glistening under the lantern above his head.

"The farmer…" Viktor said, the incredulity vivid in his eyes.

For a moment, John thought the man would attack him, blaming him for the capture of the princess. Instead, Viktor's gaze was one of surprise and perhaps even a hint of deference towards the young farmer's endurance.

Viktor turned back to face Jossiah. "You didn't tell me he lived…"

There was a sudden spark radiating from Viktor's eyes, as it would often happen whenever he was blessed with an idea.

* * *

"I'm not hungry," Margot protested.

"I don't care. Eat your stew," Robyn responded, silently admitting to herself that she had indeed performed poorly; the stew was thick and somewhat overcooked, but she had certainly done worse before.

"I *hate* stew," Margot said, throwing her wooden spoon on the table.

Her brother Melvyn ate without objection, more out of loyalty to his older sister than out of hunger. "I don't mind it."

"I do," his sister stuck out her tongue.

"Remember what mum said. You mustn't be ungrateful," Robyn lectured her. "Somewhere out there, there's a poor bastard locked in a cell that would give anything to have that bowl of stew."

"*This* stew? Then he truly is a poor bastard," Margot said.

Robyn threw her own wooden spoon at her sister, who just managed to duck before it struck her. Melvyn giggled. But the commotion did not last long, as a heavy knock on the cottage door silenced the three of them.

Robyn leapt to her feet first.

The twins hid behind their older sister, as she approached the door.

"Is it mum?" Melvyn whispered. And Margot hushed him with a pinch in the arm.

"Shut up, both of you," Robyn hissed at them.

The moon had risen, bringing with it the chilly winds of the late evening. The only warmth and light was coming from the fireplace and a few lit candles around the cottage. Visitors were not so rare in the evenings, but after the news of the attack on the royal palace Robyn hesitated to turn the doorknob.

She came back to her senses when a familiar voice called out for her.

"Robyn? Are you there?" it said.

And immediately the girl closed her eyes and sighed with relief. When she opened the door, there was a loud shriek and a black shadow flew into the room, startling them all. Robyn yelped loudly, and then the twins giggled and mocked her.

"Damn it," Robyn straightened herself. "I *hate* that crow."

Mister Beckwit walked inside the cottage and closed the door behind him as Robyn took his coat. "Ahh, don't fret over old Nyx," he said, as Melvyn pulled a wooden chair closer to him. "He means well."

"For others, perhaps. Doesn't seem to like *me* very much," Robyn mumbled.

"And how do you know? Have you ever gotten a chance to know him?"

"I think befriending someone old enough to be my grandfather is odd enough," Robyn smiled. "I can only imagine what mother would say if I started talking to animals."

"Have you heard from John?" young Melvyn asked eagerly.

"I heard Missus Aelyn say he killed a thief!" Margot said, sipping on the last of her stew with no objections, out of fear of seeming childish to their mentor.

"He did no such thing," Mister Beckwit answered honestly. "I'm sure our John is fine. All there is to do is pass the time until we hear word from him or your mother."

"But he did *fight* him, didn't he?" Robyn asked.

There was a pause, as Old Man Beckwit noticed the look of wonder and amazement in the girl's eyes. At only 17 years of age, Robyn had a quality about her that spoke of greatness; she was a defiant soul, and more capable than anyone, including her own mother, would give her credit for. And she was fearlessly loyal, the kind of friend that would rather risk death before leaving you behind.

"He fought Blackwood?" Robyn asked again, as if the old man had forgotten the question.

Mister Beckwit couldn't help but smile. "That is what they're saying, yes…"

"That's bloody brilliant," Robyn's eyes seemed to glow from the enthusiasm.

Margot and Melvyn moved closer to the fire, sitting merrily side by side, petting and feeding breadcrumbs to the one-eyed crow. In truth, Old Man Beckwit had heard word of the invasion in the palace, but he remained unsure if John Huxley was alive or dead. Yet he could not find it in his heart to say a word about it to the children.

"Look at 'im," Robyn said, glancing over at Nyx and the twins. "Stupid crow just hates my guts."

"Give him time," Mister Beckwit chuckled. "He's friendlier than you would think."

"That's exactly what mum says about Robyn," Margot said, to which her sister scowled.

* * *

A splash of pumpkin juice stained the wooden table in the servants' quarters, as Viktor Crowley slammed the tankard down in anticipation. John Huxley sat eating a plate of leftover duck and steamed vegetables, slowly regaining his strength. He took the pumpkin juice and gulped it down as Viktor took a seat across from him.

"Tell us everything you know, Huxley," the golden knight said, leaning in with a tankard in his own hands, only this one smelled of something much stronger than pumpkin juice. "Every moment counts, every detail matters."

"What good will it do, Viktor?" Jossiah Biggs asked bitterly, sitting near the fire with his legs resting on a wooden stool. "The lad's half-dead. He's probably tired and delusional."

"*You've* been tired and delusional for nearly ten years, old dog," Viktor replied mockingly, the ale beginning to show traces of the man behind the title. Jossiah didn't take the comment lightheartedly but Viktor hardly took notice, focusing instead on John's words as if his life depended on it.

"I tried to fight them off," John said. "But… there were so many of them."

"I'm sure there were, lad," Viktor said. "Did you recognize any of their faces?"

There was a crumb of marinated duck skin on John's lips but he was far too distracted to notice, his eyes drifting away as he recalled every bit of the incident, now that he had the energy for it. The two men waited patiently, both of them eagerly looking to him for answers. And it was making John feel sicker by the second. "It all happened so fast," he said. "But I do believe I saw…"

"Yes?" Viktor leaned closer, his eyes narrowing.

"Ser Harrok Mortymer," John said. "The Butcher of Haelvaara."

"Aye, son," Viktor nodded, as if confirming what he already knew. "What else?"

"Horse shit," Jossiah Biggs snarled, taking his feet off the wooden stool and walking towards a nearby table where there rested a fresh jug of ale. He poured himself some and spit on the brick floor resentfully. "The Butcher was killed in battle years ago," he said. Not that the man was very pleasant to begin with, but now that his knighthood had been revoked, he felt even less of a need to act amicably.

"I can assure you he wasn't, old friend," Viktor remarked. "He was very much alive when he swung his axe at me."

Jossiah's eyes narrowed. "Piss off," he said in disbelief.

Viktor turned back to the young farmer, fairly eagerly. "Was there anyone else you recognized? Or a name you might have heard?"

"There was a man…" John said. "I-I… I can't recall his name, it all happened so fast… But I remember his face. And the Butcher called him *My Lord*."

"Did he take anyone else?"

"I think we would've noticed," Jossiah hopped into the conversation again.

"I do believe I was asking the boy," Viktor said.

"Just the princess, sir," John muttered. "And a boy… A *friend*."

He felt a deep sadness overcoming him suddenly. Thomlin had been an innocent bystander, dragged into the middle of an attack. And now, because of him, he might have been dead somewhere.

"I tried to protect them," John went on, tears building up in his eyes from the guilt. "And I… I…"

His voice began to break as he tried desperately to hold himself together.

His gaze lowered. He breathed inward and outward, slowly and heavily.

"What is it, lad?" Viktor asked, his eyebrows lowering as if he felt pity for John.

The farmer fought back the knot in his throat and breathed heavily. He felt almost ashamed of his tears, especially in front of the famous Sir Viktor Crowley.

"I *killed* a man, sir…" he admitted out loud for the first time, and he felt a great weight lift from his shoulders. "I killed him…"

Viktor sighed deeply and took a good sip from his drink. He backed away and leaned against his chair as he thought of what to say. He was so wrapped up in his own thoughts that he had forgotten he was talking to a young lad. "First one?" he asked.

And John, unable to speak further, gave him a gentle nod.

"Well," Viktor sighed, acknowledging the farmer's naivety. "There isn't much to say, son... You were doing what needed to be done to protect her majesty."

"But I *didn't* though, did I?" John said, his eyes conveying sorrow and despair. "I *failed* her..."

At that moment, something happened that John would never have expected.

He felt a comforting hand on his shoulder that nearly made him twitch. It was the hand of Viktor Crowley, a man known as the bravest knight in all of Vallenghard, who carried the reputation of an emotionless man, though this was mostly due to the fact that he often saved his true persona for his king and comrades-in-arms.

"Keep your head up, son," Viktor said. "The world isn't kind to the good-natured... You have to stain your hands sometimes for the good of your kingdom. And it will most certainly take a toll on you... But you must fight it. You *can't* let it consume you... You understand? You did your best and that's all that matters."

Viktor's words somehow eased the knot in John's throat. After two decades of serving the king, Viktor had grown used to losing comrades in battle and the face of a farmer was surely not one he would typically make an effort to remember.

But he remembered John...

There was something in the farmer's eyes that made it impossible for Viktor to brush away. He saw reckless bravery, above all else, as well as ingenuousness. What the knight had seen, perhaps, were the remnants of a time decades past in which he had the same precise look in his own eyes.

"Wasn't enough though, was it?" Jossiah Biggs mumbled coldly, his lips pressed against his tankard.

John felt the sting of the man's words, but he tried not to dwell on them.

"Stand back, old boy," Viktor said, his brows lowering.

"What? You know I'm right. It makes no difference," Biggs replied as a drop of ale dribbled down his less-than-elegant beard.

"I said stand back..."

"You can pat the boy's arse all you want, it won't bring the princess back."

"Enough!" Viktor slammed his tankard down on the table, causing John a bit of a fright. Viktor's chair slid and fell backwards as the man leapt to his feet and confronted his lifelong friend. "Shut your bloody mouth, old boy, or I will shut it permanently for you. Because from where I stand, it seems to me that this young lad, a *sheep farmer*, was doing a far better job at protecting her majesty than *you* were... You! A royal fucking knight."

"Ah, so it was *my* responsibility now, eh?!"

"It was *our* responsibility! And we *all* failed, so it's time you stopped throwing the blame around and began focusing on how in gods' names we're coming back from this."

"There's *no* coming back! You're not a knight anymore, Viktor, *face* it!"

Jossiah's words stung his old friend harder than any dagger could. Something in Viktor's expression had changed. Some of the hope was gone, replaced by sorrow and dread but not yet desperation. The only sounds in the room for a few moments were from the cackling of the fireplace and the muffled clattering of the cook preparing dinner in the next room. And the silence only grew more painful by the second.

Jossiah sighed deeply and gradually, which was the closest thing to an apology the man could ever give anyone. "I've had enough of this rubbish," he said, his voice much calmer than before. "If you'll excuse me, I'm going to take as much gold as I can fit into a rucksack, perhaps a wineskin or three, and be on my way. I suggest you do the same."

Jossiah headed for the door, but came to a halt when his old friend spoke again.

"No..." Viktor said, and the silence that followed allowed for the word to nearly echo.

"No?" Jossiah asked with a raised brow.

Viktor nodded his head from side to side, an expression of fortitude in his entire façade. He had a hand on his belt and the other he used to wipe the sweat from his forehead and brush the hair from his face. The man even began to pace, almost involuntarily as if the blood pumping heatedly through his veins was keeping him from standing still. "I *will* fix this," he said. "Mark my words, old friend, I will."

"I think you've had enough for the night, Viktor," Jossiah said. He then turned to John and added, "Do take the ale from him before he passes out, will you?"

Viktor Crowley slid the tankard off the table so swiftly that it slammed against a brick wall and the remaining ale splashed all over the brick floors. "No!" he said, his voice rising. "I'll be damned if I'll allow this to be how it ends."

"Viktor... with all due respect, old friend, it's useless to dwell. I'm afraid this is a calamity we won't be able to move past from."

"It's a setback, is what it is."

"You *know* that it isn't..."

"Elaborate?"

"Sure, you might have a lead now. But you haven't the funds and you haven't the men. Hell, you haven't even the title anymore!"

"You have some connections, how much do you suppose we can borrow?"

"As Sir Viktor Crowley, plenty. As a mere peasant, not much I'm afraid."

"To hell with it," Viktor said, the smell of the ale starting to tarnish his breath. He only had three tankards' worth and yet the knight had grown so unused to drinking that it was starting to affect him prematurely. "Listen to me, Jossiah, *nobody* knows about this," he said. "No one but the king and the handful of people in that room."

"You realize that *handful* of people have connections everywhere, do you? All it takes is one raven and the whole kingdom will know in a matter of days."

"Which is why the time to act is *now*!"

"You mean you plan to take the money and run off?!"

"We will hire a company. A dozen men. Two, at most. We go after these bastards and we steal the princess back."

"Have you gone mad?!"

"Damn it all to hells, old man!" Viktor raised his voice again. "Were you or were you *not* a knight of Val Havyn before today?! Why don't you *act* like it!?"

"Even if your plan didn't involve treason, which it *does*… You're talking about pursuing a man you know nothing about. You've no idea what he's capable of. Hells, you don't even know what he *looks* like!"

"*I* don't," Viktor said, and then aimed at John Huxley with his eyes. "But *he* does…"

John froze in both anticipation and thrill. It was relatively warm in the room, but it did nothing for the chills he felt throughout his entire body.

"You're shitting me," Jossiah snarled. "You're not seriously suggesting this? He's a *peasant*!"

"So were *you* once, old friend," Viktor said, much more calmly than before. "And so was I. Or have you forgotten that?"

"He's just a *lad*!"

"He's a lad that fought Hudson Blackwood and lived to tell the tale. I'd say he's *our* lad!"

"I'll do it," John Huxley said abruptly, grasping the attention of both men at once. He took a moment to breathe, easing down the beating of his heart a few notches, allowing for the idea to sink in. And then he nodded nervously at the two men. "If it'll help bring her majesty back, I'll do it… I will join you."

Viktor Crowley turned back to his companion, his eyes eagerly waiting for a comparable response.

Jossiah Biggs sighed and placed a hand to his temples.

"Even if we *tried* to do this, you haven't the title anymore, Viktor. King Rowan's already raging mad. How do you suppose he'll react the minute you try to announce this voyage?"

"We'll announce it first thing at dawn," Viktor said.

"He'll lose his mind."

"Worst case, he imprisons me. He won't have my head."

"He will."

"He *won't*," a voice interrupted them, causing every head to turn. Standing at the doorframe was a woman of middle age, brown skin, a round nose, and two streaks of grey contrasting against her oily black hair.

"What are you doing here?" Viktor asked her, his eyes widening.

"Not entirely sure myself," the Lady replied.

"What did you hear?" Jossiah asked, much more hostile than Viktor had reacted.

She hesitated, only her expression was more disconcerting than it was malicious. "Just enough," she said.

As the king's Treasurer, Lady Brunylda Clark had lived in the royal palace for several decades and yet she was sure she had never set foot in that particular room before. Dressed in that elegant turquoise gown and silver jewelry, she looked the most out of place in the room.

The Lady had a reputation of having a certain disdain for the knights of the king's court. She had gained the trust of King Rowan to such an extent that she had the freedom to pursue and carry out any and all money-related matters with any lord in Gravenstone in the king's name. And yet, when an assembly was called for, the king seemed to always favor the word and advice of his knights over her own.

The numbers were never in her favor, of course. There were seven knights and only one of her.

But there was a difference between favoring the opinion of the majority and being entirely overlooked; the latter was something the Lady had grown accustomed to during her years of service, much to her own contempt. The current matters, however, had worried her enough to let go of the feud between her and the knights. And so she stood there, fighting back the hostility and lifting her chin up as high as she could.

"If you're here to blackmail us, Brunylda…" Viktor spoke, but was unable to finish.

"I will loan you the silver," she said suddenly, and both men were unsure of just how to respond.

John had the sudden impulse to step out of the room, unsure of exactly where he might end up if he chose any particular door. One of the doors opened and the princess's handmaiden stepped in, only to be glared at by several eyes. And so Brie set the second jug of ale on the nearest table and walked back out quicker than she had stepped in. John might have followed her, had it not been for his curiosity when one of the former knights spoke again.

"She bluffs," Jossiah grunted.

"Trust goes both ways, Sir Biggs," Lady Brunylda remarked. "I'm risking just as much as you are."

"Piss off, you."

"Let's hear her out, Jossiah," Viktor said, his eyes contemplative yet wary.

"She's a viper, old dog," Jossiah said scornfully. "And there's no faster way to lose your head than by trusting a viper. Especially when *this* one serves the very man that disbarred us."

"Allow me to make one thing perfectly clear to you, Mister Biggs," the Lady said with an added weight on the word *Mister* rather than *Sir*. She took two steps towards them in such an austere manner that Jossiah nearly felt the impulse to take a step back.

"I serve no man," she said to him. "I serve Val Havyn… And right now, the man leading it is drowning himself in wine like a whimpering boy. If this city is to remain standing, then you lot might be our only hope."

Viktor and Brunylda held onto their glares for far longer than they were comfortable with. In a game of blackmail, the one that broke the silence first was the weaker one. Only the Lady was not there to blackmail.

"How much will you need?" she asked.

"Stop right there, you," Jossiah said, and placed a hand on Viktor's shoulder. "If the king finds out about this…"

"Enough to hire fifteen men," Viktor said, ignoring his friend and keeping his eyes locked on Lady Brunylda's. He saw pride there. But he also saw distress. And in desperate times, trust was often a risk worth taking.

"*Ten* men," she responded, after taking a moment to consider how much she could get away with stealing from the king.

"Thirteen."

"Twelve."

By then, Jossiah Biggs had taken a seat at the table across from John. Perhaps it was the ale that was keeping him there, but in reality the man appeared to be invested in any discussion that involved money. But his grimace was still there, as he sat judging every precarious decision that Viktor took.

"You realize we're already outnumbered as it is," Viktor said. "We might get slaughtered."

"Yes," Lady Brunylda nodded. "But you're Viktor Crowley… If any man is to ensure the princess's safe return *before* getting slaughtered, it's you."

Viktor considered it briefly, well aware that he was in a position more vulnerable than he had ever been in. And so he gave the lady a nod of agreement and a half-smirk.

"We have an accord," he said.

And then they shook hands.

* * *

Not every life is wicked, she had been told all her life.
There is goodness in everyone. It's only harder to find in certain beings.
In her short life, Princess Magdalena had seen and experienced many things.

And those that had lectured her were right, for the most part; not every being was cruel. Except, of course, for those that *were*.

She opened her eyes and, for a moment, couldn't remember where she was or what had happened to her. The first thing she felt was moisture beneath her legs; the cold kind of moisture that could bring about a fever on a frosty night. When she tried to move, she realized her hands were tied to a hanging hook, two feet above her head. She was sitting against a wall made of wood on a muddy patch of grass, surrounded by strangers dressed in torn clothing filthier than her dress, which may have been a pastel blue at one point but was now hidden beneath a layer of dirt and muck.

She was inside of a carelessly built pit, with bars of wood nailed all around to keep them confined. An excuse for a cage, it was. But there wasn't much that fifteen unarmed prisoners could do against two hundred soldiers with blades.

The strangers around her were also tied up and some were pale and shivery, to the point where they looked as if they were mere minutes away from becoming corpses. A deep sickness began to settle into her stomach and chest, as all the memories began to crawl back into her mind.

She remembered walking safely through her palace, protesting about a gown her father had asked her to wear for a man she had been betrothed to without her consent.

She remembered speaking briefly with a young farmer who had come to the palace to collect a reward.

Then came the invaders… And the chaos in the courtyard…

She remembered Sir Viktor Crowley and her father's men charging into the fight.

She remembered the young farmer trying to protect her.

And the young boy that was with him… had he survived?

Had the *farmer* survived?

And what had become of the palace?

The last thing she remembered was staring into the dark eyes of a tall beast of a man that wore a mask over his jaw; a mask lined with long, sharp, inhuman teeth. She could still feel his claw of a hand grasping her face, averting the air from her lungs.

Then there was darkness… Darkness that seemed to never end…

She dreamed she had woken up in her bed, surrounded by soft silk sheets, her handmaiden approaching with a freshly cleaned gown. She could almost feel the morning breeze on her face, almost smell the warm green tea sitting on her bedside table, and almost taste the sweet cornbread she ate with every morning meal. It was a shame to find herself surrounded by such familiarity and comfort, only to wake up to the smell of piss and shit in a place unfamiliar to her.

Nearby, she noticed a subtle glow, and her nose caught the scent of roasting meat. Men had set up camp and were huddled around a firepit near a row of tents, yards away from the prisoners. There were other fires all around, but she couldn't turn her neck all the way due to the ropes. All she could see in the distance were shadows. And before she could try to make out any of the men's faces, she became startled at the sound of whispering voices approaching the cage.

The voices sounded inhuman… deeper and much rougher than any voice she had ever heard.

"I says we snatch the bitch 'n' leave!" the first voice said; a raspy growl of a voice, it was.

"Not now," said the second voice, this one deep and disquieting. "Soon, my brothers… Soon we'll be rid of the human scum."

"You said tha' *weeks* ago, Okvar," the first voice protested. "You said we'd follow Baronkroft overseas. Now we *are* overseas. *Why*'re we still 'ere?!"

"Could I have the wee one? I'm starved," said the third, this one snorting at the end of nearly every sentence.

"Then you shouldn't have finished your share," Okvar replied.

"How can you sit there 'n' let some wretched human decide when *we* get to eat?! Like we're a bunch o' hounds!?" Gruul protested, his voice louder and angrier.

"Lower your damn voice, you stupid pillock," Okvar said menacingly. "Just a few hours 'til midnight, now. Perfect time to sneak off."

Magdalena was growing restless. Her breathing quickened against her will and the sweat began to build at her temples. Suddenly, however, she became distracted by a nervous breathing to her left, and could almost feel the heat of it in her cheek. She turned her head and her eyes widened as she stared at the smoky green face of a female orc sitting among the prisoners. She had only seen portraits of nonhumans in her short life, and never encountered one in person. And almost always the portraits were male.

The orcess looked much less menacing; she looked almost like a large woman with dark green paint all over her skin. The only thing that made her look inhuman was the pair of sharp fangs sticking out from her lower lip. She looked tired and hungry and her clothes were less filthy than the rest of the prisoners, as if she had also been recently captured. She had cuffs on her feet, and the cuffs were linked to a chain that ran along every pair of feet in the muddy cage. She held a bundle of cloth tenderly against her chest, rocking it back and forth and whispering to it, and the princess could see the horror in the orcess's expression.

"*Sneak?*" Gruul spoke again. "How low have you sunk, Okvar? Orcs do not *sneak!*"

"Have you a better idea?"

"So I *can* have the wee one, right?" *Snort*.

The incoming footsteps appeared to have suddenly startled the three orcs sitting near the prisoners. A huskily built bald man with a tattoo on his cheek and an impressive orange bush of a beard approached the prisoners' cage. He was dressed in dark furs and held a rope in his sweaty hands, dragging along the five children that were tied to it.

"What're ye lot going on about?" asked the bearded man, who was quite obviously inebriated.

"Mind your own business, human filth," Okvar replied, spitting at the man's boots.

The man with the red beard said nothing, but could see the dishonesty in the eyes of the three orcs. They were hiding something, he was sure. But in his drunken state, he was also sure that he cared very little. He continued to guide the children towards the pit. Magdalena heard something vaguely familiar in the man's accent. It was Halghardian, with perhaps a decade of foreign influence, but Halghardian nonetheless; it was there despite the drunken slurring of his words.

A traitor, the princess thought to herself. In her father's eyes, there couldn't possibly be a worst kind of coward than one who allies with a foreign force to attack his own native lands.

The man threw the children inside, shot them an intimidating glare and as he spoke, his beard moved gracefully with his jaw. "I find one of ye's missing 'n' I kill the *lot* of ye. And if anyone gets any funny ideas, one of ye bett'r squeal."

With that, the bearded man closed the wooden gate.

And it was then that the princess saw her first familiar face.

Once the man was out of sight, a young boy rushed towards the princess, his hands still tied behind him, and kneeled just beside her. His enthusiasm gave her the impression that he would have hugged her had it not been for the ropes.

"Your majesty," the boy said, his brown eyes weary and his face smeared with dirt. "Thank the gods you're alright. I thought you had…" he didn't finish.

Magdalena was perplexed. She stared at the child with awe as tears began to unwillingly swell up her eyes. Despite her upbringing, she was never known to be a naïve woman, and she was well aware of the monstrosities humankind was capable of.

But *children*? This, she thought, was inhuman to say the least.

Why? She asked herself, and at the same time doubted every single thing her father and mentors had taught her while she was growing up. Every single lecture about there being goodness in everyone was proving to be wrong right before her eyes. She was angry with them, even, for making her believe such nonsense.

"It's you…" was all she could muster to say, and even then it was nothing more than a whisper. She didn't have the heart to tell the boy she had forgotten his name. After all, she had known him for mere minutes; yet at that very moment, the princess couldn't have been happier to see the boy's face.

"*Thomlin*," he reminded her with a nod.

She remembered how he tried to pull her away from the danger. And how, when she refused, he had stood bravely by her side rather than running away.

And now he was here… because of *her*. A single tear ran down her face, leaving a cold wet trail in her cheek. "Do you know where we are?" she asked him, her voice faint and weak.

"Few miles south of Elbon," Thomlin said. "I heard word among the men we'll be heading to the shores of Roquefort. A ship's waiting for us there, they said."

"A *ship*…? A ship heading where…?"

His reaction was blank. He had no words for her.

"Did they…" the princess cleared her throat, struggling through a wall of tears. "Did they *hurt* you?" she asked.

"No, your majesty," he said. "They had me serving them supper."

"Did they feed you…?"

"They did, your majesty… Yesterday's scraps, that is."

Thomlin spoke softer and slower by the second. And his weary gaze began to lower. Then, unexpectedly, he released the soft whimper he had been holding back for hours. It was followed by a flow of tears running down his caramel-colored cheeks. As he knelt, he felt his body giving in and, before he knew it, he fell forward.

His forehead rested on the Magdalena's shoulder. And it was the first warm feeling the princess had felt since regaining consciousness, and the closest thing to an embrace that they could manage. She pressed her cheek against the curls on the boy's head and wept with him, only silently.

"Shh, it's all right," she whispered. "We're going to be all right, you'll see…"

* * *

The night had stretched on for what seemed like days.

Dawn was nearing, and Viktor Crowley's somnolent eyes struggled to remain alert as he leaned over the wooden table. In front of them was a map… the most precise and detailed map John Huxley had ever laid eyes on, where the nation of Gravenstone had been drawn out with such exquisite detail that John visualized himself inside of it, right beneath the blue hills, where there was a speck of green ink and the name *Elbon* written over it in tiny black letters. Miles of land had been lessened to mere inches on the parchment, and John realized just how small his humble little village truly was.

The right side of the map, the prosperous kingdom of Vallenghard, detailed every city, village, and keep; among them was the city of *Merrymont* on the northern coast and *Roquefort* in the south. *Val Havyn* was at the center of the kingdom and there was a petite palace drawn out over the black letters to represent his majesty's home.

A large stretch of green and blue covered the center of the map, where the

Woodlands homed nearly every living creature that wasn't human, banished like prisoners in the dark.

And on the left side of the map was the kingdom of Halghard, and beyond its western coast the parchment was coated with a shade of blue with the handwritten words *Draeric Sea* written at an angle. The southwestern edge of the map ended with the sketch of a shoreline where the continent of Qamroth began, only there were no words or symbols on it, as if the whole continent was irrelevant.

"Drahkmere?" Jossiah Biggs asked in bewilderment.

"Are you certain, John?" Viktor added.

"I'm certain. It's what they said..."

Viktor's fatigue got the better of him and he took a seat in front of the map while behind him stood Jossiah, John, and Lady Brunylda Clark.

"Yet you can't recall the bloke's name, eh?" Jossiah snarled.

John found that he was growing sweatier by the second and his hands were twitching at the memory of those haunting eyes. It was as if the strange man he'd met by the creek had sucked some life out of him through a stare.

Viktor Crowley was depending on him. In a way, the entire kingdom was. John knew this was not the time for frailty but he also refused to lie to them, knowing that if he happened to say the wrong thing the entire voyage will have been futile. "Forgive me," he said. "My mind fails me..."

"That's quite a journey," Lady Brunylda said as she leaned in and examined the map. "I'm not entirely convinced 60,000 yuhn in silver is worth risking over mere speculation."

"It's not speculation, m'lady," John said. "I may not remember the lord's name, but I am *certain* they're heading to Drahkmere."

"You were *also* certain you saw the ghost of the Butcher," Jossiah said as he sipped on his fifth tankard of ale.

"I *did*!"

"He did," Viktor reiterated. "And for the bloody *last* time, old dog, it was no ghost!" He then snatched the tankard from Jossiah's hands and proceeded to drink from it himself. Jossiah shot him a look of annoyance and then reached for the jug of ale. And when he saw no other tankard nearby, he shrugged and drank straight from the jug.

"Be that as it may," Lady Brunylda continued, "If it all happened so fast and you hardly escaped with your life, how can you entirely trust what your ears may or may not have heard, Mister Huxley?"

"I-I..."

"Perhaps if there was some proof or a more reliable witness, then we could fig-"

"What's it to you?" Jossiah asked, much less friendly than he could have been. "Truly? You said yourself you care very little if we get slaughtered..."

"I said no such thing."

"*Insinuated* it, then… 60,000 yuhn? One raven and you can get that silver back in seven days' time. Eight if the wind's not in your favor," Jossiah's relaxed demeanor changed into a more cautious one as he sat up straight and refused to let go of his glare on Lady Brunylda. "Why d'you care about it at all, then?"

There was a silence again.

The Lady broke the gaze first and her lower lip may have trembled a bit.

"I bloody *knew* it," Jossiah said as he leapt to his feet again. "She plans to tell the king!"

"I mean no harm to either of you, my offer was earnest," Brunylda argued, neither confirming nor denying Jossiah's accusation.

"Bloody viper," Jossiah growled. "I *told* you she couldn't be trusted."

"If what the farmer says is true and this… *lord* is taking the princess overseas, I guarantee you there will be far more than just a hundred men waiting for you there," the Lady said. "Now would you prefer to face them with a dozen men… or the entirety of King Rowan's army?"

"So what are *we* to you then, a scouting party for *your* benefit?!"

"Do *not* raise your voice at me, Mister Biggs. One word and I could have you imprisoned." By then, the Lady was on her feet as well and she was facing Jossiah daringly and confidently.

"Better imprisoned than to be a pawn for the likes of *you*!" Jossiah shouted back.

"*I'm* your only hope to redeem yourselves!"

"Trusting you will only cost us our heads, and I'd very much like to keep mine."

"You'll lose your heads if you *don't* trust me! You can't possibly steal the princess back if she's in Drahkmere, not without support and reinforcements! You ought to know that, you've fought in enough wars."

"Oh, what do *you* know about wars?!"

"Who the bloody hells do you think *finances* every single war you've fought in?!"

"Piss off!"

"Enough!" Viktor shouted over them. Had it not been for him, John wondered whether either the Lady or Jossiah would have resorted to physical violence; the rage in both their eyes surely made it seem that way.

"She's right, Jossiah," Viktor said, and though his friend's rage remained, the bickering diminished.

John felt as out of place as he had since he'd been taken in to collect his reward the previous morning. Realizing that dawn was approaching, he thought of his mother and siblings back at the farm. They had not heard from him in nearly a day and surely the news of the invasion would have reached Elbon by then. But he couldn't bring himself to leave the room. Never had he imagined himself in the presence of Sir Viktor Crowley for longer than minutes at the very least, and yet it was the knight himself that asked him to stay…

Suddenly, there were footsteps approaching from the corridor.

Two familiar voices were conversing, one more confused than the other.

"I do hope this is worthwhile, girl. The king requested I remain within proximity," said a gallant voice.

"I was told not to say anything until you saw for yourself, Sir," the handmaiden replied.

"So you said," the first voice spoke again. "Though why this couldn't wait until dawn is beyon-"

Sir Hugo Symmond came to a halt at the door, his armor stainless and his chestnut-colored mustache as regal as it always was. He was thrown aback at the sight of the two former knights, his mouth open with surprise.

"Hello, old friend," Viktor rose to his feet and stepped forward.

"Viktor… Jossiah…" Sir Hugo mumbled; he was glad to see them, there was no doubt. And yet he knew of the severe consequences that would occur if he didn't immediately send word back to his majesty. The king would have their heads, that much was certain; perhaps even Sir Hugo's head if he waited another second longer.

"You two should not be here…" Sir Hugo said unnervingly. "And… who is *this?*"

John couldn't help but stand and bow. "Um… John Huxley of Elb-"

"He's the brave lad that took care of Blackwood for us," Viktor interjected, and Sir Hugo gave John a head nod and a gaze of slight admiration.

"What are you doing here still, Viktor?" he then asked.

"Please sit," Viktor said. "Would you like some ale? Or you, Brunylda?"

"Never mind the ale," Brunylda said as she took a seat. "You! Girl! Fetch me a bottle of Roquefort liqueur."

Brie left the room for what seemed like the hundredth time. John felt bad for the girl, having to remain awake to serve them during a meeting that was not supposed to be happening to begin with; not that Brie would have been able to sleep that night, anyway, she was so rattled.

"I don't think it would be appropriate for me to drink at this hour," Sir Hugo said worriedly. "Particularly, considering the circumstances. I-I'm sorry, Viktor, but if his majesty finds out that you're still here, h-"

"You will keep your mouth shut about it," Lady Brunylda said, much to everyone's surprise.

Viktor and Jossiah looked at one another briefly, before turning their attention back to the Lady. Sir Hugo may have felt a bit bothered by her tone, but the mild reaction from both former knights kept his curiosity intact.

"I've had enough of *his majesty*," the Lady said, and though such comments would often be disregarded and blamed on the ale or wine, she hadn't had a single sip yet. Nor did she need to… the Lady's candor and bold honesty was notorious. "Listen closely, all of you," she said with an intimidating pout. "*His majesty* is but a man… If there is anything to be understood here, it's that. This city will not rest, it will continue to run with or without him and if *he* prefers to cry and drink and lay in his own filth then he is free to do so… Meanwhile, *someone's* got to take matters into their own hands."

"And you think that *someone* ought to be you, then?" Jossiah snarled at her.

"I've signed consent from King Rowan himself to carry out any and all business relations," Brunylda remarked.

"That doesn't grant you much authority," Sir Hugo said, unconvinced.

"It's more authority than *you* have, Sir Hugo," she said to him, unwilling to succumb. "And you will be wise to keep all of this to yourself. Two knights have been disbarred tonight. I can very easily make that three, should the matter call for it."

Sir Hugo had no response; he merely listened to the Lady's every word.

Viktor felt something like hope fill his chest. Jossiah felt something similar, only his distrust towards the Lady was keeping his demeanor defensive.

"Here's what you will do, Sir," Brunylda went on. "You are to gather weapons and supplies, enough for a dozen men. You are to have them delivered to…" she glanced at John, who stammered and came back to his senses.

"Elbon, sir," he said. "The Huxleys' farm in Elbon."

"Elbon," the Lady reiterated. "And you are to ask no further questions about it, is that understood?"

Sir Hugo Symmond turned towards Viktor, the only person in the room he felt he could trust fully, and even then he wasn't entirely convinced.

"As a favor, old friend," Viktor begged, his blue eyes much less stern and more vulnerable than ever before. "Just… one last favor…"

Sir Hugo sighed. At the same time, the princess's handmaiden entered the room and handed the rare bottle of Roquefort liqueur to Lady Brunylda, who snatched it and drank right from it. And it was then that Sir Hugo gave them a nod. One single head nod, and it was enough to give them all that last shred of hope that they needed.

"One last favor," he said, and then stepped out of the room.

* * *

"Not a word out of you… Or I'll slice your babe's throat, you hear?" said a raspy voice, making a poor attempt at a whisper. It was followed by chuckles and snorts, and a loud *Shhh*.

Magdalena's eyes opened slightly, just enough to make out the dark shadows to her left. Young Thomlin was heavily asleep in her lap. The closest thing to comfort she could offer the boy was her velvet dress, and so his head was resting against her thigh while the rest of him laid over the mud inside the prisoner's pit.

The frightened orcess began to whimper in fear. "No… please," she begged. But then she held her tongue when one of the orcs pressed a blade against her child's neck. Magdalena stood still, hoping the orcs wouldn't notice her. She felt a deep anguish in her chest at the muffled sound of the weeping orcess. But she knew the orcs were planning their escape, and so they wouldn't think twice about killing her and Thomlin simply to avoid the attention.

When Murzol pulled the frightened orcess up to her feet, he nearly stumbled over Thomlin. But Gruul managed to grab his comrade by the neck just in time, throwing him to the other side of the cage as he mumbled an insult under his breath. Magdalena had opened her eyes briefly for a closer look, but she managed to shut her eyes again before Gruul glanced down at her.

"Will the two of you hurry your arses?!" Okvar grunted, standing at the gate of the pit. The large soldier with the red beard was snoring, sitting on his wooden stool with an empty bottle of mead at his boots. Still, Okvar had his axe handy in case the man happened to be a light sleeper.

The orcess tried to resist, but the vile orc Gruul continued to threaten her with his blade. He pressed it against the child and a drop of blood escaped its cheek. The infant began to cry, and so Murzol placed a hurried hand over its mouth, muffling its yelps.

"Walk, you trollop… or the child gets it," Gruul said threateningly, and the orcess obeyed.

"My name…" she spoke suddenly, her lip trembling, "…is *Aevastra*."

"Your *name*," he aimed his blade at her, "Is whatever *I* say it is. You're *mine* now."

"Gruul!" Okvar said a bit too loud. "Shut your damn yap 'n' let's *go*!"

The orcs left the pit as Magdalena subtly observed them.

On his way out, Murzol snorted loudly and spat on the unconscious red-bearded guard.

The man didn't so much as flinch. Magdalena wanted very much to wake him, if it meant the defenseless orcess wouldn't have to live through whatever horrors awaited her. But something prevented her from moving. Perhaps it was the fear of whatever horrors awaited wherever this ship was taking them. Perhaps it was the idea of the orcess having a better chance of escaping the grasp of three orcs rather than an entire company of men.

Still, the fear kept her awake.

And about an hour later, a dark figure approached the pit and came to a halt next to the sleeping guard.

"Hauzer!" the figure said, kicking the man's boots. "Get up, you old fat hound."

The red-bearded guard nearly stumbled from the shaky stool. "What in all hells…" he groaned.

"Wake up! It's time."

It wasn't dawn yet, and so the darkness wouldn't allow for Magdalena to see the figure clearly. And it didn't help that the figure had skin so dark that it blended against the night sky. She was close enough, however, to make out its long pointy inhuman ears. Hauzer rubbed his eyes and noticed there was snot on the chin of his beard. He wiped it, looked up at the dark figure and asked, "What the fuck's this about, then?"

"It ain't mine," the figure replied with a shrug.

Torches were being lit all around the camp and the prisoners were beginning to wake on their own without the need of the usual kick or shove. Magdalena shook her leg and Thomlin's head began to bounce against her knee.

"Thomlin," she whispered, but the boy was a heavier sleeper than she presumed.

Once the red-bearded guard lit his own torch, Magdalena was able to see that his companion was an elf with dark blue skin and silver hair. He had a much more calmed demeanor than the rest of the soldiers in the camp, however. In fact, they both did. Yet it didn't make matters any different, for they made just as many death threats only with less grit. Hauzer stepped inside the pit and grabbed hold of the end of the chain that held the prisoners together. His elf companion followed behind him. Hauzer was much larger and huskier, while the elf was thin but with his muscles firm and well defined.

"Come on, you lot," the elf began tugging at the chains of those that hadn't woken up yet. He noticed the sleeping boy at Magdalena's knee and gave him a tap on the arm with his boot. "Wake your littl' arse, boy," he said.

And it made Magdalena upset. "Leave him!" she demanded, a bit too boldly.

Then the elf got on one knee and held a blade out. He didn't press it against Magdalena's neck, but used the tip to lift her chin up into the light of Hauzer's torch. Thomlin woke up and sat up straight in a matter of seconds, his eyes widening at the sight of the elf's blade.

"I ain't seen this one before," the elf said.

"She's the highborn we snatched at Val Havyn," Hauzer explained.

"I see," the elf chuckled, calmly at first, but his expression changed when he noticed something peculiar to Magdalena's left; an empty spot on the mud, where a figure once sat. He gave the princess a stern glare before asking, "Where's the orc bitch?"

Magdalena shook her head, pretending to be confused, as the elf looked up at his comrade.

"The orcs," he said angrily.

"What about 'em?" Hauzer asked.

"They must've taken 'er…"

"Ahh, fuck 'em," Hauzer shrugged. "If the highborn is here, y'think

Baronkroft will care about three orcs runnin' off? He's got a hundred more waitin' back in Drahkmere?"

Hauzer began to drag the prisoners out of the pit as the elf frowned at Magdalena. Then he removed her arms from the hook and she felt her muscles cramping up, and they ached and throbbed as she was dragged out of the pit. She and Thomlin walked past Hauzer, who was still wiping residual snot from his bushy red beard. "Jyor?" he called.

His elf companion glanced at him with a raised brow.

"Sure this wasn't you?" Hauzer asked.

"I ain't spit on anyone in years," Jyor said, then took the chains from Hauzer's sweaty hands and pulled the prisoners onward.

Hauzer gave his shoulders a shrug and nodded bitterly. "Filthy greenskins," he mumbled, as he marched near the back of the formation, making sure none of the prisoners would attempt an escape.

* * *

"You're not serious?" Jossiah asked drowsily, drinking from a pitcher of fresh water after having nearly passed out from the ale. "The princess will be dead by the time we get there…"

"The Draeric Sea is the fastest route," Viktor replied. "If we march to Roquefort, we can hire a ship captain there. We leave tomorrow, we can get there in three days' time."

"Bollocks. That'll take four or five at best."

"Not if we limit our sleep, old friend. Besides, marching with a dozen men will be a lot more efficient than marching with an entire troop."

Watching the two men at work was nothing short of fascinating, and though John wanted very much to join in the conversation, he remained skeptical about the plan, as did the Lady Treasurer of Val Havyn, who was beginning to slur her own words after drinking a third of the bottle of liqueur.

"It won't work," she interrupted, and then she raised a finger and spoke as if reciting an excerpt from a formal contract. "Should there be conflict with an armed force, foreign or not, a Lord or Lady is sworn to send their king a raven every third and seventh day, unless granted otherwise by the king himself, detailing any and all unprecedented matters and/or unscheduled arrivals and departures of any company greater than five men."

"I thought *you* oversaw the ravens," Viktor said.

"I oversee them and send a reply. But the first pair of eyes to see them is the king. It's *always* the bloody king," she said, sounding a bit glum in her last sentence as she lifted the green bottle to her lips again. Jossiah eyed the bottle, now with significantly less liqueur, and he felt his stomach growl as if having a craving.

John's eyes were still examining the map. He felt something take over him. Something that thrilled him, as if awakening a part of himself he didn't know was there. While the other three were distracted in their conversation, he used his fingers to trace a path from Val Havyn to Drahkmere, only they were nowhere near the shade of blue labeled *Draeric Sea*.

"How long did you say the journey would take?" the farmer asked.

"Three days to march south to Roquefort. Then about a week at sea to Qamroth," Viktor replied.

"Not happening," the Lady mumbled softly to herself.

"And how long if we travel by land?" John asked.

"Now you're speaking through your arse, lad," Jossiah said, as bitter as was usual of him. "Surrounding the Woodlands means we march south then west along the coast. We'll just lose another two weeks."

"Didn't say anything about surrounding them," John said, silencing them all at once. "What if… we marched *through* the Woodlands… made it across Halghard to the western coast, and paid for a ship to transport us from *there?*"

There was an abrupt tension in the room.

The former knights appeared more baffled than anything else.

The Lady Treasurer, however, was quiet yet pensive.

"I bloody told you he was useless, Viktor, but does anyone ever listen to me? Goodness no, that'll be the day," Jossiah mumbled, more to himself than to his friend.

"Tell me, John," Viktor replied calmly. "Have you ever set foot inside the Woodlands?"

"Can't say I have," John shook his head, trying his best to appear confident.

"Ah… but you have heard that those who enter hardly get out alive, have you?"

John had no words. His eyes moved from the map to Viktor and then back at the map, until the Lady released a pensive '*Hmm*' that grasped Viktor's attention away.

"The boy might actually be right," she said. "Might be your best option yet, in fact… If you're sailing from a Halghardian coast, you can rest assured that no word will reach King Rowan, not in time at least… Not to mention, it would only be a two days' journey to Drahkmere. And considering the amount of time saved by crossing the Woodlands, you'd make it there only a day or two later than if you sailed from Roquefort."

Viktor put some thought into it, and it was making Jossiah rather nervous.

"N-Now hang on a minute," Jossiah stammered. "It's one thing to go after your princess's captors… but crossing the Woodlands is another matter altogether…"

Viktor examined the map one last time, painting a trail in his mind that would take him through that large patch of green, following a tiny blue line labeled *Spindle River* until the green paint turned brown again where Halghard began. It was a perilous path and he couldn't possibly foresee what was waiting for them inside...

But it wasn't impossible.

In fact, the more thought he put into it the more his expectations grew.

The golden knight looked at John one last time, the young naïve expression in his eyes. It hadn't yet been three decades since Viktor was in a similar position. And he remembered how others of higher authority questioned *him* all the same.

And so Viktor took a deep breath before nodding his head and smiling.

"Well that settles it, then," he said. "We journey through the Woodlands..."

V
The Thief & the Witch

Syrena, the witch of Morganna, struggled to hold the wooden bowl in her leather-wrapped hands. The old pork stew reeked as if it had been sitting out for days, but hunger overcame her and she gulped down every drop within minutes. Through the gap in the wall, she could hear the thief doing the same.

"I've never tasted anything so repulsive," Hudson said with a mouthful. "Remind me to ask the guard if he would serve this to his mother."

"You don't want it, slide it over," the witch said.

"Nice try, darling. You've got your own," he poured the rest of the cold brown stew into his mouth. He sighed, feeling the relief in his stomach immediately. A belch escaped his mouth, so loud it may have echoed a bit. But the relief only lasted for so long, when suddenly his stomach began to turn, not exactly welcoming the old pork.

"I think I might be sick…"

"Already? You disappoint me, thief," she said, hoping he'd caught the amiable tone in her voice. Syrena had always been a solitary woman. With witches banished into the Woodlands, she did not have many options for acquaintances other than ogres, orcs, or the occasional band of human raiders looking to wreak havoc.

She realized Hudson Blackwood had been the first human to ever converse with her for longer than 15 minutes without pressing a knife to her neck. Though her skepticism said it had everything to do with the stone barrier between them, part of her wanted very much to believe that not everyone in the world was as wicked. She was faultlessly aware of whom she was speaking to, and yet she found the thief's demeanor had been far more hospitable than any lord or king she had ever encountered.

"Indulge me, love," Hudson said, straightening his back against the wall as he sat. "What else are you capable of, aside from charming the minds of wanted thieves?"

She smirked, finding his attempt at flattery oddly amusing. She could hear him shuffling about and figured he was trying to find comfort among the bricks. It wasn't until she heard him spit, presumably into his wooden bowl, that she wondered what he was up to. And her inquisitiveness only grew when he continued to do it.

"I prefer not to talk about it," she said.

"What else is there to talk about down here? The weather?" he scoffed, more at the situation rather than at her. He held the wooden bowl in his hands, spitting into it without the slightest attempt at subtlety.

"Anything that won't remind me of the very reason I'm locked in here to begin with," she replied.

"You're locked in here because of the stupidity and ignorance of this city's civilians. It's got nothing to do with you, darling. We are what we are and we can't help that." *Spit*.

"Most people don't see it that way."

"Most people are imbeciles. But there's no point in sulking, love. Done my share and believe me, it never helps."

"I'm not sulking…"

"Avoiding a topic can be a form of sulking." *Spit*.

"Would you stop doing that?!" she asked, her displeasure reaching its peak. "It's not exactly nice to listen to."

"My apologies," he said. "I'll do it softer." *Spit*.

"Besides, if you're so keen on sharing stories, why don't we talk of *your* past?"

"It's quite simple, darling," he said. "I'm not *nearly* as interesting as you."

She hesitated before responding.

In her short life, she had been called many things. '*Harlot*', '*wench*', '*bitch*', even the occasional '*abomination*', which she found interesting considering witches were the closest to humans as far as "freaks" went. All her life, an assortment of names she could list had been used to describe her.

'*Interesting*', however, had never been on that list until now.

"At least answer me this," Hudson said. "Any chance you can hypnotize our handsome mute friend out there into letting us out?"

"D'you even know a single thing about witches?" she asked.

"Not exactly. But, unlike others, I at least have the courtesy of *asking* first."

She said nothing, only thought of the words she had just heard.

Letting us out, the thief had said.

Not *me*. Not *you*.

But *us*.

For once, Syrena was glad to not feel completely alone, even if it was in the company of a criminal. She had an unusual feeling in her chest she couldn't recognize. Something like optimism, but not yet hope. She became lost in thought for several moments. Could Syrena of Morganna possibly have what it took to escape the dungeons of Val Havyn?

The answer was quite simple. *Alone*, likely not.

With Hudson Blackwood at her side, however, the possibilities kept crawling into her mind.

"All right," she finally spoke. "Would you like to know what I'm capable of?"

"I'm listening."

"I can show you," she said. "But first we have to get these chains off me."

"Way ahead of you…"

Spit.

* * *

"What do you suppose will happen?" asked a husky Val Havyn guard with a gap between his front teeth and a breath that reeked of something foul.

"It's no use. If the word is true and the Butcher did take the princess, then she's done for," said his excessively sweaty companion. They were the only two guards to remain at their post at the palace gates for hours after the king's return, and therefore their stance had grown more casual by the minute as their knees began to ache and the boredom overtook them.

"It's a shame, really. She was quite a beauty," the foul-mouthed guard said as he spit on the cobblestone road. "She saw me nude once, y'know? When I was bathin' in the barracks, she watched me through her window."

"Oh, shut it. It's more likely you were drunk out o' your mind and mistook a servant girl for her."

"You're just envious that your member's never been observed and admired by royalty."

The sweaty guard scowled.

"What are you two going on about?" an elegant figure appeared out of the dark.

"Nothing, sir!"

The two startled guards stood up straighter, as if they hadn't just been offhandedly lounging about for hours. The abundance of life on Merchants' Square had by then diminished and the obscurity and gloom of the evening took its place; the only light was coming from the lanterns that hung at every ten feet along the palace gates.

The dim atmosphere allowed for the concerned expression on Sir Hugo Symmond's face to appear less drastic than it actually was. Furthermore, the few drops of sweat on the knight's face were hardly noticeable compared to the drenched face of one of the guards.

"Anything to report?" Sir Hugo asked out of habit.

"Just the usual, sir," said the husky guard with the bad breath. "Beggars and others of the sort asking for an audience with his majesty."

"Well," said the sweatier guard. "There *was* the woman…"

The husky guard shot his companion a glare, as if urging him to keep his mouth shut.

"What woman?" asked Sir Hugo.

"Well, you're looking at her, sir," said the sweaty guard.

At the center of Merchants' Square there was a tall elegant fountain made of ivory, and it was surrounded by wooden benches. There was the usual beggar woman feeding pigeons on one of the benches and another two women took the bench facing the palace. The younger red-haired woman was comforting the older woman, who was dressed in farmer's clothes and a wool coat the color of the sea.

"She was looking for her son, Sir... Said he was inside the palace. I figured she was bluffing, but then she refused to leave. She's just been sitting there since his majesty arrived."

Sir Hugo gave them a head nod and a sigh, before he cleared his throat hesitantly. "Gentlemen, I've a special task for you both. Head to guard barracks and gather weapons and supplies, enough for a dozen men. Have them ready within the hour."

"Yes, sir!" the foul-mouthed guard said.

"Has a scouting party been arranged?" the sweaty guard asked.

"That is none of your concern," Sir Hugo replied. "Now go. I'll stand watch in the meantime." The two guards scurried away, both of them perplexed at the idea of a knight taking over gate duty. Neither of them had the authority nor the nerve to question it, however, unwilling to risk being released from their duty permanently.

Sir Hugo glanced around cautiously, before approaching the center of the Square. Before he could even greet the two women, they were both on their feet and had already given him a bow.

"Greetings. May I be of some assistance?" asked Sir Hugo, his conduct as gallant and kind as it always was.

"I'm looking for my son," the older woman said. "Please, I haven't heard word of him since the attack."

Sir Hugo paused, skeptical about the situation. What he heard in the assembly room, he could not reveal to any peasant. And he didn't even want to *think* about what he heard in the servants' quarters. Yet leaving the woman in the dark about her own son was something he found he was incapable of doing.

"What is your son's name?" he decided to ask.

"John," Adelina said. "John Huxley of Elbon."

Sir Hugo turned from one woman to the other, each of them with desperation in their eyes and an apparent vivid love for the young man.

"He's alive and well," he said, carefully choosing his words, and immediately both women smiled and sighed with relief. Adelina couldn't help but weep as Evellyn embraced her once again, allowing the woman to lean against her shoulder. "He's being tended to at the moment," Sir Hugo went on. "I suggest you go home and rest, now. Your son could not be safer, I assure you."

"Thank you, sir. Thank you," Adelina suddenly threw her arms around Sir Hugo, who did not protest to it despite a moment of hesitation. He patted the woman's back and smiled at her.

"Come Missus Huxley," Evellyn said, smiling through her tears. "I'll walk with you."

Sir Hugo Symmond felt a rush of comfort, knowing perfectly what it felt like to lose a loved one. And knowing that he had given her that feeling of relief was comforting enough for him. Before returning to the palace gates, he turned back one last time.

"Ma'am?"

Adelina shifted her now joyous gaze back towards him.

"Your son is a very brave man," he said.

And all she could do was smile.

* * *

"Cover your ears, darling," the thief said.

"And just how do you expect me to do that?" asked the witch, rattling the chains on her wrists.

"Oh... Right. I forgot."

Hudson took a good strong sniff and with an almost painful force he spewed out a slimy bundle of snot into the wooden bowl, which was now overflowing with his own slobber and mucus. Syrena groaned in disgust and she swore she could smell the bowl even through the brick wall.

"Listen now. I'll be needing your help, if you don't mind," the thief said. "I need you to moan. Loudly."

"You need me to do *what?*"

"Moan and cry as if you were in pain, darling. I'll do the rest."

"*Moan?*" she mocked him. "This is your brilliant plan?"

"Do you wish to get out of here or not?"

"Fine," the witch sighed.

She positioned herself sideways on the cold floor and began to wail gently, unsure of what exactly the thief was expecting to hear.

"Put some lung into it, come on!" Hudson whispered through the crack.

Syrena scoffed at first, and then she moaned louder and much more convincingly. Through the dungeon doors, the snoring guard was suddenly scared awake, so abruptly that he barked with surprise and had a fist up, ready to strike.

"Hey! Something's wrong with the witch, mate!" Hudson shouted, after which he pressed his face as far through the bars as he could and whispered to himself, "Come on, big mate... That's it..."

He heard grunting, and some moments later the steel bars on the other side of the door were removed and the door swung open. The mute guard looked tired and hazy, the thin brown hairs on his head untidy as if he'd been resting against a flat surface. He walked towards the witch's cell, keys in hand.

"Good grief, mate, do they ever let you take a piss break?" Hudson asked.

The guard was wearing leather trousers and a studded vest over his bare chest. He had no need for armor; his arms and neck were exposed, as was his unfortunately unpleasant face.

"Or do you simply pick a corner?" Hudson grinned. "It would explain the smell."

Furiously, the guard placed both of his thick meaty hands on the thief's cell and roared at him, long enough for Hudson to notice the guard's tongue had been severed, thus accounting for his muteness.

"Relax, mate. Just making small talk. Something's wrong with the witch there," he aimed two fingers at the brick wall. "Might've been that lovely stew of yours," he added.

The guard looked at the witch curled up in a fetal position with her back to the bars. He grunted a few times and tapped the bars with the tip of his boot. Syrena was shaking; she had her hands pressed against her chest and had shriveled into a corner, whimpering softly. When she didn't respond to his grunts, the guard began fumbling with the keys. And he was so distracted that he failed to notice the hand extending out of the bars of the next cell over, right next to his feet.

Carefully, Hudson emptied the bowl of slime on the brickstone floor…

A strong swift pull was all it took, and the thief had his arm through the bars, wrapped tightly around the guard's neck. The guard tried to stand up straight, but his boots slipped against the puddle of slime and he sunk right back into the thief's clutch.

Syrena leapt to her feet instantly and tried to squeeze her head through the bars as far as she could. She could see the guard struggling and she could see Hudson's arm shaking and tightening around the guard's neck.

"Bloody hells, you're a stubborn one," Hudson grunted through his gritted teeth. The guard dug his sharp nails into Hudson's arm, but the black coat eased the pain enough for the thief to hold his grip.

The witch couldn't help but grin at the cleverness of the thief's plan. An average crook would have given up after not finding a way to pick the lock on his cell. Never in her life did she imagine she would meet a man who could escape a cell merely by salivating.

That, she admitted to herself, was talent.

After about a minute of struggle, the guard gave in. His boots slipped against the slimy brick one final time and Hudson lowered the unconscious man to a sitting position. The keys had slipped from the man's fingers, fortunately within the thief's reach. The clinking sound they made as he searched for the right key caused Syrena's heart to skip a beat. The snapping sound of the lock and the screech of the cell door as it opened was music to both their ears. And as the unconscious mute slouched against the bars, the thief stepped out into the dungeon corridor.

Hudson Blackwood was free.

"Thanks mate," he said, tapping the guard's thigh with his boot and walking over to the next cell. "Now... let's get those chains off y-"

The thief froze, gazing for the first time into the young witch's stunning eyes, the color of a warm autumn sunset. Her thick, greasy, raven-colored hair flowed down to her shoulders in knots, yet it gave her a strikingly appealing quality. Her lips were bright red and nearly gleamed in contrast to her milky white skin, and she couldn't have been older than thirty.

"Whoa," Hudson accidentally said out loud. The witch wanted very much to smile, but the thief's reaction had worried her, seeing as he was in a position of power that she didn't have.

"What?" she asked nervously.

"Nothing. It's just... You hear '*witch*' and you paint a certain picture in your mind. Never would have guessed you'd look so..."

The pause lingered on and Syrena felt compelled to finish his sentence, "Ordinary?"

"I was going to say *human*, but... same difference, right?"

He smiled and gave her a wink, which she found mildly amusing. He unlocked the steel door to her cell and she stepped out, feeling a rush of relief upon regaining her freedom. Had her wrists not been cuffed together, she might have hugged the thief. He proceeded to try every key, but none seemed to work on the cuffs on her wrists.

"Not a problem, darling. Come with me."

He pulled her by the arm towards the door from which the mute guard had entered. It led to a small chamber, with an assortment of used clothes and weapons hanging along the walls. And at the end of the corridor there were stairs that appeared to lead them to the outside. Syrena hadn't been in nearly as many dungeons as the thief presumably had and so she allowed him to take the lead. She looked at him with mild astonishment as he sifted through the weaponry until he found the stolen rapier from the saloon and his collection of knives.

He looked rather exultant, his eyes already anticipating his next move.

But after strapping his weapons to himself, his eyes broadened like an owl. He mumbled something under his breath and began sifting through the hooks again.

"What is it?" she asked.

"Hang on," he said, shoving old clothes aside and causing a mess.

Then his eyes came to a halt.

There, hanging on a high hook along the brick wall, was his beloved black hat.

"There you are, you beautiful bastard," he said, kissing it and placing it on his head.

This was the image Syrena had seen in nearly every corner of Val Havyn. The image of a longhaired man with a stubbly face, wearing a hat with a rim that nearly covered his misunderstood eyes.

"All right," he said, stepping in front of the witch with his trusty petite knife at hand.

Suddenly, the wooden door opened at the top of the stairs and two members of the royal guard looked down at them. One of them drew his sword and the other ran back out, shouting for backup.

"Oh shit," Hudson said, rushing to pick at the lock on the witch's wrists.

They heard grunts coming from the opposite side of the room and saw that the mute guard was waking up, rubbing his neck and jaw as he stumbled to his feet.

"Get on with it!" Syrena urged him.

"Give me a moment, love!"

The guards approached, weapons drawn and fury in their eyes.

"Hurry! They'r-"

Then there was a clink...

A loud, crisp, beautiful clink and Syrena's cuffs snapped open...

The cuffs fell on the brick floor and the decaying ogreskin with it. The witch's pale hands felt the cold breeze for the first time in days. She felt strong and liberated, like a lioness being released from her cage. She paused for a brief moment and locked eyes with the thief.

She could have kissed him.

He would have let her.

At that moment, three more guards approached them from the stairs and the mute guard had entered the room from the other side. And she looked down at her sweating palms, soft and free. They were surrounded, but there wasn't a hint of concern in the witch's eyes, only a grin.

She extended her arms out in both directions, her hands in a fist.

"Get behind me," she said, and the thief obeyed.

And then she opened her palms and, like a gush of wind, a roar of flames shot outward. The guards shrieked with fear and surprise, and shriveled into a corner. The room was scorching hot within seconds, as the flames soared in both directions. One of the guards by the stairs caught fire, and the other three tended to him, rubbing their gauntlets against the flames until they died.

"Stay back," Syrena warned them, her brows lowered as she beckoned the flames back to her palms.

Hudson Blackwood stared in astonishment. He placed his hands gently on Syrena's shoulders, as if using her as a shield. And the witch did not seem to mind it. The thief had gotten her out of the cells and, in return, she was to get him out of the dungeons.

"The keys," Hudson ordered them with a snap of his fingers. "Quick, now."

And one of the shivering guards tossed the keys his way.

They moved slowly towards the stairs together, and the guards moved out of their way, their swords still drawn. Syrena released a small wave of fire in warning, which made them all cringe in fear. Her hands were smooth and undamaged within the coat of fire, and her power over it was astonishing to see.

"What did you say your name was, darling?" Hudson spoke softly into her ear.

"Syrena," she said to him, and it was the last time she ever had to remind him.

Hudson's gaze shifted back and forth from the witch's strikingly orange eyes to the flames above her fingers. "Syrena," he whispered passionately, as if admiring her name. "Remind me never to leave your side..."

The witch grinned and shot him a wink, just as he had done moments prior.

And they fled the dungeons together, locking the doors behind them and trapping the guards inside.

* * *

The stars began to fade and the black sky dissolved into a calming shade of blue, announcing the approaching sunrise. Another day of hard labor awaited the farming villagers of Elbon, as if the disastrous events of the previous day had never taken place.

A pot of fresh water was boiling over the fire. A middle-aged woman with somnolent eyes scooped a mugfull and stirred in some tea leaves, as was her morning routine. She looked serene and at peace, despite the few hours of sleep that she had.

There was a familiar sound outside, the mild grunts of a young woman and the swift sound of an arrow being released into the air. The woman walked to the window, her tea at hand, only to see her daughter holding her bow firmly in hand, aiming another arrow at a chipped and splintery wooden board.

Adelina smiled.

Robyn Huxley hadn't slept at all. All night she'd spent either practicing or carving more arrows to add to her quiver, but she refused to go to bed until her brother returned home. She looked exhausted; her big round eyes were struggling to stay open. And the wet breeze in the air was making a mess of her hair. Robyn had thick black curls that reached her shoulders. She would often cut it herself so that it wouldn't get in the way of her training, but it would grow back so fast and she swore that the curls would return with a vengeance.

Unruly, her sister Margot would call it, and she wasn't entirely wrong; Robyn could not run her fingers through her own hair without finding a knot. All of the Huxleys, aside from John, had inherited Adelina's black hair. Robyn, however, was the only one to inherit her father's curls, and she both loved it and cursed it regularly.

The girl didn't notice she was being watched. Instead, she loosened the grip on her bow and dropped the arrow where she stood, gazing into the dirt road in the distance. She saw an old mule, dragging along a wooden cart. And its rider was a young man with short wheat-colored hair. The cart approached slowly, the rider's arms could only move so much. And before Adelina could set down her tea, Robyn had already thrown her bow on the grass and was running to meet her brother.

John had just managed to hop down from the cart when Robyn threw her arms around him. She was at an unfortunate age, truly. Her mother still saw her as a child, and she was often belittled because of it. And she would often withhold herself from embracing her siblings in front of anyone, out of fear of being seen as infantile. In that moment, however, she found that she cared very little.

John welcomed the embrace and tightened his arms around his sister.

"John," she wept into his vest. "I-I'm... I'm so happy you're back..."

Hearing about the attack on the king's palace while her brother was within its grounds had frightened her to an extent she didn't think possible. When she was reassured of his safety, the relief was indescribable; and even then she could not sleep, longing for her brother's safe return home.

John closed his eyes and sighed, resting his chin on the girl's black locks. Adelina Huxley, tears streaming down her face, ran and threw her arms around both her children. There were no words to be said; the peaceful silence of dawn surrounded them, shielded them within the comfort of the farm.

"Are you all right?" Adelina asked as she carefully lifted her son's sleeves and examined his wounds, stitched carefully and with precision.

"Long story," John said.

Robyn refused to let go and held onto her brother's arm as they took slow steps towards the cottage. The only thing John could think of in that moment was how pleasant it would feel to rest his head against something soft and comfortable; after all that had happened in such a short span of time, he felt as if he could sleep for days.

Before he could even sit, however, there was a pending matter he needed to discuss.

A pressure began to build in his chest, well aware that neither his mother nor his sister would accept the information lightly, or at all for that matter.

"Mum? Robyn?" said the farmer. "I'm afraid we need to talk..."

* * *

"That'll be 5 coppers for a pound of pork," said a woman with an untidy braid and a petite black mole between her nose and upper lip.

"I-I'm afraid I've only got 4 coppers, miss," replied a nervous young man, well aware that his sweaty hands were only holding 3. "Please, I assure you Mister Nottley will have the coin to pay you by the end of the week."

119

"I said it's 5 coppers, boy. Either pay up or step aside for the next customer."

Young Cedric turned back, noticing he was the only one anywhere near the woman's meat stand. "What next customer?" he asked, and the woman shot him a grimace.

Nearby, a crowd was beginning to gather to hear the morning sermon of the maddening entity that was Baryn Lawe, apothecary and self-proclaimed courier of the gods. In reality, Cedric thought, the man was a mere beggar that had discovered a clever way to score easy coins from naïve and susceptible civilians of the royal city.

"All right," Cedric said to the woman. "I'll just take a half-pound of pork and a dozen eggs."

As he handed her the 3 coppers, the woman shot him another stare of annoyance and hissed, as if to scare the young man away. Cedric found his way to the inn where Mister Nottley was being lodged, several streets away from the ashen remains of his tavern.

"What the bloody hell's this?" asked Nottley. "This is *not* what I asked for, boy."

"Seems the price of pork has gone up, sir," Cedric said nervously, hoping his guardian wouldn't notice the drops of sweat gathering on his forehead.

"Tell me boy, what use are you to me if you can't haggle your way into a deal with some dumb old wench?"

"She wasn't old, sir," Cedric cleared his throat. "*Or* dumb. She had a ledger in her lap."

Nottley gave him a groan of disgust. "Listen here," he said bitterly. "You have 'til the end o' the day to come up with some coin. Or your arse is sleeping outside with the horses. You understand?"

Cedric had no answer. He turned his gaze down at the floor, as if using his shaggy brown hair to cover up his shame. He was a timid and juvenile young man with a mask of confidence he wore merely to impress his guardian. And the smug tavern keeper felt more pity for the boy than actual affection; finding himself with a newly orphaned child over a decade past had seemed to him more as an opportunity for free labor. And so the child was to grow up the shadow of the man Mister Nottley wanted him to be.

"I asked you a question, boy. Do… you… understand?"

"I-I…" Cedric stammered, until he was interrupted by the sudden sound of trumpets announcing an important presence in Merchants' Square. It sent an instant relief into Cedric's chest, as Nottley leapt from his seat and rushed out of the inn, gawking about aimlessly.

Outside, peasants began to assemble at the palace gates. Some were rushing out of their homes, expecting to hear news about the princess. And young Cedric, curious as he was, climbed onto the fountain at the center of the square for a better look.

Viktor Crowley and Jossiah Biggs were standing at the gates, next to a nervous guard whose name nobody ever bothered to ask for. The guard had the trumpet in his hand and he appeared out of sorts, though his sweaty state seemed to be ever-present.

"What're you waiting for, old man?!" Jossiah asked in a loud whisper.

"Oh... R-Right," the guard said, and then cleared his throat so as to raise his voice to a shout. "Attention, citizens of Val Havyn!" he announced. "It is my honor to present to you his majesty's knights of the court... Sir Viktor Crowley & Sir Jossiah Biggs..."

Upon hearing the title, Viktor's chest began to pound. There were eyes and ears everywhere, he knew. And though he had the support of Lady Brunylda Clark, he knew his time was running short and he had not a single second to waste before the king heard word of the commotion on Merchants' Square that dawn. Nearly every pair of eyes in the city was either gathered at the gates or watching from their window.

Baryn Lawe was in the midst of his sermon, talking of the day the gods would send destruction upon Val Havyn for the sins of its people and how those that were loyal to them would be spared. He scowled as his audience dispersed and lost interest in him, their attention stolen by the golden knight. Several children had also climbed onto the fountain at the center of the square, next to Cedric, watching attentively over the sea of heads that blocked their view from below. There was an empty space near the top of the fountain, where a young orphan named Thomlin would sit during such instances. And some of the children whispered among themselves, wondering where the boy was.

As Viktor stepped forward, the muttering died down. He had everyone's attention, and it was clear that the man was tired and worn out.

"Hope you know what you're doing, old boy," Jossiah whispered, giving his friend a tap in the shoulder. And then Viktor took a deep breath and began.

"Greetings, citizens of Val Havyn," he said. "I stand before you today... to disclose the unfortunate tragedy that has befallen upon our beloved kingdom. The rumors that most of you have heard by now are true... Princess Magdalena of Vallenghard has indeed been taken."

The crowds began to mumble among themselves. Viktor allowed it for a few moments. But when those mumbles grew into a loud cluster of chattering, Jossiah Biggs stepped in front of Viktor and shouted, "Silence! Your knight commander is speaking!"

The voices diminished. Viktor Crowley stood firmly in place, as any man of his class would, waiting patiently until the silence overtook the square again.

"Our princess has been taken to foreign lands," he continued. "Our king... has been forced to take drastic measures in order to ensure not only the protection of our city, but that of our entire *kingdom*. If we allow for this foreign threat to continue, we will lose all that we have worked hard to achieve. Thus, we must be rid of this threat without question or delay. If it is the last thing I make certain, ladies and gentlemen, it is that those responsible for this attack *will* answer for their wrongdoings!"

The silence was broken once again, though this time the crowds chanted and cheered together in applause. Viktor Crowley raised both of his arms, asking the masses to remain attentive for a few moments longer.

"There is, however, another matter at hand," he said. "If we are to succeed and ensure the protection of her majesty Princess Magdalena, we must take every precaution necessary… A squadron of men will be sent on a voyage heading west… A squadron, which I will personally command and lead *through* the Woodlands… and beyond to the western coast of Halghard."

At that very moment, brows were lowered and smiles turned into grimaces.

And the eerie silence was perceived all throughout the city.

Not many citizens of Val Havyn had ventured into the forbidden grounds of the Woodlands, and most of the ones that did were never heard from again. The only humans among the creatures within said grounds were raiders, assassins, or merchants willing to risk their lives in order to save themselves a couple of weeks of travel. And then, of course, there were the witches.

"Ladies and gentlemen, I cannot ask you to risk your lives and fight for your king," Viktor said. "But I *can* ask that you fight for your kingdom… For your *home*… If you are willing, please step forth now. Furthermore, you will be granted an incentive for your services. 5,000 yuhn will be paid in silver to any man willing to join Val Havyn's squadron and partake in this venture. 5,000 yuhn along with meals and lodging to travel with us through the Woodlands, beyond to the western coast, sail to this foreign land, and retrieve her majesty from the enemy's hands. Ladies and gentlemen, the power now rests in your hands. Who, among you, will stand with me?"

The moment dragged on for what seemed like hours. Eyes in the crowds turned towards each other in wonder, watchful of any person that moved closer to the gates, though of course no one had the nerve to.

After about a minute, Jossiah moved closer to Viktor and mumbled, "This is rather embarrassing."

"Give them a moment, old friend," Viktor said with a confident tone.

It was then that there was a sudden movement within the herd of peasants. Two men pressed through the crowds, one with long blonde hair slicked back and a chin beard that looked stiff like dry grass. The other wore a wool cap, covering his short blonde hair, and he had brown fuzz running down the side of his jaws.

"*We'll* go," said Martyn Davenport, handing his leather rucksack to his brother Wyll, who struggled to hold on to his loose cap as he squeezed through the crowd. "We've been in the Woodlands before. We can manage."

"State your names," Jossiah Biggs said, a pen and brown parchment at hand.

"Martyn and Wyll Davenport of Falkbury."

The mumbles in the crowds had returned, some challenging others to step forth, while others praised the brothers for their bravery.

"I volunteer as well," said another voice, this one deep and hardened.

"Name?"

"Thaddeus Rexx," the man answered as he approached the gates, towering next to the Davenport brothers, his size and stature daunting as was usual. Viktor knew he recognized the man from somewhere, though in that moment his mind was blank.

"Thank you, Mister Rexx," Jossiah said, adding the man's name to the inscription on the parchment. "Anyone else?"

Among the crowds, a pair of innocent eyes watched as no one else would dare step forward. The naïve young man's teeth were grinding against each other as his jaw quivered, unsure of what he feared most… the voyage itself or the reactions of the surrounding citizens, should he decide to step forth.

Don't say a word, he said to himself. *Let someone else go…*

But the young man could fight it no longer.

He was tired of living under the wing of a man that had as much respect for him as he did the tavern dog. He knew that an opportunity as grand as this would surely never come again, at least not in his lifetime. And so, with every bit of courage he could possibly muster, he lifted his head, shut his eyes, and spoke aloud, "I'd like to volunteer."

It may have been minimal, but to young Cedric it seemed as if the whole world had shifted its attention towards him. He took slow steps towards the palace gates. People made way for him as he brushed past known and unknown faces in the herd.

The hand of a stunned Mister Nottley gripped Cedric's elbow as the boy walked by, the man's eyes asking the boy, *what do you think you're doing?*

"It's all right," Cedric said, easing his arm free of his guardian's grip.

Jossiah's hand trembled as he held the quill and parchment in his hands, unsure if he could go through with it all. "He can't be serious," he whispered in Viktor's ear.

"He looks strong enough," Viktor whispered back hesitantly, as if also trying to convince himself.

"Strong?!" Jossiah scoffed. "The boy couldn't fight off a *beggar,* let alone a raider or an orc."

"Then he can serve as a *squire*," Viktor whispered, turning his attention back towards Cedric. "State your name, young man," he asked out loud, fearing for the boy's safety as he gazed upon his young inexperienced eyes.

"Cedric," he said. "I am… M-Mister Jasper Nottley's ward."

Jossiah shot Viktor a look, as if asking for his final approval. The golden knight returned a nod and Jossiah wrote down the singular name on the parchment.

Cedric's mother, a tavern server, had died when he was a boy of seven and Mister Nottley never spoke of her house name again. And so the boy grew up a nameless orphan, save for the one name that everyone called him: *Cedric*.

"I offer my services to my kingdom free of payment," Cedric continued, baffling the crowds even further. "All I ask in return, sir, is for the repair of my guardian's establishments…"

Mister Nottley felt a heavy knot in his throat.

Something came over the old man. Something like compassion.

Though his young ward couldn't bear to look anywhere but down, his old weary eyes were fixated on him. And guilt began to crawl into his conscience, absorbing the definitive proof of the young man's loyalty to him, far greater than he had ever given him credit for.

"Consider it done, son," Viktor said with a nod.

Cedric stood among the lineup of recruited citizens. Thaddeus Rexx placed his heavy hand on the young man's shoulder and gave him a mild shake, as if praising his courage. Meanwhile, however, Cedric's eyes widened as he silently asked himself, *what the hell did I just do?*

"Anyone else?" Jossiah Biggs asked. There was a brief silence, as the crowds turned to one another, awaiting the next brave soul.

And it was at that very moment that something bizarrely unexpected happened, something that caught the attention of every single pair of eyes in Merchants' Square.

A sudden roar of flames shot upwards from the ground into the sky, bringing about a wave of heat all around.

The crowds backed away, cowering in fear.

And there, in front of the fountain, were two dark figures standing alongside one another.

Two very familiar faces, upon which Viktor Crowley stared in awe.

And a memorable suave voice suddenly asked, "Miss me, mate?"

* * *

It had all happened unexpectedly.

Dawn had arrived far too quickly and more than a few citizens of Val Havyn had begun their morning routines by the time the thief and the witch were out of the palace dungeons and slipping through every quiet path they could find.

It was the largest city in Vallenghard, and it didn't help that the palace dungeons were dozens of blocks away from the city gates. Sneaking around the precincts of the palace alone had taken them the better part of an hour, particularly after having avoided twelve pacing guards, seven drunkenly obnoxious peasants, and about sixteen merchants setting their stands before dawn.

By the time they reached the square, the crowds had grown exponentially.

The sudden sound of the trumpets had alerted them both, and by the time the herd of peasants had gathered, the path that would lead the two of them out of the royal city was entirely blocked. There was no other way but through Merchants' Square, and now it was swarming with civilians and members of the royal guard.

"We're finished," Syrena said worriedly, her bright orange eyes scanning the crowds from the corner of an empty narrow alleyway.

"Will you relax, love? This is how I make my living," Hudson said, as he brushed his long black hair out of his face and replaced his beloved black hat with a knitted merchant's cap.

"What're you doing?"

"Fitting in," he said with a wink.

The thief then flipped his black coat inside out. The lining on the inside was sewn with grey cloth, giving it the appearance of a tattered wool coat. From up close, however, one could see that the perceived coat had no pockets at all, but black fiber sewn in the shape of pockets. Hudson then wrapped and tied a dark blue cloth around his neck as he held between his fingers a pair of black fingerless gloves.

"Where'd you get all this?" the witch asked.

"Remember that foul-smelling mule of a man yelling at a poor one-legged merchant, claiming his winesack had less wine than the previous day?"

"You didn't *kill* him, did you...?"

"Goodness, no. What kind of man do you think I am? I simply stole his rucksack."

"Great... And how will *I* get out of the city? Or is this the end of our partnership, then? Because if so, I don't thin-"

"I'm not leaving you," Hudson interrupted as he slipped his hands into the gloves. "Are you joking? You're bloody magnificent! I'd have to be *daft* to part ways with you."

She smirked.

The thief then attached a thread of black fuzz between his nose and upper lip. His attempt at a disguised mustached merchant made the witch chuckle, but the thief's confidence seemed to go unchanged, which gave her hope.

"I understand your fear, darling," he said. "You're a witch. Untrusting of humans, and therefore keeping a distance from them all your life. I, on the other hand, am a sly street rat that has lived among humans all of my life. Believe me, I know just how stupidly unaware they all are. I can walk right past them unnoticed whenever I so please. I can be a guard, a beggar, a minister, a merchant transporting a witch prisoner for ransom…"

Upon his last remark, the witch grinned again, her faith in the thief growing.

"Now, let's leave this damned city," he said, adjusting his coat as comfortably as he could as the blue scarf around his neck started to itch. Then he tied the witch's hands with a piece of rope he pulled from a carpenter's window along the way.

When they reached the open space of Merchants' Square, the witch tried her best to not look anyone in the eye. The thief's head, on the other hand, was held up high, not a hint of anxiety in his expression.

He was an expert in disguise, but Syrena's face had been publicly exposed far too recently to go unnoticed. She saw a pair of eyes in the crowd noticing her. Then another.

And then Hudson came to a sudden halt, and Syrena stopped at his side nervously. They were nearly away from the crowds; she could practically see the city gates in the distance. And yet Hudson couldn't help but stop and listen to the commotion.

"What're you *doing?*" she hissed at him angrily.

"Shhh. One moment, darling."

It had been the sound of Viktor's voice offering the recompense of 5,000 yuhn in silver that made the thief stop in his tracks. It was enough to intrigue him into hearing what else the knight had to say.

Before she knew it, Syrena was being dragged into another empty alleyway. She observed as Hudson began removing his disguise in a hurry.

"Have you gone completely mad?!" she snarled at him.

"Forget what I said before, my dear," he said hastily. "I am no longer a merchant transporting a witch prisoner… I am Hudson Blackwood, cunning thief and mercenary." Upon stating his own name, he raised his chin and posture in a somewhat humorous way. "It's got a lovely ring to it, don't you think?"

"What happened to the plan?" Syrena asked.

"Oh, forget the plan. The plan was rubbish. We would've been caught immediately," he said, as he threw the knitted cap over his head and slipped on his black hat with amusing pride. "Here's the *new* plan. We join Sir Fancy's squadron and leave the city grounds *without* having to hide… How's *that* for a bit of spontaneous thinking, eh?"

"But they want you *dead!*"

"Lots of people want me dead, darling. It's the ones that *don't* that you want to keep an eye out for."

Syrena's expression went from startled to perplexed and with a doubtful sigh, she said, "That's the most stupid plan I've ever heard."

"And that's *precisely* why it is bound to work," he said with a wink.

"What makes you think Sir Fancy will even *want* your help?"

"Why wouldn't he?" he asked assertively, throwing his black coat on. "I'm Hudson Blackwood."

He moved towards the crowds, but she grabbed his elbow abruptly and pulled him back into the alley. "Hudson," she whispered, her left eye beginning to twitch from the anticipation. "Wait…"

"What is it, darling?"

"I, uh…" she hesitated, rubbing her eye to stop the nervous twitching. "I don't like crowds," she confessed. "They make me nervous… And… y-you don't want to be near me when it gets bad…"

"When *what* gets bad?"

She sighed and looked down at her hands, shivering with torment and hot as a furnace. And suddenly the thief reached over fearlessly, wrapped his hand in hers, and looked at her with his gaze warm and determined.

"I'm not leaving you behind," he said to her. "But if we're getting out of here, you'll have to trust me…"

She felt her heart skip a beat. Her hands kept shivering but her eye eased down on the twitching. And she could hardly speak, replying only with a worried nod.

"Come, love," he said with a devious grin. "Let's show these bastards what you're made of."

They waited for the opportune moment, moving through the swarm of civilians, astonishingly undetected. They found the perfect spot, in front of an elegant fountain, near a herd of attentive children. One of them caught sight of the wanted thief and made eye contact with him. The thief placed a finger over his own lips and winked, urging for the child's trust. The witch felt as if her heart would pound out of her chest from the torment. But the thief, in contrast, remained at ease.

The time had come… A young man had stepped forward, dragging with him a long silence that lingered for several moments.

The thief turned to the witch.

"Now, my dear," he whispered. "Time to put on a show…"

Syrena paused briefly, contemplating on what she was about to do. She had escaped the city's dungeons, only to expose herself once again to the same hostile civilians that wished to kill her only two days prior. Part of her urged her to run as far away from there as she could. She had her freedom and the thought of risking it made her tremble. But her conscience was leaning towards the thief, for it was he that made it possible to escape her prison cell to begin with. As insane as he may have seemed, she couldn't ignore his talent.

She cracked her neck, breathed deeply, and as she held an arm up in the air, shot out the largest wave of flame she had ever conjured. She did not restrain herself, hoping the shock of it all would grab the attention of the masses long enough for the thief to speak.

And grab their attention, it did…

"Miss me, mate?" Hudson said first, unable to resist himself, and it made Viktor Crowley as baffled as he hoped it would. Hudson stepped onto the fountain, elevating his view over the sea of heads.

"A beloved morning to you all!" he shouted boldly at the herd of citizens like a madman. "And what is *this*? The Golden Eagle of Vallenghard… Just the man I wanted to see."

The expression in Viktor's face gave Hudson a tremendous feeling of joy. There was no greater pleasure for the thief than to see his foes astounded and flustered upon his astute skills.

"Do not fret, *Val Havyans*, for we come here today in peace," the thief raised both his arms in the air the same way Viktor Crowley had done just moments before, almost as if mocking the knight.

"What is the meaning of this?!" Jossiah Biggs shouted from afar. "Guards! Arrest that thief!"

"I assure you, mate, you don't want to do that."

"And why the bloody hells not?!"

"Because from where I stand, I am the only thing standing in between you bringing home a live princess or a dead one," Hudson said, and it was followed by concerned whispers among the crowd. The thief hopped down from the fountain and began walking towards the palace gates, swaying with every step in his own unique manner, almost like a dance.

Syrena followed closely behind him as the peasants stepped away in horror, making way for them both. She was as watchful as she had ever been, her brows lowered and her eyes glistening almost menacingly. And as she walked with her arms at her sides, her palms remained ablaze, the flames dancing between her fingers.

Once the shock of it all had died down, Viktor Crowley felt a deep rage in his chest and sighed.

"Explain yourself *now*, Blackwood," he said. "Before I change my mind and order your beheading."

"Thank you, old mate," Hudson replied, tipping his hat in a quick bow. "I am here today, along with my radiant partner, to offer our services to the kingdom of Vallenghard and venture with you to retrieve her royalness."

"We do *not* negotiate with thieves!" Jossiah sneered.

"And that's quite honorable of you, old man. But *if* I heard correctly, your plan is to invade enemy grounds and *steal* the princess back from the grasp of the invaders… Seems to me like that's the work of a thief, is it not?"

"We will never accept the help of a crook!" Biggs spoke again as Viktor remained pensive.

"Sometimes, mate… It takes a crook to *fight* a crook," Hudson grinned.

The thief and the witch had by then joined the two former knights in front of the palace gates, and were at the center of attention, surrounded by watchful eyes and worried faces. As the thief paced about, Syrena was standing with her back to him, her flaming hands aimed at the herd so as to guard him. She glanced back a couple of times, curious of Viktor's reaction as Hudson worked his own magic on him.

"As I stand here before you on this fine day, my talents speak for themselves," Hudson spoke aloud, this time at the herd of peasants. "I've heard all about the Val Havyn dungeons... *Inescapable*, they called them. Figured I just had to see for myself and quite frankly I've seen better," he grinned at Jossiah Biggs, causing the crowds to mumble and some to even laugh and ridicule the royal guard.

"Now imagine what my skills can do for *you*, old mate," this time the thief was speaking directly at Viktor. "You *need* me... more than you care to admit. You cannot possibly break in and out of whatever foreign dungeons you speak of undetected and you bloody well know it... I, on the other hand, was *born* for it."

The silence spoke for itself. The thief's plan was indeed working.

"Furthermore," Hudson continued. "You cannot possibly guarantee the safety of these brave men standing before you." He motioned to Cedric and Thaddeus Rexx. The Davenport brothers hid behind Thaddeus's large frame, perfectly aware that the same witch they had captured for ransom just days prior could easily kill them with a thrust of her arm.

"There are dangers in that forest far greater than your fancy sword can handle," the thief went on. "I mean, honestly, have you considered the fact that these are the *Woodlands* we're speaking of? You're bound to face one or two creatures of dark magic and you won't defeat them with a piece of metal, old mate. No... It would take a much greater force to remain alive and protected. A much greater ally... Say, perhaps... A witch?" The reactions from the audience were a mix of consideration and protest, but all were caught in the thief's grasp and he refused to let them go.

Viktor Crowley sighed, well aware of the possible mistake he was about to make.

The thief stepped in front of him once more, keeping a foot's distance between them.

"Come on, old mate," he said in a lower voice as if in secret, his words meant only for the golden knight. "For old times' sake, yes?"

Syrena was close enough to hear, and she couldn't help but wonder what old times Hudson was referring to. When he got no reaction from Sir Viktor, Hudson stepped away once more, his loud voice returning to its rough vibrant nature.

"Sir Viktor Crowley, you are a brave and honorable man. There's no doubt in my heart about that, old mate. And that is *precisely* why I am offering my assistance... You give me and my radiant companion a chance, and I *assure* you...

I will do everything in my power to bring the princess home. *Alive.*"

It was at that moment that Viktor Crowley stepped forward, his studded boots echoing within the silence of the square. Hudson remained in place, confident and unperturbed. And then Viktor looked into the eyes of the thief... Memories of a past life he no longer held flashed before him, as the thief's grin slowly lost its coil and turned into a stern expression.

"You chose this," Viktor said.

Hudson scowled at him, baffled. "I'm sorry, what?"

"I'm just reminding you of the circumstances that you chose, Blackwood... We could have spoken privately like decent men would have, but you chose to do this publicly in the middle of your king's city."

"What can I say?" Hudson shrugged. "I *am* rather impulsive."

"That, you are," Viktor said. "So let's cut the bloody inspirational speech and jump right to our business here."

"Business is all I care about, old mate."

"Shut your damn mouth for a moment and listen."

There was a threatening look in Viktor's eyes, the kind that could frighten a man. It was the look of a soldier that had seen his fair share of horrors in his life and was willing to do everything in his power to ensure that his plan followed through as precise as possible. When he spoke, it was as if every single voice in the royal city had gone mute.

"You cross me..." Viktor said loudly, "You so much as *think* about crossing me... And I *will* see to it personally that you never cross another man again. My sword will cast upon you and that will be the end of Hudson Blackwood... Do I make myself perfectly clear?

"That you do, old mate," Hudson smiled and gave the knight a friendly tap on the shoulder, as if the moment had passed. But the golden knight ignored the tap and continued.

"You help me steal the princess back... And as the king's right hand, I will do everything in my power to convince the king to remove the ransom from your head."

The mockery in the thief's demeanor seized and his smile faded. He stared into the bright blue eyes of the golden knight, with a look that assured him no more tangible jesting. The plan had been to travel with the squadron no farther than the forest, after which he and Syrena would sneak away into the night while the rest slept...

The circumstances, however, had changed.

And Hudson Blackwood stood before an opportunity he felt reluctant to refuse.

An opportunity to stop running...

After careful consideration, and turning to Syrena for a hint of approval, the thief shot the same stern expression back at the golden knight.

"I want 10,000 yuhn," he said.

"You will get the agreed 5,000 and not a single yuhn more," Viktor replied.

"8,000 would be the most *human*, y'know?" Hudson felt the tension in his shoulders breaking, his witty contemptuous approach coming back to him. "I mean after all, I did just break *out* of a dungeon only to travel hundreds of miles to break *into* a dungeon. You can see the irony."

"This is *not* a negotiation," Viktor said. "5,000 or it's back to the dungeons and this time under more chains than you can fidget your way out of."

"Fine," Hudson said after a brief pause. "5,000 yuhn… *and* my own horse."

"Fair enough."

* * *

John Huxley packed what he thought would be of use to him into his late father's old leather rucksack. His mother stood by an open window, gazing into the distance at the approaching company of horses. She noticed there were no banners, which seemed most proper, considering they were bound to encounter a few unfriendly faces along the way. A subtle glow brightened her face as a mass of clouds blurred the setting sun that afternoon.

"The company is here," she said.

John walked over to the window and saw. 10 minutes, he figured it would take them, considering the path they were on was as familiar to him as the dry calluses on his hands.

"I'm sorry," John said, hardly bearing to see the trails in his mother's cheeks. "I have to do this, mum… You know I do."

Adelina turned to face her son. Her eyes were swelled up as she fought to keep the tears in. "I know."

"I can't sit here while they fight for our kingdom," he said. "Not when I'm the only one that has seen what the enemy looks like. It's not the way father would've wanted it. And I *know* it's not the way you want it either."

Adelina raised her right hand and grazed her son's cheek. John closed his eyes, feeling the warmth of his mother's hand, taking the moment to value it, well aware of the possibility that this may be the last time he would feel such warmth.

"I know," she said again as she kissed her son in the forehead. "Now go and speak with your sister, will you?"

Young Robyn sat crossed-legged above the stables, leaning on a pile of hay. As a child, she had asked for a tree house but her mother wouldn't allow it. She had settled for a room above the stables, which she had to reach by ladder. John climbed it towards her, and he saw her taking rocks from a nearby pile and throwing them into a tin bucket about 10 feet across from her.

"Given up on arrows, I see?" he tried to jest, but her firm expression remained unchanged.

"Mister Beckwit says it will help with my aim," she replied softly, as if she didn't care for the conversation. She managed to throw a rock inside the bucket and though she would typically smile at the very least, this time she looked unsatisfied.

"Looks like you're getting better," he smiled for her. "Guess I'll need to start training more or you'll catch up."

"Can you *please* just go?" she couldn't bear to look at him.

There was nothing but the sound of the wind between them, blowing through an open windowless square on the wooden walls of Robyn's barn room. Even the sounds of the animals inside the barn were muffled by the tension between the girl and her brother.

"Robyn, I'm sorry," he said.

"Please…" her voice began to break, and her jaw trembled as she fought hard to not appear vulnerable in front of him. "Just go."

John said nothing. He felt a hint of hesitation for a moment, well aware that he hadn't been away from home for years, at least not without a member of his family at his side. And the thought of this possibly being the last conversation with his sister left with with an ache in his gut.

A loud squawking broke the tension all of a sudden. The sound of flapping wings announced the arrival of the black crow as it flew in and landed on the wooden rim of the hollow window. Robyn looked at it, at its solitary eye staring back at her, feeling as though it was somehow judging her.

"John? Are you there? You've got visitors," they heard Mister Beckwit's voice down below.

John said no more and began climbing back down.

Robyn had always been the kind of person to seek isolation whenever something would upset her. She would sit and ponder and throw rocks at whatever target was nearest to her. She even considered for a moment grabbing a stone from the pile and throwing it at the crow so as to scare it away. But she found herself mildly intrigued as for the first time it didn't fly away once it was left alone with her.

When John met Mister Beckwit, Adelina had also joined them by the barn.

The company arrived, and Viktor Crowley was the first to leap off his white horse and greet them.

Adelina became instantly flustered and tense at the sight of a man she knew only by name. At the same time, however, some of the pressure left her chest, reckoning that her son's safety would be much more assured in the company of the Golden Eagle himself.

"Good afternoon. You must be Missus Huxley," Viktor said.

Something in the former knight had changed noticeably. Beginning with his attire, his armor was as regal and polished as it always was except the crest of the king was missing from his chest. The symbol of the golden eagle was still there, its wings spread outward all the way to his shoulder plates. The blue cape that he always wore was also gone, replaced by a bright red one, empty of any sigil. Viktor was no longer a knight, just a man in shiny armor, but his approach and demeanor was just as chivalrous as people were accustomed to.

"Please, call me Adelina."

"Viktor Crowley of Val Havyn," Viktor greeted her with an unexpected kiss on the hand.

Introductions were made, starting with Jossiah Biggs and three more of the king's soldiers who had all volunteered merely for the silver. Cedric and Thaddeus Rexx greeted them informally, as they had already been acquainted with the Huxleys, and seeing Cedric among the squadron both surprised and worried John a bit. The Davenport brothers hardly acknowledged the greetings, talking amongst themselves from a distance instead.

"And lastly," Viktor said with something like shame in his voice. "This is, uh…"

"No need for that, old mate. I can introduce myself," a voice interjected, hopping off a brown steed and walking closer, caressing the animal's neck along the way. He removed his black hat and, with a grin, gave a casual bow. "Hudson Blackwood of Raven's Keep, at your service."

John had been far too overwhelmed to notice the thief among the group, and he found himself at a loss for words. At the same time, young Robyn's interest became instantly peaked at the sound of the thief's name, and she couldn't help herself; she observed from above, careful not to make any sudden noises.

"How do you do, darling?" Hudson kissed Adelina's hand as well, in a way that was meant to mock Viktor's greeting. And after shaking hands with Mister Beckwit, the thief turned to John Huxley, who was still staring at him perplexed and bewildered.

"It's *you*…" John said, his voice dry from the disbelief.

"I'm sorry, do I know you?" Hudson asked sneeringly and gave the farmer a tap on the arm.

Feeling the need to explain, Viktor Crowley stepped forward and said, "Mister Blackwood and his companion Syrena of Morganna agreed to assist us in this expedition. Not to worry, we will assure the safety of the company remains a priority."

From above, the black crow screeched loudly all of a sudden, causing Robyn to fretfully back away from the window just in time to avoid being seen. "What is *wrong* with you?" she hissed at the crow.

The interruption was brief, but Viktor Crowley knew there was someone above listening.

"I do apologize," Adelina broke the sudden silence. "Our farm may be large, but I'm not sure our cottage has enough space to lodge all of you."

"Not a problem, Missus Huxley, so long as you will allow us to make camp here before we leave tomorrow at dawn."

"My land is yours, Sir Crowley."

Viktor smiled, and at the same time felt a tug at his chest upon hearing the word '*Sir*' in front of his name again.

* * *

The moon arrived quickly that evening, possibly hinting at an early sunrise.

The majority of the company was huddled around a fire in front of the Huxleys' barn. Four tents had been set up around it, all of them made of leather dyed with a dark shade of blue, but the golden crest of King Rowan was missing. Viktor explained that the reason behind it was to appear inconspicuous to the common traveler. In truth, however, he knew the loyalty of the company would shatter if they knew he was no longer a knight of the king's court.

A much smaller fire burned some ten yards away, where Syrena of Morganna sat biting at an ear of corn gifted to her by a young man with wheat-colored hair unknown to her. Having been locked in the palace dungeons, she hadn't heard of the farmer that confronted Hudson Blackwood, but the young man's warm hospitality gave her no reason to have any aversion towards him. The thief, on the other hand, was like a wild coyote stalking its prey, waiting for the opportune moment to pounce.

John Huxley was inside the barn, sharpening the cleanest knives he owned, or at least those with the least rust. He sat on a small wooden stool, a shiny steel blade resting between his boots. It had been given to him by Viktor Crowley himself, and looked like much too elegant a weapon for a farmer to wield. In fact, it was the first blade he owned that didn't look like it had been bought from a beggar. The blade had a hilt made of whale bone, smooth and white and polished, and the blade was sharp and thin like a saber, which made for a much faster swing.

"Every good swordsman needs a proper sword," Viktor had said back at the palace, and he picked out the blade from the same weapon stand where his was displayed, which made John wonder if the blade was previously Viktor's before he was knighted.

It was an honor, to say the least. And he'd kept it at close proximity since receiving it.

He threw the freshly sharpened knife inside his father's old rucksack and pulled out the next, when suddenly he heard wood creaking behind him. He had forgotten that Robyn was still sitting above the stables. She leapt off the ladder irately and headed for the doors, brushing past John along the way.

"Are you still angry with me?" he asked her.

Robyn chose to say nothing and instead shoved the door open.

But when she took one step out of the barn, a dark figure suddenly blocked her path. She froze, nearly yelping from the shock...

She wanted to say something, but no words would come to her. She felt even more flustered than if she had met a knight of the king's court. And instantly her mind recalled the portraits nailed to the walls of every other corner in Val Havyn. Yet, somehow, his eyes looked rather different in person. They looked more human, more conflicted.

"Go inside, Robyn," John said suddenly.

And the girl felt an even bigger impulse to stay. Slowly, she walked around the thief, unable to look away from his devious eyes. And then she scurried away towards the cottage, wishing suddenly that she stayed in her hideout just a few minutes longer.

John Huxley and Hudson Blackwood stared at each other in silence, each one unwilling to yield first.

The thief took a step forward and leaned on the doorframe, nonchalantly as if he was in his own home.

"Well... Doesn't *this* make for an unusual reunion?" he asked, looking at the farmer with that half-grin and half-scowl that only *he* could convey.

John tried to remain calm, though his chest was pounding infuriatingly. He sunk slowly back to a seat, realizing Viktor's company was close enough to intervene in the case of a skirmish.

"Don't mind me, mate. Just looking for a place to piss," Hudson said as he welcomed himself inside.

"Certainly not in here," John muttered, as he went back to sharpening his knives. His ears, however, remained attentive for any sudden moves on the thief's behalf.

Hudson began to pace around uninvitingly, examining the stables, noticing the splintering of the wood in certain areas where he presumed the young farmer had been training. "I see you've wasted no time in making new friends," he said scornfully.

"You should try it some time," John tried to match the thief's scathing tone. "It proves more useful than making enemies."

"Couldn't disagree more," Hudson replied. "An enemy's far more predictable. Furthermore, an enemy is, by definition, *incapable* of betraying you." He brushed past John, his boot grazing the leather rucksack on the dirt. And at that very moment, John rubbed the stone a bit too roughly, cutting his thumb on the knife's edge.

Annoyingly, he set both the knife and stone down. "What are you doing here exactly?" he asked the thief.

"What do you think?" Hudson replied. "Same thing every one of those poor bastards is doing. Finding trouble and making a bit of coin while at it. I could ask the same of *you*, mate. This isn't exactly a job for a sheep farmer."

"I'm a simple man, Hudson… And a man can earn coin in many ways, whether he has or lacks certain skills. That's the whole point of *earning* the coin," John said, with an added emphasis on the word to spite the thief.

"Well that's what I'm doing, mate. Earning my share."

The two men shared a look, each one unsure whether it was safe to trust the other. For one, Hudson was looking into the eyes of the man that had been responsible for his capture, and such a treat was rare for him. But, under the circumstances they were in, he wasn't sure if holding a grudge was the proper approach.

John, on the other hand, had deemed the man unworthy of being trusted to begin with, and he hadn't for one moment considered what a man of such skill could bring to the company whose mission was essentially to *steal* someone away. "We'll have to see about that," was all he could bear to say, to which the thief scoffed and continued to pace.

"Nice farm, you have here," Hudson said contemptuously. "It'd be a shame if you never saw it again."

"You know," John chuckled bravely, his attention shifting back to his knives. "I never *have* been fond of words. If you wish to threaten me, use your blade and not your mouth."

"Words are my only weapon, I'm afraid," Hudson said. "Sir Viktor Crowley has taken it upon himself to strip me of all the rest. *Security purposes*, he called it."

John scoffed. "Good to know. If you *had* a weapon, I might be more nervous. Without it, you're just a simple man who talks too much."

"You seem quite confident to know all about me for someone who met me for less than an hour."

"Am I wrong?"

"Quite so," Hudson spit on the dirt. "Well… except for one little thing."

John stopped sharpening his knife, his eyes looking up once more, almost unwillingly.

"You're right to feel nervous," Hudson said, his voice hardened. "Considering I *will* kill you someday… Not tonight, perhaps. Not tomorrow. But someday…"

Though Hudson remained at ease, his eyes spoke otherwise.

He glared down at John, as if making a threat through a stare.

"In the meantime, I look forward to becoming more acquainted, mate," he said as he lifted his right hand to his lips and bit into a green apple that hadn't been there before.

John suddenly looked down at his rucksack, noticeably emptier than it was before. He then glanced back up at the thief's grin and scowled. "How did y-"

Suddenly, an unexpected voice interrupted from outside the barn.

"Evening, gentlemen," Viktor Crowley said. "May I have a word in private with Mister Blackwood?"

"Certainly," John said, beginning to stand.

But the thief placed a hand on the John's shoulder and pushed him back down to a seating position. "Oh, no need for that," he said. "The farmer and I are old friends. Anything you wish to say to me, you can say in front of him." Something in the thief's tone didn't fully convince John that he actually meant what he said. More so, it seemed as if the thief was on the prowl for ways to spite or annoy the golden knight for sheer amusement.

"All right," Viktor shrugged. "It's about your companion, Blackwood."

"Lovely, isn't she? Quite an actress, too."

"Be that as it may," Viktor sighed. "It seems the company has come to a joint decision. The majority of them do not trust her."

"Why am I not surprised?" Hudson mumbled softly to John.

"I'm afraid they've asked that she remain in chains until we've reached Drahkmere."

Hudson's expression changed. His grin turned into a grimace as he stepped towards the knight.

"Have you gone daft?" he asked.

"It was a majority vote, Blackwood."

"*And?* What if we voted right now that you journey through the Woodlands stripped naked, would *you* bloody do it?" the thief's voice was beginning to rise. But the three men heard laughs outside; the sharp laughs of men that were certainly under the influence of liquor. And they instantly rushed out of the barn.

"Evening, poppet," said Martyn Davenport, chugging from a winesack and passing it to his brother. They walked towards Syrena with two of the king's soldiers, dragging with them a set of cuffs and chains.

"Think she'll resist?" Wyll asked, spitting into the fire and giving the witch a grimace.

"If she does, we'll break her wrists."

Syrena rose to her feet impulsively. But then a voice stopped her from attacking.

"I wouldn't try that if I were you," Hudson said as he walked closer, John and Viktor at his side.

"Shut it, Blackwood!" Martyn said, his unkempt chin beard swaying up and down as he spoke. "Here to protect your pet witch, eh?"

"Don't have to, mate," the thief replied. "You have to be the biggest moron alive to believe she *needs* my protection. But, please, by all means go right ahead and cuff her. It'll be most entertaining to watch you try."

Anxiety began to manifest in the brothers' chests as they noticed Syrena's palms exuding trails of grey smoke as she held them open at the ready, waiting for the drunken brutes to make the wrong choice. Out of fear and distress, she had been too slow to resist the previous time she was chained. And she looked prepared to fight before she let it happen again, especially by the same two men.

"Mister Davenport, I ordered you to wait until I spoke with Blackwood," Viktor Crowley said, his hand gripping the handle on his blade. The rest of the company was fast asleep in their tents, but the commotion outside was beginning to wake a few of them.

"She's a *freak*, Sir Crowley," Martyn said. "She can't be trusted among us."

Hudson had stepped in front of Syrena by then. He had no weapon to protect himself, only his words and defiant demeanor. "You call *her* a freak, mate?" he taunted the man. "I'd say that chin beard of yours is more terrifying."

"That's it!" Martyn pulled out a sharp knife.

"Oh good, you brought a shaver."

Martyn growled and raised the knife.

But then Viktor Crowley stepped between the two men, his sword drawn and determined.

"Enough!" he shouted. "If we're going to get through this, we *will* learn to work together. Believe me, there will be plenty of bloodshed soon enough, so save what little energy and sanity you've got for the *real* threat. That's an order! Is that understood?"

The silence, again, spoke for itself.

"Just bring the chains," Syrena suddenly said.

The stunned thief turned to her in disbelief, his eyes even showing a hint of sorrow. "What…?"

"It's all right," she said to him. "If it'll stop their fucking crying…"

She spit and stared at them with a glare that gave them both chills and shame.

And then they wrapped her hands in ogreskin and locked the cuffs around them.

* * *

Hudson Blackwood refused to share a tent with anyone. He slept outdoors, sharing the fire with the young witch as the rest of the company rested comfortably under their leather roofs. At some point during the evening, Adelina Huxley had approached Syrena with a change of clothes; a white blouse, a pair of brown trousers, and a black cape made of wool.

"Come, my dear," she'd said to the witch. "That dress looks like it must itch something awful. Let's get you changed. Come…"

The witch was stunned by the woman's kindness; it was as rare to her as having friends. Adelina had to take her into the barn and help her change, and John had stood guard by the barn entrance like a proper soldier. Adelina was gentle with Syrena, treated her like a sister or daughter, and even looked sad to see her in chains. She even left them additional blankets to help keep warm, and Syrena allowed the thief to take them, arguing that her gift allowed for her to remain warm and withstand the cold at night.

The thief lay, staring up at the night sky, his beloved hat resting on the dirt beside his head.

Syrena, freshly dressed and cleaned, sat cross-legged by the fire looking down at the cuffs she hated so dearly and the fresh layer of ogreskin over her palms.

"I *hate* knights," Hudson said.

"You hate everyone."

"*We took a vote*," he mocked them, and then scoffed. "The nerve of the lot. They ought to be thankful you didn't fry them when you had the chance. Bloody morons."

"It's just a stall. You've picked the cuffs before, you can pick them again."

"Not with that hog keeping watch on us all night."

Syrena didn't notice Jossiah Biggs lurking nearby. The man was pacing by the barn drowsily, smoking from a pipe of tobacco. "Can we get rid of him?" she mumbled.

"We can," the thief said. "But we should wait until we've reached the forest. Easier to lose them there." He paused for a moment and sighed. He moved his head at an angle and looked at Syrena's wrists, hidden under the thick moldy skin. "Will you be all right?" he asked.

"Not the first time I've been held down by chains," she made her best attempt at a smile. And then they nestled themselves close together, finding comfort among the grass, and closed their eyes for a good night's rest.

* * *

The Huxley twins lay side by side on the pair of bedspreads, both of them wide-eyed and enthusiastic as they always were. In the corner of the room was a wooden bedframe with two layers of cloth over it, where young Robyn lay pretending to be asleep.

"Tell us a story, mum!" Melvyn said, lying in the bedspread closest to the wall.

"It's a bit late for that, dear. Go to sleep," Adelina settled a soft, warm blanket over him.

"Please?" Margot asked, feigning a frown.

"Would you tell us the one about Prince Carlyle and his bride?" Melvyn asked eagerly.

"That story's boring," said Margot.

"It's better than *your* favorites!"

"It's a *love* story, Melvyn. No one likes love stories."

"*I* like it. It's fun."

"There, there now," Adelina said, sitting on a wooden chair between the two bedspreads. "Perhaps tomorrow, my dears. Now it's time to sleep." She kissed them both on the forehead and caressed their cheeks. And then she blew on the candle by the nightstand and headed for the door to the common room.

"Mum?" Margot called out.

"Yes, dear?"

"Will John be all right?"

She had no answer, at least not a truthful one. She walked slowly back towards her children and leaned in, the only light coming from the moonlight through the windows. "Your brother's a brave man," she said to them. "He's doing this for all of us."

"He's doing it for himself," a voice said abruptly. Robyn Huxley wiped the angry tears from her cheeks.

And Adelina could say nothing other than, "Goodnight, darlings. I love you all."

When dawn came, the men were up and ready by the time John Huxley walked out of his cottage, wearing the finest leathers he owned and the thickest boots he could fit his feet into. His brown leather vest was buttoned tightly, just lose enough to allow him to move freely. His rucksack was filled with fruit and bread and cheese, and he had secured knives to his belt and hid two in his boots. And the elegant sword that Viktor Crowley gifted to him was strapped to his belt, its aura almost giving him a sense of self-assurance.

He was as ready as he would ever be.

The company was loading the horses and eating their morning meal as the sunrise gave its first light, just enough light to begin their journey. But before John could join them in the field, he heard a loud thump and saw a shadow running after him from the corner of his eye.

Robyn Huxley wore her finest coat, made out of a coyote's pelt, and beneath it were the hunting leathers that she wore when she practiced her archery in the Blue Hills. When he saw her puffed-up eyes, John couldn't help but wonder how long the girl had been awake, or if she had even slept at all.

"John, wait!" she shouted, scampering after him, holding her beloved bow *Spirit* in her hands and a quiver of about 30 sharply carved arrows.

"What are you doing, Robyn?"

"I'm coming with you!"

"You can't," John said calmly. "You know that you ca-"

"Don't!" Robyn snapped angrily at him. "You *won't* stop me this time!"

"Mother needs you, Robyn. You need to stay here…"

"I said I'm *going*!" Robyn tried to push her way out of the wooden fence, but her brother blocked her path and held her back. She tried to pull away and head for the horses, but John simply held her tighter.

"Robyn, you *can't*!" he said.

Not only did Robyn continue to pull away, but she began throwing punches at her brother's arms and chest.

"Let me go!" she shouted. "I said I'm going with you!"

"Stop it! Listen to me!" John grabbed his sister by the shoulders and gave her a strong shake. "You're needed here, Robyn," he said. "Mum needs you… The twins need you… You must stay and look after them for me."

"And *who* will look after *you*?!" she yelled. Tears began to build at the corner of her eyes, and this time she did not hold herself back. John sighed, the knot in his throat growing. Robyn threw her arms around her brother, her tears smearing over the sleeves of his wrinkled white shirt.

John held her tightly, hoping it wouldn't be their last embrace. And Adelina watched them from the cottage window, a mug of tea in her hands. Struggling to catch her breath, Robyn mumbled something that John couldn't quite hear. "What was that?" he asked.

His sister backed away and wiped the tears from her face.

"We lost father," she said. "I couldn't bear losing you too…"

John could no longer help it and allowed his own tears to escape him.

Every single memory began to flash before them.

Every trip to the royal city together.

Every cold winter night in which John would give up his own sheets so that Robyn wouldn't suffer through the cold. Every scorching hot summer day in which she would unwillingly help John hunt and harvest crops suddenly became the best memories of her life.

When their father had passed away, he was there to comfort her. At the end of a hard day's labor, he was there to bestow a hug or a pat in the back.

Old Man Beckwit had taught Robyn to handle a bow, but it was John who helped her perfect those skills.

Despite their many disagreements, John and Robyn were more than just siblings. They were best friends.

"You won't lose me," John said, using his handkerchief to wipe a tear from his sister's face. "I promise you."

Robyn hugged her brother tightly one last time as she trembled, scared for his life.

"Take care of yourself, sister," he said, looking into her round brown eyes one last time. "And please… do try to stay out of trouble."

She smiled at him, not noticing she had dropped *Spirit* on the grass beside her.

"I… I promise I'll try to," she said.

* * *

The first few miles were the easiest. The green plains west of Elbon were vast and undemanding to travel through. The only faces the company encountered were travelers heading to the royal city or south to Roquefort. They strode through fields of green, with willows and pine trees growing in abundance by the mile.

The orphan Cedric gazed about in awe as he tried his best to guide the large horse that had been loaned to him by the Huxleys. "Is this it…?" he asked.

"Is what it?" asked Thaddeus Rexx, riding beside the young man.

"Are we in the Woodlands yet?"

There was a sudden mocking grunt coming from their left.

"Something funny, thief?" Cedric asked, trying his best to convey a hardened tone.

"Plenty," was all the thief said, and then he tapped his horse so as to ride away from the young man.

Cedric scowled. He turned back to the only friend he felt he had and asked, "How do we know?"

"Believe me, lad… you'll know," Thaddeus replied.

Cedric silenced himself as if by impulse when a certain figure rode past him.

He could almost sense her presence, and it was giving him a rush of unwanted chills. Syrena sat chained up on a mare that was tied at the nozzle to Jossiah Biggs's horse. The discomfort was vivid in her expression, and Cedric could hardly bare to look into her hauntingly glimmering eyes and instead stared at her leather-bound hands.

"I don't trust that witch," he mumbled when he thought the witch was too far ahead to overhear.

"It'll be fine, boy," Thaddeus said. "So long as she remains chained, she'll be no trouble. You'll be findin' worse things to worry about in the Woodlands."

They gazed at the long journey ahead. They could see the forest grounds in the distance, a large stretch of vibrant green beneath a bright blue sky. John trotted on his horse near them, trying to catch up to the knights leading the company ahead. And when he brushed past the Davenport brothers, they snickered nastily among themselves.

"If this little plan works, d'you suppose the king will let us spend a night with his lovely daughter?" Martyn asked his brother, his snide remark loud enough for the farmer to overhear. But John's composure and disregard for the brothers only angered them more.

"He thinks he's so mighty, does he?" Wyll snorted. "What's that he's riding, a mule?"

But John kept silent, despite the fact that the brothers' words were starting to anger him. Cedric was close enough to hear and felt pity for the farmer, having being acquainted with him for most of his life. He made brief eye contact with him and nodded, acknowledging him, though he couldn't muster the courage to stand up to the mocking brothers.

Hudson Blackwood rode ahead, surrounded by the royal guards, as if they were purposely caging him in. "Please don't tell me I'll have to stare at that nappy bundle of dry grass you call hair," he said scornfully, referring to Viktor Crowley, who was riding at the front, blocking most of the thief's view.

"Keep talking and I'll have you put in chains as well," said the former knight.

And the thief shot a glance at a stern-faced Jossiah Biggs and said, "A man can't be honest around here without everyone's feelings getting hurt."

Jossiah grunted and trotted on ahead, uninterested in any conversation with the thief.

"My point exactly," Hudson mumbled to the nearest soldier.

They continued to ride towards the greenery in the distance that marked the forbidden grounds of the Woodlands. Everyone in the company, including the thief, was brimming with awe; bearing in mind the approaching dangers that lurked within. They kept their gaze frontward, distracted and unaware of the pair of young brown eyes watching them from afar.

A girl was cautiously following them, riding a saddled farm pony

Keeping a safe distance, using the pine trees as shields, she rode unnoticed about a mile behind the squadron, waiting for the opportune moment to reveal her presence...

A moment that would never come...

VI
Unnamed

The nervous knocking on the door, just minutes after dawn, had come as a surprise. Old Man Beckwit nearly stumbled in his robes as he rushed to answer it, looking down at the eyes of a frightened young boy at his doorstep. The boy's eyes were red and swollen, and there were fresh trails on his reddened cheeks, and the old man knew that whatever was coming wouldn't be the least bit pleasant.

"It's Robyn," the boy said. "Something's happened…"

The scarred muscles on his leg did not, by any means, slow the old man's pace; in fact, young Melvyn found himself struggling to keep up for a few brief moments. When they reached the Huxley farm, Mister Beckwit's eyes were on alert. He did what he often caught John doing, when the farmer thought no one was looking. He observed. And when he did, the signs were everywhere.

The empty corner in the shed where the girl's satchel of arrows and bow used to sit…

The fresh trail of footsteps in the mud, left there by boots far too small to belong to John…

The empty stall in the barn where the roan-colored pony once stood…

The look of horror and denial in Adelina Huxley's eyes, well aware of what had happened yet pleading the gods to tell her otherwise.   ..

"She's gone, Abner," the woman said. "My girl is gone."

Mister Beckwit embraced his lifelong friend in his arms, letting his cane drop to the wooden floor, using what little strength his leg had left to keep his balance. The twins watched from afar, their own chests pounding with remorse at the sight of their weeping mother.

"Where did she go?" asked the old man.

"Where else?" Adelina replied. "She must've gone after John…"

She wept for hours, feeling the air escaping her chest, bit by bit until the image of her became nearly unrecognizable beneath her pallid, horror-stricken expression. Mister Beckwit remained by her side until dusk, sending Larz and Henrik off to fetch food for the grieving woman, which she would then refuse to eat.

"Be strong, Adelina," he tried to comfort her, but anything he said became muted by her sorrow. Knowing there was nothing left to say that would possibly comfort Adelina, the old man hoisted himself up with his cane and walked out into the sunset.

Margot Huxley watched him from the cottage window, her observant eyes wide and sprightly. The old man whistled sharply, and not a minute later his faithful black-feathered friend flew towards him, landing on the wooden fence surrounding the cottage, his sharp beak slightly open and his solitary eye looking up at his master.

"Margot, could you fetch mum some tea?" Melvyn said.

But his sister's mind was clearly elsewhere.

Something very peculiar was happening in their yard.

The old man leaned in closer to the crow, and his lips were moving as if he was whispering something into the crow's ear. The crow suddenly looked less like an animal… His head was somehow moving in the manner of a nod and his beak was gently opening and closing, like an attentive hound waiting for a treat.

Margot had never seen a bird move in such a responsive manner, and yet there it was.

Mister Beckwit's lips moved one last time, as if clarifying his words to his faithful companion.

And with that, the crow flew off into the distance, closely following the trail left behind by Viktor's company and their horses. There was no letter written on a scroll or anything of the sort; only words whispered by the old man. Before Margot could step away from the window, Mister Beckwit turned and caught sight of her.

He smiled at her.

She smiled back, and a slightly warm feeling began to build in her chest.

A feeling of hope…

* * *

Another warm day of spring had arrived. Another sunrise away from home.

The fatigue was so bad it nearly hurt to breathe. And on several occasions, our young princess Magdalena felt what she thought would be her last breath leave her body, and with it her faith for a safe return home.

The march south had been long and rocky just as she had predicted. Her captors appeared to be taking nearly every unstable terrain in their path in order to avoid being spotted by villagers and travelers. Not that they didn't encounter a few, but when they did they would either recruit or behead them. And leaving a trail of headless bodies behind was not necessarily a tactical approach in a kingdom such as Vallenghard, where the lord of every city and village was sworn to send a raven to Val Havyn, informing the king of any unprecedented incidents.

It had been several days of traveling now, sometimes going with little to no rest, and yet for Magdalena it seemed like weeks since she knew what comfort felt like. Where she found herself in could best be described as a cage with wheels… The rusty iron bars were about two inches wide and were aligned three inches apart from each other both vertically and horizontally, creating a large crate, ample enough for about a dozen people. Such cagewagons were made for transporting equipment or wanted criminals. But princess Magdalena was surrounded by neither.

She was sitting in the corner of the cagewagon, hungry and numb and lost in thought, when they came to an abrupt halt somewhere in the hills between Falkbury and Roquefort. Young Thomlin, inquisitive and clever as he was, leapt to his feet instantly and pressed himself against the bars so as to observe the commotion in the distance.

"What do you see?" Magdalena asked him.

"A dozen men on the road," Thomlin replied.

"Any banners on them?"

"None. Villagers perhaps, but they look weary. Maybe merchants?"

An old prisoner with grey hair and a sharp widow's peak sitting on the opposite end of the cagewagon scoffed under his breath. "Boy thinks he's got the eyes of a bat, does he?"

Thomlin and Magdalena paid him no mind. The rest of the prisoners tried to remain vigilant, but most were too frightened to peer and some had even lost an eye for it. During the previous day on the road they had lost two prisoners, one to starvation and the other for talking abrasively back to a soldier. Yet both Magdalena and Thomlin continued to baffle the rest of the captives in the cage; words of caution seemed only to go over their heads.

Some called it courage. Others called it stupidity.

"Get your bloody head down, boy!" the old man with the widow's peak hissed again.

"Let 'im see. What if they're here to help?" a frightened woman spoke out.

"Y'think a dozen men are gonna do anything to *this* lot?"

"Might be more coming. Perhaps they'll send a word out."

"They'll kill 'em first. And then they'll gouge the eyes out of these two for pryin'."

Magdalena wanted very much to speak out. She wanted to shout at the old man to mind himself, to tell him that not everyone was as hopeless as he was. If there was anything she still had left it was her perseverance, and the young princess had plenty of it. But she knew that at that moment she was no longer a woman of nobility. She was no different than anybody else in that cagewagon; she may as well have been a farmer or a handmaiden.

Thomlin continued to observe, moving his eyes away only to relay any useful information to the princess. The boy's clothes had been tattered to begin with, only now they had numerous stains that weren't there before and they were beginning to reek, only adding to the mixture of foul odors in the cage.

Magdalena was nearly unrecognizable. Her blonde hair was now filthy and tangled, and her fair skin was stained with a layer of dirt. What was once her elegant housedress was now messy beyond repair, filthy and torn and itchy to the point that it was irritating her skin.

"They're coming closer," Thomlin said suddenly, bending his knees so as to hide among the captives yet remaining watchful.

"Who is?" asked the princess.

"Hauzer and Jyor. They have people with 'em."

The husky red-bearded guard walked towards the cagewagon, dragging a prisoner in each of his large grubby hands. Jyor, the mercenary elf, walked alongside him with a set of keys in hand. One of the prisoners was a young man in his twenties with brown skin and thick black hair with decorative braids. The other prisoner was a tall woman with long silver hair who, though she appeared to be in her fifties or sixties, looked as if she had twice the strength of the young man she was being dragged with.

Jyor unlocked the door to the cagewagon.

Hauzer threw the young man inside. But the woman with the silver hair resisted; her hands were bound by rope but she used whatever defense technique she could muster. She spit on Hauzer's face and landed a kick to his shin, and then she pulled her arm free of his grasp.

Hauzer growled and winced from the pain. And the woman backed away from the cagewagon, as Jyor unsheathed his blade. She looked ready to run, but by then a handful of recruited soldiers had surrounded her.

"Get inside, wench," Jyor said with his blade aimed at her.

The fury was quite vivid in her glare. Had there not been four other soldiers there aside from Jyor, she would have made a run for it; though she was older, she looked agile and fit enough to outrun most of them except perhaps the elf. But she also looked smarter than that, as if she had been in a similar situation before. She gave in and stepped towards the cagewagon willingly. Jyor tried to grab her by the arm but she hissed at him and pulled away.

Hauzer cleaned the snot from his tattooed cheek as he groaned in disgust.

"The next filth that spits on me, I'll cut their fuckin' tongue off," he said angrily.

Magdalena and Thomlin observed from the other end of the cage. The rest of the prisoners would shrivel in cowardice whenever a soldier was within ten feet from them. And this particular instance was no different. They all cringed except for the princess and the boy; oddly enough, each of them felt that the other gave them the courage and strength they needed to stand up to the guards.

Once the cage was locked again, Hauzer cut the rope from the young man's hands as Jyor did the same with the woman. One thrust was all it took, and the thick rope split in two.

The piece of rope hadn't yet hit the floor yet when the silver-haired woman suddenly squeezed her hand through the gap between the bars and pulled Jyor inward by his ragged vest. She said nothing, only hissed at him and glowered at him heatedly. She was imagining the many possible ways she could kill him, and somehow the elf could read those thoughts in her eyes.

"Go on, you old wench," Jyor taunted her maliciously. "Give me a reason to kill ya… I'll do it slowly. Make a day out of it. Go on, then…"

Her glare did not change. Perhaps she may have been frightened on the inside, but her eyes spoke differently. Then the young man she had been imprisoned with placed a gentle hand on her shoulder.

"Not today, Valleria," he said.

The blade was still on Jyor's hand. It may have been too wide to stick it through the gap between the cage's bars, but he was sure it could make it far enough for the pointy end to stab her belly. She must have noticed it, for she eased her grip on the elf's vest slowly and carefully.

"Come on, Jyor. They've started to march," Hauzer said, walking away towards his horse.

The elf sheathed his blade and followed his companion, holding on to the glare with the silver woman for as long as his neck allowed it.

It wasn't long before the cagewagon moved again, pulled by two horses at the front. And the princess's eyes refused to move away from the two new prisoners. The woman had a certain fierceness to her that Magdalena had never seen in a woman her age before; at least no peasant or noblewoman, which is all she had known all her life. The two new prisoners sat alongside one another, quiet and cognizant.

"So much for help," the old man in the cagewagon scoffed again.

Magdalena and Thomlin sat back, trying their best to find comfort in the rickety wagon. The boy's eyes closed for a moment and he sighed with slight bleakness. The princess felt his head rest against her arm, and she allowed it. They were dragged along the path for several hours until the sun began to set and a cluster of tiny lights began to appear on the horizon. The princess shook the boy awake when she saw the lights. He awakened and stood eagerly on his feet. And it was the first real image of the city of Roquefort that Thomlin's eyes had ever seen.

* * *

The forest grounds were just a mile ahead when the first attack came…

Viktor Crowley had seen the signs minutes before it happened and he held himself as firmly and calmly as he could. The first sign was the quiet stillness all around them. The fields of Vallenghard were often filled with wild boar, deer, and even moose. But on that afternoon, it was as quiet as death. The others in the company were too fueled with unease as they approached the forest grounds, John Huxley included. But both the golden knight and the observant thief Hudson Blackwood knew that the silence seemed far too intentional.

The incline of the path was leading them upwards towards a hill of misshapen gray stones caked with humid green moss. And just beyond those rocky hills was where the Woodlands began. Dusk had come, and the setting sun casted long black shadows of the trees and stones that stretched towards the company, and the slightly misshapen figures among those shadows were quite obvious to Hudson, who was skilled in remaining unseen and unheard.

Clumsy or lazy, the thief thought to himself.

Either way, he was sure there were people hiding among those rocks...

Viktor tugged at the reins and brought his horse to a halt, and he removed his helmet for a better look.

Jossiah Biggs approached him. "What is it, old boy?" he asked.

"See that?" Viktor aimed at the shadows with his eyes. "Someone's up there..."

Confusion spread among the squadron. They looked at one another hesitantly, their hands gripping their weapons out of precaution. John Huxley moved closer to a pair of more familiar faces. "Why are we stopping?"

"Don't know," said Thaddeus Rexx. "He might've spotted someone..."

"Is it freaks?" young Cedric asked nervously.

"Couldn't tell ya, lad..."

Viktor Crowley considered their options... If the company deviated from their path or turned around at that point, the bandits ahead would suspect they were spotted and come after them. And turning your back on an enemy was never the wisest choice. Sending one soldier ahead would surely be a waste and a dangerous act. And yet standing still that way was perhaps the worst thing they could do.

"Want me to go on ahead, old mate?" Hudson offered loudly.

Viktor clenched his teeth with frustration. "Will someone shut him up?"

"Just thought I'd offer," Hudson shrugged. "Gods know you all find me disposable."

Viktor was sure he had gone through every possible scenario in his mind.

But nothing had prepared him for what happened next.

A loud echoing whistle with a smooth ring to it that seemed almost playful was coming from *behind* the squadron, and so they all turned their horses. Viktor drew his sword almost by instinct and gazed towards the east. Walking towards them was a single man with no horse, just far enough that his face was a blur. His only visible aspects were his reddish-brown shirt and a bundle of grey curls on his head swaying in the air with every step of his. And there was a furry brown creature about the size of a cat hopping along his feet.

"Who the bloody hells is that?" Wyll Davenport's horse stood a bit too close to his brother's. There was no answer, for Martyn Davenport was lost in thought, his trembling hand placed firmly on his sword's hilt.

The armed Viktor Crowley galloped to the front of the company, standing guard, facing the incoming man. He turned his horse halfway, taking one last opportunity to address his company privately. "Nobody speaks a word," he said. "I'm talking to *you* in particular, Blackwood. *One* word and I will have your damn tongue."

Hudson said nothing, only lifted both hands into the air as if to assert his defenselessness.

As they all waited silently, observing every move the stranger made, John Huxley's chest began pounding. Out of the whole crew, he felt the least protected. The only ones wearing steel armor were Viktor, Jossiah, and the three hired soldiers who thought they were taking orders from the king's right hand knight. The rest of them wore thick leathers, enough to prevent flesh wounds but none that could block a jab to the chest.

John looked down at his raggedy clothes, his brown leather vest being the thickest protection he could afford, and frowned at the sight of it. Should anything unexpected happen he would have to rely on his skills for protection. Suddenly, the silence was broken. The stranger in the distance whistled a second time, lifted his arms at his sides, and moved his fingers up and down as if signaling someone.

Nothing happened at first.

Viktor simply waited, and there was a strange feeling in the air as if they were being watched. Then the mysterious man whistled a final time, this time louder and much less playfully.

Out of thin air, a group of men dressed in rags and furs began to rise from the ground, shaking away the chunks of dead grass and dirt that covered their bodies. They were armed with blades and bows, and there were ten of them easily, not counting those hiding in the rocks atop the hill. They had been hidden in plain sight and were dangerously close to Viktor's company, and despite the company's expectations they all happened to be human.

"Clever," Hudson mumbled sourly.

The bandits closed in on them all, swords aimed frontward, remaining mostly quiet save for the snickers and hisses at whoever moved too quickly. And then Viktor turned his horse back towards the east as the mysterious man arrived at the scene.

He was an ordinary man with an unfortunate face, and his right cheek was marked with a burn scar in the shape of a scorpion, suggesting he had been a prisoner of the Rogue Brotherhood at some point in his life. His vest was made of brown fur while the rest of his clothes were made of red and brown linen. On his wrists were an assortment of bracelets and trinkets, which were visible from afar, but it wasn't until the mysterious man arrived that they realized what he wore were actually dozens of human teeth held together by string.

Up the man's leg, the furry creature climbed and settled itself on his right shoulder. It was a monkey, coated with a thick beige pelt, and it had sharp jagged fangs that may have been sharpened purposely by its master.

The mysterious nameless man began to clap his hands, slowly and almost threateningly.

"Well look at this now. We've got ourselves a hell of a catch, boys!" he spoke with a heavy Vallenghardian accent, his voice raspy and hoarse and with a higher pitch than Viktor had anticipated. "One hell of a catch, indeed..."

"I can't tell if they're nobles or beggars," one of the bandits said, aiming his sword directly at young Cedric, who cowered his gaze downward.

"Looks like a mixed breed lot," the nameless man in charge commented. Up close, his hair had quite obviously grown past its maturity and was now a bundle of grey locks, tangled like an unkempt bush, with a few black hairs hiding somewhere within. The wrinkles on his ivory skin aged the man at about fifty, a rather *strong* fifty, but he seemed more than fit for a fight and his confidence only redeemed him further, despite his short height.

"Why don't we start by puttin' them weapons down, yes?" he requested, his monkey hissing right at Viktor as it sat with its tail wrapped around its master's stubbly neck.

Viktor hesitated, but his recruits knew better and dropped their weapons where they stood.

John unstrapped the silver blade from his belt and set it down gently as if it were made of glass. A bandit snatched it immediately, one with a nasty grin and tattoos on his neck that were either ancient inscriptions or scribbles of gibberish. *He's not worthy of such an elegant weapon*, John thought to himself as a sickness settled into his belly.

"Your blade, chief," the nameless man said, shooting Viktor a menacing wink. "'Less you want one of my men up on the hill to shoot an arrow at one of your apes. All it will take is a wee whistle. Now drop it 'n' climb off that gorgeous beast slowly."

Viktor's blade hit the dirt, followed by his thick armored boots. There were unfriendly chuckles among the bandits as they forced everyone else to dismount their horses as well, and a few of Viktor's men shot angry stares back at them. John was startled and he was having trouble hiding it, but being surrounded by men like Viktor Crowley, Jossiah Biggs, and even Hudson gave him a mild sense of comfort. Out of the whole company, however, the thief appeared to be the calmest one, keeping his guard close to his witch companion.

"That's it. Wasn't so hard, was it?" said the nameless man as he picked up Viktor's steel blade and gave in to the unavoidable impulse to admire its gracious shine and stability. The man's appearance was far more threatening than his demeanor was. Had he not been robbing the company, he would have seemed almost friendly. His men, on the other hand, had 'trouble' written all over their glares.

"Beautiful blade, this is," the nameless man said. "Fancier than I'm used to, sure, but a man can change."

His men chuckled in unison, knowing precisely when to allow their leader to speak.

"It was a gift," Viktor spoke, much to the man's surprise.

"Ahh, I see... You look quite fancy yourself, there. Who d'you serve, chief?"

"I serve the Lord of Yulxester. He's sent us out on a hunt," Viktor's lie came almost naturally to him, as if he'd been preparing it for days.

And it was then that the nameless man's expression changed from amusement to distaste. In a manner of seconds, his near-friendly manner had vanished, replaced by a nasty scowl and a twitch of the nose. "That so?" he asked. "A hunt so far from home, eh?"

"'Tis a very particular hunt," Viktor tried to match the nameless man's ingenuity, failing.

"Ahh," the man replied. "And tell me, what kind of shit crew is *this* for a hunt?"

More laughs... And the tension was only getting worse...

"I wonder if *half* your apes can even shoot an arrow."

Viktor Crowley's jaw tightened, wishing his sword were still in his grasp. He tried his best to remain calm and keep his friendly grin to a minimum. But they were coming across as weak and there was no worse impression to convey to a group of bandits. The nameless man began to pace slowly, his seemingly sentient monkey glancing at every face in the squadron.

"It seems we find ourselves in a bit of an impasse, yes?" the man said loudly, his raspy voice only adding to his intimidating tone. "If I'm bein' honest, chief... I'm not exactly known to be a reasonable man, so to speak... But I do try me best to be fair. The way I see it, *no* one has to get hurt here... You stay friendly, *I* stay friendly... I take what I want, you get to keep your lives 'n' we all win... *But*... D'you know what I hate the *most*, chief? D'you know what *really* irks my bones?"

Viktor was silent, his amiable smirk now vanished. He was silently thinking of ways to hurt the man, but in his unarmed state the only way he could manage that was with his helmet.

"*Liars*," the man finished his thought. "See, I happen to know that the Lord of Yulxester's disappeared... It happened almost two weeks back now. Whole city's gone to shit without 'im 'n' no one's got a clue where he is. If he *did* send you on a hunt, then that's one *hell* of a long hunt to be on 'n' not be carryin' a single catch yet... So unless one of your starvin' apes ate it all or they have somethin' hidden in their trousers, I'd say you're a lyin' sack of shit, chief..."

With their best attempt at subtlety, Viktor's men threw gazes of concern at each other. Hudson's urge to speak had never been as strong, but knowing that they were unarmed and possibly outnumbered, he figured silence was a better alternative. But it didn't do much to stop the voice in his head...

One quick move, it told him. That is all it would take to pull the sword from the cross-eyed bandit to his left. One swift kick on the loose soil beneath his boots and he could blind the bandit, snatch his sword, and kill him faster than the man could remove the dust from his eyes.

The thief had become so lost in thought he hadn't noticed his hand twitching, nor did he notice the bandit noticing it. The bandit's blade moved from Syrena to Hudson. And then the witch moved her cuffed hands over the thief's, calming his nervous spasms.

"Not now," she whispered at him gently, and then the bandit grunted and moved the blade closer. Hudson could somehow feel Syrena's warm touch through the ogreskin, and it was keeping him calm for the time being.

"D'you know who I am, chief?" the nameless man suddenly asked Viktor, who chose not to respond. "Have you even the *slightest* idea who I am?" He lifted the majestic silver blade and pressed the tip against Viktor's neck.

"Can't say I do," Viktor spoke slowly, careful not to prick his chin with his own blade's edge.

"Good," the nameless man replied, his grin coming back to him. "Now… Here's what's going to happen… We're takin' your weapons, your food, 'n' your horses. And *since* I'm feelin' a bit generous today, I'll let you leave here with a warning… But do remember, chief, there here's *our* ground… We see your faces 'round these parts again, 'n' you best believe *my* pretty face will be the *last* you'll see."

All of a sudden, the man's monkey hissed sharply and unexpectedly, jumping off his master's shoulder and startling them all. He hopped between the company's feet, his nose close to the ground as if he was following a scent.

"Looks like he found something, boss," one of the bandits snickered.

The monkey stopped at Syrena's feet, his flared nostrils twitching in the air as he sniffed the decaying ogreskin on her wrists. The witch's heart began to race and her eye was twitching fiercely as the damn monkey shrieked loudly and shifted all of the attention to her, as if notifying his master about his catch.

"Ahh," the nameless man chuckled, his eyes broadening and his lips curving into a wide grin, revealing his yellow teeth. "Is that a *witch* you got there? Well, what a hell of a catch, *indeed*… I think I'll be takin' her too, chief…"

Syrena's twitching wouldn't stop, and for a moment she swore she felt the heat radiating from the ogreskin, she was so enraged. She then felt Hudson's hand tighten around hers, and he stepped in front of her, shielding her from the bandits. And the monkey at their feet hissed and scratched at the thief's black boots.

"I'm afraid I can't allow that," Viktor finally spoke again.

The nameless man took a step forward, close enough that Viktor could smell his reeking breath.

"I wasn't *askin'*, chief…"

The look that both men shared was mutual. Neither one was willing to cave.

Viktor may have set down his weapon but he would not allow for any man, much less a bandit, offend his honor. He may have had his knighthood taken away, but he would let no one take away his name. The Golden Eagle of Vallenghard took a step forward himself, ignoring the threat of the blade's sharp tip on his neck.

"The witch stays," he said.

And then there was a long silence. The bandits glanced at one another, unsure of how their leader would respond. Viktor felt the pressure on his neck ease down as the nameless man began to chuckle suddenly, his monkey hopping back towards him and climbing up his leg again.

"You've got quite a pair, chief," he said with a sigh, before his grin faded. And then he turned to his men and said, "Hold him down."

They grabbed Viktor Crowley by the arms and forced him down to his knees.

"Get your bloody hands off him, you bastard!" Jossiah took a step forward but was held back by a dagger to the neck.

"Now I *did* say no one had to get hurt, didn't I?" the nameless man chuckled. "But you lot just *don't* seem to get who's in charge here!"

Viktor tried to fight them off. It took three men to hold him down against the dirt, while the other six had their weapons aimed at the defenseless company. The nameless man held up Viktor's graceful blade, examining its beauty one last time.

"Such a beautiful blade, chief," he said spitefully. "It'll be an honor to kill you with it."

Viktor couldn't bear to glare at him any longer. He turned his head the other way, his right cheek pressed against the dirt as he faced his company. He locked eyes with every single one of them, one by one. They were all frightened, he could tell. And then he turned to the only pair of eyes that didn't share that look.

Hudson Blackwood stared right back, trying to concoct a plan through a stare.

It wasn't entirely clear if the knight was glaring at him or begging for help. Either way, the thief's reaction was far too late...

The nameless man raised the blade over his head. "Give my regards to the gods," he said, and then swung the blade down. And then the haunting sound of piercing flesh echoed all around.

The nameless man screamed all of a sudden... Every single person in Viktor's company winced as the blade missed Viktor's neck by just a few inches. The nameless man held up his arm, groaning with pain as his face hardened into a grimace.

An arrow was sticking out of it...

An arrow carved out of a willow's branch with decorative feathers on the unsharpened end...

There was a brief silence, during which every person present shared the same perplexed look in their eyes.

For Hudson Blackwood, however, this was far too great an opportunity to ignore… He cracked his neck and smiled. And it took a mere second for him to disarm the distracted bandit closest to him.

"Hey! What are y-"

Hudson slit the bandit's throat with one quick swing. And then he drew the hidden dagger in his boot and threw it at another bandit, striking him in the chest.

"Kill 'em all!" the nameless man shouted.

But Viktor's company joined Hudson and began to fight back.

There was a skirmish, and the bandits found themselves struggling. The Davenport brothers were quick, dodging attacks and countering with their own. Thaddeus Rexx hardly needed a weapon and used his fists. Cedric hid behind his horse. And Jossiah Biggs used his steel gauntlets to block the bandits' blades as he threw himself on the grass and snatched his weapon back.

John Huxley had no idea where to begin. Bodies fell and stumbled around him and blood began to stain the grass. He crouched near his horse as he looked for a weapon, when suddenly a nearby voice shouted, "Hey! Farmer!"

Much to John's surprise, it was Hudson that tossed him a blade; it was curved like a hook and heavier to wield but it didn't, by any means, slow the farmer down. He fought bravely, lunging forward and rolling on the grass the way he often would when training in his barn.

The nameless man was pulling at the arrow on his arm, unsure of where it had come from, when he noticed Viktor Crowley approaching him menacingly. He swung at Viktor, but the knight ducked and tackled the man down to the dirt, the elegant blade slipping from his grasp.

In a matter of minutes, Viktor's men had their weapons back, and there was not a single casualty among their company. Six of the raiders were now dead and the other three were on their knees, their hands held up in surrender.

The nameless man was lying back against the dirt and much to everyone's surprise Viktor was on top of him, viciously landing punch after punch with as much strength as he could muster. He looked enraged, like a man on the edge of losing his mind, and Jossiah felt compelled to step towards him.

"That's enough, old boy," he said.

But Viktor did not stop. Something in the man had overcome him. All of the rage that had built up inside his chest was being released through his fists. Jossiah had to grab him by both arms to stop him from killing the man.

"Viktor!" he shouted. "That's enough! He's done!"

The golden knight had his blade back, and the urge to stab it into the nameless man's neck was far too strong.

"Listen to your ape, chief," the nameless man coughed over the dirt, spitting out blood and a chipped tooth.

Viktor simply stood there, panting, sweating, and shivering with wrath.

155

John Huxley unstrapped his blade from the back of the kneeling bandit with the cheek tattoos. He placed his hand on the soft bone of the hilt and unsheathed about an inch of it, as if to confirm it was still there, and then strapped it back to his belt. The bandit shot him a scowl and a flicker of the nose.

It was over... Viktor's company had won...

Suddenly, however, a loud cry echoed in the distance followed by the startling sound of bones snapping.

And then a rapid wind chill began to blow from the west...

"S-Sir?" young Cedric said, rising out from behind his horse, his eyes gazing in the direction of the Woodlands. "W-What is that...?"

Viktor took a gander.

A man was running down the hill, screaming and shouting like a madman. He was dressed in rags and furs like the rest of the bandits, and he was distraught and out of breath as he shouted something along the lines of, "*Run!*"

The entire company gathered closely, their swords still drawn and their gazes aimed in the same direction. Behind the running man, something began to crawl down from the top of the hills, something inhuman... It was large and black and had eight legs attached to it.

John Huxley's jaw dropped.

And then the creature was followed by four more just like it.

"To the horses!" Viktor shouted.

Within seconds, the company got back on their horses and galloped away. The setting sun to the west was blinding them, but when they rushed around the hill, John glanced back and could see the creatures over the pasture. Spiders the size of sheep were scattering towards the fallen bandits.

"Arachnians, boss!" one of them shouted as the nameless man stumbled to his feet drenched in his own blood. There were five spiders in total, the smallest about twice as large as his monkey.

"Shoot the chief!" the man said. "We'll take care of the furry bastards."

Then the nameless man and two of his remaining men grabbed their curved blades from the dirt and faced the spiders fearlessly, as if they were used to hunting them down.

The last bandit cracked his neck and aimed at Viktor Crowley with his bow. The knight was a good distance away by then, but his white stallion and red cape made for an easy target. The bandit pulled the string back tightly, his fingers still and firm without the slightest hint of a shiver.

And then an arrow struck him...

The bandit dropped his bow and his arrow shot aimlessly into the sky. He looked down, slowly and profoundly confused... His chest was leaking red, and an arrow was sticking out of it. When he pulled it out, he saw that it was hand-carved with a wooden tip rather than steel, just like the arrow that had struck the nameless man's arm. And it had come from the east, from somewhere among the pine trees.

"S-Sir," he tried to call for help, but his voice was weak and faint like a whisper. And the blood began to pour from his chest furiously. He glanced towards the east, and there he caught the figure hiding in the distance...

A woman, perhaps still a girl, was standing behind a pine tree with a bow in her shivering hands.

"S-Sir!" he called again, but his comrades were busy fighting off the spiders.

And so he chose to approach the girl himself, one final effort before he dropped to his death.

From a distance, the girl pressed her back against a pine tree and panted heavily, her sweaty hands struggling to keep her grip on her bow. Her blonde-haired pony waited nearby, hidden behind a hefty shrub. And she wanted to run to it and ride away, but she could hardly move from the agitation. She did not want to kill the bandit; she wanted merely to slow him down.

Except now the man was approaching her, slowly but surely.

She grabbed another arrow from her quiver and stretched the string of her beloved bow *Spirit*.

She counted to three but couldn't find the strength to let go.

The bandit was coming closer...

She counted to three again. But still, her hand refused.

And so she set it down and breathed heavily and worriedly, taking the time to concentrate. When she looked back up, the bandit was slowing his pace down. He came to a halt just a few yards away as his chest continued to ooze red. And then his knees gave in... He fell frontward and his head slammed against the dirt.

He was dead.

And the girl nearly fainted from the shock. She had only ever killed rodents and wolves, and now her arrow had taken a human life. An unsettling warmth crawled up her throat suddenly and she found herself vomiting the eggs and water she ate for breakfast.

She breathed heavily, her bow still at hand.

Focus, she told herself. *Now is not the time for this...*

She placed her arrow gently back with the rest. If she was to catch up to her brother, she could not allow for any distractions. With one last glance for safety, she mounted her pony and began riding away.

Part of her wanted to turn around and ride back home. Her persistence, however, would not allow it. And she tapped her foot against the belly of the pony to make it gallop faster, as she followed closely behind her brother and the rest of the company.

The determination was as vivid in her eyes as it always was.

Robyn Huxley had come too far to turn back now.

She galloped into the darkness of the Woodlands, unaware of the horrors that would wait within...

* * *

A strange encounter took place that evening in the city of Roquefort. It was a night that changed the course of history, not only for young Princess Magdalena but for the entire kingdom of Vallenghard.

Roquefort was the farthest city in the south, and thus it was essential to the kingdom for trade and commerce with foreign nations. It was ruled by Lord Augustus Clark, whose eldest son was to inherit the throne by marrying her majesty. The engagement had been painted as a favor to King Rowan for his aid against the Aharian threat from overseas. But little was known about Lord Clark's intentions.

His eldest son, the noble but pampered Sir Darryk Clark, was given very little say in the marriage arrangement. And the lord treated his people the very same way. When the Aharians began raiding the villages along the shores, Lord Clark had given the order for inexperienced peasants and young ones to fight in his fleet, all of whom had never agreed to fight in the first place.

And so, after years of deception, the tension in Roquefort was growing more noticeable by the day. Many, in fact, accused the lord of promising Sir Darryk to the princess as a way of ensuring King Rowan's aid in the case of a revolt. And a revolt was certainly imminent.

Due to the recent struggles, the city had suffered an immense loss of life. And though King Rowan's army and Lord Clark's fleet prevailed, the city was left under great distress. And any matters in recent days, trivial as they may have seemed, became subject to speculation.

On this particular night, a raven was sent to Val Havyn with a letter addressed to the king.

It happened as follows...

The docks of the city were eerily empty and plagued with a sea of fog. A boisterous fish merchant approached a preoccupied harbourmaster, taking careful steps over the rickety wood along the harbor.

"That's the last of it," he said, removing his wool cap and wiping the sweat from his face.

"Noted," replied the harbourmaster, a man of about sixty with a grey head of hair and quite a laudable beard. He then annotated his initials on a parchment next to the fish merchant's name.

"What of the payment?"

"You'll have to report to the port's coinmaster for that," the harbourmaster grinned.

"But the day's gone. What if he ain't there no more?" the fish merchant asked confusedly.

"Well... this is why we have inns, sir."

The fish merchant scoffed and walked up the set of stone steps that would lead him to the high port where the city streets began, leaving behind his hefty ship tied to the dock. Somewhere up there in some rowdy tavern, his crew was two rounds of ale ahead of him, and he couldn't help but scowl out of jealousy. On his way up the steps, he bumped elbows with a young man in his twenties who was stumbling down hesitantly towards his master.

The day had turned into evening and, much like every other night, a fire was lit at the crown of the highest tower in the city's citadel. It was the largest and brightest light for miles around, so much so that even from afar sailors and pirates could easily spot the city of Roquefort in the darkest of nights. All they had to do was look for the ember of fire like an orange star in the black sky, shining down over the thousand tiny specks of light that illuminated the southern coast.

The young man running down to the lower docks was the harbourmaster's apprentice.

He had on an oversized coat, a lantern in his hand, and a flustered expression on his face.

"Master Wellyngton!" he called. But the harbourmaster was revising his list to assure no missteps that would cost him more than he could bear.

"Master!" the young man called again. "A company is approaching, sir!"

"Tell them the port's closed for the evening, lad. No shipments in or out 'til first light," harbourmaster Wellyngton said.

"I did, sir! They refused to accept it…"

"They did what?"

"They said th-"

At that very moment, the harbourmaster noticed a glow of light approaching them, illuminating the shaky docks with every step. There were two ways to reach the docks. The harbourmaster's apprentice had taken the shortest route, the steps made of stone that ran along the seaport wall. The longer way was the path around the harbor, which had no steps, only a long inclined ramp made of wood.

A stranger with a bald scalp, a red beard, and black tattooed symbols on his cheek reached the end of the ramp and approached the harbourmaster and his apprentice. There were more men behind him, a whole troop of them, waiting at the ramp.

"Th-That's them, sir," the young man whispered.

"Shut your mouth, boy," the harbourmaster hissed. "Let me do the talking…"

The two men tried their best to appear calm, but the stranger only seemed to get larger and scarier as he emerged from the fog. "Greetings, gents," the stranger said, attempting to sound proper.

"Good evening, sir," harbourmaster Wellyngton greeted him. "I'm afraid the port's closed for the evening. We'll have to make arrangements for y-"

It was then that Wellyngton noticed that the man and his companions were all heavily armed, and they dragged with them two rickety cagewagons covered entirely by a wrinkled brown cloth. They looked nothing like merchants. They looked weary and unapproachable and they bore many scars, the likes of which were not usual for common peasants.

"Ohh," Wellyngton said nervously. "I-I see your company's all here… Um… Did you not see the notice stating the port was currently off limits to civilians?"

"We ain't civilians," Hauzer said with a shrug. "We've direct orders to transport weapons to the Noorgard Islands. Only we're in need of a ship."

"The Noorgard Islands? Why, that seems rather unusual. Our kingdom has no treaty established with anyone from there."

"Let's just say we serve a lord that wishes to remain unnamed… After all, Roquefort honors a lord's freedom to conduct trade without being questioned, does it not?"

Hauzer and the harbourmaster continued talking amongst one another.

From afar, however, a pair of brown eyes was watching them. His hand was the only hand small enough to squeeze through the hole on the edge of the cagewagon, and so young Thomlin tried his best to move the cloth just far enough with his thin little fingers so as to remain hidden. All that he could manage was a slight slit, though he was close enough to catch a glimpse of the harbourmaster and his apprentice.

"What is happening?" Princess Magdalena whispered into his ear.

"They're just talking," Thomlin said. "They look doubtful."

"Get your hand back in 'ere, boy!" the old man with the grey widow's peak hissed from the other end of the cage. "You're going to get us all killed!"

"Shhh!" Magdalena glared at the old man.

Thomlin's hand did not move. At the dock, the harbourmaster was unconvinced and his apprentice could only hide behind him, cowering under Hauzer's looming façade.

"Yes, well, I'm afraid even if I *had* a captain at our disposal, w-"

"Didn't say we needed a captain," Hauzer interrupted. "Just need a ship."

"I'm afraid we don't have one of those either."

"What about *that* one?"

The harbourmaster turned to look at the large fishing vessel tied to the dock.

"I'm terribly sorry, sir, but this isn't quite the way we run things here in Roquefort, y'see."

"Will *this* be enough?" Hauzer asked as he tossed the harbourmaster a brown satchel, heavy enough that it nearly fell from the old man's grasp when he caught it. It was full of gold and jewels, enough to not only buy two ships but to recruit an entire crew for both of them.

Wellyngton's eyes widened when he took a peek inside, as did his apprentice's. "Oh dear," he said, gazing hesitantly in every direction. "W-Well, um… Yes, I suppose we can make certain exceptions for nobles that prefer their business relations remain unknown."

"Many thanks," Hauzer made his best attempt at a smile.

From inside the cagewagon, Thomlin shifted his worried gaze towards the princess.

"He's falling for it," he said. Magdalena's eyes were instantly wet. Though it had been days, it hadn't occurred to her just how powerless she was until that moment. In just a matter of minutes, they were to sail away from Vallenghard. She would be somewhere distant, somewhere unknown, a place where no one would even know her name let alone recognize her face.

What little hope she had before was now shattering before her eyes. She wanted to scream for help, but she knew that it would only result in the deaths of the harbourmaster and his apprentice, and possibly some of the prisoners… They were helpless, and she knew it.

She felt the tears crawling on the edge of her eyelids but she wiped them off before anyone noticed.

Thomlin, on the other hand, had tears crawling down his flushed brown cheeks. He was on the verge of sobbing when suddenly a swift pull sent him crashing against the wall of the cagewagon. He released a slight yelp, though it didn't appear to catch the attention of neither Wellyngton nor his apprentice.

The boy's chest was pounding. Someone from the outside had grabbed on tightly to his wrist and refused to let go. "D'you want to keep that hand, boy?!" a voice whispered angrily at him from the outside. "Or should I give you something to remember me by?"

It was quite dark, but Thomlin caught a glimpse of those frightening red eyes and that dark blue skin under a brown hood. Magdalena, startled and alarmed, grabbed Thomlin by the waist and began pulling back.

Jyor felt the boy's hand nearly slip from his grasp, and so he tightened his fist. And then the hissing sound of a dagger echoed throughout the docks, so loud that the harbourmaster's apprentice took notice. Thomlin couldn't help but yelp, and the princess had to press a nervous hand over his mouth as she kept pulling him inward.

Jyor gave one last fierce pull, and Thomlin could have sworn that his hand was done for.

Except it wasn't… Just before Thomlin's fingers went through the gap, an unexpected foot from inside the cage landed a heavy kick. Thomlin felt some of the blow, and the skin of his knuckles was scraped. But Jyor felt the real damage, as two of his fingers bent entirely the wrong way.

Thomlin fell into Magdalena's lap, and they both glanced at the silver-haired woman named Valleria, who was holding onto the wall of the cage as she pulled her foot back. Outside, Jyor shrieked loudly in pain as he pressed his wounded hand against his chest, his two broken fingers bent all the way back, creating an arch that wasn't meant to be there.

Magdalena and Valleria kept their gaze fixed on each other for a brief moment. The silver-haired woman gave the princess a nod, as if telling her they were on the same side without the need for words. The princess returned the nod, her watery eyes more thankful than any words could convey.

By then, harbourmaster Wellyngton and his apprentice couldn't help but notice the commotion. The hooded figure of Jyor was on his knees, holding on to his hand as he shivered and groaned.

"Is something the matter with your friend?" Wellyngton asked.

"Ahh," Hauzer shrugged convincingly. "Bloke must've cut himself. Kahrran steel, we have in there. That'll do it."

"Ohh right," Wellyngton said with a forced chuckle, as if he knew what Kahrran steel felt like. "Well I do hope he's all right."

"He'll be fine," Hauzer said. "We'll be boarding now. With your permission, of course."

"Oh yes, yes, on you go," Wellyngton said, his eyes still preoccupied examining the gold in the satchel, only this time his uneasiness overcame him. He couldn't help but pry.

Hauzer gave the men a signal, and they began boarding the fishing vessel, the only ship that was left in the docks that night. But before he could walk away, the harbourmaster's voice beckoned him back.

"You're from Halghard, yes?"

Hauzer froze where he stood. He turned slowly and unwillingly, his annoyance causing him to wonder whether it would be safe to simply kill the harbourmaster and his apprentice rather than risk him prying further. "Aye," was all he said, as the rest of the men began to pull the cagewagon full of slaves onto the boarding ramp.

"Your accent's a bit torn," said Wellyngton. "Been spending some time overseas, friend?"

Hauzer's glare changed. Something in him became suspicious of the old man, as if he had suddenly recognized him. "How'd you figure that?" he asked.

"Oh, I don't know," Wellyngton replied. "Just presuming."

"Then don't presume," Hauzer said, tossing the old man an extra silver coin. With that, Hauzer turned and followed his men into the ship.

Wellyngton and his apprentice remained in place, disturbed and thrown aback. They walked off towards the set of stairs, allowing for the men to take a ship that wasn't the harbourmaster's to sell in the first place.

"What in gods' names…?" the apprentice whispered worriedly.

"Don't say a word, just continue walking," Wellyngton replied.

"Shall I send word to Lord Clark?" the apprentice asked.

"To hells with Lord Clark," Wellyngton said. "Fetch us a raven… We're sending word straight to the king."

* * *

They galloped for the better part of an hour, heading southwest along the border of the Woodlands until they came across an opening between a wave of mysterious looking willow trees.

After nearly losing Viktor Crowley, the company had been blinded by the thrill of the fight.

And they were more concerned with fleeing than they were about what lurked within the Woodlands. They followed their knight commander along the path, until the darkness seemed to swallow them whole...

They became immersed into a whole other world... Every inch of their surroundings was crawling with plant life, and the wind was far colder and wetter than the outside. As the company moved deeper inside, the trees seemed to stretch higher and higher, eventually shielding them entirely from the night sky. The place was eerie and dark and hauntingly beautiful... Flowers they'd never seen before bloomed beneath their feet, wild life lurked through the branches high above, and the humid breeze seemed to almost glow under the moonlight.

The path curved again and again, and eventually Viktor Crowley could not figure out which direction was west. As the darkness consumed them, he came to an abrupt halt; the path disappeared into the fog, and he no longer had any idea where they were. He turned and took a moment to count heads, and sighed with relief when his count was the same as it had been that morning.

"Is anyone hurt?" he asked.

"Does an ankle cramp count as *hurt?*" asked Hudson Blackwood. Syrena trotted closer to him; it was clear that, though her horse was tied to the saddle of a soldier's horse, she preferred the company of the thief and would often try to stay close to him.

Sir Jossiah Biggs's armor had loosened and he struggled to hold on to the reins of his horse as he wiped the sweat from his brows. For a knight, the man was rather unfit; his brute strength in combat was his only advantage. He shot Hudson and Syrena an untrusting glare as he suddenly drew his blade.

The thief and the witch froze and glanced at one another.

"Your weapon," Jossiah said sternly. "Drop it..."

The thief sighed. "If we get attacked again you *will* need me, mate."

But Jossiah did not give in; his blade remained high and firm. "Did I stutter, thief!?" he growled. "You're no different than the witch here. You're a prisoner! And you've no need for a weapon."

"Do I not?" Hudson asked with great disdain. "So never mind the fact that we would all be dead if I *hadn't* been armed, eh?"

"Don't flatter yourself," Jossiah's eyes narrowed. "You're not the only one that can use a sword."

The thief shot Viktor a glance, and the golden knight gave a deep sigh and found himself siding with him, much to Jossiah's surprise.

"Put your sword down, old boy," Viktor said, still catching his breath.

Jossiah raised a brow. "What?"

"He could've fled," Viktor said with a nod. "But he didn't... And the bloody idiot's right. If we get attacked again, I'd very much prefer he was armed."

Hudson gave Jossiah a wink, but the former knight did not find it the least bit amusing judging by his scowling reaction. "Truce, mate," he said, more to spite him.

Meanwhile the rest of the company gazed all around, their bodies shivering from the fright.

Cedric, naïve as he was, had grown pale and his eyes were wide and alert; his lip trembled, but that was rather common of the boy. Had it not been for the thrill of it all, he may have vomited.

John Huxley held himself together as best he could. He found that nearly losing his new silver blade, the most elegant he's ever owned, had felt worse than the actual fighting did. Upon gazing at his surroundings and the eerily scenic path they stood on, he became overwhelmed to the point where he felt mildly lightheaded.

He approached Viktor, but his eyes were fixed on the dirt path ahead, obscured by the fog.

Perhaps if the sun were still shining, the path would seem almost beautiful.

Under the moon's light, however, it was ominous enough to give him shivers.

The sound of the sweeping wind was haunting and somber, and there were distant sounds above them that John hoped were just birds. His whole life, the young farmer had heard stories of the vast array of life in the Woodlands and the dangers that lurked within. Yet at that moment, there seemed not to be a sign of life anywhere, at least none that their anxious eyes could see, only sounds.

"We've made it," John mumbled, mesmerized by the strange beauty of it all.

Viktor had no reply. His eyes glanced all around, at the potential paths, at the trees above, at his flustered company... Everyone looked startled except for Hudson and Syrena. The witch, in fact, seemed almost at peace, looking all around at the place she called home and taking slow breaths as she found herself more comfortable than she had been in the last week.

"What now?" Jossiah asked Viktor.

"We must find a place somewhere to make camp," Viktor replied.

"Those bastards might still be after us. Shouldn't we keep riding?" Jossiah said as he glanced back towards the path from which they came.

"Not anymore. Not while we're in *here*," Viktor said, with a tension in his shoulders that was quite obvious. "Dusk has come... And we're no longer in Vallenghard, old friend."

* * *

The northern regions of the Woodlands were a mystery, even to folk who dwelled within them. Some spoke of a fabled city hidden within the forest, a city of ancient ruins known as Bauqora, ruled by a mythical elf queen who had roamed the land for centuries.

The Rogue Brotherhood, thirsty for power as they were, had sought this city out for decades but they never found a single trace of it. And traveling further into the mountains of Belmoor was not an option, for it was home to the minotauros. They were ruthless beasts that walked upright, had heads like bulls, and bodies covered in a black pelt. And they fought like a pack, aggressively and ruthlessly coordinated.

And so, unwilling to venture into the minotauros' lands, the infamous mercenary guild took to the southern regions of the Woodlands. There, they wreaked havoc until an outside force hired them. And such had been the case when they were sought out by Lord Baronkroft to sneak into the royal city of Val Havyn and kidnap her majesty from the palace grounds.

But now they were back in the Woodlands, back in the land they called home.

When the sun fell, the stench coming from the Brotherhood's camp became thicker and far more pungent. Ale and pipes of red spindle were being passed around the men, each of them slowly losing what little sense they had left for the night. Only about a hundred men were there; half of them had arrived that morning from Val Havyn and the rest were still on their way back, including the newly appointed captain. And so the mischief within the camp was growing as monotony began to overtake them all.

Three raiders sat around one of the many fires, laughing and conversing among one another. Their eyes would constantly move towards a solitary tent, a few yards away from the rest, where a fireless pit of black ashes was still radiating warm fumes of smoke.

"There I was, sittin' in the *Stumblin' Hare* tavern in Grymsbi," one of the men said after inhaling from a lit pipe full of red spindle and passing it to his comrade. "And then out o' *nowhere*, a damn *greenskin* walks in... I thought I had shit in me eyes, I tell ye. And then they *serve* the bastard. I thought I was losin' me mind, I even spit out me ale!"

"Ahh," the second man groaned. "Halghard's fallin' apart... First they start a war among themselves for a fuckin' throne. Then they start pardonin' *freaks* so's to grow their armies. What's next? They'll choose a *woman* to lead 'em?"

"That'll be the day," the third man said just before coughing out red smoke from his lungs.

"Give me that, ye dumb twat," the second man snatched the pipe from the coughing man's hands. "Virgin lungs, this one has, I tell ye."

The first man, green-eyed and shaggy-haired, became fixated on the solitary tent near their fire pit. "Speakin' of greenskins," he said, rising to his feet and realizing he was far more intoxicated than he figured. "Y'think the Beast is off huntin' somewhere?"

"What's it to ye?" asked the second man.

"I lost me blade back in Val Havyn... I always fancied the Beast's axe."

"Careful now, the bloke will kill ye if he finds out."

"Not if he ain't there," the shaggy-haired man took slow drunken steps towards the tent. And his two comrades whispered hesitantly behind him.

"Get back 'ere, you stupid fool!"

"Leave 'im. It's *his* arse."

The man walked around the black pit of ashes, squinting his bloodshot eyes yet unable to make out anything in the darkness of the tent. He then noticed, right next to an old rucksack, the Beast's sharp axe buried in the dirt with the handle sticking outward.

The man smiled and reached for it.

But it was buried deeper than he anticipated, and it took another strong thrust before loosening it. He held the axe up, admired its sharpness and beauty despite its old age.

"There! Now get back 'ere!" one of his comrades, the more concerned one, whispered.

The drunken man turned and smiled at them, holding the axe up. "Told youse it was a beauty."

But the man's smile didn't last very long; his comrades grew alarmed and frightened all of a sudden, and his smile quickly turned into a concerned grimace. He turned, only to see a large figure walking towards him from within the trees... a figure with three massive scars on his exposed green chest.

Frightened out of his drunken mind, the man held the axe out in defense.

"S-Stand back, Beast!" he stuttered. "I-I've got your axe!"

The orc came to a halt, not having realized the man was holding his weapon. Often, he would look the other way from the stupidity of his brothers-in-arms. But the orc had never been fond of people putting their hands on his things...

"S-Stand *back*, I say... Stand back! F-Filthy *greenskin*!"

The Beast froze... He could smell the ale in the man's breath and therefore had been willing to let the matter go. But there was one word that the orc could not stand... and the stupid man had just said it. And it was then that he opened his lips... And the sharp fangs rising from his lower teeth moved up and down as he spoke, and his voice was rough and beastlike...

"One swing," the Beast said, and his words petrified the frail man. The orc was known to be distant and hostile, and only about a third of his mercenary brothers had ever heard him speak. And his voice was as chilling as they had expected it to be.

"I give ye *one* swing," he said. "I won't even try to stop ye..."

The man hesitated, his face drenched in sweat and his breathing fast-paced and light. Suddenly the effects of the ale and red spindle had diminished, replaced by a blurred sense of caution.

"Go on then, lad!" his comrade shouted behind him. "He's just a greenskin!"

There was laughter among them, but the Beast paid it no mind. His yellow eyes were fixed on the man's filthy hands, holding his axe.

"P-Please..." the man said fretfully, realizing the grave mistake he had committed. "I-I'm sorry..."

"One swing," the Beast repeated. "And ye best not miss, lad... I killed a bear once, y'know... Crushed his head with nothin' but me hands. Now imagine what I'm gonna do to *you*..."

The man trembled even more, struggling to hold his grip on the heavy axe.

It was then, however, that a loud sound broke the commotion.

A horn echoed all around as a company of about seventy men approached, all bearing the same red leathers as those in the camp. It was being led by a familiar figure atop a black horse...

Captain Malekai Pahrvus looked elated and proud, his chin up high, his red captain's coat fitting just right. His company followed behind, dragging along a cart full of riches stolen from King Rowan's palace. Unlike the previous captain, Malekai didn't wear the captain's hat. His dreadlocks were too long and well decorated with beads and trinkets to be hidden away and tucked under a hat.

Riding in front of him was his second-in-command, quite inebriated, shouting aimlessly about. "Evenin', gents!" he said. "Lovely night, ain't it?"

Many of the mercenaries that had been left behind at the camp became suddenly flustered and alarmed. Those that had been intoxicated tried their best to appear proper in front of their newly appointed captain. And then they would relax at the sight of his fool of a right-hand man, a drunken raider of average skill known as Borrys.

One of the red raiders, who went by the name of Naru, was quite shocked to see such a man be appointed Captain's second-in-command. "Borrys Belvaine, you old hog," he said with a friendly chuckle and a head nod.

"Still alive, you baldin' bastard?" Borrys replied in a similar tone. "Give my regards to your poor sweet mum."

There was laughing and chattering among the men as they all welcomed their captain.

The Beast, however, was not at all amused... His eyes were locked on the drunken man in front of him, still gripping his beloved axe... The man's breathing had eased, seeing as the Beast was less likely to kill him in the presence

167

of the captain.

"Get on up, you dogs!" Borrys shouted at those who were lying in their tents. "Come out here and bow for your captain."

"That's enough, Borrys," Malekai muttered sternly.

There were whispers along the camp, some praising Malekai for his bravery. Attacking a royal city such as Val Havyn had been unheard of in the Brotherhood. In the hundred years that it had been active, no captain had done such a thing. Malekai had been the first. Other whispers spoke of treason, cursing the new captain for standing by as the former captain was slaughtered and questioning his loyalty to the rest of the Brotherhood.

The Beast may have been the only one to not be on either side of their disagreement. He kept to himself and disturbed no one. That was, of course, unless someone disturbed *him*.

As Malekai Pahrvus and Borrys Belvaine rode by, the drunken raider holding the Beast's axe saw an opportunity to swing. Any other man would have been smart enough to drop the axe and run off… But in his intoxicated state, the man seized the opportunity.

He swung at the distracted orc.

Had the Beast's reflexes been any slower, the axe would have sunk into his chest. But the orc managed a swift dart to the right and the axe swung into the air, causing the man to stumble. The Beast then grabbed the man by the jaw, placed his other hand on the back of his head and gave it a violent twist, at the same time releasing a thundering roar.

The man's head turned entirely around, his shocked eyes still wide as he felt the warmth leave his body before everything went black. The orc let go of the head and the man fell dead on the dirt next to the fireless pit.

Only a few mercenaries noticed the kill, the rest were far too distracted.

Silently, the orc took the axe from the man's stiff hands and gave it a good wipe, as if the man's hands had been filthy. And Captain Malekai was too preoccupied admiring the gazes that were thrown his way to even acknowledge what had just happened.

And so the Beast strapped the axe back to his belt and crawled into his tent for a good night's rest…

VII
Creatures of the Night

The beautiful green hills in the kingdom of Vallenghard were dimmed and blackened in the dead of night. The sky shimmered, coated with a million stars, and the fields became mere shadows for miles around. On this night, a small fire was burning and cackling just at the base of a steep hill.

Four figures sat around it.

Four figures and a crying infant.

They were far enough from the nearest roads so as to remain unseen yet close enough to attack unsuspecting travelers.

It had been several days since the orcs Okvar, Gruul, and Murzol had fled Baronkroft's company in search of the legendary free city of Kahrr. They'd heard many stories about the opportunities given to nonhumans in the free city; they could be anything from blacksmiths to merchants, or even serve in the city guard. Having served as mercenaries for most of their lives, however, had left an undeniable thirst in them.

A thirst for a good fight, or at the very least a good raid.

A thirst, as they say, for trouble…

The kidnapped orcess Aevastra sat near the fire, swaying her weeping child in her arms, whispering tenderly to him in her mother tongue. "*Calmaedo, min neno,*" she said, calming him with her soothing voice. "*Ya, ya… calmaedo. Vos aestar san e salvu prontu…*"

She sat across from Okvar, the largest and most intimidating of the three orcs. The vile gangly Murzol was not exactly pleasing to be around, only more tolerable. As for Gruul, the orc was far too preoccupied grunting and pestering the other two cantankerously to even give Aevastra much thought. That was, of course, until night arrived and that thirst within him kicked in…

Nearby lied the stiff body of a dead ox with plenty of meat still left on it, slowly becoming more infested with flies and slime. Okvar walked towards it and cut a piece of red meat with the same dagger he had used to pick his teeth with, a small thing the size of his ring finger. And then he held the wooden plate in front of the orcess.

"N-No… Not hungry," she mumbled, despite not having eaten since the previous evening.

"It ain't for you," Okvar said. "It's to shut that damn thing up."

After a moment of hesitation, she took the plate and set her baby down gently as if setting down a piece of delicate crystal. She began using Okvar's tiny knife to chop the raw meat into small bits. Okvar said nothing else and proceeded to add wood to the fire.

Gruul sat against a tree sharpening his knives. When he leaned back, the base of the trunk nearly screeched from the pressure of the orc's weight. "Ahh," he grunted and threw his knives onto the grass by his feet. "How long are we stayin' here, Okvar?"

"What d'ye mean?"

"We've done nothin' but hunt 'n' camp for days now!"

"Yeah? What else was ye expectin'?"

"*You* said we'd go to Kahrr! Soon as we left Baronkroft's troop, you said you'd take us there!"

Aevastra's eyes suddenly lit up at the mention of the free city. She had planned to go there with her child, if only to seek better work opportunities for herself. Never did she imagine the orcs were attempting the same. But, as vigilant as she was, she preferred to keep quiet and listen.

"Aye," Okvar replied. "With time, ye old fool... Kahrr is hundreds of miles to the east. How d'ye plan on gettin' there without a bleedin' horse?!"

Gruul hopped to his feet angrily, his voice rising and his fists growing shaky. "We're sittin' on our arses day after day! Waitin' 'n' waitin', I'm bloody *sick* of it! If I sleep outside like a filthy dog another night, I wil-"

"Ye'll do what?" Okvar stepped towards him.

Meanwhile, Aevastra held a piece of meat over her hungry child's lips; the baby's fangs were small but sharp enough to bite into it. The orcess's eyes however, moved back and forth between the two orcs, observing them, waiting for a window of opportunity.

Gruul felt his shoulders tense up, choosing his words as carefully as he could so as to not enrage his long-time comrade; of course, however, Gruul was not even mildly clever and never really seemed to know the line between arguing and provoking. "I did *not* cross the sea to come here 'n' live in filth, Okvar... You made us a promise. You plan on keepin' it?"

"Ye *ain't* in Qamroth no more, Gruul," Okvar replied. "D'ye even know what they do to folks like us 'round these parts? The human filth is a savage lot... They'll kill ye in plain sight 'n' say it was the work of the gods... It ain't enough to have a sharp axe. If ye don't play smart 'round here, yer as good as dead."

"*Curse* the human filth!" Gruul shouted. "I'm startin' to think you're scared of 'em..."

The giant orc froze, his brow lowering and his jaw tightening. Murzol was never one to intervene, but neither was he keen on being left alone with one of his companions, much less in a land unknown to him. He leapt to his feet and stood nervously between the two, both of them towering a half-foot over him.

"N-Now hang on," Murzol said with a snort and a nose twitch. "Let's not lose our heads."

"*I* ain't losin' mine," Gruul said angrily.

"Ye *that* sure, eh?" Okvar replied. "Shall we settle it with our axes, then?"

Gruul unstrapped his weapon and growled under his breath.

"Oi… what're you doin'…? Okvar…?"

"Shut yer damn yap, Murzol," Okvar said calmly yet frighteningly.

The two orcs confronted one another, each of them just as intimidating and determined. But after realizing he would possibly be killed, Gruul decided for once in his life to take the smarter route; at least briefly, he did.

"To hells with all of it," Gruul grunted angrily. "I'm leavin' this wretched place…"

"No one's stopping ye."

"You cross the sea to the lands of men 'n' sit on your arse all day 'n' live like *them*?" Gruul taunted him with a raised finger. "You're a disgrace to your kind, Okvar… A filthy disgrace…"

Okvar appeared hardhearted yet somewhat at ease, as if he was confident he could kill Gruul with a single strike.

"I won't follow you another day," Gruul spoke again. "I'm leavin'… And I'm takin' the orcess with me."

"No, ye ain't…"

Gruul's fury was now at its peak. He glared at his comrade with eyes that were once brown but now seemed to glisten a sharp red. "I spotted her first," he said. "She's mine by right."

"The rogue orc spotted 'er first… He didn't want 'er, she's anyone's to claim."

Murzol grew suddenly anxious and sweaty as he stood between the two angry orcs. He tried to mediate, but seeing as they were both armed and prone to impulsive swings, his words were a mere mumble. "Okvar…?"

"I've kept me mouth shut for years!" Gruul shouted. "I trusted you. Followed you. I'm *done*!"

"Good," Okvar said. "On ye go… Go 'n' get yerself hanged. Go 'n' lay in your own shit, for all I care. But the bitch stays with us."

"O-Okvar…?" Murzol interrupted again.

"What?!" Okvar growled.

"Sh-She's, um…"

"Stop stutterin' ye stupid fool! What is it?!"

"Well," Murzol cleared his throat. "Sh-She's gone…"

The three orcs glanced suddenly at the empty spot on the ground where the orcess once sat.

But she was nowhere to be seen… The only thing that remained was the old wooden plate with a half-eaten piece of raw ox on it.

* * *

The Woodlands may have been, to some extent, beautiful in the daylight. When night arrived, however, it was as dark and morose as the stories told.

It had happened quicker than anticipated… One moment, the company was galloping away from the bandits, searching for a safe entrance to the Woodlands while the sun was still setting in the horizon. The next moment, darkness took over like a great black shadow sweeping by and swallowing every bit of light for miles around.

With the darkness came the sounds… the muffled howling in the distance, the subtle cooing nearby, the rustling of the trees above… Life went on in the Woodlands, regardless of the time.

As Viktor Crowley's company stopped to rest for the night, a gush of unusual wind swept abruptly towards the camp, significantly colder than the winds in Vallenghard. And at that very moment, somewhere in the darkness, a branch snapped in half.

"What was that?" young Cedric asked hesitantly, sitting up and gazing at the trees in the distance, about a half-mile uphill from where they had set up camp. His ignorance of the outside world was too much for him to bear, and for a moment he let go of the false pretense of valor he often carried.

"Give it a rest, lad," said Jossiah Biggs, laying a bit too close to the fire for his own good.

They found a decent place to rest, underneath a cluster of cypress trees that stretched for what felt like hundreds of feet into the sky. There was a boulder, massive in size like a mammoth, high enough to shield them from any unexpected attacks from behind.

The nightlife of the forest echoing in harmony, the cold humid breeze in the air, and the vast green life surrounding them all brought about an aura in the camp that left everyone with a peculiar feeling in their gut, as if they had somehow stepped foot inside of a dream.

Cedric kept his gaze uphill at the willow trees… He swore that the leaves of the willows were rustling and moving in a most eerie way, against the wind rather than with it.

"I think there's something up there, sir," he said with that shiver on his lower lip.

"Of *course* there is, you blithering fool," Jossiah grunted. "These are the Woodlands. There's a reason why we camped down here and not up there."

"And what's that, sir?" Cedric asked.

"When you're in the forest grounds, lad, there *is* no safe place… The dark magic is everywhere. Even among the trees."

"The *trees*, sir?"

"Aye, the trees…"

John Huxley sat by the fire, quiet and pensive; the only acquaintances he had were two knights he had only just met, a thief that wanted to kill him, and a tavern boy that he knew only by name. All that he could do was to listen and try to make more friends than he did enemies. Currently, however, he had no clue as to which he had more of.

Syrena sat nearby biting into a chopped piece of venison, which she struggled to hold onto with her bonded hands. She had hardly spoken a word since the day one of the journey, save for a few whispers into the thief's ear. Her agreement with Viktor Crowley did not mean she was willing to fake her mistrust towards humans. Hudson sat next to her, leaning his head back against a tree trunk a few feet from Cedric. His black hat rested over the top half of his face, giving the impression that he was asleep.

Viktor Crowley was somewhere inside his tent, resting for the night. And it was in these rare instances that Jossiah Biggs would become even more hostile than he usually was. He was the only one of the royal guard to sit sporadically among both the soldiers and the recruits, particularly after a quarrel with Viktor. And the quarrels seemed to get worse by the day...

"When the Great War ended, you see, all of the freaks were banished here," Jossiah went on. "They were given their territory and we were given ours... But the freaks, they figured if *they* couldn't leave, why should they allow *us* to enter? So they *cursed* the willow trees surrounding their home in order to kill anyone and anything that dares enter these woods at night..."

"The trees... *kill*, sir?" Cedric asked, wincing nervously at the thought.

"Aye, they do," said Biggs. "When the moon shines upon them at night, they rise."

There was a look of dread in Cedric's eyes. "*They...?*"

Jossiah felt his own nerves start to peak. He was suddenly thankful for his armor, for it was shielding the goosebumps on his arms.

"When the moon rises, you see... The branches of the willows, they... They become something else entirely... Creatures of dark magic with mangled bodies made of wood and leaves. Hungry for anything that dares enter these grounds at night. Some people call them the Guardians of the Woodlands. Others just call them the broken ones. Either way, trust me, lad... You're far better off down here. You don't want to know the horrors that lurk up there..."

There was a silence.

Cedric was not the only one listening. The Davenport brothers were both on alert as well. Syrena heard it all, but rather than becoming nervous she had a subtle smirk on her face that only made Cedric more nervous. The torment only lasted a brief moment, however, before the silence was interrupted by a snicker and a sudden burst of laughter.

Hudson Blackwood was no longer asleep, if he ever was.

"Did I say something that amused you?" Jossiah asked.

The thief removed his hat from his face and turned towards Jossiah and Cedric; his wide eyes made it apparent that he was awake the entire time. "I'm sorry, old mate, but did I just hear you say '*the horrors* that lurk up there'?"

"Aye, you did."

"You should mind your own business, thief!" another voice spoke; this time it was that of Wyll Davenport, who carried an obvious mask of valor while the fear was tugging at his gut.

"Aye, that's a knight of Val Havyn you're talking to!" Cedric added in quite a similar form.

"Fine," Hudson said. "Now *I'm* the arsehole. That's all fine."

"That, you are," Jossiah scowled.

Hudson leaned back against the tree trunk once again, somehow finding comfort in the dirt as if he was used to it. While he did, his lips mumbled under his breath, "At least I'm not the one rambling on idiotically about the horrors of *trees…*"

It was loud enough for Jossiah to hear, and so the former knight grunted with displeasure and asked, "I suppose you're an expert on horrors, eh thief?"

"I know that there are far darker things to worry about than live trees, mate," Hudson said, no longer smirking and with a serious tone.

There was a short silence, broken only by the cackling fire and the sound of venison meat being ripped apart as Syrena struggled to eat without slobbering on herself. She tried holding down the meat with her leather-wrapped hand as she bit off a piece with her teeth, but even that proved inefficient.

Meanwhile, John Huxley became fixated on Hudson's expression.

The thief appeared to be mildly worried… It was vivid in his conflicted eyes…

John knew this because he hadn't seen that look on Hudson's face since the day of his capture, when his head was pressed against the cobblestone and he realized he was defenseless.

"W-What sorts of things?" Cedric asked after a while, his curiosity at its peak.

Jossiah Biggs did not like being challenged, let alone by a wanted thief. The former knight sighed, turned to Cedric and said, "When we won the war, w-"

"Our winning the war meant nothing," Hudson interrupted again, and this time young Cedric's attention was fully on him. "Most of the Woodlands had always been cursed to begin with, for as far back as we can remember… When the war was won, our people banished every single being, magical or otherwise, into these woods *including* those that had lived among us since the dawn of time… From the devious goblin to the half-wit ogre. Hell, even the *pixies*, docile as they are. And all for one infuriatingly stupid and simple reason… because they did not look like us."

The thief paused there, allowing for his words to sink in. His voice lowered a bit, the light of the fire only causing him to appear more menacing. "But there were others that were already here, y'see," he said. "*Others* that have been here all along."

"That's enough yapping, Blackwood," Jossiah said, feeling his anger rising.

"You think coming face to face with an ogre is bad, little mate?" Hudson asked Cedric, ignoring Jossiah's words.

"I said that's enough!"

"You know *nothing* of horrors..." Hudson said threateningly, this time directly at Jossiah, who stared right back at him but somehow was unable to speak a word, as if the thief's eyes had casted a spell over him. Cedric listened attentively, his inquisitiveness greater than his pride.

Hudson knew he had gotten the attention of them all, and he appeared to be enjoying himself greatly. "Tell me, little mate," he said to Cedric. "Before today, had you ever encountered a real live Arachnian up close?"

"A... *what?*"

"Giant horrific spiders that tried to eat you not three hours ago?" the thief replied. "Have you ever seen one up close...? Been unable to move, as it shoots its hot sticky web at you... tangling you in it... tightening its grasp... crawling slowly towards you on its eight scruffy legs...?"

"I'm warning you, Blackwood..." Jossiah spoke once again.

"Then there's *my* personal favorite, the stonewalker! Giant creatures *literally* made of stone from head to toe. They eat nothing but plant, mind you. But *killing*... Killing they do for sport."

"I said *shut it*..."

"And then, of course, there are the *tree nymphs*," the thief's scornful voice heightened so as to match Jossiah's. "That *is* the appropriate name for them, I believe. Then again, what do *I* know? I've never formally asked one as of yet. But *tell* me, Sir Jossiah Biggs, you ever face an entire clan of them all at once? You ever seen the way they use their vines to tighten every limb in a man's body, sucking his life away, allowing him to feel every excruciating second of it?"

Hudson Blackwood and Jossiah Biggs were sharing a glare, both with a blatant profound anger and despise towards one another. Hudson held onto the glare longer, before finally saying once more, "You know *nothing* of horrors, mate..."

Then there was another long silence, disrupted only by the distant sound of leaves and branches crackling, and a loud echoing cry that Cedric hoped had come from a crow. Meanwhile, the fire was beginning to burn out and Syrena seemed to have given up on eating the rest of her meal.

Cedric, uncomfortable with the stillness of the place, sighed and said, "Sir Biggs is probably right anyway... If we could sleep somewhere the trees will stand still, I'd prefer that."

"That's where you're wrong again, little mate," Hudson replied. "In my defense, I did *try* telling you all, but nobody ever listens to a thief... As if a thief has no honor."

"What d'you mean?" Cedric asked curiously.

"Do you know *why* the creatures were all secluded to a place surrounded by cities ruled by men?" Hudson asked. "Our ancestors didn't want them banished a thousand miles east, free to conjure up a scheme of attack whenever they please... No, they wanted them *here*, right in the center of everything... where they could keep a close watch."

"Enough!" Jossiah shouted, and this time it was loud enough to grasp the attention of the entire camp. "You think you know it all, do you thief?!"

"Not *all*, no... Just more than you, old mate."

"Piss off, you murderin' little shit!" Jossiah sat up and gripped his dagger. Had Viktor not been present, Jossiah might have made an attempt to kill the thief... Kill or hurt at the very least, for the man had the same fire in his eyes that he had during battle. Hudson didn't appear to be the least bit concerned. His expression remained unmoved, yet somehow beneath his half-smirk there appeared to be a trace of sorrow towards the man's words.

But the thief wouldn't dare show it...

The only trace, perhaps, was in the subtle glow in his deep brown eyes.

"You're nothing but a fraud and no one knows it better than you!" Jossiah went on furiously. "Notorious thief?! Ha! I've *shat* more potential than the likes of you... Captured in broad daylight?! And by a bloody *farmer*, no less?! You're an excuse for a fighter and an even *worse* excuse for a man..."

Hudson kept his glare fixed, unwilling to succumb to the rage in his chest. Even Syrena, who sat just a foot away, wanted very much to try to burn through the ogreskin and kill the man. But there was no attack. The thief was far smarter than that.

Realizing most eyes in the camp were on him, Jossiah scoffed and chuckled with satisfaction.

"You at a loss for words then, thief? *Finally?*" he asked.

John Huxley lay there, wishing he were asleep so as to not witness the discord. Hudson may not have been the most pleasant man to be around, but he *had* been the one to save them that day. It was his attack that allowed for their escape and John knew that somewhere beneath the name there was a simple man... Hudson was perhaps just as afraid as *he* was, only better at faking it. And had Jossiah not been one of his commanders, John liked to believe that he would have spoken out.

"Ah," Jossiah grunted and spat on the dirt. "Just as I thought... nothing but a filthy fraud. You're just another man that thinks he's a god."

"Hmm... yes," Hudson finally spoke, softly and somberly. "Rather typical of men, isn't it?"

Jossiah gave him one last glare, before rising to his feet and cracking his neck almost violently. There was no reaction, however. The former knight had heard enough. He walked off into the trees nearby to be alone, preparing himself for the first watch of the night.

John turned to his side and tried to find comfort, looking towards the trees uphill.

Cedric was right, he thought to himself. *They definitely are moving rather unusually...*

John then moved his neck so as to catch a glimpse of the sky above. The stars were nearly covered entirely behind a roof of leaves that appeared to go on for nearly a mile into the sky.

Absolutely gorgeous, he thought.

And it was... There was something about the Woodlands that one could never find in the realms of humans... It was like a beautiful escape... That was until John remembered everything Hudson had said about the creatures that lurked within those very grounds. And then the place suddenly became less beautiful and more unnerving than ever before.

"*Then* what happened...?" asked a sudden nervous voice.

Hudson glanced at Cedric with a mildly perplexed look. "What...?"

"What did you say *before*?" Cedric mumbled. "About our ancestors...?"

Hudson exhaled in the manner of a chuckle, finding the young man's curiosity entertaining.

"The conflict goes further back than just 250 years, little mate," he said, more to amuse the kid. "Our ancestors realized you could only fight poison *with* poison... So they began practicing dark sorcery, eventually becoming so powerful that they became immune to the creatures' spells... You see, only a mage can walk freely among those trees up there at night and not be harmed by them. Only a mage or a *witch*. Last I checked, we *had* one of those..."

Everyone slowly turned to look at Syrena, whose instinct was to shoot an intimidating stare right back at them all. And Hudson couldn't help but smirk at Cedric.

"Trust me, little mate," he said. "As long as *she's* with us, there's no safer place for us than up there among the willow trees... away from the real *horrors* that lurk out here..."

* * *

Young Robyn had never been a cowardly girl. Since childhood, her mother could see bravery in her eyes perhaps even greater than John's. Suffice it to say the girl didn't even know the *meaning* of the word 'coward' until she was ten years old.

But neither was she imprudent.

She knew there was just as much death in the world as there was wonder. And yet in one fateful moment, she'd forced the burden out of her mind and followed her intuition. A girl with a big heart, she was, but like everyone else she was imperfect.

Too young, they called her, more times than she cared to remember.

Too naïve, too callow, too stubborn…

She'd heard it all her life and her incessant ambition to prove them all wrong became her flaw.

She'd convinced herself that it was for John, that she dreaded the idea of his death and that she wanted to be there with him should fate decide his time had come… and now she was in the Woodlands, far away from home, and it hadn't crossed her mind until then that her dear mother could very well lose two children in lieu of one.

She sat in the darkness beneath a massive willow tree with thick roots halfway exposed. Using a sharp stone, she dug a hole at the base of the tree and arranged a thick layer of leaves over it until it looked comfortable enough to nestle in. She slumped into it, using as much of the tree's trunk to shield herself from the frosty wind. And as she rubbed her arms and shriveled into a fetal position, her shivering dry lips casted clouds of white fog into the air. Her furs were not thick enough to keep her warm, and it only kept reminding her that she had very little advantage with regards to armor should an unexpected danger arise.

She had chosen a secluded spot above a hill, right in the middle of a cluster of willows, where the height would give her the advantage. She could see in the distance a tiny spark of light where Viktor Crowley's company had set up camp for the night. And it was the only thing that was helping her keep her spirit, knowing that her brother was within her sight. She tried to lose herself in her thoughts so as to avoid thinking of the cold, except her mind kept going back to her mother and the twins.

"I-I'm s…" she whispered hesitantly, the way she often would when she was alone. "I'm sorry, mum…"

She sighed profoundly, hoping to ease the knot in her throat and failing.

Then she hardened her gaze, firm and determined, and forced the shivering in her lip to stop.

"You never abandon family," she said, as if she was talking to her mother. "It's what you always said…"

Suddenly she heard a sharp sound above, like that of a branch snapping in half.

She panted silently, the subtle dismay returning suddenly to her chest.

Her eyes searched all around… The movement was everywhere, and it was hard to distinguish which was caused by the wind and which was something else entirely. The leaves in the trees were rumbling a bit too harshly, she knew, for as cold as the breeze was it was not strong enough to cause such movement. As a child she'd heard about the tree creatures of the Woodlands, stories told by the few that had seen them and survived.

Some said they were peaceful, so long as you did not disturb them.

Others said they were vicious creatures that would kill anything that dared enter the forest grounds. The tree nymphs, or '*dryads*' as some called them, had a heightened sense of smell and could sense fresh human blood from a mile away. Working together in packs, they would ambush their prey and absorb them into their mother tree so as to keep her alive and breeding even more dryads at the roots.

The thought of it made Robyn's stomach turn.

She tried to sit still, so as to avoid being heard or seen.

She realized then just how alone she was. She had no one else other than her pony, and the poor thing was tied to the tree nearest to her left trembling and neighing gently, unable to fall asleep. For a moment she considered riding down the hill to meet with her brother. She'd traveled too far to return by then and he would ultimately have no say in the matter unless he wanted to be an inconvenience to his superiors.

Not now, she told herself. *The moment's not right yet.*

She wanted to prove to him that she could fend for herself, if only to stop him and mother from ever referring to her as '*just a girl*' again. But the fear was tearing at her insides, for it was rare of her to have such a feeling. She loathed it. At all costs, she wanted rid of it.

And yet it only got worse when there was suddenly a rustling sound coming from above, after which a few green leaves fell slowly at her feet, startling her, causing her heart to race. She tried to blame her imagination, tried to tell herself the lack of sleep was making her see things that weren't there. But the leaves kept dropping...

There's something in the trees, she told herself.

All around her, branches echoed one another almost in unison, as if communicating through sounds and movement. She felt the earth beneath her start to rumble all of a sudden, as if she was sitting on the belly of a beast. And then a chunk of earth in front of her began to move, as if something was pushing it from underneath...

The root of the willow tree began to rise above the soil.

It was moving... It was alive...

Young Robyn felt her eyes were deceiving her as she trembled to her feet. The branches above her began to move as well, the hardened wood bending in ways that no branch could ever possibly bend.

Beware the Woodlands, they told her, *for there is dark magic all around that lives.*

Now, Robyn Huxley had never seen a tree come to life, or any inanimate object for that matter.

She also, however, had never expected it to screech...

The root of the tree near her feet began cracking and turning about, until she saw what looked like a face made of wood with hollow eyes that were glowing, a bright green. The sound it made was something from a nightmare, loud and high-pitched and excruciating to Robyn's ears.

Then, as if answering the creature's call, the movement among the leaves grew stronger and closer towards her. Shadows began to hop from branch to branch, all the while growing in numbers. And at that very moment, a lightning struck in the distance that brought about a flash of bright light for a half-second. It was long enough for Robyn to see the dozens of creatures hanging from the branches, looking at her the way a predator would look at a prey. Without thinking twice, she ran…

Never had she moved so fast in her life.

The tree nymphs began to drop, one by one, staring and sniffing about.

Robyn glanced back over her shoulder. She could see them crawling on all fours slowly and beastlike near the pit where she had just been sitting. They were about the size of humans, only crouched and hunchbacked like apes. They began to swarm, protecting their claimed territory.

Distracted and panicked, she lost her step.

A massive wooden arm rose from the dirt, causing her to trip and fall chest forward on the dirt. She turned around and crawled back, as the still unborn tree nymph stretched towards her from underneath the soil, shrieking loudly and sharply. It wasn't fully bred yet, and the rest of the tree's root appeared to be holding it down, but the nymph had gotten a grip on the heel of the girl's boot. Her ankle was numb, but there was a tingling pain that she knew was likely to bruise later; if she would even be alive to see it, that is.

This can't be real, she told herself. *This has to be a nightmare.*

But she had been startled awake in the past for less. And the sting of the cold in her cheeks, the heavy pounding in her chest, and the pain in her foot as the nymph pulled her closer assured her that this was quite real.

She panicked, thinking this was how it would all end.

Above her, most of the fully-grown nymphs appeared to be watching while some became distracted by the glowing light coming from the camp downhill.

Robyn kicked. But the half-nymph only tugged harder at her feet.

The rest began to drop on the dirt all around her, crawling towards her on all fours, caging her in…

Another thunder. And this time, Robyn could see just how many there were.

She became lightheaded, as everything around her began to blur. Her whole life, these creatures were nothing but stories. And now there were nearly fifty of them within twenty feet of her. She felt her body give in for a moment, and the half-nymph on the earth pulled her in, swallowing part of her ankle into the earth.

Shit, Robyn thought as she found herself on the verge of unconsciousness.

In that moment, however, she heard another sound. An earsplitting screeching sound, but it did not come from any nymph. Robyn struggled to keep her eyelids open. All that she could make out was a blurry black shadow at the corner of her eye flying towards her.

A black crow with its sharp beak held up high plunged into the back of the half-nymph's head.

Robyn was nearly gone, but she had enough strength to pull her leg back and crawl before she fainted. The crow pulled its beak out from the now-dead dryad's head and shrieked in a most haunting unnatural way.

The creatures continued to crawl inward, surrounding Robyn and the crow.

The crow stood by Robyn's feet, extending its wings in place and shrieking at the creatures as if protecting her from them. With as much energy as she could muster, Robyn breathed in heavy puffs.

Stay awake, she ordered herself. *Whatever you do… stay…awake!*

She searched everywhere, but her bow *Spirit* and her satchel of arrows had been left behind at the willow tree where she had been sitting. She searched for a rock, a stick, anything sharp. That was, until she remembered the knife she had stolen from her mother's kitchen.

At that moment, a nymph snatched the shrieking crow by the wings with its sharp twig-like fingers. The crow tried to counterattack by biting, grabbing onto the wood with its beak and grappling about. But the nymph fought through the pain and added pressure to its stilted claw, preventing the crow from flapping.

The crow cawed loudly as its muscles became immobile.

It was defenseless, much like Robyn had been just seconds earlier.

The nymph tightened its grasp further; the bird's head was by then twitching with pain.

As it released what it thought was its last breath, a sharp piece of metal pierced the tree nymph's arm quite unexpectedly, causing it to shriek and loosen the grasp, a moment which the crow took to flap and thrust himself away back into the air.

The crow turned to see Robyn on her knees with her knife at hand.

And it was then that another nymph began to shriek, this time from high above in the trees. The rest of them turned their attention towards it. The nymph above appeared to be beckoning them away.

And then they left…

The nymph that appeared to be in charge began hopping downhill, and one by one the rest followed it.

It was the spark of light in the distance that caught their attention. There was more than one life to be taken down there. And the nymphs were always hungry for more.

Only one nymph remained, the one that had been stabbed.

It began crawling towards Robyn, who held her knife out in defense.

The nymph roared with fury and began to release its vines from its arms. They began wrapping around her legs like a snake, tightening and straining the muscles on her thighs. And then Robyn did as the crow had done and plunged the knife into the creature's wooden head. The nymph froze where it was. The glowing in its eyes diminished into nothing. And then it fell against the dirt beside Robyn, as stiff as wood should be, and its vines loosened and Robyn untangled herself from them.

She began glancing about, half-dazed and queasy, searching for the crow that had come to her aid.

She found it staring down at her from a seemingly motionless oak tree.

They shared a look for a moment... A very brief moment...

And then her body fell backwards against the dirt, her head hitting the ground and rendering her unconscious. The last thing young Robyn saw was the black silhouette of the crow flying towards her, before everything else went black along with it.

* * *

John Huxley was awakened by a cold breeze, the kind that could only mean an impending storm or something comparably as strong. A shiver ran up his spine, though he felt it wasn't entirely the wind that had caused it. He realized he must have dozed off while the others were still in conversation; only now, everyone in the camp was sound asleep. As he looked around, he noticed there were fewer bodies in the camp than before; two were missing to be precise.

Sir Jossiah Biggs had been assigned the first watch, yet he was nowhere in sight. John cared, though very little, about the callous knight. It was when he failed to spot the thief Hudson Blackwood, however, that he began to panic. Syrena was still there, lying in the same place where he'd last seen her. She moved subtly in her sleep, unable to find comfort with her restrained hands; the chain was locked to a sleeping soldier's arm as a necessary precaution in case she had the idea to run off in the middle of the night.

The thief and the witch hadn't left each other's sides since they left the farm, and it was strange to see one there without the other. For a moment, John wondered if Hudson was heartless enough to run off without her.

There was a sudden humming nearby that made him twitch.

Jossiah Biggs walked towards the camp, tying up his trousers presumably after having relieved himself. He ignored John at first, and instead glanced about in subtle distress. "Where's the thief?" he asked suddenly.

And John had no answer for him, for he was about to ask the very same question.

Jossiah gave the entire camp another glance. "Are you *deaf*, lad?!" he asked stridently, as if accusing John. "Where the bloody hells is Blackwood?!"

The former knight was then silenced by a blow to the head that knocked him unconscious. A dark figure dressed entirely in black appeared behind him, holding a thick branch.

John struggled to stand, keeping his gaze up. He searched the dirt for his blade. When he found it, however, it was too late. Hudson placed a heavy foot over it and dropped the branch.

"What are y-"

"Shhhh," Hudson silenced the young farmer, crouching down next to him. His troubled eyes were fixed on the trees uphill. "Don't make a sound, mate," he said softly.

John loosened his grip on the blade and turned his gaze to the trees as well, hunkering down next to the thief. He was surprised Hudson hadn't attacked him when he had the chance. Knowing very well that there had been plenty of opportunities, John became more uncertain of the thief's intentions by the minute. It was as if the thief was incapable of holding grudges and instead acted upon impulse without worrying about who was hurt in the process. Either that or the thief admired the farmer's fighting skills far too much to kill him just yet...

"What is it?" John asked in a whisper.

"There's something in the trees," Hudson said.

John took a moment to look back at Jossiah's unconscious body lying on the dirt. "Was that *truly* necessary?"

"He was speaking too loud," Hudson said calmly.

"So ask him to quiet down! Did you have to *hit* him in the head?!"

"*My* way's more efficient."

"It is not!"

"Well it's certainly more enjoyable."

"Where's the joy in knocking your own ally unconscious?!"

"I will do the same to *you* if you don't stop whispering so bloody loudly!" Hudson hissed. There was a muffled shriek in the distance, causing the both of them to turn their heads at once. The trees uphill were swaying, but nothing more. Both of them hoped it was just a crow. But both of them also knew better.

"Besides, he had it coming," Hudson added.

John remained silent, perhaps in indirect agreement.

There was a soft mumble behind them. Syrena was trembling while she slept and her head appeared to be twitching as if she was having a rather unpleasant dream. Hudson shrugged it off; having slept next to the witch every night since they met, he was well aware of how restless she was while she dreamed.

"What d'you suppose is up there?" John asked as they continued to observe the trees.

"Not sure."

"D'you think we're in danger?"

"Not sure."

"Then what the bloody hells are we doing?!"

"Listen, mate, no one is *forcing* you to stay awake... I simply refuse to be woken up by an Arachnian chewing on my legs. Don't know about you, but *I* very much *like* my legs. So you can either keep watch or go right on back to sleep."

"And leave *you* to keep watch? Not a chance."

"I'm keeping a *much* better watch than *that* useless guzzler," Hudson motioned to Jossiah, who suddenly began snoring, blowing dirt into the wind as his face was pressed against the dirt. John smirked at the sight, much to his own surprise. And Hudson noticed it and grinned along with him, as if silently agreeing that neither one was particularly fond of the man.

The midnight sounds filled the air. The wind blew steadily, creating a muffled whistling sound that felt almost musical, over the cackling fire and the chirping of the crickets. For a moment, it felt almost peaceful…

"Tell me… why are you here, mate?" Hudson asked abruptly.

"What d'you mean?"

"You're no knight. You're just a farmer. And you've no *debt* with the king, certainly, so why willingly risk your own life for the princess?"

"I'm not doing it for her… *or* him," John answered.

"Please, mate," Hudson chuckled. "Never lie to a liar."

John was suddenly at a loss for words. A million thoughts raced through his mind upon realizing that he had no definite answer to the thief's question. A part of him admittedly knew he wanted some form of respect. Whether it was respect for himself or for his family's name was not entirely clear.

"I suppose I can't judge," Hudson spoke again. "There are worse things in the world to fight for than a pair of breasts."

"Don't pretend to know it all," John replied harshly. "You know absolutely nothing of me."

"I know enough, mate… And you're either a very brave man or a very stupid one. If you've no explanation as to *why* you do what you do, then I'm afraid you're the latter."

"I'm *doing* this…" John snapped, "…because I'm the only one that's seen his face. This man, this *lord* who took her… There's something not right about 'im, he… He's more than what he seems. And if I *don't* do this, we… we may all be damned. And I cannot just sit by and watch it happen."

"We're all damned either way," Hudson said with a scoff. "If a war erupts, who do you think your lords and kings will try to save first? Certainly not the peasants… Y'see, we're *all* disposable in their eyes, every one of us. Farmers, thieves, soldiers, it won't matter. They look at us and all they see is pawns, nothing more. So long as *they* survive, fuck the rest. So, tell me, mate… why would you fight for a man who wouldn't put as much effort into saving *you*…?"

John felt himself sink for a moment, felt the thief's words tug at his heartstrings. But something somehow held him back.

Clever, John thought silently to himself. *His use of words…Too clever. With a talent like that, who even needs magic?*

Hudson underestimated John's persistence quite greatly. The only person John knew who was just as stubborn was his own sister Robyn. Perhaps it was a farmer thing. Perhaps a Huxley thing. Either way, John had the urge to remain hopeful, if not optimistic. Perhaps his hope would lead to his end, but the farmer was *not* willing to let it happen without giving the enemy a good fight.

"Like I said... I'm not doing this for them."

They said nothing for a moment, instead allowing for the peaceful night sounds to linger.

Damn it all to hells, Hudson thought to himself. *Caught in the act... And by the very same man that caught me before, no less.* But there was no way the farmer could have seen anything. No way could he have read the thief's thoughts. No way could he have known what was hidden in the thief's pocket...

As for Hudson, his own thoughts weren't all too clear to him either. Surely there was no hurry to kill the farmer just yet. Despite being loose about the gravity of their relationship, the thief forgot nothing. And very rarely did he forgive. But an impending fight could surely wait until his freedom did not hang in the balance. One clash of steel and the entire camp would be awake and with their weapons drawn.

The matter would have to wait...

John felt the thirst kick in. He hadn't had a proper drink since that morning. He wasn't sure, however, if it was actual thirst or if it was the guilt. He had challenged and caught Hudson without hesitation, but it was also Hudson that saved his life just hours before. He had to say something. *Anything.*

"L-Listen, Hudson... Back at Val Havyn... I w-"

Shhnnnnng.

They became suddenly startled as a silver longsword loomed in behind them.

"What exactly is the meaning of this?!"

John and Hudson turned their heads, only to see Sir Viktor Crowley standing over them with his weapon ready, as he examined Jossiah's unconscious body.

"The farmer did it," Hudson teased, rising to his feet.

"I did not!" John argued.

"Fine. He did not. But he *told* me to..."

"I said no such thing!"

"With his *eyes*, he did..."

Viktor stepped closer to the thief and shook him ruthlessly by the collar. "What are you playing at, Blackwood?!" he shouted.

"By the gods, did you check for meat in your teeth, mate? That's quite an awful stench," the thief grinned and shook Viktor's hands off him. Before he spoke, he fixed the collar of his beloved coat. "That *hound* of yours was being an obnoxious arse and nearly gave us all away."

"Gave us *away*?!" Viktor asked a bit too loud. "To *whom*?!"

Suddenly, there was a piercing shriek coming from the trees uphill.

The wind began to pick up, blowing dust and old leaves towards the camp.

Syrena, startled and fully awake, sat up and began gazing about hesitantly. When her eyes met Hudson's, the tension in her shoulders eased, though the look in her eyes remained.

The rumbling of the trees grew louder.

The leaves appeared to be moving in a wavelike manner, approaching them…

"What is that…?" asked the voice of a naïve young man. Cedric could not believe his eyes. He tried to force himself awake, wishing it were all a nightmare.

Only it wasn't… The leaves were moving, all right…

Something alive and hungry was approaching them.

"We must leave… We must leave *now*!" Viktor Crowley was shouting as he rushed to prepare the horses. He kicked Jossiah along the way and yelled, "Get up, old dog!"

Jossiah growled awake and instantly rubbed the back of his head with a befuddled expression.

"Wake up!" Cedric shook Thaddeus Rexx's shoulder and proceeded to do the same to the rest of the men in the camp. "Wake up! Quickly, now! Something's coming!"

Syrena, the witch of Morganna, knew exactly what was coming. With tension in her eyes, she approached the knight commander in charge. "Wait! You there!" she said.

Viktor came to a halt, realizing this was the first time Syrena had approached him directly. The witch spoke very little and therefore when she *did* speak, it was quite hard to ignore.

"Uncuff me," she said, her lustrous orange eyes captivating him.

Viktor's brow lowered. And it kept the sweat from burning his eyes. "Pardon me?"

"*You* gonna kill them? Because they mean to kill *you*. Now *uncuff* me!"

The shrieking grew louder. A rope snapped and three of the horses in the camp ran off into the darkness, their echoing neighs drifting away.

"Shit," Viktor grumbled. "There's no time!" He then turned to his men and shouted, "Come on, you lot! To the horses! Now!"

John and Hudson ran towards their mounts, grabbing their stuff along the way.

"Are those Arachnians?" John asked.

"I'm afraid not," the thief said. "It's something far worse."

Every soul in the camp was by then fully awake, packing and mounting their horses as fast as they could. The thunder echoed all around, but it wasn't exactly raining. What was falling was more like thick heavy droplets, just a handful every few seconds, not nearly enough to soak them.

The shadows above moved closer and closer.

And young Cedric's eye caught something at that very moment... One of the shadows hung on a branch right above them. Under the moonlight he saw it, the rough brown surface of what looked like a wooden arm. Cedric began to panic, realizing his horse was among those that ran off, and all of his belongings had been tied to that saddle. Like a reflex, his right hand moved to his belt, feeling the wooden handle of his trusty dagger.

It was all he had left, that dagger... And he felt lightheaded at the thought...

Before he could even *begin* to faint, however, he was knocked back against the dirt by something rough and woodlike... The shock was enough to wake him. He came face to face with one. A nymph, just inches from his face. It shrieked loudly at him and he smelled its fowl breath, like that of rotting leaves and tree sap.

Among the dirt Cedric crawled back, not believing his eyes as they looked up at the creature that stood before him. It had a scrawny body made of wood and its head was long, with dozens of sharp twigs sticking out at the top like hairs. It had hollow holes where its eyes should have been and its mouth was lined with sharp wooden teeth.

"N-No... no please," he begged, as the nymph inched towards him. It was showing no signs of mercy in its hollow eyes. All that was there was hunger.

"Hey!" someone shouted, and the nymph craned its neck away from the young man. Syrena of Morganna may have been cuffed, but she reckoned the nymph *had* to know... Somehow it had to sense her, feel her power through the ogreskin... At least, the witch *hoped*.

But the nymph began to crawl towards her, hissing at her hauntingly. Cedric managed to stumble to his feet and walked backwards, leaving the witch behind. She gave him a glower. She had saved him, but Cedric was far too afraid to return the deed.

"Oi, kid!" a deep voice shouted. Thaddeus Rexx was atop his horse, beckoning Cedric to come his way. Without hesitation, Cedric hopped on and they ran off into the dark path. Syrena felt the fury in her chest. Had she not been cuffed, her hands would be roaring with flames at that very moment. She swore she could *smell* the ogreskin burning away from the inside somehow. Then again, she swore she could smell it every time.

At that moment, more nymphs began to drop into the camp, and the company began struggling against them. Three of them caged in on Syrena, hissing at her, inching towards her with their claws exposed. The witch watched them in horror. But it wasn't horror at the sight of the nymphs, for this was neither her first encounter nor her last. It was the way they were looking at her... Normally they could sense her magic from yards away and they would hide, and she would be lucky to even catch a glance. But through the layer of dead skin, they sensed nothing.

Their hunger was far stronger than the rest of their senses.

She felt defenseless... But before the first tree nymph could attack, a sword sunk into its neck and the wood snapped. The nymph fell dead. John and Hudson had come to her defense, swinging their blades in such different forms and yet both of them with equal speed and polish.

"Their heads, mate! Get their heads!" Hudson shouted.

John listened and his wrist twisted in ways he had no idea were even possible. To train in a barn was one thing. But to fight for your life was another altogether.

The nymphs fell dead, one by one. The two men stood on either side of the witch with their blades held up, as if shielding her. When the last of the nymphs fell headless on the dirt, the three of them glanced at each other in turns. And they took a moment to catch their breath.

"You there!" a sudden voice shouted.

Jossiah Biggs, drenched in sweat, approached the three of them. They realized they weren't the only ones fighting. "My horse has run off!" Jossiah shouted. "I'm taking the witch's horse! One of you must take her with you!" With that, the former knight mounted said horse and trotted after Viktor Crowley into the foggy path between a cluster of trees.

"Hey! Come back! You *bloody* bast-"

"No time to sulk, darling!" Hudson Blackwood took a step towards Syrena and grabbed her by the waist. "You heard the man," he lifted her onto his horse and then leapt up to sit behind her, reaching for the reins. She sat sideways, her legs hanging over the horse's ribcage, for there was no way she could have kept her balance with her hands in chains.

"You'll have to wrap your arms around my neck!" Hudson told her, to which she grunted.

"I'll be *fine*."

"Darling, you either put your arms around me or you'll fall before riding the first mile."

"I've ridden with men before and I was *never* dropped!"

Hudson grabbed Syrena by the wrists, threw her arms above him, and tucked his head between them. Then he looked into her stunning eyes and admired their beauty for a half-second before saying, "You've never ridden with *me*, dear."

He kicked the horse's ribs, letting out a loud "*Hyah!*" and they sped after the rest of the crew. John Huxley rode closely behind them, followed by the Davenport brothers and then the three recruited soldiers.

Syrena found herself holding on tightly to Hudson's neck as his horse began to run faster than any of the others. It caught up to Jossiah Biggs and then left him behind. It caught up to Viktor Crowley and left *him* behind. Hudson, however, appeared displeased. With a half-grin, he kicked and yelled to make the horse run even faster.

Syrena couldn't help but feel overwhelmed by it all. It was the fastest she had ever ridden in her life. She could feel the warmth of the thief's breath on her cheek, but realized it did not bother her. The thrill of it all was quite new to her. It was rather interesting. *Exciting*, even. With her hands in chains, she was defenseless, yet she realized that she couldn't be safer riding with anyone other than Hudson Blackwood.

It's true what they say, she thought to herself. *It's not the horse that matters, it's the rider.*

The nymphs in the trees began to catch up with them. They hopped from branch to branch above them, at the same pace and some even faster than the horses. As their hunger grew, so did their aggression.

John Huxley dodged the trees like arrows. Each tree would appear out of the fog at the last second and he had to pull his horse in the right direction before it slammed against the trunk. He managed to reach the knights but struggled to keep their pace.

Both Viktor and Jossiah had their weapons drawn and swung at the nymphs *while* riding.

Now that, John thought, *is skill*. He tried to catch up to Hudson and Syrena but they were a good distance ahead. All that he had to guide him was the blurry black figure of Hudson's hat and the witch's legs swaying on the right side of the horse, and they were getting smaller and smaller by the second. He was getting left behind in the fog, the nymphs hopping after him.

Behind him, the farmer heard a man screaming. He tried looking back and from the corner of his eye, he saw Martyn Davenport being pulled up by 3 nymphs into the trees, his horse speeding away in fear. As the nymphs held on to each and every one of Martyn's limbs, vines began to crawl out of their arms and they wrapped around the man, tightening and cutting off his bloodflow. More vines wrapped around his neck and did the same, choking the life out of him as his skin turned a pale shade of blue.

There was no hope. Martyn Davenport was dead in a matter of seconds.

Further ahead, Hudson had ridden past everyone and he was the very first to come across the split. The path was divided into two very different routes, the trees and the fog making it impossible to know where they led.

Syrena, however, knew exactly where they led... She knew the Woodlands like she knew her palms.

One path, the one on the left, led to the trail along the Spindle River. The path on the right would lead them deeper into the Woodlands and towards the Copperstone bridge.

"Left!" she said. "Go left!"

Having mere seconds to react, Hudson pulled the rein on his left, and the horse just managed to make the turn. The fog, however, blinded both Viktor and Jossiah.

"Shit... *shit!*" hissed Viktor. Without a free hand to guide it, his horse stuck to the wider path, the one to the right. Jossiah Biggs followed him, sheathing his blade as best as he could. Thaddeus Rexx, Cedric, and finally Wyll Davenport appeared out of the fog, following Jossiah's horse on the wide path to the right of the split. The rest of the soldiers had been taken by the nymphs. Only a few were seen falling from their horses, the rest were pulled up. *All* of them, however, were certainly dead.

As the thief and the witch rode deeper down the path, the fog began to clear. Hudson could hear the sound of the flowing river in the distance, and he slowed his pace as he saw an opening that led them out of the trees. They had made it. The river was mere yards away.

Hudson came to a halt, dismounted his horse, and helped Syrena down.

He looked back at the foggy path and heard a trotting.

Shit, he thought to himself. He figured the knights had been left far behind. He even hoped some of them had gotten lost. Not eaten, perhaps... Just lost. But there was no such luck. One horse managed to trail them.

"Is it the chief?" Syrena asked.

Hudson's eyes squinted. There, riding in the distance towards them, was John Huxley.

The thief grinned at first; not a happy grin, but an amused one.

"Well I'll be damned," he said. "The mate's tougher than he looks."

As the fog cleared all around him, John could just about make out the silhouettes of the thief and the witch standing by the river. He felt the tension leave his body, even smiled for a moment.

And then a thick wooden arm reached down and grabbed him by the shirt.

He was hoisted up into the trees, leaving his horse scared and alone.

Then the panic came... He reached for his blade and began swinging, but the creatures' vines began to wrap around him. Syrena's eyes widened as she saw John's legs kicking the air as he was being dragged up, disappearing into the leaves. She had seen that same image before, the very last image of any man before she never saw them again. Only this time it was no stranger, but the kind farmer that opened his doors to her, whose mother had shown her an unconditional kindness, even brought her clean clothes and blankets for the cold. She couldn't bear the thought of leaving him behind... She wanted to run towards him. But there were about a dozen tree nymphs lingering in the path, staring in her direction. It was useless. Without her powers, there was no way she could save him in time.

Suddenly, however, she felt a tug at her wrist, followed by the sound of clinking metal. She looked down at her wrists and saw that her cuffs had been unlocked. The ogreskin leather hung loosely on her free hands. Her chains fell to the dirt and she saw the thief standing in front of her, holding a bronze key that he had hidden in his inner coat pocket. She realized he must have stolen it from

Viktor Crowley while the knight slept.

She looked up at him, at the very same man that had freed her *twice*.

"Fetch the farmer," the thief said, and then he drew his blade and charged daringly towards the nymphs.

She followed him, throwing the ogreskin on the mud and grinning with relief. The nymphs were hissing and growling, but it did not stop the thief a bit. He swung his sword, cutting off the heads and limbs of any nymph that got too close.

Syrena ran and stood underneath the large willow tree. When she looked up, she saw the farmer squirming, trying desperately to shake off the vines that had wrapped around his limbs. A vine was blocking the bloodflow on his right arm but John was far too stubborn to let go of his blade; his grip was as strong as his will to survive.

Syrena took a moment to stare at her free hands as they began to turn a bright shade of pink. Sparks began to form at the tips of every finger, one by one, as if they were candles. She smiled.

A roar of fire shot upwards at the nymphs and they began to scatter away like flies, hissing and screeching in fear at the sight of the flames. John felt the pressure in his limbs dying down and he started swinging his sword again, and vines were sliced in half and wooden limbs fell to the ground. He fought carelessly, however, soon realizing the vines were the only thing holding him up. He fell, fast and heavy, before a wooden arm grabbed him just before he hit the floor.

A nymph shrieked right at his face. And John cut its head off.

Then he fell on his back against the dirt.

It wasn't a very high fall, but the farmer felt a mild crack in his back all the same. Hudson had by then killed over a dozen nymphs, and the rest of them cringed away in fear of Syrena's magic. Now that the ogreskin had been removed, they could sense all of it. And they wouldn't dare come near her.

John, on the other hand, was not close enough to the witch to be safe.

One last nymph, a ferociously large one, hopped down from the tree and climbed on top of him. He tried to crawl back, but the pain in his back wouldn't allow him. The nymph was growling viciously as it too began to summon its vines. John had escaped death only to stare at it in the face all over again.

Then he noticed something odd…

The nymph's hollow eyes began to glow, not the usual green but a bright orange.

And then the rest of him began to glow just as bright.

Smoke fumed out of its head and there was a foul smell, like that of rotting leaves being burned. And then the nymph's head caught on fire, killing it instantly. Syrena was standing there with her hand on the creature's head. It fell forward next to the farmer, dead and stiff and smoky. And Syrena was panting heavily as if the magic had taken a toll on her.

The nymphs scattered into the trees, never to bother them again. And Hudson put his sword away and walked towards them. John breathed, slowly in and out, feeling his body grow tired and numb. He saw the two dark figures of the thief and the witch standing over him. Clear at first, then slowly blurring…

There was no time to rest, John knew, but his body told him otherwise.

His mind slipped away, his body with it, and he fell into a deep unprecedented sleep.

* * *

Young Robyn's eyelids were heavy and dry.

Her conscience returned before her vision did, and instantly she felt the throbbing gash in her head, almost as unbearable as the dryness of her throat.

The cold wind had blown dirt all over her, and so she groaned, using what little energy she had to wipe the muck from her face. For a moment, she had forgotten where she was. She'd been dreaming that she was safely back at the farm, waking up to the warm sunlight in her face and the pleasant smell of vegetable soup boiling in the common room.

She was safe and so was her brother John, away from the horrors of the Woodlands.

As her mind slowly crawled back to reality, the haunting images of the tree nymphs began to hit her. A rush of fear made her forget about the pain and exhaustion, and she sat up with an anxious gasp. She realized the life amid the trees had died down. They were still moving, though much calmer now as if dancing with the wind.

She breathed. It hurt her.

She longed for a drink. It didn't matter what it was, so long as it relieved her parched tongue.

I did it, she thought to herself. *I'm alive… For now, at least…*

She blinked, and somehow a vivid image returned to her mind in that half-second of darkness.

The crow, she remembered. *There was a crow… It came to me. I was nearly dead and then it… helped me.*

Suddenly there was an unexpected sound. Her head throbbed; she had had more than enough unexpected sounds for the night. Someone hissed at her from the trees, not a nymph, but someone resembling a person…

"*Psst!*" it called.

She blinked, over and over again, as if making certain she was fully conscious. There was blood dripping down her temples and some of her black curls had been encrusted with dark red. And she realized then that she must have been unconscious for nearly an hour.

"*Hey!*" she heard the voice again.

She hadn't imagined it... Something above was calling for her...

"*Psssst!*" it hissed, but somehow she found she was not quite startled by it.

If it were anything that wanted to kill her, it would have already done the deed. She lifted her head, felt dizzy and overwhelmed, and her blurred vision made it difficult to make out what exactly was lurking among the leaves of that massive oak tree.

"*Psst!*" she heard it again, this time louder, followed by "*Over here!*"

She cleared her arid throat as best as she could.

"Someone there...?" she called. She was on alert for any moving shadows among the branches, but everything above her seemed to be in motion with the wind. It was considerably less dark, but not light enough for her weary eyes. "H-Hello?" she called again.

"*Are you hurt?*" the deep echoing voice spoke again. It sounded like it belonged to a man, possibly in his thirties, and she could detect a hint of his urbane Vallenghardian accent.

She hesitated to reply. For a moment, she thought perhaps the gash in her head was so deep that the bold voice she would usually hear in her mind had somehow enhanced and she was now able to *physically* hear it... Except her voice sounded very much like her mother's and nothing like what her ears were hearing now.

"*Hello?*" the voice called again.

"Y-Yes," she stammered. "I-I mean, *no*! No, I'm not hurt..."

This time there was no response. She waited a few moments, sitting up and struggling to find the proper words to say. She crawled towards the nearest tree and sat against it, keeping her gaze up, the night wind blowing against her humid black curls. "Who are you?" she asked.

She heard the voice again, though this time it was nothing but a stifled mumble.

"*Y-You shouldn't be out here,*" it said.

Her interest had peaked.

Could it be a tree nymph, she wondered. *Do nymphs speak?*

"Come down from there," she said.

And the voice released something like a scoff.

"*Y-You need to go,*" it said. "*Return to where you came from!*"

But it was too late. Robyn's tenacity overcame her, and the girl had plenty of it. She lowered her brows and with a vivid poise she said, "I'll leave if you show me your face."

After what her eyes had seen, she knew not what to expect.

Is it an elf? They are expert climbers after all... Or perhaps a gnome? Or a pixie?

She envisioned a thousand things except what actually came next.

From the leaves of the oak tree, a dark shadow flew out...

With a swift flapping, it soared down towards her and landed on the dirt a mere three feet away.

It was the black crow.

As it landed, it shook and ruffled its feathers like a wet dog. And then Robyn's eyes widened as the crow opened its sharp beak and she realized the voice she'd heard belonged to no man at all.

"You know," the crow spoke. "The next time you decide to do something this stupid... You should at least make sure you're well prepared."

Robyn's jaw dropped. She found every single muscle in her body had gone numb. She'd heard many tales about the wonders of Gravenstone and beyond, but nothing could ever prepare her for this. In the span of one night, the girl felt she had seen her fair share of wonders for a lifetime.

"Are you all right?" the crow asked. "You look rather pale..."

"Heh," Robyn shivered and crawled away, around the base of the tree where she'd been sitting. She was blinking rapidly and her brows were arched. "Sh... Shit..." she whispered to herself.

"Oh... Right," the crow remarked and nodded his head in a most unnatural manner. "Pardon me, I had forgotten the effect I can have on people. Shall I, uh... perhaps give you a moment?"

Young Robyn had dreamed of leaving the farm for years. She dreamed of seeing all that she could see, visit every city and village, and meet every being dwelling within, human or otherwise. She did not, however, envision herself ever speaking to a bird...

"Y-You're... *talking*," Robyn finally said, trying hard to grasp the veracity of the situation, her dry mouth unable to close from the shock. She crawled back faster, but the crow seemed to catch up with very little effort, taking tiny steps on his claws as he rested his ruffled feathers.

"Careful now," the crow said. "Watch where you crawl... I didn't save you from a mob of tree nymphs only to have you sink into a pit of quicksand."

"*Quicksand?!*"

"These are the *Woodlands*, girl," he snarled. "Did you honestly expect it to be a peaceful stroll?"

Great, she thought to herself. *A crow that not only talks, but now mocks me as well.*

She turned and crawled away on all fours, so as to not stare at the crow any longer.

"Damn it, *damn* it all to hells," she hissed at herself.

"Come now," he said calmly. "There's a river nearby. You need water."

Robyn turned her head again in a flash. The more she tried to convince herself that she was hallucinating, the more her eyes and ears deceived her.

"S-Stop," she hissed at him, fighting through the knot in her throat. "Y-You're a *crow*... Crows don't *talk*."

Much to her surprise, the crow not only spoke again but he let out a soft chuckle as well, "You've a wonderful skill at observation."

"H-How hard did I hit me head?" she asked, caressing the gash on her scalp with her fingertips.

"Quite hard, I'm afraid," he answered. "But I can assure you this is very real."

"N-No," Robyn said, her mind clinging to any reasonable explanation it could find. For a moment she was talking more to herself than to the crow. "No, it's that *plant*, isn't it...? Yes, I-I've heard the stories! That plant, it sprays out a dust and it makes you see things that aren't there! What's it called?"

"There's no such plant," the crow said rather assuredly. "There *is* however a flower that sprays out a poison that blinds you. Now *settle down!*"

"Oh..." she said, her eyes wide and agitated.

Great. As if I needed more to be anxious about.

The look on her face amused the crow, so much so that he kept chuckling under his breath. "You're quite an unlikely one, you know?" he said. "You have the courage to enter the Woodlands, a place where death lurks around every corner, *all* on your own and yet you fret about a talking *crow*... Tsk tsk."

He flapped his wings and sprang forward, landing on Robyn's boot, almost as if to pester the girl.

Robyn froze once again and said nothing, on alert for any sudden movements on the crow's behalf.

"Now... I would advise that you get up. We've wasted plenty of time as it is," he said, with a tone that appeared to be growing more and more unfriendly by the second. "I've kept an eye on your bow. I'll show you to it, we'll get you some water, and then it's back to Elbon with you."

My bow...? Elbon...? How did you...

Then it hit her.

Her shoulders dropped, her breathing slowed, and there was even the hint of a smile in the corner of her lips. She knew she had noticed something rather familiar in the crow. The way he moved, the sharpness of his talons, the ruffled feathers, and the odd scar on his socket where his left eye used to be...

"It's you," she said. "You're Mister Beckwit's crow, aren't you?!"

"Call me Nyx," the one-eyed crow replied.

"Robyn... Robyn Huxley," she smiled.

"I know."

"Right... Of *course* you do!"

As she sat up, the sickness in her gut began to crawl back down.

"Did the nymphs hurt your hearing, girl? I said it's time to *go*," Nyx said, flapping away and landing on the nearest tree branch.

"W-Wait!" Robyn leapt to her feet enthusiastically. "You're... What *are* you?"

"Plenty of time for that later," Nyx said. "For now, we should focus on getting out of here."

He flew towards another branch. She followed him.

"I said *wait*, you!" she shouted. By then, she had forgotten all about the pain in her ankle. She found herself sprinting to catch up. "What are you doing here?!"

"Lower your voice, girl!" Nyx hissed at her. "Bloody hells, you really *are* clueless, aren't you?! And in response to your question, it would appear that Lord Beckwit cares more about you than you would think."

"He *sent* you...?"

"More like *ordered* me, really. Now come, before the nymphs return."

"Hang on," she said, coming to a sudden realization. "My pony!"

"I'm afraid the nymphs ate the poor thing."

"What? Seriously?!"

"No," Nyx chuckled. "He was startled and his rope snapped. Not sure where he's run off to. Anyhow, *that* ought to teach you to be more prepared next time. Now for the bloody *last* time, let's *go!*"

Robyn sighed. She had found herself filled with a peculiar joy, a joy to have encountered someone familiar, regardless of whether or not he was human. But the strangeness of the situation was still hard for her mind to grasp.

Could I still be dreaming? She wondered.

Did I die and just don't know it yet?

Or is this really happening? Is it perhaps the magic in the Woodlands giving the crow his voice?

A million questions raced through her mind and yet she struggled to find the courage to ask any of them. There was only one thing she was certain of. And it was the one thing she felt she had enough courage to say out loud.

"I'm not leaving..."

The crow craned his neck back at her in an almost intimidating way. "What did you say?"

"I'm not," she said sternly. "I came here to help my brother and I plan to follow through with that."

"*Help* him?" Nyx scoffed. He kept his beak aimed back at her as his body shifted in the branch in a most eerie manner. "I mean no disrespect but I don't see how allowing yourself to be eaten by tree nymphs is considered *helping*."

"I'm alive, aren't I?"

"Because I *saved* you, you ungrateful girl! You'd be *dead* if I hadn't interfered!"

"Then come *with* me..."

There was a silence. Had Nyx's beak allowed him to, he would have scowled.

"Perhaps you *did* hit your head harder than anticipated," he mocked her.

"Mister Beckwit sent you to protect me, did he not?"

"He sent me to *fetch* you, girl. A most noteworthy difference."

"Well…" Robyn paused, searching for the right words to say. "I guess… you'll just have to return to him and tell him you failed."

"Don't underestimate me, girl," he said, attempting to intimidate her. "You may look at me and see only a crow, but you haven't the slightest idea…"

"That so…? Prove it."

Nyx flew back down and landed on a branch that was just at Robyn's eye-level, and he stared at her with his single eye. The girl did not appear willing to yield, however. If anything, her stare became even more firm.

"Listen to me carefully," Nyx said. "There are dangers in these woods far greater than you know. You want to brave? You want to prove yourself to the world? Fine… You've *done* it, girl. You've more spirit than any person I've ever met, your brother included. Is that what you wanted to hear? Now, *please*… Stop being a reckless thing and go *home*…"

She thought about it for a moment.

She thought about her mother, about how much hurt she had probably caused her.

She thought about the twins, about what John asked of her when he left.

She felt the impulse to give in…

She *would* have, had it not been for the shrieks and howls in the distance that woke her up again.

There are dangers here, all right, she thought. *And my brother's here, facing them on his own…*

"For your own sake," Nyx spoke again with a sigh. "And the sake of everyone that cares for you, just… do the right thing."

Robyn's eyes moved towards the ground. She hadn't noticed she was now standing right by the willow tree where she had dug herself a bed of leaves. And there, just where she'd left it, was her bow *Spirit*, resting against the tree's trunk next to her quiver of arrows.

She leaned in, picked up the bow, and strapped the quiver to her back.

Then she gave Nyx one last glance.

"I *am*," she said.

And with that, she walked away, heading downhill in the direction where the bright glow had once been, now merely a trail of smoke heading for the stars. Nyx observed her for a moment. His impulses were killing him and yet neither his claws nor his wings would move. He realized perhaps his prior judgments might not have been entirely reasonable.

To risk your life for yourself was one thing…

But to risk it for someone else… that was something Nyx could not wrap his mind around.

He raised his beak. By then, Robyn was but a mere shadow drifting away into the darkness in the same direction the nymphs had gone. And he sighed one last time, shaking his head as if disapproving of what he was about to do.

"Gods forgive me," he whispered frustratingly, before flying off the branch and following after the girl's footsteps.

* * *

Viktor Crowley tugged on the reins of his horse and came to a halt, what was left of his company emerging behind him. They had ridden for a mile or two, or so it seemed, without hearing the thundering shrieks of the tree creatures. But it wasn't enough to calm any of them. Cedric was shivering as he held onto Thaddeus's calico shirt and Wyll Davenport nearly stumbled off his horse.

"Did we leave them behind?" Jossiah Biggs asked; he could have been referring to the creatures or the missing members of the company, but even *he* wasn't sure.

There was no answer from the golden knight. He only looked back into the darkness, seeing nothing in particular aside from a few owls amid the fog.

Wyll Davenport jumped off his horse at once and walked up to Viktor's horse, his eyes swollen red with tears. "We must go back!" he shouted, his voice breaking. "Martyn's back there!"

Viktor sighed and allowed for a moment of silence before saying, "Martyn's gone, Wyll…"

"You don't know that!" Wyll shouted. "Please…"

"Viktor's right, Wyll," Thaddeus said. "There were too many of them. They dragged 'im off his horse, I saw it… There's no way he could have made it out alive."

"No…" Wyll protested. "No, he's out there! Please, he's my *brother!*"

"I'm sorry, son…" Viktor said.

"No… NO!" he kicked the dirt and fell to his knees.

No one said a word. Wyll released a powerful cry, loud enough to cause an echo, as he dug his hands into the dirt and trembled with anger and sorrow, mourning his fallen brother. The black sky was by then a dark shade of blue, signaling the approaching daylight, which meant they were safe from the nymphs for the time being.

Viktor closed his eyes and sighed…

It had been a disastrous start, that much was evident. Perhaps the plan was damned to begin with. After all, who was to say the princess would even be there when they arrived at Drahkmere? And if she was, who was to say she was even *alive* still?

All that Viktor had was the word of a simple farmer.

And yet something in him wouldn't let go of that trust.

They had slept only for a few hours, but they couldn't let a single minute go to waste. So long as they kept the horses and journeyed through the day, they would be in civilized grounds within two or three sunsets... They *had* to continue.

Wyll Davenport remained on his knees, shaking and panting, coming to terms with the situation. And then a heavy hand fell on his shoulder.

"Let's go lad," Thaddeus Rexx said, giving in to the paternal instinct he often took with Cedric. "We must keep moving." But Wyll would not move. His tears dried up, leaving sticky smears on his face.

"We lost Huxley back there," Jossiah said to Viktor. "The thief and the witch, too..."

Viktor took a moment to catch his breath, the sweat dripping from his brow.

"I gotta ask, old boy," Jossiah went on. "Is this even worth finishing...?"

"Yes..."

"And if they're dead...?"

"Then we're gonna need a new plan..."

* * *

Searching for a safe place was like searching for a single word in a book written in an unknown language. The orcess Aevastra ran across the pasture among the hills, trying to blend with the shadows of the night. She heard angry shouts in the distance behind her that caused her a rush of panic.

"Find 'er, ye bleedin' idiot!" one of them said.

"I'll take this hill, you look south!" said another.

Aevastra found a place underneath a wisteria tree, which had long leafy vines hanging like curtains. She sat and held her crying child against her chest, sheltering it from the chilly midnight wind.

"*Shh, ya... ya,*" she whispered gently, rocking the babe back and forth, a tear escaping her eyes. "*Aestas salvu, min queridu neno... ya... calmaedo...*"

The child's whimpering diminished and for the first time in a long time she looked at him with hope. The orcess had been doing nothing but running for nearly a month now, and she was exhausted from it, so much so that she felt afraid to close her eyes, thinking her body would give up if she did. The child's bright yellow eyes glistened against its smooth olive skin and his cheeks bent in the form of a smile as he looked up at his mother. Aevastra nearly felt the impulse to smile along with him.

It was a feeling that she wished would last forever.

And yet it lasted only a mere moment, broken by the sound of boots splashing on mud piles followed by a croaky grunt.

Her heart raced...

Like an impulse, she hid her child within her shawl and pressed him against her chest. A tall figure stood nearby, just behind the hanging vines. Her poor attempt at hiding was of no use. Gruul squatted down and glared at her, his mouth exhaling puffs of fog as he spoke.

"What d'you think you're doin', you stupid wench?" he asked bitterly.

She said nothing, only trembled and struggled to hold on to her composure.

"Where will you go?" he asked her, spitting on the dirt between them. "To the *humans*? You gone stupid from the thirst, have you?"

She felt her shivers getting worse. Her babe was whimpering again, hardly able to breathe within the bundle of cloths.

"What was your name?" Gruul asked her.

She breathed heavily, eyes glowering and chin held up high.

"Aevastra," she said for what felt like the hundredth time.

Once, she had a clan... A family... A place to call home...

Now, she had nothing... Nothing except for her name, if that.

"Aevastra," Gruul repeated after her, his voice now soft and almost merciful. He leaned in closer. "D'you even know where you are? D'you know what the humans would do to you 'n' your child? Our kind is not welcome here, Aevastra... They'll hang ya 'n' feed your child to the dogs. Is that what you want...?"

In the distance, Okvar's shouts echoed, calling for Gruul and Murzol to regroup.

Gruul did not move, however. In fact, the orc appeared to be glancing in the opposite direction every few seconds. "There's no point in fightin' it," he spoke again. "D'you even know how to fight? Or hunt? You won't survive a day out there... You *need* me..."

The orcess considered it for a moment. Not for herself, but for her child.

Gruul was right. She wouldn't survive.

"Come," the orc held a hand out. "It's over."

She hesitated. Her mind was telling her *no* but her hand began to move closer to his.

And it wasn't until her child gave a loud cry that she came back to her senses.

"N-No," she said. "No... Y-You're a monster..."

"Aye," Gruul spit again. "But there's more than one kind of monster, you dumb bitch. If you ever live to meet a human, you'll see for yourself..."

The orc then snatched her by the arm and hoisted her to her feet violently.

"L-Let me go!" she shouted, her voice deepening almost like a growl.

"Shut it or I'll have your tongue!"

She struggled. Her baby cried and cried. She realized they were walking away from the shouts of the other two orcs. And she understood that Gruul meant to steal her... She pulled harder away, and it only appeared to be angering him.

"I think it's time we teach you a lesson," he growled.

"You won't hurt me!"

"Aye, I won't," he said. "So long as you don't resist."

He shook her aggressively and threw her onto the muddy grass. She felt the bones in her waist crack as she fell harshly, her arms occupied gripping her baby. Gruul threw his axe on the mud and unbuckled his dagger from his weapons belt.

Aevastra crawled back. "Stay away!" she shouted. "Leave us alone!"

But then a heavy slap silenced her.

"No one can hear you," Gruul said. "And those that *can* won't care."

He began tugging at the cloths. "Give me that child!" he growled.

She did not give in. The baby's cries grew so loud they must have hurt his young lungs. Aevastra felt a cold tear escape her eyes. A cold angry tear in between her grunts.

"W-What are you doing?"

"I'm gonna kill the littl' bastard... 'n' if I'm not satisfied, you can join him!"

This was it, she thought... She was defenseless...

It was either this or dying alone in a land unknown to her. She felt her grip loosen and her shivering diminish. And the orc noticed it and grinned.

Just then, however, the echoing shouts in the distance returned, this time far closer than before. Gruul glanced up suddenly, exposing his fleshy green neck to the orcess. His eyes were wide and vigilant, his ears high and attentive.

Gruul and Aevastra noticed two tiny black shadows approaching them in the distance.

There was no time to waste... The time to act was now...

Aevastra swung her arm at Gruul's neck.

One single jab was all it took... A half-second, in and out, and Gruul's neck began leaking red... His eyes widened as he felt his breath escape his mouth, replaced by the taste of his own blood.

Aevastra crawled back and rushed to her feet.

Gruul dropped to his knees, gripping his throat with both hands as blood gushed out, painting the grass red. He looked up... His eyes returned to that shade of fiery red, only this time he was suffocating and not shouting...

Aevastra glowered down at him. There was no more fear in her eyes. In one hand she held her child and in the other she held the small knife that Okvar had left for her to cut the raw ox meat. Gruul felt his life escaping him. He gave into it, fell forward and slammed his face against the mud as a puddle of red began to form all around him.

The orcess took a moment to ease her breathing. She'd nearly forgotten about the other two orcs. She hid the knife within her cloths again and caressed her baby's cheek so as to quiet him down.

"*Shhh*," she said softly. "*Ya, min queridu... Vos aestar salvu...*"

She turned and ran towards the hills, heading north again, unwilling to stop until she found the first sign of life. If it was human life she found, then she would figure out what to do then... For now, she ran, like a fearless lioness protecting her cub.

Okvar and Murzol noticed the body from afar and ran towards it. They found their comrade dead with an oozing hole in his neck. Okvar instantly turned in every direction, searching for any form of movement, as Murzol vomited into a bush.

"Dumb bastard," Murzol said, wiping the thick slobber from his lips. "You warned 'im, now he's been killed by the human scum. The wench must be dead somewhere too."

Okvar got down on one knee and picked up a torn piece of cloth from the grass. It was wet with Gruul's blood but the cloth hadn't belonged to him. It was soft and grey and similar to that of the orcess's robes. "No," he said, his lips curling into a subtle grin as he realized she must have used his tooth knife to defend herself.

"No...?"

"She's alive," Okvar said as he took a whiff of the cloth and tucked it into his pocket. "She must've run off. See?" he pointed at a trace of hurried footsteps on the mud leading north.

"What do we do?" Murzol asked.

Okvar spit on the dirt. "How many arrows are left in that satchel there?"

"Four. But one of 'em's broke."

"Bring 'em," he said as he began following the footsteps. "We're goin' on a hunt."

VIII
A Band of Rogues

The Draeric Sea had always been a treacherous region of the world for as far back as anyone could remember. It stretched along the southern coast of Gravenstone, separating the land from the kingdom of Ahari, and its currents were hardly safe to travel through, yet it was essential for merchants and fishermen. It was also notorious, however, for the many isles and ships that homed the most vicious and ruthless pirates one could ever possibly have the misfortune to meet.

It didn't end there, however… What made the Draeric Sea deadly were the sea nymphs…

The further west one traveled by ship, the darker the seawater would turn, until it became nothing but a black pit of thick slime and gunk that stretched for miles. This was how you could tell where in the world you were, they'd say.

If the water was still blue, you were south of Vallenghard.

If it was black, you were most likely south of the Woodlands or Halghard.

Beware the black seawater, they'd say, *for it only means certain death for all those who fall overboard.*

Much like the tree nymphs, those of the sea were said to be vicious hungry creatures, and they had blue scales all over their bodies and weblike fingers and toes that allowed them the ability to outswim even the fastest of humans. It didn't matter how strong or agile you were; once you fell into black seawater, the sea nymphs would seize you and drag you to the bottom of the sea, where if the drowning didn't kill you the bone-crushing pressure most definitely would.

It was hard to see the color of the water on this particular night; everything for miles around was as dark as the abyss. One lone ship was sailing west across a patch of dark water just south of the shores of Halghard. It was an old but rather large fishing vessel and it was sailing slower than usual due to the abundance of lives aboard. Nearly a hundred men were manning the ship above, most of them with fewer layers of armor than usual.

Two figures sat at the back end of the ship; one of them was preparing a bucket of warm water mixed with callis root, a plant that healers used to ease the pain of a cut, a wound, and even childbirth. The other figure, blue-skinned and sharp-eared, sat on a stool shivering and holding his left hand on his right as if holding a delicate rose.

"Damn rat!" grunted Jyor, the mercenary elf. "I'll kill 'im… Believe me, I will…"

"If ye were holding 'im by the neck, he couldn't have kicked ye," Hauzer replied as he dipped a cloth into the bucket.

"Well I'm killin' *somebody*." The elf examined his hand every two seconds, as if hoping his fingers would return to their normal upright state. His pinky and his ring finger were bent to a nearly horizontal position and a piece of bone was sticking out just above a dirty copper ring with ancient elven writing.

"It was the wench," Jyor grunted. "I *know* it. I'm gonna slit her throat first chance I get."

"She's a strong one. Might be useful. I doubt Baronkroft will let ye."

"Baronkroft's been sittin' on his arse in that room of his since we got on this ship! Toyin' with those spells of his, he's gonna go mad, mark my words. Fuckin' *mad*!"

"Aye, maybe... And madmen have a habit of killin' for no reason. Keep shouting 'n' ye'll be next," Hauzer took the dripping cloth from the bucket and moved it closer to Jyor's mangled fingers.

"Leave that!" the elf hissed angrily at his comrade. "I'll be fine, just snap 'em back into place."

"There's no saving 'em, Jyor... Ye *know* that. Just thank the gods it ain't yer fighting hand," he forced the cloth against the bent fingers, and Jyor began cursing and shivering, nearly falling off his stool as he winced from the pain. His jaw was trembling, and he was having quite a bit of trouble hiding it.

Then Hauzer rose to his feet and pulled out a thick dagger.

"N-Now wait," Jyor stammered.

"It has to be done, lad. We best get on with it now."

"I said *wait*! Get that bloody thing away!"

"We either do this *now*... Or we wait 'til they rot off ye..."

Jyor panted heavily. Hauzer's eyes showed hesitation and perhaps even a bit of concern. Having lost two toes and part of his left ear to frostbite, he knew that even with callis root the pain would manage to seep through. "If we don't cut 'em off now, the death will spread. Ye either lose two fingers now or yer whole hand later, lad. What's it gonna be?"

"F-Fuck," the elf shivered again, and after a moment of consideration he gave his comrade a nod. "Get on with it."

Hauzer placed the stool where he once sat in front of Jyor, and the elf placed his injured hand on it like a piece of meat ready to be butchered.

"Here," Hauzer tossed the elf an old smelly rag. "Bite down on that. Hard."

Jyor sunk his teeth into the rag and took anxious breaths through his nose, groaning and shaking and cursing.

"As soon as it's done, I'm gonna dip yer hand into the bucket," said Hauzer with his dagger at hand. He slid the elf's sleeve up all the way to the elbow and gave him a last look, as if asking for approval. And the elf gave him one last head nod and took a deep breath.

Hauzer swung down with all of his brute strength and the knife sunk into the wood, slicing through Jyor's fingers like butter. Had the rag not been holding the elf back, the scream would have echoed for miles. Blood began to seep everywhere, off the edge of the stool and onto the wooden floors of the ship's deck. A puddle formed and the blood began to ooze through the cracks of the wood, dripping down to the cargo space underneath the ship.

The cargo space held some thirty souls in chains, most of them pale and weak and shivering from the cold. Magdalena, princess and future queen of Vallenghard, sat among the prisoners in chains of her own, next to Thomlin, a peasant boy she hardly knew yet wouldn't dare leave his side unless they dragged him away to serve the soldiers their meals. The rocking of the ship was churning her stomach, or perhaps it was due to the scraps she had been fed just hours prior, or rather the green mold on them.

Suddenly, she felt a droplet on her head, cold and wet...

And when she glanced up, the blood dripped on her cheek and made her wince.

And the prisoners recoiled with both disgust and horror.

Thomlin was next to her, fast asleep, leaning against her arm as he'd done on the cagewagon just days prior, and she was careful not to wake him as she slid him and herself to the left to avoid the bloodstains. It may have been her imagination, but she could swear she saw the boy smile. She figured he was lost in his dreams, off somewhere hundreds of miles away in the comfort of his home, munching on a piece of pie, happy as a boy his age should be. The last thing she wanted was for him to wake up to *this*, a room beneath the deck of the ship so filthy and vile that it felt improper to even store cargo there, let alone people.

She fought back the vomit as the dripping blood formed a puddle near her thigh. Others, however, did not have the strength and willpower that she had. The sea was already making them sick, and the sight of the blood only worsened it. They began fighting for the waste buckets, which their captors would only empty out if they were sober enough to remember.

At that moment, a latch opened from above and Hauzer climbed down the ladder. He held no weapons in his hands this time, only keys. "Any of ye know anything 'bout tendin' a wound?" he asked, his face dripping with sweat and his red beard as dusty and tangled as it always was. "There's a plate of fish 'n' some ale in it for ye..."

There was a clinking sound among the captives and a weak trembling hand rose up into the air. It was the old man with the widow's peak that had been unkind towards Thomlin earlier that night, only now he appeared much weaker and closer to death. Hauzer approached him with the key ready, and nearly every pair of eyes in the room glanced at that key as if it was treasure... The one key that would free them, right in front of their eyes, so close and yet so distant...

"Yer name?" Hauzer asked as he grabbed the old man's bruised wrist.

"Swanworth," the old man said with a cough. "Sebastien Swanworth. I'm a healer."

Hauzer sunk the key into the man's cuffs and gave it a turn. Then he paused, taking a moment to look the old man in the eyes. "If yer lying to me, we'll have to throw ye overboard... And we both know what's out there..."

The old man looked dreadful. As nasty as he might have been, Magdalena hoped that Hauzer would actually give him the promised meal, if only to prevent him coming back a corpse.

"My name is Swanworth," the old man repeated. "And I'm a healer..."

Young Thomlin was startled awake suddenly, and the first thing he did was look to his left, making certain that Magdalena was still there. The princess gripped the boy's hand. They sat up against the wall of the ship, staring at the red-bearded soldier and the old man, the only two people standing among a herd of shivering captives.

"All right," Hauzer said as he removed the cuffs and pushed the old man towards the ladder.

"Wait!" Magdalena spoke suddenly, rising to her feet. "You... Hauzer..."

The massive soldier turned around, towering over Magdalena's thin frail figure. His eyes were not angry, but perhaps startled to hear her speak to him for the first time, as if he had never spoken to a person of nobility before. He said nothing, only grunted and stared, wide-eyed and slightly menacing.

"Please," Magdalena said, wiping the dirt and blood from her face so as to appear more decent. "These people need water. They will die soon without it."

"We *gave* 'em water."

"*Good* water," the princess said. "Not *sea* water."

"Times are hard," Hauzer turned and headed for the steps.

"I said *wait*!" she followed after him. Hauzer then turned and stepped forward, so harshly that the princess took back her steps with a mild shiver. And then Thomlin ran towards her and latched onto her dress. It wasn't much protection, but the princess took any comfort she could get.

Refusing to yield to the man, she swallowed back the fear.

"Give them water," she said. "Please."

"Listen girl," Hauzer said with a sigh. "I may have orders from Baronkroft not to harm ye... But don't ye get any funny ideas... Ye belong to *him* now, is that clear? Ye get water when *he* says ye get water. Ye get food when *he* says ye get food. Ye ain't in yer palace no more, girl. There be horrors out here, and yer lucky to have *us* 'round to take care of 'em for ye. Don't like it? Well... ye can go to Baronkroft yerself 'n' ask *him* for water..."

He turned and walked away again, a mild look of arrogance on his face, as if he'd won the argument, until he was thrown aback by the princess's persistence.

"Then take me to him," she said.

Hauzer came to a halt. He tilted his head just enough to catch a glimpse of her from the corner of his eye. *Frail, weak, smart-mouthed*, he pondered. *Baronkroft will kill ye without thinkin' twice.*

"Ye don't want that, girl."

"Why not?" she challenged him. "He's only a person, just like you and me... How bad can he be?"

He chuckled under his breath. "Bad."

With that, he climbed the ladder and slammed the latch door behind him. Magdalena and the boy shared a brief glance. His eyes were more concerned than hers were; instead hers were filled with intrigue.

"You ever heard of the name Baronkroft?" she asked him.

"A bit, yes..."

"Excellent," she said, walking back towards their little corner of cargo space among the prisoners. "Tell me everything you know..."

* * *

When dawn came, the unnerving sounds of the Woodlands began to subside. And the rich greenery all around became more vibrant with every bit of light that crept in from the east. What appeared like a grisly and disquieting nightmare of a place soon became a lurid oasis of plant and wild life, invigorating to the eye.

Robyn Huxley had been walking for hours, but her legs would not give in. By the time she arrived at her brother's camp the previous night it had been empty, abandoned, white smoke oozing from a fireless pit, and no bodies to be found anywhere.

The nymphs never left a body behind, that much was true.

But there were no satchels, supplies, or weapons left behind either, only two empty tents, or rather what remained of them. Her brother and the rest of the company must have escaped in time. They *must* have.

Robyn had no other option but to keep walking, with hopes of finding him if she only followed the horses' tracks while they were still fresh. After two days of depthless sleep, it was the only thing keeping her awake, that shred of hope. That and the one-eyed crow that decided suddenly to accompany her. And she was thankful that he did, only she was too stubborn to show it.

At first, she could not wrap her mind around it. She figured the gash in her head must have left her simple. But dwelling on it was not nearly as amusing, and slowly she began to accept the wild notion that Nyx was real, that his voice was real, and that he'd kept it from the Huxleys as a way to protect himself from the chaos that would ensue should the people of Val Havyn discover his secret.

For a head so small, Nyx had an impeccable memory.

He remembered the time she sprained her wrist but insisted on training anyway, and then her arrow flew into Missus Aelyn's cottage by mistake. He remembered the time she got lost in the Blue Hills after dark and her mother Adelina had to call for a search party. He even remembered the time she slipped and fell into Lotus Creek as a child and nearly died had it not been for her brother John; some things had happened when she was so young even *she* had forgotten all about them.

Why is it always the embarrassing moments that everyone remembers?

Nyx certainly did, and he appeared to be enjoying himself by reminding her. She didn't mind it, however. She welcomed it. Felt overjoyed by it, even. And she realized she hadn't smiled so much since she left the farm.

Nyx wasn't only clever, he was exceptionally intelligent.

Perhaps among the most intelligent minds Robyn had ever met.

And there was something the crow appeared to be hiding and wouldn't let go of, no matter how much she picked at his mind. And the girl certainly picked at it quite a bit.

"So you were... *human*? As in *actually* human, like me?" she asked.

"Over 250 years ago, that was," Nyx said, resting on Robyn's shoulder as they walked along that quiet muddy path. "And I certainly don't wish to dig up past memories of that life, pardon my candor."

Robyn said nothing more to that, for a brief moment of course.

They headed west along the path, away from Vallenghard and towards Halghard. When they had come across the split in the path just hours earlier, the horse hooves split with it, and so they ultimately decided to take the wider path to the right. The darkness may have had something to do with their hasty decision; all that she wanted in that moment was to be as far from the willow trees as possible.

By then, the sun had risen but the breeze in the air didn't seem to be warming up just yet. Robyn blamed that breeze for the goosebumps on her skin, but she knew better. She couldn't deny the fear. She'd never been in a real fight in her life, none that involved steel weapons at least. And Nyx only kept reminding her of just how unprepared she was, he was even starting to sound like Mister Beckwit.

To attack from afar is one thing, Old Man Beckwit would say. *Up close, however, it'll become a matter of speed and not precision.*

If only she had spent more time learning to use a blade instead of a bow...

Regardless, she was thankful for the crow's company; she *needed* that reminder.

Like mum would say, better to be frightened and careful than to be smug and careless.

The silence alone had been enough to trouble her; at least now she could speak to someone. Curiosity got the best of her and she allowed a brief silence before finally asking the crow, "Will you at least tell me how was it that you... *became* what you are?"

"That's a rather bold question to ask someone you just met, Lady Robyn," he replied.

"I'm quite sure I've known you for as long as I've been alive."

"I suppose that's true..."

"I *knew* crows couldn't live this long."

"Well… if you *must* know, it was a witch's doing," he confessed.

Robyn raised a brow with slight confusion. "You had a quarrel with a witch and she cursed you to live as a crow for all eternity?"

"Something like that. Sure."

Robyn felt something like pity for him. She had many questions, and they were starting to unnerve him, she could tell. If she was to get answers, she would have to be smart and ease her way in. "How'd you meet Mister Beckwit?" she decided to ask.

"I was attacked by a wolf one night, many decades ago," Nyx said. "I hardly escaped with my life. To be honest, I thought he'd killed me somehow. But luck has never been on my side, I'm afraid. I woke up soon enough in an old dusty cottage with no idea whatsoever as to how I got there. It was Old Man Beckwit that found and rescued me in the Blue Hills. He was *Young* Man Beckwit at the time, quite young. He brought me to his home and fixed my arm, showed me kindness when nobody else would."

"You mean *wing*…?"

"Pardon me?"

"You said he fixed your arm. You mean *wing*?"

"Oh… Right."

"Do you *talk* to him? To Mister Beckwit?" she cleared her throat nervously, hoping she wasn't prying too far.

"Normally, *he's* the talker," Nyx said with a lighthearted tone and a chuckle. "He hardly ever allows me the courtesy of an opinion."

Robyn smiled, feeling a warmth in her chest that she hadn't felt since she left home.

"I remember the *first* time he heard me talk. I nearly frightened him to death," Nyx continued, at first cheerful and then with a more somber tone. "Ultimately, however, we decided discretion was the best approach. It was for my own good, this vow of silence."

Robyn felt a knot in her throat. *A vow of silence. And yet… Here you are…*

"It took plenty of patience, no doubt… But it was the best thing to do. After all, we both know how dreadfully fidgety humans can get when they come across someone or something that doesn't fit into their idealistic view of the world."

"But you were *human*," she argued. "You said so yourself, you were cursed. You *belong* with us!"

There was a brief pause. Even while he stood on her shoulder, Robyn could see Nyx glancing at her with his only eye. She even swore she saw a sparkle there.

"Thank you, Lady Robyn," he said. "But I'm afraid it's useless… Not everyone thinks the way you do. Curses scare people. And if I flew into Val Havyn and spoke even a single word, they would burn me in plain sight. They wouldn't see me as Nyx, they would only see another freak."

"Well *I* think you're brilliant…"

Nyx chuckled under his breath. "You mustn't flatter me so, Lady Robyn."

Robyn couldn't help but smile. "Why do you keep calling me *Lady?*"

"Pardon me," he cleared his throat, though it sounded more like a squawk. "It's a force of habit. I'm from Merrymont, you see… Chivalry and generosity is our way of life. Our word is our bond. When requested to serve another, should you accept, they are your Lord or Lady until…"

"…until the favor is granted," Robyn finished with him. "Right, yes! Mum mentioned it many times in her stories."

"Smart woman, your mother."

"But surely Merrymont has higher standards, don't they?" Robyn scoffed, more at herself than at Nyx. "I'm a *farmgirl*. I'm not royalty. And you've signed no contract. You're fetching a girl that ran away, you said so yourself."

"I'm granting a *favor*…"

"To Old Man Beckwit…?"

Nyx gave her a glance and allowed for a brief silence, before his beak opened again and he corrected her, "To a friend who saved my life."

She said nothing else, feeling a sudden guilt for having pressured him for the better half of the last hour.

Nyx didn't appear too bothered; then again it was hard to read a crow's facial gestures. He had this way of speaking down to her, all the while paying her with respect, as anyone from Merrymont would do. She was not entirely sure of his opinion towards her, and quite honestly she didn't care much, for she preferred *some* familiar company over none at all.

Suddenly, Robyn came to a halt…

Nyx would have fallen off her shoulder, had his claws not dug into the fur of her coat. He was about to hiss something at her until his eye moved and he saw what *she* had seen…

There in the distance, was a man standing in front of the Spindle River with his back to them. He'd finished urinating and was tying up his trousers when he suddenly turned and saw them.

Robyn felt the impulse to hide, but it came far too late.

The man grew a devious grin and placed a quick hand on the hilt of his curved blade. He was of average height and his trousers were made of dark red leather, his body decorated with copper rings and tattoos. He had no shirt on, presumably because he'd just bathed, and he threw on a vest that was too small to cover his hairy chest. He had the face of a miscreant and his long black hair was patchy and uneven due to the scars all over his scalp.

Then he chuckled, exposing his horrid yellow teeth, and his voice was just as dreadful as his appearance. "Well… praise the gods' arses… what do we have 'ere?"

Robyn fought back the shivers. She hadn't seen that look in a man's eye before and it was disturbing her.

"Focus, now… And breathe," Nyx whispered calmly into her ear. "Are you afraid…?"

"Yes," Robyn whispered back hesitantly.

"Good… *Use* it."

The man in red walked closer, slowly and carefully, suddenly realizing the girl held a bow in her hand.

"Can you *shoot* him?" Nyx asked.

She considered it, but the only time she had ever shot at another human being, she had unintentionally taken a life. And somehow, at that moment, the dread would not allow her to reach for an arrow.

"I-I'm not sure," she whispered.

The man kept his nasty grin and yelled "Cap'n!"

And then he inched slowly towards them, spitting on the earth and chuckling roguishly.

"You either shoot him, Lady Robyn… Or you run…"

Robyn chose the latter. She turned back to flee in the direction from which she came, but only managed a couple of paces before her face slammed against the chest of another man…

Out of instinct, Nyx flew away and lost himself into the trees nearby, away from the danger.

Robyn was all alone again. She looked up at the man's face, a wide grin, mischief written all over his hazel eyes. He had dark brown skin and long dreadlocks, about six or seven of them decorated with beads and trinkets.

"Easy, girl," he said, with a tone that was by no means friendly. "What are you doing out here all by yourself?" Robyn noticed that his clothes were made of similar red leather as the other man's, only this one had on a long red coat that looked far too refined for his demeanor.

She glanced back; the other man was just a few paces away.

Not only was she alone now, but she was also surrounded.

"Look at wha' I found us, Cap'n Malekai, sir," the first man breathed into her.

"Stop slobbering, Borrys," replied the captain.

"She's a beauty, ain't she?"

"She's a child."

"Ahh, she's old enough," Borrys snickered.

Malekai, the darker man in the red coat, used a single finger with a sharpened nail to raise Robyn's chin upward. The girl said nothing. She could hardly bear to look back at that haunting gaze of his, like a hungry animal on the prowl.

Shit, she kept thinking to herself. *Shit, shit, shit. You're a bloody idiot. Why didn't you shoot?*

As brave as she was, Robyn had known nothing other than the comfort and security of her mother's farm. But home was a great distance away now. And that had never terrified her more than it did at that very moment, even when coming face to face with the tree nymphs.

"Who are you, girl?" Malekai asked.

Robyn still said nothing, instead tried to swallow her fear.

"You a mute, then?" the other man asked, seizing Robyn by the arms. She tried desperately to fight back with her fists as he snatched her bow away. It was clear to Robyn that Malekai was of higher authority than the first man, presumably named Borrys. But it was also quite evident that the power he held was corrupting the man, consuming him, poisoning his mind. The disconcerting look on his face was like that of a thrilled child playing with a knife he was forbidden to touch.

"She looks nervy, this one," Malekai said. "She'll make a fine pet."

Borrys eased his grip on the girl, yet his expression wasn't as warm as Malekai had expected.

"But... I saw 'er first, cap'n," he said somewhat timidly.

Malekai glared at him. "She'll go straight to my tent. And no one touches her, you hear?"

Borrys scowled, but in a way that seemed more threatening than gloomy, as if the man was unused to paying Malekai such respect.

Meanwhile, Robyn felt the nerves in her chest turn into rage.

*A fine pet...? A fine **pet**?! To hells with you, you sickening bastard...*

"Tie her up," Malekai said, and Borrys obeyed grimly, forcing her wrists together.

"Get your hands off me!" Robyn tried to resist.

"Oh *now* you're a talker, are ya?!" Borrys growled.

"The more you resist, the more pain you'll cause yourself, my pet," Malekai grinned.

Call me pet one more time, she wished she could say...

She glared at him. She was afraid of him, she couldn't deny.

Use it, Robyn... Use. It.

With as much force as she could muster, she kicked. And then Borrys screamed and let her hand slip, fell to his knees, held his groin as he shivered with pain. Then Robyn looked up at Malekai, at those hazel eyes that had intimidated her but now disgusted her, and she found the courage to spit on them.

The captain was far quicker than she anticipated. He growled, wiped his face with one hand and swung at her with the other. She yelped from the sting of the slap, so rough that she stumbled backwards.

She paced away, kept her gaze firm, reached down to pick up her bow.

Malekai wiped his hand on his inner coat and stepped forward, his eyes far hungrier and enraged.

She reached for an arrow... Whatever dread she felt before was gone, replaced by a will to survive.

Then, however, someone tugged at her bow from the other end. Borrys was back on his feet, and with one strong pull he seized the bow again. She had nothing left but her mother's kitchen knife. She pulled it out and backed away from the two men, taking careless steps along the rocky grass near the river.

Malekai drew his blade, a sharp curved thing that was five times the size of her knife.

"So nervy, you are," he said. "I quite like it."

She panicked...

Suddenly, however, a manic squawk and the sound of leaves rustling nearby startled them. A black figure flew out of the trees and charged at full speed towards Malekai's face. And the grinning captain was unable to react fast enough.

With his sharp beak, Nyx plunged into the captain's left eye...

An agonizing scream, a splash of red blood, Malekai's blade dropping to the ground... Robyn stood there in shock for a moment as Nyx flapped his wings viciously, trying to loosen his beak and pull it out of Malekai's spewing socket. And then Robyn came back to her senses, snatched the man's heavy blade from the dirt, and held it up the way she'd seen John do many times.

Malekai was shouting from the pain.

"Cap'n! Hold still!" Borrys grabbed the crow by the neck.

With one strong pull, Nyx's beak slid loose. And Malekai dropped to his knees, squealing like a frantic hog, his hand pressed against the bloody hole where his left eye had just been.

Borrys had his arm out, holding the startled crow away from his own face.

"Let 'im go!" Robyn said, aiming the blade at him with a glower.

Nyx tried to flap his way out, but the man's grip was far too strong. He was trapped.

Borrys glanced back and forth, from the distressed look on the girl's face to the angry squawking crow. And then his lips curved into a grin, remembering how the crow had been standing on her shoulder when he first laid eyes on her. He drew a dagger.

Robyn's eyes widened. Nyx had given her a slim chance to escape and so easily, she'd lost it.

"Drop the blade," he said, pressing the sharp tip against the ruffled feathers on Nyx's chest.

"W-Wait! Stop!" she cried, her breathing starting to pick up.

The man's grin was sickening. She wished she had her bow *Spirit* instead of Malekai's blade.

"Drop... it..."

Her grimace faded, replaced by a tired frown.

She threw the weapon his way… And Borrys chuckled under his breath. "Good girl," he said.

And then, with a grunt, he jabbed the dagger into the crow's chest.

"No!!"

Like a thundering whirlwind, Robyn Huxley's cry echoed for a mile. She shut her eyes and allowed her lungs to roar until they gave in, and the knot in her throat seemed to only strengthen her howl. She trembled with a rage so unknown to her that she feared it. And Nyx's cries faded and his wings stopped flapping, and Borrys threw his stiff body on the dirt.

"You bastards!" Robyn cried, landing punches on Borrys's chest before he seized her by the wrists.

She spat on him. And when he restrained her and turned her the other way, she spat on Malekai.

Nyx was dead… His feathers were coated in red, now… And she sobbed for him, a lifelong acquaintance, the closest thing she had to a friend, the only memory of home, gone…

Still on his knees, the captain removed his hands from his face and turned to the girl, hissing frenzied breaths through his clenched teeth. The entire left side of his face and neck was drenched in red, and more blood was oozing from his hollow socket. It was a horrifying sight, and it only grew worse when the captain stood up and began unstrapping his dagger. He grabbed hold of Robyn's neck and aimed the sharp tip of it right at her watery eye.

She couldn't fight him off, her arms were locked in place, and Borrys was snickering behind her and some of his spit dribbled on her neck. When she tried to scream, he pressed his filthy callused hand over her mouth, shrinking her voice down to muffled gasps.

"An eye for an eye," Malekai said.

And just when the tip of the dagger was a mere inch from her eyelid, something happened that caused the captain to pause in his tracks.

"Wyrmwood soldiers to the west!" a voice shouted.

The captain grunted and turned his attention away. Two men, wearing similar red leathers, scampered out of the trees. One of them couldn't help but recoil when he caught sight of his captain's face.

"How far?" Malekai asked, a pulsating intrigue in his tone, like a starving man stumbling across good hunting grounds.

"Couple o' miles," said the first man, trying his best to ignore the oozing blood. "They're well-armed… But we outnumber them easy."

Malekai appeared thoughtful, as if he'd forgotten about the pain. "Did you spot him…?" he asked.

His men snickered and nodded. "The Garroway bastard? Oh he's there, all right…"

Malekai's face lit up with ecstasy all of a sudden. He'd had a rocky start as a captain, and now fate had dropped an old enemy right on his lap. Wyrmwood soldiers were scarce as of late, and they weren't exactly known to be the most skilled swordsmen in Gravenstone. A single raid could buy his company more time before their next contract. And he'd have the pleasure of killing the famous Sir Percyval Garroway along the way.

He loosened his grip on Robyn's neck, and the girl could once again breathe with ease.

He took one last look at her, his eye radiating under the morning light while the empty hole on his left side was dark and hollow and redder than his uniform.

"Head back to the camp, Borrys... and throw the littl' bitch in my tent," he said. And then he walked off into the trees, ignoring the pain stabbing at his face, his men following his footsteps. Borrys headed in the opposite direction, dragging the weeping girl along.

She didn't know where she was headed next.

She knew only that whatever she faced ahead, she'd have to face it alone again. That comforting feeling that Nyx had given her had now vanished, nothing more than a temporary escape.

Beware the Woodlands, they told her. *Danger lurks in every corner...*

But she'd been blindsided by hope. And Nyx had paid the price for it.

She glanced back one last time, but saw only a black shadow on the dirt blurred by a wall of tears.

Focus, Robyn, she said to herself, fighting through the pain in her gut. *Now is not the time to mourn...*

Meanwhile, Nyx's black feathers moved with the frosty morning breeze, left behind to rot away into the earth. Borrys had stabbed him near his now static heart, close enough to take his life away.

250 years, he'd said... That's how long he lived with the curse...

So tragic it was, to be killed by a mercenary from the Rogue Brotherhood.

Not even a knight, or a squire at the very least. Just a rogue mercenary.

These were his final thoughts, as Nyx gave in to the darkness that began to consume him.

And just when Robyn and her captor were out of glance, he let go...

His life as a crow was over. He allowed for the curse to take him away.

A trail of mist began to rise into the air, grey like the smoke radiating from a piece of redwood when dropped into the fire, except it was coming from the exposed wound on the Nyx's chest... The grey smoke slowly darkened into a black cloud and then a spark appeared out of thin air, and the stiff crow was engulfed in flames.

In a matter of seconds, every bone and feather shriveled down, twisting and turning until it became nothing but a pile of ash... His entire body had vanished into the heat of the fire and then the flames died along with it. And the being known as Nyx was no longer human nor crow, but merely another mound of dust in the thick brown earth.

* * *

The halls of King Rowan's palace were cold and silent, so much so that every footstep would echo throughout the corridors. On this particularly bright day, these footsteps were those of a Lady, clean and elegantly dressed, as she made her way towards the king's personal chambers. Next to her walked a timid handmaiden, whose tattered shoes were so soft that she could walk through the halls unnoticed.

The corridors were bright and well lit; the tall glass windows allowed for the sun's light to enhance the rich colors all around. The high ceilings were an elegant red as were the marble tiles on the floors. The walls were made of blue velvet, rich and smooth, fit for royalty, and every frame on the doors and windows was painted a radiant gold. Lady Brunylda Clark, who was born into nobility, had lived in Roquefort's citadel in her adolescence, a structure made of brick that was large and graceful in its own way but not nearly as extravagant as Val Havyn's royal palace.

Sometimes, the Lady wondered how something so sophisticated and refined was built by men.

And the answer, of course, was that it *wasn't*...

As they walked, the Lady's expression was as rigid as it ever was, but her eyes showed a hint of concern. She was holding a piece of parchment in her humid hands. The Roquefort wax seal had been broken and the parchment was stained with nervous handwriting in black ink, muddled and smudged. She stopped at the ivory-colored doors marked with King Rowan's crest, the golden silhouette of a bear's head inside a blue shield bordered with red and two longswords crossing one another just underneath it.

"How long has it been?" Lady Brunylda asked the handmaiden.

"Three days, m'lady," said Brie.

"And you haven't set foot inside *once*?"

"We tried, m'lady. But when we did, he'd shout and throw things."

"For gods' sakes," the Lady grunted. She placed a clammy hand on the golden handle, took a deep breath, and opened the door...

The smell overwhelmed her almost instantly.

It was a mixture of liquor, incense, and either excess of sweat or urine, or both.

She held a handkerchief to her nose as she allowed herself inside.

Carefully she walked, having to step around worn clothes, silver goblets, and puddles of what she hoped was white wine. Two silver trays were on the floor, one of them flipped upside down with the old roasted duck still lying underneath it, hardly even touched. A mixture of food and juices that the king had refused to eat were scattered all around the chamber, covered in flies, and near the king's bed was a red puddle with chunks that reeked of both vomit and wine.

"Unbelievable," the Lady grunted under her breath, before turning towards Brie. "Gather the servants and have this place cleaned up immediately."

"Yes, m'lady," Brie closed the doors on her way out so as to keep the stench in.

Lady Brunylda walked towards the bed, which had been neat once but was now untidy with foul-smelling sheets and the figure of a motionless man lying naked underneath. His arm hung over the edge of the bed, and there was an empty goblet in between his stiff fingers that was just seconds away from slipping.

"Your majesty?" the Lady called, clearing her throat.

There was no response from the pallid man, not even a snore.

"Your majesty?" she called again, stepping closer towards him. She sat on the bed, slightly panicking. "Rowan?!" she shook him gently.

The king groaned softly, though it wasn't enough to calm Brunylda's nerves.

"Rowan, are you all right?!" she tried to lift him, but the man was twice her size.

His eyes remained closed as she pulled him up to a sitting position. The king's appearance was corpselike, his skin pale and his lips dry and purple. There was another groan, this one louder, and the Lady began to shake him and pat him in the back. "Rowan!" she called again, the concern in her voice growing.

Then there was a splash. The king opened his mouth and leaned forward, throwing up yet another red puddle onto the floors. Brunylda felt sick and nearly gagged, using her handkerchief to protect her nose from the reeking fumes.

But the king was alive, if only for the time being. He coughed and gasped for air for a few moments, before his bloodshot eyes looked up at his trusted treasurer sitting beside him. "Br... wha... Brunylda...?"

"Good to see you still live, your majesty," the Lady said, rising to her feet and taking a step back out of respect. The king kept panting and rubbed his eyes, his senses slowly coming back to him.

"What the bloody hells are you doing in my chambers?" he asked, realizing he was entirely nude underneath his sheets in front of one of his loyal advisors.

"Pardon the intrusion, sire," she replied. "A raven arrived this morning from Roquefort."

The king noticed the opened parchment in the Lady's hands, only he hadn't the energy to be angry at her for it. Instead he grunted and sighed with displeasure. "I've no interest in hearing any more about the Aharian threat. The battle was won."

"It isn't about the Aharian threat," the Lady said. "An unknown troop made sail last night from Roquefort's port. They bore no crest and held no banners.

Yet they had enough to pay for a ship and the secrecy of the harbourmaster."

The king wasn't entirely convinced, but he hesitated to shrug away the message.

"And this, you think, is the same troop that invaded the palace?" he asked.

"I don't *think*. I *know* so."

"I thought we had no leads…"

"We do now," she said, and then handed the parchment to the king. "The gold and the jewels they used for payment were the very same that were stolen from your palace, along with your daughter."

King Rowan's eyes widened. The parchment nearly slipped from his anxious fingers as he looked up the Lady Clark. "Are you certain?!" he asked.

"As the Treasurer of Val Havyn, when have I ever been wrong on any matters regarding finances?" she replied with a question of her own.

The king felt the life returning to his chest. The hunger he had lost returned suddenly to his belly with a vengeance and his throat was instantly dry and thirsty for water. He even felt something like slight hope crawling into his consciousness, and with it a pounding headache that made him regret every goblet of wine he had consumed in the last three days.

He gave the Lady a nod.

"Gather any advisors we have left. Have them meet in the assembly room in an hour."

"Right away, your majesty," she replied and headed for the doors.

"Brunylda…?" he called out.

Her hand was already on the golden handle when she stopped and turned around. The king's eyes were glistening, though she wasn't sure if it was due to the wine or the aching in his gut. He said nothing at first, only took deep breaths and allowed for the news to sink in. He gave her one last head nod, along with a look of admiration and gratefulness.

"Thank you," he said.

"No need to thank me for doing my duty," she remarked, before she left the room and headed to her chambers for a celebratory drink.

* * *

John Huxley woke up to a splash of cold water on his face.

He felt a rush of shivers, an overwhelming fatigue, the sun's aggressive light piercing his eyes…

A dark figure in a hat was squatting nearby in front of the river, ridding his hands of the dirt and muck. "Thirsty, farmer?"

John grunted and managed to raise himself up to a sitting position. His throat felt like sandpaper and with every breath he took he felt a deep painful pressure in his chest. "What happened?" he asked weakly, crawling towards the river and dipping his hands and face in.

"You fainted," Syrena said, sitting next to the thief with one leg over the other, pulling ripe black grapes out of a vine.

"Your timing was awful, might I add," Hudson said mockingly.

Syrena handed Hudson half the grapes, to which he replied with a grateful smile; if one could somehow kiss another with their eyes, this was the way. He poured the grapes into his coat pocket.

"You *almost* impressed me back there, mate," he said to John. "Should've known it wouldn't last. Who even faints over a few dozen tree nymphs? Tsk tsk."

John ignored him, instead examining their surroundings. They appeared to be alone, nothing but the sounds of the river's current and birds chirping nearby. He wondered how long he'd been unconscious. The last time he was awake, it was disquietingly dark.

With this much light, the Woodlands seemed... peaceful. *Beautiful*, even.

He tried to stand but the ground around him was still spinning, and so he took his time.

"W-We've got to go back," he said faintly. "We should find the others..."

Hudson scoffed. "*We*, eh?" he mumbled as he splashed a handful of water on his face.

John rubbed the sides of his head with his fingertips, as if trying to force himself to regain full awareness. "They can't have gone too far... There may still be a chance, if we jus-"

"Stop with this *we*, mate. There's no *we*," Hudson said, wiping his dripping face with his coat and rising to his feet. For a moment, he shrugged away the jousting tone he often carried and looked sternly down at John. "I'm afraid this is where we part ways, farmer..."

John frowned all of a sudden, looking about as vulnerable as a lost pup.

"But you gave your word," he said.

"I've given many things to many people, mate. What have I ever gotten in return?"

"Y-You swore in the name of your king!"

"You're right, mate, I did," Hudson said with a tone that could've been friendlier. "I swore that I would guide Sir Viktor Crowley and his company to the abandoned city of Drahkmere and help him sneak into its dungeons... But, tell me, *where* is Sir Viktor now? Dead in a ditch somewhere, I presume... Quite sorry, mate, but I never signed up to be the man's nursemaid either."

The thief shook the dirt from his coat and threw it back on.

Syrena was rather quiet. Her eyes appeared distracted by the silver blade near John's legs, a weapon far too sophisticated for a farmer. Something in John reminded her of Viktor Crowley, except she didn't feel that hostility that she'd felt towards the knight. She felt a shred of warmth, even, for the young farmer, and his devotion for the mission. And she even appreciated the way he would talk to her and Hudson, cautious yet civil, not like the rest of the men in Viktor's company. And being cautious was certainly no crime, particularly when you're unaware of a person's intentions.

"Not sure about you, love, but I'm famished," Hudson said to her, holding his hand out. "What d'you say to a warm meal and then off to Yulxester? I've *been* in cities with recently lost lords, it'll be chaotic. We'll be the least of their concerns."

Syrena placed a hesitant hand on Hudson's and rose slowly to her feet.

"You're just going to leave him here?" she whispered, but John was well within earshot.

"You say that like he's a child, darling... I know he *acts* like one, but he's a grown man. He'll be just fine."

She wasn't entirely convinced... It had been the plan all along to sneak away from the company when the opportune moment came. They had gotten lucky, however, and managed to separate without having to sneak. And yet the guilt overwhelmed her when she saw the look on John's face, a look of desperation and uncertainty. A look that was all too familiar to her. And ignoring it was near impossible.

"Hudson," John called, yielding to his helplessness, pleading to the thief with his eyes. "They were going to hang you... They promised you a pardon. They *trusted* you... *I* trusted you."

The thief was never one to feel much guilt. Something, however, was making him hesitate.

Perhaps it was the mutual muddle of dislike and respect that he felt towards John.

Perhaps it was his subtle empathy towards his inexperience and naivety.

Perhaps, however, it was the look that Syrena was giving him, the bright autumn color in her eyes somehow fading to a dimmer brown. For a moment he thought the witch might have been casting some form of spell on him, preventing him from walking away. Truthfully, he preferred *that* to the idea that he could possibly give in to the guilt.

He sighed, the frustration subtle yet still there.

And he took slow steps towards John with that typical sway in his walk.

"Listen, mate," he said. "You've got guts, I'll grant you that. *Too* much for your own good. Hell, I might even dare say I admire it. But you have one major flaw... D'you know what that is?"

John said nothing, only held his stare.

"Your honesty," said the thief. "You *do* see that, right? Or are you just too bloody naïve? You're *alone* in this world, mate, wake up! If you haven't figured it out on your own, it's about bloody time *someone* told you. Everyone's looking after only *one* skin and that's their *own*. They'd sell you to slavery for ten coppers and an old mule and *still* sleep soundly at night, d'you understand that...? You won't gain a *single* thing in this life by being honest, mate. Not anymore, anyhow."

John took a moment to take it all in. The austere expression on the thief's face was one of brute sincerity with perhaps a hint of pleasure at knowing he was right.

Now, the farmer may have been a naïve young man, but he was also an optimistic one... And while he was aware that the world was imperfect, he held out the hope that perhaps it could be better than it was. "I'm sorry that we disagree," he said.

"I'm sorry, too," Hudson said with a shrug.

Syrena's silence spoke louder than words. Everything she longed to say was piling up inside. Her whole life she hated humans for the horrors they were capable of. She had seen men hang witches and slay elves and orcs for the mere fact that they *could*... But John Huxley seemed incapable of such horrors. And part of her was urging her to take a risk...

"You did your best, farmer," Hudson added. "And I *mean* that. You fought like hells, mate. But there's not much point in fighting anymore. It's a lost cause."

"So what do *you* suggest, then?" John asked, trying his best to maintain his stance. "Because the world is deceitful, I should be more like *you*? A lying, murderous thief?!"

"*Murderous*?!" Hudson said with a burst of laughter. "So your reluctance towards me is due to the fact that I've *killed*, eh? Then answer me this, mate... This man, Sir Viktor Crowley, the noble and courageous, the Golden Eagle of Vallenghard, your *hero*... Have you any idea how many men *he's* killed?"

John's brows lowered suddenly, his eyes drifting into space, his throat aching with a heavy knot...

"The world is full of killers, mate," said the thief. "Your only choice is whether to be the man who kills to *survive* or the man who kills because he's *told* to."

There was a silence... The kind of silence that made a person think...

And then the thief chuckled, nodded his head, and began walking away again.

"Come along, darling," he said to the witch. "You're going to *love* Yulxester."

At that moment, John felt a burning impulse that he couldn't resist... He picked up his silver sword from the dirt, unsheathed it, and aimed it up at Hudson... And the hissing sound, like a deadly challenge, made the thief stop in his tracks. And John swore he could hear the bones in Hudson's neck cracking as he looked back.

"Put that sword away, mate."

But John simply couldn't allow it.

He thought of Viktor Crowley, of his loyalty towards him.

And it helped him keep his glare firm and his weapon straight.

"If you're not with us, then you're a fugitive once more," he said, swallowing back the hesitation. "Which means I can't let you go…"

Hudson rolled his eyes and sighed, the frustration more vivid this time.

"Put the damn sword away…"

"Why?" John asked, unwilling to yield. "What does it matter? You said you'd kill me one day, did you not?"

"Aye. And I meant it," Hudson replied. "Just… not today. The time's not right."

John stepped forward, bold and determined.

And for a moment, Hudson swore he was looking into the eyes of Viktor Crowley.

"Do as you must," John said. "But as long as I'm here, I can't let you leave…"

Hudson rolled his eyes again. And he turned to the witch with a grin.

"My apologies, darling," he said. "We should've let the fucking nymphs have 'im…"

With a ferocious speed, Hudson drew his sword and clashed it against John's.

They fought… But only for a split second, before the witch's fire startled them.

"Stop!" she shouted, her hands aflame.

The two men paused where they stood, their swords still crossed, scraping against one another.

Syrena took a long look at the thief, at his eyebrow raised in curiosity, at his fickle and unpredictable eyes. They had not left each other's sides since they met blindly in Val Havyn's dungeons, and yet when the moment came, the witch could not quite figure out whether or not she could genuinely *trust* the man. Then again, she hardly ever trusted anyone. It was her way of life, to live in isolation.

But she simply couldn't deny that feeling in her gut… That feeling of guilt, urging her to finish what had been started, for both John's sake and her own, if only to gain some form of respect, if only to force the world to let her be and accept her for who she was…

And rescuing the daughter of a king would surely accomplish that…

But the thought of doing it without Hudson at her side made her feel troubled, perturbed, and horribly uncertain…

He had freed her from the chains. Twice.

And she, in return, saved his life. Twice.

There was no debt to be paid and yet there was a certain loyalty there that she couldn't overlook. She had heard many things about the famous Hudson

Blackwood, but when she looked at him in that moment she found herself staring into the eyes of a simple man… A man who, much like her, was shunned by the rest of the world… And being away from that familiarity worried her, and she was willing to do anything to keep the thief nearby for as long as she could.

"Sapphires," she said suddenly, her voice warmer but firm all the same.

John began to lower his blade, yet his eyes watched the thief with caution.

Hudson, on the other hand, appeared distracted and, as always, intrigued by the witch.

"Sapphires…?" he asked.

Syrena's hands swallowed back the flames, and her skin was left red and smoky, and she looked at Hudson with both grit and affection, hoping it would somehow convince him to stay.

"I knew a witch once," she said. "A mind-reader who was held captive in the city of Drahkmere many years ago, when the ruins were taken over by Aharian pirates… She escaped, hardly alive. But she lived to tell the story…"

She stepped closer to Hudson, locking eyes with him, refusing to let go.

"She spoke of a secret chamber, deep in the dungeons of the castle's ruins," she said, her words charming him. "A chamber full of sapphires…"

Hudson raised a brow, looking into those dazzling eyes of hers.

The orange hue had returned… And it both startled and mesmerized him…

His knowledge of witches was limited. He had only met two of them in the flesh before Syrena, and both times they were killed before he could really get a sense of their true persona. He knew only what he'd heard from other mouths, the evils that witches were capable of, the death they would bring, the wretchedness of their hearts.

But Hudson was never the type of man to succumb to others' opinions on any matter; in fact he often opposed them for the mere sake of an argument. But as he looked into the eyes of the woman that stood in front of him, he saw perhaps only a dash of wickedness, the kind that was there out of habit rather than will. But he did not see evil… and the thief had a fair idea what evil looked like, he'd seen it all his life.

Syrena may have seemed mysterious, even a bit inauspicious.

But 'evil' was far too strong a word…

"What is your angle, love?" he asked suddenly.

"My angle?"

"We've *all* got one… The farmer here is clearly kissing Sir Viktor's arse and ultimately hoping to join the royal guard someday by making the right friends."

"You know nothing!" said John, and his anger only grew when the thief decided to mock him.

"He presumably also wants to get into the princess's knickers, which is all fine I suppose, it's a noble cause if ever there was one," Hudson said with a grin, then began pacing slowly around Syrena. "*I* want my ransom and my freedom,

I've made that clear… But *you*… What do *you* desire?"

For the first time since she met him, Syrena felt his aggression. She'd seen him direct it at others, but never had she spoken to her in such a tone, and when he did her eye began twitching again. She found herself questioning whether the thief had been sincere in any of his actions; after all he was well renowned for being a lying, cheating crook. For a moment, he wasn't the same man she met while imprisoned. And she wondered which man was the real Hudson Blackwood, if there was even a real Hudson at all.

"I want the same thing as you," was all she said.

"Oh darling, you struck me as many things, but not stupid… Do you honestly believe the king would pardon you?"

There was another silence. As much as she wanted to react against his tone, she knew that at some level he was right. As if reading her thoughts, the thief continued.

"For centuries, humans have hated every living being that *isn't* human. Not saying I agree, I'm simply stating facts… D'you honestly believe the noble ruler of a kingdom of *humans* will allow you to live, knowing you're one of *them*? If you were smart, love, which I fully trust that you are… you will do as I will and walk away…"

"If Viktor says the king will grant her freedom, then that is what he will do," John interrupted all of a sudden, out of fear of losing them both. "Both of you will be free when this is done…"

"That so?" Hudson shifted his attention to the farmer again. "And tell me, why should I trust *you*, mate? *You're* the reason I was locked up to begin with… The same farmer that turned me in to the authorities suddenly needs my help, eh?"

John's unresponsive expression said enough. He knew he had lost any leverage he had. He could have fought the man and though he was more than willing, he knew he had survived the last fight by sheer luck. "You're right," he said. "I can't ask you to trust me after what I did… And I'm sorry…"

The thief's expression shifted, his eyes softened, he became conflicted all of a sudden.

"But… if we're gonna save the kingdom," John said, "We will have to learn to work together."

The thief scoffed, hesitant to yield. "You say that like it *means* something, mate."

"Doesn't it? Really… Does it not mean *anything* to you? You would sit by and allow for some heartless bastard to come here and dictate what's right or wrong?"

Hudson was struck with awe. He closed both his eyes and sighed, unsure himself of what to do. He often loved to play the part of the emotionless selfish man but even he admitted to having a shred of humanity every now and then.

"Damn it all to hells," he whispered under his breath.

John nearly had him… It was vivid, as it *always* was, in the thief's eyes…

And so Hudson turned his gaze towards the only person he had any form of trust towards.

"Syrena, my dear," he said. "Do you *trust* this farmer…?"

John's eyes glanced immediately at the witch.

She turned back and forth between them. If she had been perfectly honest with herself, she would have said she wasn't sure. She would have turned and ran from both men, especially now that she was back in the Woodlands, in her *home*…

But something, somehow, kept her from moving.

Loyalty, perhaps? Or was it dignity? Or *worse*, honor?

Syrena of Morganna took a long deep breath and did something she would normally object to and yet she'd done more than once since meeting Hudson Blackwood. She took a risk…

"Yes," she said. "I trust him."

John felt the immediate relief in his chest.

And Hudson sighed for the hundredth time, fighting every impulse to walk away.

"Even if we *did* make it to the coast on our own, mate," he said, a dubious expression plastered on his face, the hesitation clear and poignant. "Even if we *did* make it to Drahkmere and even if we sneak into the dungeons, it won't matter… It's the way *out* that's the trick…"

"You're Hudson Blackwood," Syrena said, stepping forward, as confident as a lioness. "I *saw* you escape a prison cell with nothing but your own spit… *Nobody* can do that… And somehow *you* did."

"I've escaped many dungeons in my life, darling, but I am simply *one* man," Hudson found himself sharing more than he would with anyone he had met since childhood. And something like vulnerability was aching his chest. "I can't sneak an entire company in and out of Drahkmere's dungeons… That's a hell of a trick to pull and it is far out of *anyone's* reach."

"So you're afraid?" John asked.

"Afraid of having my head cut off? Shit, aren't *you* afraid, mate?"

John *was* afraid and he knew it… He hadn't been more afraid in his life…

Day and night, his mind kept haunting him… He kept seeing the image of Princess Magdalena, of her glistening green eyes as she questioned him back at the palace gardens… He kept seeing the image of Thomlin, of his innocence and his trust towards him… The image of both of them being captured because of him… Because he'd been so reckless that he decided to be a hero, because he yielded to his hasty impulses, because he was thinking only about himself… And now they were both gone, the princess and the boy, two innocent souls taken, because of him…

"Tell you what," John said, a look of humbleness on his face. "Come with me to Wyrmwood. Plenty of connections there, we can ask for any information on Sir Viktor Crowley... If he's dead or nowhere to be found, then... then I suppose we can part ways. And your contract will have been fulfilled."

Hudson hesitated, he could see the look of pain in John's expression, a look all too familiar to him. And the feeling in his gut only worsened when he heard the witch speak.

"Come, love," Syrena said, taking him by the hand with a subtle smile. "Let us go to Wyrmwood... And then, wherever the wind takes us..."

Hudson made a noise, conveying both his frustration and guilty conscience all at once.

It was, to some extent, even humorous.

"*Fine*," he said, nearly shouting. "But if he pulls that sword on me again, I'll gut him."

And then John Huxley smiled, sliding his blade back into the scabbard.

"Fair enough," he said.

* * *

The Copperstone Bridge was not made of copperstone at all, it was just a name.

It was hardly even a bridge, the old thing, more like a bunch of misshapen slabs of stone piled together, hardly supporting each other over the wide river flow. It had been built many centuries prior and was long forgotten, hardly ever used, and there were vines growing around the granite. And yet it was necessary to cross in order to reach the path that eventually led to the kingdom of Halghard.

Viktor Crowley, knight-turned-mercenary, crossed the bridge first to make sure it was safe enough. He walked and pulled his white horse by the bridle, gently and cautiously, while the rest of the company watched for any sign of a nudge among the rocks. He kept on until he reached the other side, immediately slowing his breathing when his steel-clad boots sunk into the dirt again.

"Come gents," he called out. "She's sturdier than you think."

Josiah Biggs went second. He unclipped his sword and shield so as to lighten the weight and tossed them at Cedric. "You drop that and I'll throw you in the river to fetch it, lad. Understand?"

Cedric nodded nervously. One by one, they crossed the ruined bridge, wary of the water below, which was flowing with a great fury between the gaps.

Safely on the other side, Viktor splashed water on his dirt-stained face. He could feel the layer of thick stubble on his jaw, like a piece of rough sandpaper, and he felt a sting when he rubbed his hand against his cheekbone, noticing a bruise he had no idea was there. In fact, there were several of them, on his face, his arms, his legs... It was a funny thing, the way he hardly ever felt the bruises until after the fact.

He wiped his wet face with his handkerchief and combed his greasy golden hair away from his brow with his fingers, taking a deep inhale and closing his drooping eyes.

His mind raced... Little silences like these were dangerous for him, for the silence had a tendency to make him overthink everything.

And when he would overthink, it wasn't long before he started to doubt himself.

And when he doubted himself, well... that's when lives were more likely to be lost.

It was the burden of being a knight commander. A bit of doubt could make all the difference.

He opened his eyes again, felt the heat of the sunlight start to bite at his face.

There was not a minute to waste, he knew. They had to keep moving west.

If John Huxley had survived, he hoped to reunite with him eventually. He couldn't say the same for the thief and the witch, it was his mistake to trust them in the first place, and the mission was far too important for futile distractions.

When he brought his gaze up, he caught something in the corner of his eye, an unusual movement in the water. And, out of instinct, he twitched, his hand gripping the hilt of his sword.

A figure was bathing along the edge of the river... A *person*, it seemed... Only the head and part of the shoulders were exposed, the rest was underwater, somehow managing to withstand the rapid current of the river. The figure was moving gently, caressing itself with the clear fresh water. From a distance it appeared human, except quite thin and pale and with straight hair as silver as the steel of Viktor's armor.

Viktor stood up gently and began taking careful steps towards the nude figure. Whatever it was, human or otherwise, it had its back to him. Out of precaution, he preferred to keep it that way. He noticed as he got closer that the figure wasn't only pale, but there was a subtle blue hue on their skin, like the color of the skies on a cloudy day.

Viktor's heart began thumping...

The figure emerged from the water, becoming suddenly taller, almost as tall as Viktor, and the water was just low enough that their back and some of their posterior was exposed. The water hadn't had a chance to warm up yet and was icy cold, but the pale figure did not appear the least bit bothered by it. Their slender shape and lack of body-hair made them appear almost female, a rather fit strong-armed female, though it wasn't entirely clear.

Viktor's feet refused to take another step, mostly out of respect, as the figure stepped out of the river and onto the earth, exposing the rest of their nude body. He felt the impulse to look away but he succumbed to his carnal desire, finding himself paralyzed by the beauty of it all, a weak man unable to resist temptation. The figure's body was smooth and hairless and pale, beautiful in its own way, unlike any body Viktor had ever seen in his life.

And when his eyes moved up, he realized why...

He could see an ear sticking out from within the silver hair, nearly twice the size of a human's ear, sharp and pointed rather than round...

A Woodland elf, Viktor realized. *An unbelievably beautiful Woodland elf...*

Had those ears not been there, they could have passed for a human. And though Viktor felt a rush of unease all over his body, he found himself unable to look away.

That was, until the elf looked in *his* direction...

Viktor hesitated. He couldn't read the elf's expression from such a distance, but their body language was not at all defensive. The elf moved gradually, reaching for a linen cloth and soaking up the water dripping from their body, gently and slowly, as if Viktor was nothing but a harmless bird observing from afar.

Behind him, the rest of the men in the company were chattering among themselves, distracted and careless. Wyll Davenport was the last to cross the bridge, his face as red as his swollen eyes. And when he reached the end of the bridge, Thaddeus Rexx gave him an unwelcomed pat on the shoulder.

"Air's warming up," Cedric made an attempt at small talk, kneeling before the river and washing the dirt and sweat from his palms.

"Aye," Jossiah spit on the ground, a bit too close to Cedric's boot for the young man's comfort. "Enjoy it while it lasts, boy. Soon you'll be sweating all over." He then tossed a bent whetstone at the young man's lap. "Here," he said. "Make yourself useful, will you? I need to piss something awful."

Cedric took the whetstone and unsheathed Jossiah's elegant blade as the former knight walked off into the trees. He slid the stone against it, softly at first, then gradually adding more and more pressure.

I can get used to this, the young man thought. *It certainly beats serving ale and cleaning up vomit.*

From the corner of his eye something fell all of a sudden, a bright leaf, twirling gracefully in the air. It looked far too green, far too young to have fallen on its own. And when two more just like it fell, he grew nervous and sweaty. He glanced up in a fright, and the whetstone slid from his fingers and fell into the river.

"Thad?" he called, a shiver in his lip.

"Hmm?"

"Do tree nymphs move during the day?"

"They can't," Thaddeus said. "The sun's light won't let 'em. Why?"

"I-I think... someone's up there..."

"You're hallucinatin', lad," Thaddeus scoffed. "Trees move. They drop leaves. It's nothin', just let it go."

But Cedric's eyes wouldn't move, his hands gripped Jossiah's sword tighter. After what they had gone through, it gave him some relief to be holding a real weapon, yet not nearly enough for he hadn't the slightest idea how to use it properly.

Then there were footsteps... And Cedric twitched and held the sword up...

It was Viktor Crowley, wide-eyed and noticeably anxious.

"We need to move," he said as he approached his horse. "*Now*, lads."

Tell him, Cedric's nerves poked at him. *Tell him now.*

"S-Sir, I believe there's something in th-"

Cedric felt a bone crack in his back as something heavy fell from the trees on top of him...

The shiny blade slid from his fingers and a hand snatched it immediately.

It was a woman, dressed in a hunting outfit made of fur, with greasy blonde braids and black paint around her vicious green eyes. Her knee was pressed against young Cedric's back, keeping him pinned against the mud, and she had a wide conniving grin like a hyena.

"Hey!" Thaddeus ran towards them, but the woman held Jossiah's blade up.

"That's close enough there, tiny," she mocked him.

It wasn't the sword that made Thaddeus come to a halt, it was the serrated dagger the woman was pressing against Cedric's neck with her other hand.

"What in all hells is this?!" Jossiah stepped out of the trees, tying his trousers back up.

Viktor approached them with his sword unsheathed, ready to strike the woman down. But the woman did not look like the patient kind; her brows lowered with displeasure and she pressed the knife down harder, and Cedric released a distressing whimper.

"P-Please don't... we mean no harm," the young man begged her, speaking rapidly and nervously, a tear escaping his eyes. "Please, w-we serve King Rowan of Val Havyn... We mean no harm! Please!"

The woman looked down all of a sudden, and her eyes softened a bit, as if she hadn't realized she was pressing the knife against the neck of a timid boy and not a man.

"Let him go," Viktor said, calmly yet standing his ground. "He's only a squire. If you want to start trouble, start it with me..."

He took a step forward.

And it was the last step he took before a piece of cold steel pressed against his own neck.

"Drop it," said another voice behind him.

Viktor didn't look back. He dropped his sword where he stood.

It was a man, also dressed in a hunting outfit made of fur, quite similar to the woman's. He had short blonde hair at the top of his scalp, slicked neatly back, and the sides of his head were shaved, revealing an assortment of decorative black tattoos. His green eyes were eerily similar to the woman's, as were the rest of their faces, except for perhaps his more robust jaw.

The woman whistled. And, out of the trees, about a dozen bows appeared.

And every single archer was a blue-skinned elf...

Everyone in Viktor's company fell silent, nothing but the sound of the river's flow between them.

"What do you want?" Viktor asked the woman, assuming that she was in charge due to her rigid manner. But the woman said nothing, only whistled loudly again.

"Please," Cedric kept begging, his face twitching amid the dirt.

The woman found herself easing the pressure from the dagger. And Cedric took the opportunity to look up as far as his neck would allow him. The woman had numerous scars along her cheeks and jaw. The braids on her head were messy and the black paint around her eyes was smeared with sweat.

A raider, Cedric guessed, for the Woodlands were crawling with them.

"That's my sword you're holding," Jossiah sneered.

"Is it now?" the woman spat on the dirt. "Come get it, then."

Taking it as a challenge, Jossiah took a step forward, his face wrinkled like an angry hound.

"Stay where you are, old boy!" Viktor ordered him, the blade on his neck itching at his stubble. The two raiders shared a look and a half-smirk, and the elven archers stepped closer and caged the company in with their bows at the ready.

"That's a beautiful mount ye got there," the woman spoke again, her eyes admiring Viktor's white horse. "Where's she from?"

Viktor's mind was preoccupied searching for a window of opportunity. But somehow, any possibility for their survival would end with the death of their young squire. He considered it. For a moment, he nearly gave in to the impulse to kick the raider behind him and risk Cedric's life. Instead, however, he cleared his throat and calmed the twitching of his wrist.

"Raven's Keep," he said, his voice deep and croaky.

"Ah," the woman snickered. "Best horses in the world, they are. I'd recognize one anywhere. Always wanted one..."

Viktor felt a rage building up in his chest.

Twice, he had been disarmed that week. And both times by a miscreant.

He'd be damned if he allowed them to take off with his mount, that much he was sure of. Just before he threw the kick behind, however, another voice stopped him.

"At ease!" it said, followed by the sound of boots sliding over shrubs.

A man stepped out of the trees, and Viktor felt a great relief in his shoulders when he saw him. He was dressed in black steel armor, neatly laced and polished, and a stylish green cape, hardly the uniform of a raider. The man's hair was trimmed almost to the scalp, a thin layer of fuzz it was, and he had ebony-colored skin. His left ear was damaged; there was only a hole and the upper earflap sticking out, while a deep brown scar marked his skin where his earlobe should have been.

"Well, cursed be my eyes if they deceive me," the man said. "Is that really the Golden Eagle of Vallenghard in the flesh?" He was smiling, but it was a much warmer smile than the raider woman's.

"That depends. Who asks?" Viktor replied.

The man chuckled, a friendly kind of chuckle, as if he was an old acquaintance.

"I'd recognize you and that white steed of yours anywhere," he said, before glancing at the elves and the two blonde raiders. "Lower your weapons, all of you. These men are not our enemies."

Cedric felt himself able to breathe again, as the woman lifted her knee from his back and slid her dagger back into its sheath. And immediately, Jossiah Biggs snatched his sword from her hand and wiped it, despite the fact that her hands were cleaner than his. She gave him a devious grin, then puckered her lips and shot a kiss into the air to mock him.

The man in the dark armor approached and gave Viktor a slight bow.

"Sir Percyval Garroway of Wyrmwood," he introduced himself. "Do forgive my new recruits. They're quick with their blades but not so much with their minds."

"Piss off," the woman said, before the man that looked nearly identical to her patted her on the back and they disappeared into the trees.

"You can have a rest," Sir Percyval shouted at the two as they walked off. "Have Skye take the next watch."

There was no formal reply, except for a chuckle and the faint sound of the woman's voice saying something along the lines of '*thank the bloody gods*'.

"Sir Viktor Crowley of Val Havyn," Viktor shook the man's hand. Something like anguish tugged at his chest when he introduced himself, knowing he could very well be hanged for using the word '*Sir*' when he no longer *was* one. "This is my company," he said. "Or rather, what's left of it."

Sir Percyval chuckled. "You lot look like you've seen better days," he said.

"Any day outside of these cursed lands would be a better day."

"Aye," Percyval nodded and smiled. "Come. You must be starving. Our camping grounds are not too far from here. Let's get you a warm meal."

Viktor locked eyes with every man in his company one at a time, a look that he hoped would be encouraging but came across as more guarded than anything else. He threw a nod at them as well, hoping it would reassure them. And so they followed, one by one, pulling their horses into the trees.

Cedric, still startled and shaken, brushed the dirt from his clothes as best as he could.

"That was, um," he cleared his throat. "That was quite close…"

Jossiah Biggs shot him a glare. For a man that was supposed to be on the same side as him, he always seemed to look at Cedric more as a pest than an ally, a look that reminded Cedric of his old guardian Mister Nottley.

"You gave us all away," Jossiah said with a grimace. "You give us away to anyone again, boy… And I'll cut your damn tongue off myself."

Cedric gripped his trusty dagger, the only other thing he owned aside from the clothes on his back. And he was the last one to follow them into the trees.

Great, he thought worriedly. *Guess I'll add him to the list of things that's likely to kill me.*

Just around the river bend, two swordsmen dressed in red leathers observed cautiously. A third man in a red coat had his head submerged in the river, grabbing on to a heavy boulder so as to not let the current swallow him.

"You saw 'im, did you?" the first man asked.

"Aye. Looks like he got 'imself some new recruits. Never thought it'd be a bunch o' rabbits, though."

The third man suddenly lifted his head from the water, panting heavily from the pain as blood continued to ooze from his hollow eye socket. In his quivering fingers, he held a piece of red rag that he'd torn from his cape. He pressed it against his wound and tied it delicately at the back of his head.

"Cap'n?" one of the men called.

"What in all hells do you want?" asked Malekai Pahrvus as he adjusted the rag so it would hide the hideous wound.

"We spotted 'im, cap'n," the first man spoke again. "The Garroway bastard."

"Give the word, cap'n. I'll put an arrow in his skull."

Malekai got to his feet and tried to gaze across the river, though it was mostly a blur. His vision wasn't great to begin with, and now half of it was pure darkness. He shivered, half from the pain and half from the rage. "Do we know how many men he's got?" he asked, the ragged patch becoming damper by the second as blood leaked from his socket.

"At least a hundred, cap'n. Not countin' any scouts he's sent out."

"Piss on his name, the old bastard," the other man said. "Last time we had a quarrel with 'im, he killed o'er two dozen of us 'n' all *he* lost was a fucking ear."

"We'll make sure he loses *more* this time," Malekai grinned. "Go find the bastard's camp, both of you. Then report back to the camp."

"You not coming, cap'n?"

"Do as you're told," the captain grunted. "I have a pending matter waiting for me in my tent."

The two rogues grinned at each other and scurried off towards the

Copperstone Bridge. Malekai remained where he stood for a moment, sighing and holding a hand against his throbbing face.

A bloody mess, he thought. *A bloody fucking mess...*

And it was. There was so much blood, he had to dip his head into the water again with the rag still on. It burned something awful, and he clenched his fists and grinded his teeth together. Then he walked back towards the Rogue Brotherhood's camp, rage in his chest and mischief on his mind.

* * *

About two miles east of the Wyrmwood camp, a young woman with bloodshot eyes was being dragged against her will towards a camp that reeked of musk, ale, and red spindle. Her blank gaze was one of hopelessness and her cheeks were humid and stained with the tears she'd recently shed for her fallen companion. Her beloved bow *Spirit* was now in the hands of a stranger, one whose demeanor was repulsive and cruel to say the least.

She was defenseless, and her gutless captor looked pleased by his power over her.

The two of them walked along a muddy path in the Woodlands, with rows of brown tents set up on both sides. Robyn Huxley sighed and shut her eyes, telling herself she would make it through this somehow. She tried to ignore the pain in her wrists, which were roped together so tightly that it was beginning to tarnish her skin with rashes.

The commotion in the camp was loud and disorderly.

Robyn had heard many tales of the mercenary guild known as the Rogue Brotherhood, but she had never seen a single one of them in her life, at least none that bore the colors or the infamous tattoo of the scorpion on their wrist. She imagined large, heavily-built warriors, cold and menacing, willing to fight for the highest bidder yet still having a shred of dignity left. But she never envisioned what her eyes saw on that day...

She saw men... Neither special nor memorable, or even remotely pleasing to look at...

All around her, they circled in, their glares frightening and repulsive.

A tall man with a beer gut and wavy brown hair, and countless scars and tattoos all over his body...

A husky bald man with five or six rings on each ear and a large one hanging between his nostrils...

A man with a beard that reached his chest, another man with no hair at all, and a suspiciously-smelling lanky man with a nervous twitch.

It was the girl's first glimpse of the Brotherhood, a guild of mercenaries she had heard about since childhood, and yet all she saw were simple men... Threatening, as they might have seemed, they didn't exactly have the bearings of any soldier in Val Havyn. They were disappointing and frightening all at once, the type of drunkards she would often see lounging around Dreary Lane back in Val Havyn.

"What have we got 'ere now, Borrys?" a man asked, walking out of his tent half-nude.

There was mocking and whistling and about a dozen unpleasant stares shot at Robyn, and Borrys shoved her forward so she'd walk faster.

"Ain't she a beauty, lads?" Borrys chuckled back at his comrades, caressing Robyn's cheek unwelcomingly, to which the girl scowled with disgust. She kept her gaze forward and tried to breathe through her mouth so as to avoid smelling the men's awful breaths.

"Could I keep 'er?" asked the man with the earrings as he approached them and tried to catch a sniff of Robyn's hair. "It gets rather lonely at night…"

"Sorry, lads. She belongs to the cap'n," Borrys said, to which the men began to whine in protest and spat at the girl's boots.

Robyn had only seen about five women since she was dragged into the camp and three of them were prisoners. The other two were mercenaries, she could tell from the red leather on both their outfits; one wore it on her boots and belt, and the other wore it on her vest.

Suddenly, however, Robyn's attention shifted.

A towering figure was walking towards them… And she noticed it was no human at all, this due to his significantly larger stature and olive green skin. And when she saw the two sharp fangs sticking up from his jaw, her tearful eyes widened.

Is that a…?

It was the very first orc she had ever laid eyes on. He stood at about six and a half feet tall and had no hair on his head, but had a long black beard on the tip of his chin tied into a neat braid. His ears were pointy and twice the size of a human ear, and his hands were so massive he could've probably wrapped them around a child's head. He was dragging an entire deer by its two hind legs and was carrying no weapon, giving Robyn the impression that he had hunted the deer with his bare hands. The only red leather he wore was in his trousers. His torso remained uncovered, and he had three long scars the size of Robyn's arm running diagonally across his bare green chest.

"Where's your axe?" Borrys asked the orc.

"Didn't need one."

"You bloomin' tyke," Borrys said, a bit astounded. "They don't call you the Beast for nothin', I'll give you that."

Robyn and the orc looked at one another for a moment, a moment that terrified her, before Borrys dragged her further along the path.

They reached the very last tent in the camp, the only tent bearing the mark of the red scorpion, and Borrys shoved her inside so harshly that she fell to her knees with her hands still tied behind her.

Then Borrys bent down on one knee and began tying her feet together.

She tried to resist, but it was hopeless.

"Now listen 'ere, girl," he said. "You're to wait for the cap'n to return. For your sake, don't try to run... Don't try *anythin'* rash... You don't know Malekai like I do. Trust me," he snickered like a madman. "You don't wanna cross him..."

Robyn said nothing. She simply sat there, feeling the wet earth soaking through her ragged pants. And then the red mercenary smirked at her lack of response, blew a sticky kiss in the air at her, and headed out of the tent and towards a nearby fire.

It was then that the knot in Robyn's throat returned...

She was terrified, but she wouldn't dare show Borrys...

She began breathing heavily and grunting as the tears continued to flow out of her red angry eyes. There was even a sob, which was quite rare of her. But she couldn't help it. The mere image of Nyx flapping for his life as Borrys stabbed him mercilessly was aching at her gut.

Stupid, Robyn, she repeated to herself. *Stupid, stupid, stupid...*

The guilt was unbearable. She should have shot him, and she knew it. If she had, perhaps Nyx would still be alive. She tried hard to fight the negative thoughts that were haunting her consciousness, for there was hardly any time to be morose.

For now, the nearby Wyrmwood army had gained her some time...

Time, which she would use sensibly to plan her escape...

* * *

Sir Darryk Clark of Roquefort found himself in King Rowan's assembly room, sitting along the grand rectangular table, surrounded by faces he had never seen before who were all mumbling amongst themselves. He heard '*Roquefort*' being whispered repeatedly, as well as his family name, and the anticipation of it all was causing him to sweat under the black curls above his brow.

The heavy door opened suddenly...

Some of the nobles in the room glanced over and prepared to stand, but then slouched back into their chairs when they realized it wasn't the king that walked in.

Lady Brunylda Clark, Treasurer of Val Havyn, gave no one the courtesy of a smile. Hardly anyone ever gave *her* that courtesy, and she figured decades ago that she had no reason to give it back. There was only one pair of eyes acknowledging her and it caught her off guard.

Sir Darryk Clark sat there between the representative of the Merchants' Guild and an empty chair. She was the only familiar name in the room to him, even though he hardly knew the woman. And though he found her demeanor far from amiable, he couldn't help but cling to her like a desperate child amidst a crowd of strangers.

Lady Brunylda stared back at him for a moment.

He looks lost, the poor fool, she thought to herself.

Feeling a shred of pity, she took the empty seat next to him.

He gave her a coy smile, hoping to ease the tension. But she replied with a mere head nod, not even a friendly one, the kind of nod that someone would give to a guard for doing their duty.

On the table was a grand map with miniature wooden figurines of ships and soldiers set in place along the southern coasts, plotting the king's plan of attack. Sir Darryk was in his mid-twenties, experienced enough in minor combat, but not quite poised for a war. Examining the map, he realized the amount of preparation it took for a potential war was far greater than the customary tactics he would use in battle.

The young knight's hands were sweaty and unsettled, a feeling all too unusual to him.

He was unaware of the reason the king had requested his presence in the assembly room. Not only was he the only outsider in the room, he was also the youngest and possibly the most inexperienced in political affairs. And yet the king had asked specifically that he be invited to the assembly room.

He wiped his moist hands with his handkerchief, which was a rich yellow, the color of buttermilk. The ships on the southern end of the map, bearing the emblem of Roquefort, were tinted in the very same color. Even the emblem of the elk was there, a bright red head shining amidst all that yellow. Suddenly, he had to dry his hands again…

Lady Brunylda Clark noticed his concern and couldn't help but smirk.

Poor fool… Came to Val Havyn for a bride and now he'll have to fetch her too…

Suddenly the doors swung open again.

King Rowan's presence filled the room like a lit candle in a darkened cellar. Sir Hugo Symmond was by his king's side, holding a rolled brown parchment in his hands. The king looked weary, that much was certain, but the ill look he had just an hour prior had vanished, replaced with the same red blush on his cheeks that he had whenever he shouted angrily, which was quite often indeed.

The entire room rose to their feet out of respect.

"Sit down, all of you," the king said, quite obvious that his patience was short that day. "I thank you all for gathering on such short notice."

Sir Darryk Clark removed his hand from the table, trying his best to appear casual, as if he hadn't just been mildly distressed about the king's plan of action.

"Your majesty," the Merchants' Guild's representative bowed in his chair. "You bless us with your presence! I assure you I've sent word to all of my contacts for support w-"

"Shut your mouth and listen," the king said abruptly. He had always been the kind of man to speak candidly and with a brusque honesty, much at the expense of others' sentiments. And this day was no exception. "I can't disclose too much, because quite frankly I don't *know* very much. The facts are these... I've received word from Roquefort. There might still be hope for your future queen, but we must act *now*. The enemy has been spotted... We don't know the fuckers' names, only the direction in which they are sailing. I'll need each one of you to send ravens to your connections in Roquefort and any neighboring city in the south... Inform them that my royal troop marches today, and we are to make sail for the Noorgard Islands at once upon our arrival."

Lady Brunylda Clark felt her chest pounding all of a sudden.

She wanted to speak out. She *needed* to.

But treason is treason. And she had loaned the king's silver to a man the king himself had disbarred from his court... Men were known to be hanged for much less...

"Once we get to the Isles, we will devise a plan of att-"

"Drahkmere..." the Lady blurted out loud.

Every pair of eyes in the room turned to her. She was the only woman present and though she was accustomed to it, she felt as if it was the first day all over again.

There was something burning in her chest. Something like panic.

It was foreign to her. Bitter. She loathed it.

Not only would she have to lie to the king, but she would have to make it sound convincing to a hoard of men... And she knew how challenging that could be. She had to fight back the disgust in her expression.

"What was that?" King Rowan asked.

"They are making sail for Drahkmere," she corrected him.

The king glanced briefly at the letter in his hands.

"This message from Roquefort's harbourmaster says the Noorgard Islands..."

"I know what it says," she replied. "But *I'm* telling you it's a diversion... The enemy sails for Drahkmere as we speak."

There were doubtful murmurs in the room...

Then again, there almost *always* was whenever the Lady spoke.

"Where did you come up with a thing like that?" the king asked.

She fought back the knot in her throat.

Not now, she told herself. *Don't you dare shrivel now.*

She cleared her throat. "John Huxley... The farmer that captured Hudson Blackwood... He was in the palace grounds when the attack took place. He heard them say they were taking the princess to Drahkmere..."

The king walked towards her, his steps heavy and stern and slightly menacing.

"You withheld information from me…?"

The knot in her throat returned. She was done for, and she knew it.

But she breathed, tried her best to appear relaxed…

She would be damned if she allowed herself to be seen as the villain.

She had allowed it *too* many times before…

"With respect, your grace… your condition over the last few days did not suggest you would be willing to hear anything a *farmer* had to say…"

"You couldn't possibly know this for a fact," the council member of the Merchants' Guild accused her, just as he almost always did in the king's presence.

"I know this from *experience*," she corrected him, and then turned back towards the king. "Had I gone to you days ago and told you a *farmer* overheard something, you wouldn't have given him the time of day and you know it, your majesty… So I took matters into my own hands and hired a scouting party to seek these men out and find some form of proof, in case the farmer *was* telling the truth. Now we *have* proof. What else is there to argue about?"

"Who…?" the king asked suddenly.

"Pardon me, your majesty?"

"These scouts that you hired. *Who* were they?"

She hesitated. The king's stare was nearly frightening.

Her lips opened, ready to say the first thing that crawled into her mind.

"Common mercenaries, your majesty," an unexpected voice interrupted. Sir Darryk Clark rose suddenly to his feet. "If there's anything we've learned in Roquefort, it's that often the best way to face an enemy is by consulting with *their* enemy. And the Rogue Brotherhood has plenty of them."

The king stood in silence, his glare firm but slightly less angry.

"Have you heard back from these scouts?" he asked.

"Not yet," the Lady said. "But they are traveling to Drahkmere as we speak…"

"Oh please," one of the noble advisors scoffed, trying desperately to undermine the Lady. "Drahkmere has been abandoned for decades. You can't possib-"

"Which makes it the perfect place for a foreign threat to make a lair of, does it not?" the Lady interrupted, fighting to keep her stance on the matter.

The king gave a subtle nod, slowly falling for her words.

"You expect us to believe these scouts were willing to risk their lives for this?" the Merchants' representative asked. "Drahkmere may be abandoned but it is Qamrothian territory. Our people aren't welcome there, everyone knows that."

The Lady glanced at nearly every pair of eyes in the room…

So clever, you all think you are… But you're sheep. All of you.

"Let's just say they had a conflict of interest in this matter," she said.

There were a few murmurs, but much quieter this time. The king himself even appeared convinced. And that was all she needed. "Where is this farmer?" his majesty asked.

The Lady lowered her head. After many decades of being a diplomat, she was an expert in deceit. Never did she dream, however, that she would be using those skills against her own king. And at this point, it was useless *not* to continue.

"He died of his wounds days ago," she said.

The king nodded. One simple nod, and then turned and headed for his chair again.

"Very well," he said. "We will make sail for Drahkmere."

The chattering continued. Lady Brunylda Clark felt the tension leave her shoulders instantly. She felt lighter than air. She glanced at Sir Darryk briefly, gave him a much friendlier nod this time, before they both took their seats together.

Maybe he's not entirely useless after all, she pondered.

"Your majesty, with respect, how can we be sure this scouting party can be trus-"

"Gentlemen, if *any* one of you interrupts me again, I'll have you removed from my council. Is that clear?"

The silence returned. This time, it stayed for a while as the king spoke.

"Now... I will be appointing a Lord Regent while I'm gone. Someone to speak in my name while I'm away and look after our city."

Lady Brunylda Clark felt her heart begin to race...

While the king was away before, princess Magdalena had been left in charge...

In the Lady's opinion, the princess had behaved more like a child than a true ruler. With the princess gone, the list of people that could possibly rule in the king's name was rather extensive. The Lady was confident, however, that she was somewhere near the top of it...

"The Clarks have served me for many decades," the king said. "And they have proven their loyalty to the crown time and time again."

Her brow grew sweaty... This was it, she realized...

She heard her family name come out of the king's mouth...

All there was left to do was sign the contract...

"Therefore," the king went on. "After careful consideration, I've decided to appoint the title of Lord Regent... to none other than Sir Darryk Clark of Roquefort, himself."

The silence was far greater this time.

The Lady felt her heart slow and sink deeply.

Him?! You would trust this bloody child over me?!

Sir Hugo Symmond unrolled the parchment over the table. It was signed by the king himself, and a drop of fresh blood bore his crest at the bottom of the page.

"Let's cut formalities for a moment, Darryk," King Rowan spoke across the table. "Your father has always been a trusted friend of mine… He has proven himself to be a faithful and reliable ally, and has held his title of Lord of Roquefort for over 30 years, ruling the city in my name."

Sir Darryk struggled to keep his attention on the king's words as he realized every pair of eyes in the room had turned to him all at once.

"The question here, young sir, is do you take after your father?" the king made a pause before going on, trying hard to figure the young knight out. "I can't leave just *anyone* to rule the city during my absence. It has to be someone worthy of my trust."

The feeling in the Lady's chest grew from sorrow to rage within seconds.

"I trust your father," the king continued. "And the man may be rubbish at holding his drink but his judge of character, I trust completely… And may I say, he sure happens to think the sun shines out of your arse, lad."

There were chuckles among the nobles. And it only made Sir Darryk more perturbed.

"I'd say it's about time to put it all to the test, don't you? Sir Darryk Clark of Roquefort… can I rely on you to rule Val Havyn in my absence?"

Lady Brunylda could no longer resist. She *had* to speak out.

"Pardon me, your majesty," she cleared her throat. "With respect, surely you must consider that a city like Val Havyn requires someone with a bit more… *experience* governing it?"

"Nonsense," the king scoffed. "I can't think of *anyone* more experienced than Sir Darryk."

The words stung her… *Broke* her, even…

She felt like an unwanted rusty blade in a well-stocked armory…

Decades of loyal service, she pondered. *And for what…? For shit, that's what.*

Suddenly, she felt a strong crave for a fresh bottle of Roquefort liqueur.

"What say you, Sir Darryk?" the king asked.

The sensation in the young knight's chest was a mixture of honor and fear. As the son of Lord Augustus Clark of Roquefort, he had known nobility and power all his life, but never the chance to practice it solely. He knew very little about the city of Val Havyn and even less of his own king. The one and only familiar face in the king's council of advisors was Lady Brunylda Clark's. And one familiar face among a city of strangers was not enough to give him the necessary self-assurance. But the privilege of it all overcame the fear. He refused to allow for the dishonor of his family name. And knowing very little of what it meant to rule a royal city, he took a bow before his king.

"I am your majesty's humble servant," he said. "I will serve you to the best of my ability and will see to the protection of Val Havyn until your safe return."

King Rowan nodded and smirked at the fortitude of his future son-in-law.

"Good, lad," he said. "Your kingdom depends on it…"

IX
Soldiers & Recruits

It was two hours past midday, and the forest air was growing warmer. The chirping of the birds was more melodic than John Huxley was accustomed to, as if they were harmonizing with each other from across the river, and every now and then a wild animal, often a fox or a hare, could be spotted among the shrubs. Even in the daylight, the greenery in the Woodlands was so vast and overgrown that it gave one the feeling of being inside of something, a mystic realm of some sort, rather than outdoors. Had John not been aware that he was surrounded by death, he would have considered slowing his pace to enjoy the scenery.

Hudson Blackwood was as stubborn as an old mule. He walked a few paces ahead, pretending to be more upset than he was, unwilling to pay John any more mind than was necessary. But John did not mind, he would take anything he could get. At least the thief had agreed to follow through with the voyage; that possibility had seemed a shot in the dark at first. In fact, it *would* have been had it not been for Syrena of Morganna.

She walked next to the farmer, unbound and free, and she could see him sweating through the corner of her eye. She also noticed how he would wince nearly every time she lifted her hand to remove her greasy hair from her face. But rather than be offended, she found it somewhat amusing; she felt intimidating, which was slightly better than feeling shunned.

As they walked along the river's edge, she would move back and forth between the two men, making casual conversation with them one at a time, like a courier fetching and delivering messages. It was almost comical, the way John and Hudson were avoiding each other, like two children forced to make peace yet silently objecting to it. Though Hudson appeared to be at odds with himself about the whole situation, the witch had hope that they would eventually warm up to one another. She wouldn't have taken the risk had her faith in unlikely friendships not been recently rejuvenated.

John was rather silent. And the more Syrena glanced at him, the more she pondered.

"You look unsettled," she decided to say.

"Sorry," he cleared his throat. "I-I've never actually met a witch before."

"You met me days ago," she said.

"Yes… Quite so, but… I must admit I had my doubts."

"About me?"

"About your, um… gift."

She glanced at him with a raised brow. "*Gift?*"

"Well, you know what I mean," he chuckled nervously. "W-Which reminds me… *Thank you*, miss. For saving my life back there."

"My name's Syrena," she smiled.

"Right. Syrena."

They walked in silence for a brief moment. They could see the black figure of the thief ahead of them, getting smaller, and so they picked up their pace.

"So how'd he do it?" John decided to ask her. "How'd he get the cuffs off you?"

"You're asking how a thief managed to pick a key out of someone's pocket?" she smirked at him.

John smiled back. "He's full of surprises, that one."

"Surprises?"

"Stealing from Sir Viktor Crowley to save his own skin? That, I can see. But stealing from him to save someone *else's* skin…?"

She glanced forward, at the thief strolling just yards away, picking berries out of shrubs when he came across any. It was quite a walk he had, she admitted. So suave, with that mild sway of his, like a sly cat on the prowl for trouble simply because he was confident he could handle it.

"That man freed me from my cell in Val Havyn," she said. "I didn't even have to ask him, he just… *did* it. Because I was there. Because I was trapped just like him. He could have left me there. He would have avoided the guards, even. But he stayed by my side until I had my freedom and I owe that to him."

"He needed a way out, that's all," John said doubtfully.

She gave him a glance, the smile fading away quickly. "Doesn't explain why he refused to leave *you* behind."

John slowed his pace involuntarily. "What…?"

"Back there with the nymphs… He was the one who asked me to save you."

John's lips moved, but no words would come out. His brows raised and lowered over and over again, as he tried to wrap his mind around it.

He said he would kill me someday… Instead, he saves my life?

"You're lying," he said.

"Believe what you want," she remarked. "Won't make it untrue."

And so she picked up her pace, leaving John behind to ponder.

He was somewhat staggered, thinking about the thief's words that morning.

Everyone's looking after only one skin and that's their own, he had said.

And yet he'd already proven himself wrong. More than once, in fact.

John quickened his pace again. It wasn't exactly hope he was starting to feel in his chest. Optimism, perhaps… With a mix of guilt, certainly.

You can do this, John… Just try not to draw your sword at him again…

* * *

It may have been the hunger, but the stew was damn near perfect.

The temperature was just right, the pork was tender and savory, the potatoes were soft and exquisitely seasoned. Jossiah Biggs was nearly done with his bowl by the time they were serving Cedric, and he considered asking for a second one. The cook, a slow-moving elderly man with a permanent frown, offered Viktor Crowley a bowl but the man refused, his mind occupied elsewhere.

The Wyrmwood camp was a great deal more diverse than Viktor was expecting...

Men and women, soldiers and raiders, humans and elves and gnomes; all of them were sitting side by side sharing stories and meals and laughter as if it were as normal as breathing. There were no orcs in the camp, which Percyval blamed on the orcs' lack of trust towards humans, not that anyone could blame them.

Still, Viktor was sure he'd never seen so many non-humans in the same place all at once. Elves made up at least a third of the camp, if not more, and there were at least a dozen gnomes roaming about cautiously so as to not be trampled by drunken lumbering soldiers.

Gnomes may as well have been human in Viktor's eyes. They had plenty enough in common, if it weren't for their much shorter stature. Most of them had heads and torsos the size of the average human, only their limbs were much shorter and pudgier. The gnomes in the camp, even the younger looking ones, appeared tough and seasoned and riddled with scars. Viktor knew they lived only about half as long as humans, but he underestimated just how strong and capable they could be in their prime.

Elves had less in common with humans, their skin varying in shades of blue, from a dark ocean blue to a pale hue the color of the sky. Their body shape was perhaps their only humanlike quality, except they were always on the more slender side and had longer than average limbs that gave them the advantage when it came to climbing. Their ears were always sharp and long like the tip of a spear, even longer than an orc's, which is why people often called them 'rabbits', a term that elves despised.

Viktor's eyes were fixed on one particular elf... Sitting high above a cypress tree, much higher than Viktor himself would have been comfortable with, was the beautiful pale elf he'd unintentionally caught bathing in the Spindle River. The elf was sitting calmly, taking bites out of an apple, legs dangling and back resting against the tree's trunk, keeping watch so as to allow the recruits in the camp to eat and drink peacefully.

Brilliant, Viktor thought. *Expert climbers make for expert watchmen... Or watchwomen...*

Viktor's company stuck together like a pack of children in a crowd of strangers. As friendly as the Wyrmwood recruits may have been, the men preferred not to sit among them. Instead, there was an old cart filled with barrels of ale sitting in the middle of the camp. And there they leaned, sat, climbed on top, anything to avoid mingling with the odd assortment of recruits.

Cedric appeared the most alarmed of them all. Alarmed, yet fascinated.

"This is a *Wyrmwood* camp?" the naïve kid asked, his jaw dropping involuntarily. "It's…"

"Strange? Unfamiliar?" Thaddeus suggested.

"Sickening?" Jossiah scoffed.

"…remarkable," said Cedric.

"Remarkably sickening."

Viktor, realizing he had been gawking for what must have been minutes, turned his gaze away from the elf in the tree. "Gentlemen, I'm going to have a word with the knight commander."

"I'll come," Jossiah leapt to his feet.

"I would prefer to speak with him alone, old boy."

"Viktor," Jossiah lowered his voice, his face hardening. "You can't be serious… This place is *mad*."

"Mad?" Viktor raised a brow. "Because it's a Halghardian troop?"

"*Because* it's…" Jossiah paused as an elf and two gnomes casually walked past them. "Because it's *crawling* with freaks," the man finished with a whisper.

"There are more humans here than anything else, old dog," Viktor said to him. "If you feel *that* threatened, then… I don't know. Try making a bloody *friend* for once, perhaps?"

With that, the golden knight walked away, leaving Jossiah Biggs to frown all on his own.

On his way to the knight commander's tent, Viktor's eyes wandered about at the abundance of life. Elven recruits drank and huddled around a boiling cauldron next to human raiders, rambling and laughing at one another in the same way a group of drunken peasants would do in a tavern in Val Havyn. It baffled him and brought an odd warmth to his chest all at once.

He entered the knight commander's tent, which was old and tattered, not at all a tent fit for nobility. And instantly, he felt the discomfort overtake him… Not only was it quiet inside the tent, it was astoundingly cold, as if he had stepped foot inside of a frosty wet cave.

There were three figures inside…

Sir Percyval Garroway sat in an old wooden chair, leaning in attentively.

A sickly-looking grey-haired woman sat in front of him, lost in a trance, eyes pale and ghostlike and staring down at nothing.

And the last figure was another man in armor, tall and brown-skinned, possibly also a knight. He stood behind Percyval, guarding his back as they both listened closely to the old woman's feeble whispers.

"How many?" Percyval asked, a bit impatiently.

The woman's voice was gentle and frail, and her neck was swaying back and forth as if she was sitting at the top of a hill, gazing down at a landscape.

"Thousands," she said, her wrinkled lips dry and purple. "Four. Maybe five."

"*Five* thousand?" Percyval felt his heart speed up. "That can't be."

"Maybe he sent word to the north for reinforcements?" the other knight suggested.

"Not possible," Sir Percyval replied. "The north is neutral. Bunch of cowards just waiting for the storm to pass. Maybe they're men from overseas?"

"No…" the old woman spoke again. "Peasants. Common men."

"Yes…?"

"And children…"

"*Children*?!"

The other knight placed a hand on Percyval's shoulder, which the man shrugged away as he leapt to his feet. "He's a madman!" he growled. "A heathen! A heartless bastard!"

Suddenly the old woman began to blink rapidly. The color returned to her eyes and her movement was no longer as gentle. "I lost him," she said with a sigh, and this time her voice was more natural and much less deathlike. "He must've gone too far…"

"That's all right, Zahrra. Have a rest," Percyval said as he rubbed his temples and sighed. When he began to pace, he noticed Viktor standing by the entrance to his tent. "Sir Crowley… I didn't hear you come in."

"I didn't want to interrupt," Viktor said, still somewhat uncomfortable.

"You didn't," Percyval slouched into his actual knight commander's seat, not that it was any less old and tattered than the wooden chair, just more comfortable. "Sir Viktor Crowley I would like you to meet my second-in-command, Sir Antonn Guilara the Tenacious… Antonn, my friend, meet the Golden Eagle of Vallenghard himself."

Sir Antonn gave Viktor a head nod and a handshake, but no smile. He was of average height, strong and broad-shouldered, with skin brown as mahogany, thick black hair that reached his back, and a beard that was graying at the chin. "I've heard about you," he told Viktor. "I thought you'd be taller."

"Sir Antonn the Tenacious, eh?" Viktor remarked, having heard a thing or two about the man.

"Well," Percyval said with a shrug. "It didn't feel proper to call him Sir Antonn the Stubborn."

"Piss off," Sir Antonn grunted.

Viktor was not insulted by the knight's lack of reverence; in fact he had grown tired of being worshipped, if he was being honest. And their more casual demeanor he had expected as much, for this was not Vallenghard, nor was it even Halghard for that matter. In the Woodlands, every man and woman was more or less equal… Equal in name, equal in power, and equally disposable.

"And this… this is Zahrra," Percyval aimed a palm at the old woman. "One of our new recruits."

"Another noble," she said, eyeing Viktor up and down.

Viktor nodded at her and made his best attempt at a smile.

"Ahh," she said, squinting intensely as she fixed her gaze on his worried blue eyes. "Though not as noble anymore, it seems…"

Viktor's heart began to race as he felt a cold pressure in his chest. He cleared his throat loudly and uncomfortably. "Sir Percyval, may I have a word with you in private?"

"I'm afraid I can't allow that," the man replied. "The sight can hit Zahrra at any moment. I need her by my side at all times, should the enemy get any funny ideas."

"The… *sight?*" Viktor asked, raising a brow.

"Well, in case you haven't noticed, she's a witch," Percyval chuckled at him. "Not to worry, she's on our side. She's already proven herself worthy. Hell, we'd be dead in a ditch right now if it weren't for her."

Sir Antonn dragged the wooden chair and placed it across from Percyval's desk.

Viktor took a seat. "I'm not sure I quite understand," he stammered, then turned to the old woman directly. "You can… *see* things?"

"Only brief glances," she said, sweating and resting her back against her seat as if she had just walked a hundred miles. "Thoughts, conversations, dreams, that sort of thing."

Fascinating, Viktor thought. And then he took a risk.

"We lost a few members of our company a night ago," he said. "Is there any way you can figure out if they're alive?"

Zahrra smirked. "It doesn't work that way, I'm afraid."

Of course it doesn't… Why should anything ever work in our favor for once?

"I need a link of some sort," she explained. "A strand of hair, a fingernail, something… Otherwise, I've no way to tell a man from a dog, really."

Viktor hesitated for a moment. Then he asked, "And what's the link to the enemy?"

Zahrra smiled, revealing her less than pleasant teeth. She held out an arm, and within her ragged grey sleeve she held a small jar. It was full of a light brown fluid, and floating inside of it was a finger…

Viktor stammered, sweat building up in his face and vomit rising up his throat. "By the gods…"

"Leave her be, Sir Crowley," Percyval said. "She needs rest. And, with respect, we've a war to think of. Can't waste good talent on searching for runaways."

"They're not runaways," Viktor remarked.

The old woman set the jar down on the floor. She then sighed and closed her eyes, as if she was getting ready to sleep while sitting. Viktor looked away. He couldn't bear to look at her eerie figure any longer.

"F-Forgive me for being blunt, Sir Percyval, but…" he stammered, then lowered his voice to a thick whisper. "Is an expedition like yours... *acceptable* in Halghard?"

Sir Percyval grinned. He was known to be rather direct. Sarcastic sometimes, even. But he appeared more a friend than an enemy. And Viktor knew too well from experience the differences in conducts between the two.

"As I said, Sir," Percyval leaned in and crossed his dark callused hands over the table. "We are in the midst of war. And I believe we both know that times of war are desperate. Often, desperation leads us to question ourselves. Question our decisions, our ancestors' decisions, even our very *nature*."

Viktor kept his stare. He wasn't intimidated by the man, nor did he feel Percyval was *trying* to intimidate him. And still, he was feeling more out of place by the second.

"Let me ask you something, Sir Crowley, what do you think makes something *acceptable*?" Percyval asked. "What does the word even mean? Looking back, it's rather remarkable what has been considered *acceptable* throughout our history... Did you know dismembering a man in broad daylight was acceptable three hundred years ago? *Now*, at least, they've the decency to do it behind closed doors and even *then* it's nauseating to think of... *Five* hundred years ago, it was acceptable for children to marry. Hell, at one point, even *kilts* were considered acceptable."

Sir Antonn Guilara cleared his throat. "They still are in Ahari, Sir."

"Are they really?" Percyval raised an amused brow. "Fucking Aharians. We ought to learn a thing or two from them, y'know."

Viktor couldn't help but smirk.

"Regardless, Sir Crowley, my concern is not what is *acceptable*... My concern is looking after the good of Halghard. If we don't give it all we've got, we'll lose her to a bloody tyrant. A *pig*, who is more concerned about the good of the wealthy than of the majority. The problem is, however, we don't have the numbers... By the order of King Alistair Garroway of Wyrmwood, rightful heir to the throne, we are scouting the Woodlands for recruits. Any soldier fit for battle, human or not, we will take, the arrangement being that if and when we win the war, they are promised proper accommodation. Most didn't hesitate to join. The meals and lodging alone attracts them, I'd say."

"Wait... Are you saying you've offered them... *land?*" Viktor's eyes widened.

Sir Percyval grinned and nodded. "The realms of men are like spider webs, Sir Crowley. Connections are everywhere and rumors spread faster than the shingles. In here, there *are* no rules. One will fight for the highest bidder. Land is all we've got to offer, really. Luckily, in here, that makes *us* the highest bidder."

"And you're sure you've the land to give them?"

"This is war, Sir Crowley... Death is an unfortunate consequence that comes with it."

Viktor hesitated at first. Then he took a deep breath and said, "You *do* understand what I'm trying to point out here, right…?"

Sir Percyval's demeanor was calm but he appeared somewhat insulted.

"You think I'm a madman?" he asked.

"I did not say that," Viktor remarked. "Quite the opposite, in fact, I think Wyrmwood fights for a good cause. And y-"

"I didn't ask what you thought about our cause. I asked if you think I'm a madman."

Viktor waited a moment… Then another…

Both Sir Percyval and Sir Antonn looked about ready to throw him out. Not only out of the tent, but out of the whole camp. And so Viktor had to choose his words quite carefully.

"I believe we live in an unfair world," he decided to say. "I believe our laws are so far out of our control, it's often degrading. But I *also* believe an individual should be judged by their actions… Rather than by the way he or she looks."

"Mmm," Percyval grinned. "And can you honestly look me in the eye and tell me you've lived every day of your life under these beliefs?"

Viktor hesitated… He hadn't, and he knew it…

But he decided to answer the man with honesty.

"I've done many regrettable things in my life, Sir Percyval, more than I care to admit," Viktor said. "I've seen men hanged for stealing a loaf of bread for their starving families. I've seen women burned for using exotic herbs to try and find cures for illnesses. I've *killed* men simply because they bore a different banner than mine… I've done wretched things, *unspeakable* things, because of one thing… Because it had to be done. But I have *never* broken the laws of our kingdom. Even *talking* about breaking our king's laws can get a man killed, and we both know that. And what *you're* talking about is changing a law that has existed for 250 years. You don't seriously think it will go by unnoticed?"

Percyval allowed a moment of silence as he took Viktor's words in.

"That is a matter we will deal with when the time comes," was all he said.

Viktor's heart was racing, and it only got worse when he realized the witch Zahrra had been sitting there listening the entire time. At least, he assumed she could hear him. He couldn't really tell with the way she was sitting there in that sleeplike trance.

"Pardon me if I've offended you, Sir," said Viktor. "Do believe me when I say my heart is in the right place."

"I would expect no different from the Golden Eagle," Sir Percyval said, with an emphasis on the name. He cleared his throat. "Did you know," he went on, "There have recently been rumors, Sir, spreading all over our kingdom… They speak not only of the invasion and the missing princess, but also of your disbarment…"

Viktor moved not a single muscle. He kept his gaze firm and unmoving. He knew rumors in Gravenstone spread like wildfire, but this was more than impressive. And so, he swallowed back the angst and decided to deceive the man without actually lying to him.

"There were *also* rumors that it was Alistair Garroway, your brother, who killed King Frederic in his sleep," he said daringly. "Though what kind of man would I be to believe such rumors without any proof?"

Sir Percyval grinned again, finding Viktor's audacious response amusing. "I suppose that's true," he said. "But that's horse shit, all of it. My brother served King Frederic faithfully. After the queen and prince were killed by bandits, the king drank himself to death. Those are the *facts*. Anything else you've heard is a mere rumor spread by that bastard Balthazar Locke."

"And yet it's Balthazar that sits on the throne in Morganna, is he not?"

"Because he's got the wealth and the connections," Percyval said. "He says he deserves the throne by right, says the king would have *wanted* it that way. But firstly, the man's a damn fool. He'd rather make himself a boar made of gold to place in his common room than to feed the people of Halghard. And secondly, it was my *brother* the king chose to rule as his successor... But as I've mentioned before, humans have the tendency to act rashly and stupidly. There were plenty that chose to follow Locke, all of which were only interested in making more coin. But the truth remains, Sir Crowley. My brother Alistair is the rightful heir. He was the king's right hand knight and he served Halghard well for over two decades. He never wanted the throne, said he had no right to it. But neither does Balthazar Locke, for that matter, and that's *more* important. Now the war is reaching its climax, and we are at our last resorts. We need any and every able body we can spare on our side, if King Alistair is to bring peace and order once more to the kingdom of Halghard."

There was another silence. Viktor's expression could only be described as one of respect and admiration for the Garroways. "I wish nothing but the best for your troops and the future of Halghard, Sir Percyval."

"As I for you," Percyval gave him a nod, and after a pensive moment he asked, "Where exactly *is* your company headed to, anyhow...?"

That was the question, indeed.

The company, or what was *left* of it, sat outside among the Wyrmwood recruits patiently. It was either Drahkmere or back home, and they wouldn't know until their knight commander returned. Then, of course, there was the possibility of death along the way, regardless of the destination. And it made them all terribly uncomfortable.

The most uncomfortable pair of eyes, however, was Cedric's. His eyes would glance around almost unwillingly, as he was far too frightened to stare at any one person for too long at the risk of being threatened.

His eyes came to an abrupt halt, however, when they came across quite a peculiar pair.

It was the two mercenaries that had ambushed them by the Copperstone Bridge. The woman with the golden braids sat on a wooden stool sharpening her set of knives. She had several scars here and there, the most obvious one running down her right brow, though most of it was hidden beneath the layer of black paint around her eyes. The man that looked a lot like her sat nearby, polishing his sword.

Cedric stared at the woman, his wooden soup bowl now empty. He became lost in her scars, having never seen a woman with so many of them in his short life. She must have been a mercenary for years before the recruit, Cedric thought, given the facet of brusqueness she invoked. From the way she looked, she may have been in her thirties. But there was no way for Cedric to be sure of any of this.

Before becoming a squire he was a tavern server. He hadn't been in the company of many mercenaries in his life and he had not much to compare to, but he was quite sure that no one had intimidated him as much as she did, at least not this much without having even spoken a word.

Of course, when she finally *did* speak to him, she was as daunting as he had imagined.

"What're ye bleedin' lookin' at, then?" the woman asked abruptly.

Oh… shit. Cedric stammered, realizing he'd been caught gawking. *Say something. Anything!*

"Um… p-pardon me, miss."

"I asked ye a question, lad," the woman said. "Ye got a problem?"

"N-No. No problem at all. It's only…"

"It's only what?!"

She rose to her feet in defense and gripped one of her knives. Normally, she would encounter men who had but one of the two following objectives: stealing her gold or forcing himself upon her. Cedric, however, did not strike her as either type of man, and she wasn't sure how to feel towards it.

"I've just never seen, uh… well, I've never seen a mercenary like *you* before."

"Like *me*?" asked the woman. "And what's *that* mean, then?"

"It means he's never seen a mercenary with breasts," Thaddeus answered for him, standing next to Cedric like a loyal guardsman.

"Watch yer mouth there, tiny," the woman said menacingly. "Ye don't scare me just 'cause ye're a foot taller. Only makes ye that much slower."

They glared at each other for a moment, until a sophisticated voice interrupted.

"Relax there now, dear sister," the man next to her placed his hand on her shoulder. He strapped his sword back to his belt and began twisting the top off of a drinking sack. "The little squire's just in a bit of a shock, that's all," he said. "Why, he's probably never left the comfort of his village. He'll need some time to get used to new sights."

"He bett'r hurry on then," said the woman.

She turned to Cedric and, to her own surprise, she found his ignorance and discomfort a bit entertaining. She eyed him up and down, and the first thing she noticed was the small dagger strapped to his belt. The handle appeared to be made of ivory and it had a red stone embedded on it.

"Is that a toothpick, then?" she asked him mockingly.

"W-What's that?" Cedric replied nervously.

"That wee thing strapped to yer belt."

"Um, no, miss. It's a dagger. Given to me by me mum"

The golden-haired man held the drinking sack up to his lips and gulped on what Cedric thought to be water. It wasn't until a few drops ran down the man's chin that Cedric saw the red color. The man had never been one to like ale. Wine, however, he carried with him everywhere; often he would even refuse to fight without it. Cedric could somehow see all of this in the way the man licked his lips so as to not waste a single drop.

"That's awfully endearing," the man commented. "You wouldn't want to lose that in battle, little squire. I mean, what would mother think?"

"Actually, um… she died," Cedric said; this was followed by a moment of silence.

The golden-haired man had a sense of humor and he embraced it, but was not exactly known to be rude either. In fact, he would often pride himself in giving honor to his enemies just as much as his friends.

"It happened back when I was just a boy," Cedric added.

"My apologies, lad," the man said, his smile now gone. "I didn't know."

"That's quite all right," Cedric looked down at the dirt in embarrassment. He had not spoken about his mother since childhood. The last time he even said her name out loud was the same night he was found knocking on the doors of Jasper Nottley's tavern, begging for food and shelter. He often missed her, however, and his silence only led to a greater sorrow, which then resulted in his hostility towards anyone other than Mister Nottley, the man who had taken him in when no one else would, or Thaddeus Rexx, who was one out of two people he could genuinely call a friend.

"Hey," the woman beckoned Cedric's attention.

Cedric turned to her, to her lively green eyes.

"It's not the size or edge of the blade that matters, it's the way ye use it," she said. Her mouth then curved and she found herself smiling at Cedric, who was too surprised to smile back. "Anyway, it's beautiful."

"Thanks," Cedric replied nervously, noticing he was instinctively holding on to the dagger. He didn't grip it, however. He was simply holding it, as if it was giving him the courage to speak to the woman and her brother.

"I'm Gwyn," she said.

The nervous squire looked back up at her, a sudden glow on his face. "Cedric," he muttered.

Gwyn's brother then jumped to his feet and addressed them all, "And my name is Daryan, gentlemen. A pleasure to make your acquaintance."

"A mercenary with manners," Thaddeus Rexx said, drinking from a wooden tankard full of ale. "There's a sight you don't see every day."

"Everyone must pay their dues one way or another. That's got nothing to do with one's manners, sir."

"I suppose," said the blacksmith. "The name's Thaddeus Rexx."

Cedric cleared his throat. With Thaddeus joining into the conversation, he managed to build up the courage to continue. "So you all serve King Alistair, then?" he asked.

"We don't serve anyone," Gwyn replied. "We're fightin' for the pay 'n' the land."

"Aye," Daryan said. "My sister Gwyndolyn and I w-"

"*Gwyn!*"

Daryan rolled his eyes and continued, "We were promised a share of land in the city of Morganna."

"Once King Alistair sacks it, that is," Gwyn added.

"All in exchange for our services and the services of our merry little clan of raiders. We figured a home in the city was better than rummaging all around the Woodlands for stable land."

"How many of you are there?" Thaddeus asked.

"At the moment? Two," Daryan said. "We had more before we decided to join forces with Wyrmwood."

"You both work alone then?"

"Bett'r than followin' an arseling with an unquenched thirst for power," Gwyn said as she continued to sharpen her knives.

"*Unquenched*, eh?" Daryan grinned. "Fancier word than *you're* used to, dear sister."

"Piss off."

"Anyhow, we were affiliated with a clan of bandits a few months back," Daryan said, this time to the company. "Unfortunately, the clan was led by a rather immoral man who was more concerned for his own well-being than those of his comrades. Ultimately, we decided to part ways due to our differences."

"Fuck that crazy old sack," Gwyn mumbled angrily.

"Manners, dear sister…"

"*Fuck* manners. He was a crazy old sack. He 'n' that bloody monkey of his."

Cedric couldn't help but smile and Gwyn couldn't help but notice it. She didn't know whether it was empathy or pity she felt towards the young squire. But one thing she was sure of is the kid did not belong there, regardless of how much he wished to.

Then there was a scoff. It came from the back of the cart that Cedric and Thaddeus were leaning against. The scoff caught the attention of both Gwyn and Daryan.

"Who's the mute, then?" Gwyn asked.

"That there's Wyll," Thaddeus answered for him.

"Ahh. And who cut his tongue out?"

"Piss off," Wyll muttered sourly, to which Gwyn wasn't sure whether to react angrily or shrug off. Wyll seemed to be lost in his thoughts, or rather his mind was elsewhere and not in the conversation.

"Oh look, he talks," Daryan mocked him.

"Leave him," Thaddeus said.

"Why so somber back there, lad?" Daryan went on. "Too good for a conversation with a couple of mercenaries?"

"I said piss off!" Wyll shouted, his voice then lowering to a whisper. "Bunch o' freaks."

"What was that, then?" Gwyn stood up suddenly. "Didn't hear ye. Say it to me ear, yes?"

"Hey!" Jossiah Biggs suddenly approached them, after having been gawking around the camp for several minutes. "Have we got a problem here?"

"No problem," Thaddeus said.

"Littl' shit back there thinks he's almighty," Gwyn snapped. "Come again, lad. What'd ye call us?"

"You're *freaks*, all of you!" Wyll shouted angrily at them.

"Hey! Enough! Sit your little arse down, lad!" Jossiah snapped.

Wyll obeyed, though stubbornly so.

"And *you!*" Jossiah turned to the two raiders. "Why don't you both go and sit among your rabbit friends and leave *us* the hells alone."

"Pardon me," Daryan said grimly. "What did you just call them...?"

"Oh piss off, you. You don't scare me for a second," Jossiah spat. "I've killed men *twice* your size."

"I don't doubt you have, sir," Daryan approached him. "But have you ever crossed blades with one of our elven friends?"

"I'm a knight of the kingdom of Vallenghard!" Jossiah snarled. "I wouldn't stain my sword with elf blood. Filthy little bastards... The *only* thing worse than a greenskin is a bleedin' rabbit. They're *crooks*, all of them! All they wanna do is either kill you or steal something from you."

"Allow me to understand, Sir..."

"Jossiah."

"*Jossiah,*" Daryan began. "It is your belief that our forefathers were unmistaken in their principles, that humans are superior, and that segregation of the species is the answer to our conflicts...?"

"You're *damn* right. And I will *not* be questioned by a bl-"

"So you believe that we should segregate folks to this land of death and despair… and then you're *surprised* when they raid and rob and do what they must in order to survive in a world where *all* of the wealth and power exists in a land *forbidden* to them…?"

Jossiah opened his lips, but no proper answer would come out.

His face twisted and turned with confusion, before he grunted and walked away.

"I figured so," Daryan sat back down.

An uncomfortable silence lingered in the air, filled only with distant chattering and laughs among the soldiers and recruits.

"Typical, brother," Gwyn scoffed abruptly. "Usin' words to get rid of a man 'nstead of yer blade."

Daryan grinned at her and proceeded to drink from his winesack again.

Suddenly there was a thud nearby.

The androgynous elf from the trees hopped down, carrying with them a long straight wooden stick about as tall as a person. The elf had silver hair that was combed neatly away from their pale and perfectly symmetrical face, and a strand of it was dyed purple right above the right ear.

Cedric, Thaddeus Rexx, and Wyll Davenport all gawked as the elf walked by, too close for Wyll's comfort. Cedric wiped the sweat on his brow with his sleeve nervously, as he made eye contact with the mysterious elf, who was dressed in a grey hunting outfit except without a single weapon strapped to it.

"Amazing, don't you think?" Daryan asked, and then the three men stopped staring and turned around. "Wonderful, majestic creatures, really… It's an honor to even meet *one* of them, let alone forty of them."

"King Alistair really has gone soft," Wyll scoffed. "Who in their right mind would recruit freaks?!"

"There he goes again with that word," Daryan shook his head grimly.

"Someone oughta teach *this* one some manners," Gwyn said, the hissing of her knife against the stone in her hands only adding to her threat. "He been spendin' a lot o' time with that Jossefus bloke?"

"*Jossiah.*"

"What'd *I* say?"

"Young Wyll," Daryan walked closer to him. "Allow me to relay a bit of unwarranted wisdom… One thing you must understand when you do what *we* do… Is that when you are at war with an enemy who is much stronger and powerful than you, you will find yourself making unexpected allies…"

"I'd never ally with a freak," Wyll said coldly. "What *is* it anyway?"

Daryan tipped his head with confusion. "I believe it's quite obvious that Skye is an elf…"

"I know, but I mean… What *is* it? Is it a lad or a she-elf?"

By then, the shadowy elf was too far to overhear. From what the company had seen, it wasn't entirely clear what the elf's gender was. To begin with, there was not a single hair on the elf's pale face except for their thin brows and long curved eyelashes. There was a certain femininity there, no doubt, but the elf's jaw looked strong and firm and their voice, though rare, was on the slightly deeper side. Skye had been a mystery since day one, and made some of the soldiers uneasy at not knowing how to properly address the elf.

"You know... I don't actually know the answer to that question," Daryan said.

"Why don't ye go 'n' ask for yourself?" Gwyn muttered under her breath.

"Piss off," Wyll hissed.

"I always figured it rude to inquire about such things, but you seem *too* eager to find out," Daryan remarked.

"Let it go, Wyll," Thaddeus said.

Wyll scowled at the two raiders, before he spat on the earth and walked away towards the cook for another bowl of stew. "Whole world's gone down the pisser," he whispered angrily along the way.

Daryan found himself a bit baffled at the young man's reaction. "I've known men to want to steer away from beings that are not human," he said to Cedric and Thaddeus. "But I certainly can't say I've known one to hate them as much as you folk."

"Jossiah can be a bit hard on you, but y'get used to it," Cedric said. "And Wyll's brother was, um... Well, he was killed by tree nymphs... Just the other night."

"Shut it, Cedric," Thaddeus said to him, with a bit of harshness in his voice. "It ain't anyone's concern but his, lad."

Suddenly they felt the dirt beneath their feet shake...

Cedric's eyes went wide all of a sudden.

A large beast walked past them, holding an iron pot of soup so naturally as if it was light as a leaf. The creature was nearly seven feet tall and was covered in a thick black pelt; an upright being nonetheless, with sharp claws for hands and hooves on his feet. He was dressed in rags that covered only his chest, waist, and upper legs.

What caught everyone's attention, however, was the creature's head...

It was the head of a bull, with two massive curved horns rising out of his forehead.

A minotauro... the only minotauro in the camp... He walked onward towards his resting place, which was a pit of dirt he'd dug himself and bordered with rocks, with a small fire burning at the center.

"What in the name of the gods...?" Thaddeus said, baffled at the sight of the horned beast.

"Toro," Gwyn said with a smirk.

"A minotauro from the great plains of Belmoor," Daryan added. "Last of his clan, we believe he is. Quite a magnificent creature, don't you think?"

"You seem to fancy anything nonhuman," Thaddeus said to the man.

"I'm a man who adores diversity, Mister Rexx, *that* much I willingly confess," Daryan replied. "And *if* you paid them enough mind, sir, you would soon realize that they're just as '*human*' as you or me."

Cedric found himself gripping his dagger once again, his knee jumping up and down as it usually would when he became anxious.

Daryan threw him a friendly grin. "Perhaps to some of them, *we're* the monsters," he said solemnly. "And dare I say, sometimes I can't help but agree…"

* * *

From the moment her feet touched the earth, Princess Magdalena knew she was far from home. It felt nothing like the smooth brown powder-like sand on the shores of Vallenghard. The sand beneath her feet was a somber gray and gravelly to the point where she could feel the pebbles through her torn shoes.

From the shore she could see the abandoned city… Or what was left of it, rather…

Once the soldiers Hauzer and Jyor had unloaded them all, they began dragging the prisoners in formation like chained hounds. The walk took the better half of an hour, the prisoners marching with what little energy they had left, surrounded by armed men at every side. Magdalena no longer stood out among the prisoners. She was filthy and sweaty, her blonde hair was matted and greasy, and she reeked almost as badly as everyone else there. She had torn a piece of cloth from the hems of her dress several times to help clean someone's wound, as her dress was the closest thing to a clean garment they could obtain. Thomlin walked beside her, clutching her wrist for dear life as he observed their surroundings, his innocent brown face smeared with dirt, and his clothes itching all over.

"Y-Your majesty?"

She glanced down at him, noticing his eyes were just as swollen and wet as hers.

"I'm scared," he said.

She held his hand and gave it a gentle squeeze.

In chains, it was the closest they could get to an embrace.

When they reached the walls of the fortress, they came across a massive moat. The stench coming from beneath was insufferable; the air was hot and damp and smelled of a thousand rotting corpses. A loud horn echoed from high above the wall and a wooden bridge began to lower over the moat, slowly and carefully, old rusty chains rattling, on the verge of breaking. When the bridge was nearly flat, Magdalena and Thomlin could see the abundance of life inside the city walls. Soldiers and prisoners began making way for the incoming troop, some of them spitting and chuckling at the sight of the princess in chains.

As if the stench wasn't already bad from afar, it was even worse within the walls.

"Stay close," said the princess, and the boy remained pressed against her side as the commotion and life resonated all around them.

Metals were being melted down and forged into weapons and gear...

Hot steel was being struck, bricks were being carried, bows and arrows were being carved...

There must have been a thousand men there, over half of them with gauntlets and weapons in their hands and the rest in cuffs. Most of the towers and dwellings of the city were half destroyed, bricks missing from walls and roofs with gaping holes left behind after a battle many decades past.

Magdalena had seen many cities in her life.

Drahkmere, she felt, was no city... But merely the *ghost* of one...

And the soldiers and prisoners were like rats crawling on a carcass...

There was so much smoke everywhere that it was difficult to breathe. Many of the prisoners began coughing violently through the dust and fumes, Magdalena and Thomlin included. The soldiers, however, did not wince, as if they were used to it all... The stench, the smoke, the countless hordes of flies...

With her free hand pressed against her mouth, the princess looked up and noticed the only dwelling of the city that wasn't entirely wrecked, a grand citadel made of black stone, rising for what appeared to be a hundred feet into the sky. One of the towers was missing its head and another tower had holes on its walls as if they had been attacked by catapults a long time ago, but the rest of the citadel looked sturdy and upright.

"Come on, move it!" Jyor barked at the prisoners, tugging harshly at the chains.

But both the princess and the boy couldn't help but gawk at the citadel. There was a glow of light coming from the highest tower... Something was happening inside...

"That's gotta be it, right?" Thomlin said. "His lair...?"

Magdalena said nothing. She was far too busy plotting a strategy in her mind. *That's it, all right... I'll bet this lord is hiding somewhere up there...*

And he was, though he was doing anything but hiding.

* * *

Lord Yohan Baronkroft sat in his chamber in front of a boiling cauldron.

In the distance, he could hear it, the heels of a military man's boots tapping against the stone. The dark lord grinned, feeling his heart begin to speed up from the thrill. His guest had arrived...

Sergeant Havier Weston, fully armored but unarmed, walked through the halls of the ancient citadel heading for a chamber he had been directed towards. When he was about 5 feet from it, two gnomes hopped from their stools and opened the doors for him. This was not new for the sergeant, as all species shared the land of Qamroth. It was, however, peculiar to see gnomes on guard duty; that was unspeakable among his ranks.

He entered the empty chamber made of brick and stone, old and filthy and reeking of dampness. The gnomes closed the doors behind him, echoing so loud it startled him a bit. At the center of the room there stood a long rectangular table, large enough to sit two dozen people, with elegant goblets and plates, all of which were empty, and lit candlesticks lined up along the center.

At the very end of the table there was a parchment laid out with a vial of ink and a standing quill next to it. The Sergeant walked towards it, his curiosity rising, feeling as out of place as the graceful wooden table. He knew it *had* to have been stolen along with all of the tableware and candles. It was far too much elegance for a forgotten place like Drahkmere, even *within* the grand citadel.

And there it was… When he saw it, both of his brows raised with confusion…

His name was written at the very bottom of the parchment.

Next to it was a blank space, left there for his signature and a drop of his blood.

A contract, clearly. But a contract for what?

He leaned closer and began reading as fast as his eyes would allow it. His heart was racing, knowing very well he was in an unfamiliar place surrounded by questionable men and women. The only thing that brought him to Drahkmere was the name Baronkroft, for it was far too worthy of anyone's respect to ignore.

Suddenly, his eyes came to a halt…

His eyes came across the words "three thousand soldiers" and "at once" in the same sentence. It was a contract for troops. Though it was a number that the sergeant definitely *had*, it wasn't exactly a number he could afford. The doors opened again suddenly, and the sergeant straightened his back and stood firmly next to the chair with the parchment.

A large monster of a man walked in… A man wearing black leather pants, a brown vest over an exposed chest, and a mask lined with wolf teeth over his massive jaw. He stepped two feet inside and then one to the right, standing guard next to the torch hanging over the doorframe.

Then another man walked in, this one smaller yet strangely menacing, dressed in elegant attire and a long black coat lined with a dim silver pattern along the edges and sleeves.

"Sergeant Weston," Baronkroft said, taking slow steps with his hands crossed behind his waist. "What a pleasure to have you here, sir! Welcome to the once-magnificent city of Drahkmere… Do forgive the smell. You notice it less after a drink or two, I assure you."

The sergeant was confused. He was expecting a much older man.

The man that stood before him was not yet in his fifties.

"Pardon," he said. "I was expecting Lord *Baronkroft*...?"

"Do I not meet your expectations? You break my heart, sergeant," Baronkroft grinned as he took a seat in the chair adjacent to the chair with the contract. He then snatched one of the empty goblets from the table, held it out into the air, and gave a smooth loud whistle. This was then followed by footsteps coming from outside the chamber, echoing with the stillness of the place and the cackling of a small fire that burned in a corner chimney.

In walked a very short woman whose approaching shadow was quite deceiving. A gnome woman, about half as tall as anyone in the room, with a raggedy dress and smeared paint on her eyes and lips, approached the table holding a bottle in her hands. She reached the two men, popped the cork out and began pouring the wine on Baronkroft's goblet.

The sergeant's eyes moved from the gnome woman to the monstrous man standing guard.

"Oh, don't mind my dear friend Harrok," Baronkroft said, noticing the sergeant's discomfort. "I've never met a man more loyal than him. He won't hurt you, you have my word. Please! Sit, sit!"

The sergeant took a seat, quiet and disturbed. "I can see I must have misunderstood," he said.

"Why is that, sir?" the lord asked.

The gnome woman poured wine into a separate goblet and slid it closer to the sergeant, who took it doubtfully. "Well... If I'm honest, when I read *Baronkroft*, I was expecting Lord *Armund* Baronkroft," he explained.

"Lord Armund?" Baronkroft snickered. "No, no. That was my father, you see... No, he's been dead for... How long has it been now, my dear Harrok?"

"Seven years," the Butcher replied, a deep growl of a voice muffled behind the mask.

"Dead...?" the sergeant asked, slightly startled by the Butcher. "Are you sure?"

"Quite so," Baronkroft said. "I was the one who stabbed the dagger into his heart."

The sergeant's eyes grew wide with a sudden fright.

"Don't look so startled," Baronkroft took another sip from the wine. "It was an act of mercy, I assure you. He was struck with the plague, unfortunately. And a man thinks quite differently when blood is oozing from every hole in his body... He practically *begged* me to kill him."

The sergeant wasn't entirely convinced about the man's intentions, but seeing him sip from the wine gave him a feeling of slight relief. And so he took a sip of his own before saying, "My condolences. Now... If I may ask, what is the meaning of this here contract? I don't believe I agreed wi-"

"Tell me, sergeant, have you ever been to Kahrr?" the lord interrupted. His hostility was slowly becoming clearer, and Sergeant Weston realized he might've made a terrible mistake coming to this dark corner of Qamroth.

Distraught and thrown aback, the sergeant stammered, "N-No, I don't believe I have. Anyhow, about the contract, si-"

"Incredible place, really," Baronkroft interrupted again. "The best steel in the world comes from Kahrr... The city's moat is practically impassable... Its walls, indestructible... Far better than *this* filth, I'll dare even say. Only thing Drahkmere has is a cliff at its back and a *half*-moat that smells like death."

The sergeant took another sip of his wine, uncomfortable with the lord's persistent change of topic. The wine was bitter, but it was warm and sharp and, most importantly, it was easing the sergeant's tension.

"Really, there's only *one* thing wrong with the city of Kahrr," Baronkroft said. "It's in the wrong side of the world." Upon his last remark, the lord's expression changed into a more serious one, his eyes squinting and face softening.

Sergeant Weston, still perplexed over the discussion, sighed and asked, "You brought me all the way to Drahkmere to talk to me about some free city in the east?"

"Oh the city is the least of our concern, I just happen to be fond of it," Baronkroft said. "Quite honestly, I brought you here for a very simple reason, Sergeant Weston. I need your signature."

"My signature?" the sergeant set his goblet down. "What for?"

Baronkroft rose to his feet and with his hands crossed at his back again he paced around the chamber, calmly and nonchalantly. "I'll be needing your men for a little venture, you see... You are to sign the contract and have them march to Drahkmere at once."

"Are you *mad*?" the sergeant felt the heat of the wine give him the confidence and vigor he thought he'd lost. "Why would I do such a thing?"

"Because it is the right thing to do, I'm afraid," Baronkroft kept pacing. "You've heard quite a bit about my father, I take it... After all, the man's name was enough to bring you a hundred miles east. He had a reputation, my father. He was daring, ruthless, hard-edged, you name it... But he was also a fair man. Might even be the fairest man I've ever known to live. You see, *he* believed a man should *earn* things in life. Money, wealth, power... A title means shit if the man bearing it doesn't deserve it. This is what led him to build an army as grand as his, many decades ago. This is what led him to try and invade the land to the east... A little land called Gravenstone."

"Yes, and like many before him, he *failed*," said the sergeant, taking another gulp from the wine as if it had hooked him. "I respected your father, my lord. And thus I respect *you* for keeping his cause alive, but King Ulrik will *never* agree to provide men for y-"

"I'm not *asking* King Ulrik," Baronkroft paused and glared at the sergeant. "I'm asking *you*, Sergeant Weston. Just a mere signature, that's all it would take... What's it to you anyhow? Losing a few thousand men?"

"They are *not* your men to dispose of!" Weston said, his voice rising.

"Neither are they *yours*... And yet you dispose of them any way you see fit."

The two men stood in silence. Sergeant Weston nearly felt an impulse to attack the man. After all, they were about the same size and the sergeant had the advantage of armor. Then, of course, there was the monstrosity standing by the door. Even with armor, the sergeant knew he'd be crushed by a single blow.

"At least this way, they'll be dying for a good cause," Baronkroft added. "What say you?"

The sergeant scowled.

"This is obscene," he said angrily, his chair scratching against the stone as he rose to his feet. "I am a Qamrothian soldier and I serve King Ulrik! *You*, my lord, I've never met, much less heard of. Your *father* may have been a fair man, but you are *not* your father nor will you ever be."

Baronkroft did not appear hurt by the man's words... Quite the opposite, in fact, his grin seemed unmoving, as if he had gotten the response he was hoping for. He stared at the sergeant with those glowing eyes of his and something in them appeared off. It was as if Baronkroft's mind was no longer in the room and he had sunk into a trance, all the while his eyes remained locked on the sergeant.

Weston scoffed suddenly and headed for the door.

"I've no time for this," he said. "Now if you'll excuse m..."

He came slowly to a halt... He felt his throat start to close together, his eyes slowly turning red from the lack of air. He grabbed the nearest chair and sunk into it, both of his hands pressed against his neck. He was shaking. He felt his limbs start to grow numb and cold.

Baronkroft stepped closer, his eyes red and swollen and aimed at his guest...

"You're right, Sergeant Weston... I'm not my father," he said.

At the same time, the Butcher walked towards the table with a roll of leather.

The sergeant watched as the monster of a man unrolled the leather and revealed a set of glistening knives strapped side by side, lined according to size.

"Thank you, my dear friend," Baronkroft said, and the Butcher responded with nothing but a grunt and a head nod, after which he headed for the doors and closed them behind him.

This was it... The sergeant and the lord were alone...

Though the sergeant could no longer feel any part of his body, he was quite awake. His eyes wouldn't even blink, they were paralyzed with the rest of him. The only thing he could do was breathe, and even with that he struggled. Baronkroft had somehow gotten a grip on him without even touching him.

"You know, it's funny, sergeant," Baronkroft said as he caressed each of the knives gently, one by one, as if he were stroking the petals of a rose. "I've spoken to many men of power recently. They all appear reluctant towards me. *Hostile*, even. It's rather horrid, the way they force me to act rash. They don't quite seem to grasp what I'm trying to say here... You see, I *will* get what I want. One way or the other, I always do."

The sergeant's eyes were moving, the only part of him that *could*, back and forth, examining the lord's every movement. He was stiff and vulnerable and petrified.

Baronkroft then unstrapped one of the daggers from the leather. It was of average size and the handle was made of wood, carved beautifully into the shape of a dragon's head. The steel of the blade was damn near perfect, smooth and glimmering against the light of the fire. And the way Baronkroft looked at it was startling.

"You see this blade, sergeant?" he held it up. "It's quite dear to me... Kahrran steel, forged within the finest wielding dungeons of the city's bastion. As you can see, I have an entire collection of them... But *this* one... *This* one, I find, shines the brightest..."

Baronkroft gave the man an eerie grin, gripping the dagger with his hand delicately.

"Do you know how I'm going to use it on you...?"

The sergeant felt the sweat dripping from his face. He was paralyzed, but he swore he could feel his skin crawling, a faint feeling, like the prickling on a limb when it has gone numb.

"I always like to *start* with this one," Baronkroft said eerily. "It works beautifully, I tell you... It truly manages to expose a man. Break him. Make him reveal his true nature."

He paced slowly towards the sergeant's chair.

"I can't wait to see who you truly are, sergeant," he said, his grin slowly fading into a grim stare. "I hardly know you from shit... But I'm sure by the end of the night we'll be much better acquainted. And by the time I'm finished introducing you to my entire collection... you'll have *wished* you signed that contract..."

* * *

"Drahkmere?" Sir Percyval Garroway scratched his head with doubt.

"Horse shit," said Sir Antonn Guilara, standing guard by Percyval's shoulder as he had been for the last hour. "That place is nothing but ruins."

"It's where they're taking her," Viktor said.

"Says who?"

Viktor hesitated for a moment. The witch Zahrra was rocking back and forth in her chair, her eyes pale once again, as if she was lost in a distant dream.

"Says an ally of ours," Viktor chose to say. "An ally who single-handedly fought and captured the notorious thief Hudson Blackwood... He was there during the attack on the royal palace."

"Did you say *Blackwood*?" Percyval raised an eyebrow.

"I heard that bastard's wanted for 1,000 yuhn in Halghard," Sir Antonn said.

"I *also* heard he slept with Balthazar Locke's aunt once," Percyval shrugged. "Good lad."

"Yes, well..." Viktor cleared his throat. "My ally caught him. And he heard the enemy say the princess was being taken to Drahkmere... I'm not asking for much. All I ask is for a couple of dozen men. 15 at the very least, if possible. If we don't reach Drahkmere before the next full moon, her majesty's life might be in grave dang-"

"I have no men to give you, Sir Crowley," Percyval said brusquely. "Halghard has enough to deal with than to worry about the problems of a neighboring kingdom. Besides, doesn't King Rowan have any men to spare for the rescue of his own daughter?"

Viktor's lips opened, but he hesitated to speak, alarmed by the man's words.

Percyval's face hardened, as he nearly saw through Viktor's lies. But then Zahrra startled everyone with a sudden gasp, her head twitching as her eyes glimmered from the light of a candle. "They march," she said worriedly. "The army with the red shield banners. They march south as we speak."

Sir Percyval leapt to his feet instantly, rushing towards the witch and kneeling in front of her. "Yes?" he asked eagerly. "Yes? What else, Zahrra?"

"Catapults. Oil. Fire. They plan to torch your brother's army."

"Bastards!" Percyval grunted, sweating with a driven torment. "We must go to him... we must go to my brother at once! He needs every able-bodied soldier he can get!"

"We have nearly thirty recruits already on their way here," Sir Antonn said gravely.

"To hells with them! We must move *now*!"

"The Great Rift," Zahrra said, grasping Sir Percyval's attention once again. "The Great Rift is to their left... They march around it..."

"The mountain path?" Sir Percyval asked.

"That's a long march," Sir Antonn reassured his knight commander. "There's still time, Percyval... Better to wait and grow our numbers. Better to send him a raven."

"And tell him what?! That I *dreamt* the information?"

There was a sudden silence, after which Viktor understood why his questioning the knight had been so provoking. *He doesn't know,* he realized. *King Alistair Garroway doesn't know that his brother is recruiting non-humans...*

Percyval looked as if he was mere seconds away from breaking something, he was so restless, his mind trying to come up with a proper solution. And at that moment, another figure entered the tent, bringing with them an aura of splendor, and making the tent significantly colder than before...

Viktor Crowley was the first to glance at the figure, and immediately he became flustered.

The elf from the river...

His heart began racing, his hands became warm and clammy, and he was sweating tremendously underneath his armor... He'd never been this close to the elf and he could see every detail in their face as clear as day. The elf was tall and beautiful and riddled with ambiguity. Their hair was thin and straight like a sleek brush, silver with a dash of purple dye on the right side; their nose was long and sharp, and their purple eyes gleamed with a majestic beauty, like gazing upon the eyes of a wild caracal...

"May I have a word, Sir Percyval?" the elf spoke.

By the gods...

Viktor was astonished to hear that the elf's voice was even more serene than their appearance, soft and tender, on the deeper side yet still ambiguous, and Viktor found that it conveyed a sense of leisure in him, as if listening to this very voice could instantly put him at ease from his darkest troubles.

Percyval was pacing around his tent, still clearly troubled by the witch's revelation.

"My apologies, Skye... But I cannot leave Zahrra's side. What is it you need?"

The elf made brief eye contact with Viktor Crowley, a moment that made the man feel both nervous and tranquil all at once. "A few men were spotted by the river this morning," said the elf. "They were taking a girl prisoner... And they had the mark of the Brotherhood. Something tells me their camp is nearby. We must be wary."

"The rogues?" Percyval grew an alarmed look on his face.

"What did the girl look like?"

"Never mind that, brother Antonn," Percyval interjected, strapping a blade to his belt. "First Balthazar's troops start to march, now *this*? I'm making the announcement... We must prepare to march back to Wyrmwood *tonight*. We can't afford to lose the men we've managed to gather."

"Sir Percyval?" Viktor called. "If I may sugg-"

But the knight was halfway out of the tent before Viktor could finish.

And soon after, Sir Antonn and Zahrra followed him.

Viktor Crowley was left alone with the elf for a brief moment, and it was a moment that Viktor felt had lasted for hours. His heart skipped a beat when he suddenly realized he had not yet introduced himself.

"Pardon my manners," he leapt to his feet and held his hand out. "I'm

Viktor Crowley."

"I know," said the elf with a smile. "I'm Skye."

Their hands touched...

The elf's hand was gentle and smooth and icy cold.

Viktor's was rough and calloused and sweaty.

"Skye... what?"

"Just Skye."

"I see," Viktor said, clearing his throat nervously for what felt like the hundredth time

At that same moment, Sir Percyval walked briskly back into the tent.

"Forgot my map," he muttered. "Damn Woodland roads." He gave them a quick glance, only to see the golden eagle and the elf locked in a handshake. "Right. Pardon my rudeness. Skye, this is Sir Viktor Crowley."

"I know," the elf repeated with a subtle grin.

"Skye's an ice mage from the northern Woodlands," Percyval said to Viktor. "Recruited just a few nights ago. Best decision I ever made." And then he walked out of the tent, leaving the two of them alone again.

After a brief silence, Viktor decided to ask, "How far north?"

"Far enough..."

Viktor Crowley had never been a prejudice man. If defending the young witch Syrena from the peasants of Val Havyn felt right to him, shaking the hand of the graceful elf that stood before him felt *more* than right. He felt a rush in his spine that he hadn't felt in a long time. And he found himself, for a moment, not wanting to let go.

"It's a pleasure, Skye."

"The pleasure is mine, Sir Crowley."

"Please," he said. "Just Viktor."

* * *

Borrys Belvaine, the rogue mercenary and newly appointed second-in-command, stumbled inside the captain's tent, bringing with him a trail of stench from several days of not bathing. His eyes were bloodshot and his breath reeked stronger than usual. He slumped into an old wooden chair near Robyn Huxley, who was sitting on the dirt against a pile of junk with her hands and feet bound together by rope.

She looked up at him with her weary eyes, swollen and red from the lack of sleep, her teeth pressed together so as to suppress the outraged shivering. The man was quiet at first; he used his nail to remove something from his teeth and then took heavy gulps from a bottle of what Robyn suspected was whisky, based on his awful breath.

"Hello 'gain, beaut'ful," he said to her with that heinous smile of his, revealing the rotting mold on his upper front teeth. He then pulled out an old rucksack and began fumbling through it.

Robyn recognized that rucksack…

It was old, torn, and patched up with wool. It was *hers*.

He pulled out a sour green apple and took a bite.

"Quite tasty, this," he said, his eyes squinting. "Where'd you steal it from?"

Robyn kept up her silence.

Rot in hells, she thought.

She was waiting for any abrupt movement on his behalf, so that she could use her legs to strike him with as much force as she could muster. But Borrys did not get close to her. He placed one of his muddy boots on a nearby stool and slouched even more, the inebriation overtaking him.

He took another sloppy bite from the apple and then aimed at her with his finger.

"You don' like me," he said, as if it was new information. "I can sees it…"

Robyn felt her stomach turn. She couldn't help it. She had to say something. "You killed him…"

"*What?*" he seemed honestly confused.

"You killed Nyx," she felt a knot in her throat.

Fight it, Robyn. Don't you dare let a single tear drop.

"What, the *crow?*" he asked, on the verge of laughter. "You cryin' over a damn *crow?!*"

Had her hands not been roped, she would have leapt on him and punched him in the jaw.

"He was my *friend!*" she nearly shouted, her eyes glaring at him furiously.

"He was a stupid crow, girl! Hells, I'll fetch ya another one later."

She said nothing, finding it best not to reveal any more. Though she had known Nyx briefly, she'd felt an instant connection with him, perhaps because he was the only thing that reminded her of Elbon. He made her feel secure, as if she'd brought a piece of home with her.

Only now he was gone… *taken* from her…

Mister Beckwit had sent his loyal friend to look after her and in a split second he was dead.

The girl always had a humble heart, much like her mother and brother. All her life she had been a bold and free-spirited soul, but she never dreamed she would one day long to kill another human being.

After that day, however, something within her had changed…

There was a deep hatred in her heart that seemed to be growing by the second.

She wanted Malekai dead. She wanted Borrys dead.

She wanted an arrow to pierce through their hearts and she wanted to be the one to shoot it. She wanted to watch them as they died, the same way they watched as Nyx gasped for his last breath. She remembered the way Old Man Beckwit would say that she often doubted herself and that this was the reason for her mishaps during training. At that very moment, however, there wasn't the faintest sign of doubt in her heart. She had never felt more ready...

Suddenly there were footsteps approaching just outside.

The sun was still out, and Robyn could see the looming shadow of the man, approaching the tent.

Captain Malekai Pahrvus stepped in, eye bandaged and dagger at hand, looking deadlier than he ever had. Both Robyn and Borrys froze in silence, and the mercenary sat up straighter, slightly panicking, trying his best to appear sober.

"Er... Just keepin' an eye on her, cap'n, like you asked," Borrys said, his nose twitching nervously upon realizing his poor choice of words.

"Leave us," Malekai said to Borrys, but his eye was fixed on Robyn. "And fetch us a bucket."

The man scurried out of the tent, leaving the captain and the young archer alone.

Robyn could smell the hot blood on Malekai's face from a distance.

She was afraid, she knew that much. But the rage in her chest was far greater.

He was glaring at her, and she returned the glare right back.

Say something, you bastard, she thought to herself. *Go on... Say something...*

Except he didn't, his silence was far more menacing and he knew it.

He walked closer to her, dagger still at hand. Robyn's neck could only bend so far and so her eyes became lost for a moment, as Malekai towered over her.

Stay away from me, you filth...

Once again, it was as if Malekai could read her thoughts and did exactly the opposite. He bent down on one knee, close enough so that she had no choice but to stare right at his face, half of it smeared in red just underneath the drenched cloth covering his left socket.

He moved the dagger closer to her. Her heart raced.

What are you doing? Get away!

She pressed her eyes shut and breathed heavily from the angst. Only, there was no pain. All she felt was a tug and then suddenly she could feel her wrists again. Malekai had cut her loose and was doing the same with her feet, carefully so as to save most of the rope. She felt confused for a moment, but she didn't fight it.

Good, she thought. *It'll make killing you far easier.*

"Cap'n?" Borrys Belvaine's head peeked inside the tent. "Where do I leav-"

"Just drop it anywhere," Malekai growled. "Now go prepare the iron."

Here it is, Robyn. Here's your chance.

Borrys dropped a bucket half-filled with water on the ground and left.

Meanwhile, Robyn's hand moved slowly towards the dagger.

She underestimated the captain's speed, however. Malekai gripped her wrist before she could even touch the cold blade. He snarled at her, pulled her up to her feet, and threw her across the tent with a force so strong that Robyn felt her knees scrape open as she fell.

Too slow… Damn it all to hells, why are you so bloody slow?

She sat back, caressed her wounded knees, looked up at the vile man almost as heatedly as he was looking down at her. Malekai reached into his satchel and pulled out a smelly old sack, about the size of a coinpurse, and he tossed it at her feet.

"Stir it," he said.

Robyn did nothing at first, her eyes examining the tent.

There must be something. Anything.

Except there wasn't… Unless a quill could kill a man, she had nothing. And Malekai was blocking the entrance so running was not an option…

Not that the girl *wanted* to run just yet.

Soon, yes… But he dies first… Then, I run…

"Are you deaf, girl?" he took a step closer. "I said… Stir. It."

She snatched the smelly old bag from the dirt and knew what was inside it before she even untied the knot on the string. Callis root, just like the kind her mother kept back at the farm in the case of a wound. She stirred some into the bucket of water as Malekai dragged a wooden chair closer to her, sat on it, and untied the drenched rag from his head.

Robyn was far too distracted to notice. Her eyes were on the bucket and her mind was elsewhere. It wasn't until Malekai threw the bloody rag at her and it splashed over the water that she looked up at him, and she nearly yelped from the shock. She didn't know what was more repulsive, the bloody socket or Malekai's other eye glowering at her, the hatred and hunger almost radiating from it.

"Clean me," he ordered her.

Robyn felt her stomach turn again. *Clean yourself, you filthy pig.*

He placed his dagger on the table next to him; the girl's eyes followed it. When she didn't obey him, he leaned in gently, rested his elbows on his knees, and said, "I can make this very easy for you, girl… Clean me. *Now*. Or you'll be cleaning your *own* blood off the floor…"

Robyn fought through the rage. She had underestimated the patience she would need with a man like the captain. She dipped the bloody cloth into the bucket, tried to clean it as best as she could, but there was still plenty of blood on it when she drained it. Malekai rested his back against the chair, waiting patiently for her.

She got to her feet, her weakened knees shivering, and stepped closer.

His odor was sickeningly overwhelming, a pungent blend of sweat and blood.

She pressed the wet cloth against the tender skin around his socket.

He hissed from the pain, shivered mildly, bit his own tongue to keep himself from shouting... Robyn knew too well the effects of callis root, having been treated with it many times. The sting was unbearable at first, it took minutes to numb the wound. Malekai, however, appeared slightly annoyed from the sting, at best.

Used to pain, are you? I'll make sure to fix that...

She rubbed harder. Some of the blood on his cheekbone had dried and turned into scabs. She picked at them until his bruised skin was clean, dark brown tainted with a purple hue, and she could tell he was in pain, his hands shaking as he gripped his own knees. For a moment, she was confused by it all... this power he had given her over him, how easily she could have made the pain worse, how effortlessly she could have poked at his already horrid wound. Perhaps it was a trial of some sort, to see how bold she was, how impulsive...

Focus, Robyn... Don't let him meddle with your mind...

Every movement of hers was gentle and careful, but her eyes were glancing all around, from the wound to the water bucket, the dagger on the table, even Malekai's wrists... She saw it there, the infamous tattoo... The mark of the Brotherhood, the Aharian scorpion, just as she had imagined it after all of the stories her mother had told her. Malekai must have noticed her staring at it, for he shot her a sudden grin.

"You know this mark?" he asked her, his tone softening, as if it gave him great pleasure to see her frail and meek. "It's usually the last thing people see before they die, this mark. You should consider yourself lucky."

Robyn refused to give him the courtesy of a response. She was so fueled by rage, she could hardly stand to listen to his voice. She pressed at the wound harder, but the callis root had started to take effect, and there was no sign of a reaction from Malekai.

"Do you know the story behind it?" he asked.

I don't care.

"It goes back a hundred years or so," he went on. "Captain Halbard Elkerim, the very first captain of the Rogue Brotherhood, was bitten by an Aharian scorpion."

Good. And now he's dead. Just as you'll be, very soon.

"They're said to have the deadliest poison ever known to man. Elkerim should've died. Only, he didn't."

Shit.

"People thought he was a devil of some sort. *'Made a pact with death'*, they said. But there was no pact. The Aharians figured it out ages ago, the only cure strong enough to kill the poison... It's how he managed to survive and go on to form the Brotherhood. But folks will believe what they want to believe. So the scorpion became the mark of the guild as a way to remind the people... You don't meddle with the Brotherhood. And if you do? Why, you're just as dead as if you were bitten by an Aharian scorpion."

Robyn had nearly finished cleaning the wound. Her hand wouldn't stop, however. Time was a gift in situations like these, and she was concerned about what would happen next once she finished.

"You going to say anything, girl?" he asked, his patience running short.

She ignored him at first, focusing her attention on the wound. It may have been nauseating at first, but slowly she began to accept it. As menacing as he looked, he was nothing more than an injured man. And seeing him as anything more than that certainly wouldn't help her. She breathed, slowly and calmly, before finally deciding to speak.

"If you're going to kill me anyway... Save me the speech and get on with it."

Her words stung him, she could tell. Even with one eye, it was obvious.

Malekai Pahrvus did not like being challenged. Then again, Robyn had never met a man that *did*. Despite the pounding in her chest, she tried her best to remain observant. If she was to get out of this alive, she would have to be smarter than him, she would have to learn to manipulate him.

His reaction was calm...

First there was his usual grin, then a chuckle, and finally a scornful head nod, as if undermining her. "*Kill* you? Now, why would I do a thing like that, girl?"

"If you don't, you will regret it," she challenged him even further. "Because when I get out of here, I'm going to kill *you*."

Malekai did it again... A grin, a chuckle, and a head nod...

You're new at this, I can tell, she realized. *You don't intimidate me for a second.*

"You're more stupid than you look if you think you're ever escaping," he said.

Is that all? My mother scares me more than you, you bastard...

"Face it, girl," he licked his lips. "You're done for. You belong to *me* now."

"I belong to no one."

"Oh, but you do," he chuckled. "You will clean my boots when I tell you to, shine my blade when I tell you to, if I'm thirsty you will fetch me ale."

"I'll spit on it."

"Mmm. And I'll cut your tongue off to make sure it doesn't happen again."

Robyn's hand began shivering, and so she threw the cloth back into the bucket to prevent him from noticing it. "I'm done," she said.

Malekai began to feel the damage with his fingertips. It was a brief moment, but it was one that Robyn took to gawk at the dagger sitting on the table.

One move, she thought. *Just one swift move and I'll have him.*

"I'll have you moved to another tent to start making me supper," he said, his mind preoccupied examining his tender wound. "And *if* you're good, perhaps I'll let you eat the scraps."

This is it... Grab the dagger, Robyn...

"Otherwise, I'll have to cut off a finger for every time you try to run."

You'll run out of fingers, you sick bastard...

"And if you *keep* running, then I'll start taking toes. We'll see how fast you run *then*," he chuckled, loudly and overly confident as he wrapped a piece of clean black cloth around his head.

Grab. The. Dagger. NOW!

And so she did... One rapid move and she snatched it, pressed it against his bare neck, and glared down at him... She stopped in her tracks. He didn't appear surprised at all, as if he had set her up and she had fallen into his trap. In fact, the edge of his lips began to curve slightly again.

She wanted to cut him... Every one of her muscles urged her to...

Every single one except her wrist...

From afar is one thing, she repeated in her mind. *It all seems too easy when your target is the size of your thumb.*

Her hand began shivering again...

You have him! What are you waiting for?!

To make matters worse, Malekai's brow lowered and he scoffed.

"Go on then," he taunted her. "Do it..."

But she couldn't... And she was furious at herself for it...

The image of the bandit from the hills, the one she had unintentionally killed, kept haunting her... She could practically *see* him again, falling to his knees, an arrow in his hand, *her* arrow... And as she looked down at Malekai, she felt that same jab in her chest, that jab of horror upon realizing she was now a murderer. That eye, Malekai's eye, may have been cruel and wicked, but there was a life there all the same. And she didn't have the heart to take it away. Not again.

"Cap'n Malekai, sir?"

Borrys Belvaine's voice made her lose focus... And in that brief second, the captain seized her wrist and tightened it so hard that she heard a crack. And the dagger slipped from her hand and fell to the dirt. She yelped, her chest pounding and her palms dripping with sweat.

Stupid, Robyn... Stupid, stupid, stupid...

"How disappointing," Malekai said, tightening his clasp on her wrist.

Don't struggle. Fight it.

"And here I thought you were more nervy than that," he grinned.

Like John would say... Fight through the pain, show them no fear...

But the girl's hand was turning a violent shade of red. His grip was far too strong and Robyn's jaw couldn't help but shiver.

"Cap'n?" Borrys called again.

It was then that she caught a whiff of it...

An odd smell, like that of hot metal, *dreadfully* hot...

Borrys stepped into the tent. He was holding a branding iron in his hand and the tip of it was brightly lit and sizzling.

No...

Robyn's eyes widened. Malekai seized her by the other wrist and leapt to his feet, and with immense force he threw her across the tent again. She felt her knees scrape even more. She was right back where she started, in a muddy corner surrounded by cloth and leather but nothing sharp, nothing that could help her fight back.

She crawled away, both men walking towards her.

Borrys was grinning, his twitching hand holding the blazing iron loosely.

What are you doing?! Stop...

"Hold her still," Malekai said, taking the hot iron from his comrade's hand.

And Borrys obeyed him like a subservient hound, chuckling and dribbling enthusiastically.

Don't touch me, you sick pig!

Borrys grabbed hold of her as Malekai took a gulp from a bottle of whisky.

"N-No! Stop!" Robyn resisted, but Borrys was larger and stronger and his lock on her arms was nearly unbreakable. She remembered the other prisoners she'd seen in the camp, and that they all had scars on their faces, the mark of the scorpion... And the image of them was only making her more restless...

"No," Malekai said suddenly. "Over the table. Wouldn't wanna ruin such a pretty sight."

"Cap'n?" Borrys raised a brow.

"Shut your mouth and do as you're told."

Borrys scowled. He shoved and pressed Robyn against the captain's table, while the girl twisted and turned in protest, landing punches and kicks on both men repeatedly.

But it was no use... She was trapped...

Malekai grabbed her arm and stretched it across the flat splintery surface, while Borrys pulled her sleeve up, exposing her soft pale skin.

"I don't have to do this, girl," the captain said, leaning in mere inches from her face. "I'll give you a chance... I won't mark you, so long as you say the word. Just the one word. Say *Please*."

She breathed heavily, fighting through the rage.

She could no longer fight the tears swelling up her eyes, that much was inevitable.

But the girl had never begged in her life, except to her mother, and she did not plan to start now. And certainly not with a rogue mercenary...

"Go on, girl," Malekai whispered into her ear, his hot breath causing her to shiver with disgust. "Say the word. I want to hear you say it."

Don't do it, Robyn, she told herself, over and over again. *Don't.*

"My patience is running short, girl..."

"My name's *Robyn*!" she growled angrily, and then instantly wished she hadn't said it.

"Ahh… And are you really *that* stubborn, Robyn? It's only a word… Now, go on. Say it."

Don't you dare… Fight through the pain, show them no fear…

"No?" Malekai asked.

Robyn looked up at him… There it was, that sinister smirk. The sizzling brand was in the shape of the scorpion, about half as long as her palm, and when she realized she was going to have that scar for life, her shivering worsened…

She opened her lips suddenly. And Malekai's ear waited eagerly.

"Eat… shit!" she said.

And then her heart dropped…

A moment passed… Malekai's eye twitched, he was so stunned…

And then he did it again… A grin, a chuckle, and a head nod, as always.

"What'd I tell you, Borrys?" he said. "Quite nervy, this one."

And with that, Captain Malekai Pahrvus violently slammed the hot steel onto Robyn's forearm. Robyn screamed, and it was a scream that echoed all through the camp.

"Shut her up!"

Borrys pressed a filthy hand over her mouth.

Robyn's face was a vicious red. The tears escaped her eyes unwillingly as she watched the iron melting her skin like butter. The smell of sweltering flesh began to fill the tent, as the sound of Borrys's laughter loomed over her muffled screams.

Then, after several seconds, Malekai removed the iron.

And Borrys released her from his grip.

Robyn slid off the table and shrunk to her knees into the mud, holding her bleeding trembling arm against her chest. Her face was a hot mess of sweat and tears and snot. She took a moment to examine herself. And the sight was more dreadful than she had imagined. The scorpion was there, slightly misshapen from the blood and blisters, about four inches long across her forearm.

Her entire arm was numb.

She wondered if she would ever be able to shoot an arrow properly again.

It's over. Breathe, Robyn… Just breathe…

"Tie her back up," Malekai ordered, giving the girl a look of displeasure.

Borrys, loathsome and snickering as always, did as he was told. He grabbed Robyn by the arms and pulled her to that same filthy corner of the tent where she sat before, as the captain headed towards the outside.

"I'm going to kill you…" she muttered suddenly.

Malekai's foot sunk into the mud. He bent his neck to look at her.

Robyn's glare was almost frightening. And Malekai's response only angered her further.

A grin, a chuckle, and a head nod…

"The next time you *try*, be sure to follow through with it," he said. "Otherwise, I'll give you to my men. And, believe me, they're not nearly as kind and patient as I am."

And with that, he left the tent. And Borrys followed behind him.

Robyn sat there, her mind racing with a million thoughts, distracting her from the throbbing pain, considering every single possibility...

Fight through the pain, show them no fear, she said to herself.

Fight through the pain... Show them no fear...

X
Desperate Times

In a constantly changing world, where wealth and power are more influential than morality, the painful truth is often blurred, hidden, buried beneath a mantle of lies and deception. Nobody ever talks about the things that happen in the dark, for how easy it is to turn the other way, to pretend there's nothing there, if only for a peace of mind.

But reality is much darker, much more cruel, and much more rotten…

It is difficult to turn the other way when one is living through such hardships.

It is difficult to ignore, say, the sound of a soldier getting lashed, the sound of a weeping mother who's recently lost a child, or the gut-wrenching stench of a pile of burning corpses…

Such was the reality for Princess Magdalena, and she never imagined it would ever come to this. She was on laundry duty when her nose caught the smell, and the wet sheets slipped from her grasp when she saw the black cloud rising to the skies.

Hauzer and Jyor, the two guards assigned to look after the prisoners, stood before a pile of them. Prisoners who had either given up or were beaten to death were stacked over one another in a dark corner, away from the crowds, among the heaps of decade-old rubble. They poured oil over the pile and Hauzer threw a lit torch, and instantly it lit up in flames, swallowing every bit of dead flesh all around.

The red-bearded man and the elf scurried off as quick as they could, trying their best to breathe through their mouths to avoid the smell, as pointless as it was every time. The stench was pungent and disturbing and too often one of them ended up vomiting all over the dirt.

"I tell ya, Hauzer," Jyor groaned as they walked side by side towards the crowded center of the dead city. "One day… *One* day, I'll have enough. That sleazy bastard thinks he can treat me like a pet hound."

Hauzer grunted. "If Baronkroft didn't notice ye before, he sure as hells ain't noticin' ye now that ye're half-handed."

Jyor kept glancing at his left hand, as if making sure his fingers were actually missing or if he had dreamt it all. But they were gone, all right. His hand was wrapped in a bloody cloth and it was entirely numb… He loathed it. He'd felt belittled before already, and now the other soldiers were laughing at him, at the fact that an old woman prisoner had done that to him. And his dream of one day becoming a commander was shattering before his eyes.

"I'll *make* 'im notice!" he growled.

"Settle yerself, Jyor."

"He treats us like scum, Hauzer! Makes us do his dirty work and for *what*?!"

"I say settle *down*, ye stupid lad…"

"For his own good, that's all!" Jyor wasn't settling down. "So long as *he* grows and grows, to hells with the rest of us, right? Well *I* say to hells with *him*!"

"Curse yer stupid tongue, lad!" Hauzer came to a halt just before they reached the main city grounds. They could hear the commotion coming from the set of tables where the soldiers were having their first meal of the day. And Hauzer had to speak low so as to not be overheard. "Are ye lookin' to get yerself killed?!" he gave the elf a shove. "If so, tell me now so I can stay the hells away from ye!"

Jyor allowed it… *Once*. But he was watchful for a second shove.

Hauzer may have been large and broad-shouldered, but Jyor was faster.

An altercation between the two could end with either one of them dead.

"Don't touch me again…"

"I've had 'bout *enough* of yer whinin', ye dumb fool," Hauzer growled at him.

"As if *you* don't think the same thing?! I've *seen* you. You loathe your job. And yet you stay quiet and let 'im *shit* all over you."

"Of *course* I'm sick of it!" Hauzer said, nearly shouting. "But ye don't hear *me* cryin' over it… Look, ye want power 'n' riches, I get that. *Every* bloke with an arse wants that!"

"Aye, well *some* of us don't go lookin' for it outside of our homelands like *you*!"

That was the last straw… Hauzer tolerated many things from the elf, but this was low even for him… He swung his fist and landed a heavy blow to Jyor's jaw. And the elf grunted and fell back, spat blood on the dirt, then looked up at his companion with a frantic glare.

"Listen 'ere ye little shit!" Hauzer said, his voice frightening and his expression even more so. "That place we're invading? *I* came from that place, *you* didn't… Ye have *no* idea what it's like in there… They call Baronkroft crazy. But ye know what *I* call crazy?! *Separatin'* folks like they're fuckin' animals…"

Jyor's angry panting began to die down, his angry glare beginning to shift.

"Look at me," Hauzer took a step forward. "*Look* at me!!"

Jyor growled and hopped to his feet, swinging his arm forward, but his fist missed Hauzer's jaw. The man caught the elf's arm just in time, stared him right in the eyes, mere inches from his face.

"Are ye an animal, Jyor?" he asked.

The elf didn't answer at first, only pulled his arm back.

"Are ye an animal?!"

"Fuck you!"

"*That's* right! *Fuck* me!" Hauzer barked back. "I look at ye 'n' I see no animal, Jyor… I see a hard-tempered stubborn little shit, sure. *Not* an animal…

And ye got brothers 'n' sisters out there who are bein' treated like they *are*...
Like it or not, Baronkroft is the only man with the power to *fix* that place. And
yeah, he may be a heartless bastard, but he's *all* we've got!"

Jyor's breathing slowed back to normal, and he felt the rage leave his chest.

Hauzer was right, he knew, as much as he hated to admit it...

The chattering from the nearby tables became rather palpable all of a
sudden, and the two men realized how loud they had been, how easily they could
have been overheard. When they shifted their glances they noticed a boy, dark-
skinned and weary-looking, standing nearby with an empty tray in his hands; it
was obvious he had been listening.

"What're you bleedin' looking at?!" Jyor snapped at him. "You done?!"

The boy nearly dropped the tray, he was so startled. "Y-Yes, sir."

"Stupid littl' bugger," Jyor took a step towards him.

"Sit yer arse down 'n' pour yerself a damn drink," Hauzer gave the elf a
shove again, then turned to the boy. "Ye got two more battalions to feed before
ye're done, lad."

Young Thomlin set the empty tray down and the red-bearded man escorted
him to a different part of the city, where the other battalions were lodged. It was
a long day, and by the time the boy finished serving them all, he was famished.
After being fed scraps, he was taken back into the half-standing brick dwellings,
down towards the dungeons, where the prisoners were kept when there was no
need for labor.

It was in this dungeon, where the sun's light was utterly nonexistent, where
our indomitable princess Magdalena sat, rocking back and forth in a dark corner,
fueled with dread and despair after having witnessed the burning earlier that day.
She could still see the black cloud, could still smell the appalling fumes of
scorching dead flesh. And it didn't help her sanity that the prisoners' dungeon
was so near the torture chamber, where at least three out of five nights somebody
would be either punished or beaten for interrogation, and their bellowing cries
would reverberate through the corridors.

This was one of those nights...

Baronkroft was plotting something, and he needed information. Prisoners
were being taken every few hours and not many were ever seen again. The few
that were brought back had been horribly beaten, some were missing a hand or
two, and others were left to bleed out in the darkness of the dungeon.

Hauzer walked in at one point and the prisoners scattered away in fear,
avoiding his gaze, hoping to prolong their lives as long as possible. He dragged
young Thomlin inside and unlocked his cuffs. And the boy instantly darted
towards Magdalena, who waited for him with open arms. They embraced and
proceeded to shrivel and disappear into a corner, so as to avoid Hauzer.

But the red-bearded guard noticed her still. It was difficult for him not to
notice a princess from his own homeland. She may have looked like any other

prisoner, but to him she stood out like a block of gold among a heap of black coal. He walked right past her, for he had specific orders from Lord Baronkroft to not harm her, 'not yet' at least.

He paced along the chamber, as if searching for someone, and his feet came to a halt when he locked eyes with a man, young and strong-built, whose clothes were once regal but were now filthy and tattered like Magdalena's dress. Hauzer grabbed him and pulled him up. And then a much older man leapt to his feet and began pulling at the guard's sleeve.

"No! Not my son! Please, not my son!" he begged.

But Hauzer was far too strong. Without a word, he shoved the old man away and dragged the younger prisoner out of the chamber, the iron door shutting behind him.

The old man fell to his knees, cried angry tears, his hands in fists, wishing he could break something. Several captives had recognized him but were too afraid to get near, for many had heard of his wrath and his authoritarian ways. Lord Olfur was his name, and he was from Yulxester, a city in the southern coast of Halghard where the streets were made of water and citizens traveled in boats instead of horses and carriages. After the death of King Frederic, which brought about the war in Halghard, Lord Olfur found himself at liberty to rule Yulxester at his own bidding, and having never had so much power in his life he used it to his own advantage.

Of course, Lord Olfur was no fool...

He recognized royalty when he saw it...

And through his tears he spotted the trembling figure in the corner...

"You... I know you," he said, lifting himself up.

The princess looked up at him. There may have been a subtle glint in her eyes, but her expression was not at all a timid one.

"You're Princess Magdalena... The motherless daughter of King Rowan," Lord Olfur said as he towered over her menacingly, his anger taking full control of him. "Aren't you?!"

Magdalena and Thomlin were still wrapped in each other's arms. The boy was more frightened than she was, though he tried his best to mimic her sense of valor.

"Stay away from us," Magdalena ordered.

"I'd recognize you anywhere," the old lord said, spitting nastily at her feet. "You must have your mother's eyes. You look nothing like your cursed father. If he even *is* your father, the old bastard."

Magdalena was much too exhausted for such folly, but there were eyes watching her, *expectant* eyes, and she simply could not allow for her reputation to be stained this way. She let go of Thomlin and stood up, glaring right back at the old lord. There wasn't much she could say to calm him, the old man was speaking through his rage, yet his words stung her all the same. For years, the rumors of *King Rowan's Curse* stained her, tarnished her name, and several nobles questioned whether she was indeed the rightful heir to the throne, seeing as the cursed king could father no son.

But she was certain that she was. The matter was infallible to her.

And the proof was there, from the birthmark on her right shoulder to the raging temper she had inherited from her father; the only difference was she knew how to control it better.

"Answer me, you little wench!" the lord shouted. "Are you or are you not the princess of Vallenghard?!"

Magdalena could feel the tension in her shoulders rising. She knew she would shout back, or even strangle the man if he pushed her further; not that she had ever done such a thing but she'd be lying if she said the thought had never crossed her mind. Certainly, such acts were not fit for a person of royalty, and thus she often held her temper back. But no one had ever confronted her quite so strongly before.

She *had* to say something…

Before she could speak, however, another voice interrupted and silenced them all.

"What did you just call her?" the voice said; it was that of an older woman.

Princess Magdalena and Lord Olfur both turned at once.

The woman was possibly in her late fifties, dressed in torn leathers, strong and agile despite her graying hair. At the thought of being challenged, Lord Olfur's brows lowered even further, to such an extent that Magdalena thought was not humanly possible.

"Who the bloody hells are *you* to try t-"

"I asked you a question, you old hog," Valleria said, rising to her feet and approaching the corner of the chamber where Magdalena and Thomlin stood.

"Ahh," Lord Olfur groaned and spat once again. "I should have known the princess of Vallenghard would have secret allies everywhere."

Valleria stepped even closer, in a way so menacing that Lord Olfur's knees trembled unwillingly where he stood. "I'm not her ally," she said. "I hardly even *know* the girl… I'm talking to *you*, you old fool. What was it you called her? I want to hear you say it…"

Lord Olfur groaned crossly and said, "What does it matter? Those blind bastards, don't they realize who they have in their own dungeon?! They would spare *her* but take my son?!"

"What in all hells are you talking about?" Valleria asked.

"*She's* the daughter of a King!"

"And *I'm* the daughter of a baker. We're all the sons 'n' daughters of someone, you stupid man. What're you getting at?"

"Do you know who you're talking to?!" Lord Olfur shouted.

"I don't believe I've had the dishonor, no."

"I'm Lord Olfur Millhurst of Yulxester!"

"Congratulations. No one cares," Valleria said, taking yet another step towards him. She was at eye level with the old lord, which meant she was nearly 6 feet in height. She looked stronger than him, in fact; stronger than his son, too.

"You don't dare speak to *me* that way, you old wench!"

There was a silence. The woman's jaw tightened and her nose twitched, as she shot the man quite the intimidating glare. "My name's Valleria," she said. "You either call me by me name or you don't call on me at all."

"I'll call on you as I damn well please!"

"Stop it!" Magdalena interrupted, stepping between the two. Young Thomlin stuck close to her, standing firmly by her side like a faithful knight; if it were common for a knight to latch on to a princess's sleeve, that is. "We must not fight amongst ourselves!" she said. "We must work *together*!"

By then, all eyes in the chamber were on them.

"You're not in charge here!" Lord Olfur snapped at the princess. "We oughta give *you* away to them! I'm sure they'd be quite interested."

"If they *wanted* her, they would've taken her by now," Valleria said. "Are you some sort of halfwit? D'you really think Lord Baronkroft is so senseless to not know the face of the daughter of King Rowan? They obviously need her alive."

"Then *I* say we threaten to kill her and bargain for our freedom!"

"You won't touch a single hair on the girl's head," Valleria said threateningly.

Once more, there was a silence. The scared hungry eyes of every prisoner in the chamber were locked on the commotion in that dark corner. None of them had the courage to intercept, of course. They simply observed, like vultures eyeing a prey.

Lord Olfur took another step closer, the closest he could get without touching the woman, and tried to appear firm and confident. "Or you'll do what, exactly?" he asked. "Who are *you* to threaten a Lord?"

"Careful who you taunt, old lord," Valleria warned him. "You may've been high 'n' mighty in Shitchester, or wherever the hells it is you're from. But down 'ere, you're just another captive."

"And what are *you*, old wench?"

She grew angrier, clearly bothered by the one word the lord was keen on using repeatedly. "I'm a sellsword," she said calmly.

The old lord hesitated before saying anything else. He then figured the woman was bluffing and he chuckled out loud. "*You*? A sellsword? You don't fool me for a moment."

Valleria had fought many men in her life and killed most of them. And the old lord's words were picking at her nerves so much that she wished she still had her sword at her side.

"Besides," Lord Olfur said, spitting at Valleria's boots. "A sellsword with no weapon is about as useless as an old barren wench!"

Valleria could no longer resist…

With all her might, she bashed her forehead into the old lord's nose.

The crack may have echoed… Lord Olfur fell to the floor, his nose twisted to the left, blood gushing out of both holes. He moaned in agony, blending with the echoing cries of the prisoners being tortured in the distance. "She broke it!" he cried. "The wench broke it!"

Valleria towered over him and pressed a boot to his neck to shut him up. "Next time you threaten anyone else in here, I'll hit you where it will *really* hurt, you limp hog…"

No one in the chamber moved. Lord Olfur held on to his nose, struggling to stop the bleeding. Valleria cracked her neck and headed back towards her corner.

"Wait," Magdalena called out, and the woman paused where she stood. "Valleria, is it?"

"It is…"

"Magdalena," she gave her a head nod, and the woman stood in silence as if expecting more. "How much do you know about this Lord Baronkroft…?"

Valleria sighed, deeply and somewhat despairingly.

"You don't want to know, girl."

"And what if I do?"

Valleria suddenly found herself half-smirking. She walked over to Magdalena and Thomlin's corner and took a seat on the black stone.

"What d'you want to know?"

"Anything," Magdalena said. "*Everything.*"

Valleria sighed deeply. "It's quite a long story."

"We have nothing *but* time."

"Aye… that's true," she said, resting her head against the wall. "I just wish we had a bottle of liqueur for it, that's all…"

* * *

"What in all hells?" John Huxley muttered, his mouth wide with bewilderment like a child.

In front of him was a tree, if one could even *call* it a tree…

It was the most massive tree John had ever seen, perhaps the largest in the world, for all he knew. The base of its trunk was immensely wide, roughly fifteen to twenty feet. A porch had been built into it, as well as a set of three rocky stairs that led to a wooden door. John had never seen a tree with a door before, much less one with windows all around it. There was music and commotion coming from the inside and crowds of drunken individuals of all species were stumbling in and out.

"What's wrong?" Hudson asked. "Never seen a tavern before?"

"I…"

John couldn't conjure up any words. His mouth was dry and his eyes felt deceived. He was not as troubled to see orcs and elves there, not like when he saw the orc at the royal palace; he *expected* to see them in the Woodlands. What troubled him more was the giant ogre sitting next to the tavern door, guarding it. He must have been about ten feet tall, large and hulking like an elephant, with fists big enough to wrap around a man's waist.

"We're staying *here?*" Syrena asked.

"I'm not a fan of crowds myself, love," Hudson replied. "But I smell a storm coming. We wouldn't want to risk it. Besides… They've got *ale* in there."

The witch smirked.

A pack of diverse drunkards stumbled out of the tavern, some six or seven of them. Before Hudson could walk around them, however, an inebriated woman with excessive lip paint and a messy head of blonde hair approached them. She placed her hand on Hudson's shoulder, though John and Syrena couldn't tell if it was out of coquetry or so the woman could keep her balance.

Probably both, John figured.

"Why 'ello there, handsome," the woman said, her smile not nearly as awful as her breath was. "Care for a littl' company tonight?"

Hudson removed the woman's hand gently from his shoulder.

"I'm flattered, my dear. But I'm afraid I'll have to decline the offer."

"Hmm," the woman giggled. "Ye scared?"

"Not quite," Hudson said, fighting the urge to scowl at her breath.

"What's wrong, then? Ye ain't into shagging?"

"Oh, believe me, I am. You're just not exactly the type to intrigue me."

"Hmm," she giggled again. "And how *do* ye like 'em, then?"

"Oh, you know… Smart-mouthed, manipulative, clever, hard to please," the thief took a moment to clear his throat. "…*Brunette*," he added.

John glanced at Syrena, whose cheeks were suddenly red.

"And *yes*, everything on that list is a requirement, I'm afraid," Hudson said, before he walked around the woman and towards the tavern. Along the way, the woman scowled at Syrena, but the witch paid her no mind, she only kept smiling.

John was careful when he reached the porch. The massive ogre looked at him suddenly and grunted. And the farmer walked nervously up the rickety steps, leaning as far away from the ogre as he could. "Hello," he said, his lip shivering.

"Hmm," the ogre nodded back.

It's all fine, John. All fine, he tried to calm himself, rushing through the door when he came to it. Taking the first step inside the tavern was like stepping into an unknown realm, distant from the reality that John had known all his life. For a moment, he was unsure whether the tavern had been built into the tree or if the tree had grown around it, he was so overwhelmed…

The room was completely round and the floors were slightly uneven. It was as if someone, a gnome perhaps, had carved their way inside the tree, allowing for the natural curvature of the trunk to become the tavern walls. There were several lodging rooms above, just like any other tavern or inn, and a set of spiraling stairs lined along the walls, where leafy vines had started to grow, as if the tree was claiming back its territory. And there was a strange smell in the air, like that of fresh wood and leaves, a pleasant aroma blending in with the awkward smell of sweat and body odor.

The counter was on the first floor, where tables and chairs had been set up all around, filled with the most diverse handful of beings that John could ever possibly think to imagine.

Humans, orcs, gnomes… All of them sitting side by side, drinking and conversing amiably with one another…

An orc playing a card game of *Mercy* with a human traveler…

A band of goblins, a pair of elves, all of them sitting next to a minotauro…

A posse of mining gnomes, next to an open wall where an orc girl sat on a stool, singing happily while playing a wooden harp…

Syrena noticed the look of perplexity in John's face and gave him a friendly tap on the shoulder. "You'll learn to adjust," she said, but she was wrong.

John was besieged and amused all at once. He'd hardly ever encountered any nonhumans since he was born, and seeing them together in the same room overwhelmed him with a strange feeling, one of both angst and joy, like the time he found out he was going to be a brother for the first time. He smiled, knowing that there was so much for him to see and all of his life ahead to see it.

He didn't *want* to adjust.

He wanted to hold on to that feeling for as long as he could.

"Leave this to me," Hudson cracked his knuckles, more out of habit than necessity. It wasn't clear whom he was talking to, perhaps no one in particular, perhaps it was a sort of impulse, like a knight swinging his blade at the air before a fight. The thief had been avoiding John lately, hardly ever speaking to him directly. And when he did, he didn't call him 'mate' anymore, not like he used to.

Still, the farmer had hope… And the witch hoped with him, if only for her own sake, so that she wouldn't have to continue playing the part of the messenger.

Hudson walked towards the bar where there stood, wiping the counter, a middle-aged woman with graying hair, a red housedress, sharp nails, and more energy than the young drunk merchant snoring and drooling over the counter. "Evening, love," the thief said. "What's the cost for the night?"

"10 coppers," the woman said gruffly, and out of habit she spat into an empty vase.

"Let's make it 5, shall we?"

"No, let's make it 15."

"I'm sorry," the thief said, his brows suddenly twisting with confusion. "D'you actually understand how bartering works?"

The middle-aged woman looked up at him.

John Huxley, who stood a good distance behind the thief, was able to see it all. The soft wrinkles on her face, marking her age... The darkness around her eyes, signs that the woman had hardly slept recently, or perhaps at all... John realized this was the woman's life, much like farming was *his* life. She lived within the Woodlands out of *choice*, knowing that she could very well be accepted into human civilization whenever she pleased. The fact that she would choose the Woodlands over a kingdom like Vallenghard was baffling to the young farmer.

"All my rooms are taken, sonny," the woman snarled. "If you want to steal one, I better get somethin' extra for it." She spat into the vase again.

John and Syrena kept their distance, observing the thief at work... His elbow rested on the bar, his smile was firm, his eyes just a tad bit squinted, as if planting doubt into the woman's mind, his right leg was held at ease while most of his weight rested on his left...

Every movement mattered. Every detail was essential.

The smallest mistake could make all the difference.

"Miss Rayna!" a voice suddenly interrupted. An elf girl, tall and thin, with indigo-colored skin and a head of silver curls, approached the bar with an empty tray. "Miss Rayna, ma'am!"

"What now?!" the older woman snapped.

"Rahl's been sneakin' out to smoke that red spindle again."

"Damn it, I *told* the littl' shit I didn't want that stuff near my tavern!"

"I told 'im that, Miss Rayna, but he seems t-"

"I'll handle it later, girl. Now go."

The elf girl gave Hudson and his two companions a confused glance before walking away, as if she knew they were outsiders.

"And Kiira?" the woman added. "If he tries anythin' on ya, have Edmund deal with 'im."

"Yes, Miss Rayna!"

The woman began wiping down the rest of the counter, as if Hudson was no longer there. He cleared his throat to get her attention back and she turned to him with a roll of the eyes.

"What?!" she snapped at him.

"Listen, darling," Hudson leaned in closer, still attempting to persuade her. "I can see you're quite a busy woman, so I'll make this quick... I'm not sure if your hearing's quite as good as mine, but since I walked into this room I've managed to overhear quite a few intriguing details."

"Humor me," Miss Rayna set the rag down and crossed her arms, keeping the vase close for her to spit on.

"Well, first of all, there's the group of raiders sitting to my right," Hudson muttered quite rapidly, as if time was of the essence. "All of them are visibly armed and if I know a raider, I know that there's only two things on their minds: gold and sex. And when they don't get one or the other, they tend to get a bit restless."

John took a peek at the raiders, but Syrena knew better.

"Then there's the twitching goblin sitting at the first table left of the door, who is very clearly suffering from heightened delusions due to the red spindle he recently smoked, hence that awful rotting leaf stench just outside the door. And I do believe I just heard you say you're not a fan of it either."

Miss Rayna couldn't help but glance at the goblin, more out of curiosity than actual precaution.

"And *finally* there's the enormous orc sitting in the corner next to the bard, staring directly at the blue elf across the room drinking with his goblin friends. I *know* that look, darling. Believe me, he's not in love with the elf. He's just letting him have one last drunken hurrah before beating him senseless, slicing his throat, *possibly* eating him? I'm not quite sure, has he ordered anything?"

"What's your point?" Miss Rayna asked, not quite as amused as Hudson had hoped.

"My *point* is that it's only a matter of time before something goes wrong in this place and we both know it," Hudson said with a mildly convincing grin. "And when it does, you might just wish you had someone with a few skills staying under your roof for the night."

Miss Rayna released an unexpected burst of laughter.

The thief scowled, having never been laughed at so directly in his life.

"You think all that rubbish *scares* me?" she asked. "'Cause I'm some defenseless old wench that has a tavern in the wrong side of the world? Is that it?" *Spit.*

John couldn't help but smirk. He had a certain liking towards Hudson, despite his own bad decisions, for he always seemed to have a good point or at least make a solid argument for one. But the baffled look on the thief's face was laughable. He looked like a nervous child all of a sudden, a rascal being lectured by his mother. And John found it amusing to see that side of him, to see that the man was not always faultless.

"Well I'm *not* some old wench, sonny. I am Miss Rayna and this is *my* tavern," Miss Rayna said boldly. "First of all, one of those raiders happens to be my son Grum. And yes, he *does* love gold and sex. And someday either one of those will probably be the death of 'im. But he 'n' his friends are no threat to *me*. And the orc sitting over in that corner *does* want to kill the elf. *You* would too if the elf owed you fifty coppers and you saw him here drinking 'n' pissing his money away." *Spit.*

Hudson cleared his throat embarrassingly, removed his elbow from the bar, and changed his stance, realizing his leverage in the situation was gone.

"Anythin' you say to me, I can probably tell you a story that can match it," Miss Rayna said. "Seems 'bout an average night 'round these parts. I'm here to sell them drinks, I'm no threat to them… They can do to each other as they damn well please so long as they don't cross *me*."

"What makes you think they won't?" Hudson tried to challenge her. "Having one raider son isn't much protection."

"I've *two* sons. You passed my son Edmund on your way in." *Spit.*

At that moment, the music stopped. The twitching goblin by the door hopped over the wooden table and began attacking a blue-skinned elf across from him. The mumbling throughout the place lowered down to soft hums as many turned their heads at the commotion. The goblin's eyes were dark and bloodshot, the red spindle inadequately taking its toll on him in a way that it didn't do with humans. He was vicious, angry, raging mad, biting at the air as the elf held him by the neck.

The chair suddenly slid and they both fell back.

Miss Rayna then rolled her eyes and exhaled sharply. "Edmund!!" she shouted, with a demeanor so calm that it made John wonder if fights like these were more common than they seemed.

Upon hearing the name, the tavern door swung open.

A massive arm reached in and pulled the goblin off the elf.

John's mouth dropped… Edmund, the ogre, dragged the goblin out of the tavern and then closed the wooden door. For a moment, everyone in the tavern could hear the goblin shrieking outside, followed by the snapping of a neck, the squelching of flesh, and the ogre's grunts as he began chewing.

The sounds were haunting…

But Miss Rayna cleared her throat casually and then the bard started singing again, picking up exactly where she'd left off in the song. And the rest of the guests carried on drinking and laughing as if nothing had just happened.

"I'm sorry," Hudson said, somewhat nervously. "Your other son is… an *ogre?*"

"One doesn't have to be related to an infant to be its mother," Miss Rayna grinned. "And, by the way… Good news for you and your friends, sonny. It seems a room's *just* opened up." She held up an old key made of copper, before spitting into her vase once again.

Hudson took the key hesitantly. "Don't do that. That's disgusting, y'know," he said, referring to the spitting, knowing very well that Syrena was certainly grinning behind him.

John handed the woman the 10 coppers, and then the elf girl Kiira guided them towards the rickety spiraling stairs. The room itself was rather small, but Kiira moved a few things around and made enough room for all three bedspreads.

John sunk into one of them, rested his back against the cloth, but could feel the cold hard wood beneath it. There was a lit candle on a sole wooden stand that only had room to hold one tankard of ale at a time.

After about ten seconds in the room, Hudson felt confined and crowded.

"Don't know about the two of you but I'm heading down for a drink."

"Please don't go looking for trouble," Syrena said, sitting in one of the bedspreads.

"No trouble," Hudson replied with a smirk. "Don't mind me, love... I've had a rather rough couple of days, what with the dungeon escape, the attacks, and a stupid farmer guilting me into staying on this deemed-to-fail journey."

John was standing just feet from the thief, but he may as well have been on the other side of Gravenstone. For the last couple of days he'd done that, talked as if John wasn't there. But rather than be insulted, the farmer was starting to find his banter somewhat amusing.

"Frankly, I'm surprised *you* don't feel the need to wind down, darling."

"Not now," Syrena said. "Maybe later."

"Suit yourself," the thief said. "If I don't come back up within the hour, I'm either dead or drunk. Either way, don't disturb me." He took a step towards the outside.

"Hudson?"

The thief stopped in his tracks.

John sat up, reached into his pocket, and tossed a silver coin into the air.

Hudson caught it just in time and then froze, his brow raised with confusion.

"For your drinks," John gave him a nod. "As a 'thank you'..."

Hudson didn't know what to say. He waited a few seconds before the discomfort overtook him and he left the room without speaking a word. And then John and Syrena gave each other a glance during that moment of silence.

"He'll warm up," the witch said with a friendly grin. "Give 'im time."

John smiled and rested his back against the bedspread again. Downstairs, they could hear the orc girl playing and singing a fast-paced rendition of *The Tale of Jonah 'Peg-leg' Roderick*. After what seemed like an hour inside of the tavern, John began to enjoy the music and the ambiance of the place. As odd as it was, he felt less out of place than he did when he first stepped in. He began to see the appeal that Miss Rayna must have felt upon deciding to stay and live there.

"Is this always what it's like out here?" John asked, staring blankly up at the ceiling.

"Always," Syrena replied softly. "The names 'n' faces change, but the life is all the same."

John smiled. The witch was at home, he knew, and for a moment he almost envied her for the amount of freedom that seemed to exist out here.

"Well... *Almost* the same," Syrena added. "It's not every day you meet a woman who names her birth son *Grum* and her adopted ogre son *Edmund*."

They laughed together. And John felt a sudden warmth in his chest. He didn't have many friends in Vallenghard, outside of his family and his casual acquaintances in Elbon.

Is this what it's like? He wondered. *To have friends?*

He kept smiling. It gave him joy to know there existed a place like this, so vastly different. A place where humans and elves and orcs and gnomes could all share a drink and a laugh, so affably and neighborly. It was different and refreshing. It was *thrilling*.

"John?" Syrena called for him.

"Hmm?"

"Have you any more coin?"

"Sure…"

"D'you, uh," she cleared her throat. "D'you want to go join Hudson for a round?"

John sighed, his lips still locked in a grin. "Hell, I'll join him for *two*."

* * *

Sir Darryk Clark of Roquefort sat uncomfortably in the king's chair, feeling more overwhelmed and unprepared than he did upon accepting such responsibility from the king himself.

He was the Lord Regent of Val Havyn now… Yet he had no support, no guidance, and he hardly knew anyone in the city that he could rely on. He'd sent a raven to his father in Roquefort but assumed he was far too busy making preparations for his fleet to make sail.

He was alone… And the thought of it was unnerving…

The velvet patterns on the assembly room walls, the silver crown on his head, even the cushion on his chair felt unfamiliar to him, and the map of Val Havyn on the table even *more* so… he may as well have been looking at a map of some distant city in Ahari or Qamroth.

"How many sets of gates?" he asked.

"Three, my lord," said the sweaty guard to his left, pointing to the map with his finger. "The central gates are located in the south, in front of Merchants' Square. The eastern and western gates are much smaller, and they remain closed unless otherwise requested."

"And in the north?"

"The guard barracks, my lord. There are gates there but no roads, only the creek surrounding it."

"Very well," Darryk said. "Post three men at every gate, except for the barracks."

"*Three*, my lord?" asked the husky guard to his right.

Darryk cringed, though he wasn't entirely sure if it was due to the guard's breath or if it was due to hearing them address him as '*Lord*'. It was certainly a title he dreamed of having one day, though not quite yet and definitely not in a city unknown to him.

"We've only 25 men at our disposal, gentlemen," Darryk said sternly. "And this city is far too grand for only 25 men, we all know it. Post three men at every city gate and three on every palace gate. The rest will be placed on patrol duty, covering different sectors of the city."

"Yes, my lord."

"As for you two... I need one of you to draft a notice for hire. We need more soldiers and we need them now, while the peace remains."

"We're to hire... *peasants*, my lord?" asked the husky guard.

"W-What my companion *means* to say," added the sweaty one, "Is that inexperienced men won't make for suitable members of the royal guard."

"Then you'll train them."

"Yes... with all due respect, my lord... with *what?*"

Darryk gave him a perplexed glance.

"I'm afraid we are rather short of weaponry and equipment, what with the impending battle and all. The king's troops stripped the barracks nearly clean. There's hardly anything left."

"Then we purchase more."

"The king's trusted blacksmith was Mister Thaddeus Rexx, my lord... But I'm afraid he's recently ventured out of the city. No one has seen or heard from him. His shop's being looked after by his apprentices. But, if I may be honest, they're both rubbish."

Darryk took a moment to think it through. Already, he could feel the tension in the back of his neck growing, aching at him, wearing him down. The two guards that had been assigned to him looked just as out of place as he did, if not more. And it somewhat eased his nerves a bit to know he wasn't the only one that felt unprepared.

"Very well," he said to the husky guard, trying his best to appear confident and lord-like. "*You* draft the notice for hire."

"Yes, my lord," the guard replied and left the room.

"And *you*," Darryk turned to the sweatier guard. "I have a special task for you... What did you say your name was?"

"Hektor, my lord," the guard answered tensely. "Pardon me. If I may ask... Who is to be appointed knight commander, now that Sir... Um... Now that *Viktor Crowley* is no longer with us?"

Darryk raised a brow. "I thought *you* were commanding the troop..."

"Well I am, my lord," Hektor said. "But only because I was the highest-ranking soldier left behind. Normally the position is held by... well, a *knight*."

Darryk sighed and gave him a nod. "Well... You've been doing a fair job so far. We'll have to make do for now. *Desperate times* and all that."

Hektor closed his eyes and nodded affably, as if honored to be trusted with such a task, even if indirectly. "I will serve you to the death, my lord…"

"Thank you, Hektor," Darryk said, and then his expression shifted to a more honest and concerned one. "Now… *Please* tell me you know of at least one decent blacksmith in this damned city…"

* * *

The hammer struck down on the anvil, sending pulsating rings into the air as Evellyn Amberhill held up the sizzling steel and examined it closely, feeling the warmth radiating from it.

She smiled… It was one of her best works, that sword…

So many hours of labor, it felt almost a shame to have to sell it. The problem was you couldn't survive off steel. If you could, the Amberhill family wouldn't be going hungry the way they so often did.

Little Alycia stepped out of the house, a stained apron wrapped neatly around her waist. "Supper's ready," she said.

Evellyn shot her sister a smile. "I'll be in soon." She wiped the sweat from her face and untied the lace holding her messy bun in place. A tumbling wave of red fell down to her shoulders and back; under the afternoon sun, it glistened like fire. She set the hammer down and hauled a bucket of water towards the sizzling sword.

She was laboriously focused, as she always was with any of her work.

Too focused to notice the two men standing just outside the old wooden fence surrounding her wielding yard. One of them was dressed in tarnished guard's armor. The other was wearing a silver crown, small but sophisticated, and dressed in a rich blue tunic embroidered with a gold design on the sleeves and edges. His pants and boots however, were not nearly as elegant.

The man wasn't from Val Havyn, it was obvious… His skin was brown like cinnamon, his black hair short and curly, his hands and face rough and scarred and callused. Such was the image of a warrior, not a nobleman. And the expression on his face certainly made it clear that he preferred to be in a field instead of lounging about in a palace.

"Pardon our intrusion, miss?" the man said.

Evellyn turned to them suddenly, confused and thrown aback.

"Good day," she said with a forced bow. "May I help you?"

"Yes, miss. May I speak with your master?"

Evellyn fought back the urge to roll her eyes. Instead, she picked up the hammer and began slamming it against the sword again. Not that the sword needed more work, but speaking to nobles always made her uncomfortable and so she often found the first thing to keep her occupied to avoid looking into their patronizing eyes.

"I've no master," she spoke over the sound of ringing steel. "Only my father."

"May we speak with *him*, then?"

She paused, hammer in midair, and turned back to them with a mild scowl.

"He's resting... If you wish to purchase something, you can speak to me."

"Very well," the man cleared his throat somewhat tautly. "Have you any armor at your disposal? We're looking to purchase."

"And who're you?" she asked.

The man cleared his throat again.

"Sir Darryk Clark of Roquefort," he said. "Appointed Lord Regent of Val Havyn."

"Sir Darryk Clark?" she asked. "I'm sorry, I've never heard of you, m'lord."

"Nor should I expect you to have heard of me," he smiled, a warm smile, like an outsider looking to make a friend. "I hear your father is among the best blacksmiths in the city."

"He is," she nodded. "Or *was*, rather... For now, it's only me."

"Very well. How many pieces of armor have you for sale?"

She hesitated for a moment. Nobles made her uncomfortable, all right. But Sir Darryk's demeanor was far more amiable than she would have expected. It became clear to her that the man was not the average noble. In fact, had he not been wearing the crown and the tunic, he could almost pass for a peasant. *Almost*... If peasants could only speak as elegantly as he did...

She set the hammer down again and sunk the tip of the sword into the bucket of water to cool it down. Then she approached the wooden fence, wiping her hands on her apron.

"Overall?" she said. "Twelve pieces of chest armor, fourteen sets of gauntlets and boot plates, and nine helmets, all of it the finest steel in Val Havyn."

"Not better than Kahrran steel, I'm sure," Hektor remarked.

"We don't live in Kahrr, sir."

Hektor shut right back up and wiped the sweat from his brow.

Sir Darryk gave her a head nod and a friendly grin. "How about weapons?"

"Plenty," she smiled. "Nineteen sets of swords and shields. Working on a twentieth now."

"Good," he replied. "What was your name?"

"Evellyn Amberhill, sir."

"We'll take it all, Miss Amberhill..."

Her eyes widened. Her heart began racing. "I'm sorry... *all*?"

Sir Darryk Clark examined the wielding yard. Most of the equipment was old and worn down, but it seemed reasonably durable. And the equipment had little to do with anything, it was the craft of the blacksmith that mattered. He gave Hektor a head nod, and the guard reached into his heavy satchel and pulled out an overflowing sack made of neat leather.

"1,000 yuhn in silver and copper for all of it," Darryk said. "I can have a few men come and gather the equipment within the hour. Do we have an accord?"

"Y-Yes... yes!" Evellyn said, still unsure if the man was playing some sort of trick on her.

But there was no trick... The guard handed her the heavy sack, and it nearly fell off her hands from the weight. Darryk gave her a smile.

"Excellent," he said. "Now... Should we require more, can we count on you to continue providing us with the necessary gear?"

"You can count on me, m'lord!" she smiled.

"A pleasure doing business with you..."

And that was that. The two men walked away, leaving Evellyn alone in her wielding yard with more coin than she had earned in the past two seasons combined. In a matter of minutes, the Amberhill family had enough to feed themselves for a month and still have plenty left over.

"Evellyn?" a soft voice called.

"What?" she turned around, still staggered and overjoyed.

"Soup's getting cold," her sister said.

Evellyn smiled. "You have it," she said as she approached the house. "I'm going to head to the bakery and fetch us some fresh bread."

Alycia's jaw dropped at the sight of the coin.

"Come. We'll store this somewhere safe. The royal guard will be here to gather a few things soon. And then I'm gonna need you to look after father for a few hours."

"Where will you go?"

"To Elbon. I won't be long, I promise."

"What's there to do in Elbon?"

Evellyn's face was dirt-ridden, but it was beautiful all the same. She wiped herself with her apron, and there was a new trace of hope there, vivid from the sparkle in her eyes to the warmth in her cheeks. She untied her stained apron and pulled 5 coppers from the leather sack, admired them for a moment, and then hid them in one of the pockets of her red housedress.

"I've a debt to repay the Huxleys," she said with a smile.

* * *

Val Havyn during sunset was something from a dream.

It was spellbinding, the way the sun would cast shadows of the arched red-bricked roofs over the cobblestones, and the way the light reflected from the stained glass windows of the royal palace, as the cloudy sky blended into a serene blue.

It was as peaceful as it could get.

Lady Brunylda Clark, treasurer of the royal city, sat in a beautifully decorated armchair that she had specifically requested be moved to the outdoor balcony that morning. Her bedroom was in the highest tower of the palace, nearly a hundred feet above the city streets. The view from her balcony would have been astounding for the common peasant, but to the Lady it was nothing out of the ordinary. In fact, it frequently reminded her of the responsibility she held over the people of the grand city and therefore she found herself unable to sit out there longer than ten minutes without a drink at hand.

She sat there that afternoon sipping from an elegant goblet, savoring the taste of the dark and bitter Roquefort liqueur, which was far too strong for most people's taste and yet to her it was as light and smooth as water. The wind on her face was causing her eyes to become watery and so she closed them, sighing deeply and exhaustedly, allowing for the heat of the liqueur to burn her chest...

She welcomed the burn, embraced it, felt almost completed by it...

Finally some rest, she thought to herself. There were no sounds except for that of the wind and a whistling hummingbird standing on the edge of her balcony.

She peeked at it.

How nice he must have it, she thought. *To be able to fly away, wherever his heart takes him. What joy that must be. What luck the little bastard has.*

When she closed her eyes, she did not want to open them again.

Without the view of the landscape, she could have been anywhere.

One moment she was in the royal city of Val Havyn... And the next moment she was in Roquefort, a young naïve girl with high hopes and distant dreams...

A Lady only speaks when spoken to, her father would say.

A Lady does not argue with her superiors, her mother would advise.

It wasn't until Lady Brunylda Clark was of age thirteen that she realized what her mother really meant was '*A Lady does not argue with her superiors who are men*'.

Forty years later, the Lady found that not much had changed...

Whenever she remembered it, she found herself beckoning for the nearest servant to fetch her another bottle of liqueur. Not that the drinking slowed her down, by any means; in fact, the Lady at her *worst* state often proved to be remarkably smarter than most of King Rowan's advisors at their *best*.

She breathed, slowly and deeply, her eyes growing heavy and drained.

It wouldn't have been the first time she dozed off in her balcony. In fact, during the worst of days, she preferred it. There was a soft knock on her door, however, that brought her back before she could sink into a deep sleep.

"Come in," she spoke loudly.

Brie, the former handmaiden to the princess, walked in nervously.

"Sorry to bother you, m'lady..."

"What do you want, girl?" she asked, evoking her displeasure through her words.

"Sir Dar... Umm... pardon me, *Lord* Darryk Clark wishes to speak with you, m'lady."

Lady Brunylda took a good sip from her goblet and with a scowl said, "*Lord* Darryk Clark may walk himself here if he wishes..."

At that very moment, the door hinges screeched delicately and a heavy boot stepped inside the Lady's bedroom... Darryk felt the discomfort before he could even speak. This was the second time in his life he had visited Val Havyn, and never did he envision himself ruling it. The man stood there, wearing a silver crown that felt more unusual to him than the elegant silk clothing the king had ordered made especially for him. He was 25 years of age and yet he looked more like a frightened boy turning towards the nearest familiar face for guidance.

The Lady was merely a distant aunt he knew by name yet never by face...

To him, she was the only connection he had to Roquefort...

To her, he may as well have been Aharian, for she cared very little that they shared a house name. House Clark had shown her what it meant to be a person of nobility and the amount of power and status one could earn by making the right decisions. That was, of course, exclusive to the Clark *men*.

As a young girl, she would often question why... And all she would get in response was something along the lines of '*A Lady does not question her superiors on their way of life*'.

"Thank you," Darryk said to Brie. "Would you leave us alone for a moment?"

"No," the Lady interrupted. "Stay, girl. Pour me another drink."

Brie chose to obey the Lady, and Darryk remained in place, as if waiting for the girl to finish and leave. Lady Brunylda, however, seemed to care very little about the privacy of whatever matters the knight-turned-lord had to discuss.

"To what do I owe the pleasure, my *Lord*?" she asked as she held out her goblet for Brie to fill.

Darryk cleared his throat, approaching her tentatively. "I have come to request your assistance with a particular matter, my Lady."

"I gathered that much," she scoffed. "No one ever comes up here unless they require my assistance. What can I do for you, my *Lord*?" Before the handmaiden could walk away, Brunylda snapped her fingers and beckoned her back. "I said *stay*, girl... Take a seat. I might need you."

Brie could do nothing but nervously obey, unsure if the Lady actually wanted her there or if she was simply doing it to spite the young lord. Darryk knew the Lady was never one to succumb to pressure, and so he gave Brie a head nod of acknowledgement before stepping out into the elegant balcony, taking a moment to appreciate the view.

"As you may be aware," he said. "We appear to have a shortage of men at our disposal."

She scoffed again. "The world is short of many things, my Lord, but men is not one of them."

"It *is* in Val Havyn, I'm afraid... I can't keep the city safe with such few guards, my Lady. The potential for an unprecedented threat is too great. Our guards need proper rest if they are to do their job and they can't very well leave the palace unguarded... It is our responsibility to find replacements so th-"

"*Our* responsibility?" she interrupted him. "I don't recall *my* name written on the parchment when his majesty signed your contract... I am merely a humble advisor. But please, do go on, my Lord."

There was a short silence...

Darryk resisted the temptation to argue, mostly out of unease...

"Please," he cleared his throat. "Call me Darryk."

The Lady said nothing, only continued to sip from her goblet.

It had only been days since Darryk was assigned the king's responsibilities and already his eyelids were starting to show signs of weariness, black and wrinkled in contrast to his smooth caramel skin. But despite it all, he appeared to be holding himself together quite well. His false confidence was irreproachable when in the presence of the king's advisors. In the presence of the Lady, however, the man felt the weight of expectation lift from his shoulders, replaced by something else entirely... Something like intimidation, if not fear...

"There is a gentleman from the city of Kahrr in our city grounds," Darryk said. "Count Raoul Jacquin is his name. I plan to meet with him in the morning to discuss the possibility of sending a few dozen men to Val Havyn."

"I see," the Lady said, keeping her eyes on the landscape. Since the knight-turned-lord arrived at her door, she hadn't even given him a glance. Darryk may as well have been nude and she wouldn't have noticed. "I wish you the best of luck, my Lord... Don't be at all surprised if he treats you like a common peasant. It's quite typical of Kahrran men. 'Tis why we shouldn't have free cities."

There was another silence that followed, during a moment of hesitation on Darryk's behalf. He felt his palms grow sweaty as his heart began to race. And with a deep sigh, he took a risk and said, "I would like for you to accompany me when I meet with him..."

"Is that an order or a request, my *Lord*?"

It was then that Darryk felt an impulse to become defensive. The only thing he ever knew of ruling is what he had seen in his father, and Lord Augustus Clark had never been a patient man. Darryk had always felt, in a sense, that he would do things differently should he find himself in a position of power. He simply didn't expect he would be put to the test quite so soon.

"It's a request... my *Lady*," he tried to match her contemptuous tone, and much to his surprise she half-smirked.

"I see," she said. "And what do you need *me* for? You're the Lord Regent of Val Havyn, are you not?"

"Well... My knowledge of the world outside of Vallenghard is not as grand as yours, my Lady. Eventually, there will be negotiation with Count Jacquin. And, as you are the Treasurer of the royal city, I would feel much better having you by my side."

"Ahh... Foreigners intimidate you, do they?"

"They do not, my Lady... But I know when my expertise lies elsewhere. I am a soldier, not a diplomat. And do forgive me for being blunt, but... A man makes mistakes, whether he's a peasant or a king. Perhaps his majesty didn't entirely consider the possibility that there may be another person more qualified than me to rule this city."

Lady Brunylda was thrown aback all of a sudden... She hadn't considered Darryk's feelings towards all of this. Sure, the knight had the look of a confused child when he was appointed Lord, but never did she contemplate that he would feel disinclined to accept the offer.

"Where will this Count Jacquin be staying?" she asked.

"Er... That there's a matter I've yet to figure out. I have two guards asking questions and th-"

"The Emerald Rose Saloon," a soft voice mumbled.

Both the Lady and the Lord glanced back.

"What was that, girl?"

"Um... The Emerald Rose Saloon, m'lady," Brie said, slowly rising from her chair out of respect. "M-My sister's a servant to Madame Sybil... Sometimes I visit her in the evenings."

Sir Darryk's brow was half-lowered and half-raised, in a way that hadn't seemed possible to Brie until that moment. "A-Are you certain?" he asked her with a hopeful tone.

"Yes, m'lord."

"I-I... Thank you..."

There were no words from Lady Brunylda at first, only a chuckle.

"What is it?" Darryk asked.

"A noble's first mistake is not realizing that servants have an entire society of their own. In some ways, their connections are somewhat greater than ours."

Darryk turned his attention back to the handmaiden. "What did he look like?"

"Don't know," she replied. "I didn't actually see him... but I did see his name signed on the guest list for a two-night stay. And he's paying quite a bit of coin."

"Excellent," Darryk smiled. "Excellent work!"

"Hang on a minute," Lady Brunylda set her goblet down on the glass table next to her armchair. "What did you just say...?"

Brie was both startled and confused. She wiped her sweaty palms on the waist of her green housedress. "I said my sister's a serv-"

"No, no, *after* that, girl. Regarding the guest list…"

Brie wasn't sure of what else to say. As a handmaiden, she was used to being invisible. In fact, this may have been the first time the lady stared right into her eyes for that long without giving her an order.

Lady Brunylda Clark wasn't exactly smiling… It was more of a look of amusement and perhaps a hint of newly found admiration. Regardless, it was a look that was far different than any other look she had given Brie before. There was more warmth there.

"You can *read?*" the Lady asked.

"Oh… Um… *yes*, m'lady," Brie could feel the sweat building up in her brow, just beneath a forelock of greasy brown hair, the rest of which was tied in an unkempt bun with a copper pin.

And suddenly there it was… An actual smile, plastered over the Lady's face…

"Very well… I will meet you in the assembly room at dawn, Lord Darryk," she said, to which Darryk smiled with surprise.

"My sincere thanks, my Lady!" he said with a head nod.

"Anything else?"

"Not at all, my Lady! That will do," he walked out of the Lady's bedroom, a new trace of hope in his expression. And when the door closed behind him, the Lady broke the silence first.

"As for you, girl…"

Brie's eyes left the carpet and looked up as if expecting a lecture.

"Be sure to get proper rest tonight. I want you on your best in the morning."

"Y-Yes, m'lady… Shall I bring your tea *here* or to the assembly room?"

"Fuck the tea," the Lady said unexpectedly. "Have someone else fetch it."

Brie's jaw dropped slightly. It wasn't that the Lady didn't curse, she certainly did, especially when there was liqueur involved. It was the new look she was giving her… It wasn't at all how servants were typically looked at…

"If you can read, I trust you can write, yes?"

"Um… Yes, m'lady."

"Good… You'll be coming along with us. A good diplomatic meeting will require a good bookkeeper," the Lady picked up her goblet again with a grin.

"Y-Yes… *Thank* you, m'lady!" Brie said, her face lighting up with wonder.

"Go on, girl," the Lady snapped her fingers, though Brie found it to be far less intimidating than before. In fact, the handmaiden had a concealed smile and a shiver of excitement.

"A *proper* rest, girl, remember… I need you sharp. Can't be too careful with Kahrran diplomats, they can *smell* weakness. You will wear the finest dress you own, is that clear?"

"Yes, m'lady!"

"Good. And, by the gods, will you do something about that hair?"

* * *

It was a pleasant afternoon in the farming village of Elbon.

Or, at least, it *began* as one…

The sun was setting, the air was cooling down, the grassy fields were dancing with the wind, but there was something lurking among the greenery. And for the first time in a long time, fate was to bring a great misfortune to the Huxley family.

Just before nightfall, the twins Margot & Melvyn were scampering through the fields, using sticks as swords, happy as children their age should be. But the boy began to feel anxious as his sister ran further and further away from the comfort of their mother's farm and towards Lotus Creek.

"Margot, wait!" he shouted.

But the girl's thirst for exploration always got the better of her. They ran until they reached the top of a hill, the view of their farm as beautiful and serene as it was every spring, like a charming portrait in a nobleman's study.

"Remember what Mister Beckwit said," the girl aimed at her brother's feet with the stick. The boy's eyes moved absentmindedly, and Margot then jabbed him underneath the ribcage.

He grunted. "What was *that* for?!"

"Keep your eyes on the enemy!" she grinned.

"Why, you…"

He ran after her, but Margot's speed was unmatched, as she had proven it many times before. She frolicked downhill, dangerously away from the farm, hopping over sharp stones and patches of swampy grass.

"Get back here!"

"*Make* me!"

"It's not funny, Margot! Mum said to stay close!"

"We'll be fine!"

She did what her heart told her to, which would often lean towards that which her mother objected to. She ran until she could see that dark shade of blue in the distance, until she could hear the rapid waters drifting by and could feel the breeze against her face. She came to a halt right at the river's edge, and aimed her stick up at her brother, her other arm held up in the air as if she were carrying something on her shoulder.

"Do you *dare* challenge me?!" she spoke in a deeper voice, as if imitating a gallant knight of some sort. "No man that ever challenges *me* has lived to tell the tale, sir."

Melvyn was not very impressed. "We have to go back, Margot. Mum won't like it if w-"

"D'you want to get better or not?" she asked, this time with her normal voice and an eye roll.

He hesitated. But then her sister gave him a smile.

He smiled right back and crossed his stick over hers as if they were crossing blades.

"I do in fact challenge you, Margot Huxley of Elbon!"

They clashed sticks, again and again. Margot, agile and unflinching as she was, climbed onto the stones along the river's edge, unafraid of falling into the current. But the boy was more wary, sometimes holding back on his swings out of fear of making his sister lose her balance.

"Come on, you swine!" Margot said, again in her fake knight voice. "Is that all you got?!"

"Just warming up!" Melvyn swung again.

"You fight like a farmer, lad. Who trained you?!" Margot's swing was suddenly fiercer than before, and so the boy dropped his stick. She held hers up to his neck. "Certain death," she smiled.

He was out of breath. But she could have gone on for an hour.

He pushed her stick away with mild annoyance.

"Someday," he said. "I'll get you."

Suddenly, the girl's smile faded and her eyes sunk... Something behind Melvyn had caught her eye. Something leathery and brown caught in between two stones just down the stream. She threw her stick on the mud and ran towards it, her curiosity at its peak.

"Margot? What are you doing?!"

She bent to her knees and, while holding onto a loose boulder, reached into the water.

It was a blade, old and rusty and still sheathed on a tattered leather case.

She became lost for a moment, her lips curving into a smile.

And then her other hand slipped... Her arms sunk into the water, but before the current could hit her face, Melvyn's hand grasped the back of her dress and gave a strong pull.

"*What* are you doing?!" he said, but his eyes widened immediately when he noticed the rusty blade she had fetched from the river. "Whoa... brilliant!"

For a moment, their innocent eyes became immersed with wonder. They were far too inexperienced with a blade to ever be allowed to hold one just yet. Often when they asked, they'd get lectured by their mother or Old Man Beckwit. *A blade is not a toy,* they'd say. *It's all fun and games until someone gets hurt...*

But their inquisitive little hearts could not resist. The blade, however tarnished and worn out it might have been, was like treasure to them. And not having held one in their lives made them completely oblivious to the fact that it was in fact their brother John's old blade, the very same one he'd used to fight and capture a wanted thief, the one he had lost when he threw himself into the creek just a week prior.

"Could I see...?" Melvyn asked.

"*I* found it first," she held the blade out of his reach.

"I know, but could I jus-"

"Wait, shh!" she silenced him, her ear catching something rather peculiar.

"What?"

"D'you hear that...?"

It was a high-pitched cry, like that of an infant, somewhere within a cluster of bushes nearby. They began walking towards it. Margot led the way, much like she always did, her long black hair swaying with the wind.

"W-Wait, Margot..."

He grabbed her by the elbow, but she shook herself right off.

"Let go!" she hissed at him.

"Yes, but what if y-"

"If you don't want to come, then stay back."

But he didn't... He *couldn't*... Much like any other child, his curiosity won him over, despite the fact that he was frightened out of his mind. They followed their ears, the muffled whimpering growing louder and louder with every step they took. Then, as they stepped in between two shrubs, they came across a pile of leaves pressed together into a bed, and on top of it was a bundle of cloth... Something within the cloth was moving...

Margot bent down and, with a cautious hand, revealed what hid underneath.

Her jaw dropped slightly. "By the gods..."

It was an infant orc... Tiny, olive-skinned, and sharp-fanged, but oddly endearing all the same. Melvyn searched all around for any sign of life, but there was no one. "Y-You think someone *left* it here...?"

The babe stopped crying all of a sudden and looked up at Margot, his glossy yellow eyes blinking gently, and gave her something like a smile. She smiled right back and with wonder in her eyes she reached a hand out to touch him...

"Stop!"

She bounced from the fright. "*What?!*" she hissed at Melvyn.

"What if... I-I don't know, what if it gets you *sick*, or s-something?"

"Don't be stupid, it's only a baby!"

"I-I know, but... y'know what they say. They're... *dangerous*, aren't they?"

"When has a *baby* ever hurt you?" she rolled her eyes.

Melvyn was sweating, despite the cool breeze. Margot would've been lying to herself if she said she wasn't a bit rattled herself. It was, after all, the first time they'd ever seen a baby orc.

"Fine," she said, leaping to her feet. "I'll go get mum! You stay here."

"What, *alone*? With... *it?*"

"You'll be *fine*! Stop being childish! Here, take this," she handed him the rusty blade. "Make sure nothing harms it. I'll be back!"

"W-What if *I* go get mum?!"

"You're too slow. *I'll* go!"

"Wait, M-Margot!"

But she was gone before he could protest, leaving him alone and nervous within the bushes... Alone with a babe whose mother was nowhere to be seen...

Evellyn Amberhill hopped off the cart and tied her mule to the pole just outside the Huxleys' barn. She could see Adelina Huxley harvesting corn from the field and filling baskets until there was no more room in them. With a smile, she walked over. There was a deep sadness in the Adelina's somnolent eyes. Having not heard from either of her children in a week, she hadn't gone a single night with a good sleep. There was still hope there... For a mother, it was nearly impossible to give up hope entirely.

Evellyn reached her, but the woman was lost in her thoughts. And so the blacksmith cleared her throat, startling her.

"Evellyn!" she said, wiping the sweat and dirt from her forehead. "What a pleasure it is to see you, my dear."

"Hello, Missus Huxley," Evellyn replied with a smile.

"For goodness' sake, how many times must I tell you? It's *Adelina* to you." They shared a warm hug.

"I came by to give you this," Evellyn reached into her pocket and drew the 5 coppers.

"And what's this for?"

"Oh... John didn't tell you? We couldn't afford last week's vegetable order. Business has been rather slow. He insisted we keep the food and pay you when we can," Evellyn smiled shyly.

"Sounds exactly like him," said Adelina.

Evellyn could see past the woman's false smile and could almost sense her grief. Adelina had, in fact, shed tears every night since John and Robyn left the farm. And she was having difficulty getting out of bed in the mornings.

"How are you?" Evellyn asked.

"I'm fine..."

"Honestly," Evellyn placed a gentle hand on her shoulder. "If you need anything... anything at all... please let us know."

Adelina felt the knot in her throat start to grow and before she knew it, the tears she was fighting so hard to hold back started to pour. Evellyn couldn't help but lend her a shoulder. Seeing the blacksmith only reminded Adelina of John. She still saw them as the two children they once were, running and chasing each other through the fields. She *longed* for those days, truthfully. At least her John was safe back then. Now, he could be lying dead or wounded somewhere and there was no way for her to know for certain.

"Mum!" a voice echoed in the distance. Margot Huxley had never run so fast...

Adelina turned, suddenly alarmed upon seeing one of her children without the other.

"Mum!" Margot kept shouting.

Adelina ran towards her, nearly tripping over the basket of corn, and Evellyn followed closely behind. "Margot?! Where's your brother?!"

"He's fine," Margot slowed to a halt. "Quick... By the river! There's something you have to see..."

Melvyn Huxley could hardly bear to be near the orc child.

Be brave, damn you, he thought angrily to himself. He was not like the rest of his siblings, never had been. He was always the timid one, always the one hiding behind his mother's dress while someone else stepped forward and took the lead. His lip shivered as his eyes kept searching the fields, his snooping feet inching forward. Then he glanced nervously at the tiny orc's face, as if glancing into a pit of poisonous snakes.

Truth be told, it looked like any other baby, only with olive green skin and tiny fangs sticking out of its lower lip. It looked harmless, *nothing* like the 'fierce creatures' he'd been told about all his life, just a small innocent thing.

He's just a child, Melvyn repeated in his mind. *Just a child, nothing more...*

He took another step closer, a bigger step...

And it was then that he saw the incoming shadow...

Just around the shrubs, an orcess approached holding a sack of river water in one hand and a bundled cloth in the other. Her clothes were ragged and torn and wet, as if she had recently swam across the creek. Her shoulders, arms, feet, and part of her belly were exposed where the cloth had been ripped, and her shawl was now gone, her long black knotted hair loose and wild, like the thick mane of a mare.

Aevastra looked like any other woman, except perhaps taller than average, and much like the baby the only exceptions were her fangs and the color of her skin. When she saw the farmboy standing too close to her son, she felt the hairs in the back of her neck rise. She gave him a sudden snakelike hiss and her hands dropped. The sack of water splashed on the grass and the fresh berries stumbled out of the unwrapped cloth.

Melvyn stumbled backwards in fear. "S-Sorry, I..."

Aevastra reached into her waist belt and pulled out a hidden knife, a *tiny* knife, the likes of which Melvyn's mother would use for butter, except sharpened to a thin edge. She aimed it up at Melvyn, taking careful steps towards her child, shielding it, protecting it like a wolf mother would protect her pups. It wasn't the boy that scared her, it was the rusty blade he was holding against his chest; it was still sheathed, but he looked mere seconds away from using it. She opened her lips, a rough grunt escaping with every exhale.

"Go…" she said.

And much to his surprise, her voice was soft and kind like his mother's. Her eyes may have been wary and fierce, but in a way that *also* reminded him of his mother.

"Go!" she said louder, swinging the knife gently as if trying to scare him.

A moment passed… Melvyn was petrified by the fear…

"I-I'm s… I'm so sorry," he said, easing back slowly. He loosened his grip on the blade and held it to the side as if showing her that he meant no harm.

She approached the bed of leaves.

"Back!" she grunted, knife held up in defense still.

"Y-Yes… yes, okay," he stepped back. "We were just looking after it… *Him.*"

She dropped to her knees and caressed her babe's cheek, checking for any wounds. But the child was looking up, eyes gleaming and lips curling. He was safe and unharmed, and it eased her nerves a bit.

Melvyn watched in awe. For a couple of 'fierce creatures', they appeared more human than anything else. He found that while he was still nervous, he was not exactly afraid anymore. He had a strange warm feeling, like gazing upon a mother bird feeding her chicks. Behind him, however, were a couple of more worried faces…

"Melvyn… Get back here…"

The boy turned, only to see his mother's firm eyes beckoning him back. "M-Mum…"

Adelina, Margot, and Evellyn Amberhill stood there with open mouths and befuddled looks on their faces. By impulse, Aevastra's hand swung up again, knife still at hand. And Melvyn ran to take cover behind his mother. Margot, on the other hand, stepped valiantly forward with a look of shock and wonder.

"Margot! Get back here this instant…"

But the girl's curiosity was far too great to obey.

"Hi," she said to Aevastra. "I'm Margot…"

Aevastra glared back… The girl's eyes were friendly, she could tell. The orcess hadn't seen friendly eyes in a long, long time. Her mother and the other woman, however, seemed to be more guarded.

"Margot Huxley," the girl reiterated. "I-Is, um… Is your baby hungry?"

Upon hearing Margot's words, Adelina looked down at the bundle of cloth. Not that she hadn't noticed it before, but she had failed to notice the movement within it. And suddenly, she understood the orcess's overly protective manner.

"It's okay," Margot said. "We have food… I-If you want?"

It was then that Aevastra lowered the knife. She was a rubbish huntress and she knew it. And though she wasn't at all trusting of humans, her child mattered more to her.

"What's your name?" Margot asked.

The orcess picked up her child and held him against her chest, swaying him gently.

"Aevastra," she said. "My name is Aevastra."

Adelina was hesitant to speak. Something inside her was burdening her with doubt and uncertainty. Seeing a desperate mother with a starving babe in her hands was not entirely new to her. The world was regrettably full of desperate mothers and starving babes. And though her heart knew what to do, her mind wouldn't allow it. Not again.

"Mum?" Margot muttered. "Please? I think she's lost…"

We're all lost, Adelina thought. *And that is not my child to care for…*

She felt a knot in her throat. She loathed herself for having such thoughts. But she had always been a survivor. And she knew that with both John and Robyn gone, the burden of the labor would fall entirely on her. And there was no way she could possibly provide food for two more mouths.

That is not my child to care for, she kept on, as if trying to convince herself.

But it was still a child… And the fact that it wasn't hers hadn't stopped her before…

"Please, mum…"

Adelina looked at the orcess one last time. She saw the fierceness in her eyes, the will to survive. It was far too familiar to her, and she couldn't simply ignore it. And so, with a sigh, her lips curled into a hesitant smile. And she saw Aevastra's own lips start to curl as well.

It was a pleasant moment… Quite pleasant… Until it *wasn't*.

The sudden sound of piercing flesh startled them all. An arrow flew in out of nowhere and struck the orcess in the back. And the sharp tip managed to stab through and burst out of her collar bone.

The orcess roared. And for a moment, the twins realized where the word 'fierce' came from, in the stories. Aevastra's roar was like that of a wildcat…

Adelina sprung forward and managed to catch the orcess before she fell to her knees.

Margot grabbed the baby and immediately carried him back towards the bushes to safety.

And it was then that they all saw the two pairs of sinister eyes staring from across the creek. Two orcs, standing side by side with eerie grins plastered on their faces. One of them, the massive one, was holding a bow in his hand and reached for a second arrow.

Adelina's eyes opened wider than ever before, realizing her own children were still there.

"Get back to the farm!" she shouted. "All of you! *Now!*"

They ran.

* * *

Robyn Huxley never thought she could sleep while leaning against a pile of junk.

She also didn't think it possible to dream, and yet she did.

She dreamt of Nyx... She dreamt that he still lived and that they were back at the Huxley farm, laughing and talking about the misadventure with the tree nymphs. She didn't want to wake. If it were up to her, she would've slept forever. Something, however, woke her up.

Perhaps it was the guilt.

Perhaps it was the pulsating rage in her chest.

Perhaps it was the throbbing and agonizing pain in her arm. With her hands tied behind her, she couldn't see the burn wound. But she could feel it, all right... It itched and stung like all hells...

She heard voices outside, a blend of friendly chatter and angry drunken shouts.

Nighttime had arrived, and though she now knew the horrors that lurked within the Woodlands at night, she preferred to be out there, free and imperiled. Anything could be better than this. The pain and exhaustion had gotten the better of her, and so she'd ended up sleeping for hours.

What a day, she thought. *What an awful cursed day...*

She heard footsteps approaching. Very familiar footsteps, the girl realized.

Welcome back, you bastard...

Captain Malekai Pahrvus entered the tent, looking as hostile as ever but slightly more worn out. "You done crying, girl?" was the first thing he asked, and already she couldn't bear his presence. He dropped a fresh bucket near her roped feet and a bit of water splashed on her boots. She didn't give him the courtesy of a reply, nor did she meet eyes with the man. She simply waited, her neck turned away from him, her eyes locked on her bow resting over a pile of scrolls.

Malekai bent to his knees and began untying her feet.

"Still quiet, eh?" he asked. "So eager to use that tongue before. What's the matter now?"

Her jaw shuddered from the rage. Part of her was prepared to kick the man as soon as her feet were free, knowing very well it wouldn't end great.

Breathe, Robyn, she told herself. *Be patient... Be smarter than him...*

"Look at me, Robyn," he said, then waited a moment before untying her hands.

When she refused to turn to him, he forced her by clasping her jaw viciously.

He could feel it trembling, and she was worried he would mistake it for fear.

"*Look* at me, I say!" he growled. "So nervy, you are... It's starting to irritate me."

305

"I have nothing to say to you," she finally spoke, though her throat was so dry it came across as more like a whisper.

"I don't believe you," he shook his head. "I remember the first man that ever scarred me. Believe me, I had *plenty* to say to him… I wanted to kill the fucker. It was a shame someone got to him first."

He tightened his grip on her jaw, his sharp fingernails sinking into her skin. She was mere seconds away from spitting on him. And if it hadn't been for that sinister eye of his, she would have done it already.

"I'm gonna break you, Robyn," he said menacingly. "Sooner or later, you'll warm up to me…"

Robyn waited a moment. Her feet were now free and she could very easily have landed a kick. *Either he's stupid or he's testing you,* she told herself. *Either way, don't do it… Not yet… Use your words instead.*

She opened her lips. His eager ears waited patiently as he grinned.

"I'll never stop," she said, and her eyes were honest, firm, and unyielding. "You can burn me… You can hurt me… You can keep me roped and chained, but I will *never* stop running…"

It was not the answer the captain was hoping for. And some of his grin lost its flare.

There it is again. The grin, the chuckle, and the damn head nod… Is that all you know how to do?

Suddenly, something caught her eye…

Night had arrived, and all she could see through the small opening of the tent was a sea of grey shadows. She was sure, however, that something was lurking just outside.

She could see its legs… Not *human* legs…

They were thinner and furrier, and there were *four* of them…

"You stupid, stupid girl," Malekai said. Robyn had entirely forgotten he was there for a moment; her eyes were far too distracted. "Whatever shall I do with you?" he asked.

Then the four-legged shadow came back.

It was standing just outside the tent…

A wolflike figure, only smaller… It growled softly, its sharp teeth exposed and ready… It bent down on the dirt as if ready to pounce and attack…

Robyn's heart raced. She tried to disguise her expression as a distressed one, but the intrigue in her eyes was far too vivid. And Malekai noticed it, for how couldn't he? He followed her eyes, but the wolflike shadow suddenly ran off into the darkness as if it had been scared away… And then Robyn realized why when her nose caught that awful smell of sweat and body odor.

"Cap'n Malekai, sir?" Borrys Belvaine approached the tent.

Malekai grunted frustratingly. "What?!"

"They're waiting, sir," Borrys peeked his head inside. "What do I tell 'em?"

"I'll be out in a moment, I *told* you not to interrupt!"

"Y-Yes, sir…"

Malekai turned his sinister glare back at Robyn, who appeared distraught and frantic. "When I get back here we're having a heart to heart, me and you," he said. "You aren't at home anymore, Robyn… I'll see to it that you warm up to me… 'cause, like it or not, I'm the only friend you've got out here…"

He grinned. And then slowly he leaned in and pressed his head against her cheek.

She winced and recoiled from the disgust as he caught a whiff of her hair.

"See you in a few hours, Robyn," he said. Then he stood up, threw on his red captain's coat, and stepped out of the tent to a roar of cheers from the two hundred mercenaries waiting for him just outside. "Alright, shut it, you lazy dogs!" she heard him say, and then there was a rumble of laughs and chants.

She sighed exhaustedly and lowered her head. For a moment, she felt helpless and defeated. Suddenly, however, she felt a heavy pounding in her chest as her eyes examined her loose feet…

He forgot, she realized. *The blind fool forgot about the rope…*

She began panting heavily, a broad grin of hope plastered on her face. So power-hungry, the captain was, that he overlooked something so simple and yet so vital. With her hands tied together at her back, Robyn bent and twisted her legs, then threw herself forward. She fell as gently as she could, her forehead touching the dirt as she shifted her legs to a kneeling position. Her boot slammed against the mountain of junk and there was a loud noise as a wooden shield fell from the pile. She froze, thinking she was done for… But outside, the drunken cheers only grew louder. Malekai was speaking to them all, addressing them before the raid they would soon embark on, but she could hardly lend an ear from the anxiety.

Focus, Robyn… It's now or never.

The left side of her face was blemished with sweat and dirt. She managed to push herself off the ground, so abruptly that she felt a crack in her backbone. But she did it… She was on her knees… And a second later she leapt to her feet, her hands stuck to her waist, as she carefully searched for anything sharp.

I must've missed something. I always do.

She looked everywhere, in corners she had overlooked and under places she couldn't bend to look before. Her heart was pounding so heavily inside her chest, she thought she would faint from the panic.

Come on… There must be something…

It was then that Robyn spotted her quiver of arrows. She ran towards it and bent on one knee. It was right next to her bow *Spirit*, smooth and beautiful as always.

She smiled. It brought tears to her eyes.

She had to cut the rope somehow, perhaps if she could use the tip of an arrow to poke at the thread. For a moment, she was so distracted that she had her back to the entrance of the tent. And she failed to see the shadow standing there, the wolflike shadow, staring at her, its only eye glistening beneath the light of the lit torches...

Robyn's ear caught the sound, gentle footsteps inside the tent.

No... she thought. *Not again. I won't allow it again.*

She closed her eyes and sighed deeply, preparing herself for the worst, her legs ready to kick and attack with as much force as she could muster.

And then she heard it, a familiar voice right behind her...

A deep, smooth, calming voice with a dash of wit...

"The next time I ask you to shoot that man... *Please* shoot."

She felt a chill rushing up her spine, her skin crawling with goosebumps as if she had just heard the voice of death itself. Never had her neck turned so quickly. She felt a crack, even, as she stumbled and fell back on her posterior, her eyes wide, her mouth open with disbelief.

Standing there was a fox... A fox covered in a beautiful grey pelt all over his back and tail, while the fur on his neck and feet was a scenic shade of orange with a few white specks here and there. What sent a smile to Robyn's face, however, was when she realized the fox was missing his left eye.

Her lip shivered nervously as she spoke. "Nyx...?"

And then she heard it, that chuckle of his; it was like music to her ears.

"Oh... right," he said to her. "I *may* have forgotten to mention one small but very important detail about the curse... It doesn't allow me to *actually* die, y'see."

Robyn had no words. Her eyes began to swell with tears, much like they had several times that day, only this time she *welcomed* them. "Y-You're... Nyx, you're..."

"Yes, yes, no time to waste, Lady Robyn," Nyx interrupted, his new sharp set of teeth shifting up and down as he spoke. "Let's get you out of those ropes!"

Robyn shifted eagerly to her knees again, her wrists held out for Nyx. He had grown so unused to having teeth, much less fangs with which to rip anything so easily. He was sloppy at first, but in less than a minute Robyn was free.

"Now," Nyx said, "Shall w-"

He paused where he stood as something unexpected happened...

Robyn Huxley threw her arms around him, gripping tightly onto the soft grey fur on his neck and sighing heavily into his ear. She was trembling, he could feel it. Not out of fear, but out of joy.

"Oh Nyx," she said, a tear escaping her eyes. "I-I'm *so* happy to see you..."

Nyx did not know what to say. He simply stood there, his whiskers flickering, his heartbeat speeding up. It felt strange to him, that warm feeling in his chest, one that he'd forgotten he could feel, the feeling of being cared for. It made him slightly uncomfortable.

"Yes, well," he cleared his throat. "None of this would've happened if only you listened."

It was typical of him, to resort to hostility whenever he felt uncomfortable. Yet Robyn found herself smiling all the same. She backed away from the hug, but kept her hands around his furry cheeks, caressing them softly with her thumbs as she took a moment to observe him carefully.

"It's you... It's really you," she said with a brightly lit face.

The fox looked thoughtful for a moment. He looked like any other grey fox in the world, and yet at the same time something about him reminded Robyn of that crabby old crow. It wasn't only his missing eye, it was his voice and his demeanor and the way he became flustered whenever someone took an interest in him, as if he was not used to the attention.

"Gather your things, Lady Robyn," he said. "Let's leave this damned place."

Robyn gave him a smile and a head nod and immediately began gathering her belongings as Nyx ran to the tent's entrance to keep watch. She picked up *Spirit*, caressed it for a moment, and then tied her quiver of arrows and her rucksack onto her belts. There was no food left; Borrys had taken and eaten it all. But there was still some coin in there and a bit of callis root.

She hurried over to the entrance and squatted down next to the fox.

"What's going on?" she whispered anxiously.

"They're getting ready to raid a nearby camp," Nyx replied. "When I give the word, follow me. Are you ready?"

"Yes!" she said eagerly. "Yes..."

She stared at him while he wasn't looking. *So different and yet so humanlike.*

With a piece of home at her side, she felt unstoppable all over again.

They listened attentively, watching closely as Captain Malekai Pahrvus addressed his hoard of drunken sloppy raiders. He was standing in a muddy patch of dirt, wearing his captain's coat, a blend of red and black leathers with the mark of the scorpion on his back. He *loved* that coat, dust and patches and all. It was clear in that grin of his.

Robyn's brows lowered, the rage in her chest returning...

She found herself reaching for an arrow...

"Don't," Nyx stopped her. "It's not worth it..."

Robyn's hand dropped. Nyx was right, and she knew it.

As much as she wanted to, the matter would have to wait.

"Listen here, lads," Malekai was saying. "The war in Halghard is reaching its climax... Nearby, we've spotted a camp! The banners and colors are Wyrmwood's. And serving as the knight commander of the troop, is none other than Sir Percyval Garroway, himself!" There were angry shouts from the crowd, men cursing angrily and spitting at the sound of the knight's name.

"That crooked old shit!"

"Freak-loving bastard!"

"*Coward!*"

The captain raised both arms into the air. "All right, settle down, gents… Wyrmwood has gone desperate, yes. They have resorted to recruiting *freaks* for their armies."

"It's hardly an army. Just a giant batch of pigs in armor," a raider with patchy hair and a few missing teeth yelled from the crowd, to which the rest of the men laughed in unison.

"Careful there, lad," Borrys said. "They ain't to be taken lightly."

"What's the problem?" the raider replied. "Intimidated by a few gutless apes with swords?" Another round of laughs roared among the crowd.

"You stupid shit," another one said. "They've got a *mage* with 'em…"

Then there were confused and startled murmurs among them. Robyn and Nyx waited eagerly for their moment, but Malekai was far too close to the tent. There was nothing to do but wait.

"What kind o' mage?"

"A bleedin' *rabbit*," the man growled. "An ice mage from the north!"

"Clive's right! I saw the elf with me own eyes. They've also got a horned one!"

"A minotauro?!"

"Aye. A big bastard, he is."

"Well *we* have the numbers," Captain Malekai said, attempting to bring his men back together. "It matters not whether they are men or rabbits or greenskins. Are we *not* the Rogue Brotherhood?!"

The men chanted and cheered together.

"Tell me, lads, when King Frederic fell, who was it that raided the town of Grymsbi and took all of its coin?!"

"*We did!*" the men chanted.

"And tell me, when the freaks from the lost city of Bauqora banded together to get rid of the Rogue Brotherhood, who was it that won the battle?!"

"*We did!*"

"That's right, *we* did! Don't you bloody forget it!"

As Malekai paced further away, Nyx saw a window of opportunity.

"Now!" he said to Robyn. "Follow me."

Then they ran, scuttling from one tent to another, using them as shields. Among the chaotic ambience, no one seemed to notice them. They were mere shadows in the dark, overlooked by the raiders' drunkenly impaired sights. Nyx ran ahead, looking for a subtle trail that would lead them into the safety of the trees. There was a gap among the tents, the last couple of them isolated from the rest, some fifteen feet away, a *risky* distance.

Nyx went first. He was low enough to the ground that no one saw him. And even if they had, he was only a fox, easily shrugged off as harmless.

You can do this, Robyn told herself. *You're almost out of here. Only one tent left.*

But something stopped her all of a sudden…

From the corner of her eye, she saw them… Two slaves were tied together near a lit fire, the same slaves she had seen when she was first dragged into the camp. One of them was a woman and the other a young man, both of them with a red scar on their faces, the mark of the scorpion. They were branded just like her, shackled just like her, and they had that look of both sorrow and rage on their faces, just like her…

Her feet wouldn't dare move towards the trees…

Instead, she turned and darted towards them.

"Lady Robyn?! What are you doing?!" Nyx hissed.

She wasn't thinking at all. In that moment, nothing else mattered. Even if she escaped, she could never live with the guilt, knowing she'd left others behind to suffer the same fate she would have suffered. She reached them and hid behind their frame. They were nearly unconscious, nearly passed out from the hunger and thirst, but they were alive. She tugged at their wrists, untied their ropes, and they were suddenly startled awake, their eyes wide with disbelief, as if trying to convince themselves they weren't dreaming. Nyx was keeping watch. Fortunately, the rogue raiders were drunk and distracted, long enough for Robyn to free both slaves.

"Thank you, m'lady," the woman cried, her eyes tear-stained and weary, looking at Robyn as if she was some sort of Lady Knight coming to their rescue. "May the gods bless you, m'lady… Thank you…"

Robyn gave the woman a nod. "Free the rest of them," she told her. "Make sure that no one gets left behind."

"Yes, m'lady!" They armed themselves with a couple of knives they found in a rucksack near the fire, knowing very well where to look. "Thank you, m'lady," they kept saying. "Thank you…"

Robyn smiled. She felt a great relief in her chest, and with it came the will to escape.

Now or never, Robyn… She took a deep breath and started running. She glanced over her shoulders several times, so as to make sure no one was watching. And when she reached the last tent, where Nyx was waiting for her, she stumbled clumsily. Her boot slammed against something hard and rigid, and she fell face forward on the dirt.

She failed to spot the axe… It was smooth and shimmering and dangerously sharp, and the blade of it was sunk halfway into the ground, the handle sticking outward. Robyn's heart had already been racing, only now she felt chills and the hairs on the back of her neck rising.

A frightening figure walked out of a tent. The torch that hung at the entrance illuminated his olive green face. Her eyes suddenly met his. She froze from the fear.

Damn it all to hells…

The Beast looked grim, though he almost always did. He glared at her for several moments, and then his eyes moved away as Nyx crawled slowly towards them, growling gently like a hound.

Nyx stood next to Robyn like a loyal guardsman, his sharp teeth exposed.

Robyn could see, behind the Beast's looming figure, the other slaves freeing themselves and running into the darkness. Somehow, it sent a mild relief to her chest.

I'm caught, she realized. *But at least they're free... At least there's that...*

The Beast's eyes were hard to read. He certainly recognized her. It hadn't been long since she arrived at the camp. He knew that she was not supposed to be out of the captain's tent, much less untied. But as his eyes moved away from Robyn and towards his comrades, he looked more confused than angry.

Much to Robyn's surprise, something peculiar happened...

The Beast made not a single fuss. He gave her a muffled grunt, a sign of annoyance, and then he grabbed his axe and gave it a good wipe. He didn't care for her. He only cared for his axe. And when he made sure it wasn't harmed, the large orc simply turned the other way and walked off.

Robyn and Nyx looked at each other in disbelief for a moment.

"Come," Nyx said, clearing his throat nervously. "We must keep moving."

Robyn stumbled to her feet and they ran into the safety of the trees.

She had made it... She was free, if only for now...

And ever since that day, something changed within her.

She was still Robyn Huxley, that humble farmgirl from Elbon, bold and nervy and resplendently loyal. But there was one thing she was now certain of, should she ever find herself in an unlucky situation.

She would never miss an opportunity to shoot again...

XI

The Raid

When one tells a story, it is important to relay every fact and every element, however tragic it may be. To live every day in a shell of comfort must be charming, to witness the atrocities of the world through a curtain of safety and assurance, what a life that would be. But life is quite different for the voiceless and the downtrodden. For them, these atrocities are merely a cold reality, a naked truth. For them, there is no shell of comfort, no curtain of safety, there is only life. And life, unfortunately, is no fairytale.

The sounds of steel clashing against steel rang and pulsated throughout the Wyrmwood camp. As the hours went by, sellswords and archers were being enlisted, ravens were being sent, and numbers were growing significantly. The rest of the troop had not much to do but wait, spending endless hours training and strategizing plans of attack.

A war's afoot, the sergeants would say. *No better way to pass the time than to train.*

Or, in the case of the Woodland recruits, *train and drink.*

Near a shabby old tent made of sticks and stained fabric, the twin mercenaries Gwyn and Daryan practiced their techniques, his sword clinking against her knives repeatedly as she ducked and darted out of the way as if her life depended on it. Gwyn was one hell of a fighter. Her knives may have seemed powerless compared to Daryan's blade, but she had twice the speed and agility, and she certainly knew how to use that to her advantage.

Cedric observed them carefully, examining every maneuver, every block, and every pivot, gripping his dagger while at it. Next to him, Thaddeus and Jossiah Biggs were gawking as more recruits arrived at the camp, half of them human and the rest elves and gnomes. There was even a goblin at one point, and its smell had apparently made Jossiah feel queasy, or so he argued.

The goblin was an ordinary one; a green-skinned halfling with an oversized head, a long sharp nose, and triangular ears like those of a bat. Most goblins were about as short as the average gnome, except their bodies were often bony and gangly, and some had never learned to speak properly outside of small words and gestures.

"Unbelievable," Jossiah grunted, gawking over the array of life in the camp.

"It's pointless to dwell," Thaddeus said to him.

"Are you telling me you don't feel sick to your gut?"

Thaddeus Rexx didn't give him the courtesy of a reply. Instead he turned his gaze the other way, towards the twin raiders. Gwyn was darting out of the way, when she swiftly clashed one knife against her brother's sword and the other to his neck. There they paused, shooting each other a smile.

"Ye gettin' slower," she said.

"Nonsense," he panted. "Just *drunker*. Forgive me."

They chuckled. He sipped from his winesack as they took a moment to catch their breath. Gwyn noticed Cedric staring again, only this time she responded far friendlier than she had before.

"Oi, toothpick!" she called for him. "Care to giv' it a go?"

Cedric stammered. "Oh… No, s-sorry I really shouldn't, I…"

"Get over here," she demanded.

"Leave him be, sister," Daryan took a seat on a nearby boulder. "He's only a squire."

"Ye wanna be a squire yer whole life, then?"

Cedric fought through his nerves and walked over to her, a trembling hand on the ivory hilt of his dagger. "I'm sorry. I've never exactly… *done* this before."

"No shit," she said. "Come on. Giv' us a jab."

Cedric drew his dagger. He was almost certain he was holding it wrong. Still, he did as he was told, waited for the opportune moment, and swung the sharp end at Gwyn. With minor effort, she clashed one of her knives against his and pressed the other gently against his neck.

"Eyes on me hands, toothpick. Don't let 'em get within a foot of ye. Got it?"

Thaddeus Rexx observed the two of them. He'd known Cedric since he was just an orphan boy mopping up the floors of Nottley's Tavern. And here he was, that same boy, all grown up and crossing blades with a Woodland raider. Thaddeus couldn't help but smile.

Cedric gave a careless swing, far too close for Gwyn's comfort, and so she impulsively darted to the side and kicked him in the ankle. Cedric fell face-forward on the dirt, his dagger sliding out of his palm, his wrists scraping against the mud.

Daryan gave his sister a concerned half-grin, as if saying *'Go easy on him'*.

"Stop dartin' forward, lad," she said. "Jab 'n' step back. *Always*. Let us hear it."

Cedric winced from the pain. There was a small cut on his left wrist and a fresh layer of mud on his pants. He pushed himself up to his feet. "Jab and step back," he repeated.

"Trick is, though," she grinned, placing a hand on his shoulder. "Ye don't jab 'til yer enemy's jabbed a couple o' times. Let the fucker get tired. When they're tired, they're sloppier. *Then* ye jab. Got it?"

Despite the pain, Cedric found himself smiling back.

He was used to pain, sadly. At least now he was learning from it.

"Let them get tired, then jab. Got it."

"Good lad. Now let's try it again."

Cedric knew he was making a fool of himself. Truth was, however, he hadn't had so much fun in years. He waited, as Gwyn paced around him like a wildcat striding around a prey. She darted forward with a jab, and Cedric took a step back, trying to match his pace with hers.

"Good," she said. And then she jabbed twice.

Cedric stumbled a bit, but he dodged both attacks.

"Think quick, toothpick," she grinned at him.

They went on for a few minutes as the men in Viktor's company sat and watched. The sun was starting to set, and Jossiah Biggs was growing more restless than usual. When he heard nearby footsteps approaching, he leapt to his feet desperately. Viktor Crowley did not look very happy. And Jossiah sighed and prepared himself for the worst. "What's happened, old boy?"

"We're to march with them to Halghard," Viktor replied. "There, we'll have to figure something out."

It was vague, but they had known worse conditions in the past.

"Looks like you lot are getting acquainted," Viktor leaned against the cart full of ale barrels.

Jossiah scoffed. "This whole place is a bloody freak fest."

Viktor grimaced. Despite their years of friendship, he knew Jossiah to be rather ill tempered and riddled with chauvinism. And while he knew the man was no halfwit, he learned that looking the other way often proved more effective than arguing, for there was no changing a mind like Jossiah's. Not easily, at least.

"Settle yourself, old dog," Viktor said. "If you gave it a chance, you'd see it's not as bad as you make it out to be." Jossiah scoffed again. Viktor ignored it; instead, he stared into space, as all around him soldiers were starting to put out fires and roll up their tents.

It must nearly be time, he thought.

And then, as if reading his thoughts, a soft voice startled him.

"I'm sensing a fight…"

Viktor turned around. "Oh… Hello," he said, stunned and thrown aback by that striking face. Skye, the silver-haired elf from the river, smirked as if being able to sense Viktor's fervor.

"Can you spare a moment, Sir Crowley?"

"Certainly," Viktor cleared his throat. He gave his friend one last glimpse. Jossiah, as expected, had a scowl on his face. "Excuse me, old friend."

Viktor walked off with the elf, firmly yet quite obviously flustered. He couldn't help but pry through the corner of his eye. In their hand, Skye carried a staff, as casually as if it were any other stick. It *looked* very much like any other stick, except it was carved beautifully into a straight pole while the top of it remained jagged and split into four thick stems.

But in the end, it was no more than that, a *stick*.

There was no glow, nor anything suggesting it could cause any harm.

Unless, of course, Skye were to whack someone with it.

As they walked, Viktor tried to be as furtive as he could, but his demeanor couldn't hide his astonishment. His eyes moved back and forth from the sword on his belt to Skye's wooden staff, from his steel armor plates to Skye's ragged grey hunting outfit.

No weapons. No armor. And yet not a single scar on that face, Viktor thought. *How intriguing.*

They walked towards the outskirts of the camp, where the commotion was far less lurid and the crowds diminished to a few sober soldiers here and there. They approached a grey-haired figure dressed in frayed brown robes and a loose grey shawl.

"Zahrra," Skye called out to her.

The witch turned to them, her eyes back to their natural green color.

"Ah... The man who used to be a knight," she said.

Viktor grew a sudden wall of defense. "What's this all about?" he asked as he placed a hand on the brim of his sword.

"Easy, Zahrra," Skye said. "Just say what you have to say."

The elf was somehow calming Viktor's nerves with minimal effort.

"I've plenty to say," Zahrra grinned. "But very little that he *wishes* to hear, I'm sure."

Viktor allowed for a moment of silence before scoffing. "I've no time to waste on speculation. Forgive my bluntness."

"It's not speculation," Skye intervened. "Zahrra's visions are quite real... In fact, they've saved me more times than I can count."

Viktor's foot nearly made way for the camp, but the elf brought him back. The witch, he didn't trust. That much, he was sure of. But something in him refused to walk away from Skye. "Very well," he sighed.

Zahrra grinned again. But it wasn't entirely an eerie grin anymore. Not only did she know many things that he was unaware of, but it gave her pleasure to, it seemed. She closed her eyes, visualized it all one last time, took a deep breath, and then said, "He lives."

Viktor's eyes moved confusedly from the witch to the elf. "Pardon me?"

"This ally of yours?" she said. "The sheep farmer? He lives..."

And there it was... Viktor became hooked, if only for the time being... He had mentioned John Huxley back in Sir Percyval's tent, but at no point was it specified that he was a sheep farmer. "How did you..."

"He travels with a thief and a witch," she went on. "They walk to Wyrmwood as we speak... It is where they plan to meet you. And quite a ways ahead of you, I'm afraid."

Viktor's heart raced. He felt the place grow suddenly colder, an icy cold where it was only lukewarm at best. It frightened him, alarmed him, gave him chills in his spine. "How can you possibly know?"

"I've told you," she said, somewhat coldly. "They just come to me. They're short but clear."

"*How* clear?"

"Clearer than you are right now," she snapped at him. "He wears farmer's clothing and a silver sword with a handle made of whale bone. Too fancy for him. I assume you gifted it to him?"

Viktor was dumbfounded. He didn't know what made him more anxious, the witch's words or the fact that he was starting to believe them.

He lives...? John Huxley lives... That tough, resilient little runt, he lives!

As much as he wanted to believe it, as much hope as it gave him, he couldn't help but doubt. He was, after all, only a man. "Are you *absolutely* certain?"

Zahrra's eyes rolled so far back, it seemed almost painful.

"Viktor Crowley, I don't know you," she said with a deep sigh. "And if you died right at this moment, I wouldn't bat an eye. That's how meaningless you are to me... But that also means I've no reason to lie to you. Doubt me all you'd like, but I'm *telling* you he's alive. They're *all* alive. And if you want to see them again, you've some catching up to do."

With that, the witch walked away.

Viktor was quiet, but there was a glow in his eyes that wasn't there before.

"What do you plan to do?" Skye asked him.

Viktor hesitated, but his lips were starting to show traces of a hopeful smirk.

"Catch up," he said.

* * *

Robyn Huxley walked beside her cursed companion Nyx, deep in the heart of the Woodlands, along a wet dirt path that reeked of fresh dung.

A good sign, she hoped. *Where there are droppings, there are sure to be horses... or ogres...*

The half-moon emitted a dim light through the roof of leaves and the chilly midnight wind was picking up. And yet for a change, Robyn found herself almost entirely at ease. Her fear of the dangers of the Woodlands had diminished, and she had come to the realization that danger was imminent in any direction, even among humans. She looked down at Nyx and for a brief moment she was jealous of his grey fox pelt.

"You never told me you were a soldier," she said, attempting to make conversation so as to avoid the silence.

"I never told you I was a human either," Nyx said, his shaggy feet fortuitously skipping a step every few yards due to the many years he had spent living as a crow. "Not that it matters. It was a life I once knew and will never return to. And I made my peace with that about a hundred years ago."

"What did you look like? *If* I may ask…?"

"Oddly enough, I can't remember," he said. "I've had so many faces, my human face is no more than a blur."

Robyn felt a tug in her chest. She was thrilled to have him back, that much was certain. But she had almost forgotten how much her prying troubled him. She tried to keep her questions simple, but the energy and vigor she felt was beyond compare. Nyx was back… And the more she came to terms with the idea, the wider her smile grew. They walked towards a hidden cave to rest for the night, but she knew she wouldn't be able to sleep a single minute. She was far too overjoyed for sleeping.

"I'm terribly sorry," Nyx said after a long silence. "About your arm, that is…"

Robyn's forearm was wet and warm beneath a layer of cloth. She had coated it in callis root once they were a good distance from the camp, but she'd done it in a hurry. And while the blood seemed to soak through the cloth, the pain was far less agonizing than before.

"The callis root is helping," she said. "I'll be fine."

Nyx was unsure of what else to say. Part of him felt guilty about stopping her from shooting the vile captain back in the tent. He knew that if he had allowed her, however, there was no chance of escaping with their lives. The only option at the time was to live to fight another day.

"Do you remember much?" Robyn asked abruptly. "About the Great War…?"

Nyx sighed. Though he felt reluctant to reply, he also felt he owed her an answer.

"Regrettably so," he said, losing his gaze into the distance. He even chuckled for a moment, a sad chuckle. "I can't remember my own face and yet the *war* I remember as if it had happened yesterday… It's funny, the way the mind works. It's always the bad memories that stay the longest with us…"

"How bad?"

"Dreadful… Every city and village was raided. Every day, hundreds were dying. Soldiers marched into our homes under the king's orders and dragged out every boy and girl over the age of fifteen. They threw a sword and shield into our hands and took us away in carriages in the dead of night. Many of us were never heard from again."

"Did you not have a say?"

"If we resisted, they would call us rebels. They would kill our families and make us watch."

Robyn allowed for a brief silence, mostly for herself as she took it all in.

"I'm so sorry, Nyx…"

"A war brings about desperate times, Lady Robyn," he replied, more at ease than she had expected. "Anyway, it's in the past… I was a dumb boy, praying to

the gods day after day, asking them to keep me alive for as long as they could."
He paused for a chuckle. "Perhaps I should have chosen my words more
carefully."

She tried to smile down at him but he hardly took notice, as he appeared to
be lost in thought, reminiscing on the memories of the young man he once was.

"What were you like?" she asked. "Before all of this?"

"I was merely an ordinary carpenter's son," the fox said. "Ignorant, naïve,
wishful... I lived a simple life. Can't say I had much talent for carpentry, really.
My father was the one with the gift of craftsmanship. I wanted to be a knight of
the king's court, as many boys dream to be at some point in their lives. Though
once the war started and a blade was actually shoved into my hands, I wanted
nothing more than to escape from it."

"Was that the first time you held a blade?"

"It was not," he said. "My father had been long acquainted with the
blacksmith that crafted swords for the king's army, you see. He gave me one as a
gift when I turned sixteen. You can imagine how thrilled I was at the time."

Robyn chuckled, imagining what Nyx would have looked like as a young
inexperienced lad swinging a rapier at a sack of hay. "Were you any good?" she
asked him.

"Goodness, no. I was rubbish," he replied, to which she chuckled louder. "I
never had a mentor of any kind. I was simply a lad with big dreams, toying
sloppily with a weapon I knew nothing about. But I was put to the test soon
enough. One night, while I was stumbling home drunkenly, I happened upon a
very much sober man violating a girl in a dark empty road. Fortunately I had my
sword."

"Did you kill him?"

"I did not. In fact, he disarmed me and pinned me down. He nearly killed
me, if it hadn't been for the girl hitting him in the head with an empty glass
bottle."

Robyn couldn't help but smile a bit. Nyx did not mind, in fact he'd laughed
about it once or twice himself. "Yes, it was rather embarrassing. Though it did
teach me quite a valuable lesson."

"And what lesson was that?"

"You can fantasize all you'd like, Lady Robyn, but when it comes to a real
fight in which your life is at risk, it all comes down to what you really are and not
what you *pretend* to be."

His words sunk in deeply, and Robyn took a moment to consider them. She
knew she was not a cowardly person. However, her confidence was not enough
to face a raider or a mercenary in armed combat, and she was very well aware of
that now.

"And so it was," Nyx continued, "That every night from that moment on I
practiced for hours on end until I made certain that no one would ever disarm me

again. That's how I survived all those battles during the war, you see. Stayed alive until the very end. And it was after that final battle when I was struck with this vile curse."

They walked around the base of a large hill, and it wasn't until they reached a patch of grassless dirt that Robyn realized the hill was actually a cave. There was a cold breeze coming from the inside, the only sign of life inside that dark abyss.

"Is this it?"

"It is," Nyx said, strolling casually inside. "Not to worry, it's only a goblin cave."

She hesitated. *Oh... really? That's all? Great...*

"No need to fret," he said, as if reading her thoughts. "They're mostly cowards and tricksters. Worst thing you have to worry about is if they stole from you in your sleep. I'll keep watch for the night, you get some rest."

She stepped inside, walked a few feet until she was no longer comfortable, and took a seat against the smooth brown stone. The night sky was still visible a few yards away, which eased her nerves a bit.

But she simply couldn't keep her eyes off Nyx.

So calm, he appeared... So unafraid of death, as if it were no different than life...

To Nyx, it was all the same. He was like an ancient stone stuck beneath the surface of the earth, never moving, never changing, watching as everyone else around him lived their lives the way it was *meant* to be lived, here for a moment and then gone, leaving behind nothing but a trail of memories.

"How did it happen?" she decided to ask him, her curiosity getting the best of her. "The curse? That is, *if* you're comfortable telling me..."

He lowered himself on all fours and sat across from her.

For a fox, his movements were so humanlike they were almost eerie.

"It happened after the Battle of Morganna," he said. "The last battle of the Great War, 250 winters ago. Ironic, really... the way luck allowed me to survive through a war, only to be cursed with immortality the second it was all over."

She said nothing, only leaned back and listened respectfully, as it became clear he hadn't told the story to anyone in a long time.

"Do you know the worst part of every battle, Lady Robyn?" He looked up at her with that unmistakable sorrow in his solitary eye. "It's not the killing... Morose as it may be, that's the simplest part... Your primal sense of survival kicks in and you find yourself killing enemies one after the other... The worst part is *after* a battle, you see. Walking around the battlegrounds, looking at all of the damage that you caused, all the lives that you took, the aftermath of your own doings... When the Battle of Morganna was over and we had won the war, our knight commander ordered us to burn the bodies of the enemy's casualties. I had only one eye by then. I was a bloody mess. I wanted to get back home and forget all of it had ever happened... Anyway, I scattered away from the crowds for a moment of silence. I walked all around the battlegrounds, surrounded by death... And it was then that I happened upon an old witch lying in the fields, shivering and groaning, still very much alive. She had survived by hiding... Sitting under a wrecked carriage, she was waiting for the opportune moment to sneak away into the Woodlands... I made the mistake of looking into her eyes. They looked to me as if they were on fire, only... Only the color was off. A glowing purple hue, it was. And suddenly something happened to me. I felt every one of my muscles become paralyzed right where I stood, as if she was keeping me chained down using only her glare. I can still see them sometimes. Those haunting unblinking eyes of hers... She approached me, whispering all sorts of things in a language unknown to me. She damned every one of us for killing her witch sisters. I wanted to tell her that it was not my fault. That it was either fight or be killed by the king's men for being a rebel. I wanted to tell her how deeply sorry I was for what I'd done. But I couldn't speak, couldn't move, couldn't even blink..."

Robyn cleared her throat nervously. "That's awful..."

"There isn't a day that goes by when I don't regret it, Lady Robyn. I *deserve* this curse.... Every single second of it..."

He lowered his head onto the cold stone, shutting his eye for a brief moment. He exhaled. And there was that pain he felt in his chest whenever he reminisced on those memories. It had been decades since he talked about it, and yet something about the girl was giving him the courage.

Quite unexpectedly, he felt a warm hand rub against the fur on his face...

His eye opened, startled and thrown aback, and he raised his head once more.

Robyn was caressing him, though not in the way one would caress an animal, more like the way one would comfort a friend. She'd crawled closer and was now sitting next to him, staring into his humanlike eye. On the left side of his face, there was that empty socket and that scar running down his eyelid, except now it was furry rather than black and feathery. Though he was a fox, she felt a connection upon looking at him, as if she could see the person he once was hidden there, somewhere on the inside.

"You are *good*, Nyx," she said.

"I am not..."

"Yes you *are*... I know it and so do you. You can't possibly think you're evil."

"There's a very dim line between good and evil, Lady Robyn," he said solemnly. "Sometimes you can't tell one from the other... But a man that has killed hundreds of innocent lives simply because they didn't look like him? You might call him many things, but 'good' wouldn't be on that list."

"You were just like them," Robyn said, pressing her palm gently against his soft white cheek. "Forced to fight a war that wasn't yours to fight in the first place…"

Nyx's whiskers twitched nervously. There was something like fondness in the girl's eyes and it made him feel uneasy. He'd seen everything he loved vanish. All those who were close to him had died or had been killed. And the thought of losing even *more* terrified him.

"You, uh… You should sleep," he said, clearing his throat.

She smiled, and then gently removed her hand from his face. "I'll try," she said, and then settled herself against the stone. Her eyes, however, remained slightly open, staring at him with bewilderment.

A moment passed. Then another. And when he could no longer hide it, Nyx turned back to her and asked, "What is it?"

"Nothing," she smiled. "It's just… You look good as a fox, that's all."

"Don't get used to it, Lady Robyn."

* * *

"Gather the recruits at once."

"Yes, sir… Are you absolutely certain we're to march *now*, sir?" asked the stroppy soldier. "It's not yet midnight, it'll be hours before first light. Surely, w-"

"Don't argue with me, lad, just do as you're told!" said the noble Sir Percyval Garroway, and then his soldier stammered and darted out of the tent. Percyval was sitting with his arms held firmly at his sides like a scarecrow while his squire, a gnome with a boyish face and a mop of brown hair, laced the chest armor onto his torso, tightly and carefully.

"No sign of the bastard yet," said Sir Antonn worriedly. "But his goons have spotted our camp, no doubt. Won't be long 'til *he* finds *us*."

Sir Percyval could do nothing but hold still and listen, as his squire and his second-in-command prepared him for the worst. The black leathers, bestowed to him in Wyrmwood, were robustly thick and the dark steel plates over his chest and arms were a piece of art. And yet the man couldn't help his aching nerves, burning up his insides. The Rogue Brotherhood was notorious for a reason; if armor could protect a man from them, they wouldn't have such an appalling death count. And Percyval dreaded the idea of losing the numbers he'd worked so hard to acquire. "I've never heard of this Pahrvus character," he said. "I thought the captain of the Brotherhood was some rugged old bloke."

"He was 'til recently," Sir Antonn replied, re-reading a scroll sent by one of their contacts. "The word is this Malekai Pahrvus was the captain's second-in-command 'til he betrayed him and took the company for his own."

"Sounds like an opportunist."

"Sounds more like a coward."

"That's even worse, I'm afraid," Percyval sighed despairingly. "Cowards don't hesitate to strike you from behind when you aren't looking. If they attack and we're unprepared…"

"We're screwed," Sir Antonn grunted. Then he turned to Zahrra with a bitter expression, more bitter than usual. "I don't suppose *you* can help out a little?" he asked coldly.

"Haven't I before?" she replied with a glare.

"Not when we've needed you the most. All you do is sit on your arse."

"Enough, you two," Percyval scowled, the torment radiating from his eyes. "F-Fuck," he hissed under his breath. He was thankful there were no recruits in the tent aside from his squire. So odd it would have seemed to the average soldier, so disappointing, to see their knight commander broken down to such a nervous state, so unlike a knight. It was a state of mind that Percyval would only unveil in the presence of his closest companions. And often Sir Antonn's rough demeanor would bring him back to his senses; in fact it was for this very reason that he chose the man as his second-in-command to begin with.

"Keep that chin up," Antonn grunted in that coldhearted manner of his. "You're a damn knight, not a priest. Act like it."

Outside, recruits were rushing to leave the camp. Armor was being laced, tents were being rolled, horses were being gathered and prepped, and fires were being put out. In a matter of minutes, the camp seemed far less crowded than before.

It wasn't hard for Viktor Crowley to spot his men. Even when they roamed away from their usual rest area, they were easily the three most confused faces in the camp.

Twelve, he had in his company… And now this was all he had left…

Cedric, a naïve squire with little experience.

Thaddeus Rexx, a blacksmith with a need for the gold.

And Jossiah Biggs, his friend and former brother-in-arms.

Truthfully, Viktor had nearly given up hope until the witch Zahrra came along. Despite his doubt, the man couldn't help but keep his optimism. He had survived many times before in dire situations, worse than this one in fact. And his brute determination was about the only thing the man had left.

The journey hadn't been kind to Jossiah Biggs. Sweat and dirt ran down the sides of his face and he smelled as if he hadn't bathed in weeks. He approached Viktor the way he usually would, with a scowl and a wrinkled face, quite clearly about to complain about something.

"What the bloody hells is going on, old dog?!" he asked, a clear agitation in his voice. Thaddeus and Cedric listened closely from a distance as best as they could. Leaving in the middle of the night was never a good sign, and they had all learned that the hard way. Something had to be wrong.

"Rogues," Viktor replied honestly. "They've been spotted. We can't risk an attack. We must march now."

"The Brotherhood?!" Thaddeus asked, for the first time looking slightly

323

worried.

Cedric, in contrast, was mortified.

"Then why are we still sticking with *this* lot?!" Jossiah snarled. "They're not our problem and we aren't *theirs*. I say we cut our losses and get out of here before we get caught up in the middle of their mess."

"Patience, old friend," Viktor said. "The only way to reach Qamroth is by ship. And King Alistair's got plenty of them. The more allies we make, the better our chances of getting through this voyage alive. We're low in numbers as it is."

"But *these* people?" Jossiah took a second to glance around him, and then he spoke in an even lower voice. "It was one thing to ally with Blackwood and the witch. But you mean to tell me we're fighting alongside *freaks* now?"

Viktor's brows lowered and his jaw tightened. He felt the impulse to strike the man, but decades of friendship held him back. And when he spotted Skye watching from a distance, it was the last push that he needed to finally speak up. "Jossiah, with respect, you need to start thinking twice about when it's best to shut that yap of yours."

Jossiah appeared both startled and slightly enraged. He wasn't fond of being challenged or talked down to so directly, unless it was by King Rowan. And yet in the last few weeks alone Viktor had done it on numerous occasions. "What did you say to me...?"

"You heard me clearly," Viktor stepped forward. "We aren't in Vallenghard anymore, Jossiah. It's about time you *wake* up!" Viktor's voice was nowhere near subtle, and Jossiah was growing restless, knowing they were bound to be overheard.

"*I* need to wake up?!" Jossiah hissed, his watchful eyes gazing about every few seconds. "*I* need to?! Viktor, they're *changing* you... They're corrupting you. They're meddling with your mind, don't you *see*, old boy? They *want* you to warm up to them, they're only trying to push their own luck. Are you *that* blind?!"

Viktor's silence stung Jossiah like a dagger. His stare was no longer friendly. They had been like brothers for nearly two decades and though they had their differences in the past, Viktor had never shown Jossiah the hostility he was showing at that moment through a simple stare. And when Viktor finally spoke, it wasn't only to Jossiah but to Thaddeus and Cedric as well.

"Listen here, all of you," he said unsympathetically. "This journey isn't over yet. And I intend on finishing what I started... I'm marching with Sir Percyval and his troop whether you like it or not. You can join me or you can stay behind and die."

There was a brief silence. By then, many eyes in the camp were watching in awe, both humans and nonhumans. Cedric was the first to step forward. Looking as startled as a lost pup, he stood by the golden knight with his hand at his dagger. "I'll join you," he said, not as confidently as he hoped to sound but firmly all the same.

Viktor gave him a nod of acknowledgment before turning to the two other men.

"And the two of you?"

Jossiah scowled, exhaled sharply, nodded his head ungraciously...

"You've gone soft, old boy," he said sourly. "I never thought it would come to this."

Viktor said nothing. Jossiah was talking down to his friend in a similar form as he had talked to Hudson Blackwood. And Viktor fought hard to hold back his fist.

"Marching with the enemy," Jossiah said as he spat on the dirt near Viktor's boots. "How low have you sunk?"

"Shut your mouth, Jossiah," Viktor stepped forward.

"Or what? You're going to fight me to defend a bunch of *rabbits?*"

"I said shut it..."

"They're *freaks!*"

Then it happened... Viktor's fist moved almost on its own and he struck Jossiah's jaw. Jossiah was a large man, and it was the only thing that kept him from losing his balance. Instantly, he lit up with fury and reached for his sword. He would have unsheathed it, but then Thaddeus Rexx held him back.

The two former knights glared at each other, each one equally as enraged.

"Call them freaks again and it won't just be my fist I'll strike you with," Viktor said, softer yet loud enough so that many ears in the camp were able to overhear. "They welcomed you into their camp. They fed you. And you dare stand there and call them freaks? Call them the 'enemy'?"

Viktor took another step forward.

Jossiah kept his stance but he was at a loss for words. Never in the twenty years that he had known Viktor had they quarreled physically. And yet there he was, with a chest full of rage and a throbbing jaw that was bruising purple.

"I'll tell you who your 'enemy' is, you blind bastard," Viktor said. "He, who raided your kingdom. He, who took your princess hostage. He, who decided to walk into your city and piss on your doorstep. And tell me, old boy... Was he an elf?"

Jossiah said nothing. There were raging fumes radiating from his eyes.

By then Thaddeus had let go, but he remained close, ready to intervene again.

"I asked you a question, Jossiah... *Was* he a bloody elf?" Viktor asked. "Or an orc, for that matter? A gnome? A bloody pixie?! No... He was a *man*. A walking, breathing, fucking *man*. And those you call *freaks*!? *They* might be the only difference between you living or dying."

Viktor paused there to catch his breath.

He was shaking from the rage, a rage he wasn't aware he had until that moment.

After a brief silence, he scoffed. "We're marching with them," he said. "If you're not with me, then… then get out of my bloody sight, I'm done with you."

With that, the golden eagle walked away.

Jossiah stood there firm and motionless, his hand still gripping the hilt of his sword. He remained that way for several moments, before sighing and walking to the nearest barrel of ale.

Thaddeus and Cedric were left alone, and so they looked at one another for a moment, each unsure of what to say.

"Y-You coming?" the young squire asked nervously.

Thaddeus sighed and took a gander at their surroundings. "I don't know, lad…"

Cedric bit his lip. Thaddeus Rexx was the only familiar face in the company. In a way, he was the only friend Cedric had left. Without him, the young man would be lost, squire to a knight he hardly even knew. He nearly begged the man to come along, except something stopped him. A loud voice broke the silence. A voice that gave Cedric yet another shred of desperately needed hope to cling onto.

"Oi, toothpick!"

Cedric felt a blow to his chest. Something heavy and rough slammed against him and he was able to catch it just in time. It was a piece of rusty chainmail, too slim-fitted for any soldier in the camp.

"Throw this on under 'em rags. Make 'em *work* for it, yes?" said Gwyn, shooting him a smile and a wink of the eye.

Cedric tried to smile in return, but Viktor's words echoed in his mind.

The Rogue Brotherhood, he'd heard him say. And the name alone gave him chills.

Fretfully, he removed his ragged shirt and threw on the chainmail. It was heavy and was sure to slow him down. And it nearly frightened him to death.

"Think fast, Mister Rexx," Daryan said.

Thaddeus nearly stumbled, but caught the piece of steel just in time. "I don't like shields, they slow me down."

"This ain't a street duel, tiny," Gwyn snapped. "A battle's stirrin' up."

It was then that Thaddeus and Cedric realized how nearly empty the camp was. Even with the few hundred recruits standing about, the tents and the stands had all been put away. And it shrunk the size of the camp significantly.

As Cedric threw on the chainmail, Gwyn was able to catch a glimpse of Cedric's bare chest and arms and noticed the several scars and bruises on his lanky torso. Cedric did not strike her as a fighter, and she was caught by surprise because of it. The young man, of course, panicked and his face became flushed when he noticed her staring.

"You'll be needing this, little squire," Daryan handed Cedric a sharp rusty blade.

Cedric stuttered nervously, wiping the sweat from his face. "I-I've never used a sword b-"

"It'll be alright, toothpick. Just ye watch," Gwyn said, giving him a friendly tap on the back, though the squire could see the pity in her expression. "It's just like a knife, yes? Only bigger," she shrugged. "Anyway I'll be right there with ye. We'll watch each other's backs, yes?"

Then there was a thundering shout that rounded up the herd.

"Attention! Gather 'round!" Sir Antonn Guilara stood next to a cart full of tents and banners.

As the crowds gathered closer, Cedric and Thaddeus were pushed inward, and they remained close to the twins Gwyn and Daryan for comfort. Viktor Crowley was standing near Sir Antonn, a head of bright golden hair among a sea of greasy mops. Jossiah, in return, wouldn't dare stand with them; instead he stood far to the side with a tankard of ale in his hand and a frown on his face.

"Attention! Your knight commander wishes to speak!" Sir Antonn shouted, and then stepped off to the side. Sir Percyval Garroway, knight commander of the troop, climbed onto the back of the cart so that his soldiers could get a better view of him. He was nervous and he was having trouble hiding it, though he almost always did before a potential fight.

And so, with a deep sigh and a crack of the neck, the knight began his speech.

"Greetings, my fellow bastards!" he shouted, and in return there were a few laughs and silent smiles. Upright and with a confident poise, Percyval stood. His eyes were moving all throughout the camp as if trying to address each of his recruits personally, one at a time. There were nearly three hundred of them now, with at least a hundred elves and gnomes dispersed amidst them all. That, no doubt, was a sight you could only see in the Woodlands.

"It has been quite an evening, I tell you," Percyval went on, wishing he had more space in the back of the cart to pace around. "I would like to take a moment to thank you all for your patience and your fortitude during this expedition. And to those of you that have reached out to your connections in attempts to grow our numbers, I cannot thank you enough... In just a week, we have gathered a strong enough troop to enhance our defenses in Halghard significantly. When the time comes, and make no mistake, brothers and sisters, it *will* come, we will be more than ready... We will rise victoriously and start a new life in Halghard, as promised."

Viktor expected cheers from the crowd. Instead there was a doubtful silence.

To start anew in Halghard was a dream many nonhuman beings dreamed of. But it was nothing more than that... A *dream*...

Viktor knew it. And he knew that Percyval knew it.

The elves and gnomes were smart enough to expect some resistance. Truthfully, many of them doubted the knight commander. And quite reasonably, at that, for until recently an elf could never cross into Halghard without finding some trouble.

"Aye, if we don't get out throats slit for it, that is," a doubtful elf shouted from the crowd, and a few murmurs followed.

Percyval kept his stance firmly. "They'll have to go through me first, my brother," he remarked. "I promise you... If it is the last thing I do, I will make *certain* you get what you were promised."

"And if they kill *you*?" said another, this one louder and far more provocative. "You're *one* man. Won't be too difficult. What then?"

Percyval hesitated, but he tried his damned best not to show it. He knew that if he lost them now, there would be no turning back, and everything he worked so hard to build would shatter before him. Allowing the murmurs to die down, the knight closed his eyes briefly and cleared his throat one more time.

"Listen, I know you don't fully trust me, ladies and gents," he said, with a voice so confident it gripped everyone's attention with little trouble. "I don't blame you, quite honestly, I'd doubt me too if I was in your shoes... But answer me this, how many of your brothers and sisters have died in this treacherous land...? How many of you have been spit on and broken down to bits in this living hell and been unable to do something about it...?"

The silence lingered on. For a moment, Percyval felt as if all of Gravenstone was listening.

"What I'm offering you is a chance to fight *back*... To stand up for yourselves and say '*Enough!*'... To start a new life, a *better* life... for yourselves, your children, your *children*'s children... Brothers and sisters, I know you don't know me... But believe me when I say we've more in common than you think... I come from a place where, with enough coin, a bloody tyrant can do anything and everything he desires with little consequence. Where children can be sold as servants and folks are killed for a loaf of bread and nobody will bat a fuckin' eye about it..."

Viktor looked around. Percyval's words were starting to make them all think.

To make one listen, to *truly* listen, wasn't an easy thing to do.

But Percyval was doing it, all right...

"Brothers and sisters, I'm exhausted... I'm exhausted from living in a world where people starve to death while a fat wine-guzzling bastard eats his weight in bread and throws the rest of it to the rats... A world where we turn the other way from these atrocities and then we point our fingers at those who don't look like us and call *them* evil... You all want freedom, I get that. *I* want freedom, too. But no one is going to give us freedom... No one is going to give us peace and equality. We must *take* it for ourselves... *Together*. That is the *only* way we will achieve it... For the path to freedom is *not* an easy one, I assure you, but we can journey through it *together*. We will move in no other direction but forward *together* and no matter what they say or do to us, we will *keep* fighting. They can break our spirits, but we will *keep* fighting. They can break our bodies, but we will *keep* fighting. They can call us sinners, freaks, whores, and bastards. And we will look them in the eye and say 'damn right' and we will *keep* fighting!"

Then it came, a great roar of cheers that may have echoed for a mile.

Percyval did not smile. He kept his stance like any true leader would.

"We march tonight, brothers and sisters... To Halghard, a kingdom of humans. And we will do it without fear and without hesitation. Times are changing, mark my words. Cities and towns have already started to welcome others from the Woodlands, that much is true. But it is *not* enough! The day the entire kingdom welcomes you... The day all of Gravenstone welcomes you... *That* will be the day we stop fighting!"

More cheers, and this time Viktor Crowley joined in.

Percyval took a moment to wipe the sweat on his forehead, smiling at his troop.

"Brothers and sisters, we've marched through rivers and rain. We've climbed mountains and dug through caves. A little darkness won't stop us. We march *now*. And if we must fight, we will. Now gather the remaining supplies an-"

Suddenly, an arrow flew in from the darkness...

It slammed against the steel on Percyval's chest, leaving a scratch and ricocheting off into the dirt. Had the arrow been just a few inches higher, it would have struck the knight in the neck.

All throughout the camp, heads turned and eyes widened.

Percyval was not hurt, but the horror in his eyes was there all the same.

Sir Antonn Guilara picked up the arrow from the ground; it was steel-pointed and decorated with red feathers. "They're here..."

The murmurs began, as the recruits gripped their shields and glanced about.

"Sir!" a voice shouted from the trees. Skye was climbing higher for a better view, and then they glanced back towards Percyval. "Rogues! To the east!"

It was then that they all saw it... A storm of arrows flew into the camp, striking soldiers in the arms, legs, and chests, some falling to a quick death.

There was not a moment to waste.

"Shield wall!" Percyval ordered, leaping off the cart, his face suddenly drenched in sweat.

"SHIELD WALL!!" Sir Antonn repeated in a shout.

The troop gathered closely together. A first line was formed, consisting of about twenty soldiers. They lowered themselves to a squatting position side by side and held their shields above their heads.

"Move it, let's go! Shield wall!"

"Come on, toothpick!" Gwyn dragged Cedric by the shirt.

They all joined into the formation, line after line, in groups of twenty or so. They held their shields up and pressed them close together, forming one wide barrier of wood as arrows began to rain over them. The shields varied, some of them round while others were oval or squared, but they made their best attempt at joining them together, avoiding as many gaps as they could.

"Ready, now?! Together, lads!" Percyval shouted. "Forward!"

They took a step, keeping the shield wall intact, a crawling rectangle of wood and steel.

"Again! Forward! Stay together!"

They marched ahead. Some of the arrows were splintering through the old wood, the sharp ends just inches from hitting some of the soldiers' heads.

Cedric looked up. He could see the arrows raining through the small cracks between the roof of shields. He felt like throwing up. He *would* have, if it hadn't been for the raider woman Gwyn shouting into his ear. "Ye gonna be fine, toothpick! Think of it like hail!" she said.

It did not help.

"Keep moving, don't you dare stop!" Percyval shouted, as he started to make out the shadows within the trees. Dark shadows with a hint of red, firing arrows at them one after another. There was something peculiar in their numbers, however. There may have been more, but Percyval swore he saw only a couple of dozen archers.

And then his ears caught something, leaves rustling, from both his left and his right. Beneath his shield, Percyval craned his neck. And there he spotted it, a curved blade creeping out from the edge of a tree, and a veiny arm with red sleeves was holding it.

"Shit," Percyval hissed.

The man raised his blade and shouted, "Now!"

And then a mass of swordsmen, all of them dressed in red leathers, ran in from the left and right sides of the Wyrmwood troop, caging them in, attacking them from both sides like a scorpion's pincer.

"Break wall!" Percyval shouted. "BREAK WALL!! Swords out! Attack!"

Many of the Wyrmwood recruits were killed instantly, distracted by the arrows and caught off guard by the blades. The shield wall was broken and the Wyrmwood recruits had no choice but to scatter and fight back.

Within seconds, the place turned into a bloody battlefield. Though the Wyrmwood recruits were keeping their stance, rogue mercenaries were running out of the trees in dozens. And then more began to hop down from the branches above.

Right in the middle of it all was Cedric... He stood there, frozen in fear like a field mouse, his shivering hand struggling to grip the rusty sword. His eyes were struck with horror as all around him, throats were being sliced and chests were being stabbed.

To the young squire, these weren't humans. They were monsters.

He wanted to join the fighting, but he *couldn't*. His feet wouldn't allow it.

Almost involuntarily, he ran towards the nearest cart instead and crawled underneath it, his knees scraping against the rocks as he slid into safety.

And from there, he saw it all... Bodies were falling all around, some thirty of them and counting. In the front lines was Sir Percyval Garroway, fighting and protecting his fellow recruits. But there was only so much that blades could do against arrows. The Brotherhood archers were still shooting, and they had more quivers of arrows ready at their feet, dozens of them, each with at least 15 arrows.

Skye hopped down from the tree, a fall of about twenty feet, and managed to land gracefully on both feet like a cat, right in between the fight and the Brotherhood archers. They were thrown off guard by the pale elf's bravery, and they hesitated to shoot. And Skye took that opportunity to summon a spell from the staff. The elf whispered something in a foreign tongue and then the tip of the staff began to glow, forming a cloud of frost around it like an orb. A wall of ice was erected from the ground, nearly fix feet tall and about fifteen feet wide, and it was thick enough that no arrows could possibly shoot through.

The archers were baffled. They shouted at one another, picked up their quivers, and walked around the fight, where the wall of ice could not stop them. But Sir Percyval Garroway had his eyes on them. "The bows, lads!" he shouted. "Get th-"

Suddenly, a red raider with a swinging blade ran towards Percyval. The raider's blade was just inches away from striking him, but then a silver longsword pierced through his back and out his chest. The raider fell to his knees and the longsword slid out of his back. And standing there was Viktor Crowley, fighting alongside Percyval like a trusted soldier.

"Lead the way, Sir," Viktor said.

Percyval nodded back. "With me, lads! Let's go! Get the archers!"

Percyval, Viktor, and about seven elven recruits made way towards the trees, using the trunks and branches as shields. They reached the archers and began hunting them down, one by one.

Meanwhile, with Skye forming barriers of ice, the Wyrmwood recruits were starting to gain the advantage. The twin raiders, Gwyn and Daryan, fought side by side with such dexterity, as if having practiced together for years. Gwyn's agility and her brother's drunken brute strength gave them an advantage over the red raiders' thirst. She ducked beneath her brother's arm, shielded his back as he shielded hers. They were so well coordinated that their shadows were almost *one*, an unstoppable force, slicing down any red raider that got too close.

It only lasted for a few moments, however. Just as the twins felt they had the lead, more red raiders began to ambush them, some nine or ten of them. Gwyn and Daryan turned to one another, both of them equally as overwhelmed. They had been outnumbered many times in the past but never by this many blades. The red raiders closed in on them from every direction, snickering and swinging their weapons in the air as if taunting them.

Suddenly, however, there was a deep thundering roar... The red raiders turned immediately, only to gaze upon a large beast with horns charging furiously towards them.

"Toro," Gwyn whispered with a grin.

"Oh shit," one of the raiders said, before he was stabbed in the chest by one of the minotauro's horns. Toro swung his heavy fists madly, killing red raiders as easily as if he were killing rats, breaking off a man's jaw and slamming another against an oak tree. One by one, he killed them, until there was only one man left, one small frail man dressed in red, his broken foot dragging lifelessly over the mud as he crawled away with horror.

"N-No!" the man cried. "I'm sorry... Please, I'm s-"

The minotauro slammed his hoof on the man's face, crushing his skull like an egg.

And Gwyn and Daryan stood there looking stunned, as Toro gave them a glance.

Unsure of what to say, Gwyn cracked her neck and tried to act naturally.

"I had that," she said to the minotauro, who grunted in return.

Close by, there was a sudden scream that distracted them. A Wyrmwood soldier was struck in the chest by an axe. It was by far the sharpest axe in the bloody field, due to its owner's habit of sharpening it daily... A green hand gripped the handle and gave it a strong pull, and the axe broke off the dead man's torso. It was an orc, about six and a half feet in height, with three red scars running diagonally across his chest and a black chin beard tied into a braid.

"Oi! Beast!" a rogue raider shouted from afar. "Get that horned bastard!"

The Beast locked eyes with Toro and cracked his neck, taking a moment to genuinely admire the minotauro's grace and posture. He had fought many foes in his life, a variety of species, yet he had never seen a minotauro so up close before. Toro stomped his hoofed feet where he stood, his weaponless hands held out at his sides as if challenging the Beast.

The Beast growled and threw his axe on the dirt, as if accepting the challenge.

Then he took the first step... Toro took the second step...

They began sprinting towards each other...

Hidden underneath the cart, young Cedric watched with the expression of a stunned child, as the orc and the minotauro charged in at full speed. When they collided, there was a loud bash that echoed throughout the forest. Toro's fist smashed against the Beast's scarred chest, taking the orc's breath away instantly. The orc was thrown into the air, smashing against an oak tree a mere 2 feet away from Cedric. Had the Beast turned while he laid face down on the dirt, their eyes would have met.

Cedric kept watching…

The Beast lost no time. As the minotauro approached him, the orc got to his feet and dodged the heavy black hoof. The orc landed a punch on Toro's face and for a moment, he felt a sting on his virescent knuckles. Little to his knowledge, a minotauro's skull was easily three times as tough as a human's.

The Beast and Toro then fell into an ambitious battle, landing constant kicks and blows as each one of them tried recklessly to keep up with the endurance of the other. They were the only two souls in the camp fighting only with their fists.

All around, blades were clashing and arrows struck soldiers and raiders alike.

Nearby, Viktor Crowley fought like he always did, with such precision and posture that one could never mistake him for anything other than a knight. For a moment, the man had become numb to his actions, killing men one after the other as if they were nothing but roaches. He even failed to notice his long-time comrade Jossiah Biggs fighting amidst the chaos.

There was a glowing eye in the dark, however, that found Viktor's finesse with a longsword particularly admiring… So alluring it was, that it beckoned him for a challenge… Captain Malekai Pahrvus dropped his bow and unsheathed his curved blade. He walked towards Viktor Crowley with a fierce hunger in his expression.

Viktor turned and caught sight of him. He had never seen the man, nor did he know anything about him. All he knew was that the man meant to kill him.

Malekai swung his blade first. Viktor blocked it, along with three more blows, and then darted to the side to catch his breath. Malekai was attacking fiercely, twisting his wrist in a circling motion and his blade mirroring it like a wheel.

"Take 'is head off, boss!" Borrys Belvaine shouted from afar.

Viktor stepped backwards and the heel of his boot felt the cold barrier of ice behind him. He felt trapped all of a sudden. He had been in combat many times in the 46 years that he'd been alive, and after fighting countless men of skill far below his, he seldom became worried about losing his life. On this night, however, the former knight had grown worried.

Malekai was not only agile, he was remarkably vicious. And Viktor's arms were starting to get tired and numb. Malekai, on the other hand, seemed to not sweat a single drop. The captain only kept his eyes locked on Viktor's face, as if being able to read his next move and blocking it by instinct without having to look down at their weapons. Viktor, however, took this to his advantage and tricked the captain, making a swinging motion but not landing a blow. And then Malekai jabbed forward and Viktor darted to the side. And the captain's blade sunk into the ice and became stuck there; he was suddenly unarmed.

Viktor charged at him with his longsword. But Malekai left his blade on the ice and rolled away on the dirt, and then three of his red raiders came to his defense.

Viktor was angry. For a moment, he nearly admired Malekai's skill. However as he gazed upon the captain now, grinning behind a wall of his own men, Viktor realized he'd been fighting a crooked coward.

The Golden Eagle was now surrounded, his sword held up at the ready as the three red raiders paced around him and two more ran in from around the wall of ice.

"Look here," one of them snorted. "Such shiny armor, there. *I* get it."

"Whoever *kills* the bloke gets it," said another.

Viktor glared at each one of them with a heated rage, turning as quickly as he could without keeping his back to a single one for too long.

Come on, you bastards. One of you make a move… I dare you…

Except they didn't. They simply mocked and taunted him.

Move, you cowards… Try and strike me…

And then one did. He jabbed, but Viktor darted out of the way just in time.

Then, however, he felt a sting in his calf. A rogue raider behind him landed a kick that bent Viktor's knee. And the Golden Eagle fell forward, tasting the bitter earth as he splashed onto a puddle of mud. He could hear the rogue raiders laughing at him, snickering through their yellow teeth.

"That *it*? I thought he had a pair on 'im."

"Go easy on 'im. He's just an old bloke tryin' to play hero."

Viktor felt the rage grow in his chest. He gripped the mud with his nails and began to hoist himself up. They kicked him… The blows were softened by his steel armor, but they bruised him all the same. He tried to stand up again, but they simply kept kicking, cowardly and in a pack.

Just then, however, Viktor felt a sudden rumble that petrified him…

The earth was cold beneath his palms but there was a mild quiver there, like that of a heavy footstep. Viktor held an ear out… Through the rogue raiders' nasty chuckles, he was able to hear them… The footsteps were heavy and deep…

Whatever was approaching was large. *Quite* large.

"What's wrong with 'im? Looks like he's seen a ghost!"

Suddenly a massive shadow emerged from the trees…

"Oh damn it all to hells…"

A thick branch snapped, as if something had pushed it off the tree with minor effort. And then a piercing roar echoed all around.

Viktor Crowley's mouth dropped… All of their necks craned towards the sound…

A massive foot, as big as an elephant's, stepped out of the darkness. Then another.

And then a loud shout came from one of the watchmen… "Ogres!!"

Another roar, this one louder and far more fierce. The large humanlike beast, some ten to twelve feet in height, began charging towards the battle. The red raiders turned and faced it in horror.

Viktor Crowley chose to follow his instinct. One leap and he was on his feet, running and snatching his longsword from the mud along the way. The rogue raiders tried to fight back, but within seconds the gigantic ogre had killed all five of them.

"Retreat!!" Captain Malekai Pahrvus shouted from afar.

And at that moment, three more ogres charged into the battlefield and began swinging their wooden clubs at the men as if swinging at rodents.

It was then that Viktor realized just how fast ogres could catch up. He found himself dodging them and darting left and right, running away as the massive beasts stepped around him.

It's nothing, Viktor kept telling himself. *Nothing. Nothing at all. They're just practice posts…*

Over three decades of experience were able to save the man.

He sprinted, hopped between trees, ducked beneath brushwood…

He dipped, ducked, rolled away… He ran, swung his sword at incoming red raiders, threw them at the ogres as bait, and then ran some more…

Nothing at all, he told himself. *They're all in your mind… Your mission's not over. This is **not** how you go… Today you live, Viktor… Today, you fucking live, you understand?*

And then, Viktor had a moment of hesitation…

One brief stupid moment of hesitation in which he chose to look back…

There it was, the massive beast charging after him, crushing raiders along the way.

Had he been paying attention in front of him, he would have seen the tree root. A large root, rising about a half-foot from the ground, just high enough for Viktor's boot to bump and snatch his balance away.

Viktor skipped a step and fell forward, and there was a moment of horror in which he realized what he was falling into…

There was a pit of quicksand there. In a matter of seconds, Viktor was swallowed nearly full. The ground rose higher than he had expected. Some pits were thick like mud, but this one was brutally thin and deep. And instantly, Viktor felt his body grow cold and wet and stiff.

He groaned with panic as, all around him, raiders and soldiers were fleeing.

"H-Help!" he shouted, but it was no use. Viktor may as well have been invisible.

He tried to swing his arms around but they were only making him sink faster.

His heart raced…

No... No, no, no, he told himself.

*This is **not** how you go, Viktor... Today you live...*

He felt the cold sand swallow him bit by bit, until the wetness reached his neck.

You can't... Not like this... For fuck's sake, fight back...

But the more he moved, the faster he sunk. And the faster he sunk, the less anyone around him even noticed he was there.

And so, bit by bit, his arms began to give in.

His stiff body stopped moving and his breathing slowed.

Viktor Crowley could taste the wet mud between his dry lips.

Fight back, you old dog... f-fight... back...

* * *

Breathe, she told herself, but her stubborn lungs could only manage was a tense wheezing. Fate hadn't been too kind to Adelina Huxley, and it was about to get a lot worse.

She glanced back, at the weak orcess limping down the hill. She didn't know what it was that kept her from lending a hand. Her mistrust was too ingrained, too deeply rooted within her, and she was tired of living a life in which all she did was give, and yet she never received anything in return. But none of this was Aevastra's fault, and Adelina was aware of that, and it was tearing at her insides.

Move it, damn you... Move it!

But she couldn't fight a wound. Aevastra was weak and slow, even with the blacksmith Evellyn Amberhill lending her a shoulder. Margot was still carrying the child, unworried and unafraid, confused as to why her mother was refusing to help, after all of her years of careful advice.

But family came first for Adelina Huxley, always.

You never abandon family, she'd tell her children. *However bad it may be, family is everything.*

And Margot's innocent mind couldn't help but question, '*what about those who don't* **have** *family?*'

It had been years since Adelina felt that pressure in her chest, that feeling of dread, remnants of that fateful night 10 years back... That cold winter's night in which she went from being the Huxley Widow to Adelina Huxley. She'd made the mistake back then of locking herself inside her cottage without sending for help. But it hadn't been an option then and it wasn't an option now.

She had the twins to think of... She couldn't leave them...

And she couldn't take the risk of sending one of them to Val Havyn on their own.

Perhaps if John and Robyn hadn't left her, hadn't *abandoned* her, they would've had a better chance. Perhaps then, nobody would've died...

"Run ahead!" she yelled at her children. "Go!"

And the twins darted towards the farm.

Adelina glanced back, again and again. She saw them... The two orcs were running down the hill towards them. Great big shadows they were, unmistakably inhuman, armed and covered in hunting furs from neck to toe, their skin tone rich green like olives.

Adelina was never one to hide her fear. *Better to be frightened and careful than smug and careless,* she would always tell her children. And in that moment, she was horrified. After several moments of hesitation, she finally lent her own shoulder to Aevastra, and together with Evellyn they dragged her across the field towards the farm, as the blood from the wound oozed over all three of them.

They reached the safety of the cottage, and Adelina slammed the door shut behind them and locked it. "Margot!" she said. "Take the babe into my bedroom! Melvyn, fetch the nails and start hammering every window shut!"

The twins did as they were told.

Adelina was panting and sweating by then, trying desperately to keep calm. *You can do this,* she told herself. *Gods know it wouldn't be the first time...*

There was a look of desperation in Aevastra's eyes. "He'll be safe," Evellyn assured her. "I promise you." But the orcess looked exhausted and unconvinced, drained of all her hope. She shuddered and winced as the loud creaks and thumps resonated all around her. Adelina pushed a hefty oversized cabinet in front of the door, the twins were hammering nails against the windowsills, one after the other, until they were fixed shut. Adelina grabbed pieces of old wood from the corner near the fireplace for additional support against the windows. She had forgotten all about the pot of boiling stew that was still hanging over the fire.

Evellyn handed Aevastra a wet cloth. "Press this against yourself!"

The orcess obeyed, recoiling from the pain as she applied pressure.

"Keep your hand there," Evellyn said. "I have to help them..."

Wiping the sweat from her twitching brow, the blacksmith approached Adelina, wary and nervous with every step. "Have you any weapons?"

"Only kitchen knives. There's a hatchet out in the shed, but..."

Then there was a loud thump and a violent rattle.

Someone was trying to open one of the windows from the outside.

Adelina and Evellyn stood shoulder to shoulder, firm and determined, like two soldiers standing guard. They looked at the rattling window, at the dust clouds forming at the edges, both of them preparing for the worst. Then came the snickering voices, angry and hoarse, like men deathly sick with the plague.

"Find a way in! I'll go 'round the front!"

The orcess Aevastra began heaving and panicking, viciously and beastlike. She hadn't heard Okvar's voice in days, and it was as haunting as she remembered it. "It's all going to be fine," Evellyn assured her again.

Adelina seemed more concerned about the invaders than she did about the orcess. She knew the only way to survive was to outsmart them; sitting and crying would be of no help. And so she emptied her shelves of anything sharp and brought it all over to the kitchen table.

There was a grunt and an eerie snigger just outside. "We knows you're in there, my pet!" Murzol shouted through the cracks in the wood. "I can smell ya!" *Snort.*

The front door began rattling too. The entire room fell silent, every pair of eyes gawking at the creaking wood, as a heavy fist began pounding against it from the outside. And then they heard a brash thundering voice that petrified them all. "Open the door, scum…"

Okvar was standing on the outside, glancing over his shoulder, making sure no Elbon farmers were in sight. "Listen 'ere," he said. "We don't knows ye… We just want the bitch 'n' the babe. Ye give 'em to us 'n' ye won't ever see us again…"

Adelina turned to the orcess, who sat there rocking back and forth, startled and restless.

She couldn't do it… As much as she was thinking of her children, Adelina simply could not allow it. She couldn't live with herself knowing she could have done something to stop it.

"Leave my farm immediately!" she shouted.

Outside, Okvar was growing more heated by the second. He rolled his eyes and chuckled, as his companion came stumbling from around the corner of the cottage.

"They nailed 'em all shut!" Murzol said. "There's no way in." *Snort.*

Okvar sighed heavily, the rage in his chest growing.

"This here's yer last chance, human scum," he said, and Adelina knew that he was speaking directly to her. "I'm gonna say it one more time… I don't want yer wee ones. I don't want yer farm. I just… want… the bitch."

Inside the cottage, every pair of eyes turned to one another in turns.

Damn it all to hells, Adelina shivered internally. The longer the silence lingered, the more dread she felt and the more horrifying consequences her mind would conjure. She had to say something.

Stand your ground, Adelina… Don't give in…

She opened her lips, without the slightest idea of what to shout back.

But before any words came out, something quite unexpected happened.

"Leave my child," Aevastra said suddenly, rising gently to her feet, legs quivering, face drenched in sweat. "Let him live," she said, tears swelling up in her eyes. "And you can have me…"

Adelina's eyes widened. *What the bloody hells are you doing…?*

There was a chuckle just outside. "Fine," Okvar said. "Now open the damn door."

Aevastra closed her eyes and sighed for a moment. A tear escaped her face as she took a step towards the door. This was it... She wouldn't live to see another day and she knew it... If the orcs didn't take her life, she might have ended up taking it herself. One thing she knew for certain was she was tired of running. She would not run again. Never again.

She took another step towards the door.

"No!" Adelina placed a hand on Aevastra's shoulder. "She stays... They *both* stay..."

Evellyn dragged the chair closer and helped a stunned Aevastra back to her seat.

"Now, leave my farm immediately, I will *not* ask again..."

Aevastra shared a look with Adelina Huxley. Since they met, not a single word had been exchanged between the two, and yet that one look said it all. Aevastra felt something she'd forgotten she could feel. Something like trust.

The silence lingered. Adelina fought through the nervous breathing, clenching her shivering jaw as she kept her eyes on the door. Outside, Okvar was no longer angry. He was far beyond that, his mind crawling to its darkest corners. He craned his neck towards Murzol, who appeared somewhat frightened by him.

"Torch it..."

Murzol was slightly baffled. In the distance he could see the trails of smoke rising from the chimneys of Elbon. "B-But... won't the human filth see the flam-"

"*Torch* it, I says!" Okvar growled.

Adelina Huxley felt her skin crawl upon hearing the orc's words...

"Torch it *all*," he said. "They won't let us in? We'll *force* 'em out... TORCH IT!!"

* * *

The ogres had caught them all by surprise. For creatures so large their stealth was rather impressive; they used the trees to their advantage, their rough brown skin blending in with the wood. Four ogres, they were, and yet within minutes they had killed dozens, soldiers and rogue raiders alike.

Jossiah Biggs may have once been a brave knight of Val Havyn... But bravery in a human civilization meant nothing compared to the nerve necessary to survive in a place like the Woodlands. And so Jossiah found himself hiding behind trees and shrubs, shielding himself, cowering like an old hare as he gawked with terror at the ogres trampling over everyone.

Leave it to the big bastards to fight for the sake of fighting, he thought.

At that very moment, the man wanted nothing more than to be far, far away, drinking his weight in ale in some smelly old tavern. Still, he didn't run, he refused to be that person. It wasn't exactly bravery he felt, more like stubbornness, a last attempt to save some face. He wiped the sweat from his brow and blinked repeatedly, as if trying to snap himself back into reality.

As his eyes glanced all around, he realized just how alone he was.

The only men near him were dressed in red leathers. Those that were *alive*, that was.

It wasn't until he spotted an elf hiding nearby that he felt somewhat relieved. The elf wasn't wearing red leathers, just dirty brown rags and silver gauntlets. A Wyrmwood recruit, he had to be.

Cursed be these lands, Jossiah hesitated. He then sighed and stepped towards the elf.

"Oi! You!" he shouted, and felt a rush of adrenaline run through his spine.

The elf flinched; he looked so young, so afraid and alone, Jossiah almost felt pity for him.

Damn it all to hells, the man thought, suddenly trying to fight the hostile voice in his mind.

"With me now, lad," he said to the elf. "Watch my back, I'll watch yours. Ready?"

"Y-Yes…"

Jossiah gave him a heavy smack on the shoulder as they stepped forward together.

Come on, you damn rabbit… Don't you dare let me down…

The ogre was massive, but that was where Jossiah and the elf had the advantage. They danced between those hulking elephantine legs, swinging their blades left and right. Jossiah's blade sunk into a piece of bone and got stuck there, and he had no choice but to let go of it and dart to the side. And meanwhile, the elf was moving so fast that his arms were a blur, a rapid shadow as he sliced at the ogre's ankles again and again. The ogre roared ferociously.

That's it, come on you little bastard, Jossiah found himself grinning. *Keep it up!*

The ogre fell, and it fell hard. Some thousand pounds, it had to weigh.

But then Jossiah felt a tug at his chest when he realized the elf was still underneath it.

"Out o' the way, lad!"

But the elf was frozen in terror. The massive ogre fell back and crushed him.

The impact made a tremor in the earth, and Jossiah's eyes widened from the shock.

No… No, you stupid little rabbit bastard… The former knight ran towards him, stepping over the ogre's meaty arm. The elf's head was still intact and his eyes were open but lifeless. And Jossiah fell to his knees and lifted the lad's dead chin so as to make sure. Then he fought back the vomit.

Bloody fucking hells…

Jossiah panted heavily, his eyes closing for a moment and his arms shivering.

All around him, bodies were falling. Soldiers, recruits, red raiders, there was no difference.

Jossiah became lost in a horrified trance, his ears muffling the agonizing screams and desperate cries for help. He tried to stand, but he felt his knees weakening. He stumbled over to the dead ogre's legs and pulled his blade loose. *We should've stayed in Val Havyn... We never should've left...*

He panicked. His mouth was so dry, he could hardly breathe properly.

Damn them, he told himself. *Damn them all to hells... Let them die for their beliefs if they wish. But they won't have me. No, they won't have me...*

He slid his sword back into its scabbard. His feet began to regain some warmth, as he prepared himself to run. Before he could, however, a voice beckoned him back... A muffled voice, shouting his name...

"*Jossiah!*"

At first, the man thought he was hearing things. He thought perhaps he'd gone mad from the panic.

But then he heard the voice again. This time, it was followed by "*Help!*"

He followed the sound, his ears still ringing, deadening the sounds of death all around him.

And then he spotted his friend... Viktor Crowley's head was sticking out from a wide pit of quicksand; the rest of his body was hidden, buried, vanished into the earth.

"Jossiah!!" Viktor shouted again, looking desperate and vulnerable. "Help!!"

Viktor... Bloody hells, is that... is that you?

Jossiah took a step forward, his eyes genuinely worried and eager to save his friend.

Then, however, an ogre stepped towards him... There were red raiders trying to fight it, but the ogre was smashing their heads in one by one, as the Brotherhood captain shouted "Retreat!"

Jossiah felt a knot in his throat. His eyes moved back and forth, from Viktor to the ogres. And he felt the panic return to his chest, his temples became drenched in sweat, his entire body went cold and numb...

"Help me!!" Viktor kept shouting.

But it did not help. Jossiah appeared frightened out of his mind. And the more he glanced around him, the worse it got; heads were being smashed, limbs were being torn, blood was spewing into the air from every direction. It wasn't just horrifying, it was inhuman.

To hells with them... to hells with them all...

And it was in that moment that Jossiah Biggs, former knight of Val Havyn, did something unworthy of knighthood... He fled.

Cowardly, Jossiah turned and ran as fast as his feet would allow him, further and further away from his longtime friend and brother-in-arms. And as he was trapped in the pit, Viktor had no other option but to watch as his closest friend betrayed him.

Once, they were allies, fighting side by side for their king.

Once, he trusted this man. He called him his brother, in fact.

And there he was, the same man, hurtling away into the darkness, nothing but a glimmer of silver in the distance, leaving Viktor Crowley for dead.

The former knight found, unexpectedly, that he was no longer afraid...

He felt his arms give in as he closed his eyes and took a deep breath...

His head finally sunk. The sand had swallowed him whole.

This is it, he thought. *This is the end of you... Your last mission, and you couldn't even finish it... May the gods curse you, you stupid blind fool...*

He felt the air escape his lungs, bit by bit. He opened his mouth and rapidly it filled with wet dirt and muck. He tried opening his eyes but they stung like all hells, and all he saw was darkness. There was a pressure building up throughout his body, a painful pressure as he sunk lower and deeper into the earth.

He gasped for air, but all he got was more dirt.

He shivered; the quicksand was crushing the life out of him.

His mind raced with a million thoughts, as many often said it did just before death.

He felt everything around him get suddenly cold... An *icy* cold, in fact...

His last thought was that his body had died and his mind was still awake somehow. Except he was wrong... The ground was, indeed, freezing...

A hand reached into the sand and gripped him by the gauntlet on his forearm.

What is this...?

Viktor felt a swift pull. And then the pressure began to loosen around his body.

Pull yourself with it, he thought desperately one last time.

Today, you live... Come on, you old dog...

His feet twisted and kicked and his arms reached up for nothing in particular. A pair of hands was pulling him back into the world above. Before he knew it, Viktor was vomiting out mud and sludge, gasping for air.

A gentle hand was patting his stiff back.

You're alive, old dog, he told himself. *Today, you lived...*

Viktor crawled away from the quicksand and fell back against firm ground. He breathed hoarsely, his chest throbbing, welcoming the fresh air into his lungs like they had never done before. He wiped his face as best as he could and opened his eyes, the filth dripping down every inch of his skin.

He felt life coming back to him, his body growing warm again as he gazed into those glimmering purple eyes. Skye, the pale elf from the river, had rescued him... The staff in the elf's hand was glowing and the dirt beneath them both had a thin layer of ice over it.

Amidst the chaos, Viktor Crowley did something he didn't expect to do.

He smiled.

Nearby, the Wyrmwood troop was not doing very well. Only about half of the recruits remained, and the rest were struggling to keep their defenses strong. Cedric hid underneath the ale cart, fighting through his own shame as he watched it all happen.

Somewhere amidst the herd were the blonde twin raiders Gwyn and Daryan. The man was saying something to his sister that Cedric couldn't quite overhear. And then Gwyn darted unexpectedly towards the cart, dodging an ogre and four red raiders along the way.

She hopped on top of the cart, not realizing Cedric was trembling underneath.

"Come on, come on," she was mumbling to herself, sifting through the supplies. There were clothes and shields and other sorts of rubbish. The satchel full of gold, however, was nowhere to be found.

Suddenly she spotted a movement. Something was hiding just underneath a cloth in the back of the cart. Gwyn unsheathed one of her knives and carefully moved her other hand towards it. With one swift motion, she pulled the cover off.

Lying there, scared out of his mind, was Wyll Davenport.

And in the coward's hands was the missing satchel she was searching for.

"Give it 'ere, you shit! Now!" Gwyn said fiercely, snatching it away from Wyll's quaking hands. She took a peek inside, as if assuring all the gold was still there.

Then there was a roar, a *ferocious* roar, followed by more tremors. An ogre charged at full speed towards the cart. Gwyn wasted no time. She hopped off and crawled through the tall grass, inching her way towards a row of shrubs. Wyll Davenport remained in the back of the cart, shriveled into a fetal position, when he felt a hot sticky fluid drip on his head and neck. Something was standing above him…

There was a growl, and it was frightening enough that Wyll opened his eyes.

He stared into a pair of pitch black eyes, wide and bleak and full of hunger.

Amidst the shrubs, Gwyn finally noticed the figure hiding underneath the cart. The young man was lying face-down, trembling and praying to the gods for salvation.

Her eyes widened. "Toothpick…?"

But she noticed far too late. The ogre slammed his fists down and Wyll released one last yelp, before he was crushed like an insect. With the impact, the wooden wheels broke into pieces and the entire cart fell apart. The barrels were smashed open and the ale began to pour down through the rubble.

The ogre smashed his fist down again, then a third time. And then, upon seeing the lifeless mangled body of what used to be Wyll Davenport, the hulking monster walked off to wreak more havoc.

"No," Gwyn muttered with a horrified expression. "Toothpick…"

And there he remained, the poor inexperienced squire known as Cedric, bloody and unconscious, drenched and buried beneath a pile of wood and mud.

* * *

Every room in the Huxley's cottage turned into a pit of smoke within minutes. Though the flames remained on the outside at first, they were spreading faster than Adelina could devise a plan.

"What do we do?!" Evellyn asked, coughing through every word.

There was no response.

Think, Adelina… Think…

She would always tell her children to do so, but when the time came to do it herself, she always hesitated. Too many thoughts would race through her mind all at once.

Margot and Melvyn. Evellyn Amberhill. The orc woman and her child.

Several lives depended on her. *Too* many… And if she failed?

What would happen to Robyn? And John?

They would come back to Elbon to nothing but a pit of ashes and death.

If they came back, that is…

The room grew suddenly hotter. A piece of roof fell into the common room, breaking into pieces as it hit the floor, sparks of ember spattering outward. Evellyn stomped on them so that the floorboards would not catch on fire.

"To the bedroom window!" Adelina ordered them. "Now!"

The twins ran in first and they used kitchen knives to pry the nails out.

Evellyn helped Aevastra to her feet. "This way!" she said to her. "It's gonna be fine, you'll see… You're gonna be fine…"

Except they weren't fine.

Before the last two nails were removed from the windows, the sharp edge of an axe broke through the wood, startling them all. The twins stepped back and Adelina grabbed them by the shoulders and shielded them, hid them behind her dress.

Outside, there was a deep roar.

The axe slammed against the wood repeatedly, splintering through it.

"Go back out!" Adelina pushed them back towards the common room.

The hole that Okvar made was small, but it was enough for someone smaller to crawl through. "Get 'em!" he snarled, and Murzol snickered and twisted his way in, splintering his arms along the way.

When he was halfway inside the room, he saw them. Adelina stared back into those hungry eyes, before she slammed the door shut, caging him inside the bedroom. Murzol growled, his legs slid through the hole, and he fell to the floor. "Get back 'ere, human scum!"

Murzol leapt to his feet and walked towards the door. He rattled the knob, but something was bolting it from the other side. And so he began to pound his shoulder against it.

"Open up, you bitch! I'll kill *all* of ya!"

Outside, Evellyn and the twins were pressed against the door. "We can't hold it much longer," the blacksmith grunted, coughing as the black smoke poisoned her lungs. They could hear Murzol yelling and cursing from the other side. He growled one last time before he gave his shoulder a rest and started swinging his axe. The first swing hardly made a dent. The second swing, however, broke through to the other side, and the blade was just inches away from slicing Evellyn's face.

"All right..." Adelina said. "Now!"

Evellyn and the twins scattered out of the way.

And then Murzol landed a heavy kick against the door and it swung open.

With a grin, he stepped into the common room. And the first thing he saw was Adelina Huxley holding a black pot in her hand. With a defiant stare, she threw the pot at him and the boiling stew splashed all over his face and neck. Murzol released an animal-like howl of pain. He fell backwards on the bedroom floor, his hands pressed against his seared face as hot steam oozed out of it. And then Adelina slammed the door shut again.

By then, the bedroom window was destroyed and Okvar peeked his head in.

"Where are they?!" he growled, ignoring Murzol's pain.

Meanwhile in the common room, Adelina and Evellyn moved the heavy cabinet out of the way. It was so massive that the twins had to help. When they pulled it about three feet, the door was able to open slightly, leaving just enough room for everyone to squeeze their way to the outside.

"To the cart!" Evellyn said. "Go!"

The twins went through first and ran into the grassy yard, away from the flames, as Margot carried the baby orc in her arms. Then went Adelina, who lent a shoulder to Aevastra. And finally, there was only Evellyn left. She still had a kitchen knife in her hands and she wouldn't dare leave it behind.

Suddenly, a piece of roof fell from right above her...

She took a step back. The flaming wood missed her face by just a few inches.

With a rush of fear, she leapt over the scorching rubble and squeezed her way out. The hem of her dress caught fire for a moment, but she crawled on the grass and patted herself down until the flames died. She felt the cold night air strike against her face like arrows.

It was over... They had made it out...

She got on her knees and took a moment to catch her breath, coughing out dust and smoke, over and over again, her eyes red and swollen with tears due to the heat of the fire. Then, from the corner of her eye, she saw a massive shadow approaching her. Her eyes widened...

Nearby, Adelina was helping the orcess and her baby onto the back of Evellyn's cart, when she turned and saw the blacksmith crawling away from the enormous orc.

"Ye shoulda listen'd," Okvar growled. "Now I'm goin' to crush ye like a rat."

Evellyn Amberhill felt her skin crawl as Okvar became bigger and bigger with every step. All she had in her hands was that kitchen knife, and it was nothing compared to the size of the orc's axe.

Still, she could not back down… She refused to…

She leapt to her feet as she heard Adelina shouting "Evellyn!" behind her.

She ignored it. She knew that if she ran, the orc would only come after her and the Huxleys. If she could slow him down, perhaps the Huxleys could have a chance of surviving.

"Go!" Evellyn shouted. "Get out of here!"

With a grin and a roar, Okvar gave his first swing. With the speed of a wildcat, Evellyn darted to the side, her eyes taking in the orc's massive size and weight. Okvar lifted his axe again and swung it but Evellyn was smaller and therefore faster. The axe cut deep into the wooden fence and Okvar struggled for a moment to pull it back out.

An idea rushed through Evellyn's mind all of a sudden… She ran back into the yard, closer to the fire, where there stood the Huxleys' tool shed. She opened the door. Behind her, she could hear Okvar, grunting as he yanked his axe free from the wooden fence. And then her eyes caught it… the hatchet that Adelina had mentioned before…

She snatched it and faced the orc valiantly.

"Ye don't know when to give up, do ye…"

He swung again. She toppled back, her knees scraping against the grass for only a second, before she stumbled back to her feet. She took the opportunity to swing, but the orc caught her arm with minor effort and squeezed. She felt her wrist bone crack and the hatchet slipped from her hands.

So quickly, it was over… She was defenseless…

The orc was far too large and powerful.

They stared into each other's eyes; hers were anxious and his were hungry.

Then he lifted his axe high above his head again.

She closed her eyes, ready to take the hit…

But then a loud earsplitting scream distracted him. Murzol stumbled out of the front door of the cottage, the bottom half of his clothes on fire. He was squirming and fidgeting about like a madman as the flames swallowed him up.

"Help!" he cried. "Okvar! *Help*!!"

The lanky orc stumbled forward onto the grass. And then, behind him, another large piece of roof fell, the only thing holding the walls of the cottage together. There was a loud creak as the front wall began to sway with the wind.

Murzol patted himself down, managing to kill the flames on his trousers. Then, however, he looked up, and the last thing he saw was the wall of the cottage looming over him. He screamed, a loud piercing scream, before the wall crushed him completely.

If the wall didn't fully kill him, the flames surely would finish the job.

Realizing Okvar was distracted, Evellyn Amberhill took the opportunity to land a kick. The orc's grasp loosened and Evellyn snatched her wrist away. She grabbed the hatchet from the grass and darted away, taking backwards steps as she kept her eyes fixed on Okvar.

With a growl, Okvar charged towards her. And then something unexpected happened. An arrow flew in out of nowhere, piercing Okvar's arm and causing him to growl with rage.

Evellyn turned back... Standing in the distance was Old Man Beckwit with a bow in his hands, and his farmhands Larz and Henrik were running towards them with swords and shields.

"Inside!" Mister Beckwit shouted at Adelina and her children. For a moment, he was stunned to see it was an orcess lying in the back of the cart. With Adelina there, however, he didn't bat an eye. The twins rushed into the old man's house. And with a struggling knee, he and Adelina helped Aevastra off gently.

Meanwhile, in the distance, the farmhands struggled to catch their breath as they ran towards the burning cottage. They could see him, the massive monster known as Okvar, six and a half feet in height and built like a bull. He was everything humans ever feared and more.

Okvar swung his axe again and again, and Evellyn was struggling to block the attacks with the hatchet. Then the orc managed a deep cut on her arm, and she fell back with a cry of pain. He took a step forward, hunger in his eyes. And she looked up at him, the raging flames illuminating her worried face, blinding her as his massive shadow towered over her.

Okvar was mere seconds away from killing her when a blade suddenly swung at him. Larz and Henrik had reached the yard and were dancing around him, distracting him.

"Get to Beckwit's!" Henrik helped Evellyn to her feet. "We'll handle this."

But Evellyn refused to run.

She remained in place as both Larz and Henrik attacked the wild orc.

Nearby, Adelina felt her chest pound as she watched. She had to do something. She refused to stand there safely while Evellyn and the farmhands risked their lives for her. By then, Aevastra and her child were safe inside Old Man Beckwit's cottage. And the twins Margot and Melvyn were watching the fight from the doorframe.

"Stay here!" Adelina said to them. "Don't you move!"

And then she ran off... The wind was blowing violently, and Adelina had to fight through it to keep running. Even from afar, she could see the farmhands struggling. Larz and Henrik were doing their best, but it was of no use. Okvar was large and powerful and monstrous, and it didn't help that the men had been drinking just minutes prior. As they struggled, Evellyn sneaked by and tried to reach for the hatchet, but it was dangerously close to the Okvar's feet.

Henrik went in with a jab, but the orc landed a heavy kick to his chest, forcing the air out of him. Larz watched as his friend fell to his knees and gasped for air, and he felt the rage grow in his chest. Unfortunately, rage did not suit the man well at all. It made him sloppier.

He attacked, but the orc blocked his blade with the steel handle of his axe.

And then with a powerful thrust, Okvar struck Larz's blade so hard that it slipped from the man's hands. The orc grabbed him by the neck and began squeezing, draining the life from him as he glared into his eyes.

Okvar then lifted him…

A strong beast, he had to be, to lift the man by the neck a good two feet from the ground.

Adelina was just seconds away from the yard. As fate would have it, however, mere seconds was all it took for Okvar to have the advantage.

Larz died first… Okvar had unsheathed a dagger from his belt and stabbed it into the man's belly. And the poor man had no choice but to stare into the eyes of the orc as he took his last breath. To ensure his death, Okvar twisted the dagger inside, causing Larz to shiver like an injured animal before his eyes closed for good.

Okvar threw the man's lifeless body onto the dirt.

Then there was Henrik. He grew horrified and enraged at the sight of his friend lying dead on the grass. He lounged forward and tried to attack but Okvar sliced him in the chest with the dagger and kicked him back to the ground, then placed a boot over his neck.

"Stupid bastard," Okvar spit on Henrik's face. "At least make me work for it."

Henrik trembled, frightened for his life. *This is it*, he thought, and then turned his neck towards his fallen friend one last time before closing his eyes and accepting his own demise.

Before Okvar could kill him, however, a hatchet swung down and cut into the thick green flesh on his arm. He growled, loudly and ferociously. Evellyn swung the hatchet again, this time with a force strong enough that it sliced clean through the orc's arm.

With a raging growl, Okvar confronted her again…

He stared at her, taking a moment to remember her face…

Those bright green eyes, that fiery red hair, those lips, red as blood…

Okvar was never one to remember a face. But he knew then, as he glanced at his missing right hand, his *fighting* hand, stiff and wet over a puddle of mud… He would never forget Evellyn's face…

He landed a heavy blow to her jaw with his left hand.

She fell to her knees on the mud, the hatchet nearly slipping from her grip.

She felt the throbbing pain in her jaw, and as she opened her mouth a dribble of blood oozed out. She looked up. Okvar picked his axe up from the mud with his left hand.

A growl and a powerful upwards swing was all it took…

Oh no… Please, no…

She saw her life flash before her very eyes. She took a step back, but Okvar's axe hit her with a vengeance. Even as she bent her neck back, she couldn't avoid it.

She felt it, the cold sharp steel slicing her face…

Blood splattered into the air as Evellyn stumbled back, her mouth carved open and swelling with a throbbing pain.

She was hit… And she was hit *badly*…

She felt her face grow suddenly boiling hot as blood began to drip everywhere, blinding her eyes with a curtain of red.

She was done for.

One of the last things she saw was Okvar grinning down at her, only he was nothing but a dark and blurry shadow by then.

And then there was one last roar. A roar of agony.

The sharp tip of a sword cut through Okvar's chest.

She saw Adelina Huxley standing behind him. And then the orc fell forward.

Adelina was holding Larz's sword in her trembling hand. When the orc fell stiff onto the grass, she had no choice but to let go of the sword, as it was stuck to Okvar's spine and refused to come out.

And just like that, Okvar was done for…

Adelina dropped to her knees in front of Evellyn.

The blacksmith could see her. Blurry and red, but she knew Adelina's face when she saw it. Only the woman wasn't smiling… She was horror-stricken…

Mister Beckwit and Henrik approached them, both with a similar look on their faces, a look of despair and shock as they gazed upon Evellyn's face.

Evellyn could bear the pain no more… She felt her body grow tired and heavy…

And then her eyes closed…

"No… No, no, stay with me! Evellyn, stay with me, my dear!" Adelina cried. "What has he done to you? By the gods, what has he done…?"

* * *

The last ogre fell. There were nearly twenty arrows stuck to his back, and in the end it was a blade to the neck that killed him. Sir Percyval Garroway had swung his sword at just the right time, when the ogre slipped and fell back. A mere second too late and the ogre would have risen again.

The battle was over...

Sir Percyval walked around the bloody battlefield, shaking the dirt from himself as best as he could. "Gather 'round!" he shouted.

Aside from a few grunts nearby, the place had gone suddenly quiet.

The recruits began to gather, or at least what was *left* of them.

The knight did not look happy. Even as he counted in his head, he knew his expedition had failed. His only achievement was walking into the Woodlands with a hundred men, losing half of them, and unintentionally replacing them with nonhuman recruits. Suffice it to say the knight needed a drink, and *desperately* so.

"Come on, gather 'round!" Sir Antonn Guilara shouted from nearby.

Just then, however, two heavy figures smashed against an oak tree, breaking the silence. While over a hundred souls stood watching, there were two that were still locked in combat, a minotauro and an orc.

Both of them were tired and bloody... Both of them were violently stubborn...

"That's enough!" Percyval shouted.

But the two beasts did not wince. They punched and kicked and wrestled one another as if they were the only two souls present in the field.

"Your knight commander says *enough*!" Sir Antonn shouted.

Toro then landed a heavy punch to the Beast's jaw.

By then, the Beast was the last of the red raiders present and he knew it. If he was dead either way, he preferred to fight... He growled and charged forward. But the minotauro was waiting eagerly for him. One heavy punch was all it took. Toro's fist smashed against the orc's jaw, and the orc fell back, and he felt the earth beneath him get softer and mushier all of a sudden...

His entire body sunk into a bottomless pit of quicksand.

The Wyrmwood recruits watched as the orc struggled to crawl back to firm ground.

Viktor Crowley could hardly bear it, having just been stuck in the very same pit just minutes prior.

The Beast was roaring angrily, and the Wyrmwood troop simply stood and watched. Just before the orc's shoulders sunk, however, he was able to grip a nearby stone. It was loose, but it was the only thing keeping him from sinking entirely.

Toro stepped towards the pit, his horns ready to attack.

"No!" Sir Percyval said. "Leave him..."

Toro craned his neck. Though he didn't speak, he didn't *have* to.

His eyes were filled with rage and stubborn determination.

"Easy now," Skye said from afar. The minotauro began to calm down, his large black muscles loosening. "It's over, Toro... You don't have to fight anymore..."

And with that, the minotauro walked away, leaving the Beast to die a slow death in the pit of sand. There was a long silence all around as the troops locked eyes with one another, some searching for their comrades, most of which were dead.

"What now?" Sir Antonn asked his knight commander.

"We must unite forces with my brother in Halghard," Percyval said, though his voice was now weary and bleak, a hoarse whisper through heavy pants. "Otherwise we'll lose the other half of our troop come morning..."

Viktor heard him and felt a relief in his chest. He tried to wipe the mud from his brows, but it was of no use. He was an utter mess. He had to jump into the river fully armored to remove all of the muck from his body. Regardless, he was calm now, calmer than he had been for days, in fact.

The mission is not over. You must keep fighting, old dog. Keep fighting...

He felt he could lie on the dirt and rest for hours, he was so exhausted. Then, however, a soft voice startled him, as it always did. Startled him and yet filled him with life all over again.

"I loathe ogres..."

Viktor attempted his best smirk, but it came across as more sad than lively.

"You fought well," he said to Skye. "Do try and stay nearby next time."

The elf raised a brow. "I never imagined I'd ever hear a knight say such a thing."

"Yes, well..." Viktor cleared his throat. "It isn't every day my life is saved by an elf."

Skye wasn't insulted by the comment. In fact, they shared a smile for a moment.

"Buy me a glass of wine and we can consider ourselves even," the elf said.

"In that case," Viktor smiled. "I might just buy us *two*."

The recruits were mumbling amongst themselves as their weary knight commander Percyval walked around to examine the damage, with no one but Sir Antonn at his side.

Viktor took a moment to search for his men as well.

For a moment, his mind went straight to Jossiah, and he felt his heart start to race.

To hells with him, he told himself. *Don't give him a moment's thought, Viktor...*

He walked, chin held up high. And then he noticed a familiar face nearby. The raider woman with the blonde braids was sifting through a pile of rubble viciously with a panicked look in her eye. A few more recruits approached her, and among them Viktor saw the large figure of Thaddeus Rexx, with only a flesh wound on his left arm.

"Sister?" Daryan called, but Gwyn ignored him and kept digging.

There were smears of blood on her outfit, possibly hers, but they didn't seem to be slowing her down. "Come on, come on," she was mumbling anxiously like a madwoman.

And then Viktor and Thaddeus Rexx were able to see the rags beneath the rubble.

"Toothpick!" Gwyn mumbled. "Come on, say something..."

Viktor and Thaddeus began to help her, and within a minute they dug Cedric out.

The squire was a complete mess. He was covered in mud and drenched in ale from the barrels that the ogre had smashed. He had looked up at the wrong moment and his left eye was bruised purple and swollen shut from the blast.

"Cedric!" Thaddeus said as he dragged him away from the wreckage.

"Toothpick!" Gwyn dropped to her knees and shook the young squire's shoulders. "Still there? Toothpick!?"

They lifted Cedric to a sitting position, blood oozing down the side of his face. There was a deep cut on his purple lip and the bruises had stained him all over. But the young man was surprisingly alive, and he somehow managed a weak mumble... "G-Gwyn..."

The woman sighed with relief, a look of dread in her eyes. Thaddeus hoisted Cedric into his arms and carried him towards the nearest cart, his thin legs dangling weakly in the air like a wooden puppet.

"Don't talk, lad, we'll get you cleaned up..."

Gwyn was hopping along next to them, with real and genuine concern in her expression, like an older sister caring for her brother. Viktor Crowley was just a few steps behind, beckoning someone urgently for a jug of fresh water.

"Th-Thad..." Cedric said weakly, specks of blood moistening his lips.

"I said don't talk, lad. Not 'til we fix you up."

"Ye'll be fine, toothpick. Stay with us!"

Cedric felt his entire body grow numb.

I'm alive, he told himself, almost as if trying to convince himself of it.

By the gods, I'm alive...

XII
Ogres & Stonewalkers

Sitting calmly by the river bend, somewhere within the Woodlands, John Huxley and his two traveling companions were having their first meal of the day. Roasted wild rabbit, like the day before, and a handful of elfberries that Hudson managed to steal from the tavern counter when Miss Rayna was looking the other way. John wasn't entirely thrilled by the idea of eating stolen berries, but they were many miles from the tavern by then and it was difficult to protest when his belly hadn't been properly fed for the past week.

"These are incredible," John struggled to keep the blue juice from oozing out of the side of his mouth. "We definitely don't have *these* in Vallenghard."

Hudson nodded back. "Banish an entire race of elves into the confines of the forest and you're irrefutably bound to omit yourself from a few perks, mate."

John glanced at the thief with a slightly baffled expression and said, "That was rather impressive, I'll admit."

"What was?"

"You have a way with words, I meant."

"I'm a thief, mate, not an uncivilized arseling."

"You mean like peasants?"

"I mean like kings."

John couldn't help but smirk at Hudson's quick responses. The thief must have noticed, for he elaborated soon after, "Say what you will, but kings are often the most barbaric. It's the power, mate. Too much of it can be toxic. Just ask Lord Ethelbert van Kurren."

"But he's dead…"

"Precisely."

They sat in what appeared to be a safer part of the forest.

There was nothing around them but trees, dirt, and more trees.

Behind them was a large mound of stone, about ten feet high and several meters wide. John figured they could use it to their advantage, so as to prevent an ambush, and so they sat side by side near their dimly lit fire, their backs to the stone, keeping an eye on their surroundings. Syrena had taken a walk near the river, not too far from them. John tried to object, but Hudson reminded him that the witch knew a great deal more about the Woodlands than he did. She was, after all, home at last.

Hudson continued to bite into the crisp rabbit's leg. He had taken only a few of the berries himself and let John have the rest. The farmer figured the thief had somehow eaten that morning without being noticed. In reality, however, Hudson never did trust the berries much.

"Seriously, these are unbelievable," John said. "Mum would certainly love to get her hands on these. I'm sure she'd find a way to turn them into a nice sweet tea."

"I doubt that very much, mate," Hudson remarked. "They're perfectly safe when eaten cold. But you should never boil them. Not unless you want to die young."

"What d'you mean?"

"The hotter they get, the more dangerous. The acid can burn through your skin."

It may have been the surprise of it all, but John swore he could feel his stomach turning as the juice of the berries mixed with the hot rabbit meat. His expression made Hudson chuckle.

"How do you think I got this scar?" Hudson pulled his sleeve up to his elbow. A cluster of wrinkled spots marred the flesh on his forearm, craggy and brown, about the size of an apple and darker than the thief's naturally tanned skin.

"Childhood accident?" John asked.

"You can say that," the thief replied. "I suppose we're all still children at sixteen… There was a lovely girl back in Raven's Keep that grew rather fond of me. When she found out I'd been chatting with another, she grew rather enraged. She grabbed whatever was nearest to her and threw it at me. Just my luck, it happened to be a tankard of boiling elfberries her mother would use to keep rodents away from her garden." He released a lighthearted sigh and added, "Ah, young love…"

John found himself chuckling.

Despite everything, he was finding comfort in Hudson's company. The night at Miss Rayna's tavern, it had taken about three drinks before the thief had warmed up to him; after a good half hour of acting like a stubborn child, he found himself arguing with John about anything and everything. From a debate about how a double-edged longsword was absolute rubbish compared to the speed of a single-edged rapier to a discussion about exactly how many husbands Queen Lyza of Ahari had in reality as opposed to what they've written in history scrolls.

And now, two mornings later, it was as if there had been no quarrel between the two men to begin with. Hudson even started calling him 'mate' again, which John was thankful for. It made the farmer feel more at ease, as if he wasn't traveling through the Woodlands with foes, but rather amiable acquaintances; he didn't know whether to call them 'friends' just yet.

Then, of course, there were the stories. If Hudson had anything good to contribute to the journey aside from a good stance in a fight, it was a good story. And oddly enough, they all began the same way… With a question.

"Have you ever shagged, farmer?"

The question nearly made John choke on his last berry, the sour juice giving him a slight sting in his throat. "I-I'm sorry?"

"You heard me perfectly."

John stammered for a bit, trying to find the right words to say, and Hudson was finding his reaction rather amusing. "W-Well I can't say I'm very experienced, no... After father died, I became far too busy helping mum tend to the farm. Not much time to think about marriage."

"Who said anything about marriage?" Hudson remarked. "I asked if you've ever shagged."

John tried to clear his throat, but he had nothing to wash down the knot of food with. And much to his embarrassment, his cheeks had turned a bright shade of red.

"D-Don't say that so bloody loudly!"

"Don't say what? *Shag?*"

Suddenly, and to make matters worse, Syrena appeared out of the blue from around the large grey boulder. "What're you two going on about?"

John panicked slightly. "Um, *Combat techniques...?*" he said, his voice overlapping with Hudson's as the thief said "*Stringed instruments.*" The two men glanced at one another and then back at the witch.

"*...And* combat techniques," Hudson lied. "I was just, um, *explaining* how to play a mandolin while fighting. Neat trick."

"Well *that's* funny," Syrena said. "Sounded like you were talking about sex."

The redness in John's cheeks had by then spread all around his face.

Hudson smirked and said, "I'm appalled you would think that of me."

Syrena sat on the other side of the thief, cross-legged and with her back to the boulder. "You think because I'm a woman, I can't know a thing or two about it?"

"*I* don't think that," Hudson replied. "But Sir Huxley here seems a bit ashamed of not having ever partaken in such an endeavor."

"There's no shame in that," Syrena smirked at John. "In fact, some say that witches who've never done it often end up a great deal more powerful than those who have. In some ways you can say, it, uh... *weakens* us." She winked.

John looked uncomfortable and startled. With a grin, Hudson pulled a winesack from somewhere within his coat and handed it to him.

Immediately, John took it. The presumably stolen wine was far stronger than any he had ever had. He felt the warmth of it in his chest almost instantly; it seemed to almost cleanse him. Hudson was whispering something into Syrena's ear and they laughed together. And seeing just how relaxed they were, John somehow felt a weight lift from his shoulders. It wasn't exactly something he felt comfortable talking to his mother about, or anybody else in Elbon for that matter. It simply wasn't talked about much.

"Actually," he decided to speak out after a brief silence. "There was...the *one* time."

He took another sip of wine, before he realized the thief and the witch had shifted their gaze towards him, both of them more than intrigued.

"But… It's, uh… Never mind, it's not really very interesting," John said bashfully.

"Mate, you've opened your mouth. Too late to shy away now."

"You either tell us, or we'll get you drunk enough until you do," Syrena added.

John smiled. They smiled back.

It was a nice feeling for a change.

"Fine," John said, his eyes beginning to drift. "She's, uh… She was a girl from back home. A blacksmith."

"Excellent so far," Hudson said, snatching the winesack from John's hands and stealing a sip, before handing it to Syrena.

"Her family and mine have been lifelong friends," John went on. "So she and I saw a lot of each other growing up. Then one evening, during Elbon's autumn festival, she, uh… She was acting rather strange with me. Timid, quiet, nothing like herself. Turns out, she had stolen a bottle of liqueur from her father's cabinet and was waiting for a moment to drag me away… Anyway, we managed to stray from the crowds and climbed up to the rafters of our family's barn."

"I thought you said that was your sister's hideout," Hudson raised a brow.

"Well she wasn't *there*," John said. "And with everyone in town for the festival, it was the only place we could go to be alone." The farmer took a moment to chuckle softly upon reminiscing on the one memory he hadn't spoken of to anyone since the night that it happened. "It was the first time I ever had a drink. Didn't have anything to compare it to, but the taste was quite awful."

Syrena chuckled.

"No one cares about the liqueur, mate," Hudson said, his eyes genuinely intrigued. "Skip to the interesting part."

"She was the one who pulled me closer first," John said. "I hardly knew what I was doing. It was… peculiar. She was, after all, my best friend… And yet there she was lying with me, the both of us fully unclothed. It felt so wrong yet so right all at once." John paused and his gaze lowered, the expression on his face beginning to change.

"What was her name?" Syrena asked.

"Evellyn," John replied. "Evellyn Amberhill."

"What happened to her?"

John's smile was no longer there, as if the regret in his chest wouldn't allow it.

"I still see her now and then… Few weeks later, my father became ill and died. She and I never spoke about that night ever since."

John said no more. It had been ages since he spoke of that night to anyone, and yet here he was sharing it with two most unusual companions. For a brief moment, the river flow was the only sound for what may have been miles.

"Well that took a painfully sad turn," Hudson said as he took the winesack back from Syrena and took a gulp. He then handed the wine back to John, who took it rather willingly.

"You want to hear *sad?*" Syrena said as she wiped the wine stains from her chin. "The only man *I've* ever been with was *hanged* for lying with a witch. How's *that* for a dramatic turn?" Syrena did not appear bothered to share. In fact, she was grinning from the irony.

Though it may have been the wine taking effect, John managed to smile with her. He realized he hadn't been this calm since before the journey began. He kept the winesack for another few sips. "What about *you?*" he asked Hudson. "Care to share another of Hudson Blackwood's tales of mischief?"

"Not really," the thief answered. "They're all about the same."

"Well who's the one shying away now?" John teased him. It was then that he realized the wine was most *definitely* taking effect.

"Have you ever been in love?" Syrena asked somewhat suddenly, and for the first time since meeting him, Hudson did something rather odd... He hesitated.

"I, uh... No... No, I can't say I have..."

He snatched the winesack from John's hands and took another gulp. A large one.

"Came close to it *once*," he went on, wiping his lips with his sleeve. "She was a beautiful woman. Daring and mischievous, too. And she made the best damn meat pies in all of Merrymont. Normally, I don't pay anyone much mind. If I get an urge, I find someone who has the same urge and we shag. Simple as that, no complications. But this woman was different. I was more... *invested* in her. Then, one frosty winter's night when we were lying there in her bed, I realized the sensation in my chest was still there even after we had finished. I told myself it was the wine, but as good a liar as I am, I couldn't deny to myself that I just might be falling for this woman..."

John and Syrena remained silent, pondering on the idea of Hudson Blackwood romancing a woman. It was quite an image. And suddenly John felt empty of any resentment, realizing the thief had a human side after all.

"Anyway, I was gone before I got a chance to tell her anything," Hudson sighed.

"Too embarrassed?"

"Not at all, mate... Actually, her *husband* walked in and all hell broke loose."

The three of them shared a laughed. It felt good to remind themselves that they were human. For a moment they had entirely forgotten they were on a journey to steal back a princess. And John had even forgotten that, just a week prior, these two people he was laughing with were his enemies.

Because in that moment, none of it mattered...

He wasn't John Huxley, the farmer. The other two were not Hudson the thief and Syrena the fire-conjuring witch. They were just three simple people having a conversation by the river.

It was quite a nice moment, while it lasted.

"If you'll excuse me," Hudson leapt suddenly to his feet.

"Where to?" John asked.

"Nature calls, mate."

The thief walked off into the trees. And John leaned his head back against the stone, closed his eyes and took a breath, allowing for the warmth of the wine to consume him. "You know," he said, "I think I'm starting to like him."

Syrena smiled earnestly. "Me too," she said, feeling somewhat shy about saying it out loud. She proceeded to dig through her rucksack for anything that wasn't berries or wine.

John opened his eyes again and admired the beauty all around him. He felt at peace for a change, the afternoon breeze cool against their skins. The verdure of plant life and moss-covered wood radiated under the sunlight, what little could trickle through the roof of leaves. John now understood how a place like this could be home to a vast array of others just like Elbon was home to him.

Then, however, something caught his eye, something that broke his peace.

A familiar figure was approaching in the distance...

"Syrena?" he said, somewhat worried. "Do you see that...?"

She turned and saw the figure.

Too familiar, it looked, as if she had seen the same exact figure just days prior. It was the figure of a man with curly grey hair, and on his right shoulder was a brown gangly-tailed little beast.

Her eyes widened. Her shoulders tensed.

"Oh shit..."

* * *

Even from a half-mile away, Captain Malekai Pahrvus swore he could smell the awful odor coming from the Rogue Brotherhood camp. Anywhere they traveled, it seemed they couldn't camp in one single place for too long without that damn smell coming back to haunt them. He had half a mind to order all of his men to hop into the Spindle River for a bath.

He walked, more exhausted than he had ever been. His band of raiders followed his lead, or rather what was left of them. A measly fifty men or so, that was all. A bloody disaster, it had been. Their first raid with him as captain and it was more chaotic than he'd hoped. So sure, he was, that they would take over the Wyrmwood camp. He was to face Sir Percyval Garroway himself and slice his throat. That was the plan.

It would have turned out fine, the captain thought. *If it hadn't been for those damn ogres...*

The only good things they had gained from the raid were a few bags of gold and about a dozen horses. But it was nowhere near enough to make up for the loss of life. Malekai's own horse had run off, and when the ogres arrived he'd mounted the first horse he could find. A beautiful white stallion, it was. Its seat was made of black leather and attached to it were several bags of coin and leather armor undergarments.

A knight's horse, no doubt, Malekai thought.

Little did he know that it was Viktor Crowley's horse he had stolen amidst the chaos.

The morning sun's light was piercing his eye. He tried to squint, but it only sent a sting to the tender wound on his hollow eye socket. He could see the camp just ahead, the row of tents set up just the way they left them. There was a scoff just next to him, which he chose to ignore. He was far too infuriated to even talk.

"Damn it all to hells," Borrys Belvaine said. "What now, cap'n? If we go after 'em, w-"

"By the gods, shut the fuck up, Borrys..."

They reached the camp, each raider silently heading to their own tent to either rest or mourn or both. Malekai walked towards the captain's tent, the only tent in the camp with the sign of the scorpion. Normally, it would bring a grin to the man's face, that reminder of how far he'd come. At that moment, however, it enraged him.

The last time there was a defeat this bad, the Rogue Brotherhood had rebelled and chosen a new captain, and the prior captain had been killed in the dead of night. But Malekai refused to allow that to happen; he was to sleep that night with a blade under his pillow. He figured he could send word to one of the other Rogue Brotherhood clans in the southern Woodlands, a request for more men, in which he would avoid any ugly details. But there were only 5 clans, and he'd nearly wiped out one of them overnight with his poor leadership. Questions were bound to be asked, he knew.

He entered the tent, and immediately his eye moved towards the corner...

He saw nothing... Nothing but that pile of junk of his...

His eye then glanced all around, under his desk and his butchering table, in the corner near his bed, but still there was nothing, no sign of her...

He felt his heart start to race. His brows lowered. His teeth started to grind.

"Cap'n?!" Borrys peeked a head inside. "Th-They're gone, sir! The slaves... they've escaped!"

"Get... out..."

Borrys noticed the empty tent, his eyes widening.

"Oh... I see... s-sorry, cap'n, I didn't mean t-"

"GET OUT!!"

Borrys took a nervous step back, but he didn't leave. He watched as the captain growled with rage and flipped his desk over, kicking and slamming and destroying anything and everything in front of him with his swinging blade. His chair broke into pieces, as well as his desk. The pile of junk in the corner became a pile of rubble.

Malekai then fell to his knees, shaking violently from his wrath. He breathed, slowly and heavily, welcoming the pounding in his chest like it gave him the vigor he needed. Too much had gone wrong. *Far* too much. Any further, and the man was surely to lose his mind.

Borrys Belvaine cleared his throat. "I-I'm sorry, cap'n… I'll bet it was her… She must've freed 'em. She's the only one nervy enough to do it."

The captain said nothing; his mind was preoccupied obsessing over the girl that had managed to slip from his grasp when no one else had before. This girl, Robyn Huxley, who had nothing but a bow and a quiver, not even a dagger.

Outsmarted by a farmgirl, he kept thinking, and his dry fists shook, reddening with fury. There was a long uncomfortable silence in the tent, as Malekai lifted himself to his feet, slowly and menacingly, his sole eye staring blankly into space, like a man who's lost any heart he had left in him, what little of it there was.

"Tell them all to gather their tents and supplies," he said at last. "We must prepare to march west."

Borrys cleared his throat again. "*West,* cap'n?"

"Aye," Malekai said. "We'll make way to Grymsbi. There, we will recruit as many blades as we can and get our numbers back. Tell them we march at noon… And if *anyone* sees that little bitch… She's *mine.*"

* * *

The grass was just as green. The dirt was just as thick and brown.

The birds sang just as harmoniously and the sun's glow was just as splendidly lucid.

It was the *smell* that was awfully different… It smelled like death…

With every step that Robyn Huxley took, there was a shiver. With every breath, there was a scowl. Slowly, as she walked, the greenery of the Woodlands became stained with red. And when she walked around a pile of rubble that may have once been a cart, her tired feet froze where they stood. Her muscles went numb suddenly and her knees were aching, shivering, struggling to keep her balanced. For a moment she doubted her eyes; she figured she had to be imagining things.

By the gods… Is it real?

"What on earth happened here?"

"The Brotherhood happened," Nyx replied, his fox whiskers twitching as his nose examined the air. "This was a Halghardian troop's camp. See the banners?"

"They're... *madmen*."

"No, Lady Robyn. They're just men..."

Anywhere she turned, there was a corpse. They were scattered throughout the ruined field, stiff and mangled and unmoving. Her stomach began to turn and as much as she tried to breathe through her mouth, the foul smell managed to sneak into her nostrils.

Nyx's nose suddenly latched onto a peculiar scent and he turned to follow it, walking carefully through the field, hopping over puddles of mud and chopped limbs; his orange tail seemed to drag behind, as if he still wasn't used to it. After the sickness settled down a bit, Robyn tried to adjust her sight so as to purposely blur every face in the field.

Breathe, Robyn, she told herself. *They can't hurt you...*

She couldn't possibly imagine a more horrifying sight. Bodies were stacked against other bodies, some bent and broken beyond recognition. It was a sight Robyn was unused to and would only ever see in her darkest nightmares. However intriguing life outside of Elbon may have seemed to her before, if this was the reality of it, she wanted no part of it, not anymore. Her frightened eyes followed Nyx, as the fox brushed past a body, a familiar bald man dressed in red leathers, except now his throat had been slit.

"Looks like the Brotherhood lost a good deal of their own," Nyx said.

Robyn felt her heart race. *Malekai? Borrys?*

She immediately searched for any signs of them. The beaded black dreads on Malekai's head, his red captain's coat, the black rag he wore as an eyepatch... And Borrys's lanky figure, his thinning chestnut hair, his red vest and old patchy trousers...

But there was nothing. Red raiders, there were many.

Malekai and Borrys, however, were nowhere to be found.

Damn it all to hells...

She wasn't exactly sure of what she felt.

Perhaps it was anxiety at the thought of her captors still being alive.

Perhaps it was relief at the thought that she could still be the one to kill them.

Either way, she felt uneasy and disturbed. She realized she'd spent so much time gawking that Nyx was a good distance away now, his nose twitching instinctively as he followed the scent he'd caught. He walked past a tipped carriage with dead horses still attached to it, and hanging along the sides were the banners of Halghard, torn into pieces and stained with dirt and blood.

Robyn examined the symbol on the banners, or what remained of them. There she saw it, the image of the infamous serpent wrapped around a lit torch. It was indeed a Halghardian banner, she realized, except the colors had been changed. The banner was a moss green instead of red, and the serpent was now gold rather than silver. It was no longer the late King Frederic's banner, but an imitation of it, an homage.

"Oh dear," she heard Nyx say from afar; his voice was so shaky that it startled her. He hardly ever sounded concerned unless it was for *her* life.

"What is it?" she approached him, but as she made a left turn at a thick oak tree, Nyx placed a heavy paw on her boot as if warning her not to take another step. The dirt felt suddenly softer, like mud. And when she felt her boot sink a half-inch, she took back a step.

The pit of quicksand in front of her was about six feet wide.

And right at the center of it was a head…

An *orc's* head, eerily familiar to her, covered in dirt and muck, but she could still make out the olive green skin around his eyes and cheeks. The orc's eyes were closed, his entire body was buried beneath the earth, and the only thing keeping him from sinking was his rigid arm gripping a nearby rock that appeared rather loose. Robyn recognized him immediately. This was the orc she'd come face to face with at the Rogue Brotherhood camp.

What an awful way to die, she thought. *To have to choose between sinking or starving…*

Nyx cleared his throat nervously. "Perhaps it's best if we moved along…"

She nodded, the sorrow obvious in her expression.

Suddenly, however, the orc's head began twitching…

He's alive, she realized, startled and wide-eyed. *Well, shit… He's alive!*

There was grunt, followed by a rapid blinking and a shiver. For a moment, the orc's yellow eyes appeared solemnly woeful, like an injured animal fighting for its life.

"H-Hello," Robyn's lips trembled.

He released another grunt, the frustration clearer in this one. It was as if he had forgotten where he was, as if he'd drifted into a deep sleep with hopes of waking up and realizing that it had all been an unpleasant dream.

"It's okay," Robyn tried to calm his nerves. "We're not here to hurt you." She took a moment to clear her throat and think of what to say, her hand unable to loosen its grip on her bow out of precaution. "Y-You're the orc from the Brotherhood camp, aren't you?" she asked. "The one they call the *Beast?*"

The orc slowed his breathing, and bit by bit he grew that shield of hostility that he often carried. It took a great deal of stubbornness, Robyn thought, to act adversely towards a person who was only trying to help.

Talk to me, she begged him silently. *You can trust me…*

But the Beast's stare became suddenly just as intimidating as it had been back at the camp. He opened his quivering lips, and his voice was as beastlike as Robyn had imagined it.

"What're ye doing 'ere?" he asked, specks of dirt trickling out of his lips as he spoke. "Ye shoulda gone back to yer shit-village by now."

Robyn felt a sudden dash of disappointment. Then again, she wasn't sure what she was expecting from the orc, considering what she'd already seen of him. At the very least, he seemed to have recognized her. "I-I can't," she said. "I'm not going home, I'm… W-Well, it's not important…"

"Then *go!*" the Beast growled. "The fuck ye waitin' for…?"

His words stung her like a dagger, but his utterly despondent façade spoke otherwise. The nervous twitching of his green pointy ears, his trembling fingers struggling to keep their grip on the loose stone, the forced breathing, and the desperate look on his face as he drew in dirt into his lungs with every breath… The orc was afraid. She knew *too* well what fear looked like.

"Lady Robyn?" Nyx called, looking up at her.

But the girl refused to leave. Something was holding her down.

"Why'd you let me go?" she asked him suddenly, her tone firm and intrepid, as if purposely trying to provoke him. "You're a member of the Brotherhood… and yet you see your captain's prisoner escaping and you do nothing about it. *Why?*"

"Not my prisoner… Not my problem," the Beast muttered. "Plain 'n' simple."

Something in the orc's eyes absorbed her; aside from the yellow rings on them and the green of his eyelids, those eyes could have belonged to anyone back in Elbon. And the same went for the rest of his face. His nose was larger and wider, but its shape was that of any human. He had two sharp fangs rising from his bottom lip, thick like ivory, but his jaw and even the black braid on his chin could have been a man's. And if he had *anything* in common with a human, Robyn refused to believe the Beast was missing a conscience.

"That can't be all," she said.

He scoffed at her. "Stupid littl' scrap… Think ye know it all, do ye? If ye were *my* prisoner, ye'd be dead already."

At that point, Nyx was no longer at Robyn's feet but off somewhere in the bloody campgrounds, sifting through the rubble for supplies. Robyn wanted to follow, her mind kept telling her to walk away, but her feet simply wouldn't move. It was as if the earth had grabbed hold of her as well, and she had to graze the moist dirt with the heel of her boot to make sure that it hadn't. She sighed, unsure of what to do, knowing very well that time was running short, that the Brotherhood would arrive at their camp at any moment now and Malekai would realize she was gone.

"Do you, um," she cleared her throat somewhat nervously, her eyes moving left and right, examining the pit of quicksand. "Do you need some help?"

The Beast exhaled sharply. "I don't need help from a stupid farmgirl…"

"But you'll die if y-"

"I said SCRAM!"

The agitation in his voice seemed to drag him another inch deeper into the soil. He shook even more as he tried desperately to keep himself above ground.

The stone in his right hand began to slide inward, killing him slowly, and Robyn nearly jumped in by impulse. But the orc's brute strength was somehow keeping him up, keeping him alive.

Robyn stepped away and began searching all around. She walked over to a fallen tree nearby and broke off a thick branch, the loosest she could find. She held it at one end and aimed the other at the orc. "Grab onto this," she said to him.

The Beast's glare was a blend of fury and hope, if that were even possible.

"Get that away from me," he grunted.

Robyn was shaken for a moment but she kept herself together and insisted. And Nyx was observing her from afar, wishing he were something larger than a fox in case the orc got any funny ideas.

"Just grab the branch, will you?" she said with a sigh.

"Get it *away*, ye dumb scrap…"

"I'm not leaving until you grab it."

"I don't *need* yer help!"

"Just grab th-"

"*LEAVE* ME!!"

"Oh will you *stop* it already?!" Robyn shouted fearlessly at the top of her voice.

A look of surprise overcame the Beast's face. His eyes even glowed for a moment, giving Robyn the impression that he was on the verge of tears. Still, the orc said nothing… His arm did not move from the stone, partly out of fear of sinking, but mostly out of persistence. Robyn threw the thick branch to the side and then knelt on the soil, as close as she could get to the Beast's face without sinking herself into the pit. For a moment, Nyx was just as startled as the Beast was at the girl's astounding nerve.

"You *spared* me!" she said with an unyielding tone, for a moment sounding almost like her mother. "Back at the camp when you saw me escaping… You could've stopped me at any moment, but you *spared* me instead! You did that for a reason… You might call yourself a crook and a killer, but no matter how tough you try to appear, nothing will *ever* change the fact that you spared me. That *means* something… It means somewhere inside, beneath that shield of rage you carry, you have a heart… And d'you know *why?*"

The Beast said nothing, growing more and more unsettled by the second.

Much to his surprise, however, Robyn leaned in even closer.

"Because heartless people don't *spare* you," she said, and then she grabbed the thick branch again. "Now will you *stop* being a stubborn thing and let me help?!"

The Beast *wanted* to, it was obvious. But years of hostility held him back.

"Get out of 'ere… *Now*, scrap…"

"I will not… Not until y-"

The roar could have belonged to a bear, for it echoed louder than any sound

Robyn had ever heard in her life. But it had come from no bear... It was the sound of an orc's temper, so powerful that it sent a hot, sticky breeze that blew a few of Robyn's black curls out of her face.

Angrily, she threw the branch to the side as hard as she could and yelled, "Fine!"

She then leapt to her feet and stormed off, the frustration quite clear in her rapid pace. Her face had gone red from the fury and she was mumbling under her breath, cursing through her whispers, the same way she would do after one of her mother's lectures.

The Beast closed his eyes and sighed, well aware that the girl could have been his last opportunity to survive. It was only a matter of time before the muscles in his arm gave in and his body would merge with the soil. He had already begun to accept it, in fact.

But he greatly underestimated just how stubborn Robyn Huxley could be...

When he heard the soft footsteps coming back, his chest began to pound again. He opened one eye slowly, just enough to see the figure of the girl kneeling nearby with an old rope in her hands. She was tying it around the trunk of a sturdy oak tree that stood a few feet away, and then she threw the other end into the pit of quicksand, just at the Beast's reach.

"There!" she said bitterly. "Now you can get *yourself* out!"

And with that, Robyn walked away.

Often, she would hesitate and look back. This time, she didn't.

The Beast watched her with awe. He had been traveling with the Rogue Brotherhood for nearly a decade, and not a single one of his mercenary brothers had shown this much consideration for his life; all he'd ever been to them was a weapon.

But the girl, somehow, had looked at him as more than that.

She saw *him*, not what he was, and it concerned him. *Frightened* him, even.

His eyes moved towards the strand of rope next to his arm. It was the only thing standing between him living or dying, that rope. And yet his stubborn hand wouldn't move.

Robyn kept walking away until she found Nyx sniffing around the pile of bodies, his nose twitching, still fixated on that unknown and peculiar scent.

"Can we leave?" she asked, her nose becoming more and more overwhelmed by the second. Suddenly, she longed for a nice warm bath.

"What happened back there?" Nyx asked.

"I don't want to talk about it..."

They walked away. For a moment, Nyx struggled to keep up with Robyn's angry pace.

"I did try to tell you, Lady Robyn... Orcs can be rather persistent."

"I've only met the *one* and already I can't stand them," she said sourly.

"You'll be all right. They're not all the same, you know."

"Are they not?" she exhaled nastily.

"That's like saying all *humans* are the same. Would you place John in the same league as the Captain of the Rogue Brotherhood?"

Robyn felt a sudden guilt upon hearing his words. Nyx was right, she knew, though it wasn't enough to ease the aggravation.

"Besides," Nyx said. "You will find far worse out here than orcs."

"Yeah? Like... what...?" her voice trailed off as she came to a sudden halt.

As they came across a bend in the road, Nyx realized at last what that peculiar scent had been... In front of them was an ogre, a great hulking thing about ten feet tall, sitting on the dirt with a wooden club at his side, digging into a pile of bodies as if they were served on a platter. There was blood smeared all over his jaw and chin, and chunks of dead flesh hanging between his teeth.

To Robyn and Nyx, the place was a graveyard. To the ogre, it was a feast.

"Back away... *slowly*," Nyx whispered.

Robyn's mouth had gone dry. With every step she took backwards Nyx was able to take three, his slim catlike legs made for sneaking, and she envied him for it. They hid behind a row of trees to the left of the path, but the ogre's nostrils had flared, latching onto their smell as if they were walking steaks.

Once out of sight, Robyn began panting silently.

"What now?" she asked Nyx, her brows arched with distress. She didn't think twice before confronting an orc, but fighting an ogre would be like a wolf trying to tame a mammoth.

"Wait for my signal," whispered the fox. "You will head east. I'll go west."

"W-What?" she stammered.

"We must circle the area, one tree at a time. It'll confuse him."

"*Confuse* him?!"

"He can't follow *both* our scents, can he?"

"He can *try*! What if he..."

"You give ogres far too much credit, Lady Robyn. They're halfwits, believe me, I've encountered plenty."

"Did you *see* his legs?! If he sees one of us..."

"He won't, just *trust* me!"

Suddenly a large drop of drool fell between them, thick and slimy, enough to fill half a tankard. They were so preoccupied conjuring up a plan that they didn't realize how loud they'd been whispering. There was a soft growl coming from above, and when they looked up the massive ogre was towering over them, slobber dribbling from his blood-smeared lips.

"Never mind the plan," said Nyx. "RUN!"

Robyn's feet had never moved so quickly, even when being chased by tree nymphs. The ogre moved slower due to his size, but every step he took was equal to five of Robyn's steps. Nyx was faster, and so he took the lead by a few meters before he spun around and gritted his teeth furiously.

"Keep running!" he shouted as Robyn brushed past him.

But the young archer slowed her pace reluctantly; she glanced over her shoulder, watched as the ogre's eyes became fixed on the fox, and she couldn't help but come to a halt. She refused to flee; she'd tried that option before and it resulted in chaos. Her mother had taught her many lessons, the most important of which was that you *never* abandoned family. And Nyx had proven his loyalty by tracking her all the way to the Brotherhood camp. He may have been over 250 years old, but to Robyn he was family.

"Come on, you dull bastard," Nyx was growling, keeping the ogre's attention on him. "Follow me, that's it." He was taking careful backwards steps towards the trees, waiting for the opportune moment to pounce away. With a growl, the ogre lunged forward, his hand ready to bind the fox in a tight clutch. But Nyx took the leap just in time, a backwards leap that saved him from the ogre's reach, and then he ran through the trees with intense speed and landed a bite at the ogre's ribs while the hulking monster was busy pulling his heavy arm back.

Nyx bounced right off and scurried away to a safe distance, ready to repeat the attack. The ogre looked more aggravated this time, blood dripping from the fresh wound on his belly.

"That's your final warning," Nyx said, as if the ogre could somehow understand him. "Your move." But the ogre simply shook the pain away and stepped forward, his back in a hunch, ready to reach down. Nyx did it again; he pounced back into the trees at the last moment, dodging the ogre's hand, then ran around and landed a bite, this time on the ogre's leg. But for a moment his tooth became stuck on that thick flesh, and the ogre landed an unexpected punch.

The blow sent Nyx into the air; he landed on a puddle of mud with a yelp of pain.

The ogre was slower now, walking with a limp, but he reached Nyx with little effort.

Nyx was calm, looking up at the great beast with a fearless glare, as if prepared to die, hoping he would come back as something bigger. *Get it over with,* he thought.

The ogre was growling, lifting his heavy arm into the air, ready to strike. But then an arrow flew in and pierced into his lower back all of a sudden. He released an echoing shriek, arched backwards, and moved his hand towards the arrow.

Nyx was staggered for a moment, snapping back to reality after having prepared his mind for death; he moved away towards safety as he frantically searched the area. He found Robyn hiding behind a row of shrubs, drawing back another arrow and aiming it at the ogre.

"Lady Robyn! Don't!" he shouted.

She let go… She was aiming for the ogre's eyes but the hulking monster blocked it with his hand. And then the ogre spotted her, his gaze hardened, threatening her without the need for weapons. Robyn darted away, an arrow held prepared against the string on her bow, and the ogre followed her footsteps.

"No," Nyx muttered. "No, no, look at *me*, damn you! Look at *me*!"

He wanted to run after them, but the muscles of his paw were now sprained, and he couldn't move fast enough, couldn't fight through the throbbing pain. "Run!" he shouted. "Run, Lady Robyn!"

She rolled away and squeezed through the trees, but the ogre either broke through them or found a way around them. She kept running; the fear pumping through her chest was unlike anything she had felt before, it was almost *thrilling*. But it didn't last very long... She was so distracted peeking back at the incoming ogre that she didn't notice there were more bodies lying ahead. Her boot bumped against the tattooed head of a dead raider and she lost her step, fell face-forward on the dirt, her knee bumping against a grey boulder.

Groaning from the pain, she crawled forward frenetically.

Stupid, Robyn, she told herself. *Pull yourself together...*

Her bow had slipped from her hands at some point, and she couldn't spot it anywhere nearby. She was weaponless, save for her mother's kitchen knife. And as she searched desperately for a place to hide, a hot puff of air blew suddenly from above.

No... Shit...

The ogre was standing over her. She had escaped tree nymphs and the Rogue Brotherhood only to be killed by a damn ogre... She was almost angry with herself for not being careful enough. Too horrified to look up, she kept crawling, but it was far too late... She could see the ogre's shadow, and his fist was already in the air, ready to slam down against her spine.

It's over... Damn it all to hells, it's over...

She wrapped her arms around her head, closed her eyes, and prepared herself for the pain...

But before the ogre could strike her, a sharp stone smashed against his jaw, causing him to spit out blood and broken bits of teeth. Robyn was stunned for a moment; there was no way Nyx could have lifted such a heavy stone, much less thrown it at the ogre with such strength...

She glanced to her left and felt her eyes were deceiving her.

The orc known as the Beast was out of the quicksand and was charging at the ogre, roaring ferociously with his arms at his sides, like a warrior charging into battle. He hopped on top of the boulder that Robyn had stumbled over and used it to boost himself into the air.

Robyn's jaw dropped. *Beast...?!*

When the orc came down, he landed a heavy blow to the ogre's jaw, stunning him instantly. The ogre was thrown off balance and fell back over a puddle of mud, and then the Beast climbed on top and began slamming his fists down viciously like an animal. Robyn leapt to her feet and backed away, her eyes wide with disbelief.

"Get out o' here!" the Beast shouted.

She obeyed at first, running back towards Nyx, and she found her bow hidden among the shrubs along the way. But she looked back again, unwilling to flee while others protected her. She was growing sick and tired of everyone telling her to run.

"L-Lady Robyn," Nyx approached her with a limp.

She fell to her knees and embraced him. "Oh Nyx! Are you okay?"

They watched as the orc wrestled the ogre, pinned him down, landed punch after punch. But the ogre was more resilient than all of them combined. There was no defeating him unless it was with something sharp.

"We have to help!" Robyn said.

"Stay back, Lady Robyn! I demand it!"

But she couldn't do that, not again... Her eyes moved left and right, looking for any form of leverage. Perhaps if she climbed a tree, she could use the height to her advantage and shoot arrows down. But they were moving too fast and she feared she would strike the Beast by accident. Perhaps if she lured the ogre away... but to *where*?

She searched hesitantly until something caught her attention, something shiny standing out amidst all the filth... There on the dirt, next to a broken down cart, was the Beast's beloved axe... The sharp steel edge glistened from yards away, the black leather was tightly wrapped around the long silver handle, and the pommel at the tip was sharp and diamond shaped... She would have recognized the axe anywhere.

"Stay here!" she said to Nyx.

"W-Wait! Where do you think you're..."

She ran dangerously near the fight, ducked and rolled on the dirt to dodge the ogre's frantic swinging arms, and reached the broken cart within seconds. And at that very moment, upon gazing at the girl from the corner of his eyes, the orc was thrown off his guard. The ogre was weak and bloody but his strike was still powerful, and he sent the Beast flying with a punch.

"Damn it," Nyx muttered, stepping closer, ready to jump in if necessary.

The orc had fallen face down on the mud. He grunted, panting heavily with rage, feeling every bone in his body cracking as he lifted himself back up.

"Hey! Beast!"

The orc glanced to his right. Robyn stood just four feet away, holding the heavy axe in her hands. She tossed it to him, and the orc caught it with a fierce determined glower, giving it a good swing to warm up. "Back off," he growled at Robyn, and this time she did it without a fuss, holding an arrow ready between her fingers just in case.

The ogre was on his feet now, taking slow limps towards them...

"Come 'ere, ye bastard," the Beast muttered under his breath. "Give my regards to the gods…" The ogre stumbled forward, bruised and bloody, attempting to put up one last good fight. But the orc was faster and much more agile, and within seconds the sharp axe took one of the ogre's feet, and there was a rumbling in the earth as the ogre fell on his belly. The Beast darted forward fearlessly and swung his axe down. And then the ogre closed his eyes, never to open them again.

One strike and it was all over. The axe had broken through the skull.

Nyx and Robyn felt the tension diminish, like an overwhelming boulder being lifted from their shoulders. They were safe at last…

There was a sudden silence in the air. Nobody said a word, they were all far too busy catching their breaths and wiping off the dirt and sweat from themselves. The fox was panting; his paw was hurt but there was no blood on him. And yet Robyn bent down to embrace him as if he were dying all over again.

"N-Nyx… You must sit, have a rest…"

But the old fox did not look the least bit pleased.

"Damn it all to hells, girl! Have you lost your bloody mind?!" he barked at her, with a tone that could have been friendlier. He was chiding her the same way her mother and Old Man Beckwit would often do. And she felt strange suddenly, *betrayed* almost, as if being scolded by a close friend, as if being scolded by John.

"I told you to *run*," he said. "W-Why… Why on earth did you not run?!"

She gave him space, a sudden look of guilt and shame in her eyes.

"I-I'm sorry… I was just… I was *scared* for you!"

"I'm 278 years old, girl!" he shouted angrily. "How many bloody times must I say it?! I'll be *fine*…"

She looked down, a sudden knot building in her throat. When Nyx properly caught his breath and the silence lingered between them, he felt it again, that tug in his chest… He was not used to people caring for him, and it baffled him every time that Robyn did.

"*Thank you*," he said abruptly, though it was no more than a croaky whisper.

She didn't smile, not this time. But, at the very least, the knot began to subside.

Suddenly, behind her, she heard a grunt. She was so overwhelmed, she had almost forgotten the Beast was standing there. At first she was unsure how to react, her mind hardly able to adjust to the sudden shift of atmosphere. The Beast had saved her, that much was true. But his demeanor was as rough and hostile as always, and he towered over them like a bear. And before Robyn could conjure up any words, the Beast surprised her by speaking first.

"What the fuck are ye?" he asked, his eyes wide with bewilderment as he looked up and down at the fox. Robyn and Nyx glanced at each other briefly.

"It's uh… It's quite a long story," Nyx chuckled slightly.

The Beast grunted. It wasn't a grunt of disapproval or liking, just a grunt...

There was a brief moment in which the Beast and Robyn locked eyes with one another; the subtle discomfort in both their expressions was obvious. Somehow the orc's face never seemed to change from its austere humorless form and the girl wondered if it was willingly or if the orc had had the same expression since birth. Surely, the sharp fangs on his bottom lip didn't help it.

Robyn knew she had to say something...

She *wanted* to; if only a simple '*thanks*' for having saved them...

But before she could even open her lips, the orc started walking away, without so much as a '*farewell*', yanking his axe out of the dead ogre's head along the way.

"Um... L-Lady Robyn?" Nyx tried to protest, but the girl had already darted ahead, following the orc's footsteps. He felt a dash of shame at having lectured her, particularly because the girl looked at him as a friend and not as a mentor. And he realized then that his cold remarks had not had the best timing, or the best tone. "Damn it," he hissed disappointedly at himself, before he limped after the girl and the orc.

"Wait!" Robyn was shouting, running and hopping over piles of mud to catch up.

The Beast kept on, his scowl fixed in place as he wiped the ogre's blood from the edge of his axe. His entire body was filthy and smeared with mud but he hardly paid it any mind, focusing instead on keeping his axe clean and shiny.

"You there!" Robyn said as she caught up to him. "Wait!"

"Piss off," the Beast grunted, taking a moment to spit out some of the dirt still left in his mouth.

"Where are you off to?" she asked inquiringly, walking briskly at his side.

"Ain't yer business," said the Beast.

Robyn had to walk at twice her usual pace just to stay a stride behind, like a mouse attempting to keep up with a hound. And Nyx dragged along at the back, moving as fast as his numb paw would allow him. "You're heading *west*?" Robyn asked.

"North," the Beast said, though it was hardly more than a grumble.

"*North?*" Robyn raised a brow. "What's up north?"

"Bauqora."

She scoffed under her breath; very few things irked her more than brief responses.

"What's Bauqora?" she asked.

"Will ye just piss off, already?!"

"I'm only trying t-"

"Did that ogre bite yer damn ears off?!" the Beast snapped at her as he came to a halt. He wasn't exactly angry. More like irritated, if anything. Still, it was fascinating to Robyn to see an orc behaving in such a way.

Humanlike, was all she could think to describe him. *Heated and vicious, perhaps, but plenty of humans act the same way...*

"Listen 'ere, scrap," said the Beast, breathing infuriatingly through his sharp green nose. "Don't get any funny ideas... Ye saved me, I saved ye... Debt's been paid. Now for the last time... *Piss. Off.*"

The orc walked away, and Robyn and Nyx locked eyes for a brief moment. But before Nyx could say anything, she grew a look of wonder on her face. The raised brow, the widening of the eyes, the hint of a smirk... An idea had crawled into her mind and before she knew it, she was running again.

"Hey! Beast!" she shouted. From where she ran, she couldn't see the Beast rolling his eyes nor could she hear him cursing under his breath. "Have you heard of Grymsbi?" she asked when she was at his side again.

"I don't care..."

"Well, you *should!*" she said. "They're allowing orcs there now, y'know?"

"Lady Robyn..." Nyx called, as if warning her to be cautious, but she ignored him entirely.

"I-I'm not saying it's perfectly safe, but... but it's *something*," she said. "You could come with us! You could... I don't know, find a caravan heading north, perhaps? It beats traveling through the Woodlands alone."

The Beast came to a halt again. His brow, however, had arched in such a way that suggested he was at the very least mildly intrigued. "What the fuck's Grymsbi?" he asked.

She hesitated; she hadn't exactly thought the most persuasive argument through.

But she had his attention, if only for the moment...

"I-It's a village in Halghard," she said, and then the Beast exhaled sharply.

"A village?" he asked. "A village of human filth?"

"Well... Yes, it's in *Halghard*... But there's no ban there, not anymore!"

"Horse shit," he said doubtfully. "Humans nev'r change... If I set one foot there, they'll shoot me down at first sight."

"They *won't*," she assured him. "I promise you. Times are changing. They're welcomi-"

"Ye think I'm stupid?"

She stopped speaking for a moment... She knew from experience that the best way to persuade someone into following her plan was to challenge them...

"You saw them... didn't you?" she glared at him. "The elves and the gnomes? The ones at the Wyrmwood camp, the camp *you* raided? You saw the knights, you saw the banners... They were *recruiting* nonhumans to take back to Halghard... Do you refuse to believe your own eyes, then?"

She stopped there, trying hard to maintain her stance.

She could feel Nyx's presence at the height of her knees and even then, she was nervous. As much as she tried to hide it, the orc was among the most intimidating beings she had ever encountered. She was hardly over five feet and he towered a good foot and a half over her, if not more, so much so that she felt her neck would start to ache if she bent it in that upward angle any longer.

The Beast sighed, but it was a sigh that gave Robyn hope. Little to her knowledge, the first image that crawled into his mind was the minotauro he'd faced in combat... He'd faced enemies of other races in the past, but never any that rode with a human troop... That much was unspoken of, at least with any troop from the human realms...

"If I go with ye 'n' it turns out ye were playin' tricks... I will gut yer littl' friend 'ere. And *you* after."

"I'm no liar," Robyn said, her jaw clenched and her eyes narrowing with anger.

"We'll see," the Beast said with a nod. He then aimed her with the tip of his axe as if he was pointing his finger. "And I'll make this clear, scrap... I *ain't* lookin' after youse..."

"And I'll make *this* clear," she said boldly. "We don't *need* to be looked after..."

Robyn's response alerted Nyx. Her tone should have been friendlier, not only if she wanted to make an ally of the orc, but if she wanted to avoid certain death by his fist. Robyn brushed the black curls away from her face and added, "We've made it *this* far on our own, haven't we?"

"Aye, ye did," the Beast scoffed. "And ye got snatched up by a couple o' rogue swords."

Robyn felt a sudden heat in her chest. "I'm not afraid of Malekai!" she felt the need to say.

"Good," the Beast said. "Ye shouldn't be... He's a gutless littl' shit that thinks with 'is cock. But that's what makes 'im dangerous."

There was a brief silence again. The tension had lessened, that much was certain.

But Robyn would have been lying if she told herself it wasn't still there.

The Beast looked uncertain. Truthfully, he had never been fond of humans; in fact, there'd been some nights when he contemplated killing a man merely for snoring too loudly. But the girl that stood before him had a courage he hadn't seen in a human before.

It intrigued him. It also scared him.

Robyn knew nothing of the Beast's past but if she did, she would have known that she wouldn't gain his trust so easily. Then again, she didn't *need* to. She had his curiosity, and that was enough for the time being.

The Beast released one last groan of annoyance. "Fine!" he said, then rolled his eyes as if he was already regretting his decision. "Which way's this Grymsbi?"

Robyn smiled; her eyes lit up with hope. "We must head west..."

And so she carried on with her journey, more sure of herself now, her party now made up of three... She looked down at poor old Nyx, still limping along with his injured paw; they hardly spoke to each other for the rest of the day, unless it was to make a decision. But at the very least they were still alive, still together, and she was thankful for that.

It will all be fine, Robyn... Just fine...

Every step she took from that moment on was a more careful one. Every few minutes, she would look over her shoulder to make sure they were all still safe. She had escaped death more times in the last week alone than she ever had in her entire life. She would be lying if she said the torment had gone away. But she would *also* be lying if she said she wasn't thrilled by it at the same time.

Perfectly fine, Robyn, just you wait and see... With an orc and an immortal fox by your side, what could possibly happen next that could surprise you?

* * *

Old Man Beckwit pressed the last bandage against Evellyn Amberhill's face, carefully so as to prevent the adhesive from smearing over the cut. The blacksmith was unconscious, pallid and weak from the loss of blood, but she was alive, at least for the time being. Every minute or so, her body would shiver and spasm, and her dry purple lips would mumble faint gibberish.

"Stitches are done," said Mister Beckwit. "She'll live. But she'll need more callis root and some mauve treacle if she's to keep that wound from infecting. I haven't got any, I'm afraid."

Adelina stood over the old bed, her eyes unwilling to accept that this was in fact Evellyn Amberhill. She'd always been a charming and joyful young woman, strong and determined and full of life. And here she was now, ghostly pale and close to death, the entire left half of her face hidden underneath blood-soaked bandages.

"I'll take care of her," said Adelina. "What about Aevastra?"

The orcess sat on Mister Beckwit's armchair, shivering like a newborn doe, the green skin on her shoulder bruising a dark purple around the rough bandage. The twins sat nearby, Melvyn quite perturbed and Margot preoccupied swaying the baby to sleep.

The look on Old Man Beckwit's face wasn't a pleasant one.

The orcess noticed it, and she knew before he spoke what was coming.

"The tip of the arrow was coated with poison..."

Adelina felt the air escape her chest. "What kind of poison?"

Mister Beckwit gave a sorrowful sigh. "I've seen bruises like that before," he said. "That's Aharian scorpion venom. If she doesn't treat that wound immediately..."

Adelina began to panic, her head twitching left and right. She didn't let him finish, for she knew what his next words would be. She inspected his table, sifted through his array of herbs and remedies. "There must be a way… There *must* be…"

"I have nothing for it, Adelina…"

She refused to accept it… She had just met the orcess and somehow she found herself on the verge of tears. Aevastra didn't deserve this, she didn't deserve to die this way… And what would become of the baby? He would become yet another motherless child left behind to fend for himself. The thought alone was a burden.

"I will go into the city!" said Adelina. "I'll go to the nearest apothecary and come back as soon as I-"

"She doesn't have that kind of time," Mister Beckwit interrupted. "She'll be dead by the time you return… The only way she'd survive is if…"

He paused there, wiping the sweat from his brow with an old cloth.

"*If…?*"

The old man sighed one last time. "…if you take her *with* you."

The room went silent. Margot Huxley turned to the orcess, whose breathing was beginning to weaken and eyes were growing dark and heavy.

"I-I can't," Adelina stammered. "I-If they see her, they'll… they'll *kill* her!"

"And if you don't, she'll die here. At least if we take her, she has a chance…"

Adelina gave it some thought. Not only would Aevastra be killed at first sight, but her family might suffer the consequences for even being seen with the likes of her. And in a city like Val Havyn, it was near impossible not to be spotted. They'd have to be more than wary; they'd have to be practically invisible.

"We can go to the royal palace," Old Man Beckwit suggested. "Sir Darryk Clark has been appointed Lord Regent. I knew his father Augustus quite well during my years of service in the royal guard. I'm sure the lad would be willing to help."

The baby orc gave a whimper. And it only distressed Adelina further.

In one night alone, she'd lost her home and nearly lost her youngest children.

The thought of losing what little she had left sent a throbbing pain to her temples.

"Very well," she said. "We must leave at once…"

They loaded Evellyn and Aevastra onto the back of the cart and Old Man Beckwit covered them with a large blanket. Nearby, Henrik was grunting and sobbing quietly as he shoveled dirt into a hole in the ground. And in that hole there was a body wrapped in a sheet. The poor farmhand wiped the sweat and tears from his red face as Mister Beckwit approached him.

"I'm awful sorry, Henrik…"

The farmhand said nothing, only kept shoveling.

"For what it's worth, Larz was one of the two best damn farmhands I've ever hired… And the lad fought like hells…"

Still nothing. Henrik could hardly bear to look up, his eyes fixated on his dead friend. Mister Beckwit placed a warm comforting hand on his shoulder. "I'll return in a few hours. We'll have a drink in his honor."

And so they made way towards Val Havyn, preparing to face the worst. Adelina and Mister Beckwit sat in the front, guiding the mule. And the twins sat in the back with the two wounded women. Young Margot Huxley allowed Aevastra to hold her babe during the ride, for she knew there was a possibility she wouldn't live to hold him another day. All there was to do was wait and hope.

"He's got your eyes," said the girl, hoping to lift the orcess's spirits.

Aevastra replied only with a half-smile.

"What's his name?" Margot asked.

The orcess exhaled weakly. It was as if the poison had ripped her of her ability to speak.

"Does he not *have* one…?"

Aevastra gave her a shake of the head, a very weak one, but Margot got the message.

The girl remained dismally thoughtful. She didn't know what would become of the orcess or her child. It had only been a day since she stumbled upon them along the edge of Lotus Creek, and yet she felt a peculiar warmth in her heart towards them both. If Aevastra died, who was going to give the child a name? *Every child deserves a name*, the girl thought.

"How about… *River?*"

Aevastra looked back up at her and smiled, more lively this time. And then the babe whimpered softly and looked up at them with twinkling eyes, so warm and yellow like buttermilk, so similar to his mother's.

"He likes it, I think," Margot caressed his cheek again. "Hello there, River…"

* * *

John and Syrena should have seen the attack coming. From the moment they sat down to eat, they should have known the silence was far too peaceful for it to have been a mere coincidence. But that malevolent crook and his gang of bandits seemed to have a knack for keeping quiet, as any skilled predator would.

Fleeing was pointless by then. They could see him in the distance, the man with no name, and his blurred figure alone was enough to give them both chills. The wicked monkey hopped off its master's shoulder and skittered on all fours towards them.

John tried to stand, his knees shivering, as he prepared for a good fight.

But then a cold sharp blade pressed against his neck from behind.

"Stay down, boy…"

He froze.

Syrena of Morganna was startled. She leapt to her feet with her hands at the ready. But the man had a determined look on his face and a grin that was not to be toyed with.

"One move, witch… And I'll slit his pretty littl' throat…"

Syrena couldn't bring herself to attack. She could've easily burned the man down with a single thrust of the arm, but she could not guarantee John would remain unharmed. She hesitated. And during that single moment of hesitation, another blade approached from the other side. She felt the cold sharp edge on her neck before she could even protest. And the bandits shoved them both down to their knees.

"Hands up. *Now.* And keep yours closed, witch."

They obeyed. Having no other choice, they succumbed to them, the very same bandits that had attacked the company right at the border of the Woodlands, before the spiders came.

"Go on then," said the one pinning John down, and then the other bandit seized Syrena's wrists violently and began wrapping them in a piece of brown skin that was still moist with blood and reeked awfully.

No, the witch thought to herself. *Not this again… You cowardly bastards…*

She tried to resist, but the vile man was stronger than she expected. She'd told herself that if anyone tried to wrap her hands in ogreskin again, she would light them up in an inescapable hellfire without thinking twice. And yet there she was, her wrists tightened together all over again, and there was nothing she could do about it.

John tried his best attempt at a cold stare, but he couldn't hide his fear. In everyone else's eyes, he was a boy stuck in a man's world, away from the safety of his farm. He loathed it and was thankful for it all at once.

Use it, John, he thought. *Let them underestimate you and use it to your advantage…*

The sharp-fanged monkey arrived first, hissed at them, paced around on all fours, examining every detail. His gaze was low and his nose was sniffing the ground, and John wondered if the tiny beast had somehow remembered their scent and that's how they were tracked. When its master arrived, he brought with him that same grin from several days prior. A slow dishonest clap and a snicker, and then more laughs among the other two men.

"Wha' a lovely surprise to find you two here," the nameless man said, as he paced around them with a bow strapped to his back and a blade on his belt. "Thought you could run away from fate, eh…?"

You sure do love to talk, don't you? John thought, and then wondered how that could work to their benefit.

The man turned from John to Syrena and then nowhere in particular as he spoke. "Where's everyone else run off to, lad?" he asked. "Did the chief finally grow a pair 'n' cut off the dead weight?"

John said nothing. The monkey was sniffing the satchel by his knee and it was making him uneasy. As much as he loved animals, he couldn't help but think that if the elfberries inside were hot enough, he'd feed them to it, and then the little beast would be no more.

"They cut off your tongue, or what?" the nameless man spoke again. The more the silence lingered, the more impatient he appeared. "You gonna answer me?"

Syrena closed her eyes and sighed. She had the chance to burn them all but she'd lacked the nerve to take it. She felt her body grow hot with rage, feeling as if it was seeping out of her eyes, nose, and ears. Even from her fingertips, she felt it, which was odd. She would always feel the warmth in her hands diminish upon first contact with the ogreskin; they would turn cold and dry, and her power would cease to be.

Perhaps it was that the skin had been freshly cut...

Perhaps it was that her anger was greater than she thought it was...

Or perhaps it was, and she had considered this since the reeking fumes hit her nose, that the skin around her hands was not ogreskin at all...

"Alright," said the nameless man. "Seems I'm talkin' to myself then... Fine, I can talk... I can tell you that things won't end well if you don't tell me what I wanna know. I can tell you all of the awful things me 'n' my men will do to the both of you if you don't squeal... But, tell me, where's the fun in that?" His yellow smile was nauseating to look at. It was the smile of a man that had succumbed to the lowest form of human possible and hardly felt any shame in it.

"We don't know where everyone else is," John finally spoke. "We got separated."

"Did you, now?" the nameless man asked, brimming with displeasure. "How sadly inconvenient. I was lookin' forward to capturin' the chief myself, to be honest. Torture him, kill him, skin him, the usual."

More laughs from the bandits...

That's it, John... Just keep him talking...

Syrena, however, didn't say a word, as was usual of her. She was far too distracted pondering about her hands. But John had suddenly found their window of opportunity. His naïve eyes were narrowed, but there was hope behind them, as he kept his gaze ahead towards the nameless man... and towards a shadowy figure in a black hat sneaking through the trees...

"You would sell a man's skin?" John asked, as an effort to keep the man talking.

"Shit, no. Skinning him's for me own pleasure. Old habits 'n' all that," the nameless man laughed, and this time his words made John's skin crawl. "The chief's armor would have gotten us a pretty coin, though. His blade, too. And that hair would've made for a nice wig for some balding arse-faced nobleman."

John Huxley was no longer listening. His eyes met his thieving ally in the trees, and he was vigilant for any signs or gestures. He was so distracted that he didn't realize the nameless man had bent down on one knee in front of him, so close that he had no option but to take in that awful breath.

"You kind of remind me of the chief," he said, his expression hardening. "Both of you talk like you got something else on your minds... Tell me, what's on yours, lad?"

John tried to look away, but the nameless man clutched him by the jaw and forced him to make eye contact. "I'll tell you what's gonna happen, lad... I'm gonna take your pretty little gal here over by the river for a bit. Whatever you hear, you're gonna ignore it, yes? Pretend she's just... *laughing*, if you will. We'll just be down there havin' a laugh. You *say* anything, you *try* anything, 'n' my men will slice your throat, yes?"

The fury in Syrena's chest was nearly excruciating. It may have even been made of flames, for all she knew. Her magic was something that not even *she* could fully comprehend. She was born with the gift and it was all she had known since childhood. Over the years it still surprised her from time to time... And on that day, she swore that the more she shook from the rage, the warmer and sweatier her palms were getting, despite the ogreskin...

The nameless man got to his feet and grabbed Syrena by the arm.

She tried to fight it, but it was of no use.

"Sir?" called one of the bandits. "Will you be able to shag her with her hands tied that way?"

"Ain't the first time," the nameless man chuckled.

"If it rips, I've got more goblinskin in my rucksack."

There was a brief silence...

Syrena looked down at her wrists. She knew the skin had felt different...

Its stench was different, it was thinner, it was softer... It wasn't ogreskin at all...

Well shit, she grinned.

Suddenly, she released that rage she'd built up inside, and with little effort her hands burned through the wet leather. The nameless man backed away instantly, his sleeve suddenly caught in a flame. And then Syrena stepped towards the other two bandits, her eyes furious and indomitable. She held her hand out and the flames roared out like dragon's fire.

"Someone get 'er!" the nameless man shouted.

But the two bandits had shriveled in a panic. John Huxley darted out of the way and crawled back, as Syrena stepped in front of him like a shield-maiden. The nameless man felt the sudden need to act; he unsheathed his blade sloppily and stepped towards the distracted witch, but he froze where he stood as the cold tip of a single-edged rapier poked at his back.

"Put it down, old mate. Slow and steady," said Hudson Blackwood.

But the nameless man was more reckless than John. He turned and swung his blade, sending the thief jerking backwards. There was a skirmish between the two, as Syrena's fire roared out of her hand.

"I-I yield! Please! I yield!"

The last bandit was down on his knees, shivering with fright, next to a black charred skeleton that used to be his comrade. Syrena's hands were still lit, the flames coating them like infernal gauntlets, and her auburn eyes were both deadly and stunning. "Stay down," she warned him.

"Coward!" the nameless man shouted angrily. "Get up 'n' fight!"

But it was over. Their advantage was lost.

He was disarmed by a thief, outsmarted yet again.

"You filthy street rat!" he shouted. "Don't you know who I am?!"

Hudson grinned. *Of course I do, old mate. You're just another 'son of who'.*

Suddenly, there was a rumble beneath their feet, as if something heavy and massive was being dragged over the earth. It was followed by a deep sound that may have been a grunt, only a hundred times as loud as a man's. They all turned their gazes, slowly, afraid to make a sudden move.

John was on his feet by then, gripping the bone hilt of his silver blade. The sound had come from the stone they had chosen to sit against, a boulder the size of a house. It looked like any other stone, except now it had started to move... Bit by bit, it began to uncoil itself from its rotund shape and it was rising from the ground like a beast waking from its slumber. Hudson's face hardened, his witty demeanor entirely gone, replaced by something else entirely. Something like fear...

"Stand... perfectly... still," he said, softly, as if hiding beneath the whistling of the wind.

There was a loud hissing sound, like that of an exhale, except aggressively loud. And a gush of wind blew against them all. The massive stone shifted and turned, its shape becoming more beastlike by the second. It was *alive*. Its head and torso was massive and its limbs were short and thick. And when it opened its eyes, they were black and crystallized like obsidian. It looked as if a fifteen-foot tall ogre had been struck with a curse and turned into an living, breathing stone.

John Huxley's jaw dropped. "What in all hells..."

"Don't move, mate," Hudson muttered at him. "Don't even speak."

The stonewalker was just five feet away but when it turned its eyes towards them, it could see nothing. So long as they didn't move, they were practically invisible to the strange creature, just a chunk of flawed earth. It exhaled again and then its mouth opened. The sound was like a lion's roar, only higher-pitched and hollow.

If that's its yawn... I imagine what its growl must be like, John thought as he struggled through the knot in his throat. He was standing in between Syrena and Hudson, all of them careful not to tremble too much. The two bandits, however, made an attempt to crawl away, both with their eyes full of terror.

"Don't! I said *don't* move!" Hudson hissed at them, for a moment sounding almost indifferent towards them, as if they were mere acquaintances rather than enemies. The stonewalker sniffed and turned its head again. He spotted them... its neck bent in an eerie way and the sound of stone grinding against stone filled the air. The bandit was on his knees still, shivering and whimpering quite loudly. He was closest one to it, and when the stonewalker began to sniff him, the warmth in his chest grew and his whimpers turned into cowardly moans.

"No," he made the mistake of speaking. "No, please... no..."

Shut up, shut up, shut your damn mouth, Hudson thought to himself.

But it was of no use. The stonewalker roared again, this time viciously like a predator. Briefly, the shivering bandit stopped whimpering and looked up with horror-stricken eyes. And the last thing he saw was the stonewalker's massive fist slamming down, crushing him and killing him instantly.

"Sh-Shit... Retreat!" Hudson shouted.

And so they did... John, Hudson, Syrena, and the nameless man ran as fast as they could, heading back east. Meanwhile, the stonewalker took its time rising from where it sat, as it had just woken up from a long and deep sleep. It stood on all fours like an ape and pounded its fist down, causing a tremor in the earth that may have spread for a mile.

The nameless man had somehow gotten the lead, the bow strapped to his back loosening as he ran. John knew to keep his eyes ahead, but his fear urged him to look back every other second. In the distance, he could see it; if it were to stand up straight, the stonewalker must have been almost 20 feet tall. Crouched and on all fours, it craned its neck and targeted them, four figures scurrying into the distance towards the trees.

It scratched the dirt back with its fists like a bull and prepared to charge forward.

John stumbled from the fright; the thief and the witch stopped and helped him to his feet.

The nameless man had vanished somewhere within the greenery when they came across a split in the path. They paused for a moment, realizing they would have to either lure the stonewalker back towards Miss Rayna's tavern or follow an entirely different path, a path unknown to them.

"W-We have to hide," John panicked, attempting to take the lead. "*This* way!"

"You don't want to do that," Syrena said.

"Why not?"

"Swamps," Hudson answered for the witch.

"Then what do we do?!"

"We need to get to the other side of that river, mate."

"The river?!"

"Stonewalkers hate water," Syrena answered for the thief.

The ground started shaking; the stonewalker was charging towards them on all fours. Its movement was slower, but every leap brought it a good five feet closer. John felt his heart skip a beat, knowing there was no outrunning the giant stone beast.

At that moment, a leaf fell suddenly from above and landed on Hudson's shoulder. When they looked up, they saw the nameless man climbing the old cypress tree like his life depended on it, and his shrieking monkey was oddly clinging onto his shoulders for dear life.

The thief smirked. "Climb!" he said.

"Are you insane?!" John shouted, but Hudson had his hand on a branch already.

"Will you for once in your life, mate, *listen* to the thief?!"

And so they climbed... For the first time, John was moving faster than both Hudson and Syrena. Years of practice, climbing trees and cottages with Mister Beckwit as a child, were now being put to good use. For a moment, Hudson even had a smirk on his face; he tried to hide it, but the thief was intrigued by the farmer's climbing skills. The thought even crossed his mind that John could have done well had he resorted to a life of thievery instead of a farmer's life.

There's potential there, no doubt. If only the mate wasn't so bloody reckless.

They climbed until they were at a safe height, safe enough at least to be out of the stonewalker's grasp. The creature was dangerously near; they didn't even have to look down to know it. It was charging towards the tree and was not slowing down.

"Hold on to something!" Hudson shouted. The thief and the witch locked arms with one another and gripped the nearest branch with their other arm. And John had no option but to lie on his belly and wrap himself around the wood like a monkey.

He closed his eyes. *Here it comes, John...*

The stonewalker smashed against the tree, and the impact shook every branch violently.

John stumbled, lost his grip, and fell... He swung his arms in the air and managed to snatch a branch at the last opportune moment, hanging dangerously low. He could see the giant beast below him, watching him, almost *savoring* him. A mere second felt like a minute.

You're done for... You bloody idiot, what did you get yourself into...?

With a roar, the stonewalker reached up, determined to kill; its rough hand brushed against the heel of John's boot. But then John felt a hand grip him suddenly by the forearm.

"Come on, you clumsy bastard, reach up!" Hudson said, and then gave a strong pull. John swung his other arm up for Syrena, and then the thief and the witch pulled him back up together. The stonewalker shrieked furiously and smashed against the tree again. John was panting and sweating, ruffled after having stared death right in the eye, and looking down wasn't helping the ache in his belly.

"We're trapped," Syrena spoke under her breath.

"Keep climbing!" the thief gave her a push, hoisting the witch onto the nearest branch. The trunk of the tree was about three feet wide, but it was no match for the strength of the stonewalker. With every impact, the tree was loosening its clasp with the earth. "Climb! Climb!" Hudson kept shouting.

One last time, the stonewalker struck the tree, this time taking a few steps back for a stronger impact. There was the loud sound of wood snapping, before the tree itself began to tremble where it stood. John, Hudson, and Syrena stared at one another. Even the nameless man looked down at them in shock, as the tree swayed gently from side to side. The roots gave in… The hundred foot tall tree had come to its end…

"Brace yourselves, mates," Hudson said, wrapping his arms around the tree's trunk.

The tree began to tilt. The three misfits held on for dear life as they watched the world slanting bit by bit. To John, it was terrifying and thrilling all at once. He realized then what Hudson's plan had been all along. The tree fell, the sound of the impact echoing for miles around, and there it laid on its side over then river, creating a bridge from one side to the other.

You're welcome, the thief thought. "Run! Head to the other side!"

The three of them hopped to their feet over the fallen tree and rushed across the river as quick as they could without slipping. The massive trunk felt steady enough, but hopping over every oversized branch along the way was proving challenging.

Behind them, the stonewalker roared angrily, unwilling to step near the water.

And it sent a relief into John's chest, knowing they were safe at last.

"Hurry now, mate," Hudson said. "We need t-"

But he couldn't finish… A sharp arrow flew suddenly into Hudson's chest and ripped through to his back. Syrena and John went silent.

Hudson fell back with a groan and nearly slipped into the river, but John managed to grab hold of him just in time. "No! Hudson!" he cried. "Stay with me… Hudson!"

The thief gasped for air and looked down…

The arrow was close to his heart, he knew. *Dangerously* close.

It sent shivers throughout his entire body…

Standing just feet away on the tree's trunk was the nameless man, grinning as he held his bow in his hands. His monkey was hissing at them as it perched itself on its master's shoulder and wrapped its tail around his neck. "Thought you was finished with me?!" the vile man shouted.

Syrena felt the rage return to her chest and her auburn eyes glistened sharply.

"Have you *any* idea who I am?!" the nameless man went on like a madman.

John held Hudson tightly in both arms, panicking, shivering with him. While the arrow was holding most of the blood in, Hudson was wheezing for air, looking vulnerable for the first time since they met.

"Y-You're all right. You're all right, it's nothing," John whispered, again and again, more to himself than to the thief. "It's nothing... Just a scratch..."

The nameless man pulled out another arrow.

"This is it, lads!" he spat on the river. "I'll let *you* choose your own deaths."

The thief's eyes were alarmingly red. He was looking up at John and could see the terror in his naïve gaze. He tried to say something... *Anything*... But he could hardly breathe, let alone speak...

Silently, he cursed himself for following John when he should have walked away.

He cursed himself for caring, for thinking he could somehow make it work.

Every second felt like an hour... Every breath felt like his last...

Though a life of thievery was a life that would surely end with a violent death, Hudson had never envisioned it would end this way. He imagined a more grandiose death, perhaps in the middle of a battle, surrounded by a thousand enemies that were there for the mere purpose of watching him dying.

You stupid idiot... You stupid fucking idiot... Why were you not more careful?

The blood stained him, trickled down his chest and arms, ripped the warmth right out of him.

In those last moments, a hundred questions raced through his mind.

*Is this really your end...? An arrow through the chest, shot by an unnamed bandit with awful breath and a false sense of authority? One simple arrow...? Not even a **dozen** arrows...?* If Hudson were being honest with himself, he would have preferred to die by the stonewalker's fist. At the very least, it would have made for a damn good story.

He gasped again, the sharp pain stinging him with every inhale. He would always pride himself in his courage. Only now, Hudson felt scared and uneasy, and *ashamed* for feeling scared and uneasy. The last thing he saw was Syrena standing over him with her arm held out in front of her. He felt the warmth of the fire hit his face; he watched as the flames shot directly at the man that had wounded him.

The look on Syrena's face wasn't just of rage, it was of passion.

Hudson could even swear he saw the hint of a tear there.

It was the last thing he saw before he closed his eyes and gave in to the pain.

Not a bad last image, he pondered. *Farewell, my dear Syrena of Morganna... You beautiful, vicious, magnificent thing, you…*

At that moment, everything went black. But he could still hear the shrieks of the monkey and the nameless man as they became engulfed in flames from head to toe.

"Hudson?! Stay with us!" John Huxley tried to lift his unconscious ally, when he heard another roar coming from behind. The stonewalker was sniffing around the edge of the river, as if confronting its fear of the water. It lifted one of its fists and placed it on the trunk of the broken cypress tree.

No… No, no, no, please don't, John's face hardened.

The tree shook, and the water splashed against it and sprinkled over the stonewalker's feet. It roared again, this time more cowardly, and ran back into the trees like a frightened dog. But its prying had done its horrid deed… The tree began rolling out of place, shifting with the river's current.

"Hold on!" Syrena said as she crouched down next to John and Hudson and wrapped her arms around both of them. The nameless man slipped, pulling his sharp-fanged monkey along with him; both his screams and the flames were silenced by the water as the river swallowed them both whole. The trunk was dragged away by the current, drifting the farmer and the witch away from the land and leading them towards an impending waterfall…

John felt helpless and unsettled. It was as if a part of him was lost when Hudson closed his eyes, when his *friend* closed his eyes…

"What do we do?!" he asked Syrena, pleading to her like a frightened child.

The witch was struggling to keep her balance as she stood on the moving trunk and watched at what lay ahead. "I-I don't know," she panicked.

They looked at one another. Perhaps there was nothing else *to* do.

Their options had run short and without their cunning thief, so had their ideas. They could have jumped, but there was no way they could swim through the vicious current *and* drag Hudson's unconscious body safely away.

"Damn it all to hells…"

Syrena bent to her knees again on the wide trunk and hugged both of her companions. If she knew the Woodlands, she knew that the impending drop led them to a cluster of sharp rocks at the very bottom. And if the fall didn't kill them, the rocks were likely to finish the deed…

As if reading her thoughts, John said nothing and simply closed his eyes.

May the gods be with us, he thought to himself.

They fell…

XIII
Small Minds

Count Raoul Jacquin was as corrupt and boorish as Lady Brunylda Clark had predicted, though she at the very least expected him to be slightly good-looking. Instead, what she saw before her was a stocky red-faced man with uneven teeth and a balding head. He had a round shriveled nose, eyes grey like mist, and he kept his hair long at the sides and back, which was not at all a good look for him.

I do hope he wears a hat upon occasion, the Lady thought to herself. *If only to hide that glistening red scalp.*

And she was right; it did shine quite a bit, despite the dim lighting in the room. It was as if all of the hair from his scalp had given up and the rest of his body decided to catch up. He had refused to meet with the Lady Treasurer and the newly appointed Lord Regent, putting the blame on a busy schedule, and instead had them meet in his private suite at the Emerald Rose saloon.

Lady Brunylda knew that Kahrran men had the tendency to be classless and vile in nature, but what came next was a spit on their faces, to say the least. When they entered the room, they felt the odor itch at their noses instantly, like that of feet and sweat blending awfully with cheap perfume. The count was lying nude inside a tub made of grey marble, with a thin layer of foamy soap that was dispersed so unevenly that most of his body was exposed. He sat there with a grin on his face, as if it gave him pleasure to see their unpleasant reactions. There was a young woman dressed in revealing robes massaging his thick shoulders, and though she tried to keep a straight face she could not hide her discomfort when the count looked the other way.

Poor girl, the Lady pondered. *You couldn't pay me enough coin to hold back the vomit.*

"Well, well, well… Sir Darryk Clark of Roquefort," Count Jacquin grinned as the woman behind him held up a spittoon for him. "Or shall I call you *Lord* Darryk Clark now?"

"Sir Darryk will do. It is a pleasure to have you here, Count Jacquin."

"Please, please, have a seat. Make yourself at home," the count spit onto the vase, after which the woman set it back down next to the tub. "And what is *this?* You've brought an entourage, I see."

The Lady gave no curtsy, only a head nod and a forced smile.

"Lady Brunylda Clark, Treasurer of Val Havyn," she introduced herself.

Meanwhile, the woman in the revealing robes began pouring two goblets of wine, all the while gawking at the Lady Treasurer as if she hadn't been in the presence of a woman with so much power before.

"Another Clark, eh?" the count chuckled and wiped a bit of slobber from his scruffy chin. "I sure hope it's by blood and not marriage. A young lord like *you* ought to be shagging someone a bit more like *this* one." He placed his wet hand on the robed woman's posterior; she hardly winced, as if she was used to it.

Lady Brunylda scowled and felt a grumbling in her stomach.

Whatever she's getting paid, it can't possibly be enough...

"The Lady Brunylda's a distant relative, nothing more," Darryk said, keeping his calm character quite well, taking the goblet and sipping from it scarcely. It wasn't yet mid-day, but the count appeared to already be in the midst of inebriation. Perhaps it would prove easier to negotiate with him in such state, perhaps more difficult. It all depended on the Clarks' demeanor.

"Well, in *that* case," the count glanced at Brunylda. "I may just ask for a few minutes alone with the Lady Treasurer, after we discuss business... I've never shagged a Clark woman before. Always wondered what that'd be like."

The Lady's reaction was mild; a subtle exhale through the nose and a minor tilt of the head, nothing more. Her eyes, however, spoke very differently... If one could somehow say *'Fuck yourself'* through a stare, that would have been it.

"We are here to propose a negotiation, Count Jacquin," Darryk said, hoping to ease the tension in the room and shift the conversation back to business.

The count, however, appeared distracted and uninterested. "What kind of name is *Brunylda* anyway?" he chuckled sloppily. "It's not really a name fit for nobility, is it? Lacks the class. I once met a tavern dancer with a more elegant name than that."

There was a short silence, unfamiliar to the count. It appeared to have caused him a touch of discomfort, as if he was accustomed to having servants laugh along with his remarks.

"As you might know," Darryk cleared his throat. "His majesty, King Rowan, has left Val Havyn in order to march with his troop to the southern shores."

"Aye," the count spat to the side, hoping to hit the spittoon and missing. "It's all the gossip these days, the missing princess. I've a wager that she'll turn up dead before autumn, in fact."

"A wager?" Lady Brunylda spoke again. "You disappoint me, Count Jacquin... Betting money on the death of the future queen? I've known peasants to do that, certainly, but it seems a bit low for a count."

"She isn't *my* future queen," the count chuckled. "And I didn't bet money. Lord Helmuth Larrehly of Raven's Keep is a dear friend of mine. If the girl dies, I gain one of his estates. Always wanted an estate north of Kahrr. Land's more fruitful up there. I plan on starting my own vineyard. Lady Clark, you look like a woman of proper taste. Have you ever tried Kahrran wine?"

"I sure have," the Lady gave him a nod, straight-faced and calm. "I'm afraid it's shit... I prefer something with a bit more bite."

Count Jacquin's grin lost some of its flare, as if he was playing a game of *Mercy* and the Lady was suddenly in the lead. "Yes, well, we're all entitled to our opinions, however wrong they are," he said.

The Lady grinned genuinely for the first time since arriving.

Go on, you bald bastard. You're not the only one who can play this game. Where's your smart mouth now?

"Back to the matter of discussion," Darryk interrupted the sudden silence again. "I'm afraid Val Havyn is a bit short of soldiers at the moment. We've enough guards to keep the palace safe, only we've resorted to hiring a few inexperienced men to patrol the city streets. I'm sure we both know the implications *that* can bring should an unprecedented incident occur. Therefo-"

"All right, all right," the count interrupted and chugged more of his wine, as if he had been challenged by the Lady on his ability to hold himself sober. "You aren't the first man to beg for help and you won't be the last, Sir Darryk. You want able-bodied men from Kahrr to come serve you, I see. But let's talk of *your* end of the negotiation, shall we?"

Sir Darryk glanced at Lady Brunylda, as if handing her the reins.

The Lady snapped her fingers and the robed woman answered the gesture by heading towards the door. "With the possibility of an impending war," Brunylda began, "I'm afraid our funds are rather delicate for the time being. Not to say we haven't friends in high places. We can offer the basic necessities for any soldiers you can send. Food, lodging, weapons, armor, you name it… all the while, we can provide payment for your services in portions."

At that very moment, the door creaked open and a girl no older than seventeen walked in. She carried a thick brown book under one arm and a leather bag with ink and quills in the other. She was dressed in an auburn red dress that was not nearly as elegant as Lady Brunylda's, but still quite nice. Her brown hair was mostly loose over her shoulders, with two neat braids running along the sides of her head and tied neatly behind her. There was a thin layer of powder on her cheeks and she wore a silver necklace with a ruby that she had borrowed from the Lady Treasurer. Overall a decent-looking young woman, only she looked about as uncomfortable and timid as a lost child; her hands shook as she took a seat and placed the thick book on her lap.

"We've enough currency in silver to send to you every seventh day," Lady Brunylda went on. "We propose 500 yuhn to start, with a gradual increase over th-"

"All right, enough," the count snapped his fingers. It was as if it gave him joy to interrupt others. "I've no use for money, Lady Clark, I've plenty of it."

Something in the count's eyes was disconcerting to Brunylda; his attention had drifted away from the negotiation and was now solely on the princess's former handmaiden sitting to the side. Brie did not dare look back; instead her eyes were on the thick book, now opened widely on her lap with a never-ending list of names and numbers on its brown pages.

"If you want to conduct business with me, you'll have to offer me something better," the count added, his hungry eyes still gawking at Brie.

"What did you have in mind, Count Jacquin?" Darryk asked him.

The woman in robes held the spittoon up again but the count sent her away with finger snap, hardly even giving her a glance.

"What's your name, my dear?" he asked.

Brie's hands shivered as she held a quill ready in her hand. Her worried brown eyes moved back and forth from Lady Brunylda to the drunken graceless count.

"What's the matter?" the count asked, more at the Clarks than at the girl. "You've a mute bookkeeper? You lot really *are* on the verge of falling to shit, aren't you?"

"Brie," the handmaiden exclaimed suddenly. "My name is Brie…"

The count's eyes lit up again. "Ahh Brie… Now *there's* a proper name. Fit for beauty," he grinned, his attempt at flattery falling flat. He lifted his hand and snapped his fingers again, after which the robed woman brought over a sophisticated red robe, similar to the color of the private room's wallpaper except without the golden lining. The count lifted himself to his feet, soap and water dripping from every inch of his naked body, and took his time sliding into his robe. The smirk never left his face, as he examined the disgusted reactions of the Clarks and their new bookkeeper.

"Er… Would you, um, perhaps prefer to be paid in supplies and mounts?" Darryk asked, his wide eyes suddenly finding the golden pattern on the carpet exceptionally interesting.

"We've enough farmland in Elbon and other villages up north to transport crops as payment," Lady Brunylda added. "Furthermore, we happen to have a contract with your *friend* Lord Helmuth of Raven's Keep. Everyone knows the fastest horses in all of Gravenstone are bred in Raven's Keep. If I send a letter today, we can arrange f-"

"Fuck the horses," Count Jacquin grunted. "And fuck the crops."

As he slouched himself into a chair, he beckoned the robed woman for his pipe, which she then brought over and held a lit match to. "Leave us," the count said, and the robed woman headed for the doors. The count managed to graze her posterior one last time before she left and once again there was no reaction on her behalf.

The doors closed…

The count took a drag from his pipe and blew the smoke out carelessly.

He grinned again, this time at the Lady Treasurer of Val Havyn.

"May I be blunt with you, Lady Clark?" he asked.

"I expect nothing less, sir."

"Good. Now," he sighed and rested his dripping feet on a cushioned stool. "I know very well that you lot look at me and can't help but have your judgments… You look at me and all you see is a man that *pretends* to be what you are. Only… What *are* you? You wear your pretty jewels and your fancy clothes, savoring the wealth you were born into like a pig splashing over a pile of shit. It's all you've ever known. I *earned* the money I have, I didn't inherit it. And *now* look at me… I'm no Sir Darryk Clark, I'm well aware, but with enough money I can be the most handsome man in all of Val Havyn. And you? You've absolutely no power over me and it drives you mad. Funny, the way power works, isn't it?"

He took another drag from his pipe.

"I can see that we haven't much to offer that you desire, Count Jacquin," Darryk said with a sigh. "Perhaps you'd care to enlighten us with a request?"

The count blew the smoke out in front of him, grinning like a hyena. The Lady Clark kept her gaze firm and unyielding, despite the reeking scent of red spindle filling the room.

"I'll take your offer," the count finally said. "I'll send word to my contacts in Kahrr… You can have three dozen men for the price that you offer. I've more silver than I can spend now, but perhaps after I win this wager with my old friend Helmuth I could use the coin for my vineyard."

With a rush of thrill, Brie began to write on the thick book, her very first inscription as bookkeeper for the Lady Treasurer. And there was also the hint of a smile on Brunylda's lips, and a much wider one on Darryk's.

"Thank you, Count Jacquin, that is most generous of you!" Darryk said.

"On *one* condition," the count added abruptly, before taking one last drag from his pipe and blowing the smoke out through his words. "I get to keep *this* one." He glared at Brie… The girl's lower lip quivered again, her hand suddenly unable to finish writing the count's name on the parchment.

"Pardon me?" Lady Brunylda asked, her eyes hardening.

"You heard me, Lady Clark," the count grinned. "I will agree to this contract *if* the girl comes with me, back to Kahrr, where she will serve as my new accountant… among *other* services."

Brie's face hardened into a frown and her eyes swelled with fear. "I-I…"

"*No*," Lady Brunylda said firmly as she stood from her seat. "I'm sorry, sir, but I'm afraid our offer is *not* negotiable."

"Then I feel disinclined to accept it…"

Darryk Clark was at a loss for words. He didn't have the nerve to accept the count's condition, but neither was he particularly inclined to leave without a signed contract. "N-Now wait, let's not bicker over such-"

"There's no bickering, my Lord," Lady Brunylda interrupted, maintaining her glare on the vile, grinning man. "I'm afraid the count's demands are unreasonable. The girl is no slave to be traded, she is my bookkeeper… And she will be treated with respect, like such."

Immediately, Brie felt the weight leave her shoulders and she couldn't help but sigh.

"I never called her a *slave*. She'll be *paid* for her services," the count chuckled.

But there was no change in the Lady's expression; she turned to Darryk, as if waiting for him to rise from his chair. And so he did...

Before leaving the room, however, the Lady picked up the goblet of wine, full and untouched, from the table between them. She took a great sip, upon which the count grinned profoundly.

It didn't last very long, however...

The Lady scowled and proceeded to spit all of the wine back into the goblet.

She then set it down on the table so harshly that some of the wine spilled out.

"Well," she said, wiping the red tint from her lips with a handkerchief. "It's *still* shit, just as I remember it... Good day to you, Count Jacquin."

* * *

What few supplies and mounts the Wyrmwood troop recuperated were hardly enough to sustain the amount of survivors. For the sake of efficiency, horses had to be shared, gnomes were paired up with others, and some of the sellswords rode in the back of carts. Once they'd regained their senses, Sir Antonn Guilara had gathered them all for a head count.

One hundred and nineteen had survived.

Thirty-nine were soldiers from Wyrmwood.

Forty-two were human archers and sellswords from the Woodlands.

As for the nonhumans, there were twenty-six elves, eight gnomes, and one minotauro.

And then, of course, there was Viktor Crowley and his squadron, which now consisted only of one hired muscle and one inexperienced squire. They had fought alongside Sir Percyval Garroway's troop and for this, the knight was grateful and allowed them to stay.

But at this point, they were fighting for a lost cause. Three men traveling alone to Drahkmere with hopes of breaking a princess out of a dungeon? They were hopeless and Viktor knew it, almost as hopeless as Sir Percyval Garroway if he thought his Woodland recruits would be openly accepted into his brother's army...

Sir Percyval was riding ahead, leading the way down a vast green hill, surrounded by a stretch of trees that were smaller in height and had blue-green leaves that looked almost like clovers. For once, the dirt road in which they traveled appeared to have an actual destination rather than leading them deeper into an endless maze.

Viktor Crowley rode alone, lost in his thoughts. He sat on a borrowed horse that felt strange to him; it wasn't only its brown hair, it was the way it walked and the grumbled noises it would make, so unlike his majestic white stallion. There was a brown wool blanket over Viktor's shoulders and still the wind gave him shivers. He hadn't yet dried up after having washed all of the mud from his body in the river. His armor was off, safely stored in the cart behind him, and he was wearing only his trousers and white undershirt. And without that layer of steel, he felt exposed and weak; it was almost unnatural for him.

Once the thrill of the fight was over, Viktor felt an invisible weight overcome him. He began to realize the bleakness of his situation, and it made him sink into a solemn daydream.

The Davenport Brothers were both dead. John Huxley may have been alive, but it had been a half-day since Zahrra had the vision, however right or wrong it may have been. And many things could go wrong in a half-day, he knew. And the same went for Hudson Blackwood and Syrena of Morganna, if he could even trust that they followed through with their word at all.

Then, of course, there was Jossiah Biggs... The mere thought of the man's name made Viktor's jaw clench and his fists tighten. He refused to allow Jossiah the courtesy of a single thought. Instead he sat and rode on quietly, concentrating on his path ahead and shoving the dark thoughts aside.

His eyes were heavy and glum, his cheeks had sunk, and there was a thick layer of scruff on his face. It was not at all the image of the handsome and valiant Golden Eagle.

He felt empty now; a former hero, a fallen warrior, a soon-to-be-forgotten legend...

Surely, he would live to see the day when people eventually questioned whether he was actually real or if he was merely another story...

"All's well, I hope?" a soft voice suddenly startled him.

Viktor tried to respond with a smile, but it was a rather morose one. Skye, the pale elf, rode beside him on a spotted grey mare with a scar across its furry cheek.

"Would you like the honest answer or the rubbish one?" Viktor asked.

"Honest."

"Well," Viktor sighed. "I'm tired, I'm hungry, I haven't slept well in days... My company is down to a fourth of what it was, and my back may have been injured during the battle. If you can call *that* great... Then I'm doing just swell."

Skye allowed for a brief moment of silence, before saying, "Sounds like a hell. Wish I could do something to help, but... all I can really offer is *wine*."

Viktor glanced at the elf with a raised brow. "You don't say...?"

With a smirk, the elf reached into one of the pockets on the mare's saddle and pulled out a winebag. Viktor took it instantly and poured it down his throat as if it were apricot juice.

The elf then took the opportunity to examine the former knight... There were several scars on his arms and chest, some of them fresh, and his scruffy face was ruggedly handsome yet drained of most of its life. Back in the cart his silver armor rested, dented and scratched, the golden lining on it hardly noticeable save for the design of the eagle on the chest plate. That eagle there may have been the only thing holding on to the regal image that was Sir Viktor Crowley, for the rest of him was merely a shadow of him now.

"Thank you," he said at last, holding out the winebag for the elf.

"You keep it," Skye said. "I've no need for it."

"Oh... thanks."

They rode in silence for a moment, before Viktor ultimately decided to give in to his impulse to pry. He cleared his throat and asked, "Where did you say you were from?"

"I *didn't* say."

"Right... care to indulge me?"

Skye exhaled through their nose and grinned, a beautiful subtle grin it was, marking a perfect dimple just beneath their left cheekbone. "Why would Sir Viktor Crowley suddenly have an interest in a Woodland elf?"

"Please," he chuckled. "Just *Viktor*."

"Right. I'd forgotten."

"And besides... Where I come from, I don't often cross paths with the likes of you... N-Not that I'd exactly protest," he stammered subtly. Even after watching the elf in combat, he had no idea what to make of them. The softness in their voice, that smooth glowing skin, that thin body frame and those luscious pink lips, *all* were traits he often considered to be feminine in nature... But the way the elf carried themselves, their mannerisms, and the sharp shape of their nose and jaw seemed almost masculine...

But he couldn't ask, he knew. His lips wouldn't allow it.

"Well if you *must* know," Skye smiled confidently. "My clan hails from the ice-capped mountains northeast of Merrymont. So cold and high, no human has ever traveled so far without freezing or starving to death."

"Are they still up there? Your people?" Viktor asked, genuinely intrigued.

"Can't ban us if your people never set foot in the land to begin with, can you?"

Skye's accent was rather interesting, a blend between the exotic accents from overseas with perhaps a decade or two of Halghardian influence. The warmth and softness in the elf's voice was pleasant to Viktor's ears, that much had been evident from the start. But the former knight noticed a hint of sadness in the elf's eyes, as if touching unwelcoming territory in their mind. Still, Viktor's curiosity grabbed hold of him, and so he chose his words carefully.

"Why did you leave?" he asked.

"I had a... *disagreement* with my clan. Ultimately decided it was time to part ways."

And that was that. Viktor knew better than to ask further. For a moment, he thought he saw Skye's mare pick up its pace by a step and he ran through a hundred questions to ask so as to not end the conversation there.

But he had hesitated blindly... The mare slowed down again and before he could choose what question to ask, Skye turned to him and said, "You know your men were asking about me."

"Oh?" he asked, unsure how to react. "What exactly were they asking?"

Skye then glanced and locked eyes with the former knight. It was only for a brief moment, but Viktor swore it felt like minutes.

"The same thing you're asking yourself now," Skye said.

There was no point in hiding it, but Viktor tried all the same. He cleared his throat and attempted a look of confusion. "I don't know what you mean..."

Skye chuckled. "You're a bad liar, *Just Viktor*."

They rode in silence again, but unlike other sporadic conversations, Viktor hardly felt any discomfort. And if he did, Skye had a talent for easing his nerves with simple words. Viktor allowed the elf to lead the discussion wherever they felt comfortable leading it to, and Skye's direct way of speaking only continued to surprise him.

"Rather curious for a bunch of peasants, aren't they?" Skye asked.

"Curious in what way?" Viktor raised a brow.

"Brute honesty? They wanted to know what was between my legs..."

Viktor felt a drop of sweat run down his left temple, and he silently thanked the gods it was on his left, safely out of Skye's view. "Sounds like them," he cleared his throat for the hundredth time. "Try not to pay them any mind."

"I didn't."

"Good."

Another silence, this one longer. Both the former knight and the elf felt the mild tension between them and yet neither one of them appeared eager to ride away from the other.

Perhaps it was mere stubbornness. Perhaps it was out of respect.

Or, perhaps, it was the fervent heat in both their chests...

"Did you know him very long?" Skye took a risk. "Your, um... Your friend, the knight. The one you traveled with when w-"

"Don't," Viktor interrupted, somewhat coldly yet attempting to remain calm.

"Don't?" Skye arched a brow, suddenly noticing the sadness in Viktor's eyes.

"I don't w... I don't wish to speak of him," he replied. There was a profound tension there that was causing him a great distress. His teeth were grinding against each other and his brows had inadvertently lowered on their own.

"Keeping it in will only haunt you further," Skye said, trying to help in whatever way possible. And somehow it worked... Viktor sighed, closing his eyes briefly, allowing for the rage to take over and preventing his tongue from speaking in any way but candidly.

"He was m..." he began, fighting through the knot in his throat, exhaling through his nose as his eyes blinked furiously to fight back the dampness. "He was my second-in-command for nearly a decade... I *vouched* for him. Over and over again, I did... Years of service, years of friendship, and *still* he... he left me. When I needed him the most, he abandoned me... Like it all meant nothing..."

Had they been sitting and not riding, Skye would have placed a hand the Viktor's back. The look on his face was one of betrayal and sorrow, but it slowly began to change into a more hardhearted one.

"Jossiah was the closest thing I ever had to a brother," he said. "It's a pity he didn't see it that way." Viktor paused there for another sip of wine, welcoming the bitterness as if it fueled him. "If I ever see him again," he said, "I'm going to stab him in the heart."

Skye glanced at the former knight, somewhat shocked by his words.

"You're upset," said the elf. "You're not thinking clearly."

"On the contrary, I've never thought clearer in my life."

Skye hesitated, unsure of what to say in return. Choosing their words carefully, the elf sighed and asked, "So you're to kill the man because he's a traitor and a crook? Plenty of people in the world are. You can't just kill someone and justify it with the possibility that he may cause harm to someone in future. Is it *really* worth it in the end?"

There was a brief pause once again, though it was broken by a subtle exhale on Viktor's behalf. The expression on his face was honest, yet troubled and dismal all at once.

"No," he said, shaking his head, in a manner that was meant to correct the elf. "I'm not doing it for anyone else... I'm going to do it for *myself*... I'm going to kill him and I'm going to do it for *me*."

For a moment, Viktor was afraid he'd disappointed Skye. Though they had just met, Viktor felt that the elf was, in a way, closer to him than his own men. And so, with a deep sigh, the former knight chose the path of honesty over any other... If he was damned either way, he figured he might as well say out loud what he had buried in the back of his mind...

"You think I'm doing this for the good of my kingdom?" Viktor asked, with swollen eyes and a brute candor that was almost admirable. "You think I'm in the middle of the Woodlands, risking my life, as a *favor* to King Rowan? Or a favor to the princess?"

Skye had no response. But Viktor wasn't exactly expecting one.

"No," he shook his head. "I'm doing this because if I don't, *everything* I worked so hard to achieve... my entire legacy, my entire *life*... will shatter. And I will return to being no more than an old stableman in gods know where. I could have done this covertly, I could have hired twelve men, used one of the lads to do the hiring, but I *didn't*... I did it all myself. Because I *wanted* to. Because people believe more in what they see and not in what they hear... This, *all* of this, I'm doing for *me*..."

He paused there, taking a moment to breathe and allow for it all to sink in.

"And I've failed," he added. "Perhaps, in the end, I was always doomed to be a horsekeeper in Raven's Keep... My mistake, perhaps, was thinking I could ever be more than that..."

Skye felt a tug in their chest that came rather unexpectedly. Viktor felt the tension in his shoulders suddenly ease when the elf did not ride away and leave him to sulk.

"I hope you succeed, Viktor Crowley," said Skye.

Viktor nodded gently, swallowing back the angst. "Thank you," he said.

And that was that... They rode in silence for the rest of the day, admiring each other's company quietly.

Meanwhile, a few horses behind them, Viktor's company was riding among the Woodland recruits. Cedric was resting on the back of an old cart, next to a gang of elven archers. He was weak and slow and covered in bruises, but he was awake again and able to make conversation. Gwyn had been riding next to the cart for hours, smiling and laughing with the young squire, speaking to him as if she'd known him all her life. She was kind and warm towards him now, friendlier even than the young lad's only friend Thaddeus Rexx, and any hostility she'd previously shown had now faded.

"Rest easy, toothpick," she said to him. "But do tell me if I'm boring ye to death."

"Never," Cedric smiled honestly. "Tell me more."

They laughed amongst one another as she shared stories with him; from the time she chased a bandit out of her family's farm to the time she was betrothed to a middle-aged man with a bad case of body odor. And for the first time since leaving Val Havyn, Cedric looked genuinely happy, even through all of his bruises.

Meanwhile, just a few yards behind them, Thaddeus Rexx rode in silence. The man's face appeared to have a permanent scowl as it was, only this time it was more vivid than before. He didn't exactly trust the raider woman, nor did he find her particularly affable. And the fact that Cedric was so keen on opening up to her was starting to worry him. Though not exactly prejudice against the nonhumans, Thaddeus had little interest in making any friends or acquaintances. In fact, he purposely rode between two carts of equipment so as to avoid anyone else riding beside him.

Much to his disdain, however, it did not work.

Before he knew it, a horse crept up behind him and he heard the sounds of its neighs and a man sipping loudly from a winesack.

"Why so glum?" Daryan asked, catching up to Thaddeus with minimal effort.

Thaddeus gave him a grunt. It wasn't exactly an angry grunt, but it was the best he could come up with.

"Don't mind me, Mister Rexx," Daryan said. "It just seems my dear sister's taken it upon herself to make a protégé of your little squire. And drinking on my own is no fun. I'd look like a madman if I start speaking to myself. Care for a sip?"

Thaddeus said nothing still, but he certainly snatched the wine from Daryan's hands.

"You look rather well-built," Daryan said with a smile. "Tell me, how long have you been a sellsword?"

"I'm not," Thaddeus said, handing back the winesack. "I'm a blacksmith."

"Ahh. A noble profession, indeed. Any good?"

There was a brief pause. Thaddeus wished he could say '*Piss off*', but he didn't have the heart to. Instead he said the first thing that crept into his mind. "I made Sir Viktor Crowley's armor... Not that the man even remembers it."

"Is that so?" said Daryan with his brows arched high. "The armor with the golden eagle on the chest plate?"

"Aye," Thad said.

"Did you really?" Daryan chuckled drunkenly. "Is that *real* gold?"

"Don't get any funny ideas," Thaddeus threatened him subtly.

"Wouldn't dream of it," Daryan grinned. "Just admiring a good piece of art."

Thaddeus raised a brow at first, but then nodded and took the winesack back when it was offered. "Thank you," he said.

"Is that onyx?" Daryan asked. "Or just iron?"

"Fuck iron," Thaddeus said. "That there's Kahrran steel."

The look on Daryan's face was one of both awe and respect. "Piss off... Is it really?"

Thaddeus said nothing in return, and Daryan responded to his silence with a snicker.

"You know, Mister Rexx," said the raider, a genuine grin plastered over his face. "I've a feeling you and I are going to become well-acquainted by the end of this journey."

And so it was that, as simply as that, Thaddeus Rexx had made a friend.

* * *

Spring was at its warmest in the city of Val Havyn when the riot started. It was the first of many, and one that would ultimately change the law of the kingdom for ages to come. No one had seen it coming, for the day was just like any other, if not louder and livelier than usual due to the outpour of traders willing to travel into the city now that winter was over. It began when two wagons rolled into Merchants' Square; one was approaching from the south, the other from the east, both of them moving just as slowly due to the heavy crowds that filled the cobblestone roads at midday.

The one coming from the south was a rickety wooden cart, pulled by two mules, hauling a pile of what *might* have been hay hidden underneath a wide brown cloth.

The one approaching from the east was an elegant black wagon fit for royalty, with a leather roof and white-curtained windows, pulled by two of the king's strongest stallions. The curtains were shut, but there was a slight opening through which a pair of wary eyes was prying from the inside. The wagon was so clean and refined that when it rolled through Dreary Lane it stood out like a polished emerald among a pile of coal. And from the outside, dangerous-looking men and women roamed and lurked around every corner, posted along the walls of every tavern and saloon, eyeing the wagon as if it were a giant jewelry chest with wheels.

When they reached the end of the road, the curious bookkeeper was able to see the ashen remains of what used to be Nottley's Tavern; among the clutter lay two or three smoky black figures that may have once been human. Feeling her stomach turning, she sat back and shut the curtain fully, fighting back the urge to vomit. Though she was grateful for the opportunity, Brie was quieter than usual, feeling considerably out of place in the presence of the two nobles. And just as she couldn't hide any other emotion, her discomfort was overt in her childlike expression.

Next to her, Lady Brunylda Clark sat sipping liqueur from a leather flask. And across from them both, Lord Regent Darryk Clark sat, too close for his comfort and yet there wasn't much he could do in such an enclosed space; his feet were pressed together as if to purposely avoid brushing against the Lady's dress. Though they shared a house name, there was a tension between the two nobles that seemed to come and go. One moment they looked like they wanted to murder each other and the next they seemed almost like actual relatives. And though Darryk undeniably found the Lady intimidating, every now and then he would mirror her tone and hit her with the same scathing sarcasm, as if he was inadvertently learning a thing or two from her.

"You look displeased," Lady Brunylda spoke first, after an eye roll and a sip of the flask.

"We just lost our last good opportunity to keep the city properly protected," Darryk remarked with a disappointed sigh. "Pardon me if I'm not jumping with delight."

"Oh, I'm sorry," the Lady scoffed derisively. "Should I have let him take the girl and have his way with her? Is *that* how you conduct business down in Roquefort?"

Brie was sitting right there, but she may as well have been on the other side of Val Havyn.

"I'm not saying we should have given in to his demands. I'm *just* saying we perhaps could have found some middle ground."

"Men like that don't settle, *Lord* Darryk. Trust me, I've met plenty."

"Still, my *Lady*, an opportunity like that shouldn't be walked away from so hurriedly. *Especially* considering our circumstances."

"So if Count Jacquin had asked to shag *you*, would you have done it?"

Darryk couldn't quite find a proper response.

"No?" the Lady mocked. "What's the matter? Is he not your type? Too *cocky* for you, is he?"

The wagon slowed to a halt, and Brie couldn't help but peek out the curtain again. A large crowd had gathered in Merchants' Square, huddled around the self-proclaimed courier of the gods Baryn Lawe as he gave his daily sermon. The two guards driving the Clarks' wagon observed as the crowds cheered along with Baryn's provoking shouts. Though the preacher's words may have been on the side of ignorance, Baryn Lawe was indeed a clever man. The proof was there in his crowd of followers, now twice the size as it was before. He *had* to be clever to realize the power he could gain by appealing to the small-minded.

And Val Havyn was unfortunately replete with small-minded folks.

"The god of humankind is with us tonight!" shouted the despicable man. "I *feel* his presence. He speaks to me as he does to all of you! All that you must do is lend an ear and you will hear him too. Brothers and sisters, can you *hear* him? Because *I* do... He is here today and he is angry!"

The crowd reacted, some of them chanting Baryn's name while others simply mumbled and nodded among themselves.

"Our god is *furious*... *Appalled* with his sons and daughters for forming alliances with *monsters*! Our god will *not* stand for this, brothers and sisters, and it is our responsibility to do something about it!"

The crowd applauded and encouraged him. And with every wave of cheers, someone tossed a coin into the moth-ridden hat at Baryn's feet.

"You see, many centuries past, long before the age of silver, the gods ruled our world," the madman went on. "And there was a war among them, brothers and sisters. And our god created us in *his* vision and *his* name!"

"*Praise our god!*" someone from the herd shouted.

"*Blessed be his name!*"

"*May he watch over us all!*"

The more the shouts came his way, the wider Baryn's grin stretched.

"The *spiteful* ones created these vile abhorrent creatures to fight the beloved fruit of *our* god, brothers and sisters," he said. "The goddess of the woodland elves created them to destroy us all! As did the goddess of the pixies and the god of the orcs! They have been our enemy since the dawn of humanity itself! And now, my dear friends, we stand here... In the midst of our greatest days... and we sit by as the Kingdom of Halghard welcomes these repugnant monsters into their grounds, spitting on our moral values and everything we hold dear!"

More chants came from the crowds. Even people from neighboring dwellings and shacks were starting to eavesdrop from their windows, spreading Baryn Lawe's lies like a disease.

"We are witnessing the birth or a new age! And it is up to *us* to decide the fate of our world! You've seen it with your own eyes… You stood on these very streets and watched as Sir Viktor Crowley, that dreadful sinner, spat on our god's name and allied himself with a wanted thief and a *witch*! If *that* is the man that is sworn to protect our beloved city, brothers and sisters, then I fear for our future… I fear for the future of our *children*… Will we allow this man to surrender to these monsters, these *freaks,* and allow them into our homes?!"

The shouts grew, this time far louder and angrier than before.

"Because *that* is the road we are heading towards, my beloved friends and neighbors… Today, it's a witch. What will tomorrow bring, I wonder? Will *elves* be allowed to join the royal guard? Will *orcs* be permitted to purchase property in our city?! Will these creatures be allowed to live among our people?! Among our *children*?! Our god has given us his guidance for centuries, it is written in our holy scriptures, and he has made it clear that *these* are our natural enemies! Their wretched gods created them for one sole purpose and that is to kill and burn every last one of us… The only question we must ask ourselves is will we allow it?!"

The crowd began to chant, drawing more people in and wreaking havoc on the incoming flow of carts and wagons. Several expressions in the crowd were near horrifying, among them a few that conveyed such violence that was gut-wrenching to say the least. At the same time, frustrated merchants and traders started to hop off their carts, requesting for the herd to disperse, but Baryn Lawe cared very little, he only preached louder.

"Our god can't hear you, brothers and sisters!! Will we allow it?!"

Leading the elegant black wagon were Hektor and his partner, the two guards that Darryk had taken under his wing despite not even knowing their names at first. They sat with the reins in their hands, observing the mendacious preacher and his herd of faithful followers, unable to maneuver their way around.

"Can you believe that madman?" Hektor mumbled casually as they waited.

"Makes great points, don't you think?" his partner remarked.

Hektor turned away, hiding his distaste for his partner's appalling breath. "I *don't* think that, not in the slightest," he said.

"Oh please… Crowley *has* gone soft. Nobody's allied with freaks since before the Great War. The bloke's lost his marbles, he has."

"That *bloke* is your superior, you bloody ingrate!"

"Not anymore, he's not. Haven't you heard?"

"I have… Doesn't mean I believe it," said Hektor. "No official word's been given on his disbarment. Until we hear it from the king himself, he's still *my* knight commander. *And* yours."

"If you truly believe that, you're as stupid as he is."

"You want to see stupidity, Bogden? Do you? Take a gander at *this* one. Who's *he* to know what the gods did or said centuries ago? I can't even remember what *I* did a *month* ago."

"Who are *you* to *disbelieve* it?" Bogden snorted, exhaling sharply in Hektor's face.

"Listen, old lad," Hektor said, his voice hardening. "Firstly, *I'm* not *pretending* to know the mysteries of the world, *he* is. Secondly, I've met my share of 'freaks' in the past and they're not at all what he says they are. Hells, my *mother* used to purchase fur blankets from a Woodland she-elf from Kahrr when I was a wee boy and she was a lot kinder than *you* are. And lastly, if you don't exhale in the other direction, I will *personally* wash your mouth off with more than just soap. Am I clear?"

The fowl-breathed guard snorted and spat onto the cobblestones.

"Freak-lover," he mumbled.

"Arse-breath," Hektor replied.

On the other side of the herd, across Merchants' Square, the rickety wagon had also slowed to a halt. Adelina Huxley and Old Man Beckwit rode in the front while the twins Margot and Melvyn sat in the back, hiding the infant orc beneath a bundle of wool blankets.

"Perhaps we should turn around," Adelina said worriedly.

"Too late now," said Beckwit. "We've carts waiting behind us. Best thing to do now is to wait and let the old bastard finish."

Adelina exhaled deeply, hoping to calm her nerves. And though it worked for a slight moment, the tension in her chest returned with a vengeance when the infant orc began crying.

No... Not now... Please don't, she begged him silently.

"Shhh, quiet down, River," Margot tried to calm him down with gentle whispers, but it was the hunger that was aching the poor babe, and with every second that passed his cries became louder and more animal-like.

"Keep him quiet!" Adelina whispered back at her.

"I'm *trying*."

But it was far too late... Several eyes began to shift in their direction, among them a man with three very visible missing teeth and a heavyset woman with a piece of white cloth wrapped around her head so as to hide the lice. Margot Huxley began shaking, and she caressed River's cheek to no avail.

"Shhh, it's okay... It's okay..."

Only it wasn't okay. The more she swayed him back and forth, the louder the child cried. One of the two nearby peasants hissed at her to keep the baby quiet while they listened to Baryn Lawe's sermon. And it was in that unfortunate moment when the blanket slid off the baby's face, exposing his smoky green skin. The two peasants took notice, their eyes widening and their mouths dropping with outrage.

"What in all hells is that?!"

More eyes glanced their way... Impulsively, Adelina reached back and snatched River from her daughter's hands. And when she did, the sun brightened River's face, exposing him to the crowd that began to gather around the wagon.

"What've you got there?!" someone asked rather loudly, causing even more commotion to stir. The cart was then caged in by radical peasants attempting to catch a glance. Angry glares were shot at Adelina and curious mumbles began to spread.

"That there's a freak!" shouted another.

"She's brought a monster into our city!"

The mumbles grew into a wave of angry chatter, as Baryn Lawe himself hopped down from his pedestal and began approaching the cart. The crowds dispersed and made way for him as if he were some sort of lord or king. "Stay calm, brothers and sisters! Stay calm!" the preacher said.

By then, Adelina Huxley's cart was the center of attention in the entire square. Still a few yards away, Baryn could not stop his angry herd of fanatics from growing more chaotic. One of them tried to climb onto the cart, but Old Man Beckwit stood up almost intimidatingly and shoved him back with the tip of his cane. And just before Baryn reached them, a peasant suddenly reached and pulled the cloth from the back of the cart, and it made the entire place fall silent for a moment... There she was, the helpless orcess Aevastra, weak and feeble and shivering from the pain. Next to her was the blacksmith Evellyn Amberhill, scarred and unconscious; she was a familiar face to some of the peasants, except half of it was now covered with bloodstained bandages.

"Stay away!" Adelina shouted.

And the crowds certainly did. The shock was far too great for anyone to step forward.

"Well, well, well... What do we have here?" Baryn Lawe said as he walked around the cart and towards the back for a better view.

"Stand back!" Adelina kept on. But neither Baryn nor his followers paid her any mind. As he stepped forward, the rest tiptoed closely behind as if he was the head of a poisonous snake. Every single pair of eyes was locked on Aevastra, as if the poor wounded orcess was some type of animal on display.

"By the gods... it's one of them," said Baryn, softly at first but his voice heightened bit by bit into a shout. "You *dare* bring the enemy into our city grounds...?! You irreverent traitor!!"

The crowd became instantly enraged. Adelina Huxley and Old Man Beckwit hopped to the back of the cart and shielded the twins, the orcess, and the unconscious blacksmith from the rampant fanatics. Some tried to tug at the orcess's feet while others began throwing garbage and moldy fruit their way, all the while shouting obscene rubbish.

"Give 'er to us!"

"Hang the freak!"

"Away, you traitorous bitch!"

Never had Adelina Huxley been faced with such hate and violence, even when her house was being attacked by orcs. In a way, the woman could hardly tell the difference; she kicked and shoved them all away as they tried again and again to pull the orc babe and his mother down from the cart. Aevastra was roaring, both from the pain and from the anguish, and the peasants cursed and shouted at her as if she were some sort of beast.

From the other side of the square Hektor and Bogden, the two guards riding the Clarks' wagon, became suddenly restless and worried, unsure of what to do. In a matter of seconds, Merchants' Square was on the verge of a riot, and both of them knew very well that the city was dangerously unguarded for such behavior.

A head peeked out from inside the wagon, and the voice of Lady Brunylda Clark startled them both. "What in all hells is happening out there?!"

"*Orcs*, my Lady!" Hektor said. "Orcs in the city!"

The Lady's eyes widened suddenly with terror.

Immediately the wagon doors swung open and out came the three of them.

"By the gods," Darryk Clark mumbled restlessly at the sight of the screaming herd. He then turned towards his two guards and shouted, "To our sides, gentlemen! Shields up and swords at the ready!"

The guards obeyed nervously, one of them beckoning from afar for backup.

Darryk walked ahead first, the Lady and Brie following behind. They sped towards the center of the square, where things were starting to become violent. Most of the crowd dispersed on their own, while the most stubborn ones had to be shoved out of the way by the guards.

"Make way!" Hektor shouted. "Make way for the Lord Regent!"

Darryk stepped forward, quite visibly nervous yet making his best attempt at a stern glare. "What is the meaning of this?" he asked loudly over the chatter.

"Lord Regent Clark," Baryn Lawe stepped forward with a grin, talking to Darryk as if they were both of great authority. "At last we meet in person, my Lord. And may I say your timing could *not* be better."

Six more guards approached, lining up evenly with Hektor and Bogden, shielding the Clarks and their bookkeeper at both sides.

"We have here a traitor of the crown, my Lord," said Baryn. "She has brought a plague into our beloved city!"

Adelina Huxley and her family stood on top of the cart, their eyes filled with both dread and relief at the sight of the Clarks. "Please, my Lord," she tried to speak out. "If you'll allow me t-"

"Shut your mouth, you traitorous wench, you've *no* right!" Baryn shouted. "Any man or woman that dares bring the enemy into our grounds deserves to be burned along with it!!" The crowd began to shout angrily, some of them carrying wooden clubs in their hands, prepared to swing.

"Order!" Hektor shouted, and Bogden had to echo him to keep control of them all. As Darryk stepped forward, the six guards shifted and worked together to fight back the herd, slowly forming a wall of steel around the cart.

"State your name," Darryk said.

"With pleasure, sir," Baryn replied with a bow. "I am Baryn Lawe of Val Hav-"

"I was not speaking to you, sir."

"Oh…"

Darryk had a hand on his belt, near the hilt of his sword, and it was enough for the preacher to become silently intimidated and step back, his arms extended at his sides so as to move his followers with him.

Darryk and Brunylda Clark allowed for their eyes to take it all in. Aevastra appeared to be near-death, her dark green skin becoming pale and stripped of its glow, and next to her was the unconscious blacksmith, whose bandages were starting to drench and trickle. The rest appeared uninjured, but tired and filthy all the same, and the infant orc's whimpers echoed throughout the square.

"Feast your eyes, my lord and lady," said Baryn Lawe. "Feast your eyes on the plague that this wretched woman has br-"

"Oh, shut your mouth, you blithering imbecile," said Lady Brunylda with a surprising amount of poise that stunned them all. She stepped forward, her eyes glancing back and forth from the orcess to Adelina and the baby in her arms. The silence was eerie… Adelina felt as if the entire world was looking at her, and she had no idea where to even begin.

"Who are you, woman?" asked the Lady Clark, with a hint of what may have been admiration in her eyes. It was obvious because the Lady hated everyone. And such a look coming from her was more than rare.

"Adelina Huxley of Elbon, m'lady," she introduced herself with a bow.

"*Huxley?*" the Lady asked with a raised brow.

There were some murmurs in the crowd, most of which came from acquaintances or people who had heard the rumors of the young farmer that had fought and captured the wanted thief Hudson Blackwood.

Lady Brunylda's eyes did not leave Adelina's. There was an evident tension between the two women, the commendable kind, as if they could somehow read each other through a stare. They had never met before in their lives, and yet they didn't need to. All of Val Havyn knew that Brunylda Clark hardly met anyone she felt any form of empathy towards. Until *now*.

"You're… *John's* mother," the Lady said, to which Adelina responded with a tense nod.

Darryk was far too distracted keeping his eyes on the herd. His guard Hektor, however, noticed the bright red head of hair standing out against the wood of the cart.

"My lord? I-Is that..."

Darryk followed Hektor's eyes... And then a chill ran up his spine...

There she was, the very same blacksmith woman from whom he had purchased weapons and equipment just a day prior. Or rather a dreary image of her, covered in blood and dirt. "Miss Amberhill?" he said as he caught a closer look. "By the gods..."

Merchants' Square had never felt so cold and tense. Adelina suddenly regretted ever stepping foot inside the city to begin with. "M-My farm's been burned down, m'lady," she said. "Destroyed by orcs. Please, we need your help." Adelina had hardly ever begged anyone in her life. But something about Lady Brunylda's demeanor towards her was giving her the courage to swallow her pride.

"Show me," the Lady Treasurer said.

Nervously, Adelina handed the baby to Margot to hold as she climbed down from the cart. Then she took it back and presented him to the Clarks. River had stopped crying by then and was looking up at Lady Brunylda, smiling and blinking those glistening yellow eyes, the kind of eyes that could warm even the coldest of hearts.

The Clarks' expressions were not what Adelina had expected.

There was more warmth there than in anyone else's eyes for miles.

Ordinary, was all that Lady Brunylda could think to describe the child. *Ordinary and gentle in every way, the poor thing...*

"We found him by the river, m'lady," Adelina said. "A-Along with his mother."

"I knew it," Baryn Lawe spoke from afar. "The invasion has already begun... Soon, our kingdom will be *crawling* with their kind. Our very enemy w-"

A sword was drawn... Darryk Clark suddenly became the image of the Roquefort knight he was known to be. And for the first time since becoming Lord Regent, he actually felt like himself.

"Not another word, sir. It is your final warning," he said, his blade up and ready.

And Baryn certainly held his tongue, his hands up in the air so as to convey his frailty.

"Please, m'lord," Adelina said as she bundled the infant back into the warmth of the blanket. "We've nowhere else to go... Please, will you help us?"

The citizens began to speak softly among themselves, mostly in disapproval. Lady Brunylda wanted to speak out, but she knew very well it wasn't her place. Her word would only anger the crowds further, and she was aware of it. But when she turned to the Lord Regent, he appeared more frightened than anything else, even with his sword drawn.

Darryk *wanted* to help them, every one of his instincts urged him to, but he knew that his guards were outnumbered nearly twenty to one. And things grew only tenser when the crowds began shouting again.

"*Hang the orc bitch!*" they said.

"*Burn them all!*"

"*Traitorous scum!*"

Darryk Clark was suddenly covered in sweat. His guards were looking to him for guidance and yet instead his mind drifted from him, haunting him with dark thoughts, and he began shivering… Never had he shivered when he was under threat from an enemy. Being under threat from those he swore to *protect*, however, was entirely new to him. And the man had no idea where to even start.

"O-Order," he said, but his voice was far too weak. "I-I demand order…"

"*Kill them all!*"

"*Monsters!*"

"*To hells with the lot of them!*"

Lady Brunylda Clark almost felt pity for Darryk. Within seconds, the man had lost control of the situation and it was only getting worse, as angry peasants began throwing things and closing in on them all. It was like a raging storm that they'd been shoved right into the center of.

Come on, you stupid man. Do something, the Lady thought. *If you lose them now, you lose them forever. Do something!!*

Darryk was suddenly shoved by the crowd. He stumbled forward, his sword still drawn, and when he glanced back, there was a sea of hands holding old fruit and garbage that were meant for *him*. Unless he sliced them all one by one, there was no way for him to prevent the riot from happening.

Damn it all to hells, you useless dim-witted child!

And with that final thought, Lady Brunylda Clark did what she often did. She took matters into her own hands…

"Order!" she shouted, taking Old Man Beckwit's hand and climbing onto the back of the cart to stand among them. "ORDER, I say!!"

"You heard the Lady! Order!" one of the guards repeated. Lady Brunylda's brute confidence began to spread to the guards, and one by one they held their shields up firmly and began threatening the herd with the tips of their blades.

"Order!" she shouted again, using her owl-like eyes to demand their attention.

Come on, you dumb bastards… Lend me your ears just for a minute and I will show your little Lord Regent how it's done…

The herd grew calmer, their focus shifting towards the Lady.

Within seconds, she was at the center of attention…

"Order, I say! Or, by the gods, you will answer to his majesty King Rowan!"

The mumbles diminished, and the Lady could very clearly make out the dozens of nasty stares judging her silently from afar.

"This is Val Havyn, the capital of Vallenghard!" she shouted, the vein on her forehead sticking out like never before. "And we will *not* tolerate this kind of depraved conduct in our city grounds!"

"*Hang the orc bitch!*" someone shouted, and it was followed by a few barks of agreement.

"We will hang whoever calls her an 'orc bitch' again," the Lady remarked, and it was met with an eerie silence, the kind that could either turn violent or make them all think. "Have you all lost your senses?! Is *this* how low you've sunk?! Citizens of the greatest city in all of Gravenstone, acting like a pack of vultures spouting nonsense?! Is *that* the reputation you want for your city?"

Darryk Clark stood by the cart just beneath her, though he appeared more like a soldier than a Lord Regent. The sweat on his forehead was still there, but he no longer allowed it to consume him. He felt prepared for whatever came next.

"Well?! *Is* it?! The fucking disgrace!" the Lady shouted, so harshly that a few specks of spit flew out of her lips. "Rioting while your king and his army fight for you? While they risk their lives overseas for you? And you've the nerve to spit on his name by rioting in his city streets...? Give me *one* good reason why I shouldn't have you all locked in the dungeons and throw the key into the creek..."

Darryk Clark caught his breath, his frightened eyes conveying both relief and shame all at once. Next to him was Brie, who had been shielded through most of the shoving, but her hair had been stained by a foul-smelling slime that she hoped was just old egg. Both of them were frightened, it was clear. And for a moment, they were both looking up at the Lady as well. They knew that Brunylda Clark had the tendency to be harshly adamant and direct. At that moment, however, she was nothing short of marvelous...

"We *will* have peace and order, mark my words," the Lady went on. "If not by will, then by force, but we *will* have it! Until the king has returned safely, you are to greet your Lord Regent with respect or you do *not* belong in Val Havyn!"

The majority had by then calmed themselves but, as expected, a couple of rebels among the herd kept on.

"*Traitors!*" they shouted.

"*Blasphemous scum!*"

"*They brought **freaks** here!*"

"Precisely, you ignorant fools, they were *brought* here," Lady Brunylda spoke down to them. "And we will see to it that they are escorted back to where they came from, I assure you. In the meantime, there's no need to act like animals."

"*Curse you!*"

"*Traitor!*"

"*We should burn you with 'em!*"

More grunts of agreement came from the herd. But Lady Brunylda was far smarter and knew better than to lose control again so quickly.

I can do this all day, you bastards... Unlike you, I don't bark unless I mean to bite...

"You," she raised a finger at the crowd. "Step forward…"

A few of them dispersed, shifting the focus onto a buck-toothed peasant in his mid-thirties with a cap over a shaggy head of brown hair.

"What was it you just said?" she asked him directly. "Was that a threat I just heard?"

A silence followed… The peasant glanced around, realizing the stares were not as friendly as he had hoped. "W-We don't want freaks in 'ere," he said. "We just want our children to be safe… Hang the orc bitch 'n' let 'er rot in a pile of 'er own shit!"

The Lady Clark fought the urge to roll her eyes, suddenly feeling the need for a good drink. "That's quite a tongue you've got there, young sir," she said. "One more word from it and I'll have to remove it. Is that clear?"

Silence again… And this time, it remained… The Lady had to fight off a few cold stares, but she had seen more than her fair share in her life and they didn't frighten her in the slightest.

"I will *not* repeat myself, so I will ask that you all listen closely," she said, this time speaking to the entire herd. "As of *this* moment… Anyone who dares threaten the peace in this city will be punished for it. Anyone who speaks ill of the Lord Regent, anyone who even *looks* at him the wrong way, will be thrown into a cage and left to starve. Is that clear?"

The silence spoke for itself. And with one final cold stare, Lady Brunylda sighed deeply and gave Darryk a glance. "They're all yours, my *Lord*."

Darryk Clark sheathed his sword again nervously.

He did not belong there, he knew… He did not belong anywhere within a fifty miles of Val Havyn, in fact. And yet, as he looked all around, every pair of eyes had shifted their attention towards him. All eight of his guards were staring at him, awaiting his orders. He had his sword and eight more to back him up and yet Lady Brunylda had gained back control of the masses using only her words…

He felt useless and unprepared. And so, as he wiped the sweat from his brows one last time, he took a deep breath. He knew the right thing to do, even though he also knew it might be the end of him. He simply couldn't abandon them… If he did, they wouldn't survive the night and he knew it…

"Take them inside," he said to his guards, and it was followed by a few protesting mutters. "We will give them shelter until we figure out the best solution for the situation."

Six guards remained in place. The other two, Hektor and Bogden, moved towards Adelina Huxley and her companions and lent them a hand.

"Thank you," Adelina said, a tremendous relief vivid in her eyes. "Thank you, m'lord!"

Even Lady Brunylda Clark was looking at him differently.

Good, she thought. *For once, the bloody child says the correct answer.*

And so they marched… Step by step through Merchants' Square, towards the palace gates that stood just yards away, surrounded by intimidating and angry eyes but quiet tongues. Lady Brunylda Clark and her bookkeeper Brie led the way, followed by Adelina Huxley and the orc child, the twins Margot & Melvyn, and Mister Beckwit. Hektor and Bogden carried Aevastra and Evellyn towards the palace gates. And finally, there was Darryk... The man looked like anything but a Lord Regent. He may have been dressed in fancy clothes, but his expression was one of defeat and humiliation.

They stepped inside the gates. Adelina Huxley looked up at the immense height of the grand royal palace. She could fit every villager in Elbon there and still have plenty of space, she knew. It felt *foreign* to her, odd and unfamiliar, and yet it was the only place for miles where she and her children would be safe.

Now that she had been seen carrying an orc child, the rumors would soon spread and her name would be cursed by every mouth in Val Havyn and perhaps even some in Elbon. And yet when she looked down at the child, she felt a strange feeling in her chest, as if none of it mattered. She felt everything but regret.

When she heard the gates closing shut behind her, the tension left her shoulders.

At last, they were safe...

* * *

"All it takes is one strand of lotus root," Cedric said, rather lively and enthusiastically for a young man that was nearly crushed to death the night before. "You mix in a cup of vinegar and half a spoonful of black pepper and there's not a single belly in the world that can fight it. It's quite vile and painful, but it won't kill you."

Gwyn couldn't help but burst with laughter. For a woman with such a robust demeanor, her laugh was overly vigorous and with a higher pitch than Cedric had expected. "That's bloody brilliant," she said. "*And* a bit bold for a lad like ye."

"My mum taught me the trick. Said to only use it if a person deserves it."

"Smart woman, she was."

"Quite so," Cedric smiled. "Unfortunately, I'm rubbish at scheming. Mister Nottley found the rest of the lotus root in my rucksack and beat me with a lash 5 times for it. I still got the scars in me back. I had to tend to 'im for three days until he was better."

"Yellow bastard," Gwyn grunted, the expression on her face shifting instantly.

"It was worth it," Cedric said with a shrug.

"Is he the one that gave ye that thing there on yer lips?"

"U-Um..." Cedric stammered and covered his lower lip with the tips of his fingers. The scab had managed to open yet again and he could feel the moisture of the fresh blood oozing out.

"Don't lie to me, toothpick. I know wha' a bludgeon to the jaw looks like," she said. Something in her tone conveyed a certain amount of concern, and Cedric felt a tug in his chest at the thought of it; having never had any family aside from his late mother, he couldn't help but become anxious at Gwyn's demeanor, like an older sister caring for a brother.

"Was it him, then?" Gwyn asked a second time. "For that matter, how'd a scrawny lad like ye get all 'em scars? Don't tell me it was in battle. Ye couldn't even hold a blade right."

Cedric made his best attempt at a chuckle, so as to ease the tension. "Y-Yes, that would be his doing," he confessed. "But it was *also* worth it, if you ask me. He called my friend a stupid farm wench and she'd done nothing to deserve it."

"A *friend*, eh?" Gwyn asked, and Cedric felt a relief as the woman's tone eased into a warmer one. "Didn't know ye had any of *those*."

"I've got friends," he tried to protest, but loosened himself when he saw that she was only teasing him. "Granted, not *many*... Mister Nottley makes me work late evenings and early mornings, I hardly have any time left for myself. But I manage."

"Why stick with the old schmuck, then? Sounds like the type o' man I'd like to meet."

"Oh?"

"If only to see the look on 'is old face when I kick 'im between the legs."

The two of them shared a laugh, loud enough to turn a few heads around them. It seemed like ages since Cedric had even smiled, much less laughed aloud; so long, that he had forgotten what that feeling in his throat and gut felt like when he laughed too excessively. For a moment, he found himself forgetting exactly where he was and for what purpose. It soothed him.

They had reached the western border of the Woodlands by dusk and stopped to rest on the wrong side when Sir Percyval Garroway sent soldiers to scout the area and make sure an ambush wasn't waiting for them. Cedric would never have guessed the Woodlands to be a safer place than Halghard and yet there they sat, waiting for the word to either continue or deviate from the road they were traveling through.

"What's 'er name?" the question caught Cedric off guard.

"Pardon me?"

"Your *friend*," Gwyn clarified. "The farmgirl?"

A shade of pink rose to Cedric's cheeks and he stammered to speak. His right hand gripped the dagger on his belt again, though this time Gwyn hardly noticed. It had become as natural a trait as Cedric's soft murmur of a voice.

"Robyn," he said. "Robyn Huxley... She from Elbon. A village just south o-"

"I know where Elbon is, lad," she said, friendlier than the comment sounded. "I may be a mercenary, but I ain't stupid."

"N-No, I didn't mean to-"

"Relax," she chuckled.

"I'm sorry," his gaze lowered, a hint of shame in his eyes.

Gwyn lifted a dagger at him as if it was her finger. "Apologize again 'n' I'll *actually* be angry at ye." They smiled at each other again.

Nearby, there was a commotion. Two figures approached the brigade as they hid within the darkness of the trees. Viktor Crowley stood next to Percyval, along with a crowd of about ten men, all dressed in different attire. They held no torches, out of fear of giving themselves away, and their tense stance was the only thing they all shared commonly, as if ready to spring into battle at any moment.

"What do you see, Crowley?" Percyval asked.

Viktor was dressed in his undergarments and borrowed leathers, looking more like a mercenary than a knight. "No sign of any fires," he said. "The Rift of Halghard is just two miles north, I doubt there's any threat approaching from there. Not one we can't handle, at least." He squinted and managed to make out the incoming shadows in the dark. He grew tense at first, but then realized that one of the shadows was massive and had horns sticking out of his head like a bull.

"They're back," he said with a smirk. "Standby."

Percyval echoed him and the tension broke, but the conversations seized almost instantly. Skye, the elf mage, was faster than they appeared to be; Toro, the minotauro, had to walk faster to catch up. When they finally reached the rest of the troop, Percyval stepped towards them both. "Report?"

"No signs of a troop anywhere," Skye said. "Just a scouting party of about eight or nine men camped at about a mile east of Grymsbi."

"Banners?"

"Morganna's."

Sir Percyval took a moment to breathe it in. Then he nodded and turned towards his troop. "All right. Listen up!" he shouted. "King Alistair's camp is just six miles ahead... There will be food and shelter waiting for us when we get there. If we march quietly and carefully, we should avoid any unprecedented attacks. Now gather your horses and weapons. We march!"

The troop obeyed. No one lit a single torch despite the darkness consuming the place.

"Finally," Gwyn said under her breath.

Cedric said nothing. The anxiety in his chest had returned and it wouldn't allow for any words to rise up to his lips. He took a moment to hop down from the cart and give his bruised legs a good stretch when suddenly a man in dark armor approached him.

"You there!" said Sir Antonn Guilara.

Cedric had only seen the man from a far and he was horribly frightened of him; then again, he was frightened of nearly everyone. "Y-Yes, sir?" he stood up straight all of a sudden. Gwyn stood nearby, in case the ill-tempered knight became too aggressive.

"You're Sir Viktor Crowley's squire, yes?" asked Sir Antonn. In his hands, he held the reins of a pony and was dragging the poor thing along despite its protesting neighs.

"Yes, sir... that would be me, sir..."

"Good. Here," Sir Antonn threw the reins at Cedric. "We found this thing about a mile back. It was frightened half to death. Doesn't look wild, it's tame as an old hound. Reminded me of you."

And with that, the knight walked away. Cedric stood there eyeing the frightened farm pony up and down. It was roan-colored and had a few braids on its mane, and there was a handmade saddle on it that looked rather familiar, only he couldn't make out where it was from. There was also an old quiver of arrows tied to the saddle but no bow, as if the arrows were there in case the archer that previously owned the pony ran out.

"Guess today's yer lucky day," Gwyn gave him a pat on the shoulder.

"Y-Yes," Cedric nodded, caressing the pony as if he somehow knew it from somewhere. "Yes, I guess it is..."

Gwyn walked some distance away, presumably to gather some things she had misplaced. The young squire kept a close eye on her, hoping she wasn't planning on leaving him alone for the rest of the journey. Out of the whole troop, she had been among the few people he felt comfortable and safe around. And speaking to her, though mostly as a distraction, was keeping him sane.

Thaddeus Rexx, on the other hand, was more than wary... His eyes examined Cedric, and then they would move towards the woman. There was a mild discomfort in his chest, something like doubt, if not distrust towards her. He tried to tell himself to back off, but he simply couldn't help it. Before he knew it, the blacksmith was walking after her, trying his best to keep up with her brisk pace.

"Oi! You!" he said, his voice gruff and rigid.

The woman turned to face the towering figure of Thaddeus Rexx.

"*Gwyn*," she corrected him.

"I don't care," Thaddeus remarked, the hostility more than vivid in his stance alone. "What're you up to?"

"What?" she curved her brows, thrown aback by his sudden interrogation.

"You know what I mean. The *lad*. What've you been telling 'im?"

"What are ye, his warden?" she asked with a scoff.

"What if I am?"

"Ye *ain't*. His warden's an old limp bastard with muttonchops, he told me so. And ye don't strike me as the fatherly type either. So what's yer deal, then?"

Thaddeus felt his discomfort grow into resentment and he tried his best to keep his stance. "I'm the closest thing the lad has for a friend," he said sternly. "You've known 'im for two days, I've known 'im since he was a pup."

"And ye think ye know what's best for him, do ye?" Gwyn took a step towards the blacksmith, not a single trace of fear in her bright green eyes.

"I'm only lookin' after the lad," said Thaddeus. "He's a *squire*... He's already more naïve than is good for 'im and he's gonna get himself killed if you encourage 'im to be a hero."

"Calm yerself, tiny. I was just gettin' to know the lad... I wasn't *manipulatin'* 'im, if that's what ye're getting at."

"Good," Thaddeus said. "No need to be hostile, now, I was only-"

"*Hostile?*" Gwyn's tone began to change into a more menacing one.

"Do ease your tone, there."

"*Hostile?!* So *you* approach *me* and start to *accuse* me of-"

"Sister..." Daryan approached them, placing an arm around Gwyn's shoulder.

She shook him off and turned her glare at him. "Piss off! This ain't yer mess."

"No, but it is my *sister's* mess, and thus it will *become* my mess if I don't calm you," he said, his voice much more calm and composed compared to his sister's.

"I don't *need* calming!"

"There, there, now Gwyndolyn... Do you remember what happened back in Yulxester...? We don't want another incident on our hands now, do we, dear sister?"

Daryan's eyes overpowered Gwyn's, and she felt her tension lower almost instantly as she recalled in her mind the incident to which her brother was referring to. She nodded, much more calm and at ease, before turning back to Thaddeus Rexx.

"If ye really are lookin' out for his safety, ye shit... keep a better watch on 'im during battle, will ye? I won't always be 'round to save the lad meself," she said disdainfully, and proceeded to walk back towards her mount.

Thaddeus hardly knew what to say. He allowed for his distrust to guide him and there was something like regret that was giving him the knot on his throat. He turned towards Daryan and asked, "What happened back in Yulxester?"

"That might be a story for another time, Mister Rexx," Daryan said, giving the man a tap on the arm.

"Well... at least that rage of hers will be useful during the battle. Since it appears to be approaching, that is."

"A battle is inevitable, Mister Rexx," Daryan said. "If not tomorrow, then in a week, perhaps a month... A scouting party isn't as much a concern as King Balthazar's army is. Five thousand men, they say he has. It'll take a hell of a strategy to defeat an army that large."

"You seem to know a thing or two about wars, then?"

"Regrettably so."

In the distance, a thin line of smoke was rising into the night sky, where King Alistair's army had set camp. Something in Percyval's gut urged him to send a group to kill the scouting party, but he stopped himself upon examining the condition of his recruits. They had fought and they had done it bravely, and many had even died for him.

The Rogue Brotherhood had come for *him*, there was no doubt.

The lives of the fallen recruits were in his hands and there was no turning back now.

Tonight we march, Sir Percyval thought to himself.

Tonight we eat and rest... For there may not be a chance for it tomorrow...

* * *

The Woodlands were the last place in all of Gravenstone that Robyn Huxley expected to find a tavern, and yet she did. Like a tumbling wave, she was struck with a scenery unlike any she had ever seen in Vallenghard. If her eyes were not deceiving her, the tavern looked as if it had been built inside the massive base of a tree, and surrounding it was the most diverse cluster of beings she had ever seen.

A band of human sellswords, a woodland elf with skin the color of the ocean, two orcs sitting in the fruitful garden with a sleeping goblin lying still between them, or rather she chose to *believe* it was sleeping...

About six or seven gnomes vanishing into a wide hole in the dirt, one after another...

Another woodland elf wrestling a restless goblin in the mud...

An ogre, nearly identical to the one that had attacked her that morning, sitting comfortably by the tavern door biting into the raw leg of what may have been a deer...

The more she watched, the more overwhelmed she became. She hid among the shrubs between Nyx and the Beast. Quiet and cautious, they had been hiding for a couple of minutes, thinking of the proper way to approach the strange tavern.

"D'you think it's safe?" she asked.

"For you, perhaps," Nyx said, sniffing about doubtfully. "Not so much for *me*, I'm afraid."

"I'm sure they can make an exception."

"You don't know much about life outside of Elbon, Lady Robyn."

For a moment, she turned to the Beast as if expecting him to contribute, only he appeared more aggravated and inpatient than anything else. Over the span of ten hours, the Beast must have spoken about three words, and all of them had been under his breath. Robyn tried to make casual conversation with him, but it was always to no avail.

"How hard can it be?" she asked. "You're a fox, not a bear. I'll talk to 'em!"

414

"There is *another* option," Nyx said, glancing at her bow.

She hesitated. "What...?"

"It *is* a more immediate solution," Nyx said, and Robyn felt a knot in her throat at the sound of him speaking so casually about death.

She glanced at the Beast again, hoping for some form of effort.

Are you not gonna say anything? Not even a single word?

"N-No," she said. "That is absolutely mad. I'm not killing you."

"It's either you *do* or we find somewhere else to rest for the night, Lady Robyn."

"No... I-I won't do it," she said. "There must be a better way."

"Need I remind you that I can't *actually* die?"

She shook her head nervously, glancing at the silent Beast for the last time.

Still nothing? I don't think I've ever gone that long without talking myself... Say something, damn you!

She cleared her throat. "What do *you* think, Beast?" she decided to ask.

The ill-tempered orc grunted and rose suddenly to his feet. With a crack of the neck, he stepped towards the tavern leisurely, as if he had grown tired of sitting about.

"Hey!" Robyn leapt to her feet and followed him.

With a sigh, Nyx scurried after them unwillingly. "In case you care," he said, putting as little pressure on his paw as he could. "I believe this plan to be as rubbish as they come..."

Robyn frowned. "It'll be all right," she said, though she was not entirely convinced herself. The only tavern she'd ever set foot inside was Mister Nottley's whenever John had made a delivery and brought her along. She had never set foot, much less even *seen*, a tavern built into a tree before.

The three of them stepped inside, and much to Robyn's surprise, the stares they received made her feel like *she* was the outsider. She took a moment to gaze around, admiring the beauty of the tavern. There were two other orcs inside, both much younger than the Beast, one a servant and the other was playing a harp next to an elf girl who was singing a beautiful interpretation of *The Ballad of Wingless Ehryn*.

Among the others, Robyn saw more elves, gnomes, goblins, and orcs than she had ever seen in her life. But she wasn't afraid, at least not more than she was intrigued. She then noticed a middle-aged woman in a red housedress standing behind the bar; the woman *had* to have been in charge, Robyn realized, based solely on the way she was talking to some of the servers.

Breathe, Robyn... You've got this...

"Pardon me," Robyn approached the woman confidently. "I would like a room for me and my companions."

The woman scoffed before she even said anything. "What sort o' place d'you think this is?" she asked, more irritated than angry. "No animals allowed, poppet... If he was a pup, I may have shrugged it off. But a bleedin' fox?!"

"Right... the thing is," Robyn cleared her throat, realizing what she was about to say was bound to sound mad. "He's, um... He's not a *real* fox, he's um... well he's cursed."

"Well that's just as well," the woman grunted. "I won't have a bloody *cursed* thing stayin' in here. It'll bring bad fate to the place, and the other guests simply won't have it."

"Please!" Robyn said, leaning in closer to the woman. "I can't pay extra, but I *can* work!"

"No!" the woman snapped. "Why in all hells does *everyone* insist on bartering?! Miss Rayna does *not* barter! First that loud-mouthed moron of a thief and now *you*?! If you don't leave in the next 10 seconds, I *will* call my Edmund and trust me, dear, I am much more patient than he is."

Robyn's eyes widened instantly...

"Wait," she said. "A *thief*? What thief?"

"Some dumb bloke who thought he was all high 'n' mighty."

"W-What was his name?!"

"How in all hells should *I* know?!" Miss Rayna asked with a scoff of frustration.

"I'm sorry," Robyn said gently, knowing that in some situations it was easier to lie. "M-My name's Robyn... We were traveling with my brother's squadron, y'see... We were attacked by tree nymphs and got separated. I've been trying to find my brother ever since. Was this thief, by any chance, traveling with a young man? Short blonde hair, blue eyes, farmer's clothing?"

Miss Rayna had seen more than her fair share of liars in her life. She knew their tactics and tricks and had heard every phony sob story from '*My wife's thrown me out*' to '*I'm the King of Halghard in disguise*'. She knew the young girl was lying. Every single sign was there. The girl's dryness as she spoke, the nervous twitching of her lip, and the fact that she brushed her fingers through her black curls twice during her brief story.

But she also saw something else... The girl's eyes were glowing, not the way an elf's would when they were angry but the way a human's would when they were afraid. And if Miss Rayna was aware of anything, it was that with fear came love. The girl may have been lying about something, but the love in her eyes was real.

"Didn't see a squadron of any kind, dear," Miss Rayna said, her tone more affable than before. "But the thief *was* traveling with a woman and another man. Wasn't hard to tell the woman was a witch. The other man didn't really say his name... but he does fit your description."

Robyn smiled...

Miss Rayna smiled back. "Still can't rent you the room, poppet," she said warmly. "But for two coppers, I'll let you and your friends make camp in our stables if you'd like. It's the best I can offer."

Robyn's eyes lit up with something like hope.

"Y-Yes... Th-Thank you! *Thank* you, ma'am!"

"Call me Miss Rayna."

Robyn's smile gave the woman a warm feeling in her chest. Had it not been for the wooden bar between them, Robyn would have surely gone in for a hug and Miss Rayna would have surely scowled and recoiled.

Robyn left two coppers on the bar and was on her way to the door within seconds, her two unusual companions following behind. The elf girl Kiira returned to the bar with empty tankards in a tray and noticed Miss Rayna watching their new visitors with awe.

"Travelers?" Kiira asked.

Miss Rayna disregarded the question, and as she tapped on the wood of the bar with her sharp fingernails, her eyes narrowed into a squint as if she was lost in thought. "Something funny's goin' on in the west, I think," she said.

"Should I call Edmund & Grum?" Kiira asked.

"Nah... What for?" Miss Rayna asked as she casually gulped down the last of the unfinished ale that someone left behind on the counter. "Give it a week and we'll hear all about it from some drunken halfwit, I'm sure."

XIV
Unexpected Alliances

Syrena, the witch of Morganna, was the first to wake.

The first thing she took in was the breeze, cooler and significantly more humid than any night in years. The warmth struggled to crawl back into her cold pale body. She had been shivering all night due to her humid clothes; it was a miracle she woke up at all.

Her eyelids opened slightly, exposing her to a rich blend of green and blue all around her, a blurry verdant atmosphere morphing into shape. For a moment, she had entirely forgotten where she was; she *had* to be in the Woodlands still, she figured, for nowhere else could she open her eyes to such an imposing roof of leaves, shielding her almost entirely from the starry black sky. There was something rather different, even *eerie*, about her surroundings, though she couldn't quite make out what it was.

It could have been the peculiar trees, caked with a layer of thick green moss to the point where the brown of the wood was no longer visible.

It could have been the abundance of oddly shaped leaves, similar to clovers but with the middle leaf pointy instead of round, and with a cluster of little white flora adorning every stem. What little moonlight made its way through the trees was giving the leaves a strange glow, a blue hue unlike any other plant life in the forest.

It could have also been the blow to her head altering her vision... but even the *breeze* in the air appeared to be glowing. It was entrancing and dreamlike.

She sat up and rubbed her eyes with disbelief...

It wasn't at all her imagination. The droplets in the leaves, the moss, even the *soil* beneath all the greenery was alight under the moon's glow. The ambience was almost peaceful, surreal and luminous, as if she had traveled to some distant realm in her sleep. Her nose was struck with a strong aroma, a sweet blend of honey and roses, and she realized she was lying over a pile of the softest leaves her fingertips had ever touched.

There was an unconscious body lying next to her, and when she rubbed her eyes again for clarity she realized it was John Huxley, pale and motionless yet still in one piece. She was anxious for a moment, but her shoulders eased when she heard him breathe.

"John?" she whispered. She shook him gently, but he wouldn't wake.

The almost euphoric atmosphere was so quiet and peaceful that it frightened her to be the only one awake. Not knowing where she was or, more importantly, how she had even gotten there was giving her that nervous twitch of the eye she hated. Her hands grew red and sweaty, as if they had a mind of their own and were preparing for the worst.

When she heard the sudden snapping of a twig nearby, she froze...

She tried to follow the sound, but the echo made it difficult to find its source. In the distance she heard a high-pitched whistle, like that of a singing bird, which seemed strange and unusual considering no Woodland birds were known to sing under the moon's light.

She raised her empty hands into the air as if holding a pair of blades; they were so red they looked as if on the verge of exploding. With the snap of a finger, she conjured a small orb of fire about the size of an apple. It hovered just inches from her skin and moved with her hand as if it were a part of her. She searched all around, but it was as if the light of the fire was seizing the glow away from the leaves, and they went back to looking old and dry. *Where in all hells are we...?*

She heard the whistling sound again, and this time it came from right above her. She glanced up at the leaves, her frightened eyes hardening into a glower, ready to face whatever was lurking up there. *By the gods...*

There, hiding behind a thick leafy branch, she saw it...

Or was it a *her?* It was hard to tell, the creature was so small...

First, Syrena saw a pair of glistening eyes hidden within the leaves of the misshapen tree. Then she noticed a pair of trembling blue hands rising out, grasping onto the nearest leaf as if it were a shield. The tiny creature slowly revealed itself, and Syrena noticed the razor-sharp ears on its petite head.

The witch bent down and gave John another shove, this time more aggressively, and the farmer woke up mildly startled. "Mmph," he groaned, rubbing the side of his head as if he had drunk his weight in ale the previous night. The witch kept her orb of fire alight, glancing up at the tiny creature, alert and full of dread.

"John!" she whispered, her eye twitching awfully.

"W-Where are we?" he groaned.

"Shhh! Don't speak... There's something in the trees..."

John sat up, forcing himself awake. When Syrena glanced back up the creature was suddenly gone, and the strange blue glow among the leaves left with it. Her brow lowered.

It was just there, she thought. *It was staring right at me...*

"Tree nymphs?" John asked, his eyes searching everywhere for his blade.

"No... No, it looked like..."

She gasped. When she turned back around, the strange creature from the tree was floating in the air a mere two feet from her face. Her orb turned into a sudden roar of flames and it soared into the air a good four feet. "Shit!" she yelped, thankful that she didn't accidentally set any leaves ablaze. Slowly, the flames began to shrink back down to her palms, as if the fire was mirroring the witch's heartbeat.

John sat up, his eyes wide and alert and locked on the tiny creature.

It looked like a woman, only she was a mere four inches tall and she had bright translucent wings like a dragonfly. She looked like an elf, her skin a pale shade of blue, her sapphire eyes a bit too large for her head, and ears sharp like a needle. The most peculiar thing about her was her mop of red hair, floating eerily in the air as if it were submerged in water. Only she wasn't anywhere *near* water... She was flying. Or, rather, *hovering* in the air as her wings flapped with a powerful speed. And she *glowed*, as if her very essence was radiating magic.

"What *is* it?" John asked, unable to close his mouth from the shock.

Syrena lowered the intensity of her orb until it was the size of a candle's light. But the little blue creature did not move, her eyes fixated on Syrena's hand as if mesmerized by it.

"She's a pixie," Syrena spoke softly, so as to not frighten the peculiar little being. Then she slowly curled her palm into a fist and the flame died, fading into a trail of smoke. The pixie blinked repeatedly, as if waking from a trance, but she didn't blink the way a human did. Instead it was the bottom of her eyelids that moved upwards over her pupils.

"She's... *beautiful*," John mumbled.

Distracted as she was, Syrena shook away her unease and tried to force her mind to focus. "Where's Hudson?" she asked; the knot in her throat came out of nowhere. She conjured another orb of fire and the two of them searched their surroundings, but the thief was nowhere to be found. There was only the pile of leaves in which they had been sleeping, like a giant nest among the glowing trees.

"Hudson?" John called, careful not to shout. But there was no reply, only the distant whistling coming from the abundant trees. "The river might've taken him," he said nervously. "Where *are* we?"

Syrena's left eye was driving her mad, twitching endlessly as she began panting.

"I don't know," she said, then hissed under her breath, "*Damn* it all to hells..."

The whistling became sharper suddenly, and it seemed far closer than any of the faint sounds in the distance. It was coming from the redheaded pixie... Her head was tilted to the left as if she was lost in thought.

"I-Is she trying to *tell* us something?" John asked.

The pixie whistled again, quite birdlike and beautiful, and her head was turning as if she was trying to guide their gazes towards a nearby lake. Syrena took slow careful steps forward, and the pixie remained where she was, floating in the air as if she was light as a feather.

"H-Hello," the witch said, her voice dry and croaky.

"Syrena, what are y-"

"Shhh!" she hissed, and John instead focused on finding his blade.

This is stupid, Syrena told herself, but she proceeded anyway.

"We're looking for our friend," she said. "H-Have you seen him...?"

The pixie hovered forward, and though Syrena was wary and alert, she couldn't help but succumb to her curiosity. Gently, the pixie closed in towards Syrena's ear, and the witch could feel the cold radiating from those glimmering wings, sending chills into her spine. The pixie held a tiny arm out. Her fingers looked sharp like claws, but when they touched Syrena's left temple, they felt as soft as cotton.

Syrena felt a sudden rush of energy surge through her...

Never had she had such a feeling. It was as if her entire body had been engulfed in flames for a half-second and then stopped. And after that brief thrilling moment, she understood it all. It flashed through her mind, as if she had somehow *lived* it... Only it was through someone *else's* eyes...

She saw the three dark shapes falling with the white foamy cascade, the massive tree trunk stumbling to the bottom, breaking into pieces as it hit the rocks. She saw the three shapes hit the water, saw them missing the rocks by just inches... She saw *herself*, submerged in the water, the blood oozing from her head after brushing against the sharp edge of a stone. John and Hudson were also there, pale and unconscious, being carried away by the river's current.

And then... she saw the three of them getting dragged out of the water, one by one...

Her jaw dropped from the disbelief. *What in all hells...?*

She turned to face the pixie, who was staring back absent-mindedly.

"Who *are* you?" she asked. And then the pixie flew in towards her ear again. The entire place was silent; even John didn't hear a thing. Syrena, however, caught the pixie's voice as clear as day. Her voice was a mere whisper, and it was as soft and delicate as the whistling of the wind; it was trancelike.

"*Ssssivvyyyy*," the pixie said, and then backed away gently.

Syrena's brows lowered and her left eye began to twitch again. Pixies were known to be shy creatures, hiding away from anything and everything that appeared to be alive. In her life, Syrena had only seen a few of them from afar. She had never seen one so closely before, much less heard one *speak*.

"Sivvy?" the witch repeated nervously.

The pixie tilted her head to the side again with a graceful delicacy. She didn't have to speak again. It was as if the witch could read her thoughts through a simple stare.

"W-What is happening?" John asked, his eyes moving back and forth between the two.

"I haven't the slightest idea," Syrena mumbled. It took a moment for her to soak it all in. It seemed like mere minutes before she was standing on the trunk of that massive tree, with her flaming hands shooting at the pious nameless raider. And now she was *here*... lost somewhere in the Woodlands in the dead of night, speaking to a *pixie*.

Suddenly the glow vanished. Sivvy flew away rapidly like a dragonfly, leaving Syrena and John in the dark with a baffled look on both their faces.

"We should, uh," John cleared his throat. "We should probably get out of here."

Syrena was silent and struck with awe; she could hardly manage a head nod.

"Come," John motioned her to follow him. "We should look f-"

But the whistling returned all of a sudden. They could see Sivvy approaching; it was clear because the leaves would glow whenever she came near them. Her wings were flapping enthusiastically and she was carrying something... It was a dusty black hat with a rim...

Syrena and John glanced nervously at each other as Sivvy dropped the hat right at their feet, and before they knew it, they were scampering through the greenery, following after the pixie as if she was a hound guiding them towards the source of a scent. They were careful with their steps; the plant life beneath their feet was soft and pulsating with life, they felt almost ashamed for walking over it.

Sivvy led them to an unusually shaped tree, short and strewn, with thin leafy vines hanging from its every branch like curtains. With her tiny blue hands, Sivvy pulled the vines for them to walk through. The first thing that Syrena saw through the opening was a pair of legs wearing black pants and boots, and almost instantly she felt the tension lift from her shoulders. She lowered her head and stepped foot inside. John followed.

"By the gods," the farmer pressed a hand against his mouth, sighing with relief.

Hudson Blackwood was lying on another bed of the same soft leaves. His black coat and vest were resting next to his stiff body. His shirt was unbuttoned and his wound was exposed, though it had been cauterized and bandaged with more leaves. His tan skin was now slightly pallid from the loss of blood, and his lips were dry and purple and rough.

Syrena instantly fell to her knees with a look of concern...

This was the man that had helped her break away from her chains. *Twice*. He was the first person in 10 years to show her any form of kindness, in his own peculiar way. More than that, he was the first person to *trust* her when everyone else wanted her either dead or in chains. Syrena was a solitary soul, that much was certain, but if there was anyone in the world that she cared about even in the slightest, it had to have been Hudson Blackwood.

"H-Hudson," she whispered through a wall of tears that she refused to let go of. "Hudson, darling... Wake up..."

John watched them from afar, taking hesitant steps forward. Gazing upon the face of the unconscious thief, he felt the guilt sinking into his chest. Had he not urged him to continue on the journey, perhaps this wouldn't have happened. Hudson would still be awake and alert and off somewhere doubtlessly looking for trouble.

"Hudson," Syrena shook him. "Wake up, darling... Please..."

But the thief didn't move, not even a flinch, and Syrena could no longer resist. A tear escaped her eyes, leaving a glistening trail on her pale cheek. But she refused to weep; her expression was firm and steady, as if she was entirely unaware of the tears. Her sweaty palms were grasping onto the thief's shirt and she had to bite her lower lip to keep it from trembling. Sivvy, the redheaded pixie, was watching them with awe, her head tilted to the left as she floated over John's shoulder.

Come on, mate, John pondered. *Don't do this to us...*

And then the farmer gave in to his impulses, no longer ashamed to demonstrate his concern. He dropped to his knees next to Syrena, as the witch shook Hudson harder and harder.

"Hudson," she kept saying. "Wake up, darling. We still need you..."

But the thief was cold and stiff and looked almost lifeless. John placed a gentle hand on Syrena's shoulder for comfort, and then felt his own eyes swelling up at the sight of it all.

Come on, mate... I know you're still there. Wake up, damn you!

"Don't you dare," Syrena said as she fell forward gently, placed her forehead on Hudson's cold shoulder, and gripped the leaves and dirt with her fists. "No," she kept saying. "No... You can't..."

The silence seemed to drag on for hours. John closed his eyes and a tear of his own escaped his eyes. If the pain was this bad for him, he could only imagine what Syrena was feeling. He couldn't help but think of Viktor Crowley's disapproval if the man were here to see this, and yet John found that he no longer cared. This was the man who had taken an arrow for them. This was his *friend*.

Syrena felt her fingers warming up suddenly, her mind angrily coming to terms with the reality that her only true friend was gone. And then, as if mirroring her emotions, both her hands and part of her forearms started to radiate smoke. *Get out,* she told herself, knowing very well of what her rage was capable of. *Get out of here now...*

She lifted her head from Hudson's stiff shoulder and wiped the tears from her cheeks.

"I-I have to go," she rose to her feet.

"Syrena?" John tried to calm her.

"Just let me go," Syrena could no longer look at either of them. Her hands were discolored all over again, this time much darker, almost turning purple from the agitation. Just when she took a step towards the vines, however, there was the sound of a dry inhale. And so her eyes widened and she glanced back.

Hudson's chest began moving...

John felt his skin crawl as he shook him again gently.

"Hudson...? Are you there, mate? Hudson?!"

Then it happened... A shiver of the eyelids, a twitching of the nose, and a gentle breathing… The infamous thief was beginning to wake, and both John and Syrena felt a rush of energy that woke them both entirely.

"Hudson!" John repeated with a vivid joy in his voice. Syrena threw herself into the leaves again, kneeling by the thief's head, unsure of what to do or say. Hudson opened his eyes and with every struggling breath he became slowly aware of his surroundings.

"Hudson, my dear?" Syrena spoke softly, placing her warm hand on his cold cheek.

When the thief finally spoke, his voice was hoarse and dry, and he said something Syrena couldn't quite understand. It sounded a bit like "*John.*"

The farmer and the witch glanced at one another.

"*John…*"

"Y-Yes, I'm here, mate," John said, the hint of a smile on his lips.

"*Move… closer…*"

Syrena moved aside and allowed for John to lean in.

"What is it? What d'you need?" the farmer asked, tilting his ear closer to the thief's lips.

"*John,*" Hudson whispered, weakly and drearily. "*…please tell me I'm wearing trousers.*"

* * *

The fish was crisp and warm, with a savory taste that could only be achieved with years of practice. Robyn Huxley was given three plates of them, and her eyes lit up with joy at the sight of such a feast. She walked back to the stables and handed the largest fish to the Beast, who took it instantly and bit at it as if he hadn't eaten in days. Old Nyx rejected the fish at first and urged Robyn to have it, but the girl placed the wooden plate by his paws regardless.

The Beast was grumbling and moaning through every bite.

Robyn and Nyx couldn't help but stare.

"By the gods," Nyx said, sitting with his front paws resting flat on the ground. "If you don't slow down, you'll choke on a piece of fishbone."

The Beast replied with a shrug of the shoulder and a heedless grunt. He was stuffing the fish into his mouth, bones and all, and bits of it were oozing out of the corners of his thick green lips.

They sat on the dirt inside Miss Rayna's stables. Nearby, there was a long indoor corridor with over a dozen horse stalls at both sides, and an additional space at the entrance where more horses were tied to posts and stood side to side drinking water from a long container. It was in that space where they chose to rest; the smell was not very pleasant, but considering they had four walls and a wooden roof it was the closest thing to shelter they would find for miles.

"How did you pay for all of this?" Nyx asked, looking up at Robyn as she munched on her own piece of fish, just as eagerly as the Beast.

"I didn't," she said. "That Kiira girl gave 'em to me, said it was courtesy of Miss Rayna."

Robyn had never been very fond of fish, but after a week of eating nothing but berries and stale bread with cheese, she could hardly resist that tangy aroma; she welcomed the fish and savored every bite. Nyx gave in as well and devoured everything on his plate with two mouthfuls. Even as a fox, Robyn could see the human expressions on his face. He closed his only eye and exhaled with relief, and with a flicker of his whiskers he made his best attempt at a smile, like a joyful child feasting on his favorite dish.

"I had forgotten what a real meal felt like," he said.

Robyn chuckled. Sitting beside Nyx, she felt the sudden urge to run her fingers through his soft grey fur, but out of respect she held herself back. They sat in silence for a moment, taking the time to catch their breath after days of struggling to remain alive. Should they survive the journey to Drahkmere and back, nothing would ever be the same again and Robyn knew it.

She wondered what life would be like back in Elbon now that Nyx had revealed his secret to her. She wondered why, after knowing and trusting in Mister Beckwit her whole life, did the old man not confide such a secret to her. Perhaps it had been Nyx's decision, and if it was, there was no way she could ever blame him, for humans were not the most sympathetic of the races. She wondered if Nyx would be opposed to the idea of revealing his true nature to all of Elbon, and perhaps now that her brother John had become acquainted with people of nobility, to all of Val Havyn.

A thought suddenly flashed through her mind, and it hit her like a sharp stone to the temples… She had been avoiding the thought, fighting it since the day she left the farm, and it finally crept into her mind now that she was sitting safely within four walls.

She thought of her mother…

And when she did, something like guilt began to settle in her stomach and it was certainly disagreeing with the fish.

I should've told her, she thought, and then her eyes began to swell unwillingly. *At the very least, I should've left a note…*

She breathed, slowly and deeply. What Robyn had done, as with most of her decisions, she had done spontaneously. And she certainly had no time to give her decision much thought. At the time, the only thing she knew was that her brother was leaving. He was leaving without any assurance that he would ever return. And this was something she simply couldn't live with.

You never abandon family, she repeated in her mind. *Never.*

After days of struggle, she had very little time to think about her mother or the twins until now. And she was starting to regret allowing her mind to yield to those thoughts.

You never abandon family... And yet... you abandoned them, Robyn.
You left them behind to chase after John.

She breathed again. This time, Nyx placed a paw on her boot as if he could somehow read her thoughts. She tried to distract herself from the guilt, but her mind wouldn't let go of her mother.

She missed her... She missed every lecture, every shout, every argument...

She missed the way her mother would pull at her blankets in the mornings to force her awake. She missed how there would always be a cup of tea ready for her when she woke up in the morning, along with freshly made cornbread on the table.

She even missed Margot and Melvyn, as much as they irritated her.

She missed their mockery, their tricks, their defiance... She missed chasing them through the farm when they laid their hands on her beloved bow.

She missed *all* of it...

What would mum say if she saw you right now, Robyn?

How would she react if she knew her oldest daughter was traveling through the Woodlands with a cursed warrior and an orc?

Would she be angry? Or proud? Would she ever trust her own daughter again?

A single tear ran down her face, but she wiped it away before it reached her cheek.

"Are you all right, Lady Robyn?" asked Nyx.

"I'm fine," she lied. "I'm just worried about John."

"He's a brave young man. I do trust that he is alive and well."

"I hope so, too," she smiled at him, or at least *tried* to.

A loud belch interrupted them. The Beast wiped his slobbery chin with his wrist and proceeded to dunk his head into the container of water by the horses, ignoring the fact that it was infested with slobber and dead bugs. Robyn didn't know whether to scowl or chuckle, so she did both. The Beast came back up and looked more than refreshed; drops of thick, slimy water dribbled down his green jaw and black beard.

Nyx sighed deeply. "Why not," he said, and then moved towards the water himself.

Robyn remained silent, leaning back against the wood. Her eyes met the Beast's for a moment; so humanlike and ordinary they were, nothing like she had ever envisioned an orc's eyes to look like. Then again, she didn't know exactly what to picture. In her mind, she'd pictured their eyes to be either pitch black or bright red, something sinister, something from a storybook.

It baffled her how someone so similar to her could be regarded as a monster and shunned for it. Why were they the ones who were shunned, when there were humans out in the world who were far more unpleasant? Humans that would most *certainly* think twice about fighting an ogre to death in order to save some farmgirl they just met...

The Beast rested his back against the wood, a good distance across from Robyn. Now that he had washed off the dirt from his bare chest, the girl noticed just how deep and severe the scars on his chest were. The three lines ran diagonally from the upper left side of his chest, where his heart was, down to his lower right abdominal area. She had noticed them when she first saw him at the Brotherhood camp, but not this closely nor well lit. Something had given him those scars and it *had* to have been something big.

Nyx rose out of the water then, coughing and spitting out chunks.

Chunks of *what* exactly, Robyn preferred not to know.

And then something a bit unexpected happened.

The Beast *spoke*. "Refreshing?" he asked, though it sounded more like a grumble.

Robyn's eyes widened and she glanced over at the orc with a surprised grin.

Nyx spit out a bit of slime. "Sickeningly so," he replied, and then shook his head and body like a wet hound. Unsure of how to react to the orc's sudden decision to converse, Robyn sat up straight and cleared her throat.

"Sh-Should I, um... Should I perhaps ask Miss Rayna for a proper drink?" she asked. For a moment, she wasn't sure whom she was asking. And when the Beast ignored her, she turned her gaze over to Nyx.

"If by *proper*, you mean ale... then *certainly*," the fox said.

"Anything for *you*, Beast?" she beckoned for him.

The orc ignored her again, instead he unstrapped his axe from his belt and began to sharpen it the way he usually would when he was angry or nervous. Robyn felt a dash of annoyance; the fact that the orc had said four words since they met and the fact that his axe did *not* need any further sharpening didn't help. Before she could stand, however, Kiira the elf approached the stables with a tray of overfilled tankards.

"Thought you could all use a drink," she said.

"Is it *proper*?" Nyx asked.

"Hmm?"

"Never mind."

"*Thank* you, Kiira," Robyn said with a smile. Much to her surprise, the elf girl smiled back. It wouldn't have been as unexpected if the only other nonhuman Woodlander she had ever met carried a grimace that appeared to be permanent. As Kiira handed each of them a tankard, Robyn took a moment to examine her. She was more slender than most humans, and her arms were long enough that her wrists were nearly at level with her knees. Unlike the Beast, Kiira had no fangs rising out of her bottom lip; her teeth were like that of a human's. Only her sharp ears and the color of her skin were different. She was dark blue, the color of the sky on a cloudy day, and her short curly hair was dark glistening silver.

"Do I have something in my teeth?" Kiira asked suddenly.

Robyn stumbled in her words, embarrassed to have been caught staring. "Oh… N-No, I… Sorry, I was just…"

"What? Never met an elf that served tables before?"

"Never met an *elf* before…"

Kiira chuckled as if Robyn had made a joke, her mystical grey eyes glancing at Nyx and the Beast, the most unlikely pair of traveling companions. "Oh, you're not joking?"

Nervously, Robyn shook her head from side to side and drank from the water tankard.

"Huh," Kiira exhaled, squinting her eyes pensively. "You're a peculiar one… I *like* ya."

Robyn felt an instant relief, suddenly able to laugh with ease. She was so distracted that she didn't notice the folded towels beneath the tray in Kiira's hands.

"By the way, Miss Rayna asked me to bring you these," the elf smiled as she handed Robyn the white cotton towels. "Just in case you needed clean ones."

"Oh!" Robyn's eyes lit up. "I… Yes, *thank* you!"

"I get it," Kiira said with a head nod. "You're on the road long enough, you overlook a few things. Sadly, it always comes back to remind you, doesn't it?"

Robyn chuckled with her. "That, it does."

Kiira glanced at Nyx and the Beast again. It might have been the orc's scar or the fact that he was sharpening his axe, but something about him made Kiira shiver. They thanked her for the food and the drinks, all except the Beast, who hardly acknowledged she was even there.

"Oh please," Kiira said. "It's only water. It's the least we could offer."

She went back into the tavern, and Robyn tucked the clean towels into her rucksack, neatly folded. Even after Kiira left, the Beast said nothing and kept working on his axe, refusing to look up. He looked so lost in his thoughts that Robyn simply couldn't help but pry.

"So… How'd you come across that axe?" she decided to ask.

There was no answer. Nyx gave her a sudden look that urged her to stop, but it only made Robyn more curious. *Come on, say something… You've done it before, you can do it again…*

"Did one of the rogue raiders give it to you?" she asked.

Rather than answering, the Beast rubbed the stone harder against the steel as if trying to overpower the sound of Robyn's voice. His breathing became louder and heavier, and sweat was starting to build at his temples.

"Beast? Are you there…?"

There was a grunt, and then his fingers slipped. The stone fell on the dirt, stained with trickles of red. The Beast growled and held his right hand on his left; the cut between his finger and thumb was minimal but it was leaking down to his forearm. There was a startled grunt in the distance. Edmund, Miss Rayna's adopted ogre son, had fallen asleep by the tavern door and was woken up by the orc's growls.

"Gods, a-are you all right?" Robyn asked, genuinely concerned.

The Beast was glaring at Robyn, breathing heavily through his clenched teeth.

"What do ye want from me, scrap?" he finally spoke to her.

Robyn hesitated. *How does one even answer such a question?*

"N-Nothing," she said calmly. "I was... just trying to talk to you."

"Why?"

Her eyes narrowed. "*Why?*"

"What's it to ye?"

She exhaled sharply, scoffing at his unnecessary defensive tone. "Because we're *traveling* together," she said. "And I... I don't know. I was only trying to be friendly."

"You 'n' me aren't *friends*," he growled.

"Then who *are* your friends? The Brotherhood?"

The Beast's eyes widened with rage and he exhaled sharply through his nose.

"Let it go, Lady Robyn!" Nyx warned her. The look on his face was far more serious than she had expected, like someone who had seen his share of horrors in his life and knew exactly when to push and when to retreat. Robyn cleared her throat, realizing she may have gone to far.

"I'm sorry," she said.

The Beast's glare lost a bit of its ferocity. His jaw loosened a bit and his eyes softened.

"I... I didn't mean to pry," she added. "I know what it's like to love your weapon. I never go anywhere without *Spirit*. I was only curious, that's all." She gulped down the last of the water on her tankard and began settling herself into a corner, using her rucksack as a pillow.

The silence that lingered was rather uncomfortable, so much so that Nyx rested his chin against the dirt and tried to doze off so that he didn't have to sit through it. The Beast rested his back against the wall, a bit more relaxed now. He grabbed his axe and sunk the blade into the dirt the way he usually would, glancing at Robyn as if he was expecting her to sit up and keep arguing, but she'd turned to face the wall by then.

He sighed, so deeply that it sent a cloud of fog into the air.

"My *father* gave it to me," he mumbled suddenly.

Robyn sat up with a jolt. Her eyes were so shocked they may have been on the verge of tears. *Well I'll be damned...*

"I see," she said. "Well, it's *beautiful*..."

The Beast replied with a simple "Aye" and a head nod, and then rested his shoulder against the dirt, facing the wall. It was minimal, but Robyn smiled all the same. And then, with a new shred of hope in her chest, she nestled herself again and closed her eyes.

* * *

The guard barracks were far less luxurious than the rest of the palace grounds. They were simple squared dwellings made of stone, dozens of them stacked together in long rows, with wooden stairs and balconies arrayed along the brick walls, and instead of lanterns there were lit torches hanging from iron rings at every fifteen feet. Simple and colorless, and yet Adelina Huxley felt more at ease *there* than she did when she was being escorted through the elegant halls of the king's palace.

"Right this way," said the guard, a sweaty man in his forties dressed in steel armor. The uneven landscape made it so that they were already on the third floor when they reached the barracks, and below was an empty field of dirt the size of Merchants' Square, where the king's soldiers would regularly train. The stone dwellings surrounded the entire field, enough to lodge some 200 soldiers, but the Huxleys were lodged in the room nearest to the palace gardens.

As they stepped onto the wooden balcony, Adelina could see the black gates that led to the outside, to the field of green and the edge of Lotus Creek. She could almost visualize John darting out of those gates, could almost see the malignant raiders dressed in red running through the field after him. She even kept a curious eye out for footprints on the dirt but could hardly see anything under the moon's dim glow.

The guard led the Huxleys into the cold dark room; there were beds set up along the walls, six of them, all with only a single bedspread and a pillow. The rest of the room consisted of a blackened fireplace, a couple of wooden bedside tables, and half a dozen hooks on every wall for hanging coats and belongings. It wasn't entirely clean and there were spider webs on every corner, but Adelina was never one to be ungrateful. At the very least it was a roof.

As the guard hung a lantern on the inner wall, Adelina stepped foot inside, followed closely by her children. She smiled at the man as convincingly as she could; after everything they had been through, every smile was an effort. The guard appeared friendlier than the rest, as if he was one of the few that didn't entirely hate his profession.

"Thank you," Adelina said to him. "Mister…?"

"Hektor."

"My thanks, sir," she bowed.

Two other guards carried Evellyn and Aevastra inside and laid them both on a bed. Aevastra was still alive, but she looked as if any breath could be her last. Two servants entered the room, one carrying blankets and extra pillows, and the other a tray of tea. Behind them walked a young woman that Adelina had never seen before; she was dressed like a noble but her timid demeanor spoke very differently, particularly when she began helping with the tea. The room was so crowded that Adelina failed to notice the shadow outside of the doorframe, an elegantly dressed shadow with a firm posture, standing still on the wooden balcony as if she was not welcome inside. Adelina instantly recognized her under the torches' flickers, for it was difficult not to notice a presence like Lady Brunylda Clark's.

"M'lady," Adelina took a bow; she almost wanted to embrace her for what she'd done, had it not been frowned upon, and the fact that the Lady was frighteningly intimidating didn't help either

"I've sent for the curator," Lady Brunylda remarked. "In the morning, I'll have a few men sent to your farm to sift through the rubble and recover anything of value. We will also take care of the bodies for you."

"My sincere thanks, m'lady," Adelina replied with another bow. "Truly, I don't know what would've happened if you hadn't arrived. My family and I are forever in your debt. Thank y-"

"Stop doing that," the Lady interrupted somewhat coldly, though she appeared more tired and worn out than angry.

"Pardon me?"

"The bowing," the Lady clarified. "You need only do it *once*. You're a person, not a mule."

Adelina wasn't sure how to react. She wiped her sweaty hands on her blue housedress, before nodding her head and saying, "Right. Thank you, m'lady."

Lady Brunylda replied with a mere head nod, before the handmaiden-turned-bookkeeper Brie interjected. "M'lady? I would like to stay and help, if that would be all right…"

"Don't be foolish, girl, there's no need for that," said the Lady. "We'll send someone else."

"I-I *want* to, m'lady," Brie insisted, an honest glimmer in her eyes as she spoke.

The Lady gave her a half-glare, one that conveyed a small trace of respect. *Want to?* She pondered. *The girl's either simple or she's got a bigger heart than I thought.*

"It's not that I'm not thankful for the opportunity you've given me, m'lady," Brie explained. "I *met* John Huxley during the attack on the palace grounds… He protected her majesty. *And* myself. The least I can do is try to help his family in any way I can. *If* that's all right with you, m'lady."

Brunylda gave her one last head nod. "Very well," she said.

Brie smiled, bowed, and began spreading blankets over the two unconscious women. Adelina was grateful for the help, but her discomfort towards the notion of being a burden was keeping her on her feet. And when she turned and realized the Lady was looking right at her, she froze from the unease.

The Lady Treasurer of Val Havyn, herself, Adelina thought.

It was frightening to be standing in the same room with her... This was the very same Lady that had met with Lords and noblemen of every city and village Adelina could possibly think of. The very same Lady that received death threats from the Merchants' Guild due to the amount of taxes they'd been requested to pay and yet she stood her ground as brave as any knight of Val Havyn. Everything Adelina knew of the Lady was based on mere stories and rumors and yet none of them could prepare her for that feeling in her gut when she looked right into those owl-like eyes of hers.

"Your name's Huxley, is it?" the Lady asked.

"Yes, m'lady," Adelina replied, careful not to bow this time.

"That took quite a bit of nerve, walking into the city grounds with an orc woman and child," the Lady said, with an expression on her face that was too difficult to read. Adelina fought through the knot in her throat, and even Brie and the Huxley twins couldn't help but eavesdrop from a corner.

"Would you care to join me for a drink in the courtyard tomorrow evening?" the Lady asked abruptly.

Adelina felt the tension leave her shoulders instantly, a look of surprise plastered on her face. "I... I'd be honored to, m'lady."

"Very well," Brunylda remarked. "Good evening to you."

And with that, she left the room.

Adelina sighed, somewhat glad the conversation was over. It was a strange feeling, to admire and yet be frightened of the woman all at once. And she had every right to; Lady Brunylda Clark was just as deadly as any knight of the king's court, only she used her words instead of a sword. Even the way she walked was intimidating; her manner was firm and graceful and her pace was quick, so much so that servants had to scurry along to keep up whenever they walked beside her.

The Lady cut through the palace courtyard, for it was the fastest way to reach her tower. Under her breath, she cursed the never-ending spiral of stairs she would soon have to climb. However, as she made a turn along the brick path that would lead her across, her feet came to a halt.

The gardens were as elegant as usual, except for the two fountains and the statue of King Rowan that had been damaged during the attack. At the very center of the courtyard, in front of the headless statue, was a round table made of white marble with four padded garden chairs set up around it. There was a parchment and a jar of wine on the table, and sitting in one of the chairs was Lord Regent Darryk Clark, quiet and brooding and drunker than he was proud of. For a moment he was the spitting image of King Rowan, except brown-skinned, younger, and without the bushy beard.

Sulking like a child, Lady Brunylda thought to herself, fighting the urge to scoff. *Why, he's more like a king than I imagined, the poor fool...*

She sighed and kept walking, well aware that there was no way to avoid him, not that Darryk looked in the mood for any form of conversation. He looked exhausted and worn out, bags under his bloodshot eyes, a broken man, not at all the look of a knight. When he heard the footsteps behind him he craned his neck, just enough to catch a glimpse, but there was no reaction on his behalf. Normally, in the presence of the Lady, he would either argue with her or become flustered. This time Darryk did nothing; he simply sat and stared into space as he took more sips from his silver goblet.

Good... Ignore me. You're doing us both a favor, the Lady thought.

She walked past him without a word. The only sounds in the courtyard were those of the flowing fountain and Brunylda's heels. But just before she made it to the other side, Darryk spoke through his discomfort.

"Good evening," he said, his voice weak and raspy.

"It will be. Soon."

She kept on walking, but just before she reached the door to her tower her feet came to a halt again, this time upon hearing the unexpected words come out of Darryk's mouth.

"Thank you," he said.

Lady Brunylda took a moment to gather herself; every part of her urged her to hold her tongue. *He's your Lord Regent,* she had to remind herself, over and over again. With a deep breath, she turned to face him. She could hardly make out his face under the moonlight; had it not been for the lanterns nearby, he would have been nothing but a shadow.

"For?" she asked as she stepped towards him.

And then she saw it... that look of shame and despair in Darryk's eyes. It became clearer with every step. He was no longer the Lord Regent, or even Sir Darryk Clark, the knight. He was a simple man drinking his sorrows away.

The Lady almost felt pity for him... *Almost.*

"For what you did out there," Darryk clarified. "If you hadn't intervened, gods know what they would have done... And for that, I thank you."

She came to a halt across from his table. "Don't thank me," she said, a bit colder than Darryk had hoped for. "Just do your duty, my *Lord.*"

Darryk closed his eyes briefly. 'Exhaustion' was not exactly the word to describe his state that night. For only a week, he had been Lord Regent, and already he felt his head would implode from the strain. He had no idea what he was doing, and having the Lady looming over his shoulder scoffing at his every mistake was of no help. He felt enraged all of a sudden, but he fought hard to suppress it. When he finally spoke again, he was glaring at the Lady just as coldly as she was glaring at him.

"Please don't mock me," he said gruffly.

"*Mock?*" she raised a brow. "You made a fool out of yourself out there... Have you any idea how fast rumors spread in Val Havyn? Believe me, my Lord, it isn't *my* mockery you should be concerned about."

"My Lady..."

"*Never* show them weakness. Do you understand me? The *moment* you show them weakness, you lose them all... Did they not teach you that in Roquefort? Or did they pat you in the back and pamper you even when you failed?"

"I didn't ask for this," he confessed grimly. "I never wanted *any* of this. I never wished t-"

"If pity is what you're searching for, my Lord, you're wasting your precious time."

There was a brief silence. Darryk lifted his goblet to his lips and poured what was left of the wine down his throat. He then looked back up at the Lady with a frown.

"It's *Darryk*," he said, his eyes glistening. "I've asked you enough times to call me Darryk."

"I heard you," the Lady remarked. "I simply chose not to listen."

She tried to walk away. She felt irritated and tired and wanted nothing more than a good night's rest. Darryk, on the other hand, allowed for his frustration to take over... and so, in a drunken flash of stupidity, he beckoned her back in the worst way he could possibly think of.

"Did you mean it?" he asked in a rather informal way. Once again, he wasn't speaking to her as the Lord Regent, or even a knight for that matter. He was simply Darryk.

"What?" Brunylda craned her neck with a scowl.

"The deal you made with Sir Viktor Crowley," Darryk said, admitting for the first time that he'd known about it all along. "When you loaned him the coin for his journey, did you actually mean to help him win his knighthood back? Or was he merely a pawn to you?"

Lady Brunylda Clark felt her entire body grow hot with rage. Far too many times she had been doubted, confronted, treated like a crook... She'd be damned if she allowed it from her own nephew. She approached him again, this time with a far more intimidating glare.

"You doubt me?" she asked.

Darryk felt himself sink into his chair for a moment. He cleared his throat and tried to ease the tension. "I care only for Sir Crowley's well-being, my Lady. Doubt is inevitable."

"Is it now?" she asked, stepping closer towards him. "Why is that, I wonder?"

"Why...?" he raised a brow. "I just told you, my Lady, I onl-"

"No," she interrupted. "No, you did not... Look me in the eyes..."

And so he did... for a split second, until he realized he was no match for her petrifying glower. Instead, he lifted the jar from the table nervously and poured more wine into his goblet.

"Look... me... in the *eyes*," she repeated.

Darryk set the jar down, took a sip, and looked back up. He could almost feel the fire radiating from her. Suddenly he wished for his armor back.

"Why do you doubt me, my Lord?" the Lady asked him.

Darryk had no proper response. Or rather, he knew that anything he said would be the wrong answer. He only kept his eyes firmly on hers to avoid any further disapproval.

"Is it because I'm not a knight?" she asked him. "If I was wearing a suit of armor and the king's crest, would you doubt me still?"

He sighed deeply, the guilt creeping into his chest instantly. "No, my Lady…"

"Ahh," she scoffed. "So in order to earn your trust, all I need is a sigil on my chest, is *that* it?"

She took yet another step closer…

"Or do I need a cock between my legs as well?"

Her words stung Darryk's chest like a dagger. He had no reason to doubt her, he knew. Though she was his relative, he hadn't formally met her until he arrived in Val Havyn. He'd heard the rumors of her ferocity, but nothing more. And rumors were often just… well, *rumors*. He took yet another sip of the wine as he thoroughly conjured a proper response.

"I, uh… I see that I have offended you, my Lady…"

"*Offended?*" she scoffed again, staring him down as if he was a child.

"I'm sorry," he said, setting his goblet down. There was a silence, a rather uncomfortable one, as the Lady leaned in just a foot away from his face.

"I would *never* break a contract, boy," she said, much more coldly than she had ever spoken to him before. "The mere fact that you would even question that shows just how little you know of me… You may doubt me all you'd like, but my word *alone* is worth more than a thousand signed contracts."

She then took Darryk's goblet from the table and lifted it to her lips. She emptied it entirely down her throat, the whole half-goblet, and set it right back down with a cold stare.

"Do try and remember that," she said.

And with that, she walked away… leaving the Lord Regent of Val Havyn to drink himself to sleep in the palace gardens.

* * *

Hudson Blackwood looked much more alive again. The color was returning to his cheeks by the minute, he was smiling again, and he could hardly stop himself from drooling as he cut himself another slice of honeymelon. He felt the sweet juice cleansing his parched throat, bringing him slowly back to life after being unconscious for over twelve hours. Suffice it to say the man was so ravenous he felt he could eat five whole rabbits and still have enough room left for another slice of melon.

Nearby, John Huxley was on his knees digging around a pile of rubbish. He found mostly old clothes and empty rucksacks there, but there were a few gems among the clutter. He reached deep into the pile and pulled out what looked like leather armor straps only with more hooks and belts than were normal.

"Are these for training?" he asked.

"Maybe?" Hudson replied as he glanced from afar. "They might also be for torturing."

John dropped the leather straps instantly, wiping his hands on his brown trousers with a scowl. "Well... I never would have guessed pixies to be so..."

"Strange?"

"*Curious*," John corrected him, suddenly coming across a pair of boots with rusty plates still attached to them. He pressed the soles against his own boots to check if they'd fit him.

"Ah yes," Hudson said. "Inquisitive little things, they are. Really brings a whole new meaning to the phrase '*be back before sundown or the pixies will get you*'."

John smirked. He'd recuperated most of their belongings, including the silver blade that Viktor Crowley had gifted to him, and kept on sifting through the pile as if it were treasure. Some of the things *had* to have been several years old, based merely on the dust, rust, and mold. He found a few old daggers, a loaf of stale bread, three wool blankets, an emerald ring, a pair of leather gauntlets, a rusty old guard's helmet, and two purses with a few coppers still inside.

"Keep looking," Hudson said over a mouthful of fruit. "Anything worth some coin?"

"A few trinkets here and there," John said, taking a moment to admire the massive pile, enough to fill the common room in his mother's cottage. "How could they have gathered all of this? They're so... *small*."

"*That* surprises you?" Hudson chuckled. "Carrying three unconscious bodies to safety wasn't intriguing enough, eh?"

John said nothing; he hadn't stopped to consider that at all. So small and yet somehow they had fished them out of the river to safety. Or not *they*... but *her*? The aura surrounding them was eerie, that much was certain, but so far they had only seen *one* of them.

One pixie, the size of his palm, and yet she managed to save them all.

Fascinating, was all John could think to describe her.

As he dug into the pile again, the tips of his fingers brushed against something cold and smooth like glass. Out of an old sack, he pulled out a dark green bottle labeled '*Roquefort Liqueur*', still about two thirds full. The clinking must have been loud, because before he knew it, Hudson dropped the melon skin and said, "Oh, you beautiful bastard..."

John gave him a half-smirk, squinting his eyes to read the rest of the faded label. "I'm not sure it's any good," he said. "Might be a bit old."

"All the better," the thief said with a snap of his fingers, motioning for John to bring him the bottle. The skin on his shoulder was healing rather fast thanks to whatever it was the pixie had done to it, but it was still a bit tender and delicate, and the thief was careful with his movement. John walked over and sat by him on the vast bed of leaves, green and blue under the moon's unusually bright light. He removed the cork from the bottle and handed it over.

Hudson snatched it and took a good gulp. His eyes widened. He was fully awake now.

"Fuckin' hells," he said, pressing his eyes shut from the sting. "Here."

He handed the bottle back to John, who took it doubtfully.

"Is it... *okay*?"

"No," Hudson gave in and coughed loudly, his tanned cheeks tainted with a shade of red. "But the faster you drink it, the drunker you'll get and the less you'll taste it."

John smiled and, with a shrug of the shoulders, took a sip.

It was strong... *Quite* strong, more so than any whisky or rum he'd ever had.

"By the gods," he said. "Who in their right mind would drink this?"

"Nobody," Hudson snatched the bottle from him again. "Only two kinds of people drink Roquefort liqueur, mate. Cold-blooded murderers and those who are too damn smart for their own good. Either way, not people you should ever cross."

Noted, John thought.

Suddenly a bright glow flew into the scene. Sivvy, the eerie blue pixie, hardly paid them any mind. Instead she floated above the pile of rubbish and grabbed the first rucksack of clothes she saw. With a surprising amount of strength, she lifted and carried it away with as little effort as one would rip a dandelion from its roots.

The sight of her left John a bit bewildered.

Hudson, on the other hand, simply smiled and said, "Never underestimate a pixie, mate."

He handed the bottle back to John and allowed him to keep it for a few moments, his eyes suddenly becoming more troubled and distracted as the liqueur began to kick in. "What happened back there, anyway?" he asked.

"You mean after you fell to a slumber and scared us half to death?" John asked, trying his best to match the level the humor the thief would often convey. "Not to worry. We won't be hearing from that bastard or his little beast again. Syrena made sure of it."

Hudson nodded, his gaze drifting into the distance. John took a whiff of the bottle before taking another drink. The scent was strong and pungent with a hint of something sweet like cinnamon.

"How is our dear Syrena, anyhow?" Hudson asked, and John noticed the unusual look in the thief's eyes, radiating with something like concern. The witch had been gone for nearly an hour; Sivvy had taken her to a nearby pond to wash herself, and John realized this was the third time Hudson had asked about her since she left.

"She's fine, I suppose," John said, his eyes softening. "She wasn't *hurt*, if that's what you mean."

"Good," Hudson replied modestly, unsure of what else to say. "That's, um... *good*."

John smiled and decided not to comment further, realizing the thief was coming to terms with the fact that he was indeed fond of the witch. He took a careless gulp from the bottle, forgetting how strong it was, and reacted in a most shameful way; Hudson couldn't help but burst with laughter.

"Careful now, mate! I warned you. That stuff's a bit strong for a farmer."

After a few coughs, John smirked and returned the sarcasm. "Piss off," he said. "A farmer can drink. We're just as fit and able as any mercenary or knight."

"Sure. If you say so."

They continued to pass the bottle between themselves and the expression of content in both their faces grew with every sip.

"I'll bet you couldn't do *half* the things I do," John challenged him in a friendly manner. "D'you even *know* how to use a pickaxe?"

"Of *course* I do..." Hudson remarked, "...as a *weapon*, that is."

They laughed, and for a moment there was not a single concern in their minds, save for the concern of the bottle reaching its last drop. Whatever hostility Hudson felt towards the farmer was starting to fade. And the same went for John; the man had threatened to kill him and yet he'd saved him *twice* now. Suffice it to say that John hardly felt the need to keep his sword handy anymore.

Nearby there was a soft rustling of leaves, but the two men hardly paid it any mind.

Behind a row of shrubs a good fifty feet or so away, a pond of freshwater glistened under the moon's light. A beautiful crystal clear pond, it was. Its water was lukewarm and its scent was sweet and crisp, unlike any water in the kingdoms of Vallenghard or Halghard.

Syrena of Morganna stepped out of the pond, nude and dripping wet.

She closed her eyes gently, took a deep breath, and concentrated...

Not two seconds later, her entire body began to exude smoke as the water evaporated from her scorching hot skin. It was a neat trick she had learned at the age of five. *Accidentally*, of course, but her best tricks had been learned that way.

Within a minute, she was entirely dry except for her the tips of her hair, and then she felt the cold wind prick at her smooth skin like arrows. She shivered and dropped to her knees in front of her belongings. The clothes she wore had seen better days. It had been over a week since Adelina Huxley lent them to her; there were tears on the hems that weren't there before and they were starting to reek. She was about to slide into the blouse when suddenly the sound of flapping wings startled her.

Sivvy flew in from behind the shrubs, carrying a sack that was easily twenty times her size and yet she held it the same way she would have held a grain of sand. She dropped it near Syrena's feet, and the witch noticed a bundle of relatively clean clothes inside. She looked up at the pixie's eyes, so radiant and blue like the ocean.

"Thank you!" she said with a smile.

Sivvy's head tilted slightly to the left and her eyes blinked twice.

Peculiar creatures, the witch thought to herself, and then realized she preferred Sivvy's company than that of the average human.

Suddenly and by instinct, Sivvy's head twitched… It may have been minimal, but Syrena felt her heart skip a beat. Sivvy had glanced up into the trees and became suddenly frightened. Syrena noticed another bright glow coming from above; she hadn't noticed it before because the entire place appeared to be glowing. But she saw it then… A much brighter glow, it was…

There were more pixies hiding among the leaves above them. Sivvy released an almost violent hiss and flew towards them, and the other pixies scattered away like flies. After a brief moment Sivvy came back down, gently and carefree as if nothing had happened, and Syrena felt almost silly for worrying.

You peculiar thing, she thought again. *I do hope you stick around…*

* * *

Old Nyx woke up to a sudden cold breeze and instantly turned towards the spot where he'd last seen Robyn, only to find there was nothing there but dirt. He heard a soft grunt nearby and leapt to his feet, wary and alert, his nose twitching as his eyes searched everywhere for the girl. He shook the dirt from himself and took a walk, brushing past the Beast along the way.

When he heard the grunt again, he realized it was coming from inside the stables.

It wasn't so much the darkness that bothered him, but more so the idea of Robyn practicing while drunken raiders or travelers could've been lurking nearby. He walked deeper into the stables and came across a long corridor with a dozen horse stalls on each side. And there, at the end of the corridor, Robyn stood with her bow held ready, aiming an arrow at the wall.

Nyx kept quiet at first. The girl appeared lost in concentration. She had set up a bundle of hay against the stables' wall and had drawn a target on it with a piece of coal; there were two arrows already sticking out of the hay, both of them missing the target's center by just a couple of inches. When she let go, her arrow missed again and she grunted angrily for the third time.

"Can't sleep?" Nyx finally asked.

Robyn was only a few feet away, but the fox could hear the subtle gasp of surprise under her breath. She looked restless and fidgety, the way a person would look when caught in a rebellious act, and yet with a shoulder shrug and a brusque exhale she shot another arrow. She missed a fourth time, and then she threw her bow on the dirt with a groan of despair.

"Bit late in the night for that, don't you think?" Nyx asked as he cleared his throat.

Robyn slouched herself against the wood and slid down to a sitting position, all the while running an agitated hand through her tangled black curls.

"I *had* him, Nyx," she sighed. "He was sitting right there…"

Nyx took gentle steps towards her, realizing she wasn't exactly in a perfect state of mind. "The Captain?" he asked, and she replied with a hesitant nod.

"Right in *front* of me, he was," she said. "I had a knife to his throat… Why didn't I just do it? Why did I let him live?"

Nyx sat next to her the way he often would, just close enough for comfort but far enough that they weren't touching. "Would you like the jovial answer or the honest one?" he asked.

"Neither," she grunted. "I'd *like* to figure it out for myself…"

There was a moment of silence. Robyn hoped she hadn't insulted him, but she persisted all the same.

"Very well," he responded calmly. "How *do* you feel?"

She sighed. *If only it was easy to answer such a question…*

"Angry," she said first, then bit at her lip. "Restless. Impatient."

"Good," he remarked. "And have those feelings ever helped you?"

She scoffed. "See for yourself," she gestured towards the pile of hay. He didn't need to glance to see the arrows sticking out inches away from the center.

"Yes. That certainly doesn't look right," he said, still as calm as a snail.

"I can do it," she said, still trying to make an impression. "I *know* I can. I've done it before!"

"Well… what's changed since then?"

"I dunno," she stammered.

"What's missing now that wasn't before?"

"I dunno!"

"Do you not?"

"Look, it's not the same!" she snapped at him. "It's *not* the same shooting at a pile of hay than shooting a person. It's just *not*!"

Nyx remained silent. He knew the girl was smart, *too* smart for her own good, and was willing to give her the nudge that Mister Beckwit would often deny her. But he also knew that she was a unique soul… Far too stubborn to listen and learn from others' mistakes, she preferred to *make* the mistake and learn from it on her own. Robyn Huxley didn't want to be taught to survive, she preferred to *live*.

"I'm sorry," she said nervously. "I didn't mean to shout at you, I only… I just meant that it's much more different out here. I'm not shooting at wood or hay or even those damn wolves. And it's *not* the same without Mister Beckwit or J..."

She hesitated, feeling a knot building in her throat.

And there, Nyx saw it, a sparkle along the edge of the girl's eyelid.

Had he palms instead of paws, Nyx wished he could say he'd comfort her... But even then, he was far too reserved for it. The most he was willing to do was sit and allow for her to use his shoulder for comfort, should she need it. But the girl wiped her face before she allowed the first tear.

Ah, Nyx thought. *At least the girl's growing a thicker skin... Good.*

"Y'know, he never doubted me," Robyn spoke suddenly. And though she wasn't crying, Nyx could see the anguish in her glimmering pupils. "John was the *only* one who encouraged me. Always. *Always...* When mum or Mister Beckwit would only see a stubborn inexperienced child, John saw me for me."

Nyx felt a tug of his own in his chest. He had to look away and stare at the stable walls to avoid further seeing the pain in the girl's expression.

"When Mister Beckwit would scorn me for missing, John would simply smile and say '*Fetch it and try it again*'. Always," Robyn kept on, struggling through every word as if it ached her. "I would get so angry... A few years back, I nearly broke *Spirit* in half, had it not been for him... He gave me a good shove and said, '*It's not the bow's fault. It's you*'... He said, '*If you spend your whole life telling yourself that you **can't** do something, then you never will... But you can do anything in this life. Absolutely **anything**. You can save the world someday, if you try hard enough*'."

She paused there, and this time a tear ran down her cheek without her knowing.

And as she struggled through every breath, she finally said, "He told me to try telling myself *that* and see how well it worked. And... From that moment on, any time John was there, I never missed a single shot. Never."

The wind began to pick up, bringing with it a cloud of dust that made Robyn wince mildly. Nyx glanced at the pile of hay again, at the two arrows far from the center of the target.

So peculiar, it looked... So unlike Robyn...

"So what's wrong with now?" he decided to ask.

The girl sighed, brushing the dust from her face.

"Well," she said, somewhat coldly and despairingly. "John's not here anymore, is he? He's off doing great things, not worrying about anything that should ever happen to *me*."

She rose to her feet, brushing the dirt from the rest of her clothes as she fought back the incoming tears. Nyx wanted to say something... He wanted to tell the girl how strong she was. He wanted to tell her that she had no need for John, that the courage was within her regardless. Instead he said nothing, for he knew that it wasn't his place to say any of that.

"We've a long day tomorrow," she said, leaning over to pick up her beloved bow. "We should try and rest." She began walking away, but Nyx couldn't bring himself to follow her. He sat there broodingly, sighing gently, reminiscing on the memories that had long been buried somewhere in his mind.

Of course, he had suffered loss. Immortality was just as much a gift as it was a curse; having everyone you loved pass away while you sat and watched was surely worse than dying. And after decades of pain and agony, Nyx had learned to shield himself entirely from it. In that brief moment, however, there was a shred of vulnerability that he couldn't help but succumb to. He turned his gaze towards her, his sole eye glowing under the moonlight as it always did, and she came to a halt when she heard him speak again.

"Why didn't you run...?"

The question puzzled her at first. She turned to look at him where she stood.

"What d'you mean?" she asked.

"Back there with the ogre," he said. "I *told* you to run. Several times. Why *didn't* you?"

It might have been the wind, but Robyn could see that a tear was building up in the corner of his grey furry eyelid, and his blinking wasn't hiding it a bit.

"Why did you stay?" he asked again, as if her silence bothered him.

"I... I don't know," she said with a shrug.

Nyx sighed. "Every person I've met in the last two hundred years has looked at me the same way they would look at an orc or an elf," he said. "I'm no different to them. I'm just another freak... Why risk your life to save mine?"

Robyn stared into his eye far longer than she should have. She wanted desperately to hold him tightly in her arms, to show him that not everyone in the world was cruel and wicked. Instead, she responded with the first thing that crept into her mind.

"How about *friendship*?" she said. "Or *loyalty*?"

"You would be loyal to a freak...?"

Her smile was warm and affable and it seemed to lighten the tension in Nyx's posture.

"You're not a freak, Nyx," she said. "You never *have* been. You're family."

Nyx's head dropped, and the single tear he'd been holding on to for dear life fell with it. She approached him, bent on one knee, and lifted his chin up, her hands wrapped around his furry cheeks as her own watery eyes met his.

"As mum always said," she smiled. "You *never* abandon family..."

And with that, she threw her arms around him, and Nyx allowed for her embrace to overwhelm him. They remained in silence for a while, before the cold wind picked up again and made them realize how late it was.

"Come," Robyn said, and they proceeded back to their resting place.

Little to their knowledge, however, there was a pair of ears that had been eavesdropping on their conversation in the darkness. And when Robyn and Nyx went back for a good night's rest, the Beast faked a snore and tried desperately to appear fast asleep.

* * *

Every step was agonizing. Every second, an eternity.

She breathed gently through her nose, hoping it would relieve some of the strain and yet all it did was worsen it. If having to tell someone they were going to die felt this way, Adelina Huxley could only imagine what it would feel like to receive such news.

The situation was all too familiar to her... She cared far too much, and that was often her problem. She would throw herself into other people's lives and try to fix them, knowing very well it wasn't her responsibility to do so. And in the end it was always her who was left to deliver the news, to her own mother and father, to her deceased husband, to that sick peasant woman she found in her barn 23 winters ago, seeking shelter from a storm.

It was *always* Adelina Huxley that looked after them in their final moments. And there she was, in the guard barracks of Val Havyn's royal palace, on her way to deliver the news to Aevastra. She was to look the orcess in the eyes and tell her that her child would be left motherless.

She entered the dusty old room... There she was, the poor thing, lying on the rickety bed, bundled in shabby old blankets, looking mere seconds away from death. Adelina sat on a chair next to the fireplace and waited. The only other soul in the room was Evellyn Amberhill, resting on a bed in the other end of the room. Several minutes passed before Aevastra opened her eyes and began muttering in her mother tongue.

"*Min neno queridu... Duandi aestas...*"

Adelina stepped gently towards her. "Hello, my dear," she said, and realized it was the first time she ever spoke so warmly to a nonhuman before. Aevastra's weak, baggy eyes were searching the room. "It's okay," Adelina placed a warm hand on her shoulder. "He's fine. The kids took him to the kitchen for some warm milk."

The orcess's eyes sunk back to their frail weakened state, awaiting the news. She knew what was coming before Adelina even had the chance to start. "I-I'm so terribly sorry," Adelina said, her voice breaking and struggling through every word. "The Lady Clark has sent for every apothecary in the city, but... So far, none of them had the necessary ingredients for the remedy..."

And then she watched... It began with the dropping of the eyes and brows, as if the energy was already starting to fade away from her. Then came a deep exhale, a grinding of the teeth, and a shiver. Adelina tried to lend a comforting hand, but there was nothing that could ever comfort someone from death. It was an inevitable horror with no reprieve.

443

"I'm deeply sorry, my dear... Truly..."

Aevastra's yellow eyes were glistening with tears, but none were falling just yet. She looked up aimlessly at the brickstone ceiling, blinking again and again as she took it all in.

"They say there might still be hope among the neighboring villages, but... The poison will have spread dangerously by the time they find someone with a cure..."

Another deep exhale, this time bringing a cloud of fog with it.

"*Nu importah lu que pasu en aeste mundoh,*" Aevastra mumbled. "*Solo recuerdus quedahn.*"

Adelina's chest began pounding with both fear and angst. The orcess looked as if she was trying to be at peace, but her expression seemed forced and full of despair. Attempting to understand, having heard many stories of the Woodland dialect, Adelina arched her brows and said, "It matters not... what happens in this world...?"

"...Only memories stay," Aevastra finished the translation for her, and then solemnly added, "Better this way."

Adelina couldn't quite find the words to say. She began caressing Aevastra's shoulder as if she were a lifelong friend. "Don't say that... There may still be hope..."

There was a brief silence in which Aevastra's breathing sunk into a painful huffing. It sounded rough and beastlike and yet mournful all at once. "Hope...?" she said, her voice faint and broken. "There is no hope..."

What does what even say in moments like these? Adelina pondered. Many times, she had lived them and yet every time she was at a loss for words. "Th-That's not true," she said. "My family and I... We've survived countless times on nothing *but* hope... It's the one thing we've never lost. Our lives depend on it."

Aevastra's neck bent as she looked right into the woman's eyes, and they remained there for several moments. Adelina couldn't quite make out the expression on the orcess's face. There was a deep sorrow there, it was clear, but there was also a hidden rage, one that the orcess fought hard to suppress. Out of both respect and caution, Adelina removed her hand and dragged a chair to sit closer to the bed.

"Your lives..." Aevastra said, "...are worth living... Not mine."

Adelina's felt her own eyes begin to swell.

"That isn't true," she said, nodding her head gently from side to side.

It felt strange to her, to feel such sorrow towards an orc woman that she had only just met, an orc woman that had aimed a knife at her upon first meeting. Strange, and yet she couldn't help it. She knew she would have done the same to protect her own children.

"You don't know," Aevastra groaned suddenly, and Adelina could do nothing but listen. The orcess struggled through every breath and yet she persisted like a resilient lioness. "You don't feel what I feel," she said. "To live *every* day... in fear... in world where they remind you of what you are.... in world where they remind you that you are not welcome... that you are less than nothing..."

Aevastra's words were interrupted by a violent cough, a painful one, and a few tears escaped her eyes at the same time. *"Hubieres dejadu qu mi llevehn,"* she said, then reiterated, "You should have let them take me."

Adelina's brows lowered. *Stop this... Stop this now...*

Her hand moved again, this time towards Aevastra's own hand. Upon first contact, the orcess opened her eyes again and looked down. She was far too weak to grip the woman's hand in return, but she didn't have to. The woman seemed reluctant to let go.

"No..." Adelina wiped her tear-stricken cheek with her free hand.

Never did Aevastra imagine she would see such concern in the eyes of a human. Even among her clan, she hadn't seen it. And, in that moment, she was thankful and at peace with the thought that, at the very least, her last moments would be in the presence of someone who genuinely cared.

"Listen to me," Adelina said firmly. "You *matter*... d'you hear me? Just like *anyone* else, you matter... You have been a mother to that child and you have protected him like *no* mother ever has. That child is living proof that you matter... d'you understand?"

Their eyes became locked on one another...

So different and yet so alike, they were, like two trees of the very same forest.

Aevastra looked away first, her tears staining her pale green cheekbones. But Adelina beckoned her back instantly.

"Look at me," she said. "Look at me and tell me... what is your name?"

The orcess opened her dry rough lips. *"Aeva..."*

"Say it," Adelina gripped her hand tighter. "What is your name?"

"Aevastra..."

"That's right," said Adelina. "Nobody can take that away from you, d'you hear me? *Nobody*... I promise you, your child will know his mother's name..."

The rage had entirely vanished from Aevastra's eyes, replaced with something else entirely, something like genuine peace.

"I'll go and get him for you," Adelina rose to her feet slowly and headed for the door.

"Thank you," Aevastra said delicately, to which Adelina responded with a warm smile.

And they were the last words Aevastra would ever speak.

* * *

It took less than an hour before John Huxley felt the world spinning around him.

The thief, on the other hand, was holding himself quite well, as was customary of him. They sat alongside one another, their words sinking deeper into a slur with every sip. Little did they know their witch companion was watching from a distance, behind the row of shrubs, the blue pixie floating just above her shoulder. The bright glow that encompassed Sivvy had also diminished, as if the pixie could somehow sense the witch's desire to remain unseen and wanted to take part in it.

"I'm impressed, mate," they heard Hudson say. "The last man I drank Roquefort liqueur with collapsed only thirty minutes in."

There was a shade of pink around John's blue pupils and the expression on his face was one of tranquility with perhaps a bit of vertigo. Suffice it to say, the young man was unquestionably drunk. He turned to Hudson, who had suddenly fallen into a silence after his laughter faded. John was unsure of what to say to him, but he knew there was something in the thief's mind that needed to be said. To think that such a man had once been his foe was now a mystery to him. The dreadful feeling in his chest just a day prior, when Hudson had been shot by the raider's arrow, was far too real to ignore.

"Did she, uh…" Hudson began, but the knot in his throat was strong and irritating, so much so that he cleared his throat and closed his eyes, as if he knew he would regret what he was about to ask. "Did she say anything to you?"

John smirked at him. It was rare for the thief to disclose any form of emotion, much less *concern* for someone, and it had come as much a surprise to Hudson as it did to John. Meanwhile, in the darkness, Syrena of Morganna felt her heart skip a beat upon hearing the thief's words; the pixie above her shoulder appeared to be just as invested in the pair's conversation as she was.

"She was, um… Well, she was worried for you," John said, his voice placid and slurred. "She may not have said it, but… She *was*. We both were."

Hudson took a deep breath. It may have been the liqueur, but he looked as if a wave of sorrow had suddenly plummeted over him, as if he was just now realizing he had nearly faced death. His eyes looked weary and his gaze wasn't set on anything in particular other than the bed of leaves in front of him. He placed the cork back on the bottle and laid it to rest beside him, all the while keeping the same troubled expression on his face.

"When that man shot me back there," he said. "Do you know what was the last thing that crossed my mind before everything went black?"

John said nothing, only listened attentively.

Hudson seemed to be in a sort of trance as he spoke.

"I thought… *'This is it, Blackwood. This is how you go'*… followed closely by… *'You should've told her how you felt when you had the chance, you insensible Son of Nobody'*…"

Syrena of Morganna's entire body was still scorching hot but she instantly felt a chill, sweat building at her forebrow and temples, a puff of fire erupting from one of her thumbs accidentally. She took a step back, deeper into the darkness, out of view from the two men.

"She's um… She's remarkable, that one," Hudson went on. "Remarkable, and she doesn't even *know* it… Her hesitation is her only weakness. She thinks less of herself than what she is. Truly, I… I must admit, I…"

Syrena fought through her nerves. She'd never wanted anything more in her life as much as she wanted to step out of the shadows at that very moment. She wanted to walk up to the thief and ask him to finish his thought. Her feet wouldn't move, however. She was caught in something of a trance herself.

No man had ever disclosed such feelings towards her, despite her beauty. The fact that she was a witch had been a curse all of her life when it came to any form of human connection. Even her own father had sold her as a child, wanting nothing to do with her. And to hear the thief speaking about her so differently, so strangely, it terrified her. Her orange eyes began to swell and the tightness in her chest was nearly unbearable. It was a feeling she wasn't accustomed to and yet she found herself half-smiling.

"D'you know what the sad part about all of this is?" John asked, breaking the silence.

Hudson glanced at him vulnerably. "What?"

"These may be the first serious words I've ever heard you speak… And yet I'm not sure I'll remember them in the morning." John stumbled drunkenly to his feet and gave his friend what he hoped would be an encouraging tap on the shoulder.

"Tell her, Hudson," he said. "I may not be the smartest man…"

"You're not."

"Shut up," John smirked, and then finished his thought. "But I *do* know a thing or two about regret… Don't waste another moment, mate."

Hudson looked up, and though it may have been mostly due to the liqueur, he smiled.

John nodded and smiled right back. After a brief moment, however, he placed a quick hand on his grumbling belly as his face went pale. "I think it's best that I lie down," he said, then walked off into the darkness.

Hudson Blackwood remained in that bed of leaves. Any other night before all of this had begun, he would have reached for the bottle next to him, but something stopped him this time. He had no need for it. He grabbed it and tossed it as far as his feeble arm would allow him. Once he did, his soggy eyes gazed serenely into the distance. He had never before seen such beautiful forest life. He knew the glowing of the leaves may have been in part due to the pixies hiding among them, but he did not mind it one bit. He was smiling.

Then his eyes caught something… There was an unusual movement among a nearby row of shrubs. A shadow stepped towards him, wearing a pair of leather trousers, boots, and a grey shirt that may have been cut out of a dress. Sivvy flew gently away into the trees and allowed the witch her privacy.

Their eyes met in the glimmering darkness. The thief was looking at her the same way he'd looked at her when they were escaping Val Havyn's dungeons together. And she felt her chest would implode from the anxiety; she had that quailing feeling she would often get when she was among a large crowd or at the center of attention. But unlike all the previous times, she didn't feel the need to run.

"There you are," Hudson spoke first. "You were starting to worry me…"

"Don't fret. I can fend for myself," was all Syrena could muster the courage to say.

"I wasn't worried for *you*, love, I was worried for *me*. Stay close will you?" he said. And then he shot her that mischievous, coquettish wink of his, a wink that she found oddly irresistible.

"Are you feeling well?" she asked, her lips curved into a smile.

"As well as I'll ever be."

Syrena sat next to him on the bed of leaves. Hidden beneath so many layers of black, she hadn't noticed just how oddly bright Hudson's white calico shirt looked on him now that his coat and vest were off.

"You certainly *look* well," she said, still unsure if the thief knew she had been listening to his previous conversation the entire time.

"You're far too kind, darling," he said with a grin. "This was my favorite shirt, you know. *Now* look at it. It's ruined."

"That, it is," she chuckled. "That blood stain surely won't wash off."

"Didn't mean the blood. If anything, it helps me look more menacing. It's the damned hole the arrow made. Even stitched up, I'll look like a filthy vagabond."

She smiled at his wit.

There was a brief pause, during which the thief couldn't quite find the proper words to say.

"Enough about me," he cleared his throat. "How are *you*, darling?"

Her hands were trembling. She could feel the eyes among the trees watching her. She could almost hear their whispers and hisses. And every now and then, she could see the shadows scattering away like flies thanks to Sivvy. Deep down, she knew she was merely glancing about, distracting herself, to avoid Hudson's gaze. She wanted very much to tell the thief everything. How she felt back in the dungeons, how she felt when he stood up for her in the middle of Val Havyn when nobody else would, how she felt when he so much as *looked* at her with those conflicted eyes of his.

But through the grating tension, all she could say was, "Fine…"

Hudson smiled and gave her a nod, suddenly wishing he still had the bottle of liqueur. For a while, the only sounds in the air were that of crickets and the flapping of wings in the distance. The sounds were like a harmony and the moon's perfect light was something from a dream.

"I just wanted to say," Syrena muttered. "I-I'm *very* happy that you're still here."

"Well… I'm not nearly as strong as *you* are," Hudson said. "But I think I have your friend in the trees to thank for that. Don't know what she used for this wound, but I'd like the recipe."

Syrena chuckled. And in that moment, it was the sweetest sound to Hudson's ears.

"That bloke wasn't too much trouble, was he?" he asked. "After I dozed off, I mean."

"Not at all," she said. "Believe me, I've encountered much worse."

"I'll bet… What *is* the worst you've encountered?"

She hesitated. The knot in her throat had returned, and this time it was sharper than it had ever been. And yet something in the thief's eyes relieved it. She saw something like genuine interest in them and it was somehow giving her the courage to speak.

"Be careful what you ask," she warned him.

"Where's the fun in that?" he grinned.

She smiled again, and with a deep sigh she began.

"I was a girl of fourteen," she said. "I was living with a clan of witches up north. They practically raised me since I was a child, after a hunter killed my mum and my father sold me into slavery. They were… *kind* to me, for the most part. They weren't the friendliest, but they had killed the slave traders that transported me and I was thankful for that. Anyhow, after nearly a decade with them, our differences got in the way. We didn't see eye to eye on many things, and so I ran away to live on my own."

She paused for a moment and closed her eyes. Her hands began to shiver. And soon after, they began to ooze a trail of smoke, as if by instinct. It may have been the rage in her heart disturbing her hands the same way they were causing that sting in her chest. Or it may have been the fear of opening up to someone. Whatever it was, it vanished suddenly after something rather unexpected happened.

Hudson placed his hand against hers, despite the intensity of the heat that radiated from them. His hand must have been blistering, and yet he showed not the slightest sign of pain, only interest. He moved closer towards her, slowly and cautiously.

"Tell me more," he whispered.

Her bright eyes stared at him with a hint of skepticism. The smoke oozing from her hands began to diminish, as if the thief's rough callused hands had somehow cooled them down. The shivering, however, was still there, along with her nervous breathing.

"No one's ever been this interested before," she said.

"Try me, love…"

She became lost in his gaze. She hadn't told her story to anybody in ten years, much less a human. What came more as a shock, however, was realizing that no one had ever touched her hands before. It was something that hadn't quite crossed her mind until that particular moment. Even the one man she had laid with had been skeptical about touching her hands.

And yet there she was… Hudson was not only holding them, but he was caressing them gently with his thumbs. Her heart was racing, but she didn't mind it at all. In fact, she wanted very much for his touch to last forever.

"It was the worst winter I've ever lived through," she went on. "Even with my gift, I couldn't keep myself warm… There were so many nights when I thought I wouldn't live to see the sunrise."

She paused. And then he leaned in even closer.

"Tell me more," he said.

"I decided to return to them," she said. "To the witches… I must've walked a hundred miles 'til I reached their cabin… Only…"

"Yes…?"

"It… wasn't there anymore. It had been burned down. To this day, I still remember that awful smell. The smell of death… Unfortunately for me, the raiders that had killed them were still nearby. They found me and put me in chains…"

They were already a mere foot away from each other and yet Hudson leaned in closer, slowly and carefully. And Syrena did the same. Their eyes were locked on one another as if caught in a spell.

"Tell me more," Hudson whispered again.

"They thought I was a peasant girl that happened to be lost. They… *teased* me. They said such horrible things… But they didn't know I was also a witch… So when they tied me down, they didn't bind my hands in leather."

She paused. Her eyes began to shine brighter than was usual and her lower lip began to quiver as the first tear ran down her cheek. The thief's hand was still on her warm humid hands. He used the other to gently wipe the moisture from her face. And then with a faint whisper he said, "Tell me more…"

"I…" she suddenly felt weak and feeble. The only thing that gave her strength in that moment was the look he was giving her. And it was all she needed. "I killed them all," she said. "They begged me… they pleaded for their lives and I just… *killed* them. I was only thirteen… Those witches were all I had left in the world and they *took* 'em from me. And I wasn't there to help… I felt such rage inside of me, I could no longer hold it back, and I… I killed them all. Mercilessly, I turned them into ashes and walked away as if it meant nothing."

Her voice had grown drier by then. For the first time in ten years, she had told someone what she did on that dreary winter's dawn. And yet there was no regret. The thief only held her hands tighter.

"Good," he whispered. "You *saved* more lives than you took, love. You do *know* that, right?"

She looked into his eyes and saw the sincerity in them.

"You are a ruthless wild beast, darling," he said. "And you should *never* apologize for it… It's what makes you bloody magnificent."

The silence lingered for several moments. Their faces were no more than three inches apart by then. She could nearly feel the warmth of his lips against hers, nearly taste them. But then her gaze lowered nervously and she chuckled softly.

"What is *this*, then?" she asked. "The famous Hudson Blackwood… flattering a *witch*?"

"Flattering a *woman*, my dear," he said, and then her gaze rose up to meet his once again. "An extraordinary woman with an impeccable gift… People hate you because they're bloody *terrified* of what you're capable of… It is not I, Hudson Blackwood, that will make history one day. It is *you*, my dear. Think of it… Syrena of Morganna, Queen of the Woodlands… Queen of all of Gravenstone, for that matter… How grand would it be?"

"How charming," she chuckled. "But who would ever follow a witch?"

"I would," he said. "I'd be *honored* to…"

The aura surrounding them seemed brighter than ever before. Little did they know the pixies in the trees were watching and listening with awe. But to the thief and the witch, there wasn't a single presence that could have mattered to them.

"I thought you didn't serve anyone," she whispered.

"I don't," he said. "But you're not just *anyone*."

Then, it happened. Hudson leaned in, and she couldn't help but do the same.

Their lips touched for the first time.

But then the witch's skepticism and intuition got the best of her. Her hands released a sudden roar of flames and the thief removed his hand and backed away from her with one swift pull. When he looked at her, Syrena's eyes were vulnerable and threatening all at once.

"If this is just another one of Hudson Blackwood's trickeries to get into my knickers," she said, "I *will* tie you down and burn you alive…"

Much to her surprise, the thief was smirking at her.

"I'm *appalled* you would think that of me," he said.

His response loosened the sudden tension in her shoulders.

"Are you, now?" she asked doubtfully. "Need I remind you that I had to bribe you with sapphires to convince you to stay?"

Hudson placed a hand back on the witch's sizzling palms and used the other to graze her cheek. "Oh darling," he said, conveying his desire for her with a single gaze. "Do you *honestly* believe I agreed to stay for some measly sapphires?"

Despite his rough, callused hands, his touch was warm and gentle.

Never before had another person touched her with such delicacy. Her breathing began to pick up its pace, keeping up with the robust beating in her chest. Her hands trembled, and when the thief felt it he tightened his grip. It was then that the witch leaned in and their lips met once again, this time for good. She laid him down gently on the bed of leaves and sat on top of him. They may have been laying somewhere amid the Woodlands, but to them there was no one else alive in the world.

No one, but the thief and the witch…

Two lost souls that somehow found one another in a world full of treachery.

Two lost souls that were complete at last.

XV

Altercations

The Woodlands were known to be rather quiet at dawn. It was the only time of day when raiders, travelers, and woodland folk alike were all peacefully resting somewhere, whether in a tent, an inn, or somewhere high above a cypress tree.

Such was the case when a company of about fifty men was traveling west through a muddy path. Their muttering and the sound of their horses' hooves interrupted the peaceful silence, and the abundance of red leather they all wore made them stand out against the greenery like a bloodstain. There was a shred of light rising from the horizon, yet it had been nearly twelve hours since the company had stopped to rest.

Captain Malekai Pahrvus came to a halt and leaped off his horse, or rather the horse he'd managed to steal during the raid. A majestic white steed, it was, stronger and faster than any horse the Rogue Brotherhood ever had at their disposal. Malekai caressed the soft fur on its cheek as he stepped away towards the grass. He appeared distracted, and his raiders were starting to notice. As they all brought their horses to a halt, they took a gander ahead at their captain, some of them cursing his name while others kept silent from the intimidation.

"Somethin' the matter, cap'n?" Borrys Belvaine asked from afar.

But Malekai was far too preoccupied to pay him any mind. He bent down on one knee on the grass when he saw the torn rag, brown and red amidst a patch of green. He would have recognized the red leather anywhere, even from a half-mile away. He picked it up and examined it. The brown cloth was rough and wrinkled, and it dimmed in contrast to the red leather, about three or four inches in length before the tear.

The captain lifted the rag up to his nose and took a whiff.

"Wha' in all hells is he doin'?" one of the rogue mercenaries hissed angrily from afar. "I thought we was headin' to Grymsbi."

"Settle yourself, Clive," Borrys gave him a cold stare. "Just give 'im a minute."

"He's losin' it," Clive grunted, spitting on the dirt. "Obsessed with that littl' twerp, he is."

"For the last time, we ain't after the twerp!" Borrys said, defending his captain's honor. "We're off to Grymsbi to recruit more blades. And *if* any of you see the twerp…"

"There it is," Clive grunted. "He's gonna get us all *killed*, is what's gonna happen."

"Just shut your arse. He's coming."

As Malekai walked back towards Borrys's horse, Clive and the rest of the mercenaries stopped whispering among themselves, their attentions grasped once again by their captain.

"Recognize this?" Malekai threw the torn cloth at his right-hand man.

Borrys examined it confusedly. "It's ours, alright."

"Aye," Malekai grinned. "And it reeks of greenskin."

Borrys raised a brow. It wasn't until he noticed the trail of footprints in the mud that he realized what was happening. Some of the traces were large, like an orc's, and the rest were small like those of a young woman. "Y-You don't think…" Borrys stammered.

Malekai was grinning, chuckling, and nodding his head in a way only he could do. "They travel together," he said, staring into the distance and catching a deep whiff of the air like a hound hot on a trail. "They were here."

Some of the mercenaries were unsure how to feel. They hadn't eaten properly for days and they weren't sure when they'd have a chance to. They trotted along the path for another half-hour or so, until their noses caught a warm scent like that of roasting meat, along with a distant chatter and commotion, not the dangerous kind of commotion but more like the drunken brute kind.

"Well I'll be damned," Malekai said, dismounting his horse a second time. "Never thought I'd see *this* place again."

It was the infamous tavern, built into a tree, run by a fearless woman and her two sons, a raider and an ogre. It was early morning, and already raiders and travelers were stumbling in and out of the tavern doors.

"Just what we needed," said the mercenary named Clive, already lifting his leg up to hop off his horse.

"No," Malekai stopped him. "You lot wait here. I've some business to take care of."

Clive did not seem happy, nor did the rest of the rogue mercenaries. The only one that appeared slightly nervous about confronting his captain was Borrys Belvaine. "C-Cap'n," he stammered. "We ain't had a good meal fo-"

"I said you're to wait here," Malekai glared at them all. "You don't know these people. They don't take kindly to the Brotherhood. I'll have to handle this on my own."

Several frowns were thrown his way, but not a single man had the guts to stand up to him. And so, with a grin, Captain Malekai Pahrvus shook the dirt from his red coat and walked towards the tavern, leaving his band of mercenaries to wait within the trees.

Edmund, the ogre, was sitting by the tavern doors, drooling and snoring loudly as ever. A few drunken elves and orcs were lying just outside, also snoring their lungs out, and a goblin or two had climbed to sleep on the nearest branch.

Marvelous, Malekai thought as he walked carefully around the ogre and snuck into the tavern as subtly as he could. *Just bloody marvelous.*

Many times, he wondered how such a tavern had come to exist. Built into a tree, it was, and yet it was astonishingly warm and cozy and attracted several from near and far. The tavern was nearly empty, save for a few drunken brutes here and there. And the bard was playing a soft relaxing tune that was most proper for a light morning meal.

With a deep breath, Malekai walked up to the counter and took a seat, looking about as confident as a knight. "Give us an ale, will you love?" he asked, calmly and chivalrously.

An elf girl with silver hair served him, but her eyes were distracted as she wiped the counters clean. Malekai cleared his throat and popped the collar of his red captain's coat, as if trying to grasp her attention. He took a good sip of the ale and looked up.

"Fuckin' hells, that is good," he lied, giving her a look that was somewhere between friendly and creepy. "Is it made here? The ale?"

The elf girl said nothing, only shot him a forced smile and kept wiping the counters. Malekai felt a sudden surge of anger. He had never been particularly fond of being ignored. But he kept his ease as best as he could and continued with his act.

"Tell me, love," he leaned in closer to her. "How does a beauty like you end up working in a piss pot like this?"

Kiira looked up at him at last. She'd paid him so little mind that she hadn't even noticed the man was missing an eye. "Miss Rayna's been very kind to me," she said, shrugging his rudeness away as nothing more than drunken banter.

"Well, she better be if she wants to keep a gorgeous thing like you around," he said as he took another sip of the ale. "What's your name, love?"

At first, she didn't respond, focusing instead on rubbing the crusty stains off the counter. Malekai tried to force her to look at him by leaning in a bit more and craning his neck up so as to meet her gaze. "You there?" he asked.

Still, Kiira said nothing. And it was starting to aggravate him.

"It's rather rude to ignore a paying customer, y'know."

Then she stopped wiping, so abruptly that it caught him by surprise.

"Listen... We don't want any trouble here," she looked right at him with a poise of self-assurance. "I'm warning you now. One shout and our Edmund *will* throw you out."

Almost as if he'd heard his name in his sleep, the ogre sitting outside the doors gave a jolting snore and scratched his nose, on the verge of waking up at any minute.

"Whoa," Malekai held both his hands in the air as if conveying his vulnerability. "Ease up there, love... I only asked for your name."

Kiira squinted her eyes suspiciously. An orc suddenly walked up to the counter and grunted something along the lines of "*Mead*". As she served him, Malekai tried his best to appear calm and upright.

"All right," the captain said to her, once the orc was out of earshot. "I can see that you're quite busy, so I won't waste any more of your precious time. I'm not looking for any trouble... Truth is, I'm here looking for someone. An orc... A very dangerous fellow, not to be messed with. Been searching for days, so I thought I'd stop here for a drink and a conversation."

He paused there, looking the girl up and down with a suppressed hunger in his eye.

"You haven't seen him anywhere, have you love?"

"My name's Kiira," she said sternly. "And I'm sorry, but '*dangerous orc*' isn't really a good description 'round these parts."

"Ahh, my apologies. He's a raging beast with a sharp axe made of steel."

"Haven't seen 'im."

"And he's got three red scars across his chest..."

Kiira became suddenly startled. And Malekai was far too clever a man not to notice it.

"Ahh... there it is," he said with a slight grin. "Any idea where he's run off to?"

Kiira hesitated, but Malekai tried his best not to scare her away.

"I'm only trying to help here, love..."

"*Kiira.*"

"Right... Kiira," he paused to take another sip of the ale.

Kiira began wiping the counters again, somewhat nervous at the thought of having served a meal to that very orc just the night before.

"This orc," she said tensely. "How dangerous is he, exactly?"

Malekai fought the urge to grin; he had her hooked and he knew it.

"Oh, he'd kill just about anyone," he said, quite convincingly. "He's a lone beast, that one. If he's keeping you alive, it's only for his own good. The moment he doesn't need you anymore, he'll gut you and leave you for dead."

Kiira was starting to believe him, it was clear. She began looking around nervously for Miss Rayna, who was nowhere to be found.

"Have you any idea where I can find him, love?" Malekai asked, and then cleared his throat in a stammer. "Pardon me... *Kiira.*"

Kiira's lower lip trembled; her mind was fixed on the farmgirl that was traveling with the orc, the girl she had fed just a night prior, the girl she'd given clean towels to so that she wouldn't be troubled while on the road. The thought of that girl lying dead in a ditch somewhere frightened Kiira half to death.

"W-Why are you after him?" she decided to ask.

"Well," Malekai sighed. "Let's just say he... *took* something from me. I admit, it's not reason enough to kill him for it, but considering how many lives would be at stake if I allowed him to live, well... I'd say I'm doing us all a *favor* by hunting him down. Wouldn't want a cold-blooded savage like *that* roaming around our beloved Woodlands now would we, Kiira?"

Kiira grew even more nervous and twitchy. And so, with a deep sigh, she leaned in and whispered, "I don't know where they went exactly... but I did overhear them saying they were heading west. To a town called Grymsbi, I believe."

"*They...?*" the captain raised a curious brow.

Kiira hesitated. For a moment, she saw a look in the man's eye that wasn't quite as friendly as he made himself out to be.

"I'm only trying to help, my dear Kiira," Malekai said when he noticed her looking at him suspiciously. "*Anyone* who travels with him is in grave danger. He absolutely *cannot* be trusted."

There was a brief silence, as Kiira searched around for Miss Rayna one last time.

Come on, I've got you... I've got you and you know it, Malekai thought to himself. *Tell me now, my love. Tell me what I want to hear...*

When she didn't speak, he released a deep convincing sigh.

"I mean, I suppose it doesn't really matter anymore," he said, lifting the ale casually to his lips again. "Whoever *was* with him is certainly dead by now."

"A girl," Kiira blurted out suddenly. "A farmgirl with black curls... Sh-She was with this orc, along with a one-eyed fox... She was very kind, that one."

"I'm quite sure she was," Malekai said with a grin. "Thank you for this information, my dear Kiira. I hope to one day return with the news of this beast's death."

Malekai lifted the tankard up to his lips and began chugging the beer like water. Suddenly, however, a loud shrill voice startled him, causing him nearly to spit it all back out.

"What in all hells are *you* doing 'ere?!"

Malekai took a last painful gulp and set the tankard down, pounding his fist against his chest a few times to release the air. He then gazed up at the intimidating figure of an angry middle-aged woman in a red housedress and a tangled bun of grey hair.

"Pardon me, do I know you?" he asked.

"No," she approached him boldly from behind the bar. "But I know *you*, you murderous bastard." Miss Rayna's eyes had never been redder. Even Kiira stepped away in fear, as the woman faced the man fearlessly. A good half-foot taller, he was, though it made no difference to Miss Rayna. Had the bar not been between them, the woman may have struck him by then, or at least her eyes surely suggested it.

"Give me *one* good reason I shouldn't have my Edmund crush you like a fly right now!"

"Easy there," Malekai stood up from the stool with his weaponless hands out in front of him. "Why so hostile, love?"

"Get out. *Now!*"

"Could I at least finish me ale first? I did pay for it."

Miss Rayna swung her hand over the bar and shoved the tankard viciously. The ale splashed all over the floor, some of it sprinkling onto the captain's boots.

"Oh, darling. Tsk tsk," Malekai mocked her as he glanced at the puddle of ale on the floor. "You'll damage the wood that way."

"Worth it. Now get the fuck out!" she raised the bar and stepped towards him.

"You're a fiery one, aren't you?"

"Tell me, is your blood the same color as your leather?" Miss Rayna asked heatedly.

"Never checked, love."

"Call me 'love' one more time and we'll see."

"Easy there..."

"EDMUND!" she shouted.

The ogre just outside the tavern doors snorted and woke up suddenly. And with one last grin, Malekai adjusted his coat, bowed his head, and scurried out of the tavern, leaving a trail of tension behind him and a silence that lingered throughout the bar. He snuck around Edmund and kept walking, and the ogre was far too muddled and confused to even notice him.

Meanwhile, inside the tavern, Miss Rayna's rage died down slowly. And it was then that she realized how many eyes were on her. Miss Rayna's tavern was notorious for many quarrels much like these, everyone knew. But it didn't make the woman loathe them any less. "What're you all bleedin' looking at?!" she shouted furiously.

Nervously, the bard began playing again and the guests continued chattering among themselves. With a deep sigh, Miss Rayna walked back towards the counter, and Kiira stood there with a nervous look in her eyes.

"What did you say?!"

Kiira hesitated. "Um... N-Nothing, Miss Rayna..."

"What did you *say*, girl?!" she asked again, as if she could read Kiira's lie through a stare.

"H-He was searching for the orc," Kiira confessed. "The one from last night. The one traveling with the farmgirl... Th-That was all, I swear! I just told him they were headin' west..."

Miss Rayna turned towards the door as if trying to relive it all in her mind. And then she sighed, a long exhausted sigh, before muttering, "Damn it all to hells, Kiira..."

* * *

They were mere miles away from Grymsbi. Nyx swore he could practically smell it.

He sat perfectly still, his eye staring forward at the tip of a sharp arrow that was aimed right at his head. Though he could tell the arrow was sharp enough to kill him, he was rather calm, staring at the jagged tip as if welcoming it.

"Get on with it," he said.

But the arrow didn't move.

Had a passerby spotted them it would have made for quite a peculiar sight, a girl aiming an arrow at a one-eyed fox from just two feet away while an orc watched from afar. And it only became more peculiar when the girl grew restless and set her arrow down, and the fox urged her to shoot him again.

"The more you think on it, the harder it will be, Lady Robyn."

Robyn could hardly hold her grip on *Spirit*, her hands were so slippery. "I can't," she complained. "Not while you're staring at me."

Nyx sighed. "Will it help if I look the other way?"

"Please."

He tried, and once again Robyn couldn't bring herself to shoot. She stretched the arrow back and aimed it right between the fox's ears.

Get on with it, Robyn. You've killed loads of squirrels and rabbits without thinking twice.

And she had… but none of them had been Nyx…

She felt her fingers start to cramp, her palms growing sweaty again. She almost let go, but her fingers slipped instead and the arrow fell to the dirt before the bowstring could thrust it.

"Damn it… Give me a moment," she said.

"Fuckin' hells," the Beast said gallingly, reaching for his axe. "Move aside girl, *I'll* do it."

"No! I have this," Robyn said with a forced determination in her eyes. They were hidden among the trees, right at the border of the Woodlands and the kingdom of Halghard. It was the farthest out of the forest the Beast had ever traveled, and for this he was rather nervous. He tried to hide his distress, but it was far too obvious. Both Robyn and Nyx could sense it, because the orc was quite talkative all of a sudden.

"Then *do* it 'n' stop messin' about!" the Beast growled.

"I *will*. I got it!"

"Ye couldn't kill a wolf if it ran up 'n' bit ye in the arm!"

"I *could*!" Robyn glared angrily at him. "I *have*! Several times!"

"All right, ease up, you two," Nyx said as he stepped in between them. "I'll come right back, Lady Robyn, I promise you. One good shot will do."

"Or one good swing," the Beast muttered under his breath.

Robyn sighed anxiously and nocked an arrow again.

Come on, you… Just let the damned thing go…

Nyx made the mistake of looking up. He could see how much it pained her to do it. Reluctantly, she found herself loosening her grip again and putting her bow down.

"I-Is this *really* necessary? Maybe we coul-"

"Gods' shite," the Beast grunted suddenly. He stepped in front of Robyn and before she could protest, he brought his axe down with a single powerful swing. Robyn gasped and looked away; all she heard was the sound of steel sinking into bone and then a body dropping to the dirt. She didn't even have to look; the mere image in her mind was haunting enough.

"I said I *had* it!" she shouted at the orc. She wanted very much to punch him but couldn't bring herself to do it. The Beast yanked his axe out of the fox's head, and the look on his green face was stern and emotionless, as was usual of him.

"Did ye?" he shot her a glare. "Looked more like ye were pissin' yerself."

"I was *focusing*!"

"If ye need stop 'n' *think* about the kill, ye shouldn't *be* killing."

As they argued, Nyx's lifeless body began to emit a trail of smoke into the air. Robyn, however, was so enraged she hardly took notice of it.

"He's *my* friend! You had no right!" she argued.

"He *asked* ye to shoot, scrap."

"And I *had* the shot!"

"Right. And we woulda been standin' here all bloody night."

It was then that Nyx's body caught on fire, but still the girl and orc were too preoccupied shouting at one another to pay it any mind. Within seconds, Nyx's body twisted and turned inward, and soon it was nothing but a pile of ash.

"He's my friend. It wasn't *your* deed, it was *mine*!"

"Yes 'n' what happens when it ain't yer friend on the other end of the arrow?!"

Robyn hesitated. The orc was right and she knew it. "I-I would've..."

"Ye'd be dead. *That's* what."

"Piss off!" Robyn finally landed a shove on the Beast's shoulder.

The orc allowed it. *Once.* But he was growing more and more enraged with every one of her shouts. His eyes moved from his shoulder back to Robyn. "Ye done?" he asked.

"No!" she shouted. "Don't you *ever* hurt Nyx again! You hear me?"

"Who?" he raised a brow.

"My *friend*!! The one you just killed!?"

The Beast scoffed and walked away to sit on the boulder where he'd been sitting before.

"Hey!" Robyn walked after him. "I'm not finished talking to you! I *had* the kill!"

"No," the Beast said as he pulled out a whetstone and began sharpening his axe again. "No, ye didn't."

"What do *you* know of m-"

"Listen, scrap!" the orc roared. "This ain't yer farm no more! Ye best grow a backbone or ye'll be dead before ye set one foot out o' this damned forest!"

Robyn took in the orc's words like daggers to her chest. The knot in her throat was reassurance that he was right. She had killed a man before out of impulse, without intending to. The thought of killing someone else willingly was haunting to say the least.

They felt a sudden gush of warm breeze at their feet, and both of them lowered their gazes down to the dirt. The fox was gone; there was nothing there but a mound of ash. But then something peculiar happened.

The pile of ash began to move. There was still smoke rising out of it, but the pile began to shift into a different shape, as if something had been buried just underneath it. Robyn stepped closer first, and the Beast dropped his axe and rose to his feet, far too curious to remain seated.

"Wha' in all hells?" he grunted.

Robyn lowered down to one knee, careful not to get too close. The pile of ash began to morph into a rope-like figure, rolled up into a pile. The first thing that emerged from the ash was a reptilian-like tail, scales as black as coal with thin white stripes running across. The tail began to move and sway from side to side, as if adjusting to its new form. Then a small head rose out of the pile and Robyn couldn't help but yelp and hop to her feet, only to bump into the Beast's broad figure towering behind her.

"What is it?" the orc asked.

Robyn's lower lip trembled; she could hardly bring herself to look down. Nyx crawled away from the ash bit by bit, slowly coming back to life. When he spoke, it was as if his pink tongue had taken a life of its own. His voice remained the same but his *S*'s seemed to linger. "Did I misss anything?" he asked.

"N-Nyx, you're..." Robyn struggled to speak, the hairs rising at the back of her neck.

"Yesss?"

The Beast chuckled and shook his head. He began walking west towards Grymsbi, spitting on the ground along the way, a bit too close to Nyx's tail for his comfort. Meanwhile, Robyn remained where she stood, wide-eyed and jaw-dropped.

"Am I *that* repulsive?" Nyx asked.

Robyn tried to chuckle, but what came out was more of a loud nervous exhale.

She bent down to pick him up, her shivering hands slippery and weak.

"Not at all, Nyx," she said. "I, uh... I've just never been very fond of serpents..."

* * *

461

It was midday in the green plains of Halghard, and yet the sun was hidden behind a sea of clouds and the raging winds threatened the Wyrmwood camp with a potential storm.

Sir Percyval Garroway and his recruits rode slowly into the campgrounds.

Already they could feel the hostility in the air. It began when one of the watchmen caught sight of the troop and ran off as fast as he could to inform the others. The camp was vast, and right at the entrance there were a few tents and fires where the assigned watchmen would rest and trade places with one another. The only reason the watchmen allowed the troop to enter was because Sir Percyval was in the front lines. As they strode along the muddy path, the tents grew in abundance, as did the men. Carts and armory stands were set up at every twenty or so feet, all of which bore the green banners with King Alistair Garroway's golden emblem.

Sir Percyval had his chin up and his gaze forward, but through the corner of his eyes he could see his brother's soldiers staring, scowling, spitting on the dirt with disgust.

Keep riding, he told himself. *Let them stare.*

As they rode by, conversations would seize and soldiers would turn their gaze up, shaken and thrown aback at the sight of the nonhuman recruits riding alongside the rest. Others were spreading the word already, shouting unwitting insults like '*rabbits*' and '*moles*' to alert their comrades of the intruders striding through their camp. As the crowds gathered, the chattering grew… It was as if Percyval's troop was some sort of spectacle on display…

Nervous and wary, the Woodland recruits rode closely together. Some of the humans even moved their horses towards the edges, shielding their comrades from the soldiers' unwelcoming glares. But there was no way to hide them all. The elves and gnomes stood out like a wine stain on an ivory mantle. With the stares, of course, came the mockery. And both Percyval and his recruits knew very well to expect it.

"*What in all hells?!*" they grunted.

"*Is he bloody joking?!*"

"*Dirty freaks.*"

Percyval sighed. He had to fight the urge to confront the men with his blade. *Let them talk… It isn't their approval you need…*

In the distance he could see it, some fifty feet away, the only tent in the camp dyed moss green like the banners, with the golden emblem of the serpent wrapped around the lit torch painted on both sides. It wasn't a very large tent, for King Alistair was never one to boast, he was a man that believed in efficiency over comfort, and he was the only man whose consent Percyval strived for.

The gods are with us, Percyval told himself, over and over again. *No one will fall tonight. No one will fall, for the gods are kind to those who serve them.*

Riding among the elves and gnomes was Viktor Crowley, his eyes much less weary than before and his face with a bit more color. He looked alive again, no longer the weak and pale figure he'd been days prior. He no longer wore any armor; instead he was dressed like a common mercenary, with brown and black leathers in place of his steel. The shirt he wore had a hole in the chest where an arrow had struck the man that wore it before him.

Dead men have no need for things, he'd told himself, in an effort to ease the sick feeling in his gut when he stripped the man's body of clothes and weapons.

The new outfit suited him. He looked like the type of man that fought for himself and no one else, all the while remaining true to his noble bearings. Even when Cedric had tried to fulfill his squire duties and sharpen Viktor's blade, the man had refused, claiming Cedric should sharpen blades for no one but himself.

"So this is Halghard?" Skye asked, as always beginning a conversation from out of the blue. Viktor was no longer startled; he'd learned to expect Skye to sneak up and surprise him. In fact, they were the few moments in his day that he truly looked forward to.

"Part of it, yes," said Viktor. "Halghard is a vast kingdom with *many* cities and villages. Why, it's almost as large as the Woodlands."

Skye rode stiffly and fretfully, glancing everywhere with only their eyes. "Does it *always* smell this way?" they asked.

Viktor chuckled in a friendly manner. "That's not Halghard. That's the men."

"Never seen so many men in one place before," the elf remarked. And it was no overstatement; there were thousands in the camp.

"Most of them have never seen so many *elves* in one place, I'm sure. So long as we stay together, we'll be fine. Just keep your eyes ahead."

Skye shot him a smile, but it wasn't all that convincing. The elf was undeniably nervous. "You're looking better," they said.

Viktor's face lit up. "You flatter me... But thank you, I'm *feeling* better."

"Good. It'll serve you well on your journey."

"Yes, well... I certainly hope Viktor Crowley, the mercenary, will have better luck than Viktor Crowley, the knight, ever did."

They smiled, riding in silence as they fought the urge to glare back at the Wyrmwood soldiers. By then, nearly every soul in the camp was out of their tents. Raiders and sellswords, they were accustomed to; they had recruited a great number of them already. But it soon became obvious that the elves and gnomes would not be welcomed as warmly.

Even Cedric felt out of place as he rode near the middle of the formation.

"They're supposed to be on our side, are they?" the young squire asked nervously. He was riding next to Gwyn, as he had been for the past few days despite Thaddeus Rexx's objections.

"Really makes ye think, don't it?" Gwyn scoffed. "When ye feel safer in the bleedin' Woodlands than out here... it's how ye know the outside world is shit."

Cedric gulped nervously. Thaddeus Rexx, who was riding just a few strides behind, must've noticed, for it wasn't long before he remarked. "Settle down, lad. We didn't come all this way only to die in Halghard." Cedric glanced back and nodded. And then he realized Gwyn was silently rolling her eyes.

They kept riding. The soldiers appeared to be closing in on them the further down they made it through the campgrounds. Sir Percyval arrived at the king's tent and turned his horse halfway, glancing at his second-in-command Sir Antonn Guilara.

"Keep an eye on them, will you?"

Sir Antonn's eyes widened. "Are you joking?"

"Just for a few moments," Percyval said. "I must speak with our king alone."

"Yes," Antonn sighed. "And while you do that, who's to stop them from butchering us all?"

Percyval leapt off his horse and shot his second-in-command a grin.

"I think you can handle them. They don't call you Sir Antonn the Tenacious for nothing," he said. "Besides, fret not, my friend. The gods are with us today."

Sir Antonn scoffed. "Are they, now? 'Cause I can't see them."

Percyval straightened himself up and cracked his neck. And then, after one last deep breath, he stepped towards the king's tent.

"Percyval," Viktor approached the man just in time. "Will you be all right?"

"He's my brother," Percyval said with a shoulder shrug. "How bad can it be?"

Fifteen minutes later, the king's thundering voice was shouting something along the lines of *"Are you out of your fucking mind?!"*

The shout must have been heard for a mile. Sir Percyval had no other choice but to sit there and take in his brother's wrath.

King Alistair Garroway was a tall hefty man in his late fifties with a wide face, ebony-colored skin darker than Percyval's, and long grey dreads of hair that he kept tied behind his head. His meaty fists were shaking from the rage and as he spoke specks of spit managed to fly out and strike Percyval in the face.

"I only did as you instructed," Percyval argued calmly.

"I *instructed* you to recruit able-bodied men! Not a pack of savages!" the king snatched the parchment from the table and threw it in Percyval's direction. Percyval looked at the parchment as it floated gently down to the ground. The name of every human, elf, and gnome that had been recruited was scripted onto that parchment, and there were a few names that had been crossed off after the unprecedented attack.

"That's an overstatement, brother," Sir Percyval said, his voice still soft and composed. "If you just got to know one or two of them, you'd realiz-"

"Have you *any* idea what we've had to deal with in the last few weeks?!" Alistair paced around the war table and stared down at his brother. He was only slightly taller but certainly larger at the sides, as he always had been since they were children. At that moment, however, the king was not looking at Percyval like a brother, *or* a knight for that matter; he was speaking to him like a child.

"I'm terribly sorry, brother," Percyval said.

"You're *sorry*?!" Alistair shouted. "I lost five hundred men up north! Balthazar's men threw their bodies into the Rift! I've had scouting parties go missing! I've had watchmen butchered in the dead of night! And where were *you*?! Wandering through the Woodlands with a bunch of *rabbits*?!"

"Hey!" Percyval raised his own voice in protest. "Those men out there hav-"

"They're *not* men!"

"They've *risked* their lives to save mine! They marched all the way here to serve *you*, and *this* is how you greet them?!"

"You *brought* them here!" Alistair raised an angry finger at his brother's chest. "I never *asked* you to bring them!"

"I only did what I felt was right, brother..."

"What you *felt* was right?!" Alistair's owl-like eyes were growing broader by the second. "This is no time for politics, Percyval! We are at war! Have you *any* idea the loss of life that we've already endur-"

"Yes!" Percyval shouted. "Yes, I do! Which is why you need *every* soul that's willing to fight by your side, human or not! What difference does it make?!"

"What difference?!" Alistair's face began to swell with a shade of red. He took a moment to catch his breath and lower his voice.

Percyval knew to expect resistance. His only mistake, perhaps, was believing his brother's conscience would allow him to see things differently. But it was of no use... From the beginning, the man knew what was at risk. The dread he felt in his chest was agonizing, and the idea of confronting his recruits and telling them it had all been a waste of time was unbearable. He did not have the heart to do it, certainly not after marching all this way.

When King Alistair finally spoke again, he sounded more exhausted than angry.

"I'm hanging by a thread here, Percyval," he said. "The people of Halghard look to me for guidance. They call me their liberator, their true king... How do you think they'll react when they see me advocating for rabb-"

Percyval shot him a glare, so sharp that Alistair did not finish his sentence.

"What I'm trying to say, brother," the king rephrased himself. "Is that it makes no difference what you or I believe. It's one thing to try and convince me, we are *family*. But the *people*...? They will *never* accept them. They would much rather join Balthazar Locke than to be allies with Woodland folk."

Percyval took a seat again, looking quite exhausted himself. "What is it you've always told me?" he asked. "Nothing brings folks closer together than fighting a common enemy..."

"Yes. But in their eyes, the Woodland folk *are* the enemy."

"Because no one has tried to show them otherwise!" Percyval argued. "If you led by example, you could make a difference! You coul-"

"We've no *time* for that, Percyval. We can't abandon one battle to fight another," Alistair rose to his feet again. "The people of Halghard have suffered enough. They *need* us! With every hour that Balthazar Locke sits on the throne, someone is dying of starvation."

"And what of the hundreds that die in the Woodlands every day?" Percyval challenged him further. "Are their lives not worth saving, then?"

"That isn't *our* fight!"

"Is it not?"

"They're not *our* people, Percyval... Those soldiers out there risking their lives, *they* are our people. Their starving families are our people. You'd sooner die for a pack of savages rather than stand by your *real* brothers and sisters?"

There was a brief moment of silence. Percyval sat there with a stern face and a chest full of dread and defeat. He knew his brother wouldn't see reason by talking politics. And so he tried a different approach.

"Do you remember what mother used to say?" he asked calmly, and he could almost see the displeasure in Alistair's eyes.

"Of course I remember..."

But Percyval reminded him anyway. "*We are all equal in the eyes of the gods,*" he said. "*Who are we to pass judgment on those who have never wronged us?*"

Alistair sighed, slouching back into his chair while rubbing the side of his temples in a circle as if he was in pain. "I always knew it would come to this," he said bleakly. "You know I loved mother just as much as you did, Percyval... But the woman was living a fantasy. She filled your head with all that nonsense, and look where it's gotten us..."

Percyval felt his fist tighten almost involuntarily. For a moment he was afraid of what he might do if his brother pressed him further.

"The real world isn't a fairytale, brother," said Alistair. "I cannot risk losing more than we've already lost. Not now... Not when we've come this far... I'm sorry."

Percyval sighed, rising gently to his feet. He walked towards the entrance to the tent and took a gander outside, his mind racing with a million thoughts. He could see them all. His recruits had been secluded to the edge of the camp and were standing about, waiting for him, guarding each other's backs like proper comrades, humans and nonhumans alike. He closed his eyes briefly.

What a fool I was, he told himself. *To think it would be so simple...*

He glanced back at his brother. By then, Alistair was already huddled over his map, plotting his next plan of attack and hardly paying him any more mind.

"What do I tell them?" asked Percyval.

Alistair didn't even look up. All he did was shrug a shoulder.

"You brought them here. You can take them right back to where they came from."

Percyval felt his gloom turn into rage within seconds. He stepped towards the war table once more. "Are you that heartless, brother?"

"This isn't about what *I* feel."

Percyval's face tightened. "You're the bloody *king*. Yet you're still behaving like a knight."

"Watch your mouth, brother…"

"These are people's *lives* we're talking about! They marched all this way to fight for you! To start a new life, a *better* one! And you would dare send them back to their deaths?!"

"Enough!" Alistair stood up.

But Percyval was not backing down. He stepped valiantly forward and addressed the king in the same form as he had been addressed. "You would turn your back on them all simply because it doesn't benefit *you* to help them?! In that case, tell me, how are you any different than Balthazar Locke?"

Alistair was no longer shaking from the rage. The question had infuriated him to the point where his body would no longer move, only his lips. "One more word, Percyval," he said, "And I will remove you from my council."

"You don't have to," Percyval said. He then untied the green cape from his chest armor and removed the golden pin with his brother's sigil from his chest. He threw them both on the nearest chair, glaring at his brother as he stepped towards the tent's entrance.

"I remove *myself* from your council," he said, and then made way for the outside.

"Percyval," Alistair called for him, but the man did not turn back.

Percyval walked, as always, with his chin held up high. He had never been one to question his beliefs, as his mother had always taught him. *The gods are with us,* he told himself again, in an effort to lift his own spirits. *So long as we serve them, the gods will never abandon us…*

"Percyval!" he heard his brother shout.

But once again, the man did not look back.

"Goodbye, brother," he said, just loud enough for the king to hear.

And so it was that, as fate would have it, this was to be the last time the Garroway brothers would ever speak to each other.

* * *

With the sunrise, much of the aura in the pixies' lair lost its glimmer. In broad daylight, it looked like any other place in the Woodlands, green and fertile and astoundingly humid.

Still, when Syrena of Morganna awakened she found herself utterly in peace, a feeling that had been quite rare as of late. She was entirely nude underneath Hudson's coat. It had a certain smell to it that she couldn't quite grasp, like a blend of leather, sweat, and sweet liqueur.

She smiled. It may not have been the most pleasant smell, but it was *his* smell.

And rather than shy away, she pulled the coat up and nestled herself in it.

Next to her was Hudson, still lost in a deep sleep, just as bare and exposed as she was. As usual, her body naturally radiated heat and when she saw the cold bumps on his bare chest, she latched onto him to keep him warm. For the first time in a long, long time, the witch was happy.

To think that only weeks prior, Hudson Blackwood was a complete stranger, a mere story, a sketched portrait… It was strange, the way it all happened. Because in that moment, he was possibly the only person she fully trusted other than herself.

Even John Huxley, she couldn't fully trust. After all, had it not been for his reckless whims, Hudson would never have been imprisoned in Val Havyn… Then again, Hudson wouldn't have met Syrena either. The witch would have either died in the palace dungeons or hanged for her alleged 'sins'. Remarkable, the way fate worked.

Hudson's breathing began to deepen, as if he was having a very pleasant dream.

She looked up at him. So calm, he looked. So at peace.

How could such a conflicted man be branded a monster? She wondered. He was a murderer, that much she admitted. But so was she, and so were most people she'd ever met. It was simply the world she was born into. Carefully, she sat up and stretched her arms and back, trying not to disturb him. Gradually, however, his eyelids began to blink and his body began to turn, his mind slowly coming back to the world. He felt the heat of Syrena's body against his. And when he finally recalled where he was, he smiled.

"Good morning," Syrena spoke gently.

Hudson stretched himself, the wound on his shoulder nearly fully sealed and recuperated. "Better than good, darling," he replied.

"Better, eh?" she said as she lay back down next to him.

"I've a tendency to awaken with plenty of regret and sorrow," he remarked. "This is quite a lovely change."

She felt the heat overfill her body, only this time she was much more in control of it. In the thirty years she'd been alive, she hadn't felt so strong and able. She felt essentially unstoppable. And, of course, it didn't hurt having the thief by her side, this simple man who looked at her as if she was a queen while the rest of the world labeled her a freak. It made her nervous and aroused all at once.

"Careful what you say, now," she said with a grin.

"I never say anything I don't mean," he replied. "Which reminds me, I didn't talk in my sleep again, did I?"

She chuckled. "Not that I remember. You did moan quite a bit, though."

"I figured so. I dreamt I was in Roquefort, feasting on a plate of their famed smoked duck."

"That sounds delightful."

"We'll go there someday," he gave her a gentle kiss on the forehead.

"Will we now?"

"Someday."

She couldn't help but sigh somewhat hopelessly. "You're a dreamer, I see," she said. "Remember what happened the last time you set foot in a city?"

"Of course," he said, and then looked down into her strikingly orange eyes. "It was the best decision I ever made."

Her heart raced all of a sudden. Unable to withhold herself, she gave in to his flattery, grabbed him by the neck and kissed him. It felt just as it did the night before… It felt right.

Suddenly, they heard footsteps approaching, boots crunching against dry leaves. John Huxley looked tired and parched, his golden hair disordered and full of grease. His face and most of his clothes were riddled with specks of dirt and muck, suggesting he had passed out under a tree somewhere.

"H-Hello?" the farmer called out as he rubbed his eyes, his knees quivering weakly with every step. When he walked through the curtain of vines, however, he took one look at his companions and quailed all of a sudden. And when he saw the pile of clothes, he realized the thief and the witch were both nude under the black coat.

"Ohh dear…" he said, and then gazed embarrassingly up at the trees. "P-Pardon me… I'll just…"

"Don't look so bloody frightened, mate," Hudson sat up, chuckling.

Syrena grinned, holding the coat over her chest and reaching for her clothes.

"I-I didn't know that, uh…" John stammered. "That is, I-I didn't *hear* anything, I swear."

"How *could* you have? Your snores were much louder than we were."

"Leave him be," Syrena placed a gentle hand on Hudson's shoulder as he began to slide into his black trousers.

"Stop me when I lie," the thief smirked. "For a moment, I thought it was a bloody ogre."

John tried to chuckle, but he couldn't hide his discomfort. He moved and stood behind the vines, turning his gaze into the distance, allowing them some privacy.

"Sleep well, farmer?" Hudson asked as he buttoned his shirt up.

John groaned and rubbed at his temples. "Me head's killing me. Is it *always* like this?"

"The less you think of it, the less it hurts, I find," Hudson chuckled. "Have I ever told you about the worst hangover I've ever had? I went drink for drink with an orc once. Massive fellow with a great scar across his chest."

"N-No," John kept gazing about embarrassingly. "No, I don't believe you've told me."

As the thief and the witch finished dressing themselves, the place became more and more illuminated by the second. It wasn't the sun, however... The trees were abundant enough to shield them. It was a more eerie blue glow, and it was coming from the leaves above. Syrena was the first to notice, a strange movement in the corner of her eye, and instantly she felt vulnerable and exposed.

"Think we'll make it to Halghard today?" John asked, oblivious to the eyes watching them.

"Don't see why not," Hudson replied. "So long as we limit our rest, we can m-"

"Hudson," Syrena whispered anxiously.

The thief gave her a glance, and as if he could read the distress in her eyes, he felt a pinch in the back of his neck as if he was being watched. He followed her eyes and soon after that, John did the same.

A herd of pixies, silent and observant, had gathered in a swarm. And as the three misfits became captivated by their ghostly stares, more and more were flying out of the holes in the trees and crowded around the rest. Their entire façade may have been beautiful, but the look on their tiny gazes was not... They were eyeing the three travelers like a swarm of predators closing in on a prey.

"Um... What is happening?" John whispered.

Hudson rose to his feet as gently as he could. "Make no sudden movements," he said, stepping forward with a hand held out behind him, as if shielding his companions. The pixies appeared to be communicating with each other, hissing and whispering among themselves, far too softly for the human ear to pick up.

Syrena finished dressing herself, slightly panicking.

The pixies began floating down from branch to branch, creeping in on them. John couldn't help but step closer to his companions. For creatures so small, the farmer was surprised to find how startling they could be. Some even flew around them, so as to keep them enclosed, like a horde of wasps gathering around a rosebush.

"I thought you said pixies were docile..." John mumbled gently between his teeth.

"They are... For the most part," Hudson replied just as softly. "You ever hear of the Tale of Wingless Ehryn?"

"No... But I've heard the tune..."

"Then you know how it ends, right?"

There was a sudden sharp hiss, like that of a scream only higher-pitched and slightly muffled. The pixies began scattering like flies, as a handful of them appeared to be caught in a struggle while hovering in the air.

"What are they doing?!" Syrena whispered as she finished lacing her boots and stumbled to her feet. She moved closer to Hudson, her hands held out and prepared to attack.

The majority of the tiny creatures were staring down at the three of them as if keeping watch. But the struggling handful flew lower and lower, until Syrena was able to see what the commotion was all about. Five pixies had their claws dug deeply into the wings of one particular pixie, one with fiery red hair and strikingly blue eyes.

Syrena's mouth dropped. "Sivvy...?"

The way the pixies were behaving was almost humanlike, if humans were silent and six inches tall. They dragged Sivvy down to the lowest branch and pinned her down violently by the arms and wings. The poor redheaded pixie was squirming, trying desperately to break loose. Though pixies were physically unable to cry, she looked as if she was on the verge of tears, shrieking angrily as the rest of them dug their claws even further so as to keep her restrained.

"Sh-Shouldn't we do something?" John asked, but the three of them were far too shocked to make any sudden movements.

Suddenly a rather large pixie, one with wild blue hair, green eyes, and skin just as blue, flew into the scene; she was glaring down at the three misfits in a most unpleasant way. Her neck bent and her nose twitched as if she was trying to catch a sniff of them. She was the queen of the horde, that much was clear, not only because she was twice as large as any other pixie, but also because the rest would back away in fear when she flew near them. She glanced at Sivvy and then flew towards her with a glare so sharp it was haunting.

The queen hissed, sounding almost like a snake, and then the whispering around her died down to nothing. The knot in John's throat was quite real; he placed a hand on the bone hilt of his blade as if somehow he could do something.

"*Sivvyyyy,*" the queen pixie spoke for the first time. Her voice was much harsher than Sivvy's, and much deeper. She then glanced down at the three human invaders, glaring at them unwelcomingly.

Sivvy looked petrified. It soon became clear what was happening. Sivvy had done something wretched, something forbidden. She had brought *humans* to their nest. And pixies were known for many things but, little to human knowledge, mercy was not one of them.

The pixies holding Sivvy down stared attentively at their queen as if awaiting orders. The queen, in return, darted closer until she was just a palm's length away from Sivvy's face, glaring heatedly into her eyes. Then, amidst the silence, the queen spoke only one word. And though a pixie's voice was soft and mumbled, there was the slight hint of an echo when she spoke.

"*Cortahr!*" she said, and then she flew away to the top of the tree to be alone.

Sivvy began fidgeting, hissing and shrieking desperately like a wounded animal, and the other pixies closed in on her in a swarm and began to yank violently at her fragile wings.

"Well, shit," Hudson said, hardly believing his eyes.

"What are they *doing?!*" John yelped.

Sivvy shrieked again, her left wing ripping along the upper edge. Syrena felt an instant rage at the sight of it all. Sivvy's deed had been a selfless one; she had saved three lives, and she was to pay an unfair price for it.

Do something, the witch told herself. *Anything!*

Without a violent twitch in her left eye, Syrena let go of Hudson's embrace and stepped valiantly forward. "STOP!" she shouted.

The place went silent again. The pixies all glanced at the witch in unison. They may have seemed beautiful before but at that moment they were utterly terrifying, like a horde of wasps with a conscience.

"Darling," Hudson gulped nervously. "What are you doing?"

Syrena ignored him; the rage she felt was consuming her.

"Let her go!" she shouted at them. "We'll *leave*, okay? Just… Just don't hurt her!"

Another pixie, one that appeared to be male except slightly androgynous, flew in towards the witch and eyed her up and down in a most menacing way.

"*Cortahr,*" he reiterated for his queen, like a faithful knave under a spell. And then the rest of the pixies whispered the word repeatedly as if echoing him.

"*Cortahr,*" they hissed. "*Cortahr! Cortahr!*"

Sivvy, looking down at Syrena with despair, released one last shriek of pain as the horde began tugging at her wings again. And that one shriek was all it took for Syrena's rage to grow out of control.

A roar of flames made the pixies scatter away, all except Sivvy, who stumbled down weakly to the nearest branch, her wings bent and wrinkled as if she'd been trampled over. Syrena stepped forward with her hands violently ablaze like a pair of torches, burning away part of the sleeves of her new blouse. Her orange eyes were bright embers brighter than the sun, and when she stepped towards Sivvy none of the pixies would dare get within five feet of them.

"Stay back," she warned them. The few rebellious ones that remained nearby were frightened off when Syrena taunted them with her flames, reminding them that she was in control. "Stay back, I will not say it again." Sivvy was looking down at her with awe. It was evident that no human had defended her in such a way before. "Come," said the witch, and Sivvy's head tilted in that peculiar way again. "Come, Sivvy… We're leaving…"

The gentle pixie flapped her wings as best as she could, only her flight was far less gracious than it had been before. She landed weakly on Syrena's shoulder, gazing admiringly into her eyes like a rescued child. Even the queen of the horde was staring down from above, too frightened to fly back down.

Hudson looked at Syrena as if he was looking at a majestic lioness, but the concern in his eyes wasn't the least bit subtle. "Darling…"

"Let's go," said the witch.

"*Darling*," Hudson said insistently. "May I ask that you think this through for a moment?"

Syrena gave him a glance; it was clear that her mind had been made up.

"Let's *go*," she repeated. "Now."

Realizing that she wasn't going to yield, Hudson and John gathered their belongings and backed away from the pixies' nest, heading towards the nearest path they could find among the trees. Syrena walked backwards with her flaming hands held out in defense, and Sivvy was on her shoulder grasping onto her blouse for dear life. When they were a good distance away from the nest, Syrena let go of the rage and the flames on her hands died, leaving her hands unpleasantly hot, clouds of smoke streaming out from them. From a distance, the horde of pixies kept watch like a pack of wolves, and Sivvy was looking back at them with both sadness and anger in her childlike expression.

"You're going to be all right," Syrena whispered into her tiny blue ears. "I'll look after you. I promise." And so the witch led the way, John and Hudson trailing behind her like a pair of noble guardsmen.

"Will she?" John asked worriedly.

"Will she what?"

"Be *all right*? In Halghard?"

With an unconvincing sigh, Hudson replied, "I damn well hope so, mate."

* * *

After nearly a decade of serving as handmaiden to Princess Magdalena, the young servant woman known as Brie had unintentionally walked towards the princess's chambers one early morning, dazed and lost in thought. She was almost at the bedroom door when she realized it, and she felt a cold chill run up her spine. Once, the halls were loud and lively with servants scurrying down the corridors carrying trays of tea and breakfast for her majesty. Now the curtains had been shut and the halls were eerily empty, quiet, and slowly gathering dust.

Brie made her way across the palace courtyard and headed towards the guard barracks. She had a bowl in her hands filled with warm water, stirred with mauve treacle and Halghardian velvet root. She nearly spilled it all when she stumbled across an unconscious figure sitting in the middle of the gardens. Nervously, she walked around him; Lord Regent Darryk Clark had never looked so sullen and miserable. On the table, there was an empty jar and a goblet that had been spilled, red wine dampening his black hair.

When Brie realized he was breathing, she relaxed and went about her business.

It was peculiar, she realized, the way she'd been a servant her whole life and never once felt the need to drown her sorrows in wine, and in the last few days of serving Lady Brunylda Clark as a bookkeeper she'd felt the tension in her neck rise. It was both a blessing and a burden, she realized, to have any form of power.

She made her way to the guard barracks, to the room in which Adelina Huxley and her family were being lodged. When she opened the door, young Margot Huxley jumped to her feet, startled and flustered. She had been sitting on the wooden chair next to a bed where there lied the unconscious blacksmith Evellyn Amberhill.

"I didn't touch it, I swear!" said the girl.

"I believe you," Brie replied with a chuckle. "Has she come to her senses at all?"

"No. She just keeps mumbling."

"Mumbling what?" Brie asked, more to amuse the girl than out of actual concern. She placed the bowl on the rickety bedside table and dipped in a freshly cleaned white cloth.

"Nonsense, mostly," Margot replied. "Though she did call for Alycia twice."

"Who?"

"Her sister…"

At this, Brie paused for a moment, holding the cloth in her hands half-wringed as warm water dripped out of it. "*Sister?*" she asked. "Is anyone caring for this sister?"

Young Margot hesitated. For a girl so young, it hadn't crossed her mind that Alycia, who was roughly the same age as her, had been left alone in the care of old Willem Amberhill, who had been bed-ridden and ill for several weeks now.

"Well," Brie came back to her senses. "No need to worry, I'm sure she's fine. I'll speak with the Lord Regent about it when he, uh… when he *wakes*."

Margot smiled at her. She had been sitting by Evellyn's side for hours, staring pryingly at the blood-soaked bandages, trying to catch a glimpse of what was underneath. And when Brie began removing the bandages gently, Margot's eyes grew wide with anticipation.

Evellyn's face was terribly scarred. It began with a minor scab on the lower lip, the blood on it now blackened and dry. Her upper lip, on the other hand, had been cut open severely, and though Mister Beckwit had tried to save what was left of the lip, the scar left an arch that was just high enough to expose three of her upper teeth, two of them chipped at the end. The wound split in two just underneath her cheek bone due to the barbs on Okvar's axe; the smaller cut ran inward horizontally, ending just a half-inch from her nose, while the longer cut ran all the way up above her brow. Okvar had missed her eye by just a hair, but the blade slid far enough to mark her forehead as well.

"By the gods," Margot whispered, placing a hand over her mouth, her eyes beginning to swell. She'd known Evellyn since she was a babe, and she always thought her to be among the most beautiful women she'd ever seen. This woman that lay in front of her now was unfamiliar to her eyes. From up close, she *looked* like Evellyn; she was dressed like her, she smelled like her, had red hair like her, but if Margot had seen her in a crowd she would not have recognized her, and it filled the girl with an overwhelming guilt all of a sudden. Evellyn stood her ground and faced an orc simply so that the Huxleys could get away. And that scar on the blacksmith's face would forever remind them of that.

Brie began to clean the scabs gently with the wet cloth. The mauve treacle did nothing for the pain, only prevented infection, and the wound was so deep that the handmaiden-turned-bookkeeper was glad Evellyn was unconscious for the cleaning.

"Will it ever heal properly?" Margot asked.

Brie turned and gave her a warm smile, but it was one that also conveyed a hint of sorrow.

"I'm afraid not," she said. "But she'll *live*... In the end, that's what truly matters."

The grief in Margot's face was clear. Even for a girl her age she was rather intelligent, and she understood much more than adults gave her credit for.

"Did you know her well?" Brie asked.

Margot nodded. "She's my brother John's best friend. She's one of the kindest people I've ever met. Always has been."

Brie smiled as she dampened the cloth in the bucket some more. "Where's your mother?"

"She and Melvyn took River out for some fresh air by the creek. Melvyn wanted some berries and mum wanted ginger herbs for some tea."

Brie lowered a brow. "Did she not like the tea from this morning?"

"She never tasted it. The servant dropped it all. Took one look at Aeva and screamed. Woke us all up, she did."

"Aeva...?"

"Aevastra," Margot glanced over at the orcess, who was resting on the bed across from them, unconscious as she had been for the last 10 hours due to the toll the poison was taking on her body. Brie nodded and brought the cloth back up to Evellyn's face, though her mind was now elsewhere.

"Sounds unsettling," she said. "Some people just scare easy, I suppose."

"What's *unsettling*?" Margot asked.

"Troubling," Brie clarified, to which Margot replied with a smirk of curiosity.

Then something rather unexpected happened. The second the wet cloth touched the stitches on Evellyn's face again, the blacksmith gasped fiercely for air and woke up suddenly in a shock.

Brie screamed. A loud piercing scream, it was. So loud that Lord Regent Darryk Clark woke up in the palace courtyard, confused and exhausted, his head throbbing with pain.

Brie backed away from the bed, allowing the blacksmith a good amount of space.

Evellyn Amberhill sat up, her chest throbbing, her eyes swollen with tears as she glanced all around in a fit of distress. She was dazed and in a shock, and the more her lips and jaw shivered the more she felt the sharp sting of the stitches. Within seconds her face was red and sweaty, and her entire body was trembling.

"Evellyn! By the gods," Margot said, half-stunned and half-joyful to see her awake.

"I-It's okay!" Brie said, hoping to help the woman settle down. "You're safe… You're in Val Havyn's royal palace…"

Evellyn's confused gaze seemed unwilling to settle on any particular thing. She appeared lost and slightly out of touch with reality, her mind trying to come to terms with what had happened.

"Well… *Part* of the royal palace," Brie clarified. "You're in the guard barracks."

Evellyn tried to force herself back to her senses. To Margot, the blacksmith appeared so unlike herself, so dazed and primitive, Brie even wondered if she'd fallen and injured her head when it all happened; there was certainly no wound on her scalp, none that the bookkeeper had noticed. Evellyn sunk into a frenzy, groaning and pressing a trembling hand against her aching tender face.

"Don't touch it!" Brie warned her, so loudly and abruptly that Evellyn yelped and shriveled into a corner. "I-It's okay! I'm only here to help y-"

The blacksmith leapt suddenly off the bed and, in a panic, headed towards the door, holding onto the brick walls to keep herself balanced.

"Wait!" Brie shouted. "Stop! You shouldn't be moving!"

"S-Stay away!" Evellyn finally spoke, her eyes wide with terror.

"Evellyn," Margot cried. "Calm yourself… You're safe…"

It must have been the shock of it all, but Evellyn hadn't noticed the Huxley girl was there until that moment. When she looked down at her, she felt a sudden ease fill her body. "M-Margot…?"

"Yes," the girl stepped closer. "Yes, it's me. You're okay, Evellyn…"

There was a brief moment in which the blacksmith appeared relieved. Margot's familiar face eased her agitation a bit, at the very least she knew *somebody* in the room. Then, however, the pain returned to her face and it reminded her of what had happened.

She glanced everywhere again, her entire body twitching and shaking. "I want to see," she mumbled, and both Brie and Margot turned to one another, unsure of what to do or say. The scar marked only the left side of Evellyn's face but it was quite deep and disturbing all the same. Brie had intentionally gotten rid of any mirrors, for she knew that such a wound would only shock the woman further. And Brie had seen a fair number of wounds in her life; enough wounds, at least, to know that Evellyn's face was fated to never look the same again.

"You should go and get your mother," Brie mumbled at Margot.

"I want to see!" Evellyn said again, her voice much louder this time.

"Y-Yes, just hang on for a moment," Brie held her hands nervously out in front. "Evellyn... That is your name, yes? Evellyn?"

The blacksmith simply stared back, absent-mindedly and distrustful.

"I'm Brie. And I'm a friend," said the bookkeeper. "You've been hurt very badly..."

Evellyn's breathing had slowed, but her mind was set only on one thing: the pain.

"I want to *see*," she said, this time with an ominous tone that was slightly aggressive.

"I-I don't think it's a good idea t-"

Before Brie could finish, the blacksmith ran suddenly out of the door.

"Wait!"

"Evellyn!" Margot ran after them both.

But it was of no use... Evellyn was never fond of being treated like a child, and she was certainly not in the mood for it that morning. With a surprising amount of energy, she sprinted through the palace grounds and headed for the gardens. Her eyes were stung by the piercing sunlight and still she persisted, searching anywhere for a reflection. She had a hand on her lips and could feel the stitches. She could feel the arch beneath her nose. She could feel her teeth through her closed lips. She began panicking again.

"Stay away from me!" Evellyn shouted, and though she had no weapon in her hands Brie was careful not to make any sudden movements.

"I-I'm only trying to help you!" she argued nervously.

Evellyn kept walking down the outdoor corridor when she saw the leafy green vines wrapped along the walls and columns, and more hanging graciously from the ceilings. And when the greenery grew in abundance, she saw the flowers. Before she knew it, she was in the middle of the palace courtyard.

"Oh no," Brie mumbled, running after the blacksmith, lifting her housedress with her hands. "Wait! Stop! Y-You shouldn't..."

"Evellyn, no!" Margot cried.

But it was too late...

"Stay away!" Evellyn shouted again, so loud that Lord Regent Darryk Clark glanced from across the courtyard and caught a glimpse of her face. His reaction was not pleasant, but it wasn't discourteous either. He was shocked yet sorrowful all at once. He even rose from his seat, despite the fact that the wine had drained most of his energy tremendously.

There was a brief silence; even the singing birds seemed to have been muffled. Evellyn Amberhill took a deep breath. There was still water inside one of the broken fountains nearby, only it was still and motionless. She leaned slowly inward, feeling her heart racing as if it would soon implode in her chest.

It began with her forehead. She could see her bright red hair, a tangled mess above a shivering head. Then, as she leaned closer, she saw the scab just above her eyebrow. Her eye had been spared, shielded by the bone around her socket. But as she leaned even closer, she saw the depth of the scar, split in two right at her cheekbone, and just underneath it was her disfigured lip, wrinkled and bruised, purple and red, exposing her broken teeth.

She felt a rush of dread fill her body at the sight of a face she did not recognize.

She began to sob, this time profoundly and desperately.

She let out a raging scream as she fell gently to her knees.

In a rush of panic, Brie ran off to alert Adelina Huxley and her son, leaving Margot alone with the blacksmith. Without knowing what else to do, the girl stepped closer gently, dropped to her knees, and placed a warm hand on the woman's shoulder.

They embraced. Evellyn cried into the girl's shoulder.

Darryk Clark, who was both startled and glad to see Evellyn still alive, began pacing closer, gently and cautiously, unsure of what exactly he could do or say to ease the woman's pain. Evellyn must have sensed his presence, for she looked up at him with a look of shame and despair. But at that same moment, however, her mind began to clear when she looked into his familiar eyes. Bit by bit she remembered everything, every unfortunate memory and every minor detail. Selling every weapon and armor at her disposal, receiving more coin than she had ever owned at once, traveling to Elbon to repay the Huxleys, leaving her younger sister behind...

When Darryk saw the horror in her eyes, he decided to speak first.

"Miss Amberhill," he said, his voice dry and croaky. "Is everything all r-"

"Alycia," was all she said, and then she stood up weakly, as if the mere thought of her sister gave her the strength that she lacked. Darryk then remembered it as well, the young girl waiting by the door the day he'd met Evellyn Amberhill... A girl no older than 12, with hair just as red as the blacksmith's, left alone to care for a dying man...

"I-I'll send for a carriage immediately!" he stammered.

"No," Evellyn argued. "No, I-I must go now!"

"You're not in the condition t-"

"I'm *going*!" Evellyn said, nearly shouting.

In the distance, Hektor was already approaching them, fully rested and armored like a proper guardsman. "My Lord? Is everything all right?"

"Hektor..." Darryk could not hide how glad he was to see the man.

"I heard screaming, my Lord."

"Have the wagon prepared at once," Darryk said. "Meet us by the eastern gate."

Hektor took one look at Evellyn and his eyes widened. "Yes, my Lord!"

Minutes later, they were riding through the city streets towards Evellyn's shop. Hektor and Bogden rode at the front while Darryk and the blacksmith sat inside, shielded from the rebellious Val Havyn citizens by curtains and a roof.

Darryk's royal blue tunic was starting to reek of body odor and spilled wine, and there was a thin layer of scruff along his jaws and cheeks. He did not look well at all. He was hungry and fatigued, and he had bags under his eyes from the lack of sleep. He'd hardly said two words to Evellyn since leaving the palace grounds, which was due in part to the dehydration but also to the shock of seeing the woman's face.

Uncomfortable, as he realized he had been silent for far too long, he cleared his throat.

"Are you, um… Are you all right?"

Evellyn hardly moved a muscle. Her eyes left the commotion of the outside and turned towards Darryk; they were violently red and swollen with tears. Through merely a stare, one could see that the blacksmith's spirit had been broken. She could hardly speak and when she did, the stitches would itch and sting awfully.

"What I *meant* was," Darryk rephrased himself. "Are you in any pain? Does it hu-"

"Don't," she stopped him.

With a sigh of gloom, Darryk nodded. "I'm sorry… Truly, I canno-"

"Please, just… *don't*," she said.

He closed his lips and added nothing further, realizing she was in no mood to talk about what had happened. He then reached into his robes and casually pulled a leather flask out. As he popped the top open, however, Evellyn gave him a glance.

"Isn't it a bit early in the day for that, m'lord?" she asked.

He stopped before the first sip. And then, as if ashamed, he placed the top back on.

"Pardon me. I forget myself sometimes," he said with a forced half-smile as he slid the flask back into his pocket. "It's funny… Often, I'd frown upon the idea that I was *actually* related to the Lady Brunylda… *Now* look at me. The resemblance must be eerie."

Evellyn said no more; there wasn't the hint of a smile anywhere.

Suddenly, the carriage came to a halt. And when it did, Evellyn leapt instantly from her seat and opened the door. Darryk followed after her, and as he stepped out of the carriage the sunlight pierced his eyes and made his head throb once again. He suddenly wished he'd brought water along for the ride.

From the moment Evellyn laid eyes upon her shop, she knew something was wrong. She froze right at the fence, noticing that her wielding tools were scattered and out of place as if someone had rummaged through it all.

"Stay here," Darryk told his guards. "Keep an eye out."

"Yes, sir," said Hektor, holding the reins atop the wagon as his fowl-mouthed companion sipped from a winebag. It was midday, and so the streets of Val Havyn were crowded with peasants and traveling merchants, and there were even a few curious heads peeking out of nearby windows. It made Darryk unquestioningly nervous.

Evellyn opened the wooden gate and stepped into the wielding yard. She had to walk around broken glass and scattered tools to reach her porch. The front door looked broken, barricaded from the inside by chairs and tables.

Someone's been here, she told herself. *Someone who was up to no good...*

Panicking, she ran swiftly up the front steps.

"Wait!" Darryk reached for the woman's elbow.

"My *sister's* in there!" she snatched her arm away from him.

"And so might whoever ransacked your yard!" he insisted.

"H-Hello?" she called out, much to Darryk's disdain. But there was no reply from the inside, nothing but silence. She took another step, and this time the wood beneath her torn boots creaked loudly and sharply. And not a second afterwards, she heard a muffled yelp coming from inside, followed closely by the sound of scattering footsteps.

"A-Alycia?" she called out, her words faint and garbled due to the stitches on her lips.

She held an ear close to the door for an answer. More silence.

Darryk tried to peek through the windows, but they had been covered by sheets and torn blankets. Then they heard the footsteps again, scurrying away towards the kitchen.

"Alycia?!" Evellyn called again. She then tried to push the door in, but something was barring it from the other side. For a moment, she swore she could hear the girl, crying and panting with fear in the darkness. Then, as her mind began reeling with unpleasant thoughts, she began slamming her arm against the door, hoping to push through whatever was barricading it.

Darryk glanced back. His guards were sitting nervously in front of the wagon glimpsing everywhere, knowing very well that any peasant would recognize them as the very same guards that had shoved them away and allowed orcs into the royal palace just a day prior. Darryk sighed heavily; he knew they had to act quickly if they wished to survive.

"Allow me," he said, and gave the door a try. He slammed his arm repeatedly against it, but all it did was give his arm a bruise. "Come on! Open up, you!" he mumbled to himself, as he began kicking and grunting against the door. Then, however, a window shattered just a foot from his ear.

Evellyn Amberhill had her wielding hammer in hand and was already climbing through the broken glass before Darryk could shove the door a single inch. She stumbled inside and realized the door had been blocked by a rickety chair and a flipped table. A very weak barricade, but it did the job.

As Darryk climbed in after her, Evellyn took a look around. The place was crawling with bugs and dirt and broken glass. And there was a pungent smell in the air; a foul smell, as if something was rotting.

"Aly?" she called out, and when she heard the soft whimpers she followed them carefully. "It's me, Aly... It's Evellyn..."

In the darkness of the cottage, she found her... hiding in a corner with a kitchen knife in her trembling hands, Alycia Amberhill was pale with fear and her red hair was a tangled mess. When the girl looked up at her sister's face, she froze. It was a face she did not recognize. That voice, on the other hand, was indeed her sister's... Slow and slurred, but it was hers...

"Aly?" Evellyn said, taking slow steps towards her, realizing then that her face might have startled her. The girl crawled out from her corner and approached slowly. Both Evellyn and Darryk lowered themselves to a crouching position.

"Hey," Evellyn spoke again, tears escaping her eyes. "It's me, Aly... It's really me..."

The knife slid slowly out of Alycia's hands. It fell to the floor, near a pile of broken shards of glass. Then, with tear-stricken eyes, the girl ran towards Evellyn and threw her arms around her.

"Oh Aly," Evellyn cried into her sister's shoulder. "I'm sorry. I'm so sorry, Aly."

The girl said nothing, only grabbed tightly onto her sister's dress as if her life depended on it. She looked as if she hadn't bathed in days, her face and clothes riddled with dirt and her hair greasy and unkempt. The kitchen looked as if a fight had just taken place there; nearly every chair was bent or broken and there was broken glass everywhere.

"What happened here?" Darryk asked.

The girl's lip trembled and, as she spoke, her voice was nothing more than a faint whisper. "Bad men," she said, and then Evellyn's eyes widened. "They took everything... The gold, the weapons... everything..."

Evellyn then grabbed her sister by the shoulders. "Father...?" she asked hesitantly.

Alycia said nothing at first, only whimpered and panted heavily. And then, as another tear ran down her face, she squeezed her eyes shut. "He wouldn't wake up," she said.

Evellyn froze where she stood. She lowered her brows and stared right into the poor girl's eyes. "What...?"

"I tried to wake him," Aly said, her face now drenched with tears. "H-He wouldn't wake..."

Darryk felt his own chest start to pound. He understood then what that foul smell had been. They walked towards the nearest room and pushed the door open, and instantly Darryk felt the vomit rise up his throat. The smell was far too overwhelming, so much that Darryk ran towards the outside and threw up on the grass.

Evellyn, instead, ran towards her father's body and fell to her knees sobbing. She wouldn't dare touch him, for he was pale and rotting, but she was mere inches from him crying hysterically into his bedframe.

Out in the common room, Darryk wiped his lips with one of his sleeves. *Focus,* he told himself. *Get the girl out of here. Now.*

He carried Alycia out into the wielding yard.

"Shh, it's going to be okay," he tried to calm her. "I promise you."

There was a sudden agonizing scream, the scream of a grieving woman, coming from inside the house. Meanwhile, peasants began to overhear the commotion. Eyes were staring at them through windows and doorframes, and people were starting to whisper.

"My Lord?" Hektor called from the carriage. "Is everything all right in there?"

"Fine," Darryk lied to him. "Just fine…"

But it wasn't fine… Even when Evellyn Amberhill returned, some 20 minutes later, she did not appear by any means *fine*… She was beyond broken. She grabbed Alycia by the hand and took her inside. "Come," she said solemnly. "We must clean up the mess."

"Miss Amberhill?" Darryk beckoned for her.

"Thank you for everything," Evellyn said, her voice now dry and full of sorrow. "Now please… I ask that we be left alone…"

"Miss Amberhill, if there is *anything* we could do…"

"Thank you, m'lord," she said. "Goodbye."

And then she closed the door behind her.

Darryk remained out in the wielding yard for a moment, his throat swollen with a heavy knot. *Do something,* he told himself. But as much as he wanted to he couldn't bring himself to intervene.

"My lord?" Hektor called.

Darryk sighed despairingly once again, then turned and walked towards the wooden gates.

"Shall we return, my lor-"

"Yes, yes, back to the palace," Darryk said, as he climbed into the carriage and slammed the door shut behind him.

* * *

All throughout the land of Gravenstone, cities and villages were known to be rich with one thing or another.

Val Havyn was rich with wealth.

Morganna was rich with rare herbs.

Yulxester was rich with fish, Wyrmwood was rich with crops, and Kahrr was rich with precious stones and rare metals. In the case of Grymsbi, a humble little village right at the border of Halghard and the Woodlands, it was *mud*… Grymsbi was rich with mud, horseshit, and more mud…

The filth was everywhere, on every road, stable, even *indoors*. Half the townsfolk regularly had mud-stains somewhere on their bodies, whether in the neck, the underarm, or behind the ear. Rumor had it that the town had been cursed by witches some four or five decades past, which caused the unusual rainfall over the course of every season. Others blamed the Great Rift of Halghard, stating that whatever caused the massive hole in the earth had contaminated the land surrounding it, leaving it barren and tarnished.

Regardless, Robyn Huxley couldn't help but feel an immense weight lift from her shoulders as she walked along the muddy road that led into the village. *Civilization at last,* she thought, but the blissful feeling only lasted until they reached the entrance.

Grymsbi, the very first in all of Halghard to be proclaimed a '*sanctuary village*', wasn't at all the safe haven they had been expecting. Though the guards did nothing to stop them, the looks they were given were cold and hostile. The Beast had never set foot in a human village before and it was obvious from the moment they arrived; he appeared more at guard than ever before, gripping the red pelt he wore as a belt as if ready to reach for his axe should he need to. His intimidating expression masked his uneasiness quite well. It all felt so strange to him, like walking into a stranger's home uninvited.

For Robyn, it had been weeks since she left the comfort of her home and she was already becoming accustomed to having more eyes on her than was usual for an ordinary farmgirl. Perhaps it had less to do with *her* and more to do with the fact that she was walking alongside a six-and-a-half-foot tall orc and a one-eyed serpent around her neck. Past every wooden dwelling, frightened villagers would scatter away in fear, some began crossing to the other side of the road so as to avoid crossing paths with her and her companions, others intentionally brushed past them and spat near their shoes, and worried parents hissed at their snooping children to get back indoors.

Wiping the sweat from her brow, Robyn looked at Nyx through the corner of her eye.

"Are you positive we'll be safe here?" she whispered to him.

"Absolutely not," Nyx replied subtly into her ear. "Safety, you'll find back in Elbon. This here's Grymsbi, Lady Robyn. Orcs are allowed, as are elves and gnomes. Hells, even red spindle is allowed. The *last* thing they'll care about is some measly serpent."

Nyx was speaking rather odd, and it had little to do with his strange new accent. Robyn figured he didn't want to alert anyone; while nonhumans may have been allowed, sorcery was an entirely different issue. Little to Robyn's knowledge, Nyx had already been to Grymsbi, some 150 years back, and he remembered it quite vividly down to the last detail.

They approached an old shabby-looking tavern with a blue sign reading *The Stumblin' Hare* and the picture of a rabbit-like creature submerged inside a foaming tankard. It was just as Nyx had remembered it, identical save for one small detail.

A second wooden sign hung below the tavern name. '*No Freaks Allowed*' it read at first, but the words had been marked over with a red *X*, and below it were white freshly painted letters that read: *Rabbits & Greenskins Welcome*. Nyx was suddenly thankful that neither Robyn nor the Beast knew how to read.

There was an elf beggar sitting on the mud near the tavern doors. He had a basket near his feet that was nearly empty except for a few coppers. Robyn walked up the front steps first, and when she didn't feel the Beast's presence looming behind her, she looked back. The orc was digging through his pockets for spare coin; all he found was a copper, but the elf beggar looked up and smiled all the same.

Robyn felt a tug in her chest; it wasn't exactly an act she would expect from someone like the Beast and yet her eyes continued to deceive her. "Ready?" she asked him warmly before stepping inside. So strong was her discomfort that she sought warmth from an orc that, until then, had shown her nothing but hostility. Even Nyx couldn't reassure her, not in his serpentine form; in a strange town like Grymsbi, she felt undeniably safer having the Beast by her side.

When they finally entered the tavern, only half the eyes in the room glanced at them. The majority of the customers were human, though there was a Woodland elf sitting in a corner among a band of raiders and another one serving tables. It was quite crowded despite it being early in the evening, and the only seats available were at the tavern bar. Robyn and her companions took a seat next to a husky red-faced man with a messy head of hair and an unkempt beard.

"Pardon me, sir? May I move your satchel?" Robyn asked, but the man was far too drunk and on the verge of passing out over the counter, and so she moved it anyway. All around them, the commotion was loud and overwhelming. The Beast was observing the room like a wolf sniffing about in unknown territory.

"You all right?" Robyn asked, and he replied only with a grunt and a head nod.

The tavern server was a scrawny young man in his early twenties, and when he turned and laid eyes on the Beast he yelped and dropped the tankard of ale he'd been holding so steadily. "Oh dear, I'm so terribly sorry," he said tensely, wiping his hands on his apron, attempting to look calm and casual. "Hello... Can ye help, err... can *I* help *you* with something?"

"Ale," the Beast grunted.

"Y-Yes," the young man cleared his throat. "Right away, sir. Make yerself a' home, sir!"

He was trying rather hard, and it was painfully obvious. And the Beast, in return, looked at the server with a contemptuous expression, as if looking at a bard who was ruining every note in a popular tune.

"Just water for me, please," Robyn smiled.

"Certainly," the lad said tautly. "The name's Seamus. Anything ye need, just ask!"

Robyn noticed his hesitance and she could tell the Beast had noticed it, too. And to make matters worse, when Seamus brought their drinks he leaned in towards the orc with a shivering lip.

"I'm deeply sorry, sir," he cleared his throat. "But they *make* me say this... Um... W-We don't want any trouble here, yes? Just... keep that in mind, that's all." With that, Seamus walked away to serve other clients, and Robyn couldn't help but glance at the Beast.

There was a look on his face she couldn't quite make out.

Discomfort? Anger? Sorrow? Perhaps all of them at once?

Robyn scowled. "What'd he just...?"

"Let it go, Robyn," Nyx hissed into her ear. It was the first time he'd called her 'Robyn' and not 'Lady Robyn', which surprised her.

The Beast drank from his ale, maintaining that look on his face. He hadn't exactly expected a warm welcome but the tavern server's words had come unexpectedly, and though they were minor they stung him all the same.

Robyn sipped her water, her mind reeling with a million thoughts. Now that she had made it to Halghard, she hadn't the slightest clue where to even begin. She knew her brother was heading to the western coast, yet she knew not what roads he was traveling through or whom he had associated with along the way. She'd acted impulsively throughout the journey, burdening her mind only with thoughts that required her immediate consideration. Escaping the tree nymphs, escaping Malekai, escaping the Woodlands... It was a miracle she was still alive and well, with only a burn scar on her arm to slow her down. But now that she was in Halghard, with only a few coppers in her pockets, she would need a different approach if she wished to make it all the way to the western coast.

She froze all of a sudden, noticing a peculiar set of eyes staring at her from afar. A young woman with brown dreadlocks and dark skin was sitting in a dark corner behind a table of peasants. She was sipping on her ale and wiping her chin with the sleeves of her burgundy velvet coat, but her eyes were solely fixed on Robyn, shooting her a less-than-friendly look as if recognizing an old enemy, though Robyn swore she'd never seen the woman before. To begin with, Robyn didn't know anyone outside of the kingdom of Vallenghard except for a few traveling merchants her mother was acquainted with. She also didn't remember seeing the woman anywhere within the Woodlands, unless she was a covert member of the Brotherhood, but there was no red leather nor did Robyn see any wrist tattoo. Still, the woman looked less like a peasant and more like a mercenary; she had several scars on her face and chest, scars that only a blade could make, and her hair was slicked back with a buckskin headband, revealing her rather peculiar earring, a jaguar's tooth pierced through her left ear.

"Where's my bloody drink?!" a drunken man shouted nearby.

Startled, Robyn's eyes moved away from the woman; even the drunken husky man next to them groaned annoyingly and wriggled in his chair half-asleep. There were several hostile stares thrown their way, mainly at the Beast, and Robyn felt the hairs rising at the back of her neck. Her angst only worsened when she glanced back towards the corner and saw nothing but an empty chair. The strange woman with the earring was nowhere to be seen, as if she had vanished into thin air.

Robyn felt sick all of a sudden, exposed and vulnerable, feeling as if the woman was still lurking about somewhere, watching her from the shadows. *Damn it all to hells, it seems like nowhere is safe out here.*

"Everything... all right?" Nyx asked her in a croaky whisper as if he was out of breath, his serpentine tongue moving in and out of his mouth unwillingly.

"Y-Yeah..." she hesitated. She gave him a look that was supposed to reassure him, but the serpent was not the least bit convinced. "Are *you* all right?"

Nyx stared blankly forward. His head was rocking subtly back and forth, gently like winded dog. He opened his scaly lips and whispered, "Hurts... to... talk."

Robyn felt a shred of guilt, realizing she must have asked him a hundred questions on the walk into town. "Oh Nyx, you poor thing," she said. "Your new mouth wasn't made for talking." She would have embraced him, but she already felt strange enough talking to a serpent in a crowded tavern. "You rest now. We'll leave as soon as we can."

She glanced around for an amiable-looking face. She had to ask someone where she could fetch a caravan south, for the only way to get to Drahkmere was by ship. She could ask the tavern server, she figured. At least *he* seemed friendly enough. But she'd have to wait for an opportune moment or until the tavern closed for the night. And so, seeing as she had time to spare and Nyx could not speak, she turned to the only other familiar face in the tavern.

"Slow down," she said, but the tongue-tied Beast did not slow down a bit; he chugged down his ale like water and demanded more, with a glare so sharp that poor Seamus hesitated to reach for the empty tankard. There was something odd about the orc's demeanor that evening. He did not appear in the mood for a conversation, but that was typical of him. Moreover, he seemed lost in thought, as if the life all around him was making him reminisce about the life he once had. In a way, he even looked *sad*.

"Bit different than you're used to, I take it?" Robyn decided to ask.

As usual, the Beast said nothing, only gave her a grunt.

Not this again, she thought. *Just talk to me, will you?*

"Have you ever set foot in Halghard before?" she asked, though she was quite sure she knew the answer. Still, the Beast only sighed brusquely and closed his eyes.

Come on, you… You've done it before. It's not that difficult.

Suddenly, she noticed the Beast's head moving subtly from side to side, and then his eyes looked to her as if his part of the conversation was done.

That is a 'no'… Very well, it's a start…

"No need to worry," she said to him. "The hounds that bark the loudest are the last to ever bite, my mum's always said. You won't find any trouble here, only loud-mouths."

The Beast sat so still, he may as well have been made of stone. His eyes were the only part of him that moved, observing the commotion all around them.

"Folks 'round these parts have it easy compared to life in the Woodlands," Robyn went on, attempting to lift his spirits. "They'll take one look at those scars of yours and know not to mess with you."

His expression shifted suddenly. He still wouldn't speak a word, but his eyes glanced down at his scars as if he'd forgotten they were there, as if trying to convince himself that she was probably in the right. If nothing else, it gave Robyn some comfort to know that he at least was listening.

"How *did* you get those scars?" she asked, knowing it may have been a risky question. Instantly, Nyx gave her a nervous glance. He knew he had to be subtle, but Robyn's brute courage often got her in more trouble than was good for her. "Beast?" she pressed further, determined to get the orc to talk.

"Fuckin' hells, scrap," he grunted, closing his eyes yet again, irritated and mentally jaded. "Ye don't know when to stop, do ye? If I answer *one* question, will ye shut yer yap 'n' let me be?"

Robyn bit her tongue. She didn't mean to offend him; if anything, she wanted to ease his nerves. Still, she swallowed her pride and gruffly said, "Sure."

It soon became clear that the Beast hadn't spoken personally to anyone before, at least not in recent years. Even among the Rogue Brotherhood he'd been a solitary soul, unwelcome and unwanted. He would sleep with a dagger beneath his pillow every night. He would hunt for his own food, for nobody would ever offer to share a meal with him. The world was cruel to him and his skin had grown so thick that he couldn't trust another soul; it simply wasn't in his nature anymore, if it ever was. When he spoke, the pain was palpable even as he tried desperately to hide it.

"I was just a lad," he said, his voice deep and raspy. Robyn had to lean in closer to hear him over the chatter. "Stonewalkers… they killed me whole clan, butchered 'em all in the dead of night. I was scared… Hadn't been in many fights, so I just… *ran*."

He paused there momentarily. Already, Robyn felt a knot in her throat; she sipped on her water to ease it back down.

"I was just a lad," he said again. "A young, scared, stupid lad..."

He released a heaving sigh, a rather angry one.

"I left 'em to die," he said. "The moment I saw the massive bastards, I jumped in the river 'n' let it take me... It dragged me so far from home, I didn't know where I was. I was lost 'n' alone. Only reason I survived is 'cause o' my axe. Me father taught me to hunt with it... But even my axe was no match for..."

He stopped there for a moment. Robyn fought the urge to place a hand on his back for comfort; the Beast didn't seem like the type for that kind of affection. Some folks, she realized, simply needed someone willing to lend an ear. "For...?" she asked.

"It was a bear that gave me this scar," he said. "A big fucker. Worst part is I almost let 'im win. I figured it was easier than goin' hungry. In the Woodlands, ye're either the hunter or the hunted... That was the day the Brotherhood found me. I saw 'em lookin' at me. A scrawny littl' bastard I was, fightin' off a bear, and *they* just... they stood there 'n' watched. Didn't try to help, they just... *watched*."

Robyn felt a sudden uncontrollable guilt upon remembering how much she had questioned the orc before. How she asked him about his 'friends', the rogue mercenaries.

"My axe was out o' my reach," he went on. "So I fought 'im with just me hands. Beat 'im right to his death, the giant bastard. But not before he left his mark on me." He took a moment to look down at his giant scar, a constant reminder of where he'd come from. "The cap'n offered me a deal right then 'n' there... He said I was the best fighter he ever saw. Said if I joined 'em, I'd have gold 'n' riches for the rest o' me days. A young lad with no family left would be stupid not to take a deal like that... And so I've been ridin' with 'em ever since."

Robyn understood then, the reasoning behind his cold demeanor. And the more she visualized herself in his shoes, the more she began to hate humans and their disgusting sense of entitlement.

"The bloody bastards," the Beast said, his eyes glistening under the lanterns' glow. "They never *once* asked me name, y'know... All I ever was to them was a weapon. When they saw me kill that bear alone 'n' unarmed, they nearly pissed themselves. All they saw was a mad beast... And that's who I became..."

The knot in Robyn's throat returned. She realized she hadn't asked for his name either, only assumed he preferred not to give it away. "What *is* it?" she decided to take the risk, and the Beast glanced at her morosely. "What's your name?"

He exhaled sharply through his nose; it would've sounded almost like a chuckle, had it not been so sullen. "I said I'd answer *one* question, scrap," he grunted, and then proceeded to gulp down his second ale.

Robyn did not pry further. She simply sat there and pondered on his story.

Even Nyx appeared out of sorts, as they sat in silence while the commotion reverberated all around them. Suddenly, however, their peace was broken by the same drunken brute that had been shouting nonsense moments prior. Stumbling towards the bar, the inebriated man was growling and hissing as if he was entitled to everything the tavern had to offer.

"Oi, Seamus!" he shouted. "I've been waitin' for me bloody drink for ages, mate."

The tavern server glanced nervously at the man, thankful there was a wooden counter there to separate them. "Y-Yes, Mister Hutner! Right away, sir!"

In a drunken stupor, the man took notice of the Beast, bending his neck as if trying to catch a glimpse of the orc's wrist. His expression shifted from a steady one to a hostile one, as his eyes moved back and forth from the Beast to Seamus. "The fuck's all this, then?"

Seamus tried to ignore the man. His intentions were not very clear, though it seemed he was barking more at the Beast than at anyone else. "We lettin' stray freaks into our town now?" he asked.

Seamus glanced at the Beast's wrist and saw the tattoo of the scorpion, but he grew nervous when he noticed that there was no permit number there. "Well, um... He did *pay* to be here just like everyone else, Mister Hutner," he tried to reason, but his words seemed to escape the drunken man's ears.

"Have you heard what they say 'bout orcs, lad?" asked Mister Hutner, his eyes still fixed on the Beast. "You know their skins used to be the same as ours? But over the years they all turned green 'cause of all their inbreeding."

The Beast drank his ale without as much as a wince; Robyn turned to him and expected more. And then something like rage began to grow inside her chest and the awful breath coming from Mister Hutner's mouth was only adding to it. Nyx looked up at her, wanting very much to calm her down and yet too afraid to speak out loud amidst so much commotion.

"Here's yer drink, Mister Hutner. This one's on the house," Seamus served him a full tankard, hoping it would sway the man away from the Beast. But the stubborn man's mockery only seemed to grow.

"I ain't drinkin' in the same room as no stray greenskin," he said.

Robyn couldn't help herself any longer. If the Beast wasn't going to speak up, someone else had to do it. She turned in her chair and looked up at the man's unusually scarred face.

Eat shit, she wished she could say. Instead, she chose the more proper path.

"Pardon me, sir, but my friend here paid his share just like everyone else in this tavern and he deserves the same respect *you're* getting for it."

The Beast muttered something under his breath, far too low to be comprehensible.

"Secondly," Robyn kept on. "By *whose* standards do you label him a freak?

Because believe it or not, he's got more in common with you and me than you think."

The Beast's mutter grew into a soft growl. "Let it go, scrap..."

"And *lastly*, sir," Robyn went on regardless. "I'm no historian. But I'm quite sure that your theory about the color of an orc's skin is a load of shit!" Robyn watched as Mister Hutner's face twisted into a raging grimace. He grabbed her violently by the coat and pulled her out of her seat, and Nyx suddenly wished he was something other than a snake.

"Listen 'ere, girl!" the drunken brute growled. "Your *friend* here is a filthy greenskin and that's all he'll *ever* be. A *freak*! And those who choose to be friends with freaks should be treated just the same!"

Suddenly, the Beast slammed his glass down with a force so strong that it shattered in his hand. He jumped to his feet, his hand gripping his axe, and towered over Mister Hutner's comparably smaller figure. "Tell me, old lad," he said infuriatingly. "Have ye ever seen up close the difference between the blood of a man 'n' the blood of an orc?"

The entire tavern had gone silent. Every single pair of eyes was on them.

Mister Hutner hesitated for a second, but his false sense of pride overcame him.

"Can't say I have," he muttered nervously.

"Is that so?" asked the Beast with a cold stare. "D'you want to *see*?"

The orc took a step forward. The entire tavern prepared for the worst. But Robyn stepped in between them before either one of them could land a blow.

"Beast, don't!" she said, placing a hand on his broad shoulder. "He's not worth it..."

The Beast's eyes moved from the hateful man's scowl to Robyn's compassionate gaze. Truthfully, he wanted to slay the brute where he stood. Realizing that he was in a sanctuary village, however, the orc calmed himself with a brusque groan. He reached calmly into his pocket, drew out a couple of coppers, and tossed them at Seamus. "For the glass," he said, and then headed for the tavern doors.

"Beast, wait!" Robyn ran after him, leaving Nyx behind to crawl at his own pace. They had captivated the attention of the whole tavern, and instantly the rumors began to spread from ear to ear. Seamus gave the bard a nervous hand signal, urging him to start singing again, and within minutes the tavern was as lively as it had been earlier that evening. Even Mister Hutner had calmed down, or rather he looked relieved at having dodged that fight; he grabbed his drink without paying and walked back towards his table.

There was one particular man, however, that appeared distraught and out of sorts towards the incident that had just occurred. It was the husky middle-aged man that Robyn had taken a seat next to... He was no longer asleep. He was startled and his eyes were narrowed, staring at the tavern doors as if trying to decipher a puzzle in his mind. He was dreadfully inebriated, that much was obvious. But he was certain that he recognized the orc and the farmgirl from somewhere... He'd seen them before, quite *recently* in fact...

An odd bunch, he thought, but the man had seen his share of oddities as of late, and he didn't think further on it. He searched aimlessly for his satchel, which had been resting on the seat next to him before he fell asleep over the counter. When he found it at his feet, he relaxed, but the look of gloom in his eyes remained.

He was acting strange, this inebriated man... What distinguished him from the crowd the most were his clothes; they were wrinkled and slightly smelly, stained with sweat and dried blood, as if he had recently unlaced a layer of armor off of himself.

"One more, lad," the man said, his voice in a slur.

Seamus served him a tankard of mead, just as the man would always order after a rough day of service. His eyes were red, but the mead was only half the reason. He could hardly keep himself up, he was so fatigued.

Coward, he cursed at himself. *Traitorous coward...*

Truthfully, even looking at his own reflection in the tankard of mead disgusted him; he couldn't look himself in the eyes without scowling. Where he came from, traitors were often hanged and made an example of.

"That'll be 10 coppers, sir," Seamus said, realizing the man hadn't yet paid for the last five drinks.

The man's hands were sweaty and shaky, which was also only partly due to the mead. When he felt no one was watching, the man looked miserable, morose, drowning his pain away as if there was no hope left for him. Half the customers in the tavern shared a similar look, but none of their expressions could possibly match the vivid sorrow in this man's face. Once he finished his drink, he reached into his pocket and tossed an entire coin purse at Seamus.

"I'll take a room as well," he said.

Seamus's eyes lit up as he held the coin purse in his callused hands. The weight alone told him it held plenty more than just 10 coppers. "Ohh dear... Yes! Right away, sir!"

"And lad?"

"Yes, sir?"

"Have you, uh," the man cleared his throat nervously. "Have you got any rope?"

"Um... *rope*, sir?"

"Aye. Rope."

"I'm sure we could find you some, sure! Right this way, sir. I'll show you to your room."

The man raised the tankard to his lips and finished the half-pint of mead that was left, before he rose to his feet and stumbled behind Seamus. He was led upstairs to a small room with nothing but an old bed and a large cabinet, and there were rafters above where a lit lantern hung from a hook. The room may have been old; the wooden rafters, however, looked solid and sturdy.

It'll do, the man thought.

"Seamus, by the way," the tavern server said suddenly.

"Pardon me?"

"The name's Seamus, sir. Anything ye need, just ask for me."

The man took a moment to respond, a long pensive moment, one that Seamus simply shrugged away and blamed on the mead.

"Jossiah," he finally said.

Seamus shook the former knight's shivering hand.

"A pleasure," he smiled. "I'll be right back with that rope ye asked for."

* * *

When dusk arrived, the village of Grymsbi was obscured by a thick layer of fog. The Beast was lost for a moment, and so he followed the dirt path that would lead him towards the village entrance; he could still see the fresh prints left by his boots just hours prior. If he just followed his own tracks, he would wind up back in the Woodlands eventually, safely hidden away from human civilization.

"Beast!" Robyn's voice echoed behind him. The young archer could hardly keep up with the orc's pace. The soles of her boots were riddled with mud, and she swore that some of it had somehow gotten into her socks. "Beast, wait!" she shouted. "Please, will you just wait?!"

But the orc kept up his brisk walk; the wet soil was no match for his thick muscular legs. The air had grown cold, as if announcing an approaching storm, and it managed to hide the dampness in the orc's eyes, swelling up with both sorrow and anger.

"I said *wait!*" Robyn shouted, and then the orc came to a sudden halt and spun around with a growl that was more beastlike than any growl Robyn had ever heard.

"What d'you *want* from me, scrap?!"

The vein above his brows was furiously thick and his jaw was tightly clenched, the fangs behind his lower lip appearing larger and sharper than ever before. Robyn was stunned and thrown aback, her timid eyes attempting to stare down the orc's.

"Y-You were just going to leave?" she asked him. "Without even a *farewell?*"

The Beast stepped forward with a sigh. "Listen, scrap… I'm gonna say it *one* last time. You 'n' me are *not* friends. We have nev'r *been* friends. And we will nev'r *be* friends."

The orc's words stung Robyn's chest like a sharp arrow. Her pride, however, would not allow her to shed a single tear. She'd tried to reason with him, she'd tried to comfort him, and she'd be damned if she was gonna allow him to spit on her good will when all she was trying to do was help him.

"Fine!" she said brusquely, talking through her rage. "*Go, then!* Go and be alone!"

"I been alone me whole life, scrap," he growled back at her. "It's been keepin' me alive so far. I'm better off that way."

"You're wrong," she argued, walking stubbornly after him. "You *choose* to be alone..."

The orc paused in his tracks again, glancing back at her with a glare so sharp that it hurt to look at. But Robyn Huxley was never one to yield. She held her stance as best as she could.

"Not everyone's like them, you know," she said. "Not everyone is cruel like the Brotherhood. You could do so much better, Beast... You could *be* so much better... But you don't, do you? You choose to shield yourself, even from those that want to help you. You act like you're all tough and mighty and don't need anyone else. And then you go and blame the *world* because you're alone. But you're putting *yourself* in that crate, Beast!"

The orc reached suddenly for his axe with a menacing growl.

"What?" she challenged him further. "You're gonna try to fight *me* now, too?"

Unable to withstand the rage in his chest, the Beast drew his axe and raised it high above his head. But rather than shying away, Robyn closed her eyes and valiantly kept her stance. She waited for the hit, a hit that would never come...

When she opened her eyes again, the orc was standing over her with the axe in mid air, shivering furiously and panting desperately as if it pained him to be holding the weapon for so long without drawing blood. His eyes were suddenly full of regret and his breathing was starting to slow. And as he stared down at the eyes of the brave archer, he felt his wrist begin to weaken.

Robyn wanted to say something, but any words she came up with died before they left her lips. She simply stood there and watched as the axe slid out of the Beast's hand and splashed over the mud. He lowered his gaze, grunting sullenly, trying to fight back his headache. And Robyn, unable to withhold herself, placed a warm hand on his shivering arm.

"You don't have to be alone, Beast..." she said.

But her attempt to sway him one last time into staying failed. He released a slow beastlike sigh and shut his eyes to fight back the swelling. "Just go," he said.

Robyn felt the tension coming back to her shoulders. Her mind immediately brought her back to that sorrowful evening at the Huxley farm, the evening in which her brother tried to talk to her and all she would say to him was "*Just go*." And yet here she was, scolding the Beast about his stubbornness when truthfully she was just as much so, if not more.

"Beast…"

"Just *go*, scrap… Please…"

The pressure in her chest was killing her. This was the first time she'd heard him say *'please'*, and she could tell that he truly wanted nothing more than to be alone. She understood, of course, for the two of them had more in common than the Beast was aware. And so Robyn turned around slowly and headed back towards the tavern. And the Beast walked into a sea of mist in the opposite direction. A single angry tear ran down Robyn's cheek, but she wiped it quickly as she noticed a serpentine figure crawling out of the tavern, several yards away. The streets were now empty. Even the guardsmen that were lounging about earlier in the evening were now gone, either resting or drinking their weight in mead somewhere.

Before Robyn made it safely back into the tavern, her ear caught a strange sound. She should've bolted towards Nyx at that moment, but she was so distraught that she paused where she stood. It was the sound of scratching footsteps she'd heard, and the fact that there wasn't a soul anywhere nearby made the hairs on the back of her neck stick out like thorns.

She glanced around nervously, but amidst the fog she could see nothing.

Nyx heard the footsteps too, and he slid down the tavern steps towards Robyn in an instant. But he wouldn't dare speak a single word, not when there was the possibility of someone lurking nearby.

When Robyn's ears caught the scratching sound again, she realized it was not coming from anywhere nearby, but rather from *above*… And when she finally looked up, it was far too late. A figure hopped suddenly down from a thatched roof, a figure with a very peculiar earring dressed in a burgundy coat.

"Robyn! Behind you!" Nyx shouted.

But before Robyn could react, the woman bashed her in the head with something rough like wood. The young archer was unconscious by the time the woman hoisted her over a shoulder and carried her away.

"No… No, no, no!" Nyx hissed under his breath, a rush of fear dashing through his serpentine body. He crawled after the strange woman as fast as he could, but the ground was wet and thick like a swamp and it slowed him down tremendously.

"Lady Robyn!!" he shouted desperately into the air, ignoring the pulsating pain he felt when he spoke. But the woman carrying Robyn disappeared into the fog, heading south along one of the village roads. Poor old Nyx began panicking, yielding to his ill torment, desperately wishing he still had his wings…

XVI

The Wardens of Grymsbi

'What is that strange smell?' Robyn Huxley sat and wondered, just moments after asking herself *'Where am I?'* and *'Why can't I move?'*

She felt drained and hungry, and the back of her head was tender and wet.

She felt her eyelids open fully and yet somehow everything remained a blur.

Chicken stew and old pie... It was her best guess and she hadn't been exactly wrong either. In reality, the smells of the room were of dust, berries, molding wood, and chewed up chicken bones from the previous day's stew left in a pot for the hounds to feed on later.

She found herself in an old cabin, all alone save for the ants and beetles crawling about. But the fireplace was lit and the pot that hung over it was close to a boil. She *wasn't* alone. Someone must've fed the fire recently – probably the same someone that tied her to that chair. She felt warm and muggy in her thick outdoor attire, and sitting so close to the fire was not helping.

Shit... What've you gotten yourself into now, Robyn?

Truly, she was getting tired of looking over her shoulder so often. The safety of her mother's farm had blinded her, habituated her into a sense of safety that she took for granted. But she didn't panic just yet. Whoever it was that tied her to that chair wouldn't have gone through all the trouble if they wanted her dead.

She batted her eyelids slowly, again and again, until her vision began to adjust. The room became a bit clearer, though she kept seeing everything doubled, which made her dizzy and sick to her stomach – *sicker*. She wondered if this is what it felt like to be drunk beyond any sense.

As she inspected the room she soon confirmed that she wasn't, in fact, alone.

A pair of green eyes was watching her from above a stairwell. She could just about make out the silhouette of what could have been a boy of eight or nine sitting on the top step. He was dressed in raggedy clothing and had short straight hair sticking out of his head like straw.

"*Ayisha!*" the boy shouted, and not two seconds later footsteps began to approach.

The wood of the stairs screeched with every step along with the voice of a young woman, perhaps in her late adolescent years. Her voice was quite loud and sharp with a thick Halghardian accent, and it towered over that of a softer-voiced young man. There was a third voice that Robyn couldn't quite make out, deeper and raspier than the other two but possibly still a woman's voice.

"Has she woken up?" asked the soft-voiced young man.

"She's been going on 'n' off for hours now," said the woman with the thick accent. "Hasn't fully come to her senses yet. Girl might've gone simple."

"*Simple?*" the young man scoffed. "Why is that?"

"I dunno. To start, she was *talkin'* while she slept."

"And?"

"That's scary as shit."

"No it's not. *Lots* of folks do that. My mum used to."

"Well it's scary as shit."

There was nothing but a chuckle from the third voice.

When Robyn saw the three shadows walking into the light of the fire, she recognized the first woman from the tavern. Her burgundy coat was now gone, hung on an old wooden rack by the cabin door. The dreadlocks on the woman's head were tied away from her face and Robyn saw that peculiar earring again, a sharp jaguar's tooth pierced through her left earlobe. The woman had on the same washed-out blouse that may have been white once but was now a tattered shade of ivory. There was a very noticeable patch sewn onto the left leg of her brown pants and she wore old hunting boots with empty dagger belts on the inner heel.

The young man was no man at all. He was a boy, no older than 15, with fair skin and curly brown hair that was starting to overgrow. His brown eyes had an innocence reminiscent of Robyn's young brother Melvyn. And whenever he spoke to the woman with the thick accent, his remarks were full of mockery, the amiable kind.

The third voice belonged to a young orcess with short black hair that was long in the front but shaved at the sides and back. Hailing from a society of humans, Robyn knew nothing of the way orcs aged but she placed her at about the same age as the first woman, which was about 18 or 19.

The three strangers scattered themselves throughout the living room, making it clear that the cabin was indeed their home. The dehydration was keeping Robyn from speaking or asking the countless questions she had in her mind, the most important of them being '*Who in all hells **are** you?*'

The woman with the dreadlocks and the thick accent leaned back against a wall with her arms crossed while the boy and the orc girl simply sat and stared at Robyn with awe.

"Are you all right?" the boy asked, not exactly nervously but cautiously.

Robyn used what little strength she had to lift her chin. The boy's face was clearer now. The peach fuzz on his chin, his flaring nostrils, the way his thick brows arched the way they did, conveying both curiosity and caution… It all began to settle in…

"W-Water," Robyn managed a croaky whisper.

The boy turned to the woman with the earring, as if requesting permission to move. After an approving nod, the boy hopped swiftly from his seat and brought over a small tankard of water to Robyn's chapped lips. She bent her neck back and let the cold water slide down her throat, and though it was tasteless she savored every drop.

"Tha's quite enough, now!" the woman with the earring barked at him. "We *need* tha' water for the soup later!"

The boy set the tankard down on the table and allowed Robyn a moment to breathe. The woman with the earring had her eyes fixed on Robyn like a livid watchdog. She looked distrustful, cold, and, to the average person, wildly intimidating. Her dark brown skin was smooth in some places and riddled with scars in others, and her eyes were considerably large and oval-shaped, which both suited her well but also *didn't*, considering she had the tendency to stare at people for far too long.

"Who are you?" Robyn finally asked.

"I'm Milo!" the boy replied jovially. "That's Ayisha."

"Shut yer bloody piehole!" Ayisha snapped at him. "We don't know 'er!"

"And that's Yuri over there," Milo said, motioning to the orc girl that had by then moved to the common room to sit and read.

"Are ye *deaf*, lad?!" Ayisha raised her voice.

Somehow, knowing all of their names made them less scary to Robyn.

"Don't worry. You're not a prisoner," Milo went on, attempting a friendly smile.

"Then why am I tied up?" Robyn asked.

"Well…"

"The *hells* she ain't one!" Ayisha growled. "What were ye doin' in that tavern, girl?!"

Robyn became suddenly startled as Ayisha charged towards her and bent to a knee in front of the chair. Meanwhile the orc girl, Yuri, was eavesdropping on the conversation, her eyes drifting to and from her book, a worn-out copy of 'The Return of Wingless Ehryn'.

"Easy there, Ayisha," Milo said. "Give the girl some time to adjust."

"She looks bloody well-adjusted to *me*!"

"Would you like some bread with your water?" Milo asked Robyn.

"No, I would like to be untied please…"

"*Shut* it, girl!" Ayisha growled loudly, sending a puff of air that blew a lock away from Robyn's cheek. "I *won't* ask again! What were ye doin' in that tavern?! Answer or I'll break yer fingers off!"

"You won't touch her," Milo said, not in a defensive way but more so to point out Ayisha's trickery. Ayisha spat at his boots, but the boy managed to dart out of the way in time. He then turned and spoke directly to Robyn. "She won't touch you," he said. "She's not allowed to touch you until Skinner gets back."

"Who's Skinner?" Robyn asked.

"He's our m-"

"Shut it!" Ayisha interrupted, rising to her feet. "She'll find out soon enough…"

She was a tall young woman, Robyn realized, not exactly thinly framed but strong and agile nonetheless.

"Look here, kid," she scolded Milo as she served herself a tankard of ale. "Ye best watch that tongue o' yers… Skinner may be fond of ye now, but don't let it get to yer damn head, ye hear?"

"I'm not," the boy took a seat near Robyn and rested his boots on the wooden dinner table. "I just think you should stop tormenting the poor girl."

"Precautions, lad…"

"Sounds more like *fear* to me," Yuri commented, her eyes returning to her book.

"Fuck off!" Ayisha barked, sipping on her ale.

"Well, that *would* explain why you felt the need to tie her up," Milo added.

"If I *hadn't* tied her, she would've ran!"

"No, she wouldn't have. *Run*, perhaps," Milo said, grinning as he always did when he properly corrected somebody.

"Cute," Ayisha glared at him annoyingly. "Correct me again 'n' see wha' happens…"

Robyn felt a sudden sense of discomfort upon being the center of a conversation that she wasn't a part of. "I'm sorry, but… *Where* am I?" she decided to ask.

"Same place ye was three hours ago," Ayisha said as she took her last gulp of ale.

"*Were*," Milo corrected her again.

With a fierce grunt, Ayisha threw the empty tankard at the boy. Her aim was more than precise, but he somehow managed to dodge her yet again.

"You mean… I'm still in *Grymsbi?*" Robyn asked nervously.

"The uglier areas, yes," said Ayisha.

"Hang on," Milo interrupted again. "Are you implying there are *pretty* areas in Grymsbi?"

"I swear I will slice yer tongue off, lad!" Ayisha glowered at him, but the boy's grin did not fade a bit. Robyn could see that he was enjoying himself and part of her believed that the Ayisha woman was somewhat fond of the boy, despite his immaturity and teasing manner. Then again, she hardly knew either of them. They could have been killers, for all she knew. And judging from the dagger straps on Ayisha's boots, she doubted it very little.

Suddenly, there was a knock on the front door…

A very particular knock, which Robyn found mildly amusing…

Four quick knocks, followed by two slow ones, and ending with four quick ones again. The sound was almost musical. It reminded Robyn of the drums that would announce the presence of an authority figure in Val Havyn, only without any horns or screaming announcers.

Ayisha opened the door and in walked a tall man with silver eyes, straight black hair that reached his back, and a hairless face that was astonishingly youthful for his age. He was dressed in hunting clothes and carried a thin single-edged blade on his back. He was about six feet in height and built like a blacksmith, arms and chest thick enough to be intimidating without any armor whatsoever.

"Took ye long enough," Ayisha scoffed at him.

"Distractions, lass," the man's voice was also softer than Robyn had expected.

"Sounds more like *women* to me," Yuri said, her eyes unable to look away from her book.

"Well... All right, *maybe*," the man replied with a grin as he began shedding layers of clothing.

"What shoulda taken ye an hour instead took *three*, eh?" Ayisha asked as she took his coat and hung it on the wooden rack next to hers. "And all for what? A fat arse 'n' a pair o' tits?"

"That's low even for you, Aldous," Milo smiled at him.

*Aldous, huh? So... **not** Skinner then*, Robyn thought. For some reason, this was a relief.

When Aldous finally noticed the stranger tied up in the corner of the room, his expression changed. His grin turned into a scowl and his eyes moved back and forth from Robyn to Ayisha. "Um... What's *this* all about?"

"I found 'er at the *Stumblin' Hare*," Ayisha said. "She was sittin' there with 'er pet snake 'n' that shit-eatin' orc that rides with the reds."

Aldous's face grew a sudden wall of distress. "The reds are back in Grymsbi?"

"Seems so," Ayisha said fretfully. "The *nerve* of the lot."

Robyn hesitated for a moment, still out of sorts with her unusual surroundings, but she was damned if she was going to let them talk about her friends that way.

"Y-You've made a mistake!" she said restlessly. "He's not *with* them!"

"The *hells* he ain't!" Ayisha snapped at her. "He wore the leather! *And* he had the mark on his wrist! I knows it when I sees it!"

"N-No, you don't understand! He's not *like* them!" Robyn argued. "They left him to *die*!"

"Ahh, and now yer so *fond* of 'im, are ye? Who's to say ye ain't with 'em too?!"

Ayisha's last remark nearly made Robyn implode with rage. She tried to stand but the ropes wouldn't allow it. Instead she remained in the chair, shivering and reddening with anger as her wrists became sore from tugging on the ropes so often.

"Don't you *ever* compare me to them!" she said, her jaw tightening like never before. "They tried to kill my friend... And *me*, they tried to..." she couldn't bring herself to finish; the knot in her throat wouldn't allow it. When the tears began to build around her eyes, Aldous couldn't help but frown.

"Bloody hells, Ayisha," he said as he unstrapped a dagger from his belt. "She's just a peasant girl."

"What in all hells do ye think yer doin'?" Ayisha stepped in between them.

"I'm untying her…"

"Not while *I'm* here, ye ain't!"

"She says she's not with the Brotherhood," Aldous argued.

"And?! *I* could say I'm the bloody Queen of Halghard, it won't make it true!"

"Then tell me what makes you so right…"

"*Many* things!" Ayisha's voice grew into a shout; her eyes were as wide as ever and her brows were raised in a manner more threatening than an unsheathed weapon. "Ye gonna be stupid enough to trust her over me? She's a stranger!"

"She's a *passerby*," Aldous said calmly.

"She's peculiar!"

"*You're* peculiar…"

"She was armed!"

"Show me one person who *isn't* armed in this damned village?"

"*A-And,*" Ayisha struggled to find more excuses. "Sh-She was talkin' while she slept!"

"Was she, now?" Aldous paused for a moment and glanced at Robyn with a raised eyebrow. "All right, well *that's* scary as shit."

Ayisha glanced at Milo, and just as she suspected the boy was chuckling under his breath.

"But it *isn't* a good enough reason to hold the girl hostage," Aldous added, before he stepped around Ayisha and knelt in front of the chair. He used his dagger to cut through the knots around Robyn's ankles.

"Stop!" Ayisha tried to protest.

Before any further commotion ensued, however, Robyn muttered, "Pull my sleeve up."

Nearly every pair of eyes turned to stare at her.

"What?" asked Aldous.

Robyn's brows lowered, her expression fearless and her hands in a fist.

"Pull my sleeve up," she said again, this time more sternly, as if it had been an order.

Carefully, Aldous gripped Robyn's right wrist and used his other hand to slide her sleeve up. He was confused for a moment, until he heard Robyn hiss under her breath from the sting. Her forearm was wrapped in a white cloth that was stained with red. Aldous used his dagger to cut through the cloth until the red scabs were exposed, forming a misshapen scorpion. The blisters on her scarred skin were so unnerving that even Ayisha couldn't help but kneel for a closer look.

"What I'll be damned," she muttered.

"They held me as their prisoner," Robyn said. "I would have died, if... if..."

"It's okay," Aldous said, using his dagger to cut the rest of the ropes. "You don't have to tell us."

The tension in the room died down bit by bit, as Ayisha began to question the shield of hostility she held against Robyn. "What of the orc?" she asked, much less angry now.

"He's not one of them anymore," Robyn explained. "He's no threat to you."

"So I'm to believ' he renounced his ways to look after a peasant girl?" Ayisha asked.

"*Renounced*? I'm impressed," Milo commented. Ayisha nearly punched the boy, had he not run off into the common room to sit with Yuri.

The ropes left red marks on Robyn's pale wrists; she could almost feel the blood rushing through the moment Aldous cut through the thick knots. "He looks after no one," she argued.

"Then why's he suddenly so friendly with ye?"

"He's not my friend," she added solemnly. "Believe me, he made that quite clear..."

"Well," Aldous sighed. "Probably best. The Brotherhood isn't the type to make friends. You're all right now. D'you *feel* okay?"

Robyn nodded slowly, as if the movement only worsened her headache.

"She hit 'er head," Ayisha remarked.

"You mean *you* hit my head!" Robyn corrected her.

"Only *once*!" Ayisha barked, crossing her arms as she leaned against a wall. "That blood there is from when ye hit the floor. Did no one ever teach ye how to faint properly?"

Robyn had no idea how to even answer such a question.

"Patience is a virtue, Ayisha," said Aldous.

"Patience is what gets ye killed. Or even worse, captured 'n' skinned alive."

Robyn caressed the scar on her forearm as Aldous strapped the dagger back onto his belt. At such close distance, Robyn noticed something peculiar about the young man. He seemed to be in his twenties, no older than her brother John. His face was symmetrical and clean and though there were a few scars here and there, it looked smoother than a child's face. But what really grasped her attention were his ears... They were round like a man's, but the upper edges were wrinkled and scarred as if...

She must have been staring for too long; Aldous cleared his throat and brought her back to her senses. "Don't worry, they still work," he said with a friendly smirk.

Robyn stammered and apologized, but his laughter eased her tension.

"He's a mutt," Ayisha said.

"A... *mutt*?" Robyn asked confusedly.

"Half human, half elf," Aldous explained.

For a moment Robyn forgot all about the throbbing pain in her scalp, she was so stunned. And though she knew it was rude, her eyes drifted unwillingly back to Aldous's disfigured ears. "*Half?*" she asked, brows arched with bewilderment. "I had no idea that was even possible..."

"'Course ye didn't," Ayisha grunted with annoyance. "Vallenghard's living decades in the past, it seems." It was obvious that Ayisha was not yet trusting towards Robyn, though her shoulders did appear far less tense than before. "Some merchant bloke down in Yulxester bought Aldous off a slave ship when he was a wee lad," she explained. "Cut off the tips of his ears so's he'll... *fit in.*"

Robyn felt a sudden wave of sickness overcome her. "By the gods, that's..."

"Awful?"

"Gutless?"

"...*Inhuman,*" Robyn finished.

Aldous nodded and smiled, a response that was much more affable than Robyn had expected. For someone with a past so dismal, Aldous seemed so jovial and cheerful it was astounding. "You think *that's* bad?" he chuckled. "Try being 22 years old with silver hair. I have to dye it black every full moon to keep it from fading."

"Praise the gods ye weren't born with blue skin," Ayisha added.

Robyn had no idea how else to respond. Never did she imagine such a thing was possible, for humans to breed with other species. If it was forbidden in Gravenstone to *befriend* a nonhuman, only the gods know what they would do if one were to have a child with a nonhuman.

Before she had enough time to take it all in, however, an upstairs door slammed against a wall and a cluster of voices overlapped in argument as the wooden stairs creaked with every one of their steps. Robyn was startled; the cabin was much more crowded than she thought it was. And, much like Ayisha and Milo, the group of misfits that stumbled down into the common room were arguing and mocking each other relentlessly as if they were all siblings.

"Do try and *season* it right this time, will you, Gibbons?"

"It's *chicken*, stupid. It ain't veal. Chicken's all the same goin' in."

"It's not the goin' in I'm concerned about, it's the comin' out."

"You disgust me."

"Your *smell* disgusts me."

Four children, all of them dressed in patchy secondhand clothing, walked downstairs in a single file line. The only one that Robyn recognized was the youngest, the boy she'd seen sitting in the stairwell when she first regained consciousness. The cook, presumably named Gibbons, was a husky kid of about fifteen. He didn't seem surprised to see Robyn and neither did the others, suggesting they'd caught a glimpse of her while she was unconscious; at most, Gibbons seemed surprised to see her free of the ropes while in the presence of

Ayisha.

The one that was arguing with Gibbons was a blonde boy of about thirteen wearing a hat made of a raccoon's fur. And the last one was a girl of about fourteen, a rather quiet girl with caramel-colored skin, a dagger belt similar to Aldous's, and chestnut-colored hair.

"Hey, watch your step! I just bought these shoes!" Gibbons shouted.

"Oh, calm your pits. They only cost you two coppers."

"Keep it down, the lot of ye!" Ayisha barked at them all. "I've a headache."

Robyn almost scoffed out loud. *You have a headache?*

"Oh... sorry, Ayisha," said Gibbons. "Skinner's back! He looks impatient. *And* nervous."

"How can ye tell? It's pitch black out there."

"Skinner *always* hits the reins with a sort of limp when he's nervous or impatient."

"I'm telling him you called him a limp," said the boy with the raccoon hat.

"Piss off, Tails!" Gibbons growled back.

"Alright, all of you, in position. Now!" Ayisha said in a shout.

The group scattered like mice, rushing to a formation in the middle of the common room. Meanwhile, Robyn had no idea what to do, and so she simply stood near the corner where she'd been tied up and observed.

Ayisha was nearest to the door, standing firmly with her hands at her sides like a soldier. The rest followed in what appeared to be a descending order according to height, starting with Aldous and Yuri the orc girl. Gibbons was beside them, and there was an empty space where Milo should have been. And finally the quiet girl, the boy with the raccoon hat, and the green-eyed boy stood at the very end.

Milo took Robyn's hand unexpectedly and pulled her towards the empty space in the formation. "Quick now!" he said to her. "You can stand here next to me."

Robyn hardly had the time to protest or say anything. She followed Milo and stood in line with the rest, when suddenly the front door opened with a slam. A shadow stood at the doorframe, the shadow of a weary but intimidating man in a large hat.

Before the man could take a single step inside, Ayisha shouted "Attention!" and the group of misfits raised their right hand to their foreheads and stomped the wooden floor with their right foot in unison.

"At ease, wardens," the man at the door replied with a salute, as he stepped into the cabin and dropped his bags by the door. The group did not move, however; they rested their arms at their sides and remained in place as if awaiting further instructions. The way they were all behaving gave Robyn the impression that this Skinner fellow was an authority figure of some sort, which made her feel even more out of sorts when she finally was able to see what he really looked like.

Skinner certainly did not have the bearings of a knight or a guardsman, not in the slightest. He looked like any other middle-aged man, save for his unique flashy style. His coat was a vibrant blue and his black hat looked like the type of hat a ship captain would wear, decorated with three feathers; a red one, a black one, and a white one with black spots.

"A pleasure to see ye again, sir," Ayisha spoke first.

"Anything to report?" the man asked, his voice petulant but wise nonetheless.

"We've reason to believe the Rogue Brotherhood has returned to Grymsbi, sir," Ayisha responded.

With a raised brow, Skinner took slow steps down the line formation, locking eyes with every one of his protégées one by one. When his eyes reached Robyn, however, he paused in his tracks. His expression wasn't exactly cold, but it wasn't entirely welcoming either.

"Well... what do we have here?" he asked.

"Ayisha found her at the *Stumblin' Hare*, Sir Skinne-" Milo tried to intervene.

But all it took was a raised finger to shut the boy up.

"I was asking the girl," Skinner said, tipping his head slightly to the left in awe.

Skinner's demeanor was calm and yet alarming all at once. He had a beard that was not fully grey but nearly there. His black hair was the same, long enough to reach his shoulders yet graying bit by bit. He must have been in his fifties or sixties, but he appeared to have the energy of a bear. What caught Robyn's attention the most, however, was the scar on the man's left cheek. A very particular scar, it was; the type of scar that only a branding iron could make. It was in the shape of a scorpion, with its pincers raised upwards and its tail curving up at the bottom.

Once again realizing she had been staring for far too long, Robyn decided to speak up for herself. "Pardon me, sir," she said, her lower lip trembling. "I'm... Robyn Huxley of Elbon, sir..."

"Is that so?" Skinner raised a brow. "A Vallenghardian, eh? Why are you so far from home?"

"I saw 'er walk into town earlier this evening," Ayisha decided to say. "She was in the company of that orc that rides with the reds. But she claims he ain't with 'em no more." Skinner's brows lowered instantly at the mentioning of the Beast, causing for a much more menacing expression.

"H-He's not!" Robyn argued, a hesitant stutter in her lip. "He's not like them... He's not here to hurt you and neither am I... I *swear* to y-"

Skinner raised a finger into the air once again, this time right at her.

Robyn couldn't help but to stop talking, as if the man was using sorcery to control her tongue. She knew, however, that he wasn't; the only sorcery the man needed was intimidation.

"You never answered my question," Skinner said, his eyes narrowing into a perplexed stare. "What's a girl like you doing so far from home, eh? More importantly, how on earth did you travel to the other side of Gravenstone all alone without dying?"

The room was silent all over again. Robyn panicked for a moment, suddenly wondering what had become of her beloved Nyx. The last she saw of him was the moment she left him at the tavern while she chased after the Beast. But the panic only lasted for so long, before she realized whom exactly she was panicking for. The dreadful feeling in her chest was replaced with reassurance, knowing very well that Nyx would rather, as he had proved it before, be killed again and again before giving up...

"I, um..." she hesitated. She realized every pair of eyes in the room was on her. And so, with a deep breath, she chose her words very carefully. "I wasn't alone," she said. "I had... *help*."

"Did you, now?" Skinner asked; this time his stare was far less hostile and much more intrigued. "Help from *who*?"

* * *

"All aboard!" the caravan master shouted.

An unusually diverse bunch climbed into the back of a hooded wagon, finding comfort among the wood and steel; a human family of three, five woodland elves, and two gnomes, to be precise. The caravan master was standing by counting coins in his hands when he was abruptly approached by a green broad-shouldered figure wearing a torn vest and trousers with red leather patches.

"Oi! You there," the figure said gruffly. "I hear ye headin' north?"

"Aye, good sir," the caravan master replied with a demeanor so calm that it surprised the orc that approached him. "Ten coppers for a ride, if you're interested. Fifteen if you're looking to go all the way up to Dehrvonshire. Though I must warn you, folks up there are rather close-minded about... *outsiders*."

The orc suddenly drew one of his daggers. He held it up at the caravan master, who panicked for a slight moment until he saw that it wasn't the sharp end that was being aimed at him.

"It ain't much," the orc said. "But it's all I got."

"Ohh," the caravan master chuckled with relief. "Pardon me, sir. But I've no need f-"

"That stone there will get ye at least fifty coppers."

The man's eyes moved towards the dagger's hilt. He hadn't noticed the shiny green stone entrenched onto the wood. "Is that so?" he took the dagger and examined it. It wasn't particularly special, but the stone was pretty enough that the man could swindle someone into thinking it was an emerald. And so the man threw it into his rucksack, shot the orc a friendly smirk, and said, "Welcome aboard, friend!"

The orc moved towards the back of the wagon. He had one foot on the wooden step when suddenly a voice beckoned him afar.

"*Beast!*" it called. A very familiar voice, it was. "*Wait… Beast…!*"

Glancing back, all the orc could see was fog. But as Nyx came closer, the curving trail in the mud became clearer; he emerged from the darkness, his voice winded as he begged for help.

"What the fuck are ye doin' here?" the Beast asked as he stepped away from the caravan for a moment. The passengers sitting atop the wagon gasped at the sight of the striped black-and-white serpent. Grymsbi was full of serpents, sure. But never had they heard one *speak* before.

"Beast!" Nyx hissed, his dry tongue slithering in and out of his mouth. "Help… Please…"

"Where's the scrap?!" the Beast asked when he didn't spot her amidst the fog.

"Taken," said Nyx, unable to speak more than a few words at a time.

The caravan master chuckled nervously from afar. "I-Is everything all right there, friend?"

"A moment!" the Beast growled, then looked back down at the serpent. "Taken by *who*?!"

"Don't know," Nyx struggled to catch his breath. "Follow… South…"

The Beast's chest began pounding, and he was caught off guard by it. Had it been any other human, he would have turned the other way at that very moment. But this was Robyn… This was the girl that saved his life when everyone else left him to die, the girl that refused to leave him behind even when he had ordered her to.

"We must… Go… *Now*," Nyx pressed him.

"Um… F-Friend?" the caravan master called again. "I see that you've got your hands tied at the moment, but we are running a bit late as it is and w-"

"I said a *moment*!" the Beast growled again.

"Beast!" Nyx spoke slowly and carefully, fighting through the pain. "Robyn… *needs* us…"

The orc sighed furiously, a cloud of grey mist gathering at his lips.

"I shoulda known bett'r," he said. "I never shoulda listened to ye…"

"What?!"

"Ye heard the scrap, didn't ye? Ye were right there!" the Beast grimaced. "She said I'd be welcome 'ere. Said in Grymsbi, I'd have me freedom. Then I come 'ere and it's just as I expected. Nothing but a shithole."

"She wanted to help!" Nyx tried to argue. "She risked h-"

"She's a reckless scrap, is what she is!" the Beast turned, as if attempting to walk away.

Nyx wished suddenly for a pair of claws, he was so aggravated. Even as a snake, he was quite fast and caught up with the orc easily. But he could do nothing to stop the orc from leaving, for that he had to rely on his words, however physically painful they were.

"And what are *you*?!" he managed to say, his voice becoming raspy as if it wasn't meant to be raised so loud. "Running like a coward... when your *friends* need you...?"

"She *ain't* me friend!"

"She's the closest thing to one you have!"

The Beast growled and gripped his axe. To any other person, the image would have been terrifying. But to Nyx, who had faced death more times than he could count, it was as if he was staring at a harmless critter. "Go on," he said valiantly. "Kill me..."

But the Beast realized exactly whom he was trying to intimidate. Such a strange feeling it was, to know you could intimidate almost anyone and yet come across someone who faced you with such boldness. First Robyn, now Nyx? Even someone as stubborn as the Beast couldn't help but be intrigued by the pair.

"S-Sir?" the caravan master called nervously again. "I'm afraid it's time now..."

The Beast did nothing this time, only sighed again, as if contemplating his decision one last time before making it.

"They left you to die..." Nyx said abruptly.

The Beast felt his hands start to shiver. He'd never felt vulnerable, at least not as far as he could remember. Such a feeling was foreign to him. As he stared down at the serpent, however, he saw real humanlike emotion in his eye; it was almost frightening.

"Th-They... left you... to *die*," Nyx struggled on, his voice full of dread and sorrow and aching him awfully. "And... *who* saved you?"

The Beast was far too dogged to answer, but he felt the sting all the same.

"Who... saved... you?"

The Beast closed his eyes and clenched his jaw. "*Robyn*..." he muttered.

"Robyn," Nyx repeated, and it was clear he was now using all of his muscle strength to speak. "I *told* her... to leave you... And *still*, she saved you..."

Memories of the disastrous raid ran through the Beast's mind. The fight with the minotauro, the attack of the ogres, the hours he'd spent holding on to that rock so that he wouldn't sink... And then there was Robyn, who had freed him simply because she couldn't find it in her heart to leave him. Trying to fight back this strange new feeling, the Beast glared at Nyx for a long time before the serpent spoke his last words.

"If you won't help... *Kill* me... Now... And I'll help her myself..."

The Beast softened his grip on his axe almost involuntarily. His yellow eyes drifted into the distance, towards the foggy village of Grymsbi. "Damn it all to hells," he grunted, and then a moment later he was walking briskly back towards the caravan master, cursing angrily under his breath the entire time.

"W-Well, hello again! I do hope everything is in order," the caravan master said tensely. "Do forgive my mistrust towards your *f-friend*, the serpent. I'm not particularly fond of the dark art of sorcery. But I'm sure y-"

"Change o' plans," the Beast said gallingly. "I'm gonna need that dagger back…"

* * *

Even in the darkness, the trees were noticeably different. No longer were they surrounded by a massive roof of greenery; the trees were starting to look like actual trees, some hardly higher than fifteen or twenty feet. There was an unpleasantly pungent smell in the air, like that of humidity and horse droppings blending awfully with incense, and in the distance trails of smoke stained the skies just above a cluster of wooden cottages.

"Ahh Grymsbi," said the thief Hudson Blackwood as he took a deep whiff.

"Smells bloody awful," John had a hand over his nose and another over his belly.

"I know. Isn't it a beauty?" Hudson grinned as he took a bite out of a green apple. "Say what you will about the fleapit of a town, but they sure know how to properly season a rabbit."

John noticed the apple and instantly pressed a hand to his satchel. When he didn't feel the bump, he locked eyes with the thief and scowled. "Will you *stop* doing that?!"

"I'll stop doing it when you learn to keep a closer eye on your things, mate," Hudson took another bite and tossed the apple back at John, who held it as if it had been slobbered on by a dog. "You *should* be thanking me, really. Think of it as free training."

John felt the rumbling in his belly again and gave in to the hunger. Having eaten only one meal that day, he couldn't afford to be finicky. He took a bite.

They could see Grymsbi getting bigger in the distance, now less than a mile ahead.

Syrena of Morganna was rather silent, as was usual of her. A sick feeling was settling into her gut, though it had very little to do with the smell in the air. Lately she had felt more confident than she had in years, it was obvious even in the way she walked. After years of isolation, the witch's only companion had been her own conscience. Except now she had *two*… And they were quite real… Two companions with whom she had deceived death more than once, and nothing frightened her more than losing them when she had only just found them.

"Easy, darling," Hudson said to her, noticing the wary look on her face. "It'll be just fine, you'll see. Grymsbi's welcoming orcs and elves now. You'll be the least of their worries, I promise you."

Syrena turned to look at him. There it was, that nervous eye twitch; it was subtle, but it was there. Her left eye, so luminously orange, flickered beneath her fidgety eyelid. "I thought we were going to *Wyrmwood!*" she said.

"We are, darling. Grymsbi's along the way."

John felt a sudden guilt at being the only one eating, and so he offered the half-eaten apple to the anxious witch. She snatched it so willingly that it surprised John. She sunk her teeth into it and chewed so quickly she bit her tongue twice and yet hardly winced. At her waist, her black satchel was twisting and fidgeting as if something was pushing it from the inside.

"Will you stop that?!" Syrena hissed, and then instantly sighed as if it pained her to convey such a tone. "You'll get us into trouble if you're seen… d'you *understand* that?"

Sivvy pushed open the lid of the witch's satchel and caught a glimpse of the outside, bringing with her that glowing blue aura of hers. She looked up at the witch and tilted her head in that curious manner of hers.

"Don't give me that look!" Syrena said. "You *have* to stay in there…"

John and Hudson looked at one another fretfully. Every time their minds forgot about the pixie hidden in Syrena's satchel, the curious little thing only came back to remind them. Hudson had tried to reason with Syrena, but she simply refused to hear it.

"*She saved our lives!*" she had argued. "*We owe it to her!*"

Hudson understood that, and he agreed with the witch. He only hoped that the people of Grymsbi were at least half as understanding.

As they got closer, John noticed the abundance of footprints along the muddy path; some of them were massive like an orc's foot, others were much smaller like an adolescent's or a young woman's. "Grymsbi's crawling with travelers, I presume?" he asked.

"Like you wouldn't believe," Hudson remarked. "Especially now that it's a sanctuary village. Folks of all sorts are migrating to Halghard and Grymsbi's the first stop. So long as we stick together, we'll be fine. And for gods' sake, do try and behave, mate."

John smirked. "I'll try," he said. He felt his stomach growling from the hunger again. The thief must have noticed it, for when Syrena handed him the apple he passed it right along to John.

And so they walked, much slower than their usual pace due to the lack of proper rest. Though there was constant banter among them, there was also a sense of companionship that hadn't been there a week prior. Old Man Beckwit would often say there was nothing like a long journey on the road to make a group of misfits either bond like a family or grow to loathe one another like adversaries. In this case, John was thankful that the outcome was the former. And the proof was certainly there, from the way they walked affably side by side, to the way they passed the green apple back and forth to share.

When they finally arrived at Grymsbi, it was darker and emptier than usual. While it was usually lively, even at night, the peasants had grown wary as of late, as more nonhumans began migrating into town. John certainly noticed the nonhuman folk; it was near impossible *not* to notice, for he had never seen one walk through the streets of a human village before. Such things were simply not permitted in Vallenghard.

They approached the nearest tavern, a shabby old thing with a sign that read *'The Stumblin' Hare'* and another beneath it that read *'Greenskins & Rabbits Welcome'*. There was a beggar sitting at the front steps, an elderly elf with a silver head of hair and a beard; his skin was a pale blue and he was dressed in old rags that couldn't possibly have kept him warm enough. Though elves were known to be on the thinner side, this one looked like he was on the verge of starving to death. He rattled a tin cup as they walked by, and John reached into his pockets for any coppers he could spare. But when he drew out the coins and threw them into the elf's cup, he noticed something peculiar.

The elf's forearm had been marked by a number... It read: 0107.

The elf noticed and pulled his sleeve back up to cover the numbers, his eyes lighting up with shame. John stood there gawking like a snooping child until Hudson pulled him by the shoulder.

"Come, mate," the thief muttered. "It's best not to get involved, trust me."

They went into the tavern and sat at the nearest empty table. It was rather lively, as it usually was later in the evenings. And there were a couple of nonhumans sitting and mingling about with the more broadminded peasants in town.

"What was that number?" John asked the moment they had some privacy, his mind still riddled with questions. Hudson sighed and his lips curved into a subtle smirk, a *sad* one, like a disheartened soul whose hope had vanished, leaving him incapable of a genuine smile.

"It does *sound* rather nice, does it not?" the thief remarked. "*Grymsbi*... the very first village in Halghard to bend the kingdom's law. The first 'sanctuary village', they named it. And I must say, it *does* roll off the tongue... But they don't tell you the nasty parts..."

"They... *mark* them?" John asked, his brows lowering and his gut turning.

"A *permit number*, they call it. Any nonhuman that migrates into the village must pay a fee to obtain one. Even the little ones. Anyone *without* it gets sent right back to where they came from."

"But that's bloody *awful*..."

Hudson exhaled. "You learn fast, mate."

Suddenly there was a high-pitched squeal coming from Syrena's satchel. She turned in her chair and pressed a hand down over the lid. "*Stop it!*" she hissed, and then immediately glanced all around. But so late in the evening, the peasants were far too drunk to notice or care.

"Need help there?" Hudson asked.

"She won't stop moving…"

And she was right. Sivvy had never been outside the Woodlands and being the curious thing that she was, she was desperate to catch a glimpse of it all.

"*S-Stop! Sivvy!*" Syrena hissed again.

Sivvy finally stopped moving when she found a hole at the bottom of the satchel, through which she was able to peek. Syrena tried to relax, but her eye started twitching again when the tavern server approached their table rather enthusiastically.

"Good evenin', folks!" the young man said with a broad smile. "The name's Seamus, at yer service! Can I get ye anything? Ale? Potatoes? A bit o' spiced rabbit?"

"Yes to all," said Hudson, and it was followed by a stroppy silence.

"Err," Seamus hesitated, eyeing the three sloppily dressed misfits up and down repeatedly. "Have ye got the coin to pay for it all?"

"He asked you a question, mate," Hudson gave John a shove.

"Oh… Um… Sure," said John. Seamus gave them all a smile and headed for the kitchens. The farmer then glanced at the thief with a scowl. "Y'know, I'm not *made* of money!"

"Yes, but you owe me," Hudson snatched a leftover mug of ale that had been sitting on the table when they arrived and gulped it down. "Need I remind you how you got me locked up back in Val Havyn?"

"You cannot hold that over my head forever…"

"Watch me," Hudson grinned. "Besides, they *did* strip me of all my coin, mate. The least you could do is buy me a meal."

"*Stripped* you of your coin?"

"All three coppers of it."

John scoffed, though in a friendlier way than he had in previous occasions. Hudson noticed Syrena's hand was still shivering, and so he placed his own hand over hers and gave it a gentle squeeze.

She turned to him. They shared a smile.

"Something the matter, darling?"

She breathed deeply, her eyes glancing all around. Most peasants were locked in drunken conversations while the rest were sloppily singing and dancing to the bard's upbeat rendition of *The Ballad of the Golden Eagle*. Even John was humming along, a joyful grin plastered on his face. No one seemed to be paying the witch any mind and yet she couldn't help but feel as if the entire world was watching her.

"I'm fine," she nodded, her eye still twitching madly.

"Ease yourself, darling," the thief caressed her hand. "I imagined Syrena of Morganna would be excited to be back in Halghard."

She chuckled. "I was only six years old when I left Morganna," she said. "Hardly remember the wretched place. And I'm sure nobody in this side of the world wants *anything* to do with me..."

"Hey... Look at me," Hudson said, feeling unexpectedly overwhelmed with empathy. When she locked eyes with him, it was as if there was suddenly no one else in the room but the two of them. "Fuck them," he whispered to her. "Fuck what they all think..."

He gripped her damp hands tighter, and she was surprised at how much it was helping. Her lips curved into an anxious smile. Had they not been surrounded by peasants, she would have undeniably kissed him. And he would have undeniably allowed her.

Some fifteen minutes later, they were feasting.

It was well past sundown and yet all they had eaten that day was a roughly cooked squirrel, some mushrooms that made them feel sick and dazed, and the green apple they'd shared between the three of them. Suffice it to say they ate until they could no longer fit anything in their bellies, and then proceeded to wash it down with ale.

Syrena may not have felt as safe as she did in the Woodlands, but at least her eye became stagnant and relaxed after every conversation. Little did she know that John and Hudson felt even safer next to *her*, after seeing what she was capable of. She kept glancing down at her satchel, so as to make certain Sivvy was well hidden. She could hardly see anything except for that subtle glow when she lifted the rucksack's lid, but it was enough to calm her.

The evening was peaceful, at least as peaceful as it had been in recent times.

Too peaceful for a place like Gravenstone, where trouble lurked around every corner.

It was nearly midnight, in fact, when the trouble finally arrived at Grymsbi. It began with a distant shout, a *child's* shout, and it caught the attention of half the crowd at *The Stumblin' Hare*. Just moments later, a boy no older than twelve stumbled in, panicked and out of breath.

"Seamus!" the boy shouted. "Where's Seamus?!"

John and Syrena both grew nervous all of a sudden. Hudson, on the other hand, kept munching on his rabbit as if he had not a care in the world.

"Seamus!" the boy ran straight for the bar.

"Calm yerself, lad. Ye'll scare away the customers," said the tavern server as he wiped ale and slobber from the wooden counter.

"Th-They're back, Seamus!" the boy said, his eyes wide with terror.

"Whoa there, settle down," Seamus pulled the kid aside so as to speak discreetly. "Relax now. Talk to me. *Who's* back?"

"The Brotherhood... I saw 'em... They're walking into town at this moment..."

Hudson suddenly froze mid-bite. Among the peasants, there were a few panicked whispers. Some even gathered their belongings in a rush and bolted for the doors.

"S-Settle down, everyone!" Seamus leapt out from behind the bar. "I-I'm sure it's all fine!"

But it was of no use. The peasants had consumed far too much ale to remain calm. They were panicking. And within seconds, the muttering grew into a chaotic clutter of fear and dismay.

"Everyone, *please*! Settle down! W-We'll lock the doors and... um..."

Seamus had lost control of the tavern by then. Some of the drunken peasants even took the opportunity to rob the lad while he was distracted trying to bring order into the room.

"What do we do?" John Huxley asked over the chatter. Syrena remained silent, her left eye twitching wildly all over again. Hudson wiped his mouth with a handkerchief, slowly and carefully, looking about as lost in thought as a child. "Hudson?!" John gave him a shove. "What do we do?!"

"Lower your bloody voice, mate," the thief said calmly.

"What? Why?!"

"Shh. Listen..."

Hudson held a finger up near his ear, as if signaling John to keep his lips sealed and pay close attention. There were snickers just outside the tavern, along with slow heavy footsteps over the mud...

"Please! Everyone, calm yerselves!" young Seamus kept trying desperately to keep the peace. At that moment, an old man burst out of one of the rooms, the skin around his eyes wrinkled from the lack of sleep. "What on earth is goin' on here?!" he shouted, his face red and sweaty.

Seamus stepped forward nervously. "Sir! Thank the gods you're awake..."

The old man scoffed. "Ye better have a damn good explanation, boy!"

"Y-Yes, sir! I've heard word, sir, that..."

Seamus suddenly froze in silence. The heavy footsteps were now coming from the wooden stairs on the tavern's porch. In unison, the voices began to die down and every head in the room turned except for Hudson's; the thief remained seated, his mind reeling and his hat hiding half his face.

"*M-Mercy, sir!*" cried a frail voice from outside the doors, a voice that sounded like the beggar elf's. "*Mercy... I beg you, have merc-*"

A dagger silenced him.

The tavern doors creaked open and a shadow now stood at the entrance, a shadow with decorated dreadlocks, a leather patch over his eye, and a bright red coat over his hunting leathers.

The entire room fell silent as Captain Malekai Pahrvus strolled in casually, wiping the blood off of his dagger. He was followed by a group of mercenaries, also dressed in red leather and also with a hungry look on their faces.

John Huxley recognized the captain instantly; he'd seen that face back in the royal palace during the attack. The man still had both of his eyes then, but John had no doubt that it was the very same man with whom he'd crossed blades with near Lotus Creek, where the princess had been taken. John turned his gaze away cautiously. Both he and Hudson were huddled over their food with their backs to the men in red.

"*Damn it!*" he whispered. Hudson said nothing still, only listened. And Syrena had her hands resting on the table when they impulsively started to ooze white smoke. She had to hide them under the table over her lap, but there was no covering that burning smell.

Captain Malekai made it to the tavern bar and placed his hands on the wood, leaning casually against it as if waiting to be served. Meanwhile, the peasants watched him; it was so quiet in the room, they could almost hear the crickets in the garden. Malekai glanced around nonchalantly, his brows lowered, his arms stretched out in the air as if he was confused. "What happened to the music?" he asked.

Nervously, the bard stammered and began playing again, this time a much softer tune. The tavern customers that remained glanced at one another with uncertainty. Malekai called for the tavern server's attention while the rest of the red mercenaries found a seat somewhere in the room. It was enough to ease some of the tension, but the presence of the Brotherhood had certainly caused a dent in the atmosphere.

"The name's Malekai Pahrvus!" the man introduced himself, holding a hand out. "Captain of the Rogue Brotherhood." Seamus stood nervously behind the bar, unsure of how to react to the captain's presence. "Where *I'm* from, lad… it is a courtesy to shake the hand of a guest…"

Seamus shook the man's hand and gulped down some water to ease his aching nerves. "H-Hello! Yes… Um, c-can I help ye?"

"Yes," the captain nodded. "You can start by serving me a drink."

Seamus did it reluctantly. By then, some fifteen rogue mercenaries had made themselves at home, sitting comfortably among the peasants and helping themselves to their food and drinks as if they had a right to it all.

"Why, this place looks more of a wreck than we last left it," Malekai snickered. "Have you no decency, boy?"

The old man next to Seamus, who appeared to be the owner of the tavern, was the only one brave enough to stand up to the captain. He leaned in, so as to not disturb the bit of peace that was left in the room. "What in all hells is the meanin' of this?!" he asked sharply.

Malekai took a sip from his ale and then glanced menacingly at the old man. "I'd watch that tone if I were you, good sir…"

"Ye don't scare me, lad," the old man replied. "Yer standin' in *our* village grounds. *One* word 'n' the village guards will be on ye like hounds."

Suddenly, it happened again... A grin, a chuckle, and a head nod, such as was usual of Captain Malekai Pahrvus. "Tell me, kind sir," he said calmly. "Are you the owner of this establishment?"

"That, I am!" the old man said. "And I will *not* tolerate a drunken madman *bursting* through my doors and breaking the peac-"

Suddenly the room went silent once again...

Without saying a word, Malekai drew his dagger and plunged it into the man's gut. He then twisted it viciously and yanked it out with a swift pull. The man fell, creating a puddle of blood around his twitching body. There was a sudden scream; a horrified woman dropped to her knees, crying frantically next to the old man's body.

Malekai grabbed Seamus's wet rag from the counter and used it to wipe the red smears from his dagger. He held it up close to his eyes to make certain it was nice and clean, and then he smiled and tossed the rag back at Seamus, who was horror-stricken to say the least.

"My apologies for that," Malekai said nonchalantly. "I'm not fond of being interrupted." He then glanced at the bard and pointed his dagger at him. "You stop playing again and you'll be next, you hear?"

The nervous bard nodded and resumed picking at his harp.

John Huxley saw nothing, but his ears had heard it all and he had to shut his eyes to distract himself from the horror. His hands were shaking from both fear and anger, wishing he could leap up and kill the rogue captain where he stood. But he knew that exposing himself was the dumbest thing he could do at that moment, especially when Viktor Crowley was depending on him getting to Wyrmwood.

"Now, where were we?" Malekai turned towards Seamus again.

"The farmgirl 'n' the Beast, cap'n," Borrys Belvaine approached the bar and sat on a stool near Malekai.

"Ahh yes," Malekai grinned. "I'm here because I'm searching for someone... Perhaps you can help me out, young sir."

Malekai was acting as if nothing out of the ordinary had just happened. Seamus, on the other hand, had frozen with fear. He was sweating awfully and had to keep wiping the counter to distract himself from his superior's dead body laying just a couple of feet away.

"I'm looking for a girl," the captain went on. "A young one... Fair-skinned, black curls, a real beauty. We believe she's traveling with an orc... An orc with a scarred chest, dressed in red leathers just like ours."

Malekai had a talent for reading expressions. And when he gazed upon young Seamus again, he knew what the look in his eyes meant. The young man had seen them, all right. And so, with a devious grin, Malekai went on.

"If you've seen them, I would appreciate any help you can offer, my good friend... The reward for your assistance would be most generous, I assure you."

Seamus stammered nervously, his lip shivering as he spoke.

"P-Please... We don't want any trouble, sir," he said.

"Nor do I... Just tell me where they went and you won't ever see me again..."

Seamus hesitated, but after taking a gander at his horrified guests he couldn't help but yield.

"They were here," he said. "But they've been gone for hours now. I-I swear..."

"Ahh I see," Malekai said, the hint of a smirk on the corner of his lips. "Any idea as to where they've gone?"

Seamus froze again; he could see the look of hunger in Malekai's eye. And he knew that, should he reveal what he knew, the girl's life might be at stake. Truthfully, it terrified him. But the young man was unfortunately more keen on saving his own skin than saving someone else's.

"Keep in mind, young lad," Malekai leaned in closer. "I *always* find out when someone's lied to me. *Always*. And when I do... Well..." He didn't finish his thought; he simply looked down at the dead man nearby lying on a puddle of his own blood.

"I-I saw a woman take the girl away!" Seamus revealed. "Ayisha is her name... Sh-She's one of Skinner's. She took her to their cabin over by the southern outskir-"

"I know where the old bastard lives," Malekai interrupted, his face a mixture of satisfaction and concern, as if he knew a thing or two about Skinner's reputation.

"Shall we go, cap'n?" Borrys asked.

Malekai spat on the floor out of habit. He then forced the grin back onto his face as if trying to look convincingly poised and glanced towards the nearest of his rogue mercenaries. "Clive!" he said. "Keep an eye on them all until I get back."

"Aye, cap'n," Clive snickered.

Before he left, Malekai glanced at the bartender one last time. "What was your name, lad?"

The young man shivered and wiped the sweat from his brow. "S-Seamus..."

"Congratulations, Seamus," Malekai gave him a heavy pat on the shoulder. "You've just earned yourself a tavern."

Seamus looked a bit relieved, though the horror in his eyes remained.

"Now do try and clean up this mess, will you?" Malekai tapped the dead body on the floor with his boot. "Your customers look rather unhappy."

And with that, the captain headed for the doors, leaving behind a room full of worried faces and subtle whispers, as Seamus proceeded to clean up the mess on the floors of his new tavern...

* * *

The chicken might have been slightly overcooked, but every bite was tangy and savory to Robyn's lips and she bit into it until there was nothing but bones left on her plate. The rest of the children had finished their supper and most of them were lounging about in the cabin. It was clear that guests were unusual in their home; most of them sat at close proximity to Robyn, especially the boys.

Osric Skinner, the commander of the peculiar crew, sat across from her at the dining room table shuffling through a dusty pile of parchments and maps. "You say it's Drahkmere you're heading to?" he asked.

"It's where my brother's heading to," Robyn wiped her lips. "I lost track of him in the Woodlands. But he can't have gone far."

"If he even made it out, that is," Ayisha muttered coldly.

Robyn didn't particularly dislike Ayisha, but the woman's pessimistic ways were certainly starting to pick at her nerves. "He *made* it out!" she argued, though her voice cracked mid-sentence. "He *must* have..."

Ayisha said nothing else this time, only shrugged and leaned in over Skinner's shoulder. Worriedly, Robyn turned her attention back to her plate and finished munching on her last piece of wing.

"So what d'you think?" the young cook, Gibbons, asked abruptly. Robyn hadn't seen him approaching and was mildly startled, nor did she realize Milo was inching closer from the other side like an eager child desperate for attention. "The chicken, I meant," Gibbons clarified. "How is it?"

"It's complete rubbish," Tails grunted, walking by with a half-eaten drumstick in his hand. "It tastes like goblin shite."

"You *would* know what that tastes like, then!" Gibbons gave his friend a punch in the arm.

"It's brilliant, Gibbons," Robyn smiled. And she meant it, too.

Gibbons smiled back, his face turning red as he leaned back casually on the dining room table. "Really? D'you really think so? Most people don't appreciate the art of cooking. It takes time and patience, and y-"

"Get your arse off the table, lad," Skinner muttered, his eyes never leaving the pile of parchments.

"Ohh," Gibbons's face turned even redder. "S-Sorry, sir..."

"Care for any more water?" Milo asked Robyn as held out a tin jar, his curiosity towards the girl more obvious by the minute.

"Never mind water," Skinner grunted, still digging through the pile. "Why don't you offer the girl some ale?"

"Um, no thanks," Robyn shook her head. "I've never liked the taste."

Skinner scoffed under his breath. "No one drinks ale 'cause they like the taste."

"How about an apple?" Milo asked with a wide grin, desperate to keep Robyn's attention.

"No, thank you," Robyn chuckled.

"Or a pear? A carrot? Some garlic?"

"I-I'm honestly stuffed, thanks..."

"A bit of tea, perhaps?" Gibbons asked from afar.

"Give her some of the grey. That spinach chive one's a real gut-wrencher."

"Bloody hells, why does *she* get all the pamperin'?" Ayisha growled with annoyance. And next to her, Yuri mumbled something along the lines of '*No one's ever offered* **me** *some garlic*'.

"Well *if* what she says is true," Skinner replied to Ayisha, his eyes finally finding the old map they'd been searching for among the pile. "*If* the princess of Vallenghard has indeed been taken... then perhaps King Alistair might benefit from an alliance with King Rowan. Halghard needs more swords and Vallenghard's got 'em. If a favor exchange can be arranged, well..."

"So ye plan on leavin' us again?" Ayisha protested. "Sir, with respect, we're n-"

"Don't question me, girl," Skinner said, though his tone was less strict than his words were. "Alistair's army is camped just a few miles south. It won't take me more than a day's journey. Besides, rumor has it Balthazar Locke's troops march south as we speak. Know what *that* means?"

Ayisha, along with the rest of the young wardens, had silenced themselves, their attention focused solely on their commander.

"It means it's only a matter of time before things get bloody messy around here," Skinner remarked. "I need you lot to stay here. Grymsbi's the nearest township for miles and raids might be inevitable. This town could use a few good swords to defend it."

"Fine," Ayisha said. "But I'm ridin' with ye!"

"Nonsense," Skinner said without hesitating. "You're in charge while I'm gone."

"Aldous can look after 'em! Ye might *need* me f-"

"The answer's '*no*', Ayisha..."

"But, sir, y-"

"You're staying here, soldier. That's an order!" Skinner snapped, and Ayisha's lips remained shut afterwards. But, as harsh as the man seemed, he had an obvious fondness for his orphaned group of miscreants. It was clear in the way he always softened the blow with a justification. "There's no need to worry about me, I'll be fine," he said. "Alistair's an old friend of mine. Believe me, the trip will be a breeze compared to that mess up north. I'll be takin' the cart. I can bring weapons and provisions to the troops while I'm at it."

"Fine then," Ayisha said reluctantly, aiming a finger at the map. "But I'm warnin' ye *now*. There's no way ye can take the path through the slopes. Damn rain's flooded the whole thing. I suggest the cliffside road."

Milo, Gibbons, and Tails, the three boys in the room that were close to Robyn's age, huddled around their commander, their eyes fixed on the map as they searched for a safer way out of town.

"What about *this* path here?" Milo pointed out.

"It's flooded, too," Tails said.

"Maybe she can stay here and wait 'til it dries out?" Gibbons suggested.

"That'll take days. Maybe *weeks*."

"Best to be safe, though, yeah?"

Skinner shoved the boys aside and snatched the old map away. He said nothing, but his expression alone made it obvious that the boys weren't used to having a lady stay as a guest before. It was amusing enough that it nearly made Robyn's cheeks flush. She dragged her chair closer and leaned in for a better look, though she had no idea how she could possibly help when she'd never been to Halghard before in her life.

The map of Grymsbi, while accurate enough, looked as if it had been sketched by a child. To begin with, the size of the parchment on which it was drawn was no larger than the size of a handwritten letter and the penmanship was lackluster as was the lack of color. Still, the worn out condition of the old map was representative of how well it had served its purpose over the years for Skinner and his merry band of wardens. The man sat there pensively while the rest of the youths joined the huddle as if they enjoyed his presence, or at least the act of devising a plan with him. They all stared at the map together, bickering and thinking out loud like a tight-knit family. The image, Robyn felt, was something out of a storybook.

"What about *that* path?" Milo reached over Skinner's shoulder to point at the map.

"Suppose it might work. It'll take an extra day though," Aldous pointed out.

"We don't have that kind of time," Skinner concluded.

No, Robyn realized, her mind coming back to reality. *No, we don't…*

"I still say the road by the cliff's yer best bet," Ayisha didn't aim a finger, but she didn't have to. It was quite clear where that road was, it was next to a great spot on the map that was shaded a darker grey than the rest. It almost looked like a wine stain that someone failed to rub off.

"What *is* that?" Robyn asked, pointing at it.

Everyone suddenly turned to her as if she'd just asked '*What are the Woodlands?*'

That was until they realized she wasn't from their kingdom to begin with.

"That there's the Great Rift of Halghard," Milo said, quite proud to have been the first to speak up.

"You ever seen it up close?" Tails asked.

"It's brilliant!" Gibbons said. "Takes your breath away. I could *take* you, if you'd like!"

"That's enough, lads," Skinner grunted again. "This ain't the time."

Robyn smiled. She had, in fact, heard of the Great Rift of Halghard. Her mother had mentioned it many times in her stories. It was supposed to be spectacular to look at. A great opening in the earth, it was, as if some enormous rock the size of three cities had fallen from the sky and left a dent in the world. Some philosophers believed that this was in fact what caused the Great Rift many centuries past, long before the age of silver. The more religious folk, on the other hand, claimed that the Rift was the ancient battleground where the gods of Nayarith once met to wage war against one another, long before the dawn of civilization itself.

Whatever the truth was, Robyn was only sure of one thing... She wanted *very* much to see this Great Rift in person.

"I don't think that road's very safe," Milo suggested. "The long route's the better option."

"Bollocks," Tails said. "It's just high, that's all." He gave Robyn a glance and a wink. "You're not skittish about heights, are you?"

Robyn shook her head. Truthfully she wasn't very fond of heights, but she was so willing to see the Rift that she fought through the unease.

"So what d'you think?" Ayisha asked her commander. "Y'think the wagon'll stay in one piece if ye hauled it by the cliff?"

"The *wagon* might," Skinner said, his eyes moving towards Robyn. "It's our guest here I'm concerned about."

"I'll manage," Robyn shrugged her shoulders, looking rather determined.

"I don't know... My father and I used to take that path on horse when he'd come into the village to trade," Milo said. "It's *pretty*, sure... But it's narrow. *Very* narrow. Dragging a *cart* through there might be asking for trouble. The longer path through the hills is much safer. It's dark and there are lots of good places to hide if you need to."

"I'll manage!" Robyn reiterated.

"You'll *manage* to stumble out of the bloody cart 'n' fall off into the Rift, girl," Skinner said, suddenly sounding like a concerned father.

"I've been in a cart before!" Robyn argued.

"Not with *me* behind the reins..."

"It's too dangerous," Milo added.

"She said she'll *manage*," Ayisha interjected suddenly. She made brief eye contact with Robyn, who was surprised to see the young woman on *her* side for a change. Ayisha then grunted and turned back to Skinner. "So what are we still dancin' around for? Just go on 'n' drag the bitch by the cliff."

"*Pardon* me?!" Robyn exclaimed.

"I was talkin' about the *cart*, girl."

"Oh..."

"H-Hang on, are we *sure* about this?" Aldous asked worriedly. "Milo's right, it *is* quite narrow. And the cart's wide, you'd have to be an *expert* to ride it without stumbling off the edge."

Skinner shot him a stern glare before asking defensively, "What in hells are you implying?"

Aldous stammered, nervous and afraid that he'd just insulted his commander.

"Oh... Um... N-Nothing in particular, sir!"

"You don't think I can handle it? Is *that* what you're gettin' at?"

"N-No, sir. Just, um... Just lookin' out for our guest, that's all."

"She'll *manage*," Skinner said, to which Robyn couldn't help but grin. "So it's settled then," Skinner folded the old map and tucked it into his coat. "We leave first thing in the morning."

Robyn felt her cheeks cramping up, she'd been smiling so much; it felt nice to smile for a change. She didn't think she would be able to sleep a single minute, she was so eager to see this legendary Rift. Whatever dangers lied ahead when she caught up with her brother were secondary. If she died, she would at least be able to gaze into one of the greatest marvels the world had to offer. She felt readier than ever.

Suddenly, a loud banging nearly made the front door drop from its hinges.

As if it had been staged, every pair of eyes in the room glanced towards the door in unison. The knock was an angry one and it was followed by a gravelly voice that Robyn found rather familiar. "*Open up!*" it said.

Almost by instinct, Ayisha drew a dagger that she had hidden in her sleeve. The quiet girl with caramel skin, whom Robyn had heard be referred to as Mallory, also drew the knives from her belt and stood next to Ayisha. The rest of the crew found whatever weapon was closest to them and held it ready in a manner that could only be attained with enough practice.

"At ease, soldiers," Skinner whispered as he rose gently from his seat. Aldous and Ayisha stood at either side of the man, guarding him. Skinner looked at the rest of the group and made a hand motion with two of his fingers; the youths proceeded to scatter away around the cabin, each in a different direction, hiding in places where they'd be out of sight yet ready to pounce if necessary.

"*Oi!*" the growl of a voice called again, banging a heavy fist against the door as if attempting to break it open. "*I said open the fuckin' door!*"

Something in the voice made Robyn twitch. She knew she'd heard it before, only it was muffled by the thick oak. She contemplated running to the nearest window to peek outside but that would have meant stepping in front of Skinner, something that none of the youths dared to do.

On the other side of the door, a green orc with a massive scar on his chest was starting to lose his patience, and a much calmer serpentine figure by his feet was looking up at him with a humanlike grimace.

"I thought we agreed to be *subtle*!" Nyx hissed.

"It's a town of human filth," the Beast scoffed. "What're they gonna do? Shake a parchment in me face 'cause I broke one o' their laws?"

"They can kill us…"

"They can *try*," the Beast growled. "I've seen more dangerous blokes in Bauqora." The orc not only knocked again, he began kicking the door as well. But from the corner of his only eye, Nyx caught the movement; a husky adolescent boy in a cook's apron was peeking down at them through an upstairs window.

"Beast," Nyx hissed.

"Hmm?"

"Look…"

The Beast took a glance, and then Gibbons darted away from the window with a fright.

"That's it, I seen enough!" the Beast growled angrily as he drew his axe and lifted his arm into the air to smash the door in. At that moment, however, the knob turned gently and the door creaked open. The dreary image of an old man that may have once been a noble warrior stood at the entrance.

"Greetings, good sir. May I help you?" Skinner asked.

The orc was thrown aback suddenly. He took a moment to lower his axe and ease his shoulders before he said, "I'm here lookin' for a girl."

Skinner couldn't help but grin. "In that case, you've come to the wrong household, lad. You want Flaherty's, in the northern part of town."

The Beast remained where he stood. He'd failed to notice the arrows being aimed at him from above, but he noticed now. Nyx saw them too, but he was skeptical about speaking out, unsure of how the old man might react to a talking serpent.

What the Beast's eyes instantly latched onto, however, was the brand on Skinner's left cheek. The symbol was all too familiar… In fact, the Beast had the same mark tattooed on his wrist. It troubled him, knowing he was staring into the eyes of a former slave of the Brotherhood's.

"I ain't toyin' with ye," the Beast said, taking an unwelcomed step inside the cabin. Impulsively, however, Ayisha and Aldous held their blades up, protecting their master. But the Beast did not wince, not even a bit.

"Not another step, ye hear?" Ayisha warned him, glancing repeatedly at the Beast's scorpion tattoo.

"The Brotherhood is not welcome in Grymsbi," Aldous added.

"At ease, soldiers," Skinner muttered.

There was a moment of silence, during which the hostility in the room worsened. But then a voice mumbled gently from a far, a voice that broke the tension almost instantly.

"Beast…?" Robyn said, her stunned eyes widening as she stepped forward. "Is that you…?"

The orc's glare softened with relief all of a sudden. Without saying another word, Robyn ran and threw her arms around him; she was so much shorter than him that her face pressed against his scars and yet she did not pull back. The Beast was unsure how to react. He simply stood there with his arms at his sides, not embracing the girl in return but also not disapproving of it. After all, this was the first time the orc had been held in such an embrace since he was a child.

Skinner cleared his throat gently. "Arrows down," he muttered. "At ease, all of you."

Robyn let go of the Beast and looked up at his slightly baffled yet warm expression.

"You came back!" she said enthusiastically.

"Hey, scrap…"

Robyn immediately looked down at her beloved Nyx, his serpentine tail wagging impulsively with joy at the sight of her.

"Lady Robyn!" he said, his humanlike eye glistening with disbelief. "Thank the gods y-"

She dropped suddenly to her knees and embraced him as well, and Nyx was not reluctant this time. He was so glad and relieved to see her that he wished he had arms so that he could hug her back. Meanwhile, every jaw inside the cabin dropped from the confusion, and they began whispering to each other behind Robyn's back.

"Did that thing just…"

"Shh! Don't interrupt!"

"But it just *spoke*…"

"Shut yer arses!" Ayisha snapped, but even *she* couldn't help but feel unsettled.

Robyn had no care in the world. She wiped the incoming tears and backed away from Nyx, keeping a warm hand on the rough scales that might have been his neck. "I can't believe you both came back," she said, unable to stop smiling.

"I thought you were scared of serpents," Nyx said; he would have smiled in return if his scales weren't holding him back.

"I am," Robyn chuckled, blissful and overwhelmed with joy. "But… I think it's about time I grew up a little."

* * *

Viktor Crowley sat alone on the grass a short distance away from King Alistair's campground. He was at the top of a steep hill that gave him an impressive view of the night sky; on this night, it was a luminous shade of violet, made only more dazzling by the iridescent stars and the massive half-moon rising out of the horizon.

A brilliant place to make camp, Viktor thought. *You could spot an enemy troop from miles away.*

In the distance, he could see the shadows of the Wyrmwood watchmen hiding among the trees, their bows with arrows nocked and ready. He both admired King Alistair's tactical skill and envied it, knowing very well that he may never be able to serve as a knight again. Not unless he brought home a living princess, and even then it was a gamble.

Sitting alone for more than a few minutes was not good for Viktor Crowley's sanity. Isolation often brought him doubt, fear, sometimes even anger. And this night was no exception.

He thought of John Huxley, the reckless sheep farmer from Elbon.

He thought of the thief and the witch he had hired merely on an impulse.

He thought of Zahrra, who had assured him that his companions were alive and would be waiting for him in Wyrmwood. Those were her words, words that were based on a mere vision, and he had taken the risk of believing them... A fool, he was, to trust in such nonsense...

They'd been in the camp for hours by then. He must have questioned about a hundred men. But he had been seen riding into camp with a troop of elves and gnomes, and therefore not many soldiers were willing to speak to him, and those that *did* were hardly of any help.

What a fool you are, he cursed himself. *You see the smallest sign of hope, Viktor Crowley, and you latch onto it until it shatters before you, as it always does... An ignorant credulous fool you are...*

His ear suddenly caught the sound of dry grass rustling underneath boots, and he smiled unexpectedly. A few soldiers had approached him already within the last hour, but none had so gentle a step.

"Any news?" Viktor asked without even looking back.

Skye took a seat on the grass next to him, legs folded underneath, wooden staff resting flat on their lap. It seemed as though Skye would always arrive at the appropriate moment, just when Viktor needed a good lift of spirits. "I won't lie to you. It's looking rather bad," said the elf. Even when delivering unfortunate news, it was incredible how soothing a presence Skye had, at least in Viktor's mind.

"Bad?" Viktor asked. "*Execution* bad or *banishment* bad?"

Skye shrugged. "I don't think King Alistair will kill his own brother for trying to help."

"Banishment, then," Viktor said with a nod. "Been there... To be honest, it's not as bad as I expected it to be."

Skye tried to chuckle, but what came out was no more than a loud exhale. "You've been banished for what? A few weeks? Less? These recruits have been banished their whole lives. How do you suppose *they* feel?"

Viktor wished he could take back his words. "I'm sorry. Truly, I meant no offense."

"I know... I'd never expect an offense from the noble Golden Eagle of Vallenghard."

"How many times must I say it?" he replied with a smirk. "It's just *Viktor*..."

Skye said nothing, only smiled back and nodded.

Viktor's gaze shifted back towards the horizon. So much open space, there was. So much rich and fertile land all around them, enough land to fit and establish every nonhuman being from the Woodlands and more. And yet it seemed as if no amount of land would suffice, for when it came to politics humans were as stubborn as they came.

"Skye?" called a voice from afar. "Skye the Frost-Hearted, is that you?"

The elf glanced back and rose to their feet when the shadow emerged. Viktor glanced as well, and then instantly wished he hadn't. He felt a pain his gut from the resentment.

Not now... For gods' sake, not now...

Zahrra approached them, stepping carefully over mud-riddled patches of grass. "There you are," she said to the elf. "Been lookin' everywhere for ya. Come. Now."

"What is it?"

"What *isn't* it?" the witch replied. "There've been threats. Rumors, cold stares, mockery. Soon enough, there will be a revolt if we don't get the bloody hells out of this camp."

"Who threatened you?" Skye sounded worried and defensive, as if Zahrra was a close relative of some sort.

"No one," the witch said. "Not *yet*, that is. But I can hear them all. The voices won't stop, it's making me sick."

Viktor had heard enough. He gave in to his temper and leapt to his feet, charging towards the witch with a cold stare. She looked at him as if he were a madman, as if she had done him no wrong, and it only angered him further. "You!" he called, despite the fact that he already had her attention.

"*Zahrra*," she reminded him, but he cared very little for her name.

"You said they'd be here!" he accused her indirectly. "*They travel to Wyrmwood*, you said to me! *Ahead of you, they are*. Well?!"

Zahrra's eyes narrowed. "*Well...?*" she asked back.

"Well?! Where the bloody hells are they?!"

"Calm yourself, Viktor," Skye said, but for the first time the elf's voice was not enough to soothe Viktor's rage; it was a rage he'd been building up since he left Val Havyn.

"I said they were traveling *to* Wyrmwood," Zahrra said, standing her ground as best as she could. "Maybe they encountered some trouble along the way."

"Or *maybe* you were lying," Viktor accused her, this time directly.

"I *never* lie," Zahrra shot a cold stare right back at him.

"Please, calm yourselves! The both of you!" Skye stepped in between them.

"Ahh that settles it then!" Viktor said loudly and sarcastically, fueled by his hot temper. "So I'm to believe every word you say simply because you dreamt it?!"

"I do not *dream* anything, you arrogant fool."

"I was a *fool* when I chose to listen to *you!*"

"You live in the dark, old knight... I don't expect you to understand, it is a matter too complicated for your small mind."

"You can hide behind your words all you want," Viktor clenched his jaw and his breaths turned into hisses. "But I know what you are. You're a cheating crook!"

Skye held back a gasp. "Viktor..."

"You're a *fraud!*"

Suddenly, Zahrra's eyes went pale, her green pupils fading into nothing. Skye took a step back, gripping their staff nervously, should anything unprecedented happen.

Viktor's expression began to change. He began to tremble as a cold chill ran up his back. It was as if Zahrra had crawled into his mind uninvitingly and Viktor could *feel* her there. For a moment neither one of them was truly there, only their bodies were.

"You wish to test me, Viktor Crowley?" Zahrra hissed coldly, her pale unblinking eyes locked on the former knight. "Go on then... *Test* me..."

Viktor felt the air turn suddenly icy cold, but this time it wasn't Skye's staff that caused it; this was entirely Zahrra's doing. Images began to flash through his mind, dark images that he had purposely buried deep within. He became lost, immersed in a daydream, locked in a trance in which he had no control.

"Loyalty, valor, a broken legacy," the witch muttered, as if reading every single one of Viktor's thoughts out loud. "And what is *this* I see...? A lost love...?"

Viktor's face went pale, almost as pale as Zahrra's eyes. It was as if the man was both conscious and *not* at the same time. He was aware of his surroundings but he couldn't move a single muscle. And when he tried desperately to speak, his lips could manage no more than a shiver.

"Ahh... not *lost*, no... A love *left behind*," Zahrra delved even deeper into his thoughts. "It haunts you to this day, I can see... You fight only to fill that gapin' hole in your heart..."

"That's enough, Zahrra," Skye tried to intervene, but Zahrra was not willing to yield so quickly, not until she made sure Viktor Crowley would never doubt her again; she kept her spell intact, waiting for the opportune moment to break it.

"You left behind a part of you," she said; for a moment, her voice sounded almost sad. "You don't fight for honor, Viktor Crowley... You fight so you can forget..."

The spell had frozen Viktor's eyes, but the tear that escaped him was quite real. The air left his chest and he was unable to breathe when the image flashed before his eyes... He could see her suddenly, the love he had left behind. 25 years it had been, and yet the image of her was perfectly clear.

Hair as golden as wheat, lips like red petals, eyes as blue as the ocean...

For a moment, she felt *real*... He thought if he reached out, he could touch her face...

Only she couldn't be... He knew it all too well, as much as his heart held on to the image of her. He knew that he was latching onto nothing. A mere memory, she was. Nothing more.

Suddenly there was a sharp hissing sound...

Viktor felt the witch release him, he felt the warmth surging through his body as if he'd fallen into an overflowing tub of boiling water, and within seconds his face became drenched in sweat. It was then that he realized he'd involuntarily drawn his sword while he was lost in the trance.

There was a long silence. It was obvious from Zahrra's expression that nobody had ever moved while locked in one of her spells before, much less drawn a weapon. Skye glanced back and forth between the two. Zahrra's eyes had gone back to their normal green state and she also began sweating and heaving as if she was exhausted.

With a crack of the neck, Viktor took a step towards the witch with a menacing stare that left her stunned. "Never do that again," he said. "Or I'll sink my blade into your heart..."

He walked away, back towards the camp for a drink. He didn't slide his blade back into its scabbard until he was a good distance away.

Skye and Zahrra were left alone for a moment. The witch seemed almost ashamed for having allowed her own anger to consume her, or perhaps she was simply too exhausted to be angry. She wasn't particularly fond of jumping into people's minds, more so because it would often take a bigger toll on her than it did on the victim. But she was also not fond of being called a liar, much less by an average human. Skye took Zahrra by the arm and guided her towards the nearest sitting log, making certain the witch wouldn't pass out from the lightheadedness.

"How *did* you do it?" the elf asked abruptly.

"Do what?"

"The vision you had before..."

Zahrra chuckled. "You doubt me as well, Skye the Frost-Hearted?"

"You know I would never do that," Skye said with a gentle smile. "It simply puzzles me how you were able to see his companions without a vessel."

They reached the log at the camp's entrance. Zahrra's feet had been dragging against the dirt as if she'd been drained of all her energy, and she was relieved to be able to sit despite the cold stares the Wyrmwood soldiers were shooting at them. "Yes, I suppose it is puzzling," she said. "I'm not quite sure I fully understand it myself. But either way, it's best not to dwell. Some matters are simply better off left in the past…"

XVII
Riders in Red

Nyx hardly spoke, his muscles ached so much. A few words here and there, but it was enough to amaze the younger of Skinner's wardens. They huddled around him, asking him all sorts of questions. In their inquisitive youthful minds, they imagined some ancient witch must've cursed an innocent snake with sentience because she was sick of talking to herself or something along those lines. Robyn wondered if she should've shattered their curiosity with the truth but she chose to let Nyx decide.

Instead, the girl remained close to the Beast. They were being fed so much, she felt almost at home again. As she sipped her tea, the Beast munched on a plate of chicken that Gibbons had served him. Skinner joined them at the table, his boots resting on a wooden footstool, chatting with them about all sorts of things as the ale began to kick in.

It was pleasing for Robyn to know that not everyone in the village was prejudice or cruel. Skinner, however strange he might have seemed at first, had turned out to be a kind man; a *strict* one, sure, but only when he needed to be and always to protect his fellow wards. He was one of the few that allowed folks of any race into his home. Others had to either seek refuge in taverns or inns, or else resort to sleeping outside in some vacant alley with enough roof to stay dry. A "sanctuary village", Grymsbi had been declared, but it soon became obvious that it wasn't much of a sanctuary after all. There was no safety for the Woodland folk; the word itself was starting to lose all meaning. But Skinner and his band of misfits refused to give up hope; they were like the one rusty nail holding up the roof of a shabby old cottage, stubbornly refusing to yield.

"I've trained kids of all sorts," Skinner shared with them, at some point between his third and fourth ale. "Orphaned children, wild elves, orcs seeking shelter, you name it. *The Wardens of Grymsbi*, they call us."

"*Who* calls you?" the Beast asked doubtfully, his mouth drooling with chicken grease.

"The townsfolk," Skinner elaborated. "In a vile place like this, the people *need* something to cling onto, you see. So we give them that. When the village guards fail to protect them, we're there. When the village is on the verge of a raid, we're there. Of course, once the kids come of age they go on about their ways. The names and faces change but the *Wardens* have always been here. It gives the people hope, you see."

The Beast responded, as he usually did, with a simple grunt. He then bit into the meatless chicken bone on his plate, crushing it as easily as if he were biting into an apple. The cracking of the bone made Skinner raise a brow with amusement, as the man eyed the orc up and down.

"That's quite an interesting pelt you got there, friend," Skinner said, referring to the red fox skin the Beast wore around his waist as a belt. "Did you kill it or was it already dead?"

"Didn't just kill it," said the Beast. "I ate the fucker."

"I see," Skinner smirked, and then turned to Robyn as he finished his last ale of the night. "So what's the plan *now*, then?"

There was a sudden silence. Robyn became nervous, her mind suddenly snapping back to reality. "I dunno," she said hesitantly. Skinner glanced back and forth between the girl and the orc. Robyn didn't know what the Beast's intentions were, and if he were being honest the Beast was rather unsure himself.

"You *could* join us, Beast," Robyn said, her eager eyes conveying a hint of hope. "You could be granted a pardon, even. If you came with us."

"Where…?"

"Overseas," she said. "To rescue Princess Magdalena of Vallenghard."

After a brief moment of tension, Skinner decided to interject. "I'm taking the girl south, first thing in the morning. King Alistair of Wyrmwood is an old friend of mine. He'll be glad to lend a hand, I'm sure."

"My brother's in Sir Viktor Crowley's company," Robyn added. "If we can *find* them, I can talk to them. Convince them to let you join the cause."

"The girl's right," Skinner said. "The world's changing… Every day, folks of all sorts are migrating into our kingdom. This *could* give you a chance for a different life. Saving the king's daughter could perha-"

"To hells with the king's daughter," the Beast grunted suddenly, but his tone was far more somber than it was angry. "What's the king's daughter ever done for *me*? Or for any other orc?"

Skinner gave it a moment's thought before responding. "I understand your mistrust…"

"Do ye?" the Beast scoffed, his eyes narrowing as he shook his head. "Is that all we are to ye? Just another blade for yer cause?"

Another silence. And no one, not even Robyn, dared to challenge the Beast, for his was a sentiment they couldn't possibly fathom.

"Ye say we're welcome here… Ye tell us that we can flee that cage of ours 'n' start again," the Beast went on, and it was clear how painfully difficult it was for him to share his thoughts on the matter. "We come here lookin' for a better future, a future where we don't have to run… Instead we find nothin' but wars 'n' conflict. And then ye try to rope us into a war that isn't ours to fight? That's not freedom… That's just another fuckin' cage…"

Robyn felt the guilt settling in her gut. After all, had it not been for her the Beast would never have set foot in Halghard to begin with.

"I'm sorry the world is shit," Skinner said somberly. "It'll take quite some time before we can fix it."

"Doesn't mean we can't start now," Robyn added. "One day at a time, one *orc* at a time."

The Beast said nothing further, only contemplated their words. Part of him wanted to join Robyn in her venture, but truthfully he'd never seen the sea in his life and sailing it terrified him. It would take more than an hour's conversation to persuade him otherwise, especially knowing what lurked within the black waters of the Draeric Sea.

After a long silence, Skinner cleared his throat to break the tension. "Well," he said to Robyn. "Looks like it'll still be a trip for *two*, then."

"Three," Nyx said from afar, and Robyn couldn't help but smile.

Well, she thought. *It's the **start** of a plan, at least...*

She relaxed, feeling for a change that the odds were finally in her favor. After all, if she had survived the Woodlands, what dangers could she possibly face in a kingdom of humans that would be worse than what she'd already seen? If anything, she felt more capable than the typical peasant in Grymsbi, and this eased her nerves quite a bit.

But some of the wardens were not too happy about their commander leaving them again. One in particular had her eyes on Robyn and her companions like a vigilant hound.

Even when she had guard duty, Ayisha stood on the cabin balcony peeking inside through one of the windows. The breeze was chilly that evening and yet the young warden fought through it without her coat. Skinner refused to let anyone go on guard duty without a partner, and the only volunteer that night had been the smart-mouthed curly-haired Milo, despite Ayisha's protests. They sat together, daggers strapped to their belts and bows resting nearby. Milo was still obviously intrigued, even *smitten* with their new visitor. Ayisha, on the other hand, was as distrustful towards her as she was with any stranger.

"What do you make of the orc?" Milo asked, biting into a fresh kiwi.

"What does it matter?" Ayisha remarked. "They'll be gone come mornin'."

"I know. But what do you *make* of him?"

Ayisha gave it a moment's thought, staring into the distance with resentment in her eyes.

"I would *never* trust a bloke in red leathers," she said, and Milo knew better than to challenge her on such matters. Instead, he remained pensive.

"The *girl's* something, isn't she?" he eventually said. "Very pretty, she is."

"Please," Ayisha scoffed. "Ye say that about *any* girl that even looks yer way, lad."

"No, no, this one's different, I can tell. She's got nerve."

"Nerve, my arse."

"She had the pluck to confront *you*. I'd say that's quite nervy."

"Wha' in all hells does *that* mean?" Ayisha glared at him aggressively.

"It means that *I* would never cross you," Milo confessed. "Not *truly*, at least. But *she* did. Shows that she doesn't scare so easy."

Ayisha said nothing in response. She was staring at the empty road that led deeper into town when suddenly something caught her eye. At night, Grymsbi always became hidden within a cloud of fog. Even from the balcony, all Ayisha and Milo could see were a cluster of thatched rooves and smoking chimneys, nothing more. But, amid the fog, the shadow of a boy began to form. He was running hastily towards them, boots splashing over the mud. Ayisha leapt from her seat instantly and stepped towards the edge, her eyes widening and her palms growing sweaty. The boy was distraught and out of breath, and he was shouting Ayisha's name.

Out of precaution, the woman reached for her bow. "It's Ethan," she realized.

"Bloody hells, he's rushing!" said Milo.

"What is it, lad?" Ayisha shouted back at the boy, who came to a halt right beneath them.

"Rogues!" the boy said, struggling to catch his breath. "Th-They're back!"

Feeling the hairs rising at the back of her neck, Ayisha's jaw tightened with anger. She ran back inside the cabin and hopped down the stairs so swiftly, it startled everyone inside. Tails stopped playing his mandolin and Skinner paused in the middle of a story. Ayisha, who was known to act brash when she was angry, began charging towards their guests with ill intentions in her eyes.

"I knew it!" she growled. "I bloody *knew* it! Ye lyin' bastards!!"

"At ease, Ayisha," Skinner stood from his seat.

"They *lied* to us, sir! Ye let 'em into our home 'n' they spit in our faces!"

"I said at *ease*, soldier," Skinner had to step between Ayisha and Robyn; the young warden was calm within seconds but the fire in her eyes remained.

"I'm sorry, sir," she breathed.

"Good. Now... *calmly*... what is happening?"

"Rogues, sir! They're back in Grymsbi!"

As if it wasn't quiet enough already, the room became soundless at the sound of Ayisha's words. One by one, they all locked eyes with one another, as if questioning each other without ever speaking. Robyn, Nyx, and the Beast felt alarmed and out of place, like innocent bystanders amidst an impending riot.

Then another set of footsteps ran hurriedly down the stairs.

"Sir!" Milo shouted, nearly stumbling at the last step. "I've spotted them! Up the road, they are! They're nearly here, sir!"

"How long?" Skinner asked gruffly.

"M-Minutes, sir..."

"How *many* minutes, lad?!"

"Two. Maybe three at the most."

Skinner's eyes began to wander, all the while the youths began mumbling amongst themselves. Three seconds, it must have taken. Three mere seconds for Skinner to concoct a plan in his mind...

Or, rather, to *choose* one…

"Attention, lads!" he said loudly, and every single one of the wardens of Grymsbi rose to their feet and stood up straight like a proper soldier. "Operation Fly Trap…"

They broke their stance simultaneously. So organized, they were, that upon hearing the words come out of their commander's lips, they knew exactly what needed to be done and how.

"*Set the bait!*"

"*On it!*"

"*Bows up high, blades down low!*"

"*Hide the gold!*"

"*Someone kill that bloody fire!*"

"*Already on it!*"

Robyn leapt from her seat and placed Nyx around her neck, as everyone rushed and scampered all around her. "What's happening?" she asked.

"Change of plans, little one," Skinner said as he stuffed bread and blocks of cheese into a satchel. "Looks like we leave *tonight*, you and I… Well, you and I and… the *serpent*."

"But what about the rogues?!"

"It's not the first time they've tried to hunt us down," Skinner grinned, strapping blades onto his belt and sliding more inside his sleeve.

"We can help!" Robyn tried to argue.

"No need, lass. They'll handle it."

"I *want* to help!"

"We'll handle it, don't fret," said a friendly voice. Robyn turned around, only to find herself looking into Milo's warm smitten gaze. "Here," he said, handing her a jaguar's tooth that was almost identical to the one Ayisha wore as an earring. "Something to remember us by!" he said, and it was then that Robyn noticed he was wearing a similar tooth as a necklace. In fact, in some form or another, every single one of the youths was wearing one.

"Oh… Thank you!" was all Robyn could think to say.

"It was a joy to have met you, Robyn Huxley of Elbon!" Milo gave her a nod, before he scurried away upstairs with a bow in hand.

By then, nearly everyone was in their proper position. Ayisha and Milo took the upstairs. Aldous, Yuri, and Mallory strapped blades to themselves and stealthily hid around the common room. Gibbons took the smallest child into the kitchen, where there was ample space to hide. The only one left was Tails, who was setting up a scarecrow made of hay in the common room's armchair, its back to the door so that it looked like a sleeping person. Once he placed the old straw hat over it, he ran upstairs to join Ayisha and Milo.

"Ready, now?" Skinner asked Robyn, who appeared distraught and out of sorts. "Let's get to the stables! Quick, now!"

But Robyn's feet wouldn't move just yet... Her eyes shifted immediately towards the Beast, who was standing nervously against the wall with his axe in hand. He looked worried and out of place, as if he wanted nothing else but to run back into the Woodlands, where he knew the land like he knew every edge of his axe.

It was all happening so fast, Robyn hardly had any time to take it all in. She stood there, lips quivering, her bow sliding from her sweaty palm. "Will you be all right, Beast?" she asked fretfully, her mind coming to the realization that she might never see the Beast again.

"Just go, scrap," he replied, much friendlier than he had ever spoken to her before. "Go 'n' save yerself. Don't ye worry 'bout me."

"But I can't just *leave* you here!"

The Beast's eyes drifted from side to side as if searching for a response. Despite his tormenting physique, he appeared almost like a lost child.

"Oi! You there!" Yuri, the orc girl, shouted suddenly from afar; the Beast glanced back and forth to assure that she was indeed talking to him. "They might need you upstairs, mate! Care to lend a hand?"

With a hesitant grunt, the Beast nodded and gave his neck a good crack.

"Brilliant," Yuri shot him a friendly grin and gestured for him to follow her upstairs. "The big guy's helping!" she shouted up at her comrades. "Get to your places!"

The Beast took one step towards the stairs, but something stopped him all of a sudden.

He looked back... Back at the girl that had saved his life...

Robyn looked genuinely woeful to be parting ways with him. And as much as he tried, he couldn't deny the aching in his throat to be parting ways with *her.* But she didn't hug him this time. She kept her distance, just as she knew he preferred. All she gave him was a head nod and a warm smile.

"Farewell, Beast," she said. And then she headed for the back door.

The Beast closed his eyes and sighed, cursing himself in his mind, fighting back the little resistance he felt in his core. Then, with as much strength as he could muster, he gave in...

"*Ignar,*" he said.

Robyn Huxley froze where she stood. She let go of the doorknob and glanced back, her eyes broad with surprise. "What...?"

"My name," he said. "It's Ignar..."

Her face lit up with both joy and surprise. Though Skinner was shouting at her from the outside, nothing could have possibly stopped her from walking back for a proper goodbye.

"Robyn Huxley," she said, holding her hand out as if they were meeting for the first time.

The orc's hands were massive compared to hers. They shook, her pale fingers reacting against his olive skin like a jasmine on a flowering shrub.

"It's been a pleasure, Ignar," she said with a smile.

And then they parted ways.

* * *

John Huxley hadn't seen much of the Rogue Brotherhood aside from the attack on Val Havyn's royal palace, but he'd heard plenty of stories. He'd heard of their lack of honor, their lack of mercy, and once he even heard they kept slaves. The rumors alone would make his stomach turn. Gravenstone had plenty of troubles as it was, it did not need another plague of crooks to make matters worse.

Captain Malekai Pahrvus had left twenty men behind at *The Stumblin' Hare* and took the rest with him. There were just as many villagers, if not a more, but none had the courage to stand up to the Brotherhood. Never had John seen such behavior before his eyes, not even from the most vulgar of peasants in Vallenghard. The rogues were scattered throughout the tavern, prattling and helping themselves to any drinks or food on the table, regardless of whether or not it had already been touched. They mocked and harassed the peasants, as if the peasants were there for the Brotherhood's amusement. The unworldly youthful bard was forced to sing songs he hadn't heard of before and the rogues threatened to cut his fingers off if he didn't make an attempt. There was even a young woman serving tables, and Clive, the red mercenary left in charge, kept grazing her whenever she was near him, knowing she'd be too frightened to repel.

The Brotherhood's behavior was repulsive, to say the least.

Hudson Blackwood had stopped eating by then; he sat there silently with his hat over his eyes, looking meditative. John waited several minutes for the thief to conjure up some sort of plan, some plot to fight back. But rather than looking sprightly, the thief looked almost as if he was stalling. And so, after much hesitation, John leaned in discreetly.

"What's the plan?" he asked.

Hudson squinted his eyes at him. "Plan? What plan?"

"You're not seriously staying put while these bastards do as they please...?"

Across from them, Syrena sat with a nervous hand pressed down on her satchel's lid. Her eye was twitching madly again and every time Sivvy yelped or squirmed, she glanced about agitatedly like a gazelle in a lion's territory. "Keep your voices down, will you?" she asked them.

"Tell that to the farmer," Hudson said.

John's mouth dropped from the aggravation. "Why am I the only one in this table acting like a sane person? Hudson, mate... You fought for us back in the Woodlands, you saved the entire company, you should be leaping up from your seat right now with your blade drawn!"

"Mate, allow me to indulge you in a good life lesson," Hudson muttered gently, his eyes examining the room as he spoke. "If a matter is none of your concern, the best thing to do is to stay *out* of it. Trust me on this. It's kept me alive so far."

"Are you *serious?!*" John whispered a bit too loudly. He glanced up warily, but none of the raiders paid them any mind; their table was far enough in the corner that it was overlooked. When he turned to look at Hudson again, he did so with a look of betrayal, as if the thief had wounded him with his sudden egotism. "Hudson Blackwood, the famous thief and mercenary, shying away from a fight simply because it *'doesn't concern'* him?!" he said in a way that was meant to guilt the thief.

Hudson shot him an unpleasant grimace, like an irritated merchant shoving a beggar out of the way. "John, do you remember that annoying thing I mentioned?"

"What annoying thing?"

"The one you're doing *now*…"

John scowled, unable to conjure up a good response.

"Bravery and recklessness, mate," Hudson said. "There's a bloody *difference!*"

"So I'm supposed to sit idly by while th-"

"Settle yourselves, *both* of you!" Syrena hissed at them with a heated dread, rubbing her eyelid to fight back the twitching. "You're gonna get us all killed!"

"You heard the lady," Hudson remarked. "Settle your arse or I'll settle it *for* you."

"Hudson, I won't just sit here whil-"

"It's *not* your fight, mate! What does it matter?! Sometimes you have to sit one out if you wish to see another day."

"But *look* at these people!" John insisted. "They're not soldiers or mercenaries! You can't just *expect* them to defend themselves against these savages…"

Hudson scoffed and glanced at Syrena. "Hear him? Thinks he's the *guardian* of peasants, this one." But the witch was far too anxious to care for the thief's mockery. With a trembling hand she reached for her ale, which was utterly untouched, and began gulping it down as if she'd die if she didn't finish it soon.

John took a moment to observe the room. Half the peasants, the more brute ones, were by then drunkenly carrying on with their conversations without a care in the world, while the other half were cowering in fear as the red mercenaries shoved at them and ordered them to empty out their satchels.

John nearly leapt from his seat, he was so angry. These villagers looked like they could have belonged in Elbon; he felt if he glanced in any direction he could have spotted Missus Aelyn or Old Man Beckwit sitting among them. It pained him to be sitting comfortably while others in the room were being robbed and harassed, especially when the Brotherhood seemed to only be pestering the weakest.

Unable to reserve himself, John leaned in towards the thief again.

"Listen, mate," he said. "If you want to spend the rest of your days sitting about, drinking the pain away, by all means do so... But life goes on with or without you, Hudson. These people have *families*! They have *children* waiting for them at home! And you sit there calmly and tell me I'm acting rash?"

"You *were* acting rash," the thief said gruffly. "Now you're acting stupid..."

"Fine," John said, rising steadily to his feet. It was painfully clear in his nervous mutter that he had no plan, but was merely acting on impulse. "I'm the stupid one," he was saying. "All right, I'll show you '*stupid*'. Better to be stupid than selfish, if you ask me."

"Sit down, John..."

"*You* sit. Have another drink, go on."

"Sit *down*, you reckless bastar-"

"I will *not*!" John snapped, loud enough this time that a few peasants certainly took notice over the music. "Fine! You want me to *say* it?! That's fine, I'll say it! You were right, Hudson... I *don't* know what I'm doing. Are you satisfied?"

John was now glaring down at the man he called his friend. Hudson, in his stubbornness, refused to look the farmer in the eyes and instead lowered the rim of his hat.

"You were right all along," John went on regardless, his voice firm and confident. "I'm *not* as strong as I thought I was. Not as fast. Not as clever. Hells, if it weren't for the sun I'd hardly know which way's east... But I *do* know one thing..."

John hesitated for a moment, as if he was coming to terms with himself.

"I was *not* born to pick vegetables and feed sheep my whole life," he said out loud for the first time. "I've missed plenty of opportunities in the past to do the right thing but, for just *once*, I... I want to *take* that chance rather than throwing it away. For once, I just want to do something *right*."

Hudson took a moment to respond, as if he was either offended or distracted. Normally, it would have thrilled him to lecture the farmer, to sit him down and tell him why he was talking like an idiot. He had every argument ready in his tongue when a sudden commotion distracted them, stealing his moment away.

"Shut your arses!" a man shouted, a mocking snicker hiding within his words. "Let the poor lad speak, will ya?"

Seamus, the bartender and new owner of the tavern, was standing in front of a table full of red mercenaries. The young lady who had been serving tables was also there, sitting on the lap of the one called Clive, as he chuckled and sniffed her hair unwelcomingly. The look on the girl's reddened eyes said she had no interest in being there, but Clive had a dagger in his hand and she was frightened of what he would do with it.

"Now, what were you saying, lad?" one of them asked.

Seamus nervously set down a tray of drinks. "Here's the round ye asked for," he wiped the sweat from his brow and took a deep breath. "Umm, Faye... I think they need ye in the kitchen," he said to the girl. Clive's grin twisted into a grimace; the poor girl took the opportunity to slide away from the mercenary's grasp and run off as quickly as she could.

"We was only talkin' to her," one of them said, laughing hysterically like a hyena.

Seamus cleared his throat. "That'll be 5 coppers for yer drinks... *please*," he stammered.

A few of them snorted drunkenly, as if it had been a joke. Clive, on the other hand, did not look very happy. "What?" asked the vile brute. "You can't offer a few drinks to your guests on the house?"

Seamus inspected the table warily. While the five mercenaries sitting there looked tired and slow, they were *armed* while Seamus wasn't, not unless a butter knife could kill a man. "W-Well," he chose his words carefully. "Perhaps I'll just keep a count for ye. And we could settle it later."

"Yes," Clive snickered. "Perhaps..."

Seamus turned to walk away, but then a boot kicked him in the heel. He stumbled face-forward, his jaw slamming against the wooden floorboards, and it was followed by a burst of laughter. To make matters worse, Seamus realized he'd fallen over the red stain from his late superior's blood and his face went pale as he fought back the vomit.

"Look at his face!" one of the mercenaries nearly choked from the laughter, his face turning almost as red as his leather armor. "Yellow bastard."

Had there been less people nearby, young Seamus probably would have sunk into tears, he was such a gentle soul. With men like the Brotherhood mercenaries in the village, there was no possible way he would survive as owner of the tavern for longer than a week. He placed both hands flat against the floorboards and pushed himself up; his cheekbone was starting to bruise and he could taste blood on his lips.

Suddenly, a pair of muddy boots approached and came to a halt in front of him.

Seamus became agitated at first, expecting a slap or a kick in the ribcage.

Instead, there was a hand; the man wasn't there to hurt him, he was there to help him up.

Seamus couldn't see the man's face, only a blonde shadow contrasting against the lanterns' glow. He took the hand and pulled himself to his own two feet. "Thank you... May the gods bless you, sir..."

"My name's John," the young man replied, and then with a determined glare he turned his attention towards the table of mercenaries. "Hey! You, there!"

The bard kept playing and the more drunken folks kept to themselves, but the commotion had certainly started to turn a few heads. Clive spat on the floor while the other mercenaries on the table watched him intently; he'd only been left in charge for an hour or so and already the man looked as if the authority was poisoning his mind. "Can we help you?" asked Clive.

"Yes," John replied confidently. "I do believe you owe this man 5 coppers…"

* * *

Better to be stupid than selfish, the thief repeated in his mind, and it sounded more and more ridiculous every time. *Better to be* **stupid**… *than* **selfish**?! *What does that even mean, you stupid farmboy? You stubborn, reckless, loud-mouthed, meat-headed* **farmboy**!

Hudson Blackwood didn't know whether he was angrier with John or with himself. He remembered that feeling in his gut, that hateful feeling, when he threatened to kill John the night at the Huxley's farm. He was feeling it again, except this time it left him with a sour taste in the back of his throat, as if he was cowardly stabbing a friend in the back.

"What d'you think you're doing?" Syrena suddenly hissed, keeping a hand over the lid of her satchel. The tavern was quieter now, and the witch had to slide over to the other side of the table with Hudson so that she could whisper to him discreetly. Hudson looked quite distracted. Not only were his eyes conflicted, as was usual of him, but there was also a glimmer there that he fought hard to suppress, as if John's words had stung him more than he cared to show.

"What do you mean, darling?" he asked, sipping casually from his ale.

"I *mean* why in all hells are you not helping him?!"

Hudson was slightly staggered. As nervous as Syrena was about being exposed, he wasn't expecting her to side with the farmer. "Because he's being a *moron*!" he argued back in a whisper.

"That's never stopped you before…"

"If he wants to get himself killed, he may do that on his own."

"Cut the shit," Syrena snatched Hudson's ale away with a shivering hand and began gulping it down herself. If the witch had been 'nervous' before, there were no words to describe how she was feeling at that very moment. She was like a panicked bard before their very first performance, like a desperate child about to confess a mischievous deed, like a tense inexperienced soldier riding into battle for the first time.

"Cut *what* shit?" Hudson raised a brow.

"You care about him," Syrena remarked. She seemed quite convinced of it, too. But Hudson chuckled under his breath as if it had been a joke.

"I think you've had enough, darling. You're talking nonsense."

"You do," she insisted. "You care. And you hate yourself for caring."

Hudson glanced from afar, as if debating with his own conscience. By then,

Clive was on his feet facing John, towering a good three inches over him. "*Lad thinks he's got quite a pair, does he?*" the rogue mercenary snickered. At the sight, Hudson realized he was in fact trembling; or at least his fingers were, as if they were instinctively beckoning him to reach for his blade. He had to curl his hand into a fist to keep it steady.

"Just *look* at him!" the thief whispered. "He's a reckless bastard trying to prove himself a hero. Men like that don't live very long and I'm certainly not letting him drag *me* down w-"

"Please," she scoffed, speaking quite rapidly as if a fight was to break out at any moment. "You went from wanting to kill 'im to sharing a bottle of liqueur with 'im."

"I don't see your point. What's *that* got to do with anything? I'm *still* gonna kill him," Hudson snatched his ale back from her grasp and took a sip, before he shrugged his shoulders and muttered, "*Someday.*"

"No you won't," the witch replied with an eye roll. "In fact, you *like* him."

Hudson shot her a scowl, as if insulted by the comment. "Piss off..."

"I'll piss off when you admit it."

"*Why* would I lik-"

"Same reason you liked *me* in the first place," she interrupted him. "You found someone who can match you in a fight and it intrigues you."

"*Match* me?!" he exclaimed, so defensively that it was almost laughable; his brows arched as if he was appalled by the comment. "That little twat is absolutely *no* match for me!"

"I thought he got you captured," said Syrena.

"W-Well," he stammered. "I-I mean... *technically*, yes. But that doesn-"

"So he *did* match you..."

"It is *much* more complicated than that."

"Will you just cut the shit already?!"

Suddenly, the commotion became worse. John Huxley was far too stubborn to yield, and so Clive turned to his goons and ordered them to '*hold the bastard down*'.

John resisted, but there was only so much he could do against four men. They pinned him down over a table, pressing his face against the wood. The bard stopped playing all of a sudden and every pair of eyes was now on them.

"Let me go!" John yelped. "Fight me yourself, you worthless coward!"

Clive laughed, a few chunks of spit spraying John in the face. "You hear 'im, lads?" he snorted, and then shook his head with a grin. "I don't fight *boys*, goldie, I fight *men*."

John became enraged and tried to fidget his way out of their grasp, but they only pressed his head down harder and drew a couple of knives against his neck. The farmer realized then that Hudson's patience was in fact the smarter route. When dealing with men who had no honor, one simply couldn't expect a fair fight.

"I don't think this one answers to words, brother," one man chuckled and tossed a sword at Clive. "You gotta teach him a different way."

At the sight of the sword, John felt the energy fuel him all of a sudden. He pushed and shoved and broke from the men's grip for a brief moment. But before he could cause any serious damage, Clive landed a blow to his jaw with a heavy fist. John could suddenly taste the blood on his lip.

"This one's squeamish," someone snickered.

One by one, the red mercenaries were landing punches and kicks. John fell to the ground defenselessly, shriveling into a ball and shielding his head with his arms, grunting with every blow he received, bruises starting to tarnish him all over his body.

Meanwhile, in the corner of the room, Syrena gave Hudson another shove. "What're you *waiting* for?!"

"The mate needs to learn his lesson, darling…"

The rogue mercenaries bruised him, not quite badly, but John would certainly be feeling the pain for days, if not weeks. He tried to fight back, but the attacks were coming from every direction, and he was getting slower after each one of them.

"All right, enough!" Clive shouted. "Pull the bastard up!"

John was lifted by the arms and pinned against the table again. This time, he could feel the pain around his left eye; he needed no mirror to know that it was swelling up. Clive toyed with his blade, tossing it from one hand to the other. Even in his drunken state, the man was undeniably quick.

"Let this serve as a lesson to the lot of you!" he shouted, red-faced and livid. "The Rogue Brotherhood owns this town now, you hear me?! You answer to *us*… And anyone who wants to challenge me will taste the wrath of me blade…"

The vile man looked down at John one last time, grinning and slobbering drunkenly all over himself. "Looks like you stepped into the wrong tavern tonight, boy…"

Then, with a huff, the man lifted his arm and swung down at John's neck!

A sharp metallic sound echoed in the room…

John lifted his gaze but he could hardly see a thing through his swollen eye; all he could see were shadows. Another blade had blocked Clive's attack, a thin sharp saber held by a hand wearing fingerless leather gloves.

"Pardon me, mate… but I can't let you do that…"

The blades slid against each other, as Clive took a step away from the table.

"Who the bloody hells are *you*?!"

Hudson gave his neck a good crack, as if he was preparing for a fight. "I'm the man that will one day kill this dumb bastard… But I'm afraid that day is *not* today. Now back off, nice and slowly."

In a panic, the red mercenaries let go of John, suddenly realizing whom they were standing in front of. Syrena ran towards the farmer and loaned him a shoulder for balance.

"By the gods!" one of the mercenaries said drunkenly. "Clive, d'you know who that is?!"

"Is it *really* him?" asked another, also drunkenly, rubbing his eyes as if he was hallucinating.

"I'd recognize that face anywhere! It's that wanted thief... Hudzer Brownworth!"

"It's *Hudson*, you blitherin' idiot! *Hudson* Brownworth!"

"I don't care who he is!" Clive took an angry step forward, his blade ready to strike, but one of his men held him back by the shoulder.

"Careful, Clive... I've heard about this one. He's not to be toyed with."

"Aye!" said another. "I heard he took down the Sawyer gang single-handedly."

"Bollocks! I thought the Sawyer gang was killed in a fire..."

"And who d'you think *started* that fire??"

"Well *I* heard he shagged one of Balthazar Locke's aunts once."

"Oh? Which one?"

"The older one with the lazy eye."

"Did he *really*? Well, shit..."

Realizing the men were inebriated past any sense, Hudson cleared his throat to get their attention back. "That was a mere rumor, gentlemen. I assure you," he said, hoping that at least Syrena would believe him.

"No, no, I *saw* you!" one of the drunker mercenaries insisted. "They chased you out of the Morganna for it. There's still a bounty out for your head, y'know?"

"Enough!" Clive shouted. "Listen 'ere, you runt..."

"No, *you* listen, mate," Hudson stepped forward valiantly, his voice rising as if he was addressing the entire tavern. "I think it's about time you and your lot pack your things and leave, yes? Before things get ugly..."

"I will *not* be talked down to by a thief!"

"Ahh... because you're so honest and well-mannered, eh?" Hudson scoffed. John unsheathed his own blade and stood next to his friend, ready to guard his back.

"Watch your tongue, lad," Clive said with a glare that would have been menacing for any man; to Hudson, however, it was laughable.

The thief glanced around and saw that every eye in the room was on him. And so, with a smirk of pleasure, he used it to his advantage. He leapt onto a table so that he'd tower over everyone. "Attention, ladies and gents!"

The peasants were drawn in as the red mercenaries around the room stumbled to their feet. Hudson could see that most of the villagers looked helpless, like bullied children waiting for an adult to come and set things straight.

He could also see that some of them were reaching for bottles, butter-knives, even *chairs*… *anything* that would aid them in a fight against the Brotherhood; they were simply waiting for somebody to start that fight.

"This here's Grymsbi!" Hudson shouted with a smirk. "And the Rogue Brotherhood is *not* welcome here!" His smirk turned into a sudden glower. He gave his saber a good spin with his wrist, as if he was warming up. "Let's show them the way out, shall we?"

Within seconds, a riot ensued in the tavern…

Hudson's brief words had managed to rile up the villagers, giving them the courage they so desperately needed. They used whatever was at their disposal to fight back; glass bottles, pots and pans, their own shoes… The rogue mercenaries may have had sharper weapons, but the ale had slowed them down significantly.

"Come on, lads!" someone shouted. "Fight the bastards off!"

Hudson remained on the table, swinging down at red mercenaries who dared to crowd up on him. They swung at his feet but he simply hopped swiftly with a smirk, as if he were dancing, as if it was all a game to him. He managed to disarm one of the rogues and snatched up a second blade with his left hand.

John joined the fight, moving slower than usual due to the fresh bruises. Mercenaries were running in from every direction, one of them aiming to strike the farmer in the back. But before he could even swing, the runner was held back violently by the neck; he was pressed against a wooden wall and he could feel the excruciating burn in his jaw.

Syrena of Morganna stood there, glaring viciously into the mercenary's eyes.

"W-What… *are*… you?!" the man struggled to speak.

The witch's eyes were so bright, they almost hurt to look at. She looked as if she was in a trance, not speaking a single word, but letting her hands do all of the talking. There was a hissing sound as the man's neck started to ooze smoke. He shrieked from the pain. When the witch let go of him, his neck was burned severely, branded with a red blistering handprint. The rogue mercenaries saw her and backed away from her, unwilling to take a single step nearer. Syrena was so fueled by her power she was almost enjoying herself. She had no need for a weapon; instead, she made a flaming fist with both her hands and began swinging at whoever got too close.

Amid the commotion, Clive was killing peasants one after the other. He was the only one of the Brotherhood crew that seemed able enough, or at least sober enough, for a proper fight. After glancing in every direction, he finally spotted John Huxley, the man that had started it all. He stepped towards him with ill intentions in his glare.

John heard the man's raging growls before he even turned to look.

He's behind you, the farmer warned himself.

Remember, now… Just like Old Man Beckwit taught you…

He waited until he heard the wooden floorboards squeaking behind him.

And when they did, he closed his eyes and bent his knees to dodge Clive's attack. The blade missed his hair by just an inch. He fell to a squat and then swung his leg across, kicking Clive's ankles and causing the man to trip backwards.

With a swift motion, John snatched a wooden shield from a dead mercenary's hands and stood on his feet. Clive got up as well and lunged forward, attacking the farmer sloppily but strongly all the same. Their blades clashed repeatedly. With every step that Clive took, John took one backward, until his back was against the wall. They struggled, their weapons sliding against one another in a tight lock.

All around them, glass shattered and chairs broke in half. The Brotherhood was losing the upper hand, and the few mercenaries that remained were starting to flee.

"*Clive!*" they shouted. "*Clive, let's go!*"

"*We won't win this!*"

One of them was running for the doors when suddenly a spear jabbed him in the gut. It was the only thing that made Clive break his glare on John.

"*Shields up!*" someone shouted from the outside.

The village guards had arrived; they were lined up around the tavern, guarding every exit.

It was over. The red mercenaries were trapped.

"No," Clive muttered, suddenly looking like a nervous child. "No... NO!!"

He swung, but his rage made him sloppy. After a few clashes, John disarmed and pinned Clive down on the floor, his knee pressed against the red leathers on the man's back. As the armored soldiers started to charge in, Syrena's eyes widened. She immediately put her hands down and killed the flames, but there was lingering smoke rising out of them like a sizzling steak. She glanced all around for Hudson, who was suddenly nowhere to be found. Instead, she dropped to her knees and used John as a shield to hide her smoking palms. The farmer had the tip of his blade pressed against Clive's neck.

"Stay down!" he said.

Clive spit on the farmer's boots. "You gonna kill me, goldie?" he snickered.

John's glare was almost menacing. He *wanted* to sink the blade in, but something held him back. He wasn't sure if it was honor or the fear of killing again, but he tried not to dwell on it.

"You're done," he said. "It's over..."

The village guards began snatching up any remaining mercenaries and shoved them out of the tavern doors. Sivvy was nearly spotted glimpsing out of the satchel had it not been for Syrena, who ran and closed the lid just in time, strapping it back onto herself after she'd left it behind in her chair.

As the guards lifted Clive up by the arms, he shot John a grimace.

"I'll never forget your face, boy," the man said, spitting on John's boots.

The farmer said nothing in return, only turned the other way as if the man did not exist.

"Take 'im away!" the knight commander growled.

"*Never*, y'hear me?!" Clive went on radically. "I'll *never* forget your face!"

John's chest was pounding. He'd faced death for what seemed like the hundredth time since the journey began. He was so edgy that he jolted when he felt the warm hand on his shoulder.

"Hey," Syrena said. "Relax. It's only me... Where's Hudson?"

John's eyes scanned the room. Injured peasants were being tended to while others were rushing to steal from the pockets of fallen mercenaries before the bodies were dragged out. Seamus was starting to clear out the mess and guards were scurrying in and out of the tavern doors.

Hudson, however, was nowhere to be found...

* * *

Over a dozen men in horses, all of them dressed in red leathers, rode cautiously through the empty road that led to Skinner's cabin. A light was guiding Captain Malekai Pahrvus towards it, a light coming from one of the windows. The white stallion, which he'd stolen during the raid back in the Woodlands, was tired and hungry, mud splattering over its legs with every step, each one slower than the last.

"Shh, easy now," he caressed the stallion's neck, his dark brown hands contrasting against the animal's snow-white pelt. Suddenly the light inside the cabin died and Malekai raised a fist into the air, signaling the rest of his men to a halt.

The captain narrowed his only eye, but through the fog all he could see were shadows.

He gritted his teeth... Every time he struggled with his sight, it only reminded him of his hatred for the farmgirl he knew only as 'Robyn'. Only *once* she'd said her name, but the man was never one to forget such things. Had it not been for her, he would still have both his eyes; such a misfortune it was that Nyx had taken the better of the two. He blamed her not only for his eye, but also for losing more than half of his men during the raid on Sir Percyval Garroway's camp.

Fueled by vengeance, he wanted her dead. And he wanted to be the one to do the deed.

They left their horses tied to a row of trees nearby and furtively sneaked towards Skinner's cabin. It looked almost entirely abandoned, save for a crow or two resting on the roof. Malekai led the way; he got to the cabin and put his back to it. He slid against the walls until he reached one of the windows for a peek. Once again, his eye failed him. All he saw were lifeless shadows, an empty dining table, and an unlit fireplace that was oozing hot smoke.

Where are you, you sneaky bastard? You couldn't have gone far…

It was then that he saw what looked like a sleeping person sitting on an armchair in the common room. He glanced at his men and silently instructed five of them to walk around the cabin and check the stables. The remaining ten remained in place awaiting further instruction.

"S-Sir?" whispered Borrys Belvaine, the captain's second-in-command.

"Shut your mouth…"

"But, cap'n, sir…"

Borrys placed a gentle hand on his captain's shoulder. Malekai took one glare at him and the man removed it instantly. "I-Is this really necessary, sir?" he asked. "Is the girl really worth all this?"

The captain unsheathed his blade. He would have killed his own man, had the rest of them not been gawking at them; even *he* knew that turning on your own was not a good way to ensure loyalty. "It's not about the girl, you idiot," he whispered. "Skinner and his goons are the one thing keeping this place safe, not the guards. We kill them all and the entire village will be licking our boots by sunrise. Do you understand now?"

"Yes, but sir… W-We've tried it before 'n' you saw what happened last tim-"

"We were *sloppy* last time," Malekai insisted. "And our old captain was a cowardly bastard."

"But cap'n, w-"

Malekai pressed the tip of his blade against Borrys's chin. "One more word out of you, Borrys Belvaine… and I'll gut you like a fish."

Borrys said nothing after that. Malekai straightened his knees and cracked his neck. He walked to the front door and began turning the knob, slowly so the wood wouldn't creak. He signaled the others to stand behind him with their blades ready.

The door was unlocked; it opened effortlessly with a single push.

And the silence that followed was eerie…

"Keep your backs to the walls," Malekai said to his men.

And then he took the first step inside.

Meanwhile, the five men sent to inspect the stables were doing a rubbish job of keeping quiet. They whispered loudly, walked briskly, snickered amongst one another as they helped themselves to anything they could find in the stables that looked like it was worth some coin.

"Not a single horse taken," one of them observed. "They must've left on foot."

There was even an old wooden carriage parked on the other side of the stable walls with two horses still tied to the reigns. It appeared empty, and so the red mercenaries hardly paid it any mind. Behind it, however, was the girl they were so desperately searching for, crouched near the back wheels with her bow in hand and her serpent companion wrapped around her neck.

Robyn caught glimpses of the rogues when they were distracted sifting through the pockets on the horses' saddles. Her eyes were searching for one particular man in red, the man that scarred her and attempted to make a slave out of her... But Malekai Pahrvus was nowhere to be seen...

Her heart slowed its pace; in truth, he was possibly the only man that actually frightened her.

"No one back here," another man said. "Should we go back?"

"No. Try 'n' find another way in! Pick the lock if you have to."

Robyn Huxley was grinning in the dark. She crawled cautiously over the mud and took a peek through a hole in the stable wall. There she found Skinner, hiding with a blade in hand between the stall door and a pile of hay, grinning at the men's complete lack of caution. He gave Robyn a wink and placed his forefinger over his lips, signaling her to keep quiet. And that, she did...

She realized then that the Brotherhood's reputation was not entirely what it was made out to be. They may have been cruel, merciless, even rotten. But they were not exactly the smartest bunch, at least most of them weren't. They were just men, sloppy and lazy, hungry for gold yet unwilling to make any added effort. If Skinner and his gang of wardens were hiding so easily from them, Robyn felt a shred of hope still that she would survive the journey to Drahkmere.

It was a strange sensation, indeed. She felt almost invincible.

* * *

"That's the last of 'em!" shouted a village guard as he dragged the rogue mercenary known as Clive out of *The Stumblin' Hare*.

"Line 'em up with the rest!" said the knight commander.

Drunk and disarmed, the rogue mercenaries of the Brotherhood were pinned to their knees with their hands on their scalps. Clive was the only one resisting, and so the guards shoved him onto the mud.

"Strip them of their weapons! And someone find the owner of this establishment..."

"Umm, y-yes sir," young Seamus approached the knight commander. "That'd be me, sir."

The commander took one glimpse of the lad and said, "You're a bit young to be a tavern owner, aren't you?"

"Y-Yes well," Seamus stammered shyly. "It was no choice of mine..."

"I see," the commander nodded grimly. "What's your name, lad?"

"Seamus, sir..."

With a nod of approval, the knight commander turned to his men. "Strip them of their gold as well!" he said. "It should help young Seamus pay for any damages…"

Seamus's eyes widened. "Ohh… *Thank* you, sir!"

"Don't mention it, lad."

One of the mercenaries was yelping and crying obnoxiously, and it was starting to draw attention from the nearby murmuring crowds. He was aiming a shivering finger at them, cursing and crying like a wild vulture.

"Beware the dark witch!" he shouted. "Ungodly, she is! Beware! *Beware!*"

Among the peasants hid Syrena of Morganna. She looked the other way, wishing she had escaped with Hudson when she had the chance. One of the guards bent on one knee and inspected the crying mercenary; there was a red handprint on his neck and his skin was blistering awfully.

"Ungodly!" the man went on. "She's *ungodly*!"

"By the gods… You ever see anything like this, knight commander?"

They examined the wound closely, and then several eyes moved towards the crowd of villagers. Syrena hid behind John, keeping her gaze away so that the orange glow of her eyes would remain unseen.

"Ahh," groaned the knight commander. "He's spouting nonsense. Take 'im away!"

Syrena felt a sudden rush of relief.

As much of a sanctuary as the village was, there was no escaping a death sentence when one was a witch. Even mages had a choice in studying magic; witches were cursed with their abilities from birth. And Syrena had unfortunately faced the gallows many times in the past.

Once when she was 16, in fact, she'd actually hung from the noose and was near death. But her body worked in mysterious ways, and when it felt the jolts she became immersed in flames. The noose burned off along with all of her clothes. She'd fallen over the mud, naked and out of breath yet still alive. The only reason she'd survived at all was because the Lady of the village had taken a liking to her at the time. And, just like any friend she ever had, that Lady was now long-gone, ashes blowing in the wind.

Ungodly? She pondered cynically. *I'd show you ungodly if I could…*

"Knight commander!" one of the village guards ran abruptly into the scene. "There's been another attack, sir!"

"How many?"

"A dozen or so, sir! They were spotted in the southern outskirts, near Osric Skinner's cabin, sir!"

The commander gave it a moment's thought, sighing as if he'd been called into duty after being drained for the day. "Very well… You lot, take them away!" he ordered half of his men. "The rest of you, come with me!"

They rode away towards Skinner's cabin as the Brotherhood mercenaries were dragged in a line towards the prisons. John watched the soldiers, feeling a sudden urge to join them, until Syrena tapped him suddenly on the shoulder.

"Look!" she whispered, a hint of hopefulness in her voice.

John followed her eyes, and then his lips curved into a subtle grin.

There, standing in the shadows, was a man in a black hat sitting on a horse. He was holding the reins of two other mounts, both with saddles made of red leather. As the villagers began to disperse, heading home for the night, John and Syrena made way for the trees. Hudson was waiting there for them with a stolen winesack and a satchel full of gold.

"Care for a ride, anyone?" he asked, winking at them in that sly manner of his.

Syrena hopped onto one of the horses. "Where did you get these?" she asked.

Hudson shrugged. "They won't be needing their rides in prison, love."

With a smile lighting up her face, the witch grabbed the thief by the neck and pulled him in for a kiss. Once said kiss was over, however, she landed a slightly heavy slap across his face. "Never leave us like that again, you hear me?!" she warned him.

"Yes, ma'am!" Hudson winked at her again, as if he quite enjoyed the slap. "And *you*, you dumb bastard," he glanced at John. "The next time you try to do something like that at least wait for my signal, will you?!"

But John was lost in his thoughts, staring at the guards' shadows riding away to the south.

"See something, farmer?" Hudson asked.

"The Captain of the Brotherhood," John said worriedly. "He's still out there... Perhaps... I dunno, perhaps we should help..."

"The village guards will take care of it, mate," said the thief with a shrug. "And we have a schedule to keep, remember? Best to get on with it... Our job here is done..."

John hesitated for a moment. Something in the back of his mind was drawing him after the guards. Perhaps it was what the Brotherhood captain had said, something about a girl he'd been searching for. There was a certain familiarity with the captain's description of her, though John had been so distracted at the time that it was starting to fade from his mind... Black curls? Fair skin? Something along those lines... Such a vague description shouldn't have troubled him so much, and yet there he was...

"Come on, mate," Hudson said, handing John the reins of the third horse. "We've gotten into enough trouble for the night, don't you think?"

John took the reins but did not move. He knew Hudson was right. He knew Viktor Crowley was probably waiting somewhere out there for them. And yet his feet hesitated to move.

"Come, now," Hudson insisted. "There's nothing to see out there, mate."

Halfheartedly, John gave in. Whatever the Brotherhood's Captain had said, it was a matter that he'd have to force out of his mind if he wished to follow through with the journey.

"You're probably right," he said hesitantly. "Nothing to see out there."

* * *

Malekai took careful steps inside the cabin like a devious wildcat. His swordsmen mirrored his every move, some of them crouching to blend in with the shadows. It was as silent as death save for the crickets and the wolves howling in the distance. It was just as it had been the last time, a deserted cabin in the outskirts of town. But Malekai was much smarter than his men, even with a wounded sight. He knew the wardens were near. He knew he and his men were being watched.

He paced towards the sleeping figure in the armchair, his gaze vigilant, glancing at every corner for any sign of movement. The rest of his men pinned themselves to the walls, sliding further inside, two of them making way for the stairs. When Malekai took another step, the wood creaked beneath his boot. He lifted his fist into the air again and his men froze where they stood.

But the person in the chair did not move. And it was then that Malekai realized something wasn't right. He poked at the chair with the tip of his blade and the straw hat fell to the floor, exposing a head made of cloth. Malekai's jaw tightened with rage. But before he could make any sudden movements, his ear caught something.

His eye may have been shit, but the man always did have quite an ear. It was a soft puffing sound, as if someone was breathing through a stuffed nose. And it was accompanied by a subtle creak, like wood being bent too far and on the verge of cracking.

Where are you, you gutless little rat?

Someone was aiming a bow at him, Malekai knew. He could almost feel the eyes on the back of his neck. Whoever it was, they were struggling to hold their grip on the arrow. Malekai felt the sudden urge to take cover, but he knew that in such cases, letting an enemy know that you're aware of their presence was like asking to be shot. But suddenly, his eye decided to aid him... In a moment of clarity, he caught a glimpse of the shadow upstairs. A girl was aiming right at him, a girl with a jaguar's tooth hanging from her ear.

Hello there, you beauty...

He was ready to dash for the stairs.

But then a sudden sound startled them all.

Just outside the front door, a teenage boy with a raccoon hat hopped down from the roof and onto the porch. Then, with the swiftness of a hare, he grabbed the knob and pulled the door shut, trapping Malekai and his swordsmen inside.

"Get 'im!" shouted Borrys Belvaine, but before any of the men could move, a trapdoor in the common room floor fell inward with a slam. A hand emerged from beneath and grabbed the foot of the nearest rogue mercenary. With a swift pull, brave Aldous dropped the man to the floor and killed him with a single jab to the throat. "*Now,* lads!" the youth shouted, and then chaos followed.

Captain Malekai Pahrvus leapt to the nearest corner for safety as arrows began flying in from above. Ayisha and Milo were aiming with precision, but Borrys Belvaine tipped the dining table over and used it as a shield for himself and three others. "In here, lads! Take cover!"

At the same time, however, Yuri the orcess leapt out of a hollow cupboard with a pair of blades and Mallory the quiet girl began spitting poisonous darts through a pipe from underneath the staircase.

"Cap'n!" Borrys shouted, hiding cowardly behind the table. "There's too many of 'em!"

Another red mercenary ran for the door, only to find that it had been locked from the outside; he was killed by an arrow before he could find cover again.

Damn it all to hells, Malekai gritted his teeth as he used the scarecrow's armchair for cover. He looked at the front door, contemplating running and slamming against it. But the doorknob began rattling on its own before he could sprint towards it.

"*Cap'n?! You there?!*" a muffled voice called from the outside. The few rogues from the stables had come to aid their men; they began breaking some of the windows and shooting arrows back at the young wardens.

"*Get the cap'n out o' there!*" one of them shouted. Some tried to force the thick wooden door open with their shoulders, and when that didn't work they used their blades. But the cabin had been solidly built for this. It was clear that the man that owned it knew a thing or two about strong defenses.

"It's too strong! Find another way in!" someone ordered.

But there was a sudden growl coming from above that distracted some of them. One of the rogue mercenaries glanced up in a fright, only to see a massive green orc glaring down at him from the balcony.

"Bloody hells... I-It's him! It's the Bea-"

The orc hopped down and landed on top of the man, breaking both his ribs and skull upon impact. The other four were stunned and horrified. They stood there with their blades in hand, staring at the frightening orc that was once their comrade, the orc they had left to die...

Ignar the Beast let out a startling roar that made them all shudder. And then, as if killing rats, he swung his axe brutally like a vicious warrior thirty for carnage.

Malekai saw it all through one of the broken windows, he saw the bodies falling one by one until all of his mercenaries were no more. He knew then that this was their last straw, seeing as he could only count five heads inside the cabin, including his own. And so, in a rush of panic, he rolled over the floor towards the back door, which looked rickety and much less sturdy than the front one.

"This way, lads!" he shouted. He used the rage he'd built up and slammed against the door repeatedly with every bit of his brute strength. The lock broke off after the third slam, and Malekai nearly stumbled into the mud. His last four men soon followed behind. They were free at last...

"Cap'n?! Are you alright?! Are you *wounded*, cap'n?!" Borrys asked with genuine concern. But before Malekai could catch his breath, there was a loud "*Hyah!*" that diverted his attention.

A cart ran past them, so swiftly that it brushed against barrels and piles of hay and caused a mess in the stableyard. Malekai was standing dangerously close; another inch and the cart would have scraped his chest. He saw Osric Skinner – known enemy of the Rogue Brotherhood – sitting behind the reins. But it did not stagger him as much as the figure sitting next to Skinner did.

It was a girl no older than seventeen, with black curls and a coat made of a coyote's pelt.

Malekai recognized her instantly, for she had that look of defiance on her devious grin.

Their eyes met, and for that fleeting moment it was as if the whole world had gone quiet. The expression on Malekai's face began to shift; he was stunned at first, his eye focusing on the girl's face while the rest of the world remained a blur. Soon, however, his face tightened with fury and drops of sweat began to form at his brow.

Robyn Huxley had fooled him, ridiculed him, driven him to a rage that made him senseless. In his mind, he had spent years climbing the ladder patiently, had become the Captain of the Rogue Brotherhood, only to see it all collapse before him because of this one girl... And there she was, the gutless thing, escaping his grasp yet again...

Without a single word, Malekai slid his blade back into its sheath and ran for his horse.

"Cap'n!" Borrys ran after him. "Sh-Shit... Come, boys! Follow the cap'n!"

The attack on Skinner's cabin was over. Eleven men were scattered over the floors, all of them red mercenaries, all of them dead. The Wardens of Grymsbi gathered on the porch, the Beast standing among them. They watched merrily as their commander rode away in the cart, safe and uninjured. Robyn turned in her seat and waved goodbye at them with a smile.

They had done it. They had escaped the wrath of the Brotherhood yet again.

Even Ignar the Beast felt his lips curving into a warm smile, which was as rare as a Vallenghardian blackbear hunting at mid-winter.

"Farewell, scrap," he muttered under his breath. "Farewell..."

It was a pleasant moment while it lasted. The young wardens patted each other's backs and shared smiles with each other. But then a white stallion rode out from the trees, speeding down the road in pursuit of the cart. Captain Malekai Pahrvus was not finished; he wouldn't rest until he saw the girl dead. When the rest of the red mercenaries galloped behind their captain, the wardens glanced at one another in a panic, unsure of what to do.

"With me, lads! We're goin' after 'em!" Ayisha said, rushing to the stables.

"Wait! Skinner ordered us to stay here!" Aldous protested, struggling to keep up with her pace. The rest of them followed in a close formation like a flock of birds.

"I *said* we're goin' after 'em!"

"The horses... they're gone!" Milo said suddenly. When they reached the stables, there was nothing but clutter and garbage.

"The bastards must've scared them off..."

Ayisha froze, her mind thinking of the worst possible outcome.

"It'll be alright," Aldous tried to calm her. "Skinner's tough. He'll make it back."

But even he wasn't certain of it...

Vengeance could drive a man insane, and the look on Malekai's face had certainly started to show it. In a moment of fury, the captain chose to trail them like a tenacious predator refusing to let a prey escape. The only thing that gave the young wardens hope was that their fearless leader knew Halghard's roads better than any of the rogue mercenaries did.

Skinner, true to his word, took the cliffside road, a majestic route that gave Robyn a spectacular view of the Great Rift of Halghard that left her speechless. It was also, however, a treacherous deathtrap for anyone traveling at full speed on horse; a single wrong move and both horse and rider would fall off the edge and plummet a thousand feet down to their deaths. The road was long and rough, and every few seconds the cart would bounce and the wheels would screech.

"Anyone on our tail?" Skinner asked, hesitant to slow the cart down.

Robyn glanced back at the murky vacant road.

"I think we lost them!" she said with a smile. "We made it!"

"Don't celebrate just yet," said Skinner. "Hang onto something, will you?"

Robyn chose to grab on to the cart's wooden backrest so that she could sit on the edge and take in the view. It was just minutes before dawn and the black sky was starting to lighten into an overcast blue hue, with just enough light to give Robyn a detailed spectacle of the grandiose Rift. Her mother's description couldn't have been more precise, she realized; it looked as if a massive object had crashed in from the sky, leaving an immense opening in the thick brown earth that stretched for miles on the horizon. It was frightening and beautiful all at once.

"Sit back, girl. It's gonna be a long ride," Skinner said.

But Robyn was so overwhelmed with curiosity, she could hardly stay in her seat. She stretched her neck for a better view of the Rift, enjoying her brief moment of bliss. It was utterly peaceful until she heard those vicious neighs echoing behind them, the neighs of a frightened horse that was being lashed and overworked.

She felt her heart quicken and her palms start to sweat. Skinner's hearing must not have been great, for he seemed concentrated on the road ahead. Robyn placed her knee on the seat and lifted herself for a better view.

"What are you doing? I said *sit*, girl!"

The fog started to clear and the sun was peeking out of the horizon. And it was then that Robyn saw him, a figure dressed in red leathers riding a white stallion. He stood out against the brown scenery like a barbed scarlet rose on a dying shrub.

"Oh shit," she mumbled, her eyes widening with panic. "Shit, shit, shit…"

And then, like a loyal pack following their alpha wolf, a group of red riders emerged from the dissolving fog, trailing behind their captain.

"Skinner! They've tailed us!" Robyn said agitatedly.

Skinner winced and tried to glance over his shoulder, but his eyes diverted back to the road when he felt the horses drift perilously to the right. "Fucking hells," he growled, gripping the reins for dear life. "How many are there?!"

"I dunno! Four? Five?"

"Which *is* it, girl? Four or five?!"

"F-Five!" she squinted her eyes. "It's five!"

Skinner's neck remained still, keeping his gaze ahead, but his eyes were gently moving from side to side as if he was contemplating their options, what little they were.

"You must ride!" he finally said to her.

"What?!"

"You heard me, girl. Take the reins…"

"But I-I've never ridden a cart bef-"

"Listen to me, girl!" he shouted aggressively at her. "If we don't fight back, we'll *die* out here! Do you understand that?! Now take the reins, I say!"

Robyn stared at the narrow road trailing endlessly ahead, the cliff just inches to the right. A mere bump, a simple twitch of the wrist, the smallest mistake could shake the wheels off track and kill them all.

"I-I can't!" she panicked.

"I said *take* the reins, girl! That's an order!"

An arrow flew suddenly into the cart. Had the wooden backrest not been there, it would have struck Robyn in the shoulder. She felt the hairs rising on the back of her neck.

This is it, Robyn, she told herself. *There's no other way…*

She breathed deeply, taking a moment to accept what was about to occur.

"What on earth are you *waiting* for?!" Skinner shouted at her.

Another breath… A *deep* one… She had to force herself to concentrate and muffle Skinner's shouts, for they were of no help to her at that moment…

If we don't fight back, we'll die out here, she repeated the man's words in her mind. Calmly, she removed Nyx from her shoulders and set him down on the seat.

"Lady Robyn?" he looked up at her.

And she replied with a nervous whisper. "I'm sorry, Nyx…"

"What are you doing?!" Skinner glanced at her with his brows in an arch. But Robyn appeared determined and lost in concentration, like a soldier charging bravely into battle.

If we don't fight back, we'll die out here…

Skinner's words kept echoing in her mind, overwhelming her, frightening her half to death. If she died out here, she wouldn't see John again. She wouldn't see her mother or the twins again. They may never even know what became of her. Malekai would throw her body into the Rift and she would be forever forgotten.

If we don't fight back, we'll die out here…

The words horrified her but she *used* them, as if they were the oil that would feed her inner fire. Another arrow flew into the cart but she managed to duck this time; it missed her hair by an inch. She glanced suddenly at Skinner with a hardened glare. "Keep riding," she said to him; it sounded almost like an order.

She forced the fear out of her chest and eased her breaths into a relaxed and gentle rhythm. She'd always been a bold soul, that Robyn… but Malekai had left a mark on her, a wound that she yielded to like a frightened child.

She loathed it… At all costs, she wanted rid of it…

And she knew that the only way to accomplish that was to face him the way she had faced every one of her fears in the past, just as she'd seen her mother do.

"Lady Robyn!" Nyx shouted up at her fretfully, panicking at the realization that in his serpent form he could do absolutely nothing to stop her.

If we don't fight back, we'll die out here…

She strapped her quiver of arrows to her back and reached for her bow. She rose gradually to her feet, maintaining her balance as best she could while the cart ran at full speed.

"Lady Robyn, what in all hells do you think you're doing?!"

She gave her neck a good crack and then gazed back at Malekai as if the man was nothing but a red target on a wooden board.

"Fighting back," she said, and then she hopped to the back of the cart.

* * *

The ruthless captain charged ahead, slamming the reins so fiercely that the poor steed neighed in pain with every strike. To Malekai's right, one of his bowmen was aiming again, his legs clasped at his mount's sides to keep himself balanced.

"Wait!" said Malekai. "Save your arrows!"

"Aye, cap'n!"

"And listen, lad!" Malekai growled. "Only *wound* her, you understand?!"

But the bowman couldn't hear; they were riding so fast that the wind was freezing his ears. "What??"

"I said *wound* her! I want the bitch for myse-"

Malekai became stunned all of a sudden, the blood rushing from his face.

A sharp arrow pierced through the bowman's neck... A *lethal* shot...

The bowman was only alive for a few seconds to see it. He felt his body grow cold as the blood gushed down his chest. And then his body sunk into a slouch and he fell to the right, dragging his crying horse off the edge of the cliff with him.

Slowly and bewilderingly, Malekai turned his gaze forward.

He saw her... Robyn Huxley was standing on the back of the cart with her bow in hand... But Malekai hardly recognized the farmgirl he had tied up in his tent. She looked fearless, aggressive, and ready to kill again. She took aim and, without hesitating, released another arrow.

Malekai pulled his horse to the left just in time and the arrow grazed the hairs on his scalp. His eyes widened, the mask of valor he once held had shattered; the girl was determined to kill him and, for the first time since meeting her, Malekai became worried for his life.

"Spread out, lads!" he shouted. "Take to the trees!"

The remaining three raiders scattered themselves, finding paths along the greenery to their left. Malekai had the road to himself, allowing him the breathing space he needed. He galloped on, drawing himself fearlessly nearer to the cart, knowing he would only make himself a bigger target. But with every arrow that Robyn shot his way, he appeared to dodge them with ease, as if he could read where the arrow would hit the moment she let go of it.

When he was a good thirty feet away, he pulled out his blade. Robyn could see him clearly now. She could see his eerie grin returning, as if he was enjoying himself, fueled by the thrill of the chase.

"Go on, you bitch!" he muttered violently under his breath. "Give us more!"

Robyn was aiming again, but she hesitated when she realized Malekai was no longer trying to catch up to her. He kept a cautious distance, but he wasn't slowing down either.

"That's it," he kept on, softly so that she wouldn't hear him over the sound of horse hooves. "You've only got so many arrows... Give us all you got..."

Something pricked at her ear all of a sudden, a violent rustling of leaves coming from her right. "Skinner, look out!" she shouted, and then the cart darted dangerously towards the cliff, and the wheel nearly slid off the edge. A rogue mercenary with a shaved head had galloped into the road and nearly crashed into them. But Skinner managed to slam the reins just in time and the man had no choice but to trail behind them. He was so near, Robyn could practically *smell* him.

She aimed right at him with her bow but the man surprised her with a shield he had strapped to his back. He swung it forward and hid behind the steel. She could hear him snickering as he galloped even closer, close enough to jump into the cart.

But then she lowered her aim a good three feet.

I'm so sorry, she thought to herself, as if the poor horse could somehow read her thoughts. She closed her eyes and let go... The arrow struck the horse on the foreleg and it gave out a bellowing cry before it fell face-forward onto the dirt. The red mercenary was thrown into the air; he rolled on the mud, trying desperately to sink his nails into something, but it was of no use. He'd been riding so fast that the horse slid over the mud and pushed the man off the cliff to his death.

Robyn took a moment to catch her breath.

Two down. Three more to go.

Meanwhile, in the front of the cart, something caught Nyx's eye.

"To your left, old man," he warned.

Skinner took a quick glance and saw the shadow galloping within the trees, catching up to the cart with ease. "No... no, no, no, come on!" Skinner hit the reins again. But before he knew it the rider had surpassed them, and just a moment later he galloped out of the trees in front of the cart. They were surrounded, a snickering mercenary with arm tattoos in the front and Captain Malekai Pahrvus in the back.

"What's the plan now?" Nyx asked.

The rider in front of them had already started to slow down, leaving Skinner no choice but to do the same. "Oi! Girl!"

Robyn held on to her arrows, realizing it'd be easier to outrun Malekai than to kill him. She glanced back and cursed under her breath when she noticed the other rider ahead, treacherously close for his own good. She drew an arrow, but Skinner held her back with a hand motion.

"Don't!" he said. "We'll crash into the dead bastard and stumble off the cliff!"

With one hand on the reins, the man reached into his rucksack and pulled a thick dagger out of it. "You've no choice now, girl! You *must* ride!"

He slid to the side, giving her room to hop to the front. Whatever fear burdened the young archer before had now diminished, replaced by a boundless thrill, one that made her feel unstoppable. It might have been her imagination, but the road looked suddenly wider, a good foot and a half of space between the wheels and the edge of the cliff.

It's nothing Robyn, she told herself. *Just think of it like riding next to a river. What's the worst that could happen?*

Nyx had curled himself on the seat like a rope, shrinking his size a good three feet, his head popping out from the center so as to keep watch, which was the only way he could be helpful in his state. "Watch the trees," he said to her.

When she took a glimpse, there was only one shadow left dashing through the greenery. *Borrys Belvaine,* she recognized him even as a red silhouette.

Skinner crouched on the front edge of the cart, keeping his balance with only his heels. A single slip of the ankle and his body would fall under the wheels, but the man was much more agile than he appeared for his age. "Don't be gentle with it! Get us closer!" he shouted at Robyn. Then he took a risky leap onto one of the horses that was pulling the cart. He nearly stumbled off, but he wrapped his arms around the horse's back and hoisted himself to a seat.

Focus, Robyn... Fight back...

Realizing what Skinner's intentions were, she smirked. She hit the reins and the cart moved closer to the red rider, the two horses closing in on his. Skinner was just two feet away, but he knew killing him from afar was not an option. If they wanted to avoid a clash, he'd have to remove the man from his horse entirely.

Skinner bent a knee and placed one foot onto his horse's back, then the other. Then, without thinking twice, he took another leap, pushing himself as far as his legs would allow him. He landed sloppily behind the red rider; a mere half-foot and he would have sprung right off and tumbled down the cliff.

They struggled... The red rider refused to let go of his horse and Skinner refused to let him keep it. Robyn slowed the cart a bit, just far enough so that she could still lend Skinner a hand, should it be necessary.

Meanwhile, Nyx glanced over the backrest of the cart.

"He's gaining on us..."

Robyn's grin faded. She'd been far too distracted, she'd forgotten about the real threat. When she glanced back, Captain Malekai Pahrvus was only a few feet away. Any closer and the man would be able to hop into the cart.

She hit the reins again, unaware of the danger that lied ahead.

Skinner was the first to notice it; his disturbed reaction made him slow, and so the red rider jabbed a dagger into the old man's leg. Skinner grunted from the pain, but rather than yielding to it he allowed it to fuel his rage. Risking losing his balance, he grabbed the red rider by the head and gave it a violent twist.

There was a crack. And then the rider slumped forward.

He'd won... But there was no time to lose, for the threat ahead was now treacherously near... "Sharp left!" he shouted so loudly, his lungs nearly gave in.

Robyn became startled... Skinner pulled his horse carelessly into an opening among the trees. They crashed into a willow and stumbled on a resting log. The horse fell hard, and Robyn hoped Skinner wasn't underneath it when it did.

When she turned her gaze forward again, her jaw dropped...

Straight ahead, the road curved sharply to the left; a wide curve it was, and beyond it was nothing but empty space. The Great Rift of Halghard was as enormous as the stories told... And Robyn Huxley hadn't even seen half of it...

Her instinct told her to jump off, but she couldn't just leave Nyx behind. Instead, she let go of the right rein and pulled on the left one like her life depended on it. The poor horses bellowed loudly, their necks bending, beckoning them to take that sharp turn. But there was nothing that could have prepared Robyn for what came next.

The horses made the turn, but there was a moment of terror in which the cart began to tip off-balance. Robyn felt the world stand still for a moment, before everything began to tilt.

The whole cart flipped... Robyn leaped and rolled over the pebbly mud... She tried to bury her nails into something, *anything* at all, but she'd been riding too fast and her grip slipped against the soil. She scraped her knees, elbows, and wrists over the wet gravel, and before she knew it she was tumbling off the cliff...

She let out a yelp of panic as her hand latched onto the only thing at her reach. A thick tree root, possibly belonging to one of the willows nearby, was sticking out of the earth, lodged along the cliff's edge like an oversized vine. The cart fell, dragging the crying horses down with it, missing Robyn's head by just a hair.

She made the mistake of looking down... She watched as the cart and horses shrunk down to the size of a whetstone, before vanishing entirely into the misty abyss that was the Great Rift. Some thousand feet deep it must have been, and Robyn had tempted fate at the very last moment.

You made it... By the gods, you **made** *it!*

But then she had a chilling realization... Nyx was still sitting next to her when the cart had flipped... In a panic she glanced up, but there was no sign of him anywhere. He might have been crushed by the cart, for all she knew. Or he might have fallen *with* it...

She had survived death again but hardly had time to rejoice; she was alone again, stranded, hanging by a vine along the edge of a cliff. And her breathing only grew hastier when she heard a neighing horse come to a halt just above her head.

She heard a faint *"Whoa,"* and a pair of boots slamming against the mud.

No... Please, no...

"Tsk tsk," she heard him, and then the footsteps approached.

Damn it all to hells, no...

Robyn was hanging a good foot below the edge of the cliff. Even if she climbed her way back up, there was no outrunning the captain... She was *trapped...*

Captain Malekai Pahrvus leaned in for a better look. His boots sunk into the dirt and Robyn's face was briefly speckled with dust and gravel. She coughed, holding on for dear life, unable to rub her eyes clean; instead she forced the dirt off by blinking rapidly. The captain had a nasty grin plastered on him. He hadn't been this close to her since that night in his tent. He began with a sigh of relief and then, just as he'd done many times before, he chuckled and nodded his head in that disdainful and patronizing manner of his.

"You have quite some nerve, you know that?" he said, and already Robyn couldn't stand to hear his voice. "Truly, you must be the most stubborn fucking thing I've ever met in my life…"

She said nothing in response. If she were being honest, the rage in her chest frightened her; she didn't know that she was capable of so much hate. Malekai turned his gaze briefly away from her, glancing at something out of her view. He bent on one knee and reached for it.

"Tsk tsk. What a mess, what a mess," he said, and then lifted his arm for her to have a look.

It was Nyx, drenched in mud and hanging lifelessly from Malekai's hand. Parts of his serpentine body had been flattened and smeared with his own blood and guts. Robyn bit her tongue to fight back the rage.

Nyx… My dear Nyx, I am so sorry…

A tear escaped her eye. She hoped Malekai would stall further, at least long enough for Nyx to revive himself. But that small shred of hope died after what Malekai did next.

"I must say, your choice of friends baffles me," he said. And then with a disapproving nod he threw Nyx's body into the Great Rift.

"No!!!" she cried, but Nyx was swallowed by the dark pit of fog within seconds; she kept her eyes on him until he disappeared into nothing. And then she sobbed, knowing she might never see her friend again. Malekai was almost touched by it all, his head tilting to the side as he stared her down.

"You brought this upon yourself, girl," he said.

Unable to resist herself, she hissed loudly at him, "My name is *Robyn*!"

"Right," he said, his tone one of subtle admiration. "Robyn Huxley… What a pity. Such a beautiful name *wasted* on a stubborn little shit like you…"

Robyn glared right back at him through her tears.

If you're going to kill me, just get on with it, she thought. But in reality, death frightened her greatly, and she couldn't find the words to say without admitting her defeat. A horse trotted to a halt nearby. Robyn silently wished it were Skinner coming to her aid, but Malekai's calmness spoke differently.

"Cap'n!" shouted Borrys, dismounting his horse. He observed the tracks on the dirt and the muddle of food and supplies that had scattered when the cart flipped. "What in hells happened 'ere?!"

Malekai did not look very happy. It was as if Borrys's screech of a voice had reminded him of the wretched reality. *Of all the good men I could have been left with,* he pondered despicably. *Why did I have to be stuck with you?*

"Where, uh... Where are the rest of our men, cap'n?"

"Shut up and get me a bow."

Robyn's heart raced. There was a bow on the grass, a humble little thing made of elven wood. Borrys snatched it and handed it to his captain. Even as Robyn hung from that angle, she recognized *Spirit* when she saw it.

"You know," Malekai sighed, spitting into the Rift and nearly hitting Robyn. "I had many ideas for how I would kill you. But I must say this way's far better than anything I could've planned."

Borrys handed his captain an arrow, and once again it belonged to Robyn. Such irony it was that she was to be shot by an arrow that she had carved herself, killed by the very same bow with which she had learned to kill.

"I know you must not think very highly of me, girl..."

"*Robyn*," she growled at him, and it only made his grin wider.

"Right. *Robyn*," he said. "You know... Regardless of what you may believe, I'm not the monster you make me out to be. Hells, in another life you might've even made a worthy comrade. I do admire a bit of nerve."

He nocked the arrow in place and pulled back the string. Robyn fought the urge to look away, as much as it pained her to see her bow in his filthy hands.

"You still *can*, you know," he said suddenly, aiming the sharp tip right between her eyes. "It doesn't have to end this way..."

Robyn wished she could have believed him, but she could read the wickedness in his eye. *Lying bastard... I'm the daughter of Adelina Huxley. Deceiving me will take a lot more effort than that.*

"All you have to do is say the word, Robyn. And then Borrys and I will pull you right back up," he said. "Just the one word... I want to *hear* you say it..."

Robyn frowned. She was certain he would kill her the moment she said it.

"No point in being stubborn this time, Robyn," Malekai went on. The sound of his voice when he said her name was so revolting, she regretted ever telling him what it was. "You either say the word or you say nothing ever again... Go on, then... Say *please*."

Robyn's grip on the vine began to loosen. Her other arm was still in pain from the brand, there was no way she could have pulled herself up with it. It was either death by fall or death by Malekai's hand. And she'd already made up her mind. She took a last glance down below at the Rift.

It's all right, Robyn... Just do it...

Malekai sighed. "Time's up," he said. "Any last words, Robyn?"

She looked up fearlessly and hissed through her gritted teeth.

"Eat... shit!" she said, and then her fingers began to slide.

Malekai felt an instant rage. He was about to let go of the arrow, when suddenly a thundering sound startled them all...

A sharp, earsplitting, high-pitched growl echoed for miles around...

Robyn's hand regained its grip, and her mind jolted her back to her senses.

She'd been prepared to let go, prepared to die, before the sound broke her from that trance. It was followed by a strong sweeping wind, the likes of which could only be brought upon by a storm.

"What on earth was that?" Malekai turned to the trees. In a panic, he had lowered the bow, glancing about for the source of the sound. Borrys was too stunned for words, his lower lip shivering and his hand on the hilt of his blade. The two men locked eyes with one another, their troubled minds in a daze. Whatever beast had made the sound *had* to have been large.

"M-Maybe we should go, cap'n..."

But there was no chance of it, not yet. Malekai was so fueled by vengeance, it blinded him. He walked back to the edge of the cliff with Robyn's bow in hand. Robyn's wrist was aching; she'd slid down so far, she was practically holding onto life with her fingertips.

"Cap'n!" Borrys shouted, his eyes glancing in every direction, startled half to death. "Cap'n, just leave her! She's not worth it, cap-"

"Fuck off!" Malekai snarled, his hands determined to kill. He was ready to take aim again when the sound arose. A sweeping sound, like that of a ship's sails thrusting heavily against the wind, resonated from underneath them, from somewhere within the Great Rift.

With it came another roar, this one loud and alarmingly near...

Robyn watched as the blood drained from Malekai's face, as if the man had come face to face with death. He was looking in her direction, at the shadow rising out of the misty depth. She craned her neck down... and the corner of her eye caught a glimpse of the winged beast...

Malekai was startled off balance when it flew past them, a massive creature the color of coal, with scaly reptilian skin and giant wings like a bat. With an ear-splitting roar it flew into the great blue sky, casting its shadow over them, soaring with the wind like a thousand-pound bird.

"By the gods..." Borrys exclaimed, his face pale and his tongue suddenly as dry as sandpaper. "I-Is that a... a...!"

Malekai stumbled back to his feet, his hair ruffled and his eye-patch hanging loosely out of place. He yanked it off and threw it over the mud, gazing into the skies at the massive creature, astonished beyond words. He'd never seen such a creature in real life, only heard the stories, and even then he'd doubted they were anything more than myths. Yet here he stood staring at one.

The winged creature circled back around and flew towards them at great speed. And it was then that Malekai wakened from the shock. "To the horses! Now!"

They ran to their mounts and galloped away. But the creature was brutally fast; it was getting bigger and bigger as it neared the cliff again. Borrys whimpered like a frightened child, spouting devout nonsense as if he were suddenly a man of faith that deserved to be spared.

Malekai wasted no time. He was more concerned about saving his own skin, he figured Borrys could serve as bait and slow down the great beast. It flew past the edge of the cliff, overlooking Robyn along the way as if she was not a worthy prey for it. The creature's gaze was instead fixed on the two riders. It was here for *them*.

Robyn forced herself back to her senses. Whatever that thing was, it had given her a fighting chance. Using what little force she had left, she pulled herself up and used her free hand to grip the earth as best she could.

Her mind was distracted, astonished by the winged creature. She had to be careful, had to force the dark thoughts out of her mind; if that thing circled back towards her, she was certainly done for.

Concentrate, Robyn... Push, now... Give it all you got!

Her heel found a sturdy-enough stone along the cliff's wall and she used it for additional force. Before she knew it, her eyes were at eye level with the ground. She could see Malekai and Borrys scampering off down the road from which they came. Too many trees were in the way, and so the giant creature flew in the open space along the edge of the cliff, trailing the two men like a great eagle chasing after a pair of field mice.

Now's your chance, Robyn. Don't you dare waste it.

Somehow, she managed to grip the loose soil long enough to pull her knee up to the flat ground. Once she did that, she felt a release of tension all over her. One good push was all it took before she was crawling over the mud again. She cared so little about all the filth that she lied there face-up for a moment, catching her breath, stroking the mud with her fingertips as if it was precious.

You did it... You bloody did it... You're alive...

Her eye caught sight of her bow *Spirit*, filthy and wet over a nearby puddle. Malekai must've dropped it on the way to his mount, she figured. Immediately, she reached for it, caressing it like a lost pup. She wasn't done just yet. So long as she had her bow, she would keep fighting. She found her quiver of arrows over a patch of dry grass, right next to a tattered red-leather eye patch.

He will pay... The evil bastard will pay for all he's done...

There was another roar, high-pitched and resonant, like the shrill cry of a frantic crow only deeper and much rougher. The winged creature had outrun the two rogue mercenaries. Its bat-like wings slowed to a halt and it perched itself on the other end of the road, where the path was wider. Malekai had a good lead on his right-hand man, and when the creature enclosed them, he was the first to face it. He brought his white stallion to a halt.

There it was, the big monstrous thing... Its reptilian head was five times the size of a horse's, its jaw stretched outward like a crocodile's, its teeth were frighteningly jagged like a mass of daggers. Above its forehead, the creature had a pair of horns, curved and sharp like a bull's, and its neck was a good six feet in length, which made it look even larger when it stood on its lizard-like legs.

Malekai was careful not to make any sudden movements, for this creature was not looking at him the way a predator looks at a prey. It was an expression so vicious and hostile that it was hard to believe this thing was just an animal.

It opened its massive mouth... And the captain felt the scorching heat radiating from it... "Easy there, boy," he mumbled at the creature, his face drenched in sweat. "Easy..."

A bright orange glow began to crawl up the creature's reptilian neck. When Malekai saw it, he darted frantically towards the trees. And then, within seconds, everything was aflame. Borrys Belvaine made an attempt to flee, but there was no outrunning the beast. It craned its scaly neck and the raging fire drifted with it, swallowing both Borrys and his horse like bugs.

Robyn watched in horror; she could hear their cries even from a distance. Borrys twitched frantically, the reins caught in between his fingers, and his howling horse trotted blindly off the edge of the cliff. They fell, their bodies engulfed in flames, like a pair of falling stars disappearing into the Great Rift.

A cloud of black smoke began to gather above the trees. The flames were spreading, creating a scorching barrier impossible to escape. The creature shoved its head fearlessly between the blazing trees, its scaly black skin impervious to it, like a hungry unrelenting cat hunting down a rat. As if assuring the Captain's death, the creature coughed out more flames, this time in worn-out puffs, as if it was still recovering from its last scorching breath.

Even from a distance, Robyn was sweating from the intoxicating heat.

But she wouldn't dare move... She was captivated by the creature, mesmerized by its resilience and its haunting beauty; a majestic fearless thing that had spared her life when she was in most dire need of it, like a guardian spirit watching over her...

Oh no...

Robyn's limbs were suddenly trembling. The winged creature turned on its heels and looked in her direction, as if expecting to find her standing there. Despite the heat, her body grew cold with fear... She turned and ran, faster than she thought she was capable of, cursing under her breath as her boots splattered mud into the air.

The creature dropped into the Great Rift and used the winds to his advantage, flailing its thick meaty wings and trailing her effortlessly. Frightened out of her mind, Robyn stumbled and scraped her knees even further. She was so filthy she wondered how the creature could even tell her apart from the rest of the brown earth.

Feeling the sweeping wind behind her, she tossed and turned, crawling backwards in a fit of distress. The creature landed right in front of her, triggering a mild tremor in the earth beneath her fingertips. There was no outrunning it now; her humble bow was no match for the creature's fire. She was utterly helpless.

Don't look up at it, she told herself. *Do **not** look up...*

A moment passed... Robyn shut her eyes, waiting for the heat to devour her, but the creature did nothing. It simply stood there watching her.

Don't move a muscle... Show it that you mean no harm...

She remembered Old Man Beckwit mentioning something about the way animals often fought for power, about how some would only attack when provoked, and she hoped that the majestic creature was smart enough, that it could somehow sense her frailty in its own peculiar way. Or was it a matter of sight? Could the creature not see her when she stood perfectly still?

Realizing it was not there to harm her, Robyn lifted her eyelids gently and took a moment to observe it. Its body alone was about the size of three horses, and it had a sharp tail like an alligator that added another four or five feet. Its body was smooth and glimmering like obsidian, except for the set of spikes along its neck, and it was almost entirely black save for its wings, which seemed to have a reddish hue to it under the sun's light, the color of dark raw meat gone dry.

And its eyes, they were... No... Its *eye*...

The winged beast only had its left one...

The right eyelid was empty, marked by a deep scar over the socket...

Robyn's jaw dropped. The creature opened its mouth and exhaled a puff of grey smoke, and with it came a guttural sound that was almost human. A few moments passed, as if the creature was stalling, giving the girl some time to adjust.

And *then*, well... Then it *spoke*...

A deep rumble of a voice, it had. It was deathlike and chilling, and eerily familiar to Robyn's ears. It was the voice of her beloved Nyx.

"Hello, Lady Robyn..."

She was stunned... She told herself she was imagining things, that the injury on her head was more serious than she thought. But when she looked into his eye, she couldn't help but sense that warmth, that wisdom, that familiarity.

This was no wild creature at all... This was her *friend*...

"N-Nyx...?" She rose gently to her feet, her weak knees shivering from both enervation and fright. "Is that... *really* you...?"

Nyx said nothing, only exhaled again. He looked weary and exhausted, possibly due to the flames he'd forced out of his neck. His wings had folded and settled against his scaly ribs, resting until he took flight again.

"Nyx, that *can't* be you..."

Robyn couldn't quite find the words to say. Nyx bowed his head so that he could remain at eye-level with her, and she took the opportunity to caress his cheek the way she always did. Only this time there were no feathers to touch, no fur to graze. His skin was rough and hardened like stone and the spikes running down his neck looked more like sharp black bones from such a close distance. When he opened his mouth to breathe, she could feel the heat radiating from the inside as if he was brewing up another roar of hells' fire.

"Nyx, you're... you're...!"

"Disconcerting?" he asked. "Horrifying?"

Her lips curved into a joyous smile. "*Beautiful*," she corrected him.

And though the scales on his skin wouldn't let him smile back, his glimmering eye said enough. Robyn was looking at him with a dreamlike expression, like a little girl whose wish had just been granted. Overwhelmed with emotions, she chuckled, unable to remove her hand from his face. Her whole life, she'd heard the stories from her mother, and she believed such creatures to be no more than myths and legends.

And yet here she was, standing in front of one...

A live fire-breathing dragon...

By the gods, Robyn... If mother could see you now...

"You're beautiful, Nyx," she said again, feeling the urge to throw her arms around him. Suddenly, however, there was the sound of boots crunching against leaves. Nyx's neck turned faster than the man could take another step.

It was Skinner. He was standing behind a row of willow trees, baffled out of his mind. Robyn smiled at first, until she noticed the blood oozing from the man's belly.

"Skinner!" she ran to him. He looked alive still, not yet pale from the loss of blood, but he had to lean against the nearest tree for balance. "Skinner!" she lent him a shoulder for balance. "By the gods, are you all right??"

"What in all hells is that...?" the man couldn't remove his eyes from the dragon.

"It's okay!" she calmed him. "It's all right! He won't hurt you..."

Skinner's brows twisted, his expression shifting from baffled to concerned. "You've some explaining to do, girl..."

She couldn't help but chuckle. "Skinner, I'd like you to meet Nyx..."

The dragon approached, gently so as to not frighten the man. Skinner's gaze shifted back and forth between the two of them. "The *snake*?!" he asked bewilderingly. "Y-You're the bloody crawler?!"

"Easy there," Nyx said, jokingly. "Where I come from, that term is not very polite."

Skinner exhaled, and the sound was something between a laugh and a yelp, as if hearing Nyx speak with such a powerful resonance gave him unbearable chills. "Gods strike me," he said nervously. "Now tell me, lad... Why the fuck didn't you do that *earlier*?"

Robyn smiled again, and then she drew the attention back to the more pressing matter at hand. "Skinner, you're hurt... We must get you back to the cabin!"

The man nodded, but he looked more agile than his wound made him seem.

"Looks like you won't be needing that lift any longer, girl," he said with a grin. "By the gods... Just *look* at you two..."

He was still quite mesmerized by Nyx, and the loss of blood was making him loose concentration. Robyn tried to press him, but the man seemed confident enough to fend for himself. And it only soothed her nerves further when a limping horse emerged from the trees, a horse that used to belong to one of Malekai's men.

"Come, we must take you back..."

"No need, girl," Skinner insisted, removing his arm from her and standing up straight. He kept a bright red cloth pressed against himself, one he had stolen off the body of the dead rogue mercenary. "I've survived worse than this. I'll manage... And so will my friend here." He gave the horse a soft tap on the neck.

"But you're bleeding! You can't jus-"

"I said I'll be *manage*, girl... You've a long journey ahead, you mustn't waste any more time... And besides, the cabin's only a mile back down the road."

"Are you *sure?*" Robyn asked worriedly.

Skinner chuckled. "What's your plan? To *fly* me back? That ought to be interesting... Half the folk in Grymsbi haven't seen a tree nymph in their lives, you think they'll react kindly to a... Gods strike me... to a *fire-breathing dragon?*"

She looked down at his wound. It didn't look great, but his confidence reassured her. She swung her arms forward and embraced him, causing him to grunt mildly from the pain. "Thank you, Skinner," she said. "Thank you for everything..."

He smiled down at her.

"Go on, girl," he said. "Go and find your brother..."

Robyn glanced back at Nyx. So majestic, he looked, standing there on all fours with his neck held up a good six feet high. She walked closer to him, hesitating. But she didn't even have to ask him... He lowered himself on the ground like a hound, low enough for her to climb on his back. She'd lent him her shoulder before, as a crow and a snake, and now he was to return the favor.

"Careful," he said to her.

She came to a halt right where his neck ended and his back began, placed one boot onto his shoulder, and leapt on top of him, using the spikes on his collar to keep herself balanced. She could hardly believe where she was sitting. The scales beneath her legs were warm from the heat and yet she didn't mind it. She welcomed it, even felt thrilled by it.

"Farewell, Robyn Huxley," Skinner smiled at her from afar. "And always remember... Should you ever need us, you will always find shelter with the Wardens of Grymsbi..."

She smiled back at him. "Farewell, Skinner."

And so Nyx walked towards the cliff... His steps were slow and heavy, causing resonating thumps that shook the earth beneath them. Robyn's heart began to race as they approached the depth of the Great Rift. She was both terrified and thrilled all at once. Nyx stopped right at the edge, his claws digging deep into the dirt for a good grip.

He craned his neck back. "Ready?" he asked her.

No... Not in the slightest...

She took a deep breath and gave him a hesitant nod. Then she pressed herself against his neck, gripping onto his scales for dear life. Nyx's wings stretched back as he released a thundering roar. And then his body began to tip forward...

Robyn kept her eyes open. Her gaze shifted from the blue horizon to the darkness of the Rift. They fell... And within seconds they were falling at such great speed that Robyn nearly lost her grip as she felt the air escape her lungs for a moment.

Then Nyx extended his wings... They soared with the wind, circling above that pit of darkness, defying it the way a seagull defies the ocean current. He started flapping, and before Robyn knew it they were going up again, heading for the clouds.

"Hold on," Nyx muttered.

Robyn could feel the rumbling beneath her whenever he spoke. She took a moment to admire the view; as they got higher, the trees shrunk down to the size of shrubs and the roads looked like they were just an inch wide, as if she were suddenly staring down at a map. She could still see Skinner down there, trotting gently back into town on horse, keeping his gaze up at them.

She smiled. She almost wanted to wave, but her hands were clasped tight around Nyx's spikes. As they flew ahead, she saw the people of Grymsbi starting their morning routines, only they looked like ants from so up high. She squinted her eyes, suddenly realizing that they were all starting to look up...

Folks ran in and out of their homes, staggered and thrown aback...

They were pointing, waving, dropping to their knees...

They were scattering to spread the word, climbing to their rooves for a better view, scared out of their minds and fueled with amazement all at the same time...

Robyn Huxley couldn't believe her eyes.

She felt as if she was in some sort of dream.

"They're watching us," she said. "They're all *watching* us!"

"Are they, now?" Nyx asked, bending his neck downward. "Well... Let's give them something to see, shall we?"

They flew down towards the village... Slowly the roads and the trees grew larger and larger, until Robyn was able to make out the stunned expressions in all the peasants' faces. The more frightened ones were running to take cover while the bolder ones stood and watched. They must have been as low as twenty feet when Nyx soared upwards again, and Robyn watched as the people turned their heads with amusement, pointing up at them... at *her*... Their bewildered gazes were not just fixed on the dragon, but on the woman riding it...

She smiled again. She not only felt thrilled now, she felt *invincible*.

They circled back and flew up again, away from the village, heading south. "Hang on tight, Lady Robyn!" Nyx said. "We have a long journey ahead of us."

She leaned in and embraced him, welcoming the heat beneath her ribs.

The wind grew colder with the elevation, her wolf furs hardly able to withstand it all, but she paid it no mind.

The cold struck her skin, reddened her nose, paled her face and chest, but she paid it no mind.

The height quickened her heart's pace, sent cold shivers up her spine, but she paid it no mind.

She was flying...

XVIII
The Strong & the Weak

Lord Yohan Baronkroft stood on his balcony, high above the dead city of Drahkmere, fingers tapping the black stone that bordered the terrace. He gazed over the horizon at a small company of horses, some two dozen of them, riding towards the city gates. The landscape outside of the ruined city was nothing but barren hills of black soil and rocky terrain that went on for miles. And beyond the northern hills was a dead forest, blackened and dry, trees with thick leafless branches poking out like thousands of needles. The Dead Moors, they were called, and there was no possible way to cross them on foot; it would be like trying to cross a narrow tunnel with nails sticking out of the walls.

It gave the lord great comfort to know that there was only one direction from which an enemy troop might attempt to attack the city, and that was from the hills to the west, the direction from which the small company of horses was approaching. With a grin plastered on his face, he paced back into his personal chambers, the only somewhat elegant place in all of Drahkmere, decorated with stolen furniture and tableware, none of it matching in design or color.

A red armchair with a tall backrest rested near the fireplace, and in it sat a bloody man tied down by ropes and beaten beyond recognition. He had his trousers on but no shirt or shoes, and there were small cuts all over his body, hundreds of them, as if he'd fallen inside a barrel of razors. None of the cuts were deep enough to cause him severe damage, but all of them stung brutally, and his skin was bound never to look the same again.

"My dear Sergeant Weston," Lord Baronkroft said, pacing back and forth around the armchair. "You've no idea what your cooperation means to me and my company. Truly, I must thank you. May the gods smile down at you for the rest of your days."

The lord placed a hand on the sergeant's head and caressed it like he would a hound's.

Once, the sergeant was an experienced man of great prestige and repute, a respected man in the Qamrothian royal guard. He was handsome even, in his own rugged way. Now, however, he was pale and weak and dripping blood from all over his body. His right eye was swollen shut and his tongue had been sliced off. For the last few days he'd had no choice but to sit and listen to Baronkroft, beaten down to submission, his sense of humanity all but ripped away from him.

"Now, don't you wish you had signed that contract willingly when you had the chance, sergeant?" the lord asked, gradually rubbing his palm over the brown fuzz on the sergeant's head. Strange as it was, it hadn't been the first time Baronkroft petted him that way, and the sergeant knew it wouldn't be the last. Whenever he had resisted in the past, he'd get another cut, and so the sergeant eventually yielded to it.

"How different would things have turned out between us?" Baronkroft asked, chuckling like a madman. "How funny, life is."

The doorknob rattled suddenly, the doors squeaking as they opened gently, and in walked a towering figure with a leather mask over his jaw. Baronkroft's face lit up instantly with a wide grin.

"Ah, my dear Harrok... Come in, we've been expecting you!"

The lord motioned the Butcher to another armchair by the fire, across from the bloody sergeant. There was nothing but a wooden center table between them, where there rested a tin jar and a lone silver goblet.

"I believe you've met my right-hand man, sergeant?" Baronkroft asked, well aware of the answer. "Supreme Commander Harrok Mortymer. 'The Butcher of Haelvaara', they called him once. The deadliest warrior that ever hailed from Ahari. Built like an orc, isn't he? Even now, after so many years."

A boy entered the chamber at that moment, a nervous boy dressed in rags with caramel-colored skin and matted hair full of grease. He had his head down, careful not to look anyone directly in the eyes, and headed straight for the center table. He may as well have been invisible, for the lord paid him absolutely no mind; the boy was only there to do his duty and leave. He grabbed the jar carefully with both hands and began pouring.

A red liquid filled the goblet until it nearly overflowed, a liquid that was far too bright and thick to be red wine. As if Thomlin wasn't already intimidated by the eerie tension in the room, his eyes suddenly widened upon realizing exactly what he was serving.

"Do you know why my dear Harrok wears this mask?" Baronkroft asked the wounded sergeant. "It's not for intimidation, if that's what you believe, though it certainly does help. About a decade or so ago, there was a battle in Ahari. I take it you remember it, sergeant? Qamrothian troops invaded the city of Haelvaara in order to steal something that wasn't theirs. Imagine that... And they call *me* an extremist," he chuckled. "A precious piece of treasure, it was, one that would bestow great power to the man that possessed it. Anyway, as you're well aware the Aharians won the battle. And the scriptures say that the notorious Harrok Mortymer, the Butcher of Haelvaara, was struck by a war hammer to the jaw. They say it took nearly a dozen men to kill him."

As Baronkroft spoke, the Butcher slowly raised his arms and began untying the lace on the back of his mask. Thomlin set the jar down and stepped to the side, remaining in the room so as to observe what would happen next.

"What an unfortunate fate for a warrior of such talent, don't you think sergeant?" Baronkroft asked, as he came to a halt next to the Butcher's chair. The Butcher's teeth-lined mask dropped to the floor; the face that it revealed was something from a nightmare...

The man was as pale as his own silver eyes were. His nose was chipped at the tip and the skin just beneath his nostrils was wrinkled and scarred. He had no chin; it had been entirely broken off by the war hammer. Instead there was a wide gap where his chin should be and his jaw was unfinished, leaving nothing but two pieces of bone and flesh sticking out like a set of horns. His tongue was still there along with his upper teeth, rotten as they were. He looked more like a walking corpse than an actual man.

Sergeant Weston's eyes widened with horror.

"Is something the matter, sergeant?" Baronkroft asked; even when his face was blank, there was always the hint of grin concealed within it. "You're not intimidated by my dear Harrok, are you?"

The Butcher grabbed the overflowing goblet and began pouring it slowly into his chinless mouth. Most of the blood made it down his throat, while some of it splattered over his malformed jaw and cheeks. Thomlin watched from a corner, his mouth hanging open with shock, feeling as if his innocent eyes deceived him. There was a moment in which Baronkroft noticed the boy, only he wasn't angry or upset. In fact, the eerie grin returned, splitting his face in two. The Butcher savored every last drop and then wiped his face with a wet towel, every movement slow and placid and ghostly.

"There you go, my friend," Baronkroft placed a gentle hand on Harrok's shoulder, in a similar form as he had done with the sergeant, except perhaps with more respect. It was as if the sergeant was a mere pup while the Butcher was his most trusted hound. "Feeling better, I take it?" he asked.

The Butcher placed the empty goblet on the center table and said nothing. His chinless jaw was still smeared with red and his eyes were pale and hungry.

"Do forgive him for his unlikely habits," Baronkroft said to the sergeant. "It's not my dear Harrok's fault, the poor man. He needs it."

A tear escaped the sergeant's face. So many years of service to the Qamrothian royal guard, and for what? For *this*? At that moment he knew that his life was over. He wouldn't see his family again. He wouldn't see his home again. He was to die in this forgotten city, along with many other souls under Baronkroft's rule. Accepting it all nearly calmed his nerves. *Nearly.*

"Now, if you'll excuse me, Sergeant Weston," Baronkroft began pacing away. "I've some business to tend to before your superiors arrive. They should be here within the hour, I imagine. In the meantime, try not to do anything stupid... Otherwise I'd have to cut you again... My dear Harrok could always use a bit more energy for our gathering tonight. And by the gods, does he have an appetite," he chuckled.

Nervously, Thomlin began drifting towards the doors. He was so startled and shaken that he almost wondered if it was real or if the hunger was starting to make him hallucinate.

"Leave us," Baronkroft said, and Thomlin wasted not another second.

The boy turned and fled the room as fast as he could. He closed the chamber doors behind him and took a moment to catch his breath, pressing his back against the doors as if to keep the horrors locked inside. For a boy of twelve, he had seen far more than his curious mind could bear. And once his breathing was back to normal, his feet did something unexpected... They *ran*.

Through the empty black halls of Drahkmere's citadel, he ran, his eyes scanning for anything and everything that could possibly aid him in his escape. It was a rare instance, for his hands and feet to be free of ropes or chains. There was no way of escaping the citadel grounds undetected, he knew. Guards and recruits lurked around every corner. Patience was his best virtue, and he had used it before to seek out imperfections and possible hideouts. At that moment, however, the pounding in his chest wasn't allowing him to think.

Down a set of stairs, he hopped. Across an empty hall, he ran.

Further away from the prison chambers, the citadel became more and more unfamiliar to his eyes. Eventually, he had forgotten where he was or what direction he'd come from. He entered a large dining room with wooden tables and chairs that were falling apart, ceilings and crystal chandeliers that were riddled with spider webs, and an awfully putrid scent in the air, a blend of humidity and death.

He ran through the first set of doors he could find, only to come across a tower of spiraling stairs. He heard voices about two floors above, the grunts of two men hiding and drinking somewhere in the darkness. One of them must have heard him, for he snorted and shouted, "Who's there?!"

Thomlin sped downstairs as fast as he could, hopping over sets of steps and nearly falling every time. His knees became weak, the soles of his feet started to ache, and eventually one of his heels slipped on the edge of a step and he stumbled forward. When he fell, he scraped his wrists against the black stone and began bleeding, sharp pebbles sinking into his tender skin. Had his hands not eased his fall, his jaw would have smashed against the stone and his first thought was that he would have probably ended up like the Butcher.

The boy groaned from the pain, silently so as to not be heard by the drunken men above. He pushed himself up with a weak hand, but the sting made him wince and the blood started to spread. While face down on the floor, however, something caught his eye.

He noticed a glow, a subtle spark of light coming from the wall to his left...

He craned his neck and realized there was a hole in the stone. It was small, about the size of two fingers, but it was there. The glow was coming from the other side of the wall, a crystal-like blue glimmer like that of a sapphire.

Thomlin's eyes widened...

There were spider webs everywhere on this side of the citadel and there were no men to be found, save for a few drunks or rogues that snuck away and lurked in the darkness like rats among ruins. It was an entire section of the citadel, the boy realized, that was utterly unguarded. And the room he was staring into appeared to have no door leading to the inside, at least not from the hall of spiraling stairs. Still, he was sure of what his eyes told him. For a downtrodden peasant, precious stones like these were hard to miss. Those were sapphires he was seeing, all right.

"Hey!" a sudden voice startled him.

Thomlin glanced up with a twitch. A drunken man and a green orc were standing high above the set of stairs, glaring down at him.

"Wha' in all hells are *you* doin' down here, boy?!" asked the man, a mercenary in his thirties with black hair and an excuse for a beard.

"I-I got lost!" Thomlin lied, rising to his feet and wiping his bloody hands on his shirt.

"I bet you did," the man grinned menacingly. He glanced at his orc companion for a brief second before spitting and walking down the stairs towards Thomlin. "Got any coin on you, boy? Anythin' we can sell?"

"We can sell *him*," the orc suggested.

"I, um… N-No… Lord Baronkroft sent me to the kitchens for more ale, sir!" Thomlin lied again, his chest pounding with fear.

"That so?" the man laughed. "Got any food on you?"

"We can eat *him*," the orc suggested again.

"N-No, sir. I really must be going now…"

"Slow down there, littl' bugger," the man stepped forward, cornering the poor boy. "Y'know this is exactly why you shouldn't wander off. Who knows who you'll bump into down 'ere."

Thomlin was terrified. He had no weapon, nor anything he could use as one. And even if he did, there was no way he could outrun a man and an orc at the same time, not unless he was running upstairs. He was trapped.

"Something you ain't tellin' me, boy?" the man asked.

"We can beat it out of 'im," the orc said, once again his suggestions leaning more towards the violent side.

Suddenly a door slammed open just a set of stairs beneath them, and a large husky man with a shaved head and a red bush of a beard stepped out. He had a bottle of mead in his hand, as if he was seeking a place to drink in silence, but he frowned when he noticed the boy and the two figures.

"What the fuck are ye doin' out here?" Hauzer snarled, but much to his surprise Thomlin appeared relieved to see him. The boy nervously slid his way around the man and the orc and ran towards him.

"S-Sorry, sir!" Thomlin hid behind Hauzer's towering frame. "I got lost…"

"You lose something, Hauzer?" the drunken man asked.

"Piss off, ye dirty bastard. Shouldn't ye be standin' guard somewhere?" Hauzer spat.

"We was just havin' a drink with the boy, Hauzer. Let 'im stay with us a bit longer," the man snickered.

"N-No, sir!" Thomlin immediately yelped. "I prefer to go back now…"

Hauzer gripped the boy's arm and pulled him away, giving the two drunks one last glare as he brushed past them. "Get the fuck back to work, both of ye! Or Baronkroft will have yer tongues…"

The man and the orc both snorted and made their way back up the stairs.

Hauzer left the tower and closed the door behind him, dragging Thomlin across an outdoor corridor with a pleasant view of the sea. It was dusk, and had Thomlin been anywhere else it would have been beautiful. But even a warm sunset could do nothing to fix the morose sight of the ruined city.

"They try anythin' on ye?" Hauzer asked all of a sudden.

"No, sir…"

"Ye got lucky, then… What in hells were ye thinkin', lad?" the large man closed his eyes and sighed as if he was exhausted, as if his job had started to take a toll on him. He bit off the cork on his bottle and began gulping it down as they walked without a care if anyone saw him. Though Thomlin may have been frightened of the man once, this time he wasn't. If anything, the boy was thankful for Hauzer's timely arrival.

"I'm sorry, sir," he said.

"Don't be sorry, lad. Be *smart*. 'Round these parts, if ye ain't smart, ye get killed. Plain 'n' simple."

"Y-Yes, sir…"

They walked on for what felt like an hour.

Hauzer kept his grip tight around the boy's arm as if his hand was a steel cuff.

Slowly, Thomlin's surroundings became more and more familiar. He was silent for the rest of the walk, ready to be reunited with his only friend, Princess Magdalena. He was ready to greet her with an embrace, the way they became used to greeting each other, ready to tell her what he had seen in that hidden chamber next to the spiraling stairs… A chamber full of sapphires…

* * *

Darryk Clark sat in the king's study, silent and preoccupied as he signed his name at the bottom of a newly drafted parchment. He lifted a goblet to his lips and, like the previous three sips, he'd forgotten there was nothing there but water. After several nights of heavy drinking, the man could hardly lift his head that morning. He'd stayed in bed until noon after vomiting twice and spent the rest of his day drinking water and prune juice. Then, after hours of contemplating, he began drafting the same contract over and over again until it was to his satisfaction.

Once he finished signing his name, he used the tip of his dagger to prick his thumb. He stained the parchment with a drop of his blood and pressed the Clark seal next to his name. And then he simply sat there, revising every word for the hundredth time.

Lord Regent Darryk Clark, he silently mocked himself. *Champion of Roquefort's Spring Tournament at the age of seventeen. Sworn into knighthood at the age of nineteen. Betrothed to the princess of Vallenghard at the age of twenty-five. The embodiment of success, father called you once... If only the man could see you now...*

He sat back and rubbed his left temple with a mild groan.

Be careful in Val Havyn, he'd been told. *They'll eat you alive up there.*

If only you had listened, Darryk... If only you hadn't been so careless...

Darryk Clark had grown accustomed to praise his whole life. From the moment he wielded a sword for the first time, he was told he'd been born for it.

Born to fight, born to lead, born for victory, his father would so arrogantly boast.

But that was in Roquefort. And Darryk was far from home.

Had it been up to him he would still be back there, patrolling the city streets, the streets he called home, and being gawked at with great regard simply for being himself. But all he could think about for the last two days was the chaos he had witnessed in Merchants' Square. Never had he felt so weak and powerless. He'd been so naïve and foolish to think he would be accepted as Lord Regent simply for his house name. Had it not been for the Lady Brunylda, only the gods knew what would have happened to them all. The lack of control he had over the city made his head throb.

He was not fit to be a lord, he knew...

Not two weeks had passed and already he was sick of it...

As he rolled the parchment carefully, his ear caught the echoing footsteps approaching from the hallway. They were heavy and anxiously hurried, and he could almost feel the tension in his neck rising, dreading whatever news those footsteps were bringing to him.

"My lord?" he heard Hektor call from the outside.

"Come in," Darryk replied.

Hektor opened the door but remained in the hallway, looking more distressed than ever before. "You must come at once, my lord!"

"What is it?" Darryk rose to his feet. He was no longer wearing his royal blue tunic. Instead, he wore the black leathers and steel plates he'd brought with him from Roquefort. He looked more like himself again. And though the armor was much heavier, his back was a lot straighter than it had been in previous days.

"The peasants, my lord!" Hektor said worriedly. "The peasants, they're..."

Without thinking twice, Darryk began strapping his blade onto his belt. "Yes?!"

"They're rebelling again, my lord..."

Darryk began panicking. Not a minute later, they were dashing through the courtyard and into the main hall. It was quite dark inside, darker than most evenings; every lantern had been unlit and every curtain had been purposely shut. Many of the palace servants were hiding behind the windows, glimpsing through the cracks in the curtains at the mob outside the palace gates. There were a good number of guards there, fully armored and weapons strapped to their belts, awaiting instructions from their Lord Regent.

Darryk spotted Lady Brunylda Clark among the crowd, standing there in her elegant teal gown, her face stained with a hardened grimace, and just behind her was her timid bookkeeper Brie. Adelina Huxley and her children were also there, but they were secluded in the dark, somewhat ashamed to be at the center of the impending revolt.

"What in all hells is happening out there?" Darryk pulled the curtain open slightly and took a gander. The gates were a mere silhouette, darkened by the light coming from all the torches, and through the bars he could see the mob shouting angrily and throwing garbage over the black steel railings. The gates were holding them all back, but the crowd was massive enough that it made Darryk panic all the same. Even Lady Brunylda appeared somewhat out of sorts; behind her cold expression, her eyes couldn't hide the unease.

"Stand back," Darryk told the servants; they retreated into the shadows of the corridors but their prying eyes and ears remained close. The light of the torches was beaming through the stained windows, through the cracks between the curtains, illuminating their troubled faces with a bright orange glimmer.

"They've gone mad," said Lady Brunylda as she took a sip from her flask.

"They demand to speak with you, my lord!" Hektor said. "They refuse to leave until you remove the orcs from the city grounds..."

"But she's *dead*," Adelina Huxley felt the need to speak up, out of panic. "Aevastra died this morning..."

"Yes, well... tell that to *them*," Hektor replied nervously, and then turned back to his Lord Regent. "Orders, sir?"

But Darryk could say nothing in return. Instead he glanced towards Lady Brunylda for guidance. And just as he was expecting, she was scowling before he even said a word.

"What do we do?" he asked worriedly.

"*We?*" the Lady raised a brow.

He looked at her as if he was pleading to her with his eyes alone.

"You wouldn't just throw me into the fire pit alone, would you?"

"What else am I to do? Burn *with* you?"

"*Help* me!" he said, his voice nearly a shout.

"Help you *how*, exactly?!"

Darryk was panicking again and she could see it; the mere image of him was enough to make her scoff. She turned her back on him and began walking away, but Darryk sprang and followed her like a frantic dog.

Don't do this, he begged her silently. *Don't abandon me now... I **need** you now... You can't be this heartless.* But as they walked swiftly down the corridor, Darryk found himself struggling to keep up with her rapid pace.

"Wait… I… What do I *say* to them?!" he asked desperately.

"What do *I* know?! You're the Lord Regent. Figure it out!"

"I'm not a Lord Regent, my Lady," he admitted out loud for the first time, a bit somberly at that. "I never have been a Lord Regent. I'm a *soldier*!"

"Then *tell* them that!"

"I-I can't! They'll shun me!"

"They already shun you…"

"Yes, but surely y-"

"For fuck's sake, boy!" she came to a halt and confronted him, her voice echoing throughout the dark hallway loud enough that all of the palace servants overheard. "Pull yourself together and do your duty! I am *not* your mother, I am your advisor!"

"Then *advise* me!" he raised his own voice, accepting the fact that the servants might lose whatever respect they had left for him.

"You want advice?!" she stepped closer, her eyes fuming with rage and her words once again stabbing at his chest like a dagger. "Here's some fresh advice for you… *Wake up*! Open your bloody eyes and look around you!"

He hesitated to talk back, for Lady Brunylda Clark had never been so terrifying.

"This isn't Roquefort, you arrogant child! You won't be praised and coddled here simply for being who you are," she said bluntly. "The world is *not* your playground. If you haven't figured that out on your own, it's time you learned the hard way. The world is a cruel shit-heap of a place… It will deceive you and it will defy you. And if you aren't strong enough, it will *break* you, until you're nothing more than a walking pile of forgotten dreams, drinking the pain away while awaiting death… The *only* thing that separates you from the rest is your will to keep fighting. And if you don't have the nerve to walk out there and speak to your people as a proper leader then you shouldn't *be* one!"

With that, the Lady walked off into the darkness, towards a set of spiraling stairs.

Darryk Clark had never felt more shame than he did at that very moment. He'd been a fool to think he could take on the task of Lord Regent. And when matters had gotten out of hand, he'd been an even bigger fool to expect compassion from a woman that had none.

Just before he walked back towards his guards, however, something unexpected happened. Lady Brunylda Clark came to a halt just before the palace steps. She appeared hesitant, as if fighting back the bit of empathy pricking at her chest.

"That preacher has caused enough trouble for you as it is, my *Lord*," she said, once again with that added weight on the title so as to spite him. "If I were in your place, I would take the opportunity to *silence* him once and for all…"

The Lady then walked away, disappearing into the darkness of the staircase.

Darryk sighed… He knew then exactly what he had to do…

"M-My lord?!" Hektor called from afar. "They're beating the gates down! Orders, sir!"

"*Damn them all,*" Darryk cursed under his breath. His ears were ringing from the shouts outside the palace walls. Something strange happened to him right then and there. He felt the weight lift suddenly from his shoulders. If he was alone in this, he was to handle it the only way he knew how… Like a *knight…* Somehow, the thought of it made the pressure a bit more bearable. He approached the front doors, his chin up high and an expression on his face that conveyed both sorrow and rage.

"*Orders*, sir?!" Hektor asked again.

"Round up every man we've got," Darryk ordered, slightly surprised at his own grit. "Send twenty of them out through the western gates and have them surround the crowd from the outside. Have the rest stand in formation at the gates."

"Yes, my Lord! Right away!"

"And Hektor…?"

The man looked back. "Yes, sir?"

"Come back at once… I need you by my side, should anything happen…"

"Gladly, sir."

Adelina Huxley could do nothing but watch, her twins hiding behind her dress, guarding River as if he was their own sibling. Darryk tried to give them a head nod of encouragement, but it in no way calmed their nerves. He then whispered something into Brie's ears, and the young woman ran off hurriedly towards the king's study as if to retrieve something.

"Very well," Darryk glanced at Bogden, the only guard left inside. "Open the doors."

* * *

It was an unpleasantly hot evening in the prison chambers of Drahkmere. The stench that oozed from the sewers was so awful and pungent that prisoners were vomiting into the waste buckets more often than was usual.

Princess Magdalena of Val Havyn had entirely given up on keeping herself clean. For several days they had put her to work with the other prisoners, mostly doing the easier tasks like washing pots and dishes or mopping up the floors of empty chambers while the other prisoners were stuck with the harder labor.

Never did she think she'd be eager for the days when she had laundering duty, for they were the only times when at least *part* of her body was brushed cleaned. Hauzer had taken notice of it and, much to her surprise, the red-bearded man often tried to send her along with the launderers and would almost always pair her up with Thomlin, at least when the boy wasn't serving Baronkroft his meals and drinks.

Because of this, the boy and the princess became inseparable.

She hadn't even bonded with her handmaiden Brie to such an extent.

When Magdalena argued with one of the prisoners, Thomlin was there to support her. When she wasn't up to a certain task, the boy would volunteer to take her place. Then, of course, there were the bad nights... the nights in which she felt like ripping her hairs out from the misery... Thomlin reminded her of Val Havyn; without even knowing it, the boy was keeping alive her hopes for an escape.

Valleria, the grey-haired mercenary woman, came a close second. She wasn't exactly the warmest of company; she was outspoken, aggressive, and quite intimidating. But after every argument Magdalena would have with one of the other prisoners, the woman seemed to always take the princess's side. "*You're the only one who makes any damn sense 'round here*," she once said to Magdalena, and she'd said it fearlessly in front of everyone else.

For Magdalena, these were her only two friends in all of Drahkmere. When they were reunited in the prison chambers after a hard day's labor were the only times she actually smiled. And this night was no different. Hauzer escorted Thomlin back, after the boy had finished his serving duties, and Magdalena greeted him with a warm embrace.

Thomlin wasted no time. He told the princess everything he had seen. From the eerie encounter in Baronkroft's personal chambers to the abandoned quarters of the castle, an entire section of ruins left uninhabited. And then, of course, he told her what he'd seen at the tower with the spiraling stairs. Magdalena's jaw dropped upon hearing it all. She sat on the wet black stone and took it all, all the while thinking of ways in which she could use this information to her advantage.

"*Sapphires?*" she asked, something like hope in her luminous green eyes.

"A whole chamber full of 'em," Thomlin replied, enthusiastic and eager as always.

"Are you *certain*?" Valleria asked.

"As certain as ever! Saw it with me own eyes, it's there! It's hidden under a pile of rubble, but it's *there*! I don't think even Baronkroft knows it."

"*Where*, exactly?" asked Magdalena, her mind already rolling with infinite possibilities.

"Right beneath the eastern tower, it is! A whole part of the castle left completely empty. Nothing but rats 'n' beetles down there."

"Horse shit," said a voice from nearby. Sebastien Swanworth, the imprisoned curator, sat up straight against the wall with that same look of arrogance and doubt on his face that he carried with him always. "Baronkroft's held his lair here for nearly a year. You'd have to be daft to think he hasn't ransacked the whole place clean."

"It's *there*, I tell you!" Thomlin insisted. "I *saw* it!"

"The little lad's right," Valleria added. "There are parts of the keep too dangerous to roam through. The rooves on the whole eastern half of the citadel are shit. I've seen 'em when they put me on smithin' duty."

"Horse. Shit. You've *both* lost your minds," Swanworth argued.

"Do you wish to get out of here or not?" Magdalena asked, her voice stern and unyielding.

Swanworth said nothing. Instead he slouched back with a scoff.

Magdalena looked around her. Half the prisoners in the chamber were either asleep or close to death. The other half was much too tired or scared to respond to the news.

But they were listening, all right…

It was hard not to listen when the chamber was as small as a common dining room and some fifty prisoners were cramped together inside.

"Thomlin," Magdalena said after a brief silence. "Are you *certain* of this?"

"Of *course*, your majesty…"

"*Magdalena*," she corrected him.

"R-Right… Sorry," the boy stuttered. "*Magdalena*… I would never lie."

The princess took a moment to breathe. She hadn't heard news this promising since before she was kidnapped. And even now, she had only the word of a peasant boy. Still, he was possibly the one person she trusted the most in this unknown land. She simply couldn't allow such an opportunity to pass her by merely because of her doubt. "All right," she said. "I need to see it for myself. Do you remember exactly where it is, Thomlin?"

"Of course. I *never* forget!" the boy said eagerly.

"Good," she smiled at him. "Tomorrow morning, meet me by th-"

Suddenly, there was a loud clink that resonated throughout the chamber. Normally the prisoners would have scattered in fear, except his time they were either much to weak or they were sick and near death.

Hauzer and Jyor walked in with keys at hand, and began pacing about the chamber. Magdalena felt a sudden dread at the thought that the two men had possibly overheard their entire conversation. But they didn't exactly look angry. *Serious*, perhaps, but that was nothing new. As they got closer, some of the prisoners cowered into a corner, afraid of being summoned and questioned by Baronkroft's torturers. But the two guards came to a halt right in front of the princess and her two companions.

"She's the one, yes?" Jyor asked, a bony blue finger aimed at Magdalena.

"Aye," Hauzer replied with a nod. "She's the one…"

"She looks like a common peasant," the dark elf grabbed her violently by the elbow and lifted her. "Right this way, your majesty."

Magdalena did not make a sound, not even a yelp, but instead she glared back at him with just as much ferocity.

"What's this about?" Valleria asked, rising to her feet like a loyal guardswoman. Hauzer and Jyor were always hard to read. Typically, the prisoners were all taken at once and assigned to different labor. Whenever a prisoner was taken from a chamber *alone*, however, it was unclear whether or not that prisoner would ever return.

"Back off, wench," Jyor growled.

But Valleria was more resilient than that. "Where are you taking her?!"

"I said back off!"

Valleria did not back off. Instead, she did what no prisoner would ever consider doing. She placed a hand on Jyor's forearm and gave it a yank. "What're you gonna do to the girl?!"

Jyor growled viciously all of a sudden. He threw Magdalena forward and she landed on Hauzer's arms before she hit the floor. The elf turned and landed a heavy slap on Valleria's face. So heavy, it was, that the woman stumbled down to her knees. She then glanced up, shivering with rage, her cheek starting to go red.

"Leave her alone!" Magdalena shouted.

"You'll speak when spoken to, you wretche-" Jyor had lifted an arm at Magdalena but, before he could strike, Hauzer's massive hand stopped him with hardly any effort. The elf glared at his partner furiously, the kind of glare one gives an enemy rather than a friend.

"Enough, lad," Hauzer grunted.

"Get your dirty hands off me," Jyor pulled his arm loose. "She's just a foreign bitch… Why d'you care anyway?"

"I don't," Hauzer said. "But Baronkroft does… Ye leave *one* bruise on her 'n' he'll have ye castrated. Now calm yerself, will ye?"

With a grunt, Jyor left the chamber first, leaving Hauzer behind to drag the princess along. Magdalena took one last glance back at her only two friends, and both the boy and the woman looked troubled. The princess was quite concerned herself, but she wouldn't dare show it to the two guards, for she was much smarter than that.

They took her up a set of spiraling stairs that seemed endless. By the time they reached the top, her legs were aching and shivering. They shoved her into a cold dark room that looked like a torturing chamber, with hooks hanging along the walls and a drain wedged between the stone at the center of the room. For a moment, she became frozen with fear.

"Take yer clothes off," said Hauzer.

The princess hesitated. "What for?"

"You heard 'im, girl!" Jyor growled and clutched her by the collar. "Strip!"

He gave it a good yank and the dress ripped right at the sleeve.

"Enough, lad!" Hauzer said, but the elf didn't seem to care much; he tore at Magdalena's dress until it could no longer stay on unless she pressed it against her chest.

"Stop! Stop this now!" Magdalena wailed angrily, forcing back the tears. It wasn't exactly that she loved the dress, but it was the only thing she'd brought with her from Val Havyn when she was taken. As Hauzer kneeled and mixed soap into a bucket of water, Jyor kept tugging at the dress, cursing and spitting on the princess, as if it pleased him to see her vulnerable and helpless.

"No! I order you to stop!" Magdalena cried, and then released an unintentional *"please"*.

By then, the dress was nothing but a bunch of rags. The princess refused to let go of her raggedy corset, the only thing shielding her otherwise nude body. She felt cold and exposed and angry. And she wished suddenly for a weapon, *any* type of weapon, despite the fact that she'd never had to use one before.

"Let go of it, girl!" Jyor said frustratingly. And when she refused, he growled and reached for the nearest bucket.

"That one ain't ready yet," Hauzer warned.

But Jyor did not care. He splashed Magdalena with the ice-cold water and she instantly released a shrill cry that must have echoed down a few floors.

"*That* should teach you, you dumb bitch!"

"Oi!" Hauzer shouted, getting up and snatching the empty bucket away from the elf. "What the fuck's the matter with ye?! Did I *not* just say tha-"

"The wench thinks she's in charge 'round here!"

"That '*wench*' is Baronkroft's key!" Hauzer shouted back, and the princess couldn't help but overhear. "If ye can't keep it together for just a few minutes, lad, then get outta here and *I'll* take care of it!"

"Piss off! Baronkroft left us *both* to do it!"

"Aye, 'n' just wait 'til he hears ye put yer filthy hands on 'er."

At that moment, Jyor unsheathed a dagger with his good hand. But Hauzer did not seem the least bit phased by it; he looked at Jyor as if the elf was holding a mere butter knife.

"What?" Hauzer stepped forward fearlessly. "Ye gonna *kill* me, are ye? Hmm?!"

The elf was shivering from the rage. He couldn't bring himself to swing, knowing very well that Hauzer was three times his size and could break his wrist with little effort. He took one last glance at the naked princess, wet and shivering in a dark corner, and then curtly put his dagger away.

"Fuck off, the *both* of you," Jyor left the room and slammed the door behind him. And there was a brief moment of silence as Hauzer lowered his head and sighed exhaustedly.

"Damn Rabbits," the red-bearded man whispered to himself.

Fretfully, Magdalena reached for the torn pieces of her dress and used them to cover herself up between the legs. Hauzer took a glance at her; the princess was slender to begin with, only now he could see the bones in her ribs and chest. She was pale and weak and nearly dying. And he, in return, seemed to almost pity her.

"I, uh," Hauzer cleared his throat. "Baronkroft said I have to wash ye…"

He bent down on one knee in front of the bucket of warm water and kept stirring the soap. Magdalena didn't feel safe but she also didn't feel alarmed, not the way Jyor made her feel. She wiped the cold water from her face and straightened herself up to her feet. She breathed slowly, over and over again, as Hauzer set the bucket down nearby and prepared to bathe her.

"Wait!" she blurted.

Hauzer looked at her. He appeared almost uncomfortable by her naked body.

"Please," she said, her voice dry and hoarse. "Could I… just… maybe have some privacy?"

Hauzer closed his eyes and sighed. "Can't do that, girl. Ye *know* I can't."

Magdalena took a second to think… She knew the man was not heartless; it wasn't at all hard to tell, based solely on his demeanor towards her and the rest of the prisoners. But he also wasn't dumb, and tricking him was going to take a lot more effort than that.

"Then I would like to be bathed by someone else," she said, and then felt the need to clarify, "A *woman*."

"Ain't no women in Baronkroft's troop," he muttered.

"Doesn't *have* to be from his troop…"

Hauzer thought about it for a moment, and then he grunted and said, "Wait here."

Magdalena was left alone for several minutes. She slouched to a sitting position and, once she could no longer hear the man's echoing footsteps, the tears began to flow on their own. She didn't sob, she didn't whimper, she hardly even made a noise. She simply allowed the tears to flow until they were finished. Then she used the torn cloth that used to be her dress to wipe her face clean and dry.

You'll make it through this, she told herself, aware that she may very well not.

She soon realized that this was the first time since she was taken from Val Havyn that she had any privacy at all. When she ate a meal, when she changed her monthly towels, and even when she relieved herself, there was always a guard watching her. Angrily and miserably, she pressed her head onto the filthy torn cloth and screamed as hard as her lungs would allow it, careful to muffle the sound so as to not alert any guards nearby. She remained that way for several moments, until footsteps began approaching again.

Hauzer unlocked the door and in walked a familiar face that made the princess sigh with relief. "Ye got 10 minutes," said the red-bearded man. "Make sure she's clean. I'll bring 'er somethin' to wear for the evening."

When the door closed, Valleria remained where she stood, staring down at the sad figure of the shivering nude princess. Then, with a deep sigh, she dropped to her knees and wrapped her arms around her. Magdalena returned the embrace, crying into the woman's chest.

"Those vile fuckin' animals," Valleria growled. "What have they done to you?"

"Nothing," Magdalena said, once she was able to catch her breath. "Baronkroft ordered them to have me cleaned…"

"Cleaned? What for?"

"I don't know. They said he needed me."

"What for?" Valleria asked again.

"I've no idea," said Magdalena. "But I have a feeling I'm about to find out…"

* * *

Stupid boy, the Lady cursed under her breath. *Spoiled, arrogant, **stupid** little boy…*

Lady Brunylda Clark was unsure of what exactly it was that was holding her back from retreating to her chambers. And she certainly did try, but after the first set of spiraling stairs her feet refused to go any further.

Damn him. Damn them all!

But then she heaved a sigh of fury and stepped into one of the common rooms on the second floor of the royal palace. It was quite dark all around, and the Lady very much preferred it that way. Every candle remained unlit. Every curtain was shut except for one.

She creaked the window open just enough to overhear yet remain hidden. She could see the crowd some twenty feet below, twice as large as before, holding torches and shouting nonsense as they slammed the gates with sticks, stones, and hammers. And standing right in front of them all, like the head of a snake, was the mad preacher known as Baryn Lawe.

What a fucking catastrophe, the Lady thought to herself. She was thankful that she'd brought liqueur with her from her chambers, she was so irritated. Suddenly, as she sipped from her flask, the palace doors opened right beneath her feet. She hesitated, still unsure if she should stay and watch.

It wasn't that the Lady cared much for Darryk Clark… She fought hard to reject the notion that she was feeling any form of compassion for the man, she tried to convince herself that it was no more than pity. Darryk was, after all, an outsider in Val Havyn. And the Lady knew very well what that felt like, for she felt like an outsider every time the king gathered his court in the assembly room. The rest of the advisors would often glare at her as if she didn't belong, the very same way she would often glare at Darryk, in fact.

The crowd began to roar and shout angrily when Darryk Clark walked down the front steps of the palace. Some were surprised to see him in armor, but the more radical ones cared very little. When they threw whatever rotten produce they had left over the gates, they aimed for *him* this time, and some of it splattered right near Darryk's boots.

From above, the Lady watched, feeling the ache in her chest turn into rage.

Don't you dare show them weakness, she advised the young knight silently. *Show them who is in control.*

She wished suddenly that she had said this to him personally. Then again, a proper leader shouldn't have to be told any of this.

As Darryk Clark approached the gates, his head was held up high like a proper knight. Though he was dressed in armor, he still wore the silver crown of Lord Regent over his black head of hair. He had his back to the palace, and so Lady Brunylda was unable to see his face, but she sensed that he was holding himself together, as the man often did even when he was shivering on the inside. Such was the burden of a noble; showing others your fear could shatter your reputation in an instant.

Suddenly, there was loud stomping and the clinking of metal coming from the western road outside of the palace gates. A formation of about twenty guards had marched out from the western gates inconspicuously and walked around the angry mob, lining themselves in an arch so as to cage them all in. They were armed with blades and round shields of steel, all of which had been crafted with care by the blacksmith Evellyn Amberhill. Another ten guards remained inside the gates with their swords drawn, awaiting orders from their Lord Regent.

From the second floor of the palace, Lady Brunylda Clark observed it all. The formation of the outside guards was in the shape of a half-circle, rounding up the mob like sheep against the black gates. For a moment, the Lady admired Darryk's tactical skill. The guards weren't many, and they were certainly outnumbered, but they had the advantage of armor and weaponry. And it was enough to calm a few of the rebels; the shouts diminished and no longer did they throw anything.

Meanwhile, Darryk took his time walking down the palace steps… Within seconds, the place was relatively quiet, and the Lord Regent became the center of everyone's attention.

"Lord Regent Clark! The gods smile upon us tonight!" Baryn Lawe spoke first, a mask of bravery plastered over his grinning face. Had his mob not been at his back, the man would have cowered before the royal guard.

Darryk stood firmly and intrepidly, unwilling to yield to the same mob that had ridiculed him just a few days prior. He looked at Baryn Lawe menacingly, but he chose his words as carefully as his father had taught him. "Explain yourself. Now."

"With pleasure, sire," the mad preacher took a bow. "We are all here to fulfill the wishes of our god, m'lord… We mean no harm to you or anyone else in your company, I assure you. Our demands are quite simple… We have been patient with you, as it was our king's decision to appoint you Lord Regent of our beloved city… But we will hold our silence no longer! Our safety cannot be guaranteed, so long as that filth is in our city grounds!"

The peasants shouted in agreement, some of them praising Baryn for his courage.

"We demand that they be removed at once!" Baryn added, and the chants only grew from there. Darryk appeared rather calm, as a proper knight commander would look. He allowed the mob a few moments of chatter, before he craned his neck towards his guards. His face was blank, his eyes steady and unwavering.

"Arms at the ready!" he shouted.

The sound of armor clinking in unison resonated all around, as every soldier of the royal guard stomped a boot on the cobblestone and held their weapon out in defense. Even those few inside the gates had their swords out, aimed forward next to their shields.

Within seconds, the place was silent again.

"Outer flank! Forward, march!" Darryk shouted.

The formation of guards on the outside took one step forward. The mob was pressed tightly together. Some of them were forced to kill the fire of their torches so as to avoid burning their neighboring peers.

"Again! Forward, march!"

The formation took another step forward.

This time the mob was forced so tightly together that Baryn Lawe was pressed against the palace gates. The man had his arms up at his sides, trying desperately to control his own followers, but his worried gaze was fixed on Darryk, who stood firmly with a hand at the hilt of his sword.

"Halt!" Darryk shouted, and his guards stopped where they were, their swords still up and aimed at the herd. Darryk took a moment to pace back and forth along the inside of the gates. The peasants were almost like a herd of caged hens and Darryk like a wolf eyeing them through the bars.

Every single pair of eyes was on him, even from inside the palace.

For once, Darryk appeared almost like an actual leader.

"What is the meaning of this?!" the preacher tried to protest, his face pressed between two of the black bars. "We are citizens of Val Havyn!"

"Are you, now?" Darryk asked, his brows lowered and his jaw clenched tightly. "Because from where I stand, sir, you look more like traitors of the crown."

The silence returned, and many of the gazes among the mob lost some of their confidence.

"Hektor?" Darryk called.

The loyal guard stepped forward. "Yes, my lord?"

"Remind me again what the punishment is for betraying the crown, if you will."

"*Death*, my lord..."

Baryn Lawe's face twisted into a grimace. Though the preacher was afraid, he was far too much of a pious vulture with an obsession for power, and thus he was not willing to succumb without a fight.

"We are loyal to his majesty, King Rowan!" he shouted confidently. "Not an immoral and corrupt foreigner who *pretends* to be a Lord!"

The mob began to shout angrily once again. It was quite interesting, the way a single man had the power to build up their buoyancy with just a few words. Then again, that was the way power often worked...

As the noise began to build up, Baryn's grin slowly returned.

It did not last very long, however...

Darryk turned to Hektor and gave him a mere head nod. The guard, in return, proceeded towards the gates with the keys at hand. The rest of the inner formation huddled around Hektor as the man opened the gate and pulled the mad preacher inside. There was some resistance from the mob and the gates were nearly forced open, but the guards on the inside began jabbing the tips of their swords through the black bars, injuring a few of the more persistent rebels.

Hektor locked the gates shut again and then threw the mad preacher onto the stone steps, right at Darryk's feet. Meanwhile, from upstairs, Lady Brunylda Clark took another sip from her flask, observing the young lord like a proud mentor watching an apprentice at work.

*Well done so far. You **have** them... Now don't you dare lose them...*

"Silence!" Hektor shouted at the mob as Darryk paced about quietly, glaring down at the frail figure of Baryn Lawe, utterly stripped of his power. When the voices died down, Darryk spoke again, this time directly at the preacher so as to make an example out of him.

"You should consider yourself fortunate, Mister Baryn Lawe," he said. "If this were any other city in Vallenghard, you'd be up for a beheading right at this moment. But this is the royal city of Val Havyn... And I would hate to stain my blade with the blood of a mad preaching rebel..."

Though much less confidently, Baryn couldn't help but persist and talk through his rage. "I'm a servant of our god... as is King Rowan... If he only knew what you were keeping within his palace walls, he woul-"

"I'm afraid that is none of your concern now, sir," Darryk interrupted. He then looked up at the mob, at the wary eyes and scowls, and addressed them all directly. "The matter has been dealt with!" he announced. "The orc woman has died from her wounds... She is no longer within our grounds. There is no more reason for concern or panic."

There was a sudden mumbling among the peasants. The mad preacher's face was riddled with a muddle of expressions; confusion, rage, regret, all of them vivid in his glimmering eyes.

"We have sent a caravan to the Woodlands, where she will soon be buried," Darryk lied. "Normally such matters are dealt with discreetly, but... it would appear we've a few citizens who are far too eager to get involved…"

As he spoke the last few words, Darryk glared down at the mad preacher.

What are you? The young knight asked him through a glare. *Are you truly this mad? Or is it all a ruse to rile up the crowds and make some coin?*

Baryn Lawe couldn't have been older than sixty. Though it was true that many people in Gravenstone believed in the Gods of Nayarith – the gods of the nine races – it was also true that such beliefs were more common among the elder folk. The young, particularly those who grew up motherless and fatherless, had never been properly taught about the religion and therefore scoffed at such beliefs.

Baryn, on the other hand, was a mystery to Darryk. The mere fact that he was a beggar suggested he had lived a life of poverty, as many orphans did. But his beliefs appeared far too strong to be a false pretense.

"Now," Darryk finally spoke again, as he stepped around Baryn and towards the angry mob. There may have been black-painted steel bars between them, but Darryk glared at the peasants so confidently, it was hard to imagine he would have acted any differently had there *not* been. "Do try and listen, for I will say this only once…"

And listen, they did. During that brief moment, there wasn't a single mouth talking except for Darryk's. And little to his knowledge, Lady Brunylda's lips were curving into a smile as she continued to watch over him from above.

"This city is under *my* protection," Darryk said boldly. "And such rebellious acts will *not* be tolerated… I do not care if you're a nobleman or a peasant, the king's law will pertain to any and every person within these city grounds. Anyone who dares *break* the king's law will answer to me. Anyone who plots *against* the king will answer to me. Anyone who so much as disturbs the *peace* will answer to me."

Darryk's confidence appeared to be working somehow. But, as it so often happened, the tables turned suddenly against him when the mad preacher decided to interject yet again.

"To you?" Baryn said mockingly. "To *you*?! The very person who allowed an orc into our city?!"

"The orc woman has died," Darryk responded instantly. "The matter has been dealt with."

"And what about the *child*…?"

There was a sudden silence, during which Darryk noticed every pair of eyes in the mob turn to him. And the preacher, as usual, did not resist the temptation to taunt him. "Answer us, then!" he growled. "What about the orc child?!"

Darryk felt a tug in his chest as he towered over Baryn.

Are you really that heartless, you old fool? Darryk wondered.

But it didn't matter at that moment. The only thing that *did* matter was that Darryk was at the center of attention. And anything he did could make or break his reputation.

He knew what he had to do. And, as it always happened, there was a brief moment of doubt, during which Darryk had to force himself to act with his mind rather than his heart. Once he was ready, he unsheathed his blade…

There were several gasps among the crowd. But Darryk had little time to focus on anything but the task at hand. Any image of him that the peasants had seen before was suddenly gone. He was Sir Darryk Clark again, and there was no sign of any *Lord Regent* present there.

"Hold him," Darryk said.

Hektor and Bogden grabbed the preacher and pressed him down against the palace steps. Baryn tried to resist, but it was of no use; he was pinned down with a knee to his back and his hands were held against the stone, rendering him defenseless. Among the silence, Darryk paced again with his sword in hand. He appeared so determined, even the Lady Brunylda was gawking pryingly through the curtains, suddenly thankful that she had stayed to watch.

"It appears that I am not making myself clear," Darryk said. "The peace *will* be held in Val Havyn… If I have to execute every rebel that defies the crown, then so be it! His majesty, King Rowan, has left House Clark in charge of his throne and, by the gods, House Clark will look after it if it costs me my life!"

The mob was listening intensely. And when Darryk looked upon them all, he noticed something right then. All his life, he was accustomed to gazes of respect and admiration. In the eyes of the Val Havyn citizens, however, he saw *fear*. They were indisputably afraid of him. And it was the final encouragement that he needed.

With one final exhale, Darryk made an unpredicted move.

He walked up to one of his guards and whispered something into his ear. The guard then rushed back into the palace, as Darryk turned his attention back to the frightened mob of citizens.

"*However*," Darryk spoke up again, as every ear within a mile appeared to be locked on him. "Much like many of you, I'm sure, I am a man of truth… That is to say, I *am* one to recognize my own flaws when I am in the wrong…"

He glanced suddenly at the mad preacher; such a frail shivering figure compared the confident man he had been just minutes prior.

"Mister Baryn Lawe *is* right about one thing," Darryk said, and it was such an unanticipated declaration, that even Lady Brunylda held herself back from taking any more sips from her flask.

You can do this, Darryk, the man told himself. And it was vivid in his eyes that he was struggling through the knot in his throat.

"I am *not* fit to be your Lord Regent," he said, and it was followed by several confused stares and mutters. By then, it wasn't just the angry mob that Darryk was worried about. Word about the rebellion had spread throughout the city and there were several peasants watching from afar, either out their windows or standing along one of the city streets. Within a few hours, the entire city would know about the failed Lord Regent. And, much to his surprise, Darryk Clark felt *relieved* rather than ashamed of the words he had just spoken aloud for the first time.

The palace doors opened suddenly... Brie walked out dressed in that same stylish red dress, holding in her hands an elegant silver box decorated with blue velvet on the inside. She walked down the steps towards Darryk and held the box out to him.

Come on, he told himself. *You're almost done... Get on with it...*

"I, Darryk of House Clark," he said as he gently removed the silver crown from his head. "Renounce the title of Lord Regent of Val Havyn..."

He placed the crown inside the box. Instantly, he felt the weight lift from his shoulders as his fingers brushed against the blue velvet. He knew, however, what removing the crown meant for him. He would never be crowned Lord of Roquefort, as word would most definitely reach his father of what had happened that night. He would be shunned for causing dishonor to his family and would most likely lose King Rowan's blessing to marry Princess Magdalena.

It was the one thing he had been brought up to be, a *Lord*.

And he gave it all up the moment he let go of that silver crown.

Never in his life did he wish for a drink more than he did then...

"Ladies and gentlemen, it has been an honor to serve you all," Darryk lied again. "But I'm afraid I cannot fulfill a role that I am not fit to take..."

He felt a knot in his throat once again, this time heavier than the last.

Say it, Darryk... Just bloody say it...

He took a deep breath.

"And so it is my sincere honor to appoint Lady Brunylda of House Clark... as the Lady Regent of Val Havyn."

The silence lingered for what seemed like an hour. There weren't just murmurs, there were *glares* shot at Darryk. Among them, several peasants asked each other questions such as '*Is he serious?*' and '*What in all hells did he just say?*'

Darryk, on the other hand, held his stance just as well as he had done before.

"But, make no mistake, ladies and gentlemen. The peace *will* be kept!" he said. "This city *will* be taken care of, I will see to it myself! I will serve our Lady Regent as knight commander of our city's royal guard."

He expected respect, but all Darryk got was a cluster of cold stares and worried faces. And, just when he thought it couldn't get any worse, Baryn Lawe decided to speak up again.

"Blasphemy!" the mad preacher said as he lied face down against the palace stairs. "Are you bloody joking?! Appointing a *woman* as our Regent?!" Baryn snickered, but he underestimated Darryk's resilience as a knight commander. "How dare you?! King Rowan would strike you down if he knew... You irreverent coward... No woman has *ever* been Lord Regent! Curse you *and* that wretched woman! House Clark should be burned to the ground for this!"

Darryk had suddenly heard enough. Without a moment of hesitation, he stepped towards Baryn with a frightening look in his eyes. "Hold him up," he ordered his guards. Hektor and Bogden grabbed the preacher's shoulders and lifted the man to his knees.

"W-What are you doing?" Baryn stuttered.

Another guard grabbed a fistful of Baryn's hair and pulled his head down so that the back of the man's neck would be exposed. Baryn began panicking in a way no citizen in Val Havyn had ever seen him panic. "Wait... N-No! *Please!* Mercy!" he said, his voice rising to a shrill cry.

"No!" Darryk shook his head; he'd never been fond of beheadings, particularly when the crime had merely been *speaking* too much. "His *tongue...*"

The mad preacher felt a sudden rush of relief, but it was replaced by dread just seconds later when a gloved hand grabbed the tip of his tongue and forced it out of his mouth. He tried to protest, but his voice was no more than a muffled groan by then.

Sir Darryk Clark stepped forward, his sword at hand.

"Mister Baryn Lawe," he said. "You have spoken ill of your Lady Regent... Now prepare to face your punishment..."

The preacher squealed in horror as the cold tip of Darryk's blade touched the tender pink skin of his tongue. Darryk waited a moment, his eyes looking deeply into the preacher's. *You made me do this,* he told him with his eyes.

All it took was one quick slice, and the preacher's tongue flew into the air and onto the palace steps. The crowd watched in horror as the preacher fell to the floor, groaning and holding his mouth as the blood spewed down his jaw.

Darryk took a moment to observe them all, and it was the final affirmation he needed to know that he had made the right choice. They were *frightened* of him. Frightened of what he was capable of doing.

And it was exactly what he wanted; he'd tried to gain their respect the easy way, but Val Havyn had proven to be much more of a conservative city than Roquefort was. He had to resort to behaving like a soldier again.

"It appears you all may have misunderstood me," he said, continuing to pace around a broken Baryn Lawe. For the rebelling peasants, it was as if they were looking at an entirely different man.

Darryk appeared firm and at ease, though on the inside he was on the verge of vomiting, as he always was whenever he killed or punished anyone. "The Lady Clark *is* your Lady Regent now!" he announced assertively. "And she *will* be treated with respect, as such."

From above Lady Brunylda watched, dropping both her jaw and her flask of liqueur upon hearing Darryk's words. She did not know exactly how to feel... All she knew, as she stood in that dark empty common room, was that there was no way in all hells she would be able to sleep that night...

"I was not fit to be a Lord Regent, that much I admit," Darryk Clark went on confidently. "But, make no mistake, ladies and gentlemen… I am one hell of a knight commander… I've fought Aharians, orcs, pirates, sea nymphs, you name it… And *you?*" he paused for a delicate chuckle. "You don't scare me… Not now, not ever…"

The mob watched with awe as Darryk wiped his blade with a handkerchief and slid it back into its sheath. Then, with a forced sigh, Darryk turned towards the frail figure of the mad preacher. For a moment, he felt he was getting carried away by the act. But if it was to help his reputation as the city's new knight commander, he figured it worth it to act on his impulses.

"Throw him in the dungeon," Darryk said to Hektor. "Then throw the key into the creek. He loves the gods so much? He may spend the rest of his life praying to them in solitude…"

And so, the guards dragged the sobbing preacher away. Darryk ordered the rest of the guards to retreat, and the mob began to disperse one by one.

Once it was all over, Lady Brunylda Clark retreated to her chambers, seeing as her flask was now lying on the carpet empty of any liqueur. She was shivering and her stunned face was empty of any emotion. For a moment, she had to pinch herself to know it hadn't all been a dream. And when she didn't wake up, her heart began racing…

What in all hells have you done, boy?

Her eyes were glistening, but there was no way she would ever cry. She hadn't cried since she was 13 and she was damn sure she wouldn't start now. But the sensation remained there, deep in her pounding chest, so powerful it was overwhelming.

And so it was that, as fate would have it, Lady Brunylda Clark became the first Lady Regent in the history of Gravenstone.

* * *

Magdalena of Val Havyn had nearly forgotten what it felt like to be a princess. Her skin felt cold and strange without the layer of dirt and sweat over it. Her hands were now clean, even underneath her fingernails, and her hair smelled like roses. She looked like herself again, yet she felt foreign and out of place in that green velvet dress.

Father always did say green was my color, she thought, and it nearly brought her to tears. *Made me look so much like mother, he'd say.*

An emerald necklace hung around her neck and she had two mismatching rings on each hand, one of them silver and the other gold. She sat in a clean chamber with walls made of black stone and sophisticated yet mismatching furniture that looked like it may have been stolen from various different castles and fortresses.

Valleria was there with her hands unchained, a rare instance considering her background as a sellsword, but there was no chance of escaping with the doors locked tight and the chamber being a hundred feet high above the city. The woman brushed Magdalena's tangled hair as she had been ordered to do. Meanwhile a gnome woman with cluttered makeup around her eyes and lips worked silently on the princess's nails, a smooth ivory color, one that complimented Magdalena's fair skin and blonde hair.

"Why in hells they thought *I* was fit to do this baffles me," Valleria scoffed, pulling viciously on the blonde knots with an old brush.

"They didn't," Magdalena admitted. "I was the one who asked for you."

"Me?" she asked. "No offense, but do I look like a bloody handmaiden?"

"No, you look like a friend."

The brushing stopped briefly. Valleria seemed somewhat thrown aback, as if no one had ever called her a *'friend'* before. She sighed despairingly and glanced out the balcony window. "What's the point of it all?" she asked. "Why this? What does he get out of it?"

"I know just as much as you," Magdalena shrugged her shoulders lightly.

Valleria looked down at the gnome woman, who appeared to be fully dedicated to painting the nails with great precision. "You there," Valleria called, but the gnome woman did not acknowledge her at all. Valleria may as well have been a ghost. "Hey!" she snapped her fingers to get the gnome's attention. "I'm talkin' to you, woman. You there?"

The gnome finished Magdalena's last nail and looked up...

So eerie, she looked, her face empty of any sentiment.

Lifeless, almost, as if she was caught in some form of trance.

"The good lord will set us free," she muttered. "All that is needed is bait..."

With that, the gnome woman walked away, taking with her the nail polish and a tray of empty goblets. Valleria and Magdalena locked eyes briefly, and the sellsword could see the fear in the princess's eyes.

"I didn't like the sound of that," said Magdalena.

Valleria sighed again. "How in all hells did I end up in this fucking place?"

A key rattled suddenly and the door on the other end of the chamber opened. Hauzer and Jyor walked in, and Magdalena rose to her feet instantly out of precaution.

"Take the woman back to the dungeons. Baronkroft will be 'ere soon."

"Why do *I* have to take 'er?" Jyor nagged.

"'Cause he asked me person'ly to look after the princess."

Jyor growled and cuffed Valleria's wrists again. They glanced briefly at one another, Valleria's stare firm and expressionless while Jyor's was relentless and uncouth.

"How's the face?" he asked with a grin.

"How're the fingers?"

His grin faded just as fast as it had come...

"Behave, lad," Hauzer said from afar. "We won't be doin' this for much longer after today."

With a vicious shove, the elf took Valleria away. Magdalena would have been concerned for the sellsword's safety, had Valleria not proven to her how capable she was of defending herself even without a weapon.

Magdalena and Hauzer were left alone in the chamber, and the young princess took the opportunity to observe him. He no longer carried the grimace he often did. He looked exhausted, in fact, as if he hadn't slept properly in days. A part of him even seemed troubled, in a way.

Magdalena brushed a few stray hairs from her face and bit her lip so as to suppress the shivering. *Now's your chance,* she thought. *Say something to him...*

"What's all of this for, exactly?"

Hauzer looked at her as if he'd somehow forgotten she had a tongue. His red beard was so thick that it was hard to read his lips when he spoke, as if it was the red bush doing the talking rather than the man. "I ain't supposed to talk to ye..."

Of course not... But you don't strike me as the obedient kind...

"I won't say anything," she promised him.

He closed his eyes and grumbled something incoherently under his breath. It killed the princess not to know and it killed him not to be able to tell her, she could see. "Ye'll be fine," he said brusquely, and instantly Magdalena felt her neck and shoulders loosen a bit. "Baronkroft doesn't care about ye, he only wants his army. Ye do what he says 'n' he'll let ye keep yer head."

Oh, she pondered cynically. *Just do what he says? Is that all? Well, shit...*

"Why does he need *me* to get an ar-"

"Don't push yer luck, girl," Hauzer snapped. "I've said enough already."

Magdalena's mind became riddled with questions. And with the questions came the dread and the somber memories of a home that she may never have a chance to revisit. Her father, her beloved Val Havyn, her gardens, even her handmaiden Brie, as much as she'd often bicker with her. She missed *all* of it.

So distant, it felt, the life she had... Even after a few weeks, she felt she'd been held captive an eternity. Sleeping among dirt and vomit, starving day and night, all the while not knowing why she had been taken to begin with. She had no friends other than Thomlin and Valleria, and even *they* were mere acquaintances, the only shreds of joy she could find in that wretched place.

It was a mystery to her, all of it. From the forgotten ruins to the soldiers and prisoners inhabiting it. The prisoners were all humans, and from what she'd seen they all hailed from somewhere within Gravenstone. The soldiers and servants, on the other hand, were a diverse bunch; there were orcs, elves, gnomes, and humans of every class.

Then there was Hauzer, the man that had kept guard over her since she was taken and whose accent was most definitely Halghardian. What kind of man would leave Gravenstone to join a foreign force and attack his own homeland? For what purpose?

Patience, Magdalena, she told herself. *Today's the day your questions will be answered.*

The chamber doors creaked open again, and the princess felt her body grow suddenly cold. The monster of a man that walked in was very familiar; she remembered him as the last face she saw before passing out in Val Havyn, just outside the palace grounds. Those massive hands were the very same that blocked the air from entering her lungs, and she could never forget that dreadful mask or those ghostlike eyes…

The Butcher posted himself against the brick wall, making way for the incoming figure behind him. Magdalena felt her heart skip a beat. Her breathing quickened and her eyes stopped blinking.

He's here…

It began with a shadow; the light from the torches exposed him before the Lord even stepped foot inside the chamber. The long-haired shadow approached leisurely from the corridor, calm and serene, as if he had all the time in the world to spare. His boots clanked against the brick floor, one after another like the beating of a slow drum.

And then she saw him, a tall and slender man dressed entirely in black. He had a deathly grin on his lips and his sunken eyes conveyed an eerie appetite for power. His black facial hair was trimmed neatly and reacted sharply against his pale skin. He wore several rings made of silver that glistened along with the silver thorns embroidered on the wrists and hems of his black velvet overcoat. The largest ring of them all was on his right hand, covering his index finger entirely like an embellished silver sleeve; the outline of a thorny vine wrapped around the finger while the tip of it had been molded into the shape of a sharp talon.

When he locked eyes with Magdalena his grin widened, splitting his face in half. "Your majesty!" he said nonchalantly, as if greeting an old friend. He paced towards her and she felt a sudden cold rush in her spine, despite the fact that she was standing right next to the fireplace. "By the gods, you look stunning… Absolutely stunning… An image fit for royalty, I'll dare say…"

He stopped a few strides away from her and glanced back at the Butcher.

"Thank you, my dear Harrok. You know where to go, should I need you."

The Butcher nodded and locked the doors behind him, and then Baronkroft shifted his attention back towards the silent princess.

"He sure knows how to grasp the attention in the room, doesn't he?" he asked with a snicker. He approached Magdalena again, and with every step he took the princess could feel the room grow colder somehow, as if he was bringing with him an icy aura that was invisible to her eyes.

Stop shivering, damn you. Stop it now!

"You must be wondering why I've summoned you this evening, your majesty," the lord said, pacing back and forth near the fireplace. She could smell his perfume, a strange blend of incense and something else, something hot and pungent like blood.

She kept her words to herself and he, in return, seemed almost pleased by her stunned silence. He came to a halt right in front of her, but he wouldn't look her in the eyes just yet; instead he observed the rest of her, a look of hunger and greed in his eerie gaze, as if she were a piece of treasure he had earned for himself.

"This is a significant day for us both," he brushed his hand gently through her soft yellow hair. It sickened her, and he could tell that it did. Yet he kept doing it, as if he were petting an animal rather than a person. "When the evening's over, your majesty, everything will have changed... For you, for me, for *all* of us..."

Magdalena said nothing still, she hardly even moved. She simply stood there, attentive of his every move. Even the slightest twitch could potentially reveal something useful.

"So pay close attention to what I'm about to say," he let go of her hair for a moment, his grin vanishing. "I have never been fond of repeating myself, I must warn you, so I will only say this *once*. Your job will be quite simple... You are to stand there and not speak a single word... It shouldn't be too difficult. You've done it all your life, I'm sure. The only difference tonight is that your very fate will depend on it."

Her brows lowered slightly. *What sort of game are you playing?*

In her life, she had known many men that were hungry for power. They were as ordinary to her as a beggar was ordinary to a tavern server. But *this* man... His hunger was nearly terrifying. He seemed like the type of man her father would often warn her about when it came to world politics, the type of man who would stop at nothing until his every need was met, regardless of the casualties.

"Do not fear me, your grace," Baronkroft raised his hand again, this time grazing her cheek with his right index finger, the cold silver sleeve giving her bumps in her skin. "Regardless of what you may have heard, I assure you that I am a merciful man at heart. Should you cooperate with me, I can be a most generous friend."

Her eyes glistened as if she was on the verge of tears. And when he noticed them, he grinned even more; little did he know Magdalena was grinning right back on the inside. She'd learned to hold back her blinking at the age of 5 so as to dampen her eyes, making it seem like the tears would come at any moment. She found it fascinating what she could get away with by making people believe she was some sort of delicate defenseless creature, and she'd learned to use it to her advantage.

"*However*," his grin faded. "Should you do anything to ruin this night for me…"

He paused there. This time, Magdalena felt strange and dizzy and lightheaded, as if he was somehow altering her mind through a stare. He took one final step closer.

"Well, let's just say I've killed men that I once considered family simply for lying to me… Just imagine the things I would do to you…"

With that, he stepped away to serve himself a goblet of wine. Without his overwhelming scent, Magdalena felt she could breathe again. She couldn't deny her fear, but she'd be damned if she was going to let him control her like he seemed to control everyone else.

"A word, Sergeant Hauzer?" Baronkroft beckoned him with a grin.

The red-bearded man walked over to the table and the lord whispered something into his ear. Magdalena was unable to hear a single word, but Hauzer's twisted grimace was enough to startle her.

"S-Sir?" the red-bearded man asked confusedly.

Baronkroft took a sip from his goblet and gave Hauzer a cold stare. "Is there a problem?"

"Well, I…" Hauzer appeared troubled again, clearing his throat as he thought of an appropriate response. "Sir, I just don't see the need to d-"

"Are you *questioning* me, Sergeant Hauzer?" Baronkroft looked frightening all of a sudden, not only in his glare but in the way he moved and spoke, cold and heartless like a vulture circling a near-death prey.

"No, sir… I beg your forgiveness, sir…"

"Good," Baronkroft nodded. "Then do as you're told, soldier… Unless you want to join the prisoners down in the dungeons…"

It was then that the lord left the room, a grin plastered on his face as if he was unstoppable. Magdalena could see the discomfort in Hauzer's eyes, it was clearer than the crystal goblet Baronkroft left on the table.

The princess was taken to a chamber nearby and her hands were cuffed in chains again. It felt strange to be cleaned up and made to look elegant, only to be chained down like a prisoner all over again. And through the unease, she couldn't resist her urge to pry.

"Did he tell you to do this?"

Hauzer groaned under his breath but gave her no answer. He picked up the chains and pulled her out towards the corridor.

"Where are we going…?"

His boots echoed loudly down the corridor as if he were a massive ogre, a heavy stomp compared to her soft footsteps, her feet sliding against the bottom of the oversized sandals she'd been given to wear.

"Hauzer…? Where are you tak-"

"Right 'bout now would be the best time to shut yer mouth," he said.

But she couldn't. The unease was pricking at her chest like a thorn, and the fact that she knew Hauzer couldn't harm her gave her at least a bit of unforeseen power.

"What did he say to you back there?"

"That ain't yer concern…"

"Is it not? Well it sure seems lik-"

"For fuck's sake, do ye want to keep yer life, girl?!" he came to a halt, hissing at her soft enough so as to not be overheard by the ears behind the walls.

"Y-Yes, of course…"

"Then shut yer mouth 'n' so as I say."

Magdalena could no longer fight the shivering in her lip. For a moment it was hard for her to read the man's intentions. He seemed far less cruel than before, if he ever truly was. Perhaps it was a façade all along. Or perhaps he was simply angry at the world. But being angry didn't make you cruel, Magdalena knew. Her own father was the angriest man she had ever known.

"What did he say?" she asked him again, her eyes on the verge of tears, *real* ones this time. "I must know…"

Hauzer sighed again, and his desperation was undeniable. He unsheathed a sharp curved knife from his belt all of a sudden and gripped it as he continued to drag her down the dark corridor.

"I'm sorry, yer majesty," he said.

When she inadvertently slowed her pace, he gave the chains a good yank.

He hardly looked back at her, as if it pained him to.

"Sorry for what?" she bit her lip again.

"For what I'm about to do…"

* * *

The room was dimly lit with an array of candles and a torch at every corner. Nearly two dozen men sat around the long dining room table, which was empty of any food but replete with more wine than the men could drink.

Every soul present was growing impatient and restless, sweating ruthlessly as the warm humid wind blew into the chamber from the outside. The balcony had no windows. It was hardly a balcony, the old thing. Many of the bricks were missing, as if it had been struck by catapults long ago and never fixed. The view, on the other hand, was quite impressive. Or it *would* have been, had the rocky fields in the distance not been as dark and rotten as they were.

The moon had risen at just the right time, it seemed.

It was full and vibrant when the footsteps came.

The men's chattering diminished into faint whispers when their ears caught the tapping of the boots echoing down the hall. The gnome woman that had been serving the drinks headed for the wide doors and opened them.

And then the room fell silent…

Lord Yohan Baronkroft entered, wearing a freshly sewn coat made of black ridged velvet, stripped of any decoration except for the collar, which was embroidered with a dim silver prickly vine. The rest of his clothes were graceful and stainless, a neat white shirt beneath a smooth black vest and leather pants. His black boots had steel plates over them that clinked with every single step. And his hands, pale as his face was, were replete with silver rings, one of which covered his entire forefinger.

He looked like a Lord, that much was certain.

All that was missing was a crown…

"Greetings, gentlemen!" he began with his usual grin. "What a pleasure it is to have you all here this evening."

The eerie silence lingered for a while. Every man in the room was exasperated and angry, and they were baffled at the sight of the Lord walking in entirely alone, with not a single guard at his side. Baronkroft instantly recognized the man in charge; he was the only one that genuinely seemed dangerous, compared to the rest.

"Well, cursed be my eyes," Baronkroft approached the end of the table, towards the chair closest to the balcony. "I half-expected you not to show up, knight commander."

The knight commander was in his fifties, easily. Rugged and strong, with a black beard that was greying at the roots and a grey head of hair that he kept tied behind him as any proper warrior would. His armor was black and silver, and unlike the rest of the men, he had steel-clad spikes on his shoulders and the face of a wolf crafted onto the silver on his chest.

"Lord Yohan Baronkroft, at your service," the lord bowed.

The man rose to his feet, but he did not bow in return. "Sir Gerhard Vandelour," he introduced himself, his hand on the hilt of his blade.

"Oh, I know," Baronkroft grinned. "The Wolf of Qamroth, himself. It's quite an honor, truly. It isn't every day one meets a gentleman of your talent."

"Where's Weston?" the commander asked, not a trace of affability in his glare.

Baronkroft took a moment to examine the rest of the men. All of them were dressed in armor, and it was clear that they had seated themselves in accordance to their ranks, as further down the table the glares became less firm and the hairs on their heads less grey. But there was one thing all of them had in common… they were armed and prepared for a fight, if necessary. Somehow, this pleased Baronkroft further, for his grin grew wider and his eyes hungrier.

"Patience, Sir Vandelour," he said. "We're on the same side, you and I."

"Horse shit," the knight remarked. "I'm loyal to my king. You are not. And I ran out of patience decades ago, so I will ask again. Where is Sergeant Weston?"

Baronkroft glanced at the gnome woman.

"Magda?" he called. "Would you be a darling and fetch Harrok for me? Have him bring the sergeant at once."

The gnome woman took a bow. "Yes, m'lord."

As she left the room, there was a moment of silence in which some of the men glanced at one another in confusion upon hearing the name *Harrok*.

"Feel better?" Baronkroft gave Sir Vandelour a friendly tap on the shoulder. "Now, please. Sit! The sergeant will be here soon. Sit and help yourselves to a drink!"

Sir Vandelour eased his shoulders a bit, but he kept his eyes locked on the lord, watching for any sudden unexpected movement. Baronkroft casually poured himself a drink. And soon after, a few of the men felt comfortable enough to do the same.

"You're probably all dying to inquire about the purpose of tonight's gathering," Baronkroft said, his goblet in hand, pacing around the room as if it was his playground. "Mark my words, gentlemen, tonight will mark a very important record in our history."

"Madmen do not make history," Sir Vandelour interrupted. He was the only one in the table without a drink and he very much preferred it that way.

"I beg to differ, knight commander!" Baronkroft remarked with a grin. "In fact, our history is rather replete with people who were once regarded as madmen and radicals. Ridiculed, scorned, shunned for their ideas... Sir Kristoffer Bahr was only a beggar when he led the rebellion of Kahrr. A century and a half later, it remains a free city thanks to him... Captain Genevieve Van Gault was called a traitor of the crown when she began smuggling goods and merchandise to neighboring countries for profit. Now her legacy lives on through the Merchants' Guild... Dare I even mention the stable boy that saved King Ulrik's life over thirty years ago? People laughed at the boy for thinking he could ever be more than a dung-sweeper. Now he is widely known throughout the country as the Wolf of Qamroth."

Baronkroft gazed over at Sir Vandelour, though the man did not seem at all impressed.

"Enough," the man said. "If you've a point to make, I suggest you get on with it."

"My point, knight commander, is simple!" Baronkroft grinned. "There is a very thin line between a madman and a legend. The one thing that distinguishes the two is the will to follow through with their plans."

"And what is it you need from *us*?" asked another one of the men at the table. "Weapons? Armor? Coin for your venture?"

"I've no interest in your riches, sir," Baronkroft said. "I only need your men..."

There was a brief silence; Sir Vandelour broke it with a scoff.

"And why in all hells would we comply?"

"Why...?" Baronkroft kept pacing, staring aimlessly into space. "Tell me,

Sir Vandelour… in your many years of service, how far east have you traveled?"

The knight commander lowered one brow and raised another, as if trying to figure out the purpose of the lord's questioning.

"And I don't mean Ahari," Baronkroft added. "That old shit heap means very little to me. No, the place I'm speaking of is a little place *north* of Ahari… A little place called Gravenstone…"

"I've been there," said another one of the men. "Riddled with humans, it is."

"Ahh, but it *isn't*, you see," Baronkroft went on. "It's only riddled with humans because they'd kill you if you were anything else… You see, not many people are aware of the horrors that take place in this land. And those that *are* aware would much rather turn the other way if it meant their trade contracts and treaties with the kingdoms of Halghard and Vallenghard remain intact."

"What in all hells are you getting at?" asked Sir Vandelour.

At this point, Baronkroft unveiled a map he had hidden within his coat. He unrolled it on the table near Sir Vandelour, placing a candle and a jar of wine on each end to keep it from rolling back up. Using his right forefinger, the lord tapped the center of the map with the sharp end of his silver ring.

"See that patch of land there?" he asked, and then backed away for the rest of the men to catch a glimpse. "Any civilian would take a gander and see nothing more than a vast stretch of forest. And they'd be right, for the most part. I've been there a few times myself. It's hauntingly beautiful, in fact. They call it the Woodlands."

Sir Vandelour began to comprehend where Baronkroft was headed. And he was growing rather impatient with the man's rambling.

"What *I* see, however…" Baronkroft came to a halt just before his balcony, his eyes drifting towards the darkened distance, "…is a *prison*."

A few of the men began mumbling to one another, raising brows and scowling.

"Nothing more than a filthy prison, gentlemen," Baronkroft sighed, his voice softening, his ghostly grin suddenly fading. "It is a land riddled with magic and horror. Ungodly beasts lurking around every corner, trees that come to life at night… It is a land with no boundaries and no rules. A land of death and misery. A place where the strong prey on the weak and the unlucky suffer unimaginable losses…"

Baronkroft had to fight back any sentiment, not only because it disgusted him to show any but also because he knew Sir Vandelour was not the type of man to succumb to emotion.

"Gentlemen, I would never wish upon you any of the horrors that exist in this forsaken land. I wouldn't wish it for *any* of you. To have to survive in this place, to have to fight for your lives every minute, to have to look over your shoulders or risk being enslaved… That isn't life, and we all know it. This place, it's... it's a cockpit of mayhem, where the good die young and the bad survive only to wreak havoc on those who seek only to survive..."

At this point, Baronkroft had nearly everyone's attention; everyone except the knight commander Sir Vandelour, who remained at guard out of instinct. The atmosphere in the room was eerie and abnormal, as if there were ears listening behind every wall. Little to their knowledge, however, there *were*...

The doors from which Baronkroft had entered had been left wide open, revealing a long torch-lit corridor. And in the corridor adjacent to it, hidden by the black stone wall, were two figures waiting for their moment to arise. Princess Magdalena of Val Havyn was one of them. And she had heard everything. The humans that Baronkroft was referring to were *her* people. The map that Baronkroft had revealed to them was *her* home. She wanted desperately to scream for help, to tell them all that Baronkroft was a madman. But two things prevented her from doing so.

One was the fear. Baronkroft was not the kind of man to make empty threats.

The other was curiosity. The tone in the man's voice when he spoke about Gravenstone was not a vindictive one. In fact, it was almost a tone of admiration.

"All right," Sir Vandelour stood from his chair, the wood scratching against the stone floor. "I think we've all heard enough of your nonsense. I demand to see Sergeant Weston at once."

"Patience, Sir Vandelour," Baronkroft attempted to stall. "The point I'm trying to mak-"

"I know the point you're trying to make," the knight commander interrupted. "I simply don't care for it, sir."

Baronkroft's grin lost some of his charisma. He placed one hand over the other in front of him, listening attentively to the knight commander, his expression becoming more intimidating after every word.

"Foreign laws are none of our concern, *Mister* Baronkroft," said Sir Vandelour. "Above all, not the laws of a country that we've been in quarrel with for the last two centuries. My brigade serves King Ulrik of Qamroth. *Not* you!"

"I suggest you take a seat, knight commander," Baronkroft said calmly.

"*I* suggest you cut the shit and deliver us our man!"

"I said take a seat, sir..."

"If I have to ask again, it won't be nicely!"

"Take. A. Seat."

"Where is Weston, you sick bast-"

"I said *SIT DOWN!*"

The room turned suddenly icy cold. Sir Vandelour felt a blow to the chest, as if someone had struck him with a warhammer. His knees bent unwillingly and he fell back heavily against his chair. His hands were suddenly gripping the armrests as if holding on for dear life. He looked at his body as if it was no longer his, as if something had taken control over it. The entire room turned towards Baronkroft, whose expression had changed from affable to frightening.

"I must say I'm rather disappointed," the lord sighed, rubbing his temples as if he was suddenly tired, as if a severe headache had come out of nowhere.

"W-What on earth have you done to me...?" Sir Vandelour asked somewhat desperately.

"I did ask nicely, did I not? But men often tend to challenge me, gods know why. Do you not *see* what I am trying to do, here?" Baronkroft paced around the room again. "I'm *not* the monster here, gentlemen. The *real* monsters are out there!" He aimed a finger at the map on the table. "Whatever atrocities I've committed are *nothing* compared to what they're putting people through in that place! Elves and orcs banished to a land of death, gnomes building civilizations underground for the sake of survival, and anyone who sets *one* foot outside of those borders gets decapitated simply for not being human..."

"It is *not* our concern!" Sir Vandelour argued through his fear, seeing as the rest of the men were too stunned to do so.

"Ahh... so you prefer to sit by and do nothing while injustice carries on just a few hundred miles from here?"

"And what can *we* do to change that?!" Sir Vandelour asked, rather honestly at that. "Slavery is still practiced in Ahari! Beyond the Draeric Sea, in the Noorgard Isles, women are scarred at birth, they call it 'purification'. Do you expect to fix all of *their* problems as well?!"

Baronkroft gave it a moment's thought. It wasn't that Sir Vandelour was heartless, but he was a man that cared only for the justice of his homeland.

"Well," Baronkroft sighed. "We must start *somewhere* now, mustn't we?"

As the lord paced, Sir Vandelour felt the warmth returning slowly to his body. It became clear that Baronkroft was not strong enough to hold whatever curse he had placed on the man for too long, at least not without it taking a physical toll on him. And, smart as the knight commander was, he knew better than to continue dragging the attention back towards himself.

"So tell me," Baronkroft went on. "Exactly how many men have you out there waiting beyond the hills at this moment?" The question caught all of the men off guard, so much so that the lord had to raise both arms out into the air as if awaiting an answer.

"Little over a thousand, sir," one of the lower ranking officers finally spoke, his entire body shivering with fear.

"Excellent!" Baronkroft's grin returned. "Now... here's what is going to happen next, gentlemen. You are going to bring in every single one of those men. They are going to walk through my gates willingly and with their weapons down. And then you are going to ride *back* to your city and bring me a thousand more. You will ask no questions, you will give no explanation to your superiors, and you will follow these orders in a timely manner. I will only wait for so long before I get impatient, I must warn you." He chuckled for a moment, but no one else in the room was in a jovial mood.

"And what if we don't comply...?" asked Sir Vandelour.

Baronkroft looked at the knight commander with a menacing glare. Before he could open his lips, however, two frightening figures walked into the room all of a sudden. They brushed past Hauzer and Magdalena along the way, and the young princess shivered at the sight of the bloody man that was being dragged in.

There were gasps and mumbles inside the room. Sergeant Weston was beaten and cut beyond recognition, and the monstrosity that was dragging him in looked pale and dead behind his studded mask.

Baronkroft chuckled again. "Well... I could *not* have timed that better if I tried."

The Butcher threw Weston onto the floor. Two of the men leapt from their chairs and ran to tend to the broken man, helping him up with their jaws hanging open. "Weston! By the gods, what have they done to you?!"

Baronkroft appeared almost pleased by their reactions.

"You're a monster..." one of the men muttered.

"Yes, I've heard that many times before," Baronkroft replied with a chuckle. "Frankly, after all I've lived through, I just don't see it..."

They carried Weston over to a nearby chair. Sir Vandelour remained in his seat, trying his best to hide the dagger he had drawn by his leg while Baronkroft was distracted.

"Now, gentlemen!" Baronkroft brought his hands together in a clap. "I believe we've stalled long enough... It is my honor to present to you the spectacle of the night!"

Outside the doors, Hauzer's hands grew sweaty, his fingers slipping against the rusty chains that were locked to the princess's wrists. Magdalena's heart had already been racing, only now it felt as if it was going to implode from her chest.

Calm yourself! Remember what you've learned!

"Gentlemen," Baronkroft grinned, a hand aimed out at the doors. "Her majesty, Princess Magdalena of Val Havyn..."

Hauzer took the first step. Magdalena followed closely at his side. She didn't recognize a single face in the room and yet they all seemed to have known her name. Their eyes examined her from head to toe; Hauzer even stood against the wall next to the fireplace so that the light illuminated her face like a portrait.

"Isn't she just *breathtaking?*" Baronkroft asked them all.

"What is the meaning of this?" asked one of the men at the table, his eyes gripped by the chains over the princess's wrists. "What in hells have you done, you bloody fool?!"

"Is something the matter, gentlemen?" Baronkroft asked nonchalantly. "You all look rather odd... So weak and feeble... So unlikely for gentlemen of your ranks..."

At that moment, Baronkroft walked past Hauzer and held out his hand. Almost reluctantly, Hauzer handed his dagger to him. While he did have it out and aimed at her, Hauzer did not worry the princess much, not the way Baronkroft worried her. At least Hauzer seemed much less impetuous.

"That *can't* be!" shouted one of the lower-ranking officers. "She... Blessed gods, that *is* her!"

Sir Vandelour was now sitting quietly, unwilling to draw the attention towards him again. Luckily, the rest of his men appeared willing to speak their minds now, which was buying him some time.

"Don't you touch her, you monster!" another man rose from his seat.

"Ah, ah, ah," Baronkroft glared at him with menacing eyes. "Take a seat, sir... Before you make me do something I'll regret..."

The man felt a drop of sweat run down his temple as he slowly sunk back down into his chair.

"That's it, sir... Besides, it would be a real shame to scar such a beautiful thing," he brushed his forefinger, the one with the silver ring on it, against Magdalena's cheek. "What kind of man would I be if I allowed any harm to befall her?"

He took a moment to observe the room. He had them all on the edge of their seats and it appeared to please him. He let out a loud chuckle once again and let his arms hang loose all of a sudden, as if he was only bantering with old friends.

"Look at you all!" he said. "You all look as if you've seen a ghost... It's rather funny, the way power changes you, isn't it? The way it makes you feel unstoppable, able to vanquish any obstacle...? But, with time, you forget how *small* you truly are... How *easily* your life can be taken by a blade to the *neck*."

Suddenly, he swung his arm to the right... Magdalena fought the urge to yelp as the tip of Baronkroft's dagger pressed against the tender skin below her chin...

The men in the room nearly leapt from their seats from the fright.

"I have eyes and ears in many places, gentlemen," Baronkroft glared at them all as he kept the dagger there for everyone to see. "One raven is all it would take... I could cut her majesty's pretty little throat and send a message to every single city and village in Gravenstone and tell them that *you*, Sir Gerhard Vandelour, *killed* her mercilessly by order of King Ulrik."

"You wouldn't!" shouted Sir Vandelour's second-in-command.

"Wouldn't I?"

"You're a nobody! They'd *never* believe you!"

"Then I'll send her head... Think they'd believe me then?"

"You would start a war between two countries for your own benefit?! You would sacrifice *thousands* of innocent lives f-"

"And how many lives have been lost under King Ulrik's reign?" Baronkroft asked defiantly. "And for what purpose, may I ask, if not his own?" He removed the dagger from Magdalena's neck and sunk it into the wooden table. By then, the lord was red-faced and shivering with fury. He looked like a raging madman who had just smoked three pipes of red spindle and was heading off into a battle.

"Don't test my patience, gentlemen," he said. "Or, by the gods, I'l-"

"You'll do *what*?!" Sir Vandelour had suddenly heard enough. "*Kill* us, will you?"

"Now, where would be the fun in that?" Baronkroft remarked, chuckling eerily. "No, Sir Vandelour, I wouldn't kill you… I would *break* you… Bit by bit, I would make certain that you learn what it truly feels to be nothing. Some of you will never see the light of day again, I'll make certain of it. And *you* Sir Vandelour, I would keep nearby. I would kill her majesty in front of you and let you watch me as I write a letter naming you her killer. I would make you watch as your beloved kingdom goes to war with Gravenstone. You'll be branded a traitor… Your name will become a curse to people's ears… Your children and *their* children will spend their entire lives looking over their shoulder…"

He paused there and pulled the dagger out from the wooden table. He held it up delicately and stared at it as if it were treasure. "Do I have your attention *now*, gentlemen?" he asked. "Or shall I show you just how rash I can be when you fuck with me…?"

There was a long uncomfortable silence, during which the hidden dagger nearly slipped from Sir Vandelour's sweaty hands. An entire life he'd spent building his reputation, fighting barbarians, keeping the peace, fighting loyally for his king… And yet in the end, it all came down to a single man threatening him inside of a locked room… The knight commander simply couldn't live with himself if he didn't at least make an attempt to fight.

"Well," Baronkroft straightened himself up and gave his neck a good crack. "Perhaps I'll give you all some time to think on it…"

He turned to face the door. And it was in that brief moment, when his back was exposed, that Sir Vandelour saw his opportunity. The knight commander pushed his chair back and swung his arm… The dagger flew across the room heading right for the lord's back. Magdalena was deathly near, and she could see that the lord was mildly grinning, as if he'd been expecting the attack.

Baronkroft turned back around with the speed of an elf, his right hand up in the air as if prepared to catch the blade…

But it did not touch him… It never even reached him…

Instead, the dagger slowed to a halt in mid-air, the sharp tip hardly reaching within an inch of his palm. It was as if the dagger was suddenly lighter than a feather, floating weightlessly at Baronkroft's eye level.

The men around the table watched in shock, Sir Vandelour included. Most sorcerers in Qamroth were known to manipulate the elements. But even the most powerful of wind mages could not do what the lord was doing. This was dark magic.

"I'm impressed, knight commander," Baronkroft muttered, rotating his wrist gently, his right forefinger manipulating the dagger's movement, tenderly as if the dagger was floating in water. "I've heard of your deadly aim… I've only ever *dreamed* I could one day see it for myself…"

The dagger began to turn gently in the air, the sharp tip aiming in Sir Vandelour's direction.

"It's nice to see a man live up to his reputation…"

Baronkroft's hand suddenly twitched and he hissed sharply as if he felt a sting running up his arm. The dagger flew across the room again, this time in the opposite direction, just as fast as it had been traveling before; it was as if the lord had grasped, manipulated, and stalled the dagger's energy, and then released it all with one sudden jolt.

Sir Vandelour felt his heart race as he found that, once again, he could no longer move a single muscle in his body. He was stuck there like an unmoving target. But before the dagger sunk into his chest, one of his men, a rather young one, leapt from his seat and shouted, "*Stop!*"

The dagger came to a halt just an inch from Vandelour's heart. Baronkroft's eyes drifted eerily towards the interrupting young soldier, who looked rather inexperienced and frightened.

"We'll do it!" the soldier said in a panic. "W-We'll call the soldiers in and send for more… J-Just *stop* this, please…"

Baronkroft wanted to smile. He almost did, in fact, until a fierce pain shot up his arm and into his chest. His wrist suddenly fell and the dagger fell to the floor with it. And Sir Vandelour could once again feel the warmth crawling through his veins. Baronkroft turned his back to the men, hiding from their sight as he reached into his pocket and drew a handkerchief made of black silk.

Standing that way, Magdalena had a clear view of him. The lord's nose had started to bleed and there was a soft hint of black among the red. He had also gone pale, much more pale than his usual state; he had gone from looking elegant to looking deathly ill within seconds.

Magdalena was stunned. She'd never seen such sorcery in her life. And she knew that neither had the rest of the men, for they were as startled as a bunch of children facing a ruthless beast.

Once Baronkroft wiped most of the blood away, he gave Hauzer a head nod. And without saying a word, the red-bearded sergeant dragged Magdalena away, back towards the corridor.

"Very well!" Baronkroft turned back towards the men, trying his best to regain his stance. "That settles it, then! I do thank you for your cooperation, mister…?"

The young soldier that had spoken up was suddenly startled, as if not used to having all the eyes in the room fixed on him. "Um… *Vincent*, sir… Vincent

Soriano."

It was a peculiar name, but Baronkroft reacted benevolently, as if the young man was an old friend of his. "My dear Harrok, would you be kind enough to escort young Mister Soriano to my personal chambers?"

Vincent froze with fear as the infamous Butcher of Haelvaara approached him and lifted him by the arm.

"As for the *rest* of you gentlemen!" Baronkroft took backwards steps towards the door after all of his party was out of the room. "I'm sure you must all be feeling a bit out of sorts… Perhaps a bit of time to consider things will do you some good, yes?"

Once he took the first step outside, the two goblins that were waiting by the doors slammed them shut and placed a steel bar over them. Instantly, Sir Vandelour and his men leapt from their seats and tried to find a way out. But there was no use. Baronkroft had chosen that room for a reason. The only way out was through those doors or out the balcony to a hundred foot drop.

"What has that boy done?!" Sir Vandelour asked with a vivid rage in his tone.

Meanwhile, outside the doors, Lord Yohan Baronkroft took a moment to catch his breath. He used his handkerchief to check for more blood, but his nose was now dry, as if nothing had ever happened. He grinned.

"Where are you taking me?" cried the young soldier named Vincent. "*Sir?!*"

"Thank you, my dear Harrok!" Baronkroft shouted, his voice echoing down the corridor. "Do see that the boy gets a meal!"

"*Wait… please, take me back… No!!*"

Aside from Baronkroft, the only ones left in the corridor were Magdalena and Hauzer, and they became startled when they saw the wicked grin on the lord's face. His hands were shivering from the exhilaration, his teeth chattering as if the room was icy cold all of a sudden. He looked like a madman, like a peasant who that just stumbled upon a million yuhn, like a warlock that just discovered the secret to eternal youth. Sir Vandelour and his men were pounding against the doors behind him, but Baronkroft hardly seemed to care, as if he hadn't a care in the world.

"Well!" he laughed hysterically and brought his hands together with a clap. "That was *quite* an evening, wasn't it?"

Magdalena was stunned beyond words, her face pale and ghostly all of a sudden.

"I don't know about *you* lot, but a good night's rest sounds rather lovely right about now, does it not?" Baronkroft asked.

Magdalena's jaw dropped even further; she could hardly believe her eyes. The man had gone from intimidating to friendly in a manner that no sane man could ever possibly achieve, at least not convincingly.

"Retreat!" he said with a hand signal.

Hauzer dragged the princess away. She was already formulating in her mind the story she would tell Thomlin and Valleria and the rest of the prisoners, when Baronkroft's voice stopped them suddenly.

"Whoa, stop right there, Sergeant Hauzer! Where do you think you're going?"

Hauzer glanced back with a confused expression. "To the prison chambers, sir..."

Baronkroft chuckled as if bantering with a friend.

"Come on, Sergeant Hauzer... I said a *good* night's rest, did I not?"

Hauzer raised a brow, and Magdalena was too mystified to speak a single word.

"Take her majesty to a proper bed tonight," said Baronkroft. "It's the least we could offer her."

It was then that Magdalena knew that something definitely wasn't right in Baronkroft's mind. Whatever sorcery he had used was taking a toll on him. And, being the ingenious thing that she was, she instantly began thinking of ways that she could use it to her advantage.

"Oh, and by the way!" Baronkroft shouted from the other end of the corridor.

Hauzer came to a halt. Baronkroft was looking right at the princess, and Magdalena looked right back at him. The lord's eerie grin was still there, and his demeanor was just as jarringly buoyant.

"You were astonishing back there, poppet!" he said, and then he walked off towards his chambers with a stroll so peaceful and confident, it was hard not to see how insane the man had turned in just a few minutes' time.

Hauzer and Magdalena glanced at one another briefly.

"You heard 'im," Hauzer said. "Right this way, yer majesty."

She followed him to a guest chamber that was not entirely clean but much more comfortable than the prisons. She was locked in there, of course. And when the princess sunk into the bed, it was as smooth and comfortable to her as cotton.

But she did not sleep that night... She *couldn't*, not after what she had seen...

She lay there perfectly still for hours, her mind reeling with a thousand questions. There was only *one* thing she knew for certain. There was no use in waiting any longer. Baronkroft's plan was in motion, and so she had to make sure she had a plan of her own. Waiting for a rescue was no longer an option.

For once, she could no longer sit and let her ideas flow within her idly.

For once, she had to act rather than wait to be called upon by her father.

For once, she had to take control and do *something*...

* * *

Adelina Huxley could not bring herself to sleep, as much as she tried.

It was a pleasantly warm night, not as humid as most spring days in recent years, and after several hours of lying wide-eyed in bed she decided to step outside for a moonlit walk around the palace gardens. She gave both of her sleeping children a gentle kiss on the forehead; they shared a bed with River, the infant orc that fate had placed in her family's hands. *Gods help us... what are we going to do with you?*

So much had changed for them in the last few days.

One moment, Adelina and her children had a farm.

One moment, Evellyn had a father and a blacksmith shop.

And suddenly, it was all gone... Adelina could no longer brew tea in her kitchen the way she would often do when she had trouble sleeping; her kitchen was nothing but a pile of ash now. She could no longer daydream while gazing out her window, could no longer take in the greenery in the distance or smell the pure country air. Instead when she walked outside, there was nothing but a field of dirt and gravel, empty except for a few rows of training mannequins and racks of weaponry. It almost seemed as if fate had played some sort of cruel joke on the Huxleys.

The palace gardens were just a short walk from the guard barracks and, aside from her children, that was the only thing that brought Adelina any joy. Three nights in a row she couldn't sleep, and three nights in a row she'd visited the gardens.

She liked the silence, the scents, the myriad of flowers swaying with the wind.

She liked the peace that it brought her, for peace had been so rare as of late.

But when she entered the gardens on this particular night, she realized she wasn't the only one whose mind had been shaken by the evening's plight. A woman in a beautiful teal gown was sitting there alone with a goblet in hand and a half-empty bottle of Roquefort liqueur on the table. Adelina's feet trembled to a halt; she tried to retreat back into the shadows but the solemn woman locked eyes with her, and leaving felt suddenly rude and bad-mannered.

"Pardon me, m'lady," she said. "I didn't mean to intrude..."

"You didn't," Lady Brunylda replied, her face blank and her eyes gazing at nothing.

"M-My apologies... I'll leave you in peace," Adelina gave her a nervous bow.

"Wait..."

Adelina's feet froze almost involuntarily.

The Lady Clark sighed tiresomely and bent her neck until it cracked. It became rather obvious that she may have been sitting there drinking for hours, based solely on her reddened eyes and the subtle slurring of her words. She sat up properly in her seat as if preparing for an important conference. "Huxley was your name, right?" she asked.

"*Adelina*, m'lady."

"Right," the Lady grunted. She had a slight moment of hesitation, a moment that was rather noticeable, for she was never one to hesitate to speak her mind. "I, uh… I do believe I promised you a drink?"

Adelina was unsure of how to respond. For a woman so intimidating, the Lady was speaking to her more like a peer than a peasant, though Adelina figured it may have been partly due to the liqueur. "I… um," she cleared her throat in a stammer.

"Come, woman," the Lady beckoned her with a sharp snap of the fingers. "Sit."

And there it was, suddenly. The intimidating and demanding figure of the Lady had returned. Nervously, Adelina walked over and took a seat across from her. The only light around them was from the lanterns that hung at every corner of the lavish gardens, and the only sounds were the faint distant echoes of the river's current and the night watchmen pacing restlessly in the dark.

"Don't look so bloody tense," said the Lady. "Relax. Have a drink."

Adelina glanced blankly at the table. "There's only one goblet, m'lady…"

"Oh," Lady Brunylda raised a brow. "Apologies… Here, have mine."

She poured a bit more liqueur into the goblet and kept the bottle for herself. Adelina wanted to refuse the drink, but she couldn't bring herself to do it. She could smell the Lady's breath from across the table, and it reeked of liqueur; not that she judged her, for Adelina was never one to shy away from a drink. But after everything that had happened, drinking was the last thing on her mind. Still, out of respect, she lifted the goblet to her lips and took a sip.

The liqueur was strong. *Quite* strong.

She felt the burn instantly as it made its way down her throat.

They sat there in silence for a moment and while Adelina felt a touch of discomfort, the Lady appeared dazed and out of sorts, profoundly lost in her thoughts as if reminiscing on her entire past life over the course of just a few hours.

"I saw what happened out there," Adelina broke the silence first. "Should I *congratulate* you, m'lady?

The Lady shook her head and scoffed, though more at the situation than at Adelina. There were no words or gestures from her, not even a smile. Her face was as hard as stone. It was as if she still couldn't wrap her mind around the idea that she was, by law, the Lady Regent of Val Havyn.

"Must be a lot to take in," Adelina went on. "To be the first Lady Regent ever t-"

"Stop that," the Lady interrupted. "I don't wish to think about it."

Except it was all she could think about, if she was speaking honestly…

"Apologies, m'lady," Adelina mumbled, a hint of shame in her gentle tone.

"By the gods, woman, is apologizing the only thing that you know how to do?" the Lady asked, fairly coldly.

Adelina frowned and took another sip of liqueur for confidence. "Well," she said. "I'll have to ask for your forgiveness once again. But where *I* come from, we believe in kindness and generosity over self-pride." There was a brief silence; Adelina instantly wished she could take back her words, out of fear of having insulted the Lady.

"How charming... And what of those who don't *deserve* your generosity?"

"*Especially* to those," Adelina remarked.

The Lady scoffed. "You clearly have more hope in humanity than I do."

"I *must*... My family's survived countless times on nothing *but* hope."

Adelina expected another scoff, but the Lady instead raised a brow and gave her a half-smirk, as if silently approving of her response. It was subtle, but Adelina felt a good deal more relaxed. Much like her own children, the woman had always been a fast learner, and it didn't take her very long to realize that the Lady Regent highly admired bluntness over bashfulness.

"Your children are adjusting well, I presume?" the Lady asked suddenly.

Adelina sighed. She realized then that she'd been so distracted thinking of John and Robyn and the attack on her farm to even consider how the twins were handling it all. "I do hope so," was all she could think to say.

"They seem to have grown fond of the orc child," the Lady added.

Adelina smiled. "Yes, well... children will be children."

"I'll have to take your word for it."

"Have you no children, m'lady?" Adelina felt comfortable enough to ask.

"None," said the Lady as she lifted the bottle up to her lips for a good gulp. "Never had the time. Nor the inclination, for that matter. How many do *you* have?"

Adelina hesitated, a sour feeling in her gut overwhelming her all of a sudden.

Honestly, I don't really know anymore...

"Four," she decided to say. "I have a daughter of seventeen."

"And where might *she* be?"

The discomfort in Adelina's gut turned suddenly into dread.

"She, um... She ran off," her voice became weak and shaky. "She was quite upset about John leaving. I just never imagined she would actually go after him."

After a brief silence, the Lady sighed and threw Adelina's exact words right back at her. "*Children will be children...*"

"Indeed," Adelina nodded. She found that she was no longer overwhelmed by the bitterness of the liqueur, as if her tongue had slowly adjusted to it. She took another sip. "She was always the most distant," she said, shaking her head gently from side to side. "Always so bold and stubborn... But the truth is she was the one who cared the most…"

"John's the eldest, I take it?" the Lady asked, eyeing the woman from head to toe. "But you don't look a day past forty. I take it you must've had him very young."

Adelina hesitated again. She didn't have half the Lady's confidence, and she couldn't bring herself to say that she didn't wish to think more about it. Instead, she cleared her throat and simply said, "Quite young, yes."

The Lady took a moment to properly respond. She stared intensely at Adelina as if trying to read the woman's entire life merely through observation.

"Well you've done a remarkable job," she eventually said, much to Adelina's surprise. "Granted, I only met John briefly. But he seemed like a fine enough young man."

Adelina smiled, suddenly thrilled to have been complimented by a woman of such great authority and regard. But then the Lady Clark narrowed her gaze and examined Adelina's round hazel-colored eyes. "How strange," she said, her words much less slurred than before. "He didn't quite have your eyes, though… Nor your black hair… He must have taken after his father, I presume?"

Adelina sighed first, contemplating on the memories she had of John as an infant. She remembered the first time she held him in her arms. She remembered how unworthy she thought herself to be, a girl of only seventeen caring for a child. Realizing the Lady was still waiting patiently for a response, Adelina nodded and said, "You have no idea…"

Then the silence returned. Neither woman said anything more about John, and Adelina felt the sudden need to shift the focus away from herself.

"Will you be all right?" she asked. "With everything that happened out th-"

"I said I don't wish to think about it," the Lady said coldly, closing her eyes as if it pained her to even remember.

Adelina thought before she spoke this time. The Lady certainly intimidated her, but she also appeared troubled beyond words. And it was in Adelina Huxley's core to help ease pain when she saw it. She'd done it with Aevastra, with Evellyn, with complete *strangers*, even. And, at that very moment, her tongue simply could not hold back.

"None of us *wish* to think about anything," she said. "It's the burden of the mind. The more haunting thoughts are often the loudest."

Lady Brunylda raised a brow. *Quite shrewd for a peasant woman,* she thought, and then eyed Adelina up and down again.

"All I'm saying is," Adelina cleared her throat, "I am here to listen if you ever wish to talk. It's the least I could do after everything you've done for us."

The silence lingered for several moments. The wind appeared to be picking up, but it was warm enough that it didn't cause them much discomfort. Lady Brunylda's eyes began to swell and glisten, and she hoped that Adelina would shrug it off and blame it on the dust the wind carried.

But there was no way to hide it. The Lady was not at all in a good place.

Calm yourself, Brunylda thought. *You didn't shed a single tear when father died and you won't shed any tonight.* She breathed deeply. The last person she had opened up to personally was her own mother, and it had been well over thirty years. But there was something about the peasant woman that allowed Brunylda to lower her guard. And she suddenly found herself unafraid to speak vulnerably for a change.

"You know... ever since I was a young girl," she said solemnly, "All I ever wanted to be... was *queen.*"

Adelina looked up, quite surprised at the Lady's brute honesty.

"I've known Rowan for many years, you see," she went on. "I knew him since he was just *Prince* Rowan, in fact. He was kind, caring, disgustingly dashing. Hardly the cantankerous thing he is today."

They shared a brief chuckle together. Adelina felt so much calmer, she found herself sitting back in her chair, allowing for the warmth of the liqueur to fill her chest. They even sat quite similarly, she noticed, for two women of such drastically different upbringings. Their right leg rested over their left, one hand on their right knee and the other on their drink. It was enough to dim the intimidating image of the Lady that Adelina held in her mind.

"Did you love him?" Adelina felt comfortable enough to ask. And just as she expected, the Lady Clark scoffed again. But it was at least a much friendlier scoff than she was used to.

"Goodness, no!" the Lady said, forcing back a laugh. "*Rowan?* I'd sooner love a goblin than love *him*... No, I've never loved *anyone*, truthfully. Never saw the point of it."

"That's because there *is* none," Adelina said. "It just happens."

"Well I'm certainly thankful I never had the displeasure," Brunylda remarked. "*Love*... Makes everyone stupid, is all it does."

Adelina knew too well herself what love could do to a person. The day her husband died, she had lost the love of her life. And the heartbreak that soon followed had nearly broken her, had it not been for her children; *they* had since then become the love of her life. And she couldn't possibly imagine what life must be like for a woman like Brunylda Clark, who had neither.

"Anyway," the Lady went on. "Once Rowan was of age, he became the most suitable bachelor in all of Gravenstone. Every girl in the kingdom wanted to marry him... Myself included, in fact. Not because I had any feelings for the old fool, but because I knew that it was the only way I'd have a chance to be queen."

She hesitated, closing her eyes and sighing as if the words were aching her.

"But, as fate would have it, he fell in love with another," she said. "And so I focused instead on what I knew best... Trade, commerce, managing my family's debt... By the time I reached the age of maturity, I was far too valuable to be married off to some measly lord. Instead, Rowan swore me into his service... I had to sit there at his side, day after day, watching as his pretty little wife served him his wine... She was a kind and gentle thing, truth be told, but she was bloody useless at being queen. Didn't know the first thing about ruling a kingdom, but she didn't *have* to... Because she was *pretty*. And that's all Rowan cared about. Frankly, I never saw the point of being beautiful if it's the only thing you've got."

Another silence, and this time the glimmer in the Lady's eyes returned.

But, just as before, there were no tears. The Lady wouldn't dare shed any.

With a clearing of the throat and a rapid blinking of the eyes, she took another sip from the bottle. "Anyway," she said, much less solemnly this time. "A brief year, their marriage lasted. Then the poor girl died... And Rowan never got to see his child..."

"I remember," Adelina said, a sudden sadness in her tone. "I was just a girl at the time, but I was there when she fell off the balcony. Really makes you wonder, doesn't it?"

"Wonder what?"

"About... the *curse*?"

The Lady chuckled and shook her head. "The *curse*... What a load of rubbish."

"Do you not believe it's true?"

"The world isn't a fairytale, Huxley. There are no such things as curses."

"Perhaps," Adelina's voice softened. "Still, one can't help but wonder. Specially after *three* wives and no heir?"

"No *son*," the Lady corrected her. "He's *got* an heir..."

Adelina nodded. *That is true. And yet... He may have lost that heir, for all we know...*

They heard footsteps approaching from the other end of the courtyard. A figure dressed in armor walked through the gardens, holding an elegant silver box in his hands. As he stepped towards them, the light from the lanterns illuminated his face. Like the Lady Brunylda, he looked tired and worn out, yet his appearance remained graceful and pleasing to the eye.

Adelina figured it must have been a family trait. Even at their worst, there was an undeniable elegance there; their sharp cheekbones and their black hair, thick and polished like a stallion's mane, and even the brown tone of their skin were all traits that made a member of House Clark recognizable to anyone anywhere in Gravenstone.

"Good evening," Darryk said with a nod. "May I have a private word with you, my Lady?"

"No," Brunylda scoffed. "But you're going to anyway, so you may as well sit."

Feeling as though she didn't belong, Adelina rose to her feet. She glanced at the Lady one last time with a smile, and then she lifted the goblet to her lips and finished what was left of the liqueur.

"Will you look at that?" the Lady chuckled and glanced at Darryk. "She handles her drink a lot better than you."

Darryk smiled uncomfortably, realizing the Lady was far beyond sobriety.

"Thank you, m'lady," Adelina bowed and set the empty goblet on the table. "Should you need anything, you need only ask. Anything at all."

And then the Lady did something she hardly ever did unless it was in a scornful manner. She smiled... A genuine smile that one would only share warmly with a friend...

Adelina retreated to her room to sleep, leaving the two nobles alone in the gardens. There was an uncomfortable lingering silence, as Darryk took the empty seat across from the Lady and leaned back. He sighed and stared into space much like she was doing, resting the box in his lap as if it were treasure.

"I imagine you must have questions for me, my Lady."

He had an entire speech prepared, truth be told, but Lady Brunylda stopped him before he could continue.

"What in all hells were you thinking, boy...?"

He hesitated, swallowed back his modesty, and instead fought to hold his ground. "What exactly do you mean, my Lady?"

"I *told* you to wake up," she said with a sigh of frustration. "I *told* you to stand up for yourself... to go out there and do your duty, and y-"

"I *know*," he interrupted her, as gently as was possible. "And I listened..."

She eyed him up and down. For once, the man didn't look entirely like a lost child. He looked more confident, more sure of himself, as if replacing the Regent crown with his armor had brought him back to his true nature.

"My duty, as King Rowan declared it, was to do what was best for Val Havyn," he said. "And that is *precisely* what I did."

She said nothing, only stared at him, trying desperately to figure him out.

So strange, it was, to know that he was her nephew and yet not know a single thing about him other than his name. She watched as he gently opened the box's lid; the silver crown glistened beneath the lanterns' light, brighter than any star in the night sky. His shivering hand was only inches from the silver, but he seemed reluctant to touch it, as if he didn't find himself worthy of it.

"This is quite a beautiful crown," he said, his voice weary and melancholic. "Normally, I believe there's a ceremony when it gets passed down to someone, but... considering the circumstances, well... I don't believe I was ever worthy of *wearing* it, much less passing it along..."

He placed the opened chest gently on the table and turned it so that it was facing her.

"This is yours, my Lady," he said. "It always has been..."

And with that, Sir Darryk Clark rose to his feet and retreated to his chambers for the night. Lady Brunylda sat there quietly for a moment, her eyes fixed on her nephew. She watched him until he disappeared into the shadows of the halls. And then she glanced all around, making certain that she was indeed alone. There was darkness and silence all around, nothing but crickets and night owls humming in the distance.

It was then that she glimpsed down at the silver crown.

It belonged to her...

At last, after 40 years of dreaming, the crown belonged to her...

It wasn't a queen's crown, but it was the closest she would ever get to it.

She lifted a trembling hand and touched it for the first time. She was never one to believe in magic, and yet she swore that when her fingertips touched it, she felt a spark.

And then it happened. She could hardly believe it herself.

A tear gathered at the edge of her eyelid...

The first tear she shed since she was a child...

XIX
The Voyage Continues

Sir Viktor Crowley had never been the type of man to have a drink in the mornings. He was hardly the type of man to drink at all, in fact. Luckily for him, he was no longer Sir Viktor Crowley. He was just another mercenary traveling with Sir Percyval Garroway's troop, if the man even *had* a troop left.

Nearly half of the king's soldiers had been sent up north before dawn.

The remaining half were starting to clear the camp, leaving Percyval's recruits wandering about without a clear answer as to whether or not they would be joining the fight. The rumor was that the campgrounds of Balthazar Locke's army had been spotted. And so King Alistair's plan was to attack the camp from both east and west. Naturally, he needed to make certain there would be no surprises, and so he'd sent half his men a few hours ahead to clear the path for the rest.

Not the best tactic, considering how outnumbered they are, Viktor thought silently to himself. Then again, King Alistair knew the land of Halghard better than Viktor did. For a moment he felt a hint of jealousy, reminiscing on the days he would advise King Rowan before a battle and knowing very well that he may never have a chance to do so again.

He thought briefly of his old friend Jossiah Biggs, first about the many times they'd fought side by side in a battle and then about the simpler times, the times when they were merely young soldiers in the royal guard. They would get drunk together at Nottley's Tavern after a long journey or during a day of festivity in Val Havyn. Jossiah never had a particularly warm reputation but Viktor would be lying if he said every memory of the man was a bad one. There was a time when they were as close as brothers, in fact. Or at least it *felt* that way, seeing as neither Viktor nor Jossiah had any brothers.

With a sigh of frustration, Viktor shook the thoughts out of his mind. He figured it wasn't worth getting angry over things he had no control of. In fact, there was a chance he would never see Jossiah again. The man could be dead for all he knew.

When the soldiers asked him to clear the wooden table so that they could chop it up and feed it to the fire, Viktor moved and sat on the back of a nearby cart. He heard footsteps approaching and for a moment he hoped it was Skye again. He hadn't seen Skye since the quarrel with Zahrra and was worried that he had offended the elf. When he glanced over his shoulder, however, he saw that it was Percyval Garroway who was coming to speak with him.

"Well," the man said, climbing onto the cart and taking a seat next to Viktor. "If it isn't the Golden Eagle of Vallenghard, drinking his pain away… Careful now, I could hardly tell you apart from a peasant."

Viktor smiled. Though it was early morning, he could tell by Percyval's breath that the man had also been drinking. "I could say the same of you, Garroway."

"Any word of your companions?"

"None," Viktor said, a sudden sorrow in his tone. "If I'm being honest, I... I'm not sure they even made it out of the Woodlands."

"Lighten up, Sir Crowley. Have some hope."

Viktor chuckled. "Any hope I had left in me died when I left Val Havyn."

"Ah... don't say that," Percyval placed a warm hand on Viktor's shoulder and gave it a mild shake. "There's always hope. *Always*. Even when the whole world appears to be turning its back on you, the gods are always watching over you. It's all part of their plan, my friend."

Viktor scoffed involuntarily, hoping Percyval wouldn't take offense.

"I hate to sound dull, but... After everything that's happened, I don't really think the gods like me very much."

"It's not about liking you or not," Percyval said as he reached into his coat pocket and pulled out a winebag. "The gods are kind to those who serve them humbly. And I see *plenty* of humility in you, Crowley. You need only embrace it."

"I've spent most of my life following orders," Viktor said in a grief-stricken tone. "I've fought and killed men simply because I was told they deserved to die... I'm sorry, but I don't see how that qualifies as serving the gods humbly."

"Never too late to *start* serving them humbly," Percyval shot him a friendly smirk.

Viktor said nothing in return, only gazed into the distance at the verdant fields ahead. Meanwhile, Percyval drew from his pocket his list of recruits and read them in silence, a wave of guilt and sorrow overcoming him. For two men sulking, they both appeared unprepared to quit. Some of the recruits had even started to gather nearby when they saw Percyval.

It felt like they'd been sitting silently for several minutes when Percyval finally lifted his head away from the parchment. "Could I ask you something, Viktor?"

This was the first time Percyval Garroway had addressed Crowley by his actual name.

"Go on?" Viktor replied, caught off guard by the abruptness of it all.

Percyval's face was suddenly a lot less jovial than before. "Is it true?" he asked.

Viktor raised a confused brow. "Is *what* true?"

"You know what," Percyval looked him in the eyes, not a single hint of banter in his expression. "Is it true that you're no longer a knight of King Rowan's court?"

Viktor sighed. He felt a tug in his chest, a wave of both anger and grief overwhelming him.

"Well?" Percyval pressed him, and it was clear that Viktor was not in the mood to speak much about it at all.

What do you want from me? Viktor contemplated. *You want me to say it out loud? You want me to tell the world how I failed my kingdom? You want me to tell you that my knighthood was revoked by the very same man whose life I saved two decades ago? Why don't you just kill me now and spare me the grief?*

He wanted to say it all out loud and more.

But instead he poised himself up and stood his ground. "Yes..."

Percyval remained silent at first. He had heard the rumors already, but was thrown off when he met Viktor Crowley in person and saw him wearing that famed armor of his with the golden eagle embedded on his chest, spreading its wings against the steel.

"Yes, it's true," Viktor said again, this time loudly and fearlessly, much more at peace with himself than he thought he would be.

"I see," Percyval gave him a nod. He allowed for a brief moment of thought before he cleared his throat and changed the subject abruptly once again. "Where is it you're going, again?"

Thrown off by the question, Viktor raised a brow with mild confusion. "What?"

"Princess Magdalena," Percyval clarified. "Where's she been taken?"

Viktor cleared his throat. He was so surprised by Percyval's casual response that his mind went blank for a moment. "Overseas," he managed to say. "To the ruins of Drahkmere."

"I see," Percyval nodded again, and then suddenly asked, "Any chance you could use a hundred and sixteen soldiers for your endeavor?"

Viktor glanced suddenly at him, puzzled and thrown aback. "Pardon me?"

"Well," Percyval took a sip from his winebag. "A hundred and *eighteen* if you count me and Antonn. I've yet to speak with him, but... He'll warm up to the idea, I'm sure...."

Viktor was bewildered beyond reason. "Did you not just hear what I said? I'm not a knight anymore. I'm not even a soldier. Other than my blade and a few hundred yuhn, I have nothing to my name."

"Well, that makes *two* of us," Percyval said solemnly, but there was something about his expression that gave Viktor hope. "I'll tell you something, Crowley," the man said with a deep and sorrowful sigh. "I don't know about you, but... I've grown sick and tired of listening to kings... Sick and tired, I tell you... Sometimes one has to simply trust their instinct and do what needs to be done. It isn't enough to *believe*. Sometimes you have to make the world notice. Force them to *hear* what you have to say. And I can't think of a better way to make that statement, can you?"

A hint of a smile began to form on the edge of Viktor's dry lips.

He waited… Percyval appeared to be concocting some sort of scheme in his mind…

As they sat, the recruits from the Woodlands had started to gather around them, closing in on them as if they were awaiting orders. Percyval turned to Viktor one last time, holding his hand out for a handshake.

"To Drahkmere?"

Viktor grinned. "To Drahkmere…"

They shook hands.

"Listen up, ladies 'n' gents!" Percyval shouted as he rose to his feet in the back of the cart. "Sir Viktor Crowley has a few words to say to you all…"

* * *

Cedric held his dagger up as if ready to jab forward, barely able to grip it in his sweaty palm. His eyes were fixed on a wooden target a good fifteen feet away. He would have been more confident if Gwyn, the mercenary woman that he'd befriended, wasn't standing right behind him, glancing over his shoulder and whispering suggestions into his ear.

"Am I holding it right?" he asked.

"Hold it however ye damn well please," she said. "It's yer *aim* I'm worried about. Ye couldn't hit a rabbit's arse if it was painted red."

Cedric wiped the sweat from his brow. "I'm sorry…"

"Don't be sorry, lad. Be *focused*… Now take aim 'n' throw the damn thing."

Stumbling over his fretfulness, Cedric threw the knife. It did not hit the wood. Instead, it grazed it and fell into the mud. He sighed with disappointment, as did Gwyn.

"Sorry," he said again.

"Oi. What'd I say before?"

He smiled. "Apologize again and you'll *actually* be angry?"

"Ye learn fast," she grinned back. "Now go fetch yer littl' blade 'n' take a rest."

Cedric picked up his dagger and wiped the mud off of it with his coat. Gwyn took a seat on a wooden bench nearby and poured herself some ale from one of the barrels, all the while getting cold stares from King Alistair's soldiers. They had been left alone for almost an hour now. Her twin brother Daryan had wandered off to practice with Thaddeus Rexx, and Viktor Crowley was sharing a drink with Percyval Garroway and Antonn Guilara after his big speech on the impending voyage. The only other souls nearby were gnomes and elven recruits, but after the cold welcome they'd received the day prior they seemed wary of any humans, even those within their own troop.

Cedric did not mind Gwyn's company, however. He found her much more amiable than anyone else in the camp, despite her bluntness and rough demeanor.

He took a seat next to her and she handed him a tankard of ale. He took it willingly and followed her eyes; she was staring at the Wyrmwood soldiers with something like awe. He knew she wasn't very trusting towards them, but something about her eyes spoke very differently. It was as if she was envisioning herself in armor, training amongst them all.

Cedric wanted to speak out. He wanted to ask Gwyn about her past, about where she had lived before she became a Woodland mercenary and why she became one in the first place. He wanted to ask how she'd learned to fight so well. She was as quick with her knives as she was with her tongue, and despite her being Daryan's twin sister their manners were vastly different, as if they had grown up on opposite coasts of Gravenstone.

Instead, he said nothing and waited for her to choose when to speak.

"So what's Val Havyn like?" she asked him suddenly. Even with her hardy demeanor and the black paint on her eyes and cheekbones, the woman had a rather striking smile. Cedric couldn't help but smile back.

"I don't know," he said. "Loud? Crowded? What d'you mean, exactly?"

"Is it true tha' ev'ry road is made o' stone?"

Cedric chuckled. "Um, yes… Yes, that *is* true. And the rooves are made of brick."

Gwyn looked bewildered. Little to Cedric's knowledge, she had grown up in Grymsbi, a place where roads were nothing but mud and every dwelling was made of wood with thatched rooves. Grymsbi and the Woodlands were essentially all that Gwyn had ever known.

"I've heard rumors 'bout it," she said. "But I nev'r been there meself."

"Oh?" Cedric took a sip of his ale. "What sort of rumors?"

"Like… d'you *actually* have the number o' people tha' live in yer cities written at the gates?"

Cedric couldn't help but chuckle. "Oh, you mean the population count… Yes, that's true."

Gwyn lowered her brows but kept her bewildered grin. "So… Wha' would happ'n if I *killed* someone there? Would they send some bloke with a pick 'n' hammer to change the number?"

Cedric laughed again. "I've no idea. Never thought about it."

"Well *someone's* gotta do it," Gwyn laughed with him.

Percyval's Woodland recruits were all sitting on the outskirts of the camp, away from the abundance of tents at the center. Gwyn preferred it that way, and so did Cedric; King Alistair's soldiers were treating them more like intruders than allies. Some recruits were growing restless by the hour and others had even started whispering about returning to the Woodlands. They were waiting for Viktor Crowley to give the order to march south, only the man seemed hesitant to leave, and so they passed the time the only way they knew how, training and drinking and laughing amongst themselves.

It wasn't yet noon when the travelers arrived.

Cedric's ear caught the sound of horse hooves approaching before the guards even started to gather at the camp's entrance. When he gazed over the horizon, he leapt suddenly to his feet, his eyes wide with disbelief like a gentle hound that just spotted its owner.

Gwyn got up as well, somewhat startled by his reaction. "What is it, toothpick?"

But the squire was far too stunned to answer her. He blocked the sunlight with his hand and narrowed his eyes for a better look.

Three horses approached... The riders were two men and a woman... One of the men, the more mysterious-looking one, wore a black hat with a rim and a long coat. The woman had raven-colored hair and eyes that seemed to glimmer with the sun's light. And the other man was blonde, and he was dressed in farmer's clothing.

"Well I'll be damned," Cedric mumbled, his lips curving into a smile.

With a tremendous amount of enthusiasm, the young squire started running down the hill, nearly stumbling twice. He hopped over the muddy grass and brushed past soldiers and Woodland recruits, mumbling *excuse me* at every few feet. He could hear Gwyn running behind him, except she was shouting *watch it* or *out of the way* at everyone. In the distance, Cedric saw the camp guardians speaking to the traveling trio, and there seemed to be some subtle tension between them already.

John Huxley had dismounted his horse first and stepped forward to try and reason with them. "We're not looking for trouble, sir," he was saying. "We're just here to speak with King Alistair."

"The king's busy, boy!" one of the guards barked unpleasantly. "We're at war. I suggest ye head right back to where ye came from."

"Yes, but we've important matters to discuss with him..."

"I said move it along, boy!"

"We're friends of the crown, sir! I assure you!"

"The *hells* ye are," the guard spat on the ground and then glanced at the farmer's two traveling companions. He recognized the man in the black hat and coat from somewhere but he couldn't quite figure out where. The woman, he didn't *have* to recognize; he could tell by her eyes that she was a witch. "We don't want her kind here," he said. "We've enough trouble with the rabbits and moles as it is."

John grimaced at the guard's comment. He felt the urge to punch the man but he held himself back, seeing as there was a swarm of soldiers lounging nearby with their hands on the hilt of their swords.

"*Wait!*" someone shouted in the distance.

The guards did not wince; their eyes were fixed on the three strangers. But John recognized the young squire from afar and smiled. Cedric was out of breath by the time he reached them, but the expression on his face was no less joyful and eager.

"It's all right, sir! They're with *us*!" the squire said. "They're our friends!"

But the guards did not respond as kindly as he'd hoped. One of them drew his sword and stepped towards Cedric with a menacing stare. "Back off, ye freak-loving littl' bastard," he growled.

Cedric shivered and took a step back, raising both his hands into the air. "B-But…"

"Back. *Off.*"

"He's telling you the truth!" John tried to protest, but neither guard seemed willing to yield. One of them blocked John's path while the other threatened to jab the young squire with his blade.

"Scram, boy! Before I send ye to meet the gods!"

Cedric stumbled backwards, gripping his dagger, wishing for the courage to unsheathe it. He didn't have to, however. Before he could even conjure up a response he heard another hissing sound behind him, like two blades being drawn at once.

"Oi," Gwyn stepped between Cedric and the guard. "Ye wanna threaten someone, threaten *me*!"

"This ain't yer business, lass!"

Gwyn's eyes lit up with rage all of a sudden. "Call me tha' again, I dare ye…"

"Wait, stop!" Cedric yelled. He wouldn't have been nearly as confident had Gwyn not arrived just in time to save his skin. "There's no need for this! I'll go get Sir Percyval and Sir Viktor and they'll explain it all!"

"Sir *Percyval*?" John asked.

"It's a long story," Cedric said, the smile returning to his face.

The guard raised his sword threateningly again. "If yer lyin' to us, lad…"

"But I'm *not*!" Cedric argued, once again his confidence driven by the fact that Gwyn was at his side with her knives out. "Five minutes. That's all I ask for. I'll be right back!"

The guard grunted, glancing back and forth between Cedric and the trio of strangers. Gwyn did not yield either, but rather she waited until the guard sheathed his blade first before she slid her knives back into their leather scabbards.

"Five minutes," the guard said. "If yer not back by then, I'll force 'em away with my blade."

There was a sudden snicker that broke the tension. The guard glanced over and saw Hudson Blackwood grinning beneath the rim of his hat. "You call *that* rusty thing a blade?" the thief whispered.

"Five minutes," Cedric walked backwards towards the tents. He gave Gwyn a glance and said, "Keep an eye on them for me, will you?"

Gwyn gave him a grin and a head nod. "Get on with it, lad."

John Huxley could hardly believe this was the same timid squire that he'd been traveling with. There was a new layer of confidence there, along with a few bruises and scars that weren't there before.

"It's good to have you back, John," Cedric smiled at them one last time before leaving, even at Hudson and Syrena. "It's good to have you *all* back... Five minutes! I'll take care of it!"

* * *

Princess Magdalena walked silently down the corridor towards the prison chambers. Hauzer was escorting her, quiet as he usually was, and this time she had no questions for him. She could hardly conjure up any words at all, she was so stunned from the night before.

Her father had taught her that when fighting a battle, even if the odds are greatly against you, there was always a way to overcome it all. But she hadn't the slightest idea where she could even begin to challenge a man with such power. All she could do was walk and try to find some reason behind it all. She bit at her lip nervously and scratched at her wrists, now reddened from the rusty black cuffs.

She came to a halt before the steel door as Hauzer fumbled with the keys.

The man looked tired and dreary, the look of a man who wakes only to struggle through the day. Before he unlocked the door, however, he turned towards her, eyeing her from head to toe.

"Ye hurt?" he asked as he tried to catch a glimpse of her neck.

Unsure of how to respond, she nodded gently. He placed a hand on her chin and moved it so as to get a better look. There was no blood at least, only red marks left there by Baronkroft's tight grip.

With a sigh, Hauzer grabbed the cuffs on her wrist and began unlocking them. He would always wait until the prisoner was inside the chamber before setting them loose. This time, he did not. And when she heard the clink of the lock, her heart skipped a beat.

"Sorry 'bout last night," he said abruptly, and the princess looked up with a twitch. "Didn't mean to press that dagger against ye..."

She had no words for him, nor did he expect her to. But the look they shared was strange. It was the look of a man whose mindset wasn't entirely clear. And hers was the look of a frightened captive searching desperately for a way out. It was a look the princess desperately needed in that moment, for before she knew it her mind was reeling with possibilities all over again. He opened the door to the chamber and made way for her. When she walked in, the prisoners dispersed, allowing for the princess to be at the center of attention. Finely dressed and clean, she stood out among the prisoners like a gleaming silver locket among a pile of rust.

Once Hauzer locked the steel door and walked off, the questions began.

"*Are you all right, your grace?*"

"*What happened out there?*"

"*Did you hear anything?*"

"*Who were the new soldiers?*"

"For fuck's sake, give the girl some room!" Valleria pulled her aside for a seat.

Young Thomlin was there, wide-eyed and eager to see the princess again, as was usual of him. "Learn anything?" he asked.

Magdalena looked far too puzzled, so much so that even the stubborn prisoners had huddled around her, among them the curator Sebastien Swanworth and the forgotten Lord Olfur of Yulxester.

"He's a madman..." Magdalena said in a mumble.

"We knew *that* much, girl," Valleria scoffed. "What did you *see?*"

The princess exhaled sharply.

If I told you, you would never believe me...

"Those soldiers weren't here to rescue us, were they?" someone asked from the darkness. Instantly there were several mumbles and groans of despair within the chamber.

"No... They were not," Magdalena said. "They were here answering a call... *Baronkroft's* call..."

A few among the crowd began sobbing, while others hissed and grunted angry words into the walls.

"He plans to gather an army large enough to attack Gravenstone. Soon he will have thousands of soldiers," the princess went on, and with every word the stares became more and more troubled.

"And what about *us?!*" Valleria hissed.

"With more soldiers that will soon arrive, the work will only grow," Magdalena guessed, and Valleria kicked a nearby bucket angrily, causing a messy splash of fluids in a darkened corner. For a moment, the princess swore she could see the fumes of rage rising out of the woman's ears.

"So the bastard will work us to death 'til we can't work no more?!" she growled.

"We must not dwell on such negativity..."

"More soldiers means more *mouths* to feed, stupid girl!" Valleria shouted with angry tears in her eyes. "More rags to wash, more armor to smith, more whips to lash us!"

"And more *time!*" Magdalena argued back.

For a moment, Valleria's gaze narrowed in thought.

"Time for *what?*" she asked doubtfully.

With a sigh, Magdalena took a moment to look around her. Every gaze clung onto her for an answer. Every face, young or old, had hardly any hope left in it. Realizing the moment to plant that last hope was now or never, the princess rose to her feet again so that she towered over them all. Nearly a hundred prisoners were in the room that night, most of them drained and overworked. For a moment, the princess seemed uncomfortable at the thought of being the cleanest person there. But she swallowed back the fear and looked at them the way a proper leader would.

"None of you saw what I saw!" she said, the fear vivid in her eyes. "With every day that passes, that man out there grows more powerful... And he..." she struggled through her words all of a sudden as the haunting image of the floating dagger crawled back into her mind.

"He can... *do* things... things that no man should be able to do..."

"And that scares you, does it?" Valleria asked scornfully.

The princess knew that the mercenary woman wasn't asking it to be cold, but she shot her a glare all the same.

"Of *course* it scares me," the princess said. "Hundreds of men have done unspeakable things, but... but *none* of them could do what I saw Baronkroft do..."

When she looked around again, Magdalena could see the fear in all of their gazes. And she tried desperately to push them all to use that fear to their advantage.

"That man out there has imprisoned us all like *hounds*!" she said. "He has broken us all and stripped us of our humanity as if it was *his* right... But every single one of us in this room has one thing in common... We've *survived* him this far... And if we've done it this long, we can go on a bit longer!"

"Look around you, girl!" the curator Sebastien Swanworth scoffed. "How much longer d'you think we all have left?"

"*Longer*," the princess argued. "We're *not* alone in this! There are more chambers out there. More prisoners like us."

"And more *soldiers* arriving to make sure the peace is kept," someone else argued back.

"No..." the princess insisted, nodding her head back and forth. "No, he has *blackmailed* them all. There are more coming, yes, but they have no say in the matter. They're here because Baronkroft threatened them."

"And what d'you suggest, girl?" Valleria asked doubtfully. "That we blackmail 'em all, too?"

"We don't *need* to... We have something *better*."

At that moment, the princess turned towards the peasant boy Thomlin, who was beginning to catch on to the princess's plan.

"The sapphires..." the boy smiled. A sudden silence followed, as every pair of eyes began to slowly light up with hope.

"I *know* soldiers," Magdalena said. "My father has thousands of them. And I know how to speak to them. Baronkroft has blackmail. But *we'll* have sapphires. Who do you suppose the soldiers would be more inclined to lend an ear to when we need it? Or when we need one of them to turn the other way?"

"And *how* do you propose we get to those sapphires before Baronkroft's men sniff 'em out?" Valleria asked, just as doubtfully as before.

"I don't know…" Magdalena hesitated. "We come up with a plan. Bit by bit, we can fetch them out."

"*What, so we bash a hole in the wall?!*" someone asked.

"Wouldn't have to be a *big* hole," Thomlin spoke out, standing loyally next to the princess. "*I* could climb in there, no problem…"

"*And where do you suppose we hide them all?*" someone else asked.

"*What if we get caught?*"

"*What if the soldiers won't fall for it?*"

"All right, enough!" Magdalena shouted suddenly, and then the mumbling died down bit by bit as she glared at them all. "Do you want to stay and *die* here?! Or do you want to get out there and *live?!*"

The silence lingered…

With hardly any food in their bellies, the prisoners knew they hadn't long to live. Some had days left. Others had mere *hours*. And that haunting thought was the one thing that gave them that last shred of hope.

"I'm *sick* of this!" Magdalena shouted abruptly, her eyes narrowing and her jaw tightening with fury. "I'm sick of sitting and *waiting* to be rescued… Waiting for a chance to be free… I will *not* wait, not anymore! I'm getting the bloody hells out of here and I'll do it with the help of two people, five people, or a *hundred* people. I will do anything and everything until I see it done. And, mark my words, I will *never* wait to be rescued again."

The prisoners stood there, far too stunned to speak. In the distance, they could hear muffled shouts, captives being dragged out of their chambers to be tortured. And it only echoed the princess's fury.

"Who's with me?" she asked suddenly, her eyes glancing all around the prison chamber. Nobody moved at first; they simply glanced at one another with fear and hesitation. Magdalena's chest was pounding furiously, her mind once again haunted by the image of the floating dagger. If she had to work alone, if *anything* at all went wrong, she could only imagine the horrors that would await her if Baronkroft caught her.

"Very well, girl," said a voice that brought joy to Magdalena's chest.

It was Valleria, stepping up valiantly like a true warrior.

"So tell us… What exactly *is* your plan?"

* * *

A nearby fire was flickering, and it was the only sound filling the uncomfortable silence between the traveling trio and the Wyrmwood guards. Even Gwyn was getting restless and uncomfortable, groaning and muttering insults under her breath. The farmer looked ordinary enough, but every now and then Gwyn would make eye contact with Hudson or Syrena and her eyes would narrow, as if she was trying to figure them out.

"So, uh," she cleared her throat. "How do ye know toothpick?"

John, Hudson, and Syrena glanced confusedly at one another. "Who?" the thief asked.

"*Cedric*," Gwyn clarified.

"Oh!" John chuckled. "Well, uh... we're old friends."

"*Acquaintances,*" Hudson added.

"Hey!" growled one of the guards. "No talking!"

"Oh, calm yer pits!" Gwyn snapped at him.

Hudson and Syrena grinned at each other, a hint of subtle admiration towards the woman's grit. They eyed her from head to toe, examined the many scars over her arms and face. They stared at her knife belt, at her choppy blonde braids, at the black war paint smeared over her eyes and cheekbones. It was baffling to think that such a woman would ever befriend a bashful little peasant like Cedric.

"How do *you* know him?" John asked curiously.

Gwyn smirked, the hint of a dimple on her pale cheek. "Like the lad said... 'tis a long story."

A few of the nearby guards leapt to their feet as if an authoritative figure was approaching. The rest of the soldiers in the camp were dispersing as a diverse crowd of humans, elves, and gnomes walked briskly towards the camp's entrance. The crowd was being led by three figures, none of whom John could recognize from such a distance, but he was left speechless at the sight of such an assorted troop within human realms.

"Will you look at that," Hudson grinned.

Once the crowd was close enough, John Huxley realized exactly whom he was staring at. The regal image of the Golden Eagle of Vallenghard was still there but it had blurred, almost as if the knight had died and resurrected as a new man entirely. He was still Viktor Crowley, strong and fit for a man in his mid-forties, ruggedly handsome with blue eyes that were both welcoming and intimidating all at once. But his appearance had vastly changed; he was merely a shadow of the man that had marched out of Val Havyn. His silver armor was now gone, replaced by dark mercenary leathers, but his red cloak was still there, red as bright as blood, the same color as the banners of Raven's Keep. Viktor's face was no longer clean shaven; his scruff had started to grow into beard territory, and it was just as blonde as his greasy long hair.

Well cursed be my eyes, John smiled at the sight of his knight commander alive and well.

Viktor was walking hurriedly, his face lighting up as he got closer, his eyes blinking repeatedly as if making sure they weren't deceiving him. To his left was a knight dressed in dark steel armor with ebony-colored skin and a neatly-trimmed layer of fuzz on his head. To his right was a pale silver-haired elf that could have been male or female or neither. Cedric was also with them but he was falling behind, unable to keep up with Viktor's eager pace. And behind them all were the dozens of recruits, marching closely together like a flock of birds.

Hudson and Syrena both leapt off their horses and stood next to John like a pair of guardians.

"Stand back," the Wyrmwood guards ordered.

"It ain't these three ye should tell that to," Gwyn mocked them, and then made way for the incoming crowd. Viktor didn't even acknowledge the two soldiers; his eyes were fixed on the three misfits, grinning at them as if he was staring at the faces of old friends from Val Havyn's royal guard.

"At ease, gentlemen," Percyval Garroway said to the Wyrmwood soldiers.

John tried his best to stand firmly and confidently in the presence of his knight commander. "Greetings, sir!" he said. "By the gods, it's so good to see you agai-"

Viktor placed a hand on John's shoulder and pulled him in for an unexpected hug. "You tough little bastard," he muttered into the farmer's ear. "I never thought I'd see you again..."

John knew not what to do, and so he simply stood still until the man let go of him. "Thank you, Sir Crowley," he cleared his throat and smiled nervously.

"Just *Viktor*," the man corrected him, and then took a surprised glance over at the thief and the witch. "Well," he approached them with an expression on his face that was difficult to read. "Hudson fucking Blackwood and Syrena of Morganna... I never had you two pegged as the type to follow through on a promise..."

Syrena remained silent, giving Viktor nothing but a friendly grin.

"Hello, old mate," Hudson stepped forward, reluctant to admit that he was mildly glad to see Viktor still alive. "You look different, have you finally lost some of that extra weight?"

"Careful," Viktor replied in a similar form. "I'll still beat the shit out of you."

Viktor held a hand out, and after a moment of hesitation the thief took it.

There was a silence, as everyone watched the two men locked in that handshake.

"Good to see the tree nymphs didn't get you, old mate," said Hudson.

"Likewise," Viktor nodded.

As the Woodland recruits gathered around them, there was a sense of comradery that caught John off guard. He recognized almost no one from the crowd except for Viktor and Cedric, and eventually he spotted Thaddeus Rexx amidst a cluster of elves. But despite their strange faces, they all welcomed the traveling trio with smiles and pats on the back as if they had been a part of the troop all along.

"Percyval!" Viktor called. "I've a task for you, my friend."

"Say the word, my brother," the man stepped forward. "And it shall be done."

"I must send a raven before we march south."

"A raven?" Percyval asked. "Where to?"

Viktor grinned, his chest overflowing with hope and grit.

"Val Havyn," he said.

* * *

Aevastra, the orcess from the Woodlands, had proven to be a lot more resilient than people thought she would be. Aharian scorpion venom was horribly lethal and could kill the average human within the first 12 hours. Aevastra, however, had held onto life for two days after being struck with the poisoned arrow.

Two days, Adelina Huxley told herself as she wiped a cold tear from her cheek. The wind blew the hairs away from her face, giving her a chill that made her bundle the orc child against her chest. The soil beneath her feet was loose and damp, and Henrik, the helpful farmhand, was able to dig up a grave within minutes. Aevastra's body had been loosely wrapped in a white sheet, and she was resting just inches from Adelina's feet, awaiting burial.

Two days, you knew her, Adelina... So why does it hurt this much?

In the back of her mind, however, she knew the reason. She was holding it in her arms.

When Henrik and another farmhand lowered the corpse into the pit, a stiff green hand fell out of the sheet. The farmhand stumbled back in shock and the sheet slipped from his nervous grip. Adelina felt a sting in her chest at the sight.

"Settle yourself!" Henrik barked. Once they settled the body inside, he reached for the shovel.

I'm so sorry, Adelina wished she could say to Aeva. She wished she could have given the orcess a proper burial, but she hardly had any coin left to feed her children, let alone purchase an actual casket. When Henrik shoveled the first pile of dirt over the sheet, the woman turned her gaze away. And when she did, she suddenly wished she hadn't.

There it was, the pile of black rubble that used to be her home, now unrecognizable and reeking of smoke and ash. Another tear dribbled down her cheek and this time she allowed it. She and her husband had built that cottage with their very hands, when they were nothing more than a pair of young naïve lovers. Long before John. Long before Robyn and the twins. Long before she became the Huxley widow.

Now she had nothing...

Without anyone to tend to the farm, the crops would soon rot, if rodents and thieves didn't get to them first. She'd have to sell the sheep and the horses just to make enough coin to survive through the winter. And *then* what? Was she to rent a room in a Val Havyn inn with her two children and a motherless orc child? They'd all be killed before anyone allowed it, she knew.

"We'll take care of it, Missus Huxley," Henrik said. "No need to stay and watch."

She nodded and gave him what could pass for a smile. "Thank you, Henrik..."

She was walking towards Old Man Beckwit's cottage when she felt a sudden tug on the back of her dress. "Mum?"

"What is it, dear?"

Margot aimed a finger into the distance. "Look..."

With widened eyes, Adelina handed River to the young girl and walked hurriedly towards the approaching carriage. It was a black majestic carriage with curtains and a roof, reined in by two men in armor, nothing like a farmer's cart. It was rare for such elegance to ride through Elbon, at least when it wasn't the autumn festival. One of the guards was Hektor, Adelina realized; he raised his hand to salute her from afar and then opened the carriage door.

Lady Brunylda Clark always looked regal, with her flowing gowns and abundant jewelry.

On this day, however, she didn't just look regal... She looked like a queen...

Her black hair had been styled and tied back neatly and gracefully, revealing a pair of royal blue earrings that hung a good inch below her earlobe. She wore a brand new corset, the same color as her teal gown, embroidered with a floral design that was fit for royalty. What was most different about the woman, however, was her glistening silver crown. And when the Lady approached the Huxley farm, her neck was as stiff as ever, as if she were balancing a delicate bouquet over her head.

The crown suited her splendidly. Not only did it match her silver rings, but it reacted beautifully against her dark hair and the two grey streaks that she refused to dye and instead worked into her hairdo.

"M'lady," Adelina took a bow. "By the gods, you look..."

"Exhausted?" Brunylda asked.

"*Beautiful...*"

The Lady was unsure of how to respond. Her head felt unusually heavy and it wasn't helping her headache. For the first time in a long time, she did not have a drink with her morning meal and it made her feel strange and out of sorts. There wasn't enough black tea that could have awakened her the way her liqueur did.

"So... this is what's left of it?" the Lady asked after a brief silence. "Your farm?"

"It is, m'lady," Adelina glanced at the rubble. The roof had collapsed entirely, and there was only one wall left standing, stained entirely with black soot. "My apologies. I would ask you in for tea, but..."

The Lady smiled, genuinely admiring Adelina's vigorous strength. She didn't seem to mind the mud beneath her elegant shoes much; in fact, she made way towards the filthy debris.

"Come, woman," she said. "Walk with me."

Adelina allowed the Lady to take the lead, following just a step behind as was customary for those of lower status. She was no longer intimidated by the Lady's presence. If anything, she was starting to enjoy her company; it had been too long since she had anyone to talk openly with that wasn't her children or Old Man Beckwit.

"The crown suits you, m'lady," she said warmly. "Truly, it does."

"No need to flatter me," the Lady chuckled. "No one can hear us at the moment."

They walked around the rubble and towards the cornfields. The soil was starting to become riddled with loose ears of corn, becoming more infested with worms and bugs by the day. Surprisingly, however, there was no unpleasant smell. As they walked along the green fields, the Lady seemed almost refreshed as she took in the spring aroma.

"I've come to share the news," she said abruptly. "A raven arrived this morning from Halghard. A raven sent by Viktor Crowley himself." Adelina felt the hairs rise at the back of her neck as the Lady came to a halt and faced her directly.

And?

The Lady's expression remained blank and steady. "It would appear there was an incident, during which John Huxley was separated from the company, along with the thief Hudson Blackwood and his witch companion."

Adelina's heart raced. She wasn't entirely sure where this was going, but she resisted the urge to press the Lady about it.

And?!!

"He's a rather interesting man, your John," the Lady raised a brow, her lips curving into a subtle grin. "It would appear he somehow managed to convince both the thief and the witch to follow through with the voyage... They were reunited in Halghard as of yesterday. They march to Drahkmere as we speak."

Instantly, Adelina released a sigh of relief, pressing a hand to her mouth as the tears swelled in her eyes.

Thank the gods... He's alive... My John is alive!!

"Thank you, m'lady!" Adelina said joyfully. "D-Did he mention anything about my girl…? About *Robyn*…?"

There was a brief silence, during which Brunylda's grin faded slowly.

"I'm afraid not," she said. "But if she's anything like her mother and brother, I'm sure there's hope yet…"

When Adelina smiled, she felt the warmth overwhelm her chest, for these were desperately needed good news. "Thank you!" she said again. "May the gods bless you, m'lady… Thank you!"

"Bloody hells, woman," the Lady said. "You're *too* kind, it's repulsive. Stop that."

But there was no stopping Adelina's smile. It was so contagious, even the Lady couldn't help but smile with her. They walked around the rubble and back towards the barn, where Henrik was still shoveling dirt over Aevastra's grave.

"It's quite an honorable thing you're doing here," Lady Brunylda said, referring to the burial. "Not everyone would be willing to bury an outsider within their grounds."

"Yes, well… I don't exactly have the coin for a caravan to take her anywhere."

At this last comment, the Lady glanced at one of her guards and signaled him with a gesture. "Hence why I'm here," she said.

Adelina raised a brow as Hektor approached them with a rolled parchment in his hand. "Pardon me, m'lady?" she asked.

"You don't think I came all the way to Elbon just for the scenery, did you?" the Lady scoffed, much friendlier than her remark made it seem. "He really is a remarkable young man, your John. Truthfully, now I can see why…"

The Lady smiled at her again. As Hektor walked nearer, Adelina couldn't help but feel a mild sense of discomfort. Never did she imagine she would become acquainted with someone like the Lady Clark. Never did she envision them walking through her farmgrounds side by side. And most of all, never did she think the Lady would be treating someone as warmly as she was that morning, much less a peasant.

"Before he left, John Huxley made an arrangement with me," the Lady confessed. "He was to be paid 5,000 yuhn in silver for his services, just like everyone else. And, believe me, they all took every single coin… All of them, except John Huxley. He took only what he thought would be sufficient for the voyage, which was 500 yuhn."

Hektor began unrolling the parchment.

"He asked me to look after the rest for him," Brunylda went on, as she took the parchment from the guard's hands. "He requested that, in the case of his death, the money go to his mother and siblings… As of yesterday, we know he's alive and well, but…"

The Lady took another glance at the rubble that used to be the Huxleys' cottage.

"Considering the circumstances," she said. "I believe you're more in need of the money than he'll be, should he return."

She handed the parchment to Adelina, who felt an instant rush up her back when she saw the drop of blood. The woman could hardly read, save for a few simple words. But she knew her family name when she saw it. And there it was, right at the bottom of the parchment, next to the blood.

A contract, she realized. And among other things, she saw her own name listed next to the sum of 4,500 yuhn. It wasn't a tremendous amount, but it was more coin than Adelina ever had all at once. She looked up at the Lady, her eyes stunned and her lips quivering. "M'lady, I… I don't know what to say…"

"There's nothing *to* say," the Lady remarked, as she took the contract back and handed it to the guard to keep safe. "This is your family's coin. I trust that it should be more than enough to compensate for the damage those filthy monsters caused you."

Adelina fought back the tears, mostly out of coyness.

"Thank you, m'lady," she took another bow.

With a hand gesture, Lady Brunylda sent Hektor back to the carriage.

"For safety's sake, I'll have your silver stored in the palace. I've notified the vault guards that you are permitted access to it whenever you please. I've also asked Brie to draw up a list of potential hires for the hard labor. In just a few weeks' time, I trust you'll have your cottage back. And possibly more, should you play your cards right and arrange a few trade agreements."

"But… I-I'm no businesswoman," Adelina stammered. "I've have no idea where I would even start."

"Well… I've never been one to provide counsel free of charge," the Lady said, a grin forming at the edge of her lips. "But give it a few drinks and gods know *what* sort of tips I might just happen to spew out."

Adelina felt she could have hugged the woman, but there was no way she would ever act on it, especially now that she was the Lady Regent of Val Havyn.

"I cannot possibly thank you enough, m'lady…"

"Try," Brunylda said warmly. "Good day to you, Huxley."

And with that, the Lady turned and headed towards the carriage.

Adelina remained in place, still flustered and thrown aback. Margot and Melvyn were, by then, running towards their mother, curious and wide-eyed.

"Is something the matter, mum?" they asked.

Adelina looked down at her children and smiled at them warmly, caressing their faces the way she would do every night before bed.

"Nothing, my darlings," she said blissfully. "Nothing at all."

* * *

Viktor Crowley led the way through the Falkbury trail, a Halghardian country road that ran through a vast hillscape of green. Behind him marched his new company of mercenaries, the first in centuries to be comprised of both humans and nonhumans. And as they headed towards the southern shores of Halghard, a trip that would take them a week with good weather, the former knight was slowly recovering from his fateful fall.

His days of knighthood were behind him now.

Even if he did rescue the princess and escape with his life, King Rowan wasn't known to be a very merciful man. At best, Viktor could regain his honor in Halghard. He'd made an ally out of Percyval Garroway, a man with ties to the kingdom, a visionary with hopes of bending the law.

But Viktor was a realist; a hopeful one, but a realist all the same.

Even as they rode on, Viktor knew the troop was gravely at risk, and it was picking at the back of his mind like a blade. They passed villages and forts along the trail and every time, folks looked at them all as if they'd just witnessed a massacre before their eyes. Inns closed their doors on them, merchants turned their backs, and children would stare and throw stones from afar.

To the peasants of Halghard, the troop was a walking abomination.

It made no difference that Halghard had two sanctuary villages or that more nobles and people in power were starting to think more broadmindedly. Because, no matter the effort, the smallminded would always be stubbornly set in their ways. To them, the elves and gnomes were trespassers, no better than the common criminal. They were the muck at the bottom of the barrel, the filth that humans' ancestors had fought so hard to cleanse the world of, a walking pile of unworthy scum here to permeate their land.

Viktor Crowley was well aware of it all, and still he's taken them all under his wing. He'd been blindsided by hope, the fool. He'd promised them freedom, something that wasn't in his power to endow. The rescue of the princess of Vallenghard in exchange for the right to leave the Woodlands for good. Many were hesitant to join, some even fled while they had the chance, but a good hundred of them had stayed. It was a smaller company than it had been at first but it was a hell of a lot more than a dozen, Viktor figured.

"Do you think they'll be safe?" John Huxley asked one morning, riding alongside the man he once saw as his superior. Truthfully, there was hardly much of a difference between the two of them now, save for some twenty years or so.

"I can't promise their safety more than I can promise yours," Viktor said honestly.

John kept glancing back. It was remarkable for the farmer to see the comradery between the hired swords and their elven counterparts. The gnomes kept to themselves mostly, but they rode alongside others who greeted them with a handshake rather than a glare.

"Are they... *permitted*?" John asked reluctantly, as if asking whether or not a wound was lethal and dreading the answer.

"They're not *marked*, if that's what you're asking," Viktor remarked. "It's only been days since they left the Woodlands."

"I see... And what's to stop a posse of guards from detaining them all?"

Viktor thought about it for a moment. And, once again, he chose the more honest and direct answer. "You think a hundred blades will be enough to stop them? *I* certainly think so."

John raised a brow. "But sir..."

"John, old boy, what did I say?" Viktor asked with a friendly grin. "I'm not anyone's '*Sir*' anymore. Call me Viktor."

John understood then... The doubt that was hindering his conscience was well grounded, after all. What they were doing was unlawful. Viktor had, in a sense, become a fugitive of the kingdom. And John was surprised to see the man so at ease about it. Every meter they marched was forbidden, every step they took was another reason to sentence them all to a hanging. Whether he liked it or not, the fact remained... John was marching alongside a traitor of the crown...

Viktor must have realized the perplexed look on the farmer's face, for he reached over and gave him a pat on the shoulder as if to wake him from a trance. "Something on your mind, lad?" he asked, but the look on his eyes was an affable one, like a mentor looking after a fellow pupil. "Go on, then. Speak. What troubles you?"

John fought through the sour feeling in his gut. "It's just... Won't there be *consequences*?"

He glanced back again, though the look of wonder in his expression had suddenly faded.

Viktor gave it a moment's thought; his eyes left John and moved towards the landscape. "Don't let your mind get carried away, John," he said finally. His tone had shifted, however; he sounded almost as if he was speaking to Jossiah Biggs all over again. "The time will come someday when you'll find yourself making the hard decisions. Whether it's leaving home or deciding the fate of a man behind the tip of your blade. Or, perhaps, doing something that your kingdom's law forbids because you know it in your gut to be the right thing."

John looked at the man, hardly recognizing him behind that new façade. He was still Viktor Crowley, but he was changed, much like a prisoner changes after years of captivity. Viktor's edges were rougher, his mannerisms were less like a soldier and more like a sellsword. He was more distant now, and there was even a hint of cynicism behind his grin.

But John didn't blame him. He'd heard what Jossiah Biggs had done. He'd heard it from an elf, a nimble elf with unbelievably striking features that had grown to be rather close with the former knight.

Jossiah, Viktor's lifelong friend and comrade, had fled and left the man to die...

And John could only imagine what such a betrayal could do to a person...

"I would never force you to follow in my footsteps, old boy," Viktor went on. "Nor will I speak your name to anyone, should you choose to part ways and head home... You've been loyal to the company's cause since day one, and for that I owe it to you. But I do hope that you will stay. And I hope that you see what I'm trying to accomplish here. Not just for me, but for the rest of these folk..."

Viktor took a moment to turn his horse halfway. There was a good twenty feet or so between them and the rest of the troop. The formation didn't reach too far back, about a half-mile at best. And he realized then that, while the company was his, he hardly recognized more than a dozen faces or so.

He saw Percyval and his second-in-command Antonn Guilara in front of the mass of horses.

He saw humble young Cedric riding alongside the gutsy mercenary woman Gwyn.

Next to them were Hudson Blackwood and Syrena of Morganna, possibly the only two that didn't look entirely out of place among the Woodland mercenaries, like leather next to darkened steel, one suitable with the other.

"If it's all right with you," John cleared his throat, then turned his horse halfway as well.

"Go on, lad," Viktor gave him an approving nod.

John trotted behind, casually sliding back into the formation next to the thief and the witch. Viktor found it intriguing, the way fate had played their cards. When the journey began, it seemed probable that John and Hudson would murder each other in the dead of night. And weeks later, there they were, riding next to each other and bantering like lifelong comrades. And the witch, Viktor had distrusted almost to no end, yet when he looked at her now, chainless and free, he couldn't have been more pleased to have her back.

You did one hell of a job there, John Huxley, the former knight thought, wishing he could say the same about himself. Percyval Garroway and Antonn Guilara approached, each trotting at either side of Viktor.

"Spirited lad, that one," said Percyval, glancing back at John.

"That, he is," Viktor remarked, though not as lively as he was before.

"You look troubled," said Antonn.

"Yeah, well," Viktor sighed. "Can't remember the last time I *wasn't,* unfortunately."

"Patience and faith, Crowley," Percyval said affably. "The gods will lift you from your troubles if you allow them to."

"Enough about the damn gods," Antonn grunted, wiping the sweat from his black brows.

"One shouldn't speak ill of them, brother," Percyval smiled. "They're always listening, always watching over us. Even as we speak, they're marching with us."

"To fuckin' *Drahkmere?*" Antonn mocked him.

"Aye, brother. Even there. The gods will protect you 'til you reach your grave. You need only open your heart to them."

"There's only *one* god," Antonn said. "And trust me, he's not in fuckin' *Drahkmere*."

"Enough, you two," Viktor said with a grin. Riding with both knights at his side made him feel safe again. He'd lost his closest friend, whose name he'd refused to speak again. But, in return, he'd gained more friends than he could have hoped for. For once, the world appeared to be giving him the upper hand, he simply needed to be wary and play his cards right, particularly when there were already a few souls in his company that were questioning his honesty.

One of those souls, unfortunately, was John Huxley. The farmer rode his horse quietly and pensively, observing the trio of knights from afar. His whole life, he'd thought of Sir Viktor Crowley as the man he hoped one day to become. Only now, he wasn't entirely sure. His image of the man had shattered, replaced by a sudden doubt, an inevitable qualm towards the man's intentions.

Were they, in fact, for the good of the kingdom? Were they his own?

Or were they for the good of the Woodland recruits?

What does it all mean anyway? For the *good* of anything?

Who's to say what's good and what's bad?

John felt, in a sense, awakened. The fear he had back at the Huxley farm, the dread of one day becoming a man like Hudson Blackwood, had vanished. He'd seen the man behind the hat, after all. And he learned that perhaps the cunning thief wasn't as radical as he thought. Perhaps Viktor was just as flawed and perhaps there *was* no right or wrong to anything.

People were simply *people*. And it hadn't been so clear to John as it was now.

He was no hero. Hudson's words had never struck him so brusquely before.

This was not John's story. It wasn't *anyone*'s story, in fact.

John was just another blade in the masses, lucky enough to have been roped in the middle of it.

Or *unlucky*, perhaps? Only fate would tell.

"What's wrong there, mate?" the thief brought him back to his senses.

"Nothing," John shook his head. "Nothing at all..."

"You look as if you've eaten rotten kale."

"Piss off," John grinned.

"You're right. What am I saying? *All* kale's rotten."

John chuckled. For once, he was happy to be where he was. He'd been blinded his whole life by a sense of what was right or wrong, simply because everyone else would tell him so. He felt almost invigorated by being able to decide for himself. Invigorated and frightened, all at once.

"Still tense about that dragon?" Syrena asked him.

"Not to worry, mate," Hudson patted him in the back. "We've got a dragon of our own." He shot Syrena a wink, and she grinned coquettishly in return.

"Hang on, what was that?" asked a nervous voice behind them. Young Cedric's face had gone suddenly pale. "D-Did I just hear you say...?"

"Pay 'em no mind, toothpick," Gwyn comforted the lad. "Their heads must be fried from the heat."

"Believe what you will," Syrena told the woman. "We know what we saw..."

"Horse shit," Gwyn snapped somewhat coldly at the witch. "D'you take me for a halfwit?"

"This one's got quite a tongue," Hudson mumbled to John, just loud enough that woman most certainly overheard.

"Dragons aren't real," Gwyn scoffed, hoping to ease Cedric's nerves. "What's next, then? Ye gonna tell us the fucker *talked*, too?"

Cedric wiped his dampened hands on his trousers. "I suppose you're right," he laughed nervously. "There's no such thing... There can't be..."

"Oh but there *can*," Hudson grinned. "Believe me, little mate, they're as real as pixies."

"Stop fillin' his head with shit!" Gwyn interjected. "Pixies ain't real either. This here's the *real* world. Not a bloody fairytale."

"Oh, for fuck's sake," Hudson rolled his eyes. "Where'd this one come from, anyway?"

"*This* one's got a name!" the woman glared at him. "It's *Gwyn*!"

"I don't care."

Syrena, daring as she was becoming, took a quick glance at their surroundings, making sure there were no horses nearby that were outside of their company. And then, with a devious grin, she lifted the lid of her rucksack.

Like a young bird taking flight for the first time, Sivvy stretched her wings and floated gently out, keeping a close distance with the witch as if she were her guardian. Instantly, the whispering around them seized. Every pair of eyes was drawn towards Sivvy's glow, dashingly radiant even under the sunlight.

Gwyn's jaw dropped. "What in all hells...?"

The thief and the witch glanced at one another, both of them with subtle mischief in their eyes.

"*Gwyn*, was it?" Hudson said with a sly grin. "My apologies, you're absolutely right. There *are* no such things as fairytales..."

John Huxley rode in silence, feeling about as jovial as a child. He stared ahead into the distance and could almost see the blue hue of the Draeric Sea lined along the horizon, their last stop before they sailed overseas to Drahkmere.

He took gentle breaths, his mind reeling with a million thoughts about the journey ahead. There was no way to know what fate had in store for them. Surrounded by his new friends and acquaintances, there was only *one* thing the young farmer was certain of...

If he somehow made it back to Elbon in one piece...

This was going to make for one hell of a story...

Afterword

I finish my tale, as I often do, with a celebratory drink.

But when I bring the bottle up to my lips, I realize it's empty. When did *that* happen, I wonder? I grab another bottle, yank the cork out with my few good teeth, and spit it out into a corner.

One last gulp and I'm done, I tell myself, but I know it's bollocks.

What kind of example am I setting for these children? A good one, I hope. At least the little rats seem mildly entertained.

Or, at least, they *did*. Now they're just sitting there in silence, staring at me enthusiastically as if expecting more. It's quite remarkable, the way a child's mind works. You can sit on your arse for hours telling them a story and yet it's never really enough for them, the little rats.

"*What?*" I finally grunt.

They glance at each other confusedly. It feels like they've been sitting there an eternity and yet they're wide awake and eager for more, it baffles me. Hells, they've eaten *twice* since they got here. It must be close to midnight by now. Has it ever occurred to them that an elderly man needs a break from time to time?

The elf boy, the pluckiest of the three, decides to speak first.

"So... *then* he died?"

I narrow my eyes in confusion. "Then *who* died?"

"The *Guardian!*"

"You said you'd tell us how he died," the human boy adds. He's always been the louder, more annoying one of the lot. Always trying to make his opinion known, as if it mattered more than everyone else's. "I think he's brilliant! Did you know he was the one who stole the Amulet of Varisvaara?"

The elf boy straightens himself up eagerly. "Was it long after that? When he got *eaten*, I mean?"

"You mean *decapitated*."

"Don't be stupid. Everyone knows he was *eaten*."

"Mister Barlowe, *tell* him the Guardian was *publicly executed!*"

For gods' sake, I must stop these two before they start with this again.

"Shut up, the both of you!" I exclaim, rubbing my temples gently and rolling my weary aggravated eyes.

"Was it *Nyx* that ate 'im?!"

"Don't be stupid," says the red-headed girl, the more curious one. *Wynnifred.*

I don't know why her name's the only one I remember. I suppose it's because she's the only one that truly *thinks* about the stories. Not like the other two, who just sit and listen for the thrill, so that they can hear about who was killed by whom and in what way. What's the point of a story if you overlook the lesson entirely?

"There's no way!" Wynnifred goes on. "Nyx was only a dragon until th-"

"Don't *spoil* it!" the elf boy interjects.

"Bloody fuckin' hells," I sigh, not because I'm actually annoyed but because *someone* has to stand up for the poor girl when the other two fools decide to corner her. "The *nerve* of you two! I just spent the whole bloody day tellin' you the story of how it all began, but all you care about is how the bloke *died?!*"

"I bet it was brilliant!" the elf boy adds eagerly. "I bet he died with a smile…"

"Who *was* the Guardian, anyway?" asks Wynnifred. "Was it Viktor?"

"Were you even *listening?*" her cousin snaps at her. "It was obviously John!"

"But, Mister Barlowe never said so!"

"He didn't *have* to, stupid."

"All you care about is the bloody Lady Knight!" the elf boy spits.

Well of course she does, I think to myself. *The Lady Knight's braver than any of you, you dumb pests.*

"Well she *did* ride a fire-breathin' dragon!" Wynnifred argues. "Did the Guardian ever do that?"

Good. Very good. Stick up for yourself, ginger. Don't let them have the last word.

"By the way, whatever happened to House Clark?" the elf boy asks.

Finally, a question worth answering.

"Well, some say th-"

"*I* heard they all died!" the human boy interrupts again. "That's why there hasn't been a Clark in Gravenstone for decades!"

I fight the urge to glare at the boy. He's too young to know any better and it's not his fault his attention span is rubbish. "All right," I groan. "I think you've asked enough questions for the night."

"But Mister Barlowe!"

"I said *enough*! Piss off, the lot of you!"

Without protesting any further, the children all rise to their feet and start gathering their belongings, all the while continuing with their childish arguments. I don't particularly like yelling at them, but it's the only way to get them to scram. Once they were here 'til dawn, and I had to get rid of them by leaving the house myself.

"You hardly spoke of Queen Magdalena," Wynnifred complains.

I allow it, only because it's her…

"That's because *hers* is the second half of the story," I say.

She smiles. "Will you tell us *next* week, then?"

I smile back. "Sure, ginger. But do me a favor and open that window for me. You lot have been loungin' about so long, it's starting to reek in here."

"It smelled this way when we got here," says the elf boy. "By the way, I need a piss pot."

"You have to go out back, lad."

The elf boy leaves the room as obedient little Wynnifred opens the window. Just as I expect, it's pitch black out there. Based on where the moon sits, I'd say it's well *past* midnight. How deceiving, those candles can be. But it's not the first time we lose track of time. I'm well aware that I've the tendency to lose myself in my stories. I only wonder why these little buggers' parents don't seem to care much where their children wander off to.

Thump thump thump!

Ah, there it is... A heavy fist starts hammering dramatically at my door. The door shakes, rumbles, gathers clouds of dust along the edges... A shrill voice starts shouting from the outside and both Wynnifred and... the *boy* one, her cousin, they freeze as if they just heard a hungry lion's roar.

"Open up!" the woman shouts. "I know you're in there!"

*Good gods, woman. There are people sleeping... not **here**, perhaps, but have some decency still...*

"It's mum," Wynnifred says, wide-eyed and nervous.

"Oh shit..." the boy one says.

"Oi! Language!" I bark at him.

"But I learned it from *you*."

"Well *un*-learn it!"

The girl runs to the door and opens it. In walks a full-figured woman in a blue housedress and an apron, looking about as angry as... well *me*, on a bad day. Immediately she starts to scream and I wonder if my voice is as agonizing as hers when I raise it.

"Where've you been, girl?! I've looked *everywhere*! Have you any idea how worried I've been?!"

Not very, I imagine. *They've been here for fifteen hours...*

"I-I'm sorry, mum," Wynnifred confesses timidly. "W-We only came by for a story."

"In the dead of night?!"

"It was morning when we got here," the boy says from afar.

"Don't think I forgot about *you*, boy!" the angry woman raises a finger at him. "I'm havin' a word with your mother!"

Finally she glances at me. I say nothing, only work on my second bottle and stare back at her. I wonder if the woman knows how well she fits into the image of the hackneyed villain in a children's story, what with that mole above her lip and that sharp glare the likes of which any child would cringe and cower away from. Anyway, I figure I should put the bottle down and say something. Staring for so long's not exactly proper.

"Good evening, Hilda," I give her a nod.

"Piss off, you!"

All right, well... I tried...

"How many times have I told you?!" Hilda scolds the girl. "I *don't* want you wanderin' off without tellin' me where you're goin'!"

"But we weren't doing anything wrong," the boy argues.

"We're fine, mum."

"Shut it, girl!"

"They're fine, Hilda," I intercede again, for the children's sake. "They just wanted a story."

"I said *piss off*!" she raises a finger at *me* now. I try not to let the dirt beneath her fingernails distract me, but I'm a sucker for trivial particulars. "I've *nothing* to say to you!" she shouts, despite the fact that I'm sitting just three feet away. "Filling children's heads with all that rubbish... You should be ashamed..."

Don't argue, Jack... Stay out of it...

"Dim-witted queens and knight liberators?" she scoffs. "Utter nonsense!"

*Don't argue... Do **not** arg-*

"It's not nonsense if it's true," I mumble.

Fuck...

"Are you barkin' *mad*?!" she raises her voice further, so loud it's no wonder the neighbors hate me. "Their heads are filled with rubbish as it is, they don't need any more of it from *you*!"

"Hilda..."

"They're *children*!"

"Yes! Yes, they are!" I rise suddenly to my feet and match the volume of her voice. It scares her. "They're children who, before you know it, will grow into *adults*! D'you *want* them to grow old thinking life's a fairytale? They *deserve* to know the truth..."

She's flabbergasted, because no one had ever spoken to her in such a tone... I stand my ground, because it's about time *someone* did...

Though I admitted to myself that I often got carried away with my stories, it never occurred to me to soften the blow. I told the stories the way they happened. I told them countless times, I hardly needed the notes anymore, hadn't for the last two decades. I used to tell the stories to grown folk who wanted to hear the *truth*, rather than the nonsense they were told by palace ministers.

What fault did *I* have that the only audience I had left, after all these years, were children?

And what fault did *they* have to be the only ones in this vile town with an actual mind of their own?

"Listen 'ere, you scum," she steps forward, that damn finger of hers aimed right at me again.

I expected a lecture or a couple of insults at best. Instead she freezes when the back door creaks open. The elf boy walks in as casually as always, drying his blue hands with an old rag. The woman's face goes from puzzled to enraged within seconds, and the elf boy's suddenly about as vulnerable as a pup.

"We're leaving," the woman says coldly. She grabs Wynnifred and the boy by the wrists and drags them towards the door.

"But Aunt Hilda, w-"

"I said we're *leaving*. Now!"

"What did we do?" Wynnifred asks.

"I told you countless times, girl!" Hilda hisses at her child. "I *don't* want you messin' about with their kind!"

I bite my tongue and make a fist. I know that it's not my place to tell others what to think, but it's so hard to resist when all I want to do is throw my bottle at her and call her a sheep.

"But he's our friend!" Wynnifred says, the poor innocent thing.

How is it that such a youngin' has more sense than her own mother, I wonder?

"No daughter of mine is gonna be friends with a rabbit!" Hilda shouts. "They've got *their* side of the village, we've got *ours*. End of story!"

"But *mum!*"

"*END... OF... STORY!*"

They leave the room.

The elf boy's no longer smiling, his childlike joy is replaced by a wave of melancholy. He's too young for this nonsense, he deserves so much better. In an uncomfortable trance, he starts to gather his things in silence.

Damn it all to hells...

"Hey," I stop him before he leaves.

He looks at me with those faultless little eyes of his, so naïve and innocent. What kind of person has the gall to place such blame on a child that never asked to be born?

"Don't pay it any mind, you hear?" I tell him.

He shoots me a half-smile, and a forced one at that.

"Ignorance," I say to him. "It's the one thing we can't get rid of... It's not your fault. You understand?"

He nods. But the scar remains, I can tell. "See you next week, Mister Barlowe..."

"See you next week, little lad..."

He leaves with a frown on his face.

I feel the rage sweltering in my chest, killing me slowly.

How *dare* she? The gutless bitch...

He's just a kid... but she can't see that through her willful ignorance. He comes here for an escape, to smile for a little while and not have to worry about the shithole of a nation that we live in. And she barges into my home and *reminds* him? The fucking gall...

I reach for my bottle again. It's the only thing that'll help me pass the time, the only thing that'll keep me going until next week, until the little ones come back for another story.

For me, there's no routine. There's hardly any sense of time, every day's about the same. Except for the *seventh* day, the only day I genuinely look forward to, the day I get to tell my stories just like the good old days.

On the seventh day, I get to see those smiles, full of absolute wonder and joy. The smiles that serve as proof that we *can* be better, and that someday perhaps we *will* be better. I feel the dread in my chest suddenly, knowing I may not live to see that day, knowing that one day my eyes and lips will shut forever.

But if I can spend the little time I have left making sure that those children are better than we were, I'll damn well do it. And there isn't a single loud-mouthed soul out there that can stop me.

A sudden creak makes me drop the bottle…

Wynnifred, the little rebel, enters my home one last time.

"What're you doing back here, girl?"

"I forgot to give you something," she digs through her rucksack. I expect a trinket of some sort, an anklet or necklace, some crafty little thing that children often make to pass the time.

"You best go now, before your mother gets b-"

I feel a peculiar warmth overtake me suddenly… For once, the liquor fails to keep me numb… There she stands, the curious little thing, holding a crumpled meat pie wrapped in a handkerchief. She hands it to me eagerly.

"Mum always says that if we don't eat well, we'll starve," she mutters innocently. "I don't want you to starve…"

I take the meat pie. It crumbles further in my hand.

I clear my aching throat as a strange feeling hits my chest.

"Thank you, ginger…"

She smiles again. "My name's Wynnifred."

I nod, unable to smile back. "I know…"

Her mother shouts from the outside and she darts out of the room.

I stare at the old meat pie as if I was holding treasure in my hands.

I never considered myself to be a friendly person. I hardly ever leave the house these days, in fact. Strange, what isolation could do to someone. Often I felt I was the embodiment of hopelessness. But to see such an innocent thing care so much for an old bastard like me? It's unnerving and heartening all at once.

I eat the meat pie within minutes. It fills my liquor-ridden belly.

And then I feel the exhaustion start to settle in.

I make it to my bed this time. I lie there, inebriated and cold.

Another night in hell…

At times it's difficult to tell my dreams apart from reality, they're so often bleak. I suppose that's the burden of the liberal mind.

And so I close my eyes and force myself into a deep slumber, silently wishing I could sleep forever…

Or, if not forever, then at least until the seventh day…

Character Index

Kingdom of Vallenghard

John Huxley
Age: 23, Hair: Blonde, Eyes: Blue.
Courageous, Benevolent, & Reckless.
A young farmer from Elbon with dreams of someday becoming a knight.

Hudson Blackwood
Age: 30, Hair: Black, Eyes: Brown.
Clever, Devious, & Intrepid.
A notorious thief/mercenary from Raven's Keep

Robyn Huxley
Age: 17, Hair: Black, Eyes: Hazel.
Kind, Stubborn, & Brave.
A young archer from Elbon. John Huxley's sister.

Adelina Huxley
Age: 40, Hair: Black, Eyes: Hazel.
Warm, Protective, & Good-natured.
Mother and keeper of the Huxley farm.

Margot & Melvyn Huxley
Ages: 11, Hair: Black, Eyes: Hazel.
Twins; the youngest of the Huxley children.

Nyx
Age: 306. Wise, Candid, & Loyal.
A swordsman who fought in the Great War, before he was cursed by a witch with immortality. He resurrects as a different species every time he is killed.

Sir Viktor Crowley
Age: 43, Hair: Blonde, Eyes: Blue.
Valiant, Firm, & Conflicted.
The Golden Eagle of Vallenghard.
Knight Commander of Val Havyn's royal guard.

Sir Jossiah Biggs
Age: 45, Hair: Brown, Eyes: Brown.
Distant, Cold, & Prejudice.
A knight of King Rowan's court. Viktor's lifelong friend and comrade.

Lady Brunylda Clark
Age: 53, Hair: Black, Eyes: Brown.
Candid, Fearless, & Dangerously Intelligent.
The outspoken Treasurer of Val Havyn.

Sir Darryk Clark
Age: 25, Hair: Black, Eyes: Brown.
Modest, Empathetic, & Coy.
A knight from the city of Roquefort and Lady Brunylda's distant nephew.
Betrothed to Princess Magdalena and appointed Lord Regent of Val Havyn.

Brie
Age: 19, Hair: Blonde, Eyes: Blue.
Friendly, Meek, & Intelligent.
Former handmaiden to Princess Magdalena. Bookkeeper to Lady Brunylda Clark.

Evellyn Amberhill
Age: 24, Hair: Red, Eyes: Green.
Kind, Diligent, & Proud.
A blacksmith in the city of Val Havyn and lifelong friend of the Huxleys.

Alycia Amberhill
Age: 13, Hair: Red, Eyes: Green.
Timid & Gentle. Evellyn's younger sister.

Baryn Lawe
Age: 60s, Hair: Grey, Eyes: Brown.
Forthright, Prejudice, & Deceiving.
A preacher in Val Havyn, hateful towards anyone who isn't human.

Cedric
Age: 18, Hair: Chestnut, Eyes: Brown.
Bashful, Friendly, & Loyal.
An orphan who volunteers to be a squire for Sir Viktor Crowley.

Jasper Nottley
Age: 50s, Hair: Brown, Eyes: Brown. Cruel & Greedy. Cedric's abusive warden.

Thaddeus Rexx
Age: 40s, Hair: Black, Eyes: Brown.
Discreet, Strong, & Protective.
A blacksmith from Val Havyn that volunteers to join Sir Viktor Crowley's company.
He is a friend and father figure to Cedric.

Martyn & Wyll Davenport
Age: 30s, Hair: Blonde.
Hunters/Traders from Falkbury that captured the witch Syrena of Morganna.

Mister Abner Beckwit
Age: 60s, Hair: Grey, Eyes: Hazel.
Friendly & Wise. A veteran of the royal guard; friend and mentor to the Huxley children.

Larz & Henrik
Age: 30s. Mister Beckwit's farmhands.

Count Raoul Jacquin
Age: 60s, Hair: Grey, Eyes: Black.
Spiteful, Greedy, & Selfish.
A wealthy count from the free city of Kahrr.

King Rowan of Val Havyn
Age: 50s, Hair: Brown, Eyes: Green.
The King of Vallenghard and Magdalena's father. A good leader with a strong temper,
presumed to have been cursed by a witch with the inability to father any sons.

Sir Hugo Symmond
Age: 40s, Hair: Chestnut, Eyes: Brown.
A knight of the king's court.

Hektor & Bogden
Age: 40s. Soldiers of Val Havyn's royal guard.

Kingdom of Halghard

Syrena of Morganna
Age: 30, Hair: Black, Eyes: Orange.
Fidgety, Aggressive, & Honest. A witch with the ability to conjure fire.
Though born in the city of Morganna, she has lived in the Woodlands for most of her life.

Sir Percyval Garroway
Age: 45, Hair: Black, Eyes: Brown.
Honorable, Ethical, & Avant-garde.
A knight who is sent to the Woodlands to recruit soldiers for his brother's army.
He supports civil rights for all races and believes in unity and the breaking of barriers.

Sir Antonn Guilara
Age: 48, Hair: Black, Eyes: Brown.
Tenacious, Cranky, & Loyal.
Sir Percyval's second-in-command; a foreigner with a shadowy past.

King Alistair Garroway
Age: 50, Hair: Black & Grey, Eyes: Brown.
Resilient, Seasoned, & Unyielding.
Sir Percyval's older brother. Once the right-hand knight of the King of Halghard, Alistair rose to power when he led the rebellion against the usurper Balthazar Locke.

King Balthazar Locke
Age: Unknown. A tyrannical usurper who was once the king's most trusted advisor.
Claimed the crown for himself after the king's unexpected death.

Osric Skinner
Age: 60s, Hair: Black & Grey, Eyes: Blue.
Experienced, Firm, & Protective.
A former guardsman who spends his days mentoring and providing shelter for orphaned youth,
naming them the 'Wardens of Grymsbi'.

Ayisha
Age: 19, Hair: Dark Brown, Eyes: Honey.
Sharp & Distrustful. A member of Skinner's wardens.

Milo
Age: 15, Hair: Brown, Eyes: Blue.
Kind & Smart. A member of Skinner's wardens.

Aldous
Age: 20, Hair: Silver/Dyed Black, Eyes: Green.
A half-human/half-elf and member of Skinner's wardens.

Yuri
Age: 19, Hair: Black, Eyes: Yellow.
An orcess and member of Skinner's wardens

Gibbons
Age: 15. A member of Skinner's wardens.

Tails, Mallory, & Sam
Ages: 14, 13, and 9. Members of Skinner's wardens.

Seamus
Age: 25, Hair: Red, Eyes: Green. Friendly and Good-natured.
A tavern server in Grymsbi that becomes the owner when his superior is killed.

The Woodlands

Captain Malekai Pahrvus
Age: 40, Hair: Black dreads, Eyes: Hazel.
Cruel, Megalomaniac, & Resentful.
The newly-appointed Captain of the Rogue Brotherhood.

Borrys Belvaine
Age: 35, Hair: Brown, Eyes: Brown.
Greedy & Wicked.
A member of the Rogue Brotherhood; Malekai's second-in-command.

The Beast
Age: Unknown, Hair: Black, Eyes: Yellow.
Bad-tempered, Withdrawn, & Tough.
Used to be the sole orc member of the Rogue Brotherhood, until they left him behind to die. Befriends Robyn Huxley and becomes her traveling companion.

Clive
Age: 40s. A member of the Rogue Brotherhood.

Naru
Age: 40s. A member of the Rogue Brotherhood.

Miss Rayna
Age: 60s, Hair: Grey, Eyes: Blue.
Strict, Domineering, & Compassionate. The owner of a tavern in the Woodlands, which was built into the trunk of a massive tree.

Kiira
Age: 20s, Hair: Silver, Eyes: Grey.
An elf servant to Miss Rayna.

Edmond & Grum
Ages: Unknown.
Miss Rayna's two sons; an ogre and a human raider, respectively.

Gwyndolyn 'Gwyn' Althercross
Age: 35, Hair: Blonde, Eyes: Green.
Fierce, Snappy, & Loyal.
A mercenary who was recruited into Sir Percyval Garroway's troop. She befriends Cedric, seeing him as a younger brother figure she can mentor.

Daryan Althercross
Age: 35, Hair: Blonde, Eyes: Green.
Polite, Well-read, & Drunk.
Gwyn's twin brother; also recruited into Sir Percyval Garroway's troop.

Skye
Age: Unknown, Hair: Silver, Eyes: Purple.
Reserved, Soft-spoken, & Nimble.
An androgynous elf and ice mage from the north who was recruited into Sir Percyval Garroway's troop. It is unknown whether Skye is male or female, nor do they specifically identify as any gender.

Toro
Age: Unknown, Hair: Black pelt, Eyes: Black.
A minotauro from the Great Plains of Belmoor; Skye's henchman.
Recruited into Sir Percyval's troop of Woodland folk.

Zahrra

Age: 70s, Hair: Grey, Eyes: Green.

Blunt, Aggressive, & Resentful.

A seasoned witch with the ability to read people's thoughts through a link such as hair or fingernails.

Recruited into Sir Percyval's troop of Woodland folk.

Aevastra

Age: 30s, Hair: Black, Eyes: Yellow.

Quiet, Vigilant, & Brave.

An orcess who flees the Woodlands in search of a better life for her infant son in the free city of Kahrr.

Kingdom of Qamroth

Lord Yohan Baronkroft

Age: 45, Hair: Black, Eyes: Black.

Extremist, Maniacal, & Liberal.

A lord with a dark past whose cause is to liberate the oppressed races of Gravenstone. Because he practices dark magic, his mind has been infected, thus he is violent and aggressive when challenged.

Princess Magdalena of Val Havyn

Age: 19, Hair: Blonde, Eyes: Green.

Astute, Outspoken, & Dedicated.

The princess of Vallenghard, who is kidnapped by Baronkroft and smuggled overseas.

Harrok Mortymer, the Butcher of Haelvaara

Age: Unknown, Hair: Brown, Eyes: Pale Grey

Aggressive, Heartless, & Cannibalistic.

Baronkroft's right-hand henchman, who was believed to be dead until recently.

Thomlin

Age: 12, Hair: Brown, Eyes: Brown.

Kind, Spirited, & Loyal.

A peasant boy and prisoner who befriends Princess Magdalena.

Valleria
Age: 60s, Hair: Grey, Eyes: Blue.
A sellsword and prisoner who befriends Princess Magdalena.

Sergeant Hauzer
Age: 45, Hair: Red, Eyes: Green.
A soldier in Baronkroft's army, in charge of looking after the prisoners.

Sergeant Jyor
Age: 39, Hair: Platinum, Eyes: Grey.
An elf soldier in Baronkroft's army, in charge of looking after the prisoners.

Okvar the Destroyer
Age: Unknown, Hair: none, Eyes: Yellow.
An orc who flees Baronkroft's army to migrate to the free city of Kahrr.

Gruul & Murzol
Ages: Unknown, Eyes: Yellow.
Okvar's orc goons, who flee Baronkroft's army to migrate to the free city of Kahrr.

Sir Gerhard Vandelour
Age: 47, Hair: Black & Grey, Eyes: Brown.
A knight from Qamroth who gets blackmailed into lending his army to Baronkroft.

Sergeant Weston
Age: 40s, Hair: Brown, Eyes: Brown.
A soldier loyal to Sir Vandelour who gets kidnapped and tortured by Baronkroft.

Sebastien Swanworth
Age: 60s, Hair: Grey, Eyes: Grey.
A curator and prisoner of Baronkroft's army.

Lord Olfur Millhurst
Age: 50s, Hair: Brown, Eyes: Brown.
A lord from the kingdom of Halghard and prisoner of Baronkroft's army.

Magda
Age: Unknown, Eyes: Brown.
A gnome woman and servant to Baronkroft.

End of Book One

This story will continue in…

Legends of Gravenstone
The Battle of Drahkmere

32855409R00392

Made in the USA
Middletown, DE
08 January 2019